Praise for *T.C. Boyle S*

"Who else of Boyle's generation could have assembled, by this point, a collected stories the size of the Phoenix phone book? Boyle has S.J. Perleman's affection for the absurdities of pop culture as starting point, Richard Coover's wicked sense of the flimsiness of our received cultural representations of goodness and evil, Donald Barthelme's gift for deadpan comic premises. . . . The fact that I've just negotiated [its] seven hundred pages and I'm not sick to death of it attests to its over-all inventiveness, flash, and just plain entertainment value."
—*The New York Times Book Review*

"A great fat book, by a youngish writer making his claim to Maestro status . . . reveal[s] a writer born to elegance and equipped with keen eyes, ears, and a preternatural skill at evoking the objects of his roving interest." —*Los Angeles Times*

"Varied, clever, and delightful . . . Boyle has a reputation for wit, which is evident, along with his versatility, in these tales . . . these stories are consistent in their readability and quality."
—*The Chicago Tribune*

"*T.C. Boyle Stories* gives ample evidence of Boyle's encyclopedic range . . . there are few authors who could master half as many settings . . . this often delicious collection confirms the success of Boyle's prodigious effort to resuscitate the comic tale."
—*New York Newsday*

"Each [story hops] with manic energy . . . at his vaulting, imaginative best Boyle suggests the bastard child of Flannery O'Connor and Monty Python." —*The Miami Herald*

"Boyle has utterly seduced me with his short stories . . . there's enough variety here to fill a five and dime, and enough pathos, irony, sardonicism, cleverness, humor (both good and ill), passion and despair to fuel a schizophrenic . . . furthermore, Boyle clearly wants to have fun with these pieces. . . . Boyle's more of a John Cheever: sharp, precise, masterful . . . no other writer I can think of has such a good time with this format."
—*Men's Journal*

PENGUIN BOOKS

T.C. BOYLE STORIES

T. Coraghessan Boyle is the author of *Drop City, A Friend of the Earth, Riven Rock, The Tortilla Curtain, The Road to Wellville, East Is East, World's End* (winner of the PEN/Faulkner Award), *Budding Prospects, Water Music,* and six collections of stories. In 1999, he was the recipient of the PEN/Malamud Award for Excellence in Short Fiction. His stories appear regularly in major American magazines, including *The New Yorker, GQ, Esquire,* and *Playboy.* He lives near Santa Barbara, California. T.C. Boyle's Web site is www.tcboyle.com.

T. C. BOYLE
S·T·O·R·I·E·S

THE COLLECTED STORIES OF
T. CORAGHESSAN BOYLE

PENGUIN BOOKS

PENGUIN BOOKS

Published by the Penguin Group

Penguin Group (USA) Inc., 375 Hudson Street, New York, New York 10014, U.S.A.

Penguin Group (Canada), 90 Eglinton Avenue East, Suite 700, Toronto,
Ontario, Canada M4P 2Y3 (a division of Pearson Penguin Canada Inc.)

Penguin Books Ltd, 80 Strand, London WC2R 0RL, England

Penguin Ireland, 25 St Stephen's Green, Dublin 2, Ireland (a division of Penguin Books Ltd)

Penguin Group (Australia), 250 Camberwell Road, Camberwell,
Victoria 3124, Australia (a division of Pearson Australia Group Pty Ltd)

Penguin Books India Pvt Ltd, 11 Community Centre, Panchsheel Park, New Delhi – 110 017, India

Penguin Group (NZ), cnr Airborne and Rosedale Roads,
Albany, Auckland 1310, New Zealand (a division of Pearson New Zealand Ltd)

Penguin Books (South Africa) (Pty) Ltd, 24 Sturdee Avenue,
Rosebank, Johannesburg 2196, South Africa

Penguin Books Ltd, Registered Offices: 80 Strand, London WC2R 0RL, England

First published in the United States of America by Viking Penguin,
a member of Penguin Putnam Inc. 1998
Published in Penguin Books 1999

12 13 14 15 16 17 18 19 20

PUBLISHER'S NOTE

These selections are works of fiction. Names, characters, places, and incidents either
are the product of the author's imagination or are used fictitiously, and any resemblance
to actual persons, living or dead, events, or locales is entirely coincidental.

CIP data available.
ISBN 0-670-87960-6 (hc.)
ISBN 0 14 02.8091 X (pbk.)

Printed in the United States of America
Set in Life
Designed by Betty Lew

For the editors:

Bill Buford, Dan Halpern, Lewis Lapham,

Gordon Lish, Charles McGrath, George Plimpton,

Alice K. Turner and Robley Wilson, Jr.

"Reflexes got the better of me."

—Bob Marley, "I Shot the Sheriff"

CONTENTS

III. And Everything in Between

· I ·

Love

MODERN LOVE

There was no exchange of body fluids on the first date, and that suited both of us just fine. I picked her up at seven, took her to Mee Grop, where she meticulously separated each sliver of meat from her Phat Thai, watched her down four bottles of Singha at three dollars per, and then gently stroked her balsam-smelling hair while she snoozed through *The Terminator* at the Circle Shopping Center theater. We had a late-night drink at Rigoletto's Pizza Bar (and two slices, plain cheese), and I dropped her off. The moment we pulled up in front of her apartment she had the door open. She turned to me with the long, elegant, mournful face of her Puritan ancestors and held out her hand.

"It's been fun," she said.

"Yes," I said, taking her hand.

She was wearing gloves.

"I'll call you," she said.

"Good," I said, giving her my richest smile. "And I'll call you."

On the second date we got acquainted.

"I can't tell you what a strain it was for me the other night," she said, staring down into her chocolate-mocha-fudge sundae. It was early afternoon, we were in Helmut's Olde Tyme Ice Cream Parlor in Mamaroneck, and the sun streamed through the thick frosted windows and lit the place like a convalescent home. The fixtures glowed behind the counter, the brass rail was buffed to a reflective sheen, and everything smelled of disinfectant. We were the only people in the place.

"What do you mean?" I said, my mouth glutinous with melted marshmallow and caramel.

"I mean Thai food, the seats in the movie theater, the *ladies' room* in that place for god's sake . . ."

"Thai food?" I wasn't following her. I recalled the maneuver with the strips of pork and the fastidious dissection of the glass noodles. "You're a vegetarian?"

She looked away in exasperation, and then gave me the full, wide-eyed shock of her ice-blue eyes. "Have you seen the Health Department statistics on sanitary conditions in ethnic restaurants?"

I hadn't.

Her eyebrows leapt up. She was earnest. She was lecturing. "These people are refugees. They have—well, different standards. They haven't even been inoculated." I watched her dig the tiny spoon into the recesses of the dish and part her lips for a neat, foursquare morsel of ice cream and fudge.

"The illegals, anyway. And that's half of them." She swallowed with an almost imperceptible movement, a shudder, her throat dipping and rising like a gazelle's. "I got drunk from fear," she said. "Blind panic. I couldn't help thinking I'd wind up with hepatitis or dysentery or dengue fever or something."

"Dengue fever?"

"I usually bring a disposable sanitary sheet for public theaters—just think of who might have been in that seat before you, and how many times, and what sort of nasty festering little cultures of this and that there must be in all those ancient dribbles of taffy and Coke and extra-butter popcorn—but I didn't want you to think I was too extreme or anything on the first date, so I didn't. And then the *ladies' room* . . . You don't think I'm overreacting, do you?"

As a matter of fact, I did. Of course I did. I liked Thai food—and sushi and ginger crab and greasy souvlaki at the corner stand too. There was the look of the mad saint in her eye, the obsessive, the mortifier of the flesh, but I didn't care. She was lovely, wilting, clear-eyed, and pure, as cool and matchless as if she'd stepped out of a Pre-Raphaelite painting, and I was in love. Besides, I tended a little that way myself. Hypochondria. Anal retentiveness. The ordered environment and alphabetized books. I was a thirty-three-year-old bachelor, I carried some scars and I read the newspapers—herpes, AIDS, the Asian clap that foiled every antibiotic in the book. I was willing to take it slow. "No," I said, "I don't think you're overreacting at all."

I paused to draw in a breath so deep it might have been a sigh. "I'm sorry," I whispered, giving her a doglike look of contrition. "I didn't know."

She reached out then and touched my hand—touched it, skin to skin—and murmured that it was all right, she'd been through worse. "If you want to know," she breathed, "I like places like this."

I glanced around. The place was still empty, but for Helmut, in a blinding white jumpsuit and toque, studiously polishing the tile walls. "I know what you mean," I said.

■ ■ ■

We dated for a month—museums, drives in the country, French and German restaurants, ice-cream emporia, fern bars—before we kissed. And when we kissed, after a showing of *David and Lisa* at a revival house all the way up in Rhinebeck and on a night so cold no run-of-the-mill bacterium or commonplace virus could have survived it, it was the merest brushing of the lips. She was wearing a big-shouldered coat of synthetic fur and a knit hat pulled down over her brow and she hugged my arm as we stepped out of the theater and into the blast of the night. "God," she said, "did you see him when he screamed 'You touched me!'? Wasn't that priceless?" Her eyes were big and she seemed weirdly excited. "Sure," I said, "yeah, it was great," and then she pulled me close and kissed me. I felt the soft flicker of her lips against mine. "I love you," she said, "I think."

A month of dating and one dry fluttering kiss. At this point you might begin to wonder about me, but really, I didn't mind. As I say, I was willing to wait—I had the patience of Sisyphus—and it was enough just to be with her. Why rush things? I thought. This is good, this is charming, like the slow sweet unfolding of the romance in a Frank Capra movie, where sweetness and light always prevail. Sure, she had her idiosyncrasies, but who didn't? Frankly, I'd never been comfortable with the three-drinks-dinner-and-bed sort of thing, the girls who come on like they've been in prison for six years and just got out in time to put on their makeup and jump into the passenger seat of your car. Breda—that was her name, Breda Drumhill, and the very sound and syllabification of it made me melt—was different.

Finally, two weeks after the trek to Rhinebeck, she invited me to her apartment. Cocktails, she said. Dinner. A quiet evening in front of the tube.

She lived in Croton, on the ground floor of a restored Victorian, half a mile from the Harmon station, where she caught the train each morning for Manhattan and her job as an editor of *Anthropology Today*. She'd held the job since graduating from Barnard six years earlier (with a double major in Rhetoric and Alien Cultures), and it suited her temperament perfectly. Field anthropologists living among the River Dyak of Borneo or the Kurds of Kurdistan would send her rough and grammatically tortured accounts of their observations and she would whip them into shape for popular consumption. Naturally, filth and exotic disease, as well as outlandish customs and revolting habits, played a leading role in her rewrites. Every other day or so she'd call me from work and in a voice that could barely contain its joy give me the details of some new and horrific disease she'd discovered.

She met me at the door in a silk kimono that featured a plunging neckline and a pair of dragons with intertwined tails. Her hair was pinned up as if she'd just stepped out of the bath and she smelled of Noxzema and pHisoHex. She pecked my cheek, took the bottle of Vouvray I held out in offering, and led me into the front room. "Chagas' disease," she said, grinning wide to show off her perfect, outsized teeth.

"Chagas' disease?" I echoed, not quite knowing what to do with myself. The room was as spare as a monk's cell. Two chairs, a loveseat, and a coffee table, in glass, chrome, and hard black plastic. No plants ("God knows what sort of insects might live on them—and the *dirt,* the dirt has got to be crawling with bacteria, not to mention spiders and worms and things") and no rug ("A breeding ground for fleas and ticks and chiggers").

Still grinning, she steered me to the hard black plastic loveseat and sat down beside me, the Vouvray cradled in her lap. "South America," she whispered, her eyes leaping with excitement. "In the jungle. These bugs—assassin bugs, they're called—isn't that wild? These bugs bite you and then, after they've sucked on you a while, they go potty next to the wound. When you scratch, it gets into your bloodstream, and anywhere from one to twenty years later you get a disease that's like a cross between malaria and AIDS."

"And then you die," I said.

"And then you die."

Her voice had turned somber. She wasn't grinning any longer. What could I say? I patted her hand and flashed a smile. "Yum," I said, mugging for her. "What's for dinner?"

She served a cold cream-of-tofu-carrot soup and little lentil-paste sandwiches for an appetizer and a garlic soufflé with biologically controlled vegetables for the entrée. Then it was snifters of cognac, the big-screen TV, and a movie called *The Boy in the Bubble,* about a kid raised in a totally antiseptic environment because he was born without an immune system. No one could touch him. Even the slightest sneeze would have killed him. Breda sniffled through the first half-hour, then pressed my hand and sobbed openly as the boy finally crawled out of the bubble, caught about thirty-seven different diseases, and died before the commercial break. "I've seen this movie six times now," she said, fighting to control her voice, "and it gets to me every time. What a life," she said, waving her snifter at the screen, "what a perfect life. Don't you envy him?"

I didn't envy him. I envied the jade pendant that dangled between her breasts and I told her so.

She might have giggled or gasped or lowered her eyes, but she didn't. She gave me a long slow look, as if she were deciding something, and then she allowed herself to blush, the color suffusing her throat in a delicious mottle of pink and white. "Give me a minute," she said mysteriously, and disappeared into the bathroom.

I was electrified. This was it. Finally. After all the avowals, the pressed hands, the little jokes and routines, after all the miles driven, meals consumed, museums paced, and movies watched, we were finally, naturally, gracefully going to come together in the ultimate act of intimacy and love.

I felt hot. There were beads of sweat on my forehead. I didn't know whether to stand or sit. And then the lights dimmed, and there she was at the rheostat.

She was still in her kimono, but her hair was pinned up more severely, wound in a tight coil to the crown of her head, as if she'd girded herself for battle. And she held something in her hand—a slim package, wrapped in plastic. It rustled as she crossed the room.

"When you're in love, you make love," she said, easing down beside me on the rocklike settee, "—it's only natural." She handed me the package. "I don't want to give you the wrong impression," she said, her voice throaty and raw, "just because I'm careful and modest and because there's so much, well, filth in the world, but I have my passionate side too. I do. And I love you, I think."

"Yes," I said, groping for her, the package all but forgotten.

We kissed. I rubbed the back of her neck, felt something strange, an odd sag and ripple, as if her skin had suddenly turned to Saran Wrap, and then she had her hand on my chest. "Wait," she breathed, "the, the thing."

I sat up. "Thing?"

The light was dim but I could see the blush invade her face now. She was sweet. Oh, she was sweet, my Little Em'ly, my Victorian princess. "It's Swedish," she said.

I looked down at the package in my lap. It was a clear, skin-like sheet of plastic, folded up in its transparent package like a heavy-duty garbage bag. I held it up to her huge, trembling eyes. A crazy idea darted in and out of my head. No, I thought.

"It's the newest thing," she said, the words coming in a rush, "the safest . . . I mean, nothing could possibly—"

My face was hot. "No," I said.

"It's a condom," she said, tears starting up in her eyes, "my doctor got them for me they're . . . they're Swedish." Her face wrinkled up and she began to cry. "It's a condom," she sobbed, crying so hard the kimono fell open and I could see the outline of the thing against the swell of her nipples, "a full-body condom."

I was offended. I admit it. It wasn't so much her obsession with germs and contagion, but that she didn't trust me after all that time. I was clean. Quintessentially clean. I was a man of moderate habits and good health, I changed my underwear and socks daily—sometimes twice a day—and I worked in an office, with clean, crisp, unequivocal numbers, managing my late father's chain of shoe stores (and he died cleanly himself, of a myocardial infarction, at seventy-five). "But Breda," I said, reaching out to console her and brushing her soft, plastic-clad breast in the process, "don't you trust me? Don't you believe in me? Don't you, don't you love me?" I took her by the shoulders, lifted her head, forced her to look me in the eye. "I'm clean," I said. "Trust me."

She looked away. "Do it for me," she said in her smallest voice, "if you really love me."

In the end, I did it. I looked at her, crying, crying for me, and I looked at the thin sheet of plastic clinging to her, and I did it. She helped me into the thing, poked two holes for my nostrils, zipped the plastic zipper up the back, and pulled it tight over my head. It fit like a wetsuit. And the whole thing—the stroking and the tenderness and the gentle yielding—was everything I'd hoped it would be.

Almost.

She called me from work the next day. I was playing with sales figures and thinking of her. "Hello," I said, practically cooing into the receiver.

"You've got to hear this." Her voice was giddy with excitement.

"Hey," I said, cutting her off in a passionate whisper, "last night was really special."

"Oh, yes," she said, "yes, last night. It was. And I love you, I do . . ." She paused to draw in her breath. "But listen to this: I just got a piece from a man and his wife living among the Tuareg of Nigeria—these are the people who follow cattle around, picking up the dung for their cooking fires?"

I made a small noise of awareness.

"Well, they make their huts of dung too—isn't that wild? And guess what—when times are hard, when the crops fail and the cattle can barely stand up, you know what they eat?"

"Let me guess," I said. "Dung?"

She let out a whoop. "Yes! Yes! Isn't it too much? They *eat* dung!"

I'd been saving one for her, a disease a doctor friend had told me about. "Onchocerciasis," I said. "You know it?"

There was a thrill in her voice. "Tell me."

"South America and Africa both. A fly bites you and lays its eggs in your bloodstream and when the eggs hatch, the larvae—these little white worms—migrate to your eyeballs, right underneath the membrane there, so you can see them wriggling around."

There was a silence on the other end of the line.

"Breda?"

"That's sick," she said. "That's really sick."

But I thought—? I trailed off. "Sorry," I said.

"Listen," and the edge came back into her voice, "the reason I called is because I love you, I think I love you, and I want you to meet somebody."

"Sure," I said.

"I want you to meet Michael. Michael Maloney."

"Sure. Who's he?"

She hesitated, paused just a beat, as if she knew she was going too far. "My doctor," she said.

You have to work at love. You have to bend, make subtle adjustments, sacrifices— love is nothing without sacrifice. I went to Dr. Maloney. Why not? I'd eaten tofu, bantered about leprosy and bilharziasis as if I were immune, and made love in a bag. If it made Breda happy—if it eased the nagging fears that ate at her day and night—then it was worth it.

The doctor's office was in Scarsdale, in his home, a two-tone mock Tudor with a winding drive and oaks as old as my grandfather's Chrysler. He was a young man—late thirties, I guessed—with a red beard, shaved head, and a pair of oversized spectacles in clear plastic frames. He took me right away—the very day I called—and met me at the door himself. "Breda's told me about you," he said, leading me into the floodlit vault of his office. He looked at me appraisingly a moment, murmuring "Yes, yes" into his beard, and then, with the aid of his nurses, Miss Archibald and Miss Slivovitz, put me through a battery of tests that would have embarrassed an astronaut.

First, there were the measurements, including digital joints, maxilla, cranium, penis, and earlobe. Next, the rectal exam, the EEG and urine sample. And then the tests. Stress tests, patch tests, reflex tests, lung-capacity tests (I blew up yellow balloons till they popped, then breathed into a machine the size of a Hammond organ), the X-rays, sperm count, and a closely printed, twenty-four-page questionnaire that included sections on dream analysis, genealogy, and logic and reasoning. He drew blood too, of course—to test vital-organ function and exposure to disease. "We're testing for antibodies to over fifty diseases," he said, eyes dodging behind the walls of his lenses. "You'd be surprised how many people have been infected without even knowing it." I couldn't tell if he was joking or not. On the way out he took my arm and told me he'd have the results in a week.

That week was the happiest of my life. I was with Breda every night, and over the weekend we drove up to Vermont to stay at a hygiene center her cousin had told her about. We dined by candlelight—on real food—and afterward we donned the Saran Wrap suits and made joyous, sanitary love. I wanted more, of course—the touch of skin on skin—but I was fulfilled and I was happy. Go slow, I told myself. All things in time. One night, as we lay entwined in the big white fortress of her bed, I stripped back the hood of the plastic suit and asked her if she'd ever trust me enough to make love in the way of the centuries, raw and unprotected. She twisted free of her own wrapping and looked away, giving me that matchless patrician profile. "Yes," she said, her voice pitched low, "yes, of course. Once the results are in."

"Results?"

She turned to me, her eyes searching mine. "Don't tell me you've forgotten?"

I had. Carried away, intense, passionate, brimming with love, I'd forgotten.

"Silly you," she murmured, tracing the line of my lips with a slim, plastic-clad finger. "Does the name Michael Maloney ring a bell?"

And then the roof fell in.

I called and there was no answer. I tried her at work and her secretary said she was out. I left messages. She never called back. It was as if we'd never known one another, as if I were a stranger, a door-to-door salesman, a beggar on the street.

I took up a vigil in front of her house. For a solid week I sat in my parked car and watched the door with all the fanatic devotion of a pilgrim at a shrine. Nothing. She neither came nor went. I rang the phone off the hook, interrogated her friends, haunted the elevator, the hallway, and the reception room at her office. She'd disappeared.

Finally, in desperation, I called her cousin in Larchmont. I'd met her once—she was a homely, droopy-sweatered, baleful-looking girl who represented everything gone wrong in the genes that had come to such glorious fruition in Breda—and barely knew what to say to her. I'd made up a speech, something about how my mother was dying in Phoenix, the business was on the rocks, I was drinking too much and dwelling on thoughts of suicide, destruction, and final judgment, and I had to talk to Breda just one more time before the end, and did she by any chance know where she was? As it turned out, I didn't need the speech. Breda answered the phone.

"Breda, it's me," I choked. "I've been going crazy looking for you."

Silence.

"Breda, what's wrong? Didn't you get my messages?"

Her voice was halting, distant. "I can't see you anymore," she said.

"Can't see me?" I was stunned, hurt, angry. "What do you mean?"

"All those feet," she said.

"Feet?" It took me a minute to realize she was talking about the shoe business. "But I don't deal with anybody's feet—I work in an office. Like you. With air-conditioning and sealed windows. I haven't touched a foot since I was sixteen."

"Athlete's foot," she said. "Psoriasis. Eczema. Jungle rot."

"What is it? The physical?" My voice cracked with outrage. "Did I flunk the damn physical? Is that it?"

She wouldn't answer me.

A chill went through me. "What did he say? What did the son of a bitch say?"

There was a distant ticking over the line, the pulse of time and space, the gentle sway of Bell Telephone's hundred million miles of wire.

"Listen," I pleaded, "see me one more time, just once—that's all I ask. We'll talk it over. We could go on a picnic. In the park. We could spread a blanket and, and we could sit on opposite corners—"

"Lyme disease," she said.

"Lyme disease?"

"Spread by tick bite. They're seething in the grass. You get Bell's palsy, meningitis, the lining of your brain swells up like dough."

"Rockefeller Center then," I said. "By the fountain."

Her voice was dead. "Pigeons," she said. "They're like flying rats."

"Helmut's. We can meet at Helmut's. Please. I love you."

"I'm sorry."

"Breda, please listen to me. We were so close—"

"Yes," she said, "we were close," and I thought of that first night in her apartment, the boy in the bubble and the Saran Wrap suit, thought of the whole dizzy spectacle of our romance till her voice came down like a hammer on the refrain, "but not that close."

(1987)

IKE AND NINA

The years have put a lid on it, the principals passed into oblivion. I think I can now, in good conscience, reveal the facts surrounding one of the most secretive and spectacular love affairs of our time: the *affaire de coeur* that linked the thirty-fourth president of the United States and the then first lady of the Soviet Union. Yes: the eagle and the bear, defrosting the Cold War with the heat of their passion, Dwight D. Eisenhower—Ike—virile, dashing, athletic, in the arms of Madame Nina Khrushcheva, the svelte and seductive schoolmistress from the Ukraine. Behind closed doors, in embassy restrooms and hotel corridors, they gave themselves over to the urgency of their illicit love, while the peace and stability of the civilized world hung in the balance.

Because of the sensitive—indeed sensational—nature of what follows, I have endeavored to tell my story as dispassionately as possible, and must say in my own defense that my sole interest in coming forward at this late date is to provide succeeding generations with a keener insight into the events of those tumultuous times. Some of you will be shocked by what I report here, others moved. Still others—the inevitable naysayers and skeptics—may find it difficult to believe. But before you turn a deaf ear, let me remind you how unthinkable it once seemed to credit reports of Errol Flynn's flirtation with Nazis and homosexuals, FDR's thirty-year obsession with Lucy Mercer, or Ted Kennedy's overmastering desire for an ingenuous campaign worker eleven years his junior. The truth is often hard to swallow. But no historian worth his salt, no self-respecting journalist, no faithful eyewitness to the earthshaking and epoch-making events of human history has ever blanched at it.

Here then, is the story of Ike and Nina.

■   ■   ■

In September of 1959, I was assistant to one of Ike's junior staffers, thirty-one years old, schooled in international law, and a consultant to the Slavic-languages program at one of our major universities.* I'd had very little contact with the president, had in fact laid eyes on him but twice in the eighteen months I'd worked for the White House (the first time, I was looking for a drinking fountain when I caught a glimpse of him—a single flash of his radiant brow—huddled in a back room with Foster Dulles and Andy Goodpaster; a week later, as I was hurrying down a corridor with a stack of reports for shredding, I spotted him slipping out a service entrance with his golf clubs). Like dozens of bright, ambitious young men apprenticed to the mighty, I was at this stage of my career a mere functionary, a paper shuffler, so deeply buried in the power structure I must actually have ranked below the pastry chef's croissant twister. I was good—I had no doubt of it—but I was as yet untried, and for all I knew unnoticed. You can imagine my surprise when early one morning I was summoned to the Oval Office.

It was muggy, and though the corridors hummed with the gentle ministrations of the air conditioners, my shirt was soaked through by the time I reached the door of the president's inner sanctum. A crewcut ramrod in uniform swung open the door, barked out my name, and ushered me into the room. I was puzzled, apprehensive, awed; the door closed behind me with a soft click and I found myself in the Oval Office, alone with the president of the United States. Ike was standing at the window, gazing out at the trees, whistling "The Flirtation Waltz," and turning a book of crossword puzzles over in his hands. "Well," he said, turning to me and extending his hand, "Mr. Paderewski, is that right?"

"Yes sir," I said. He pronounced it "Paderooski."†

"Well," he repeated, taking me in with those steely blue eyes of his as he sauntered across the room and tossed the book on his desk like a slugger casually dropping his bat after knocking the ball out of the park. He looked like a golf pro, a gymnast, a competitor, a man who could come at you with both hands and a nine iron to boot. Don't be taken in by all those accounts of his declining health—I saw him there that September morning in the Oval Office, broad-shouldered and trim-waisted, lithe and commanding. Successive heart attacks and a bout with ileitis hadn't slowed the old warrior a bit. A couple of weeks short of his sixty-ninth birthday, and he was jaunty as a high-schooler on prom night. Which brings me back to the reason for my summons.

"You're a good egg, aren't you, Paderewski?" Ike asked.

I replied in the affirmative.

*I choose not to name it, just as I decline to reveal my actual identity here, for obvious reasons.
†This is a pseudonym I've adopted as a concession to dramatic necessity in regard to the present narrative.

"And you speak Russian, is that right?"

"Yes, sir, Mr. President—and Polish, Sorbian, Serbo-Croatian, and Slovene as well."

He grunted, and eased his haunch down on the corner of the desk. The light from the window played off his head till it glowed like a second sun. "You're aware of the upcoming visit of the Soviet premier and his, uh, wife?"

I nodded.

"Good, that's very good, Paderewski, because as of this moment I'm appointing you my special aide for the duration of that visit." He looked at me as if I were some odd and insignificant form of life that might bear further study under the microscope, looked at me like the man who had driven armies across Europe and laid Hitler in his grave. "Everything that happens, every order I give you, is to be held strictly confidential—top secret—is that understood?"

I was filled with a sense of mission, importance, dignity. Here I was, elevated from the ranks to lend my modest talents to the service of the first citizen of the nation, the commander-in-chief himself. "Understood, Mr. President," I said, fighting the impulse to salute.

This seemed to relax him, and he leaned back on the desk and told me a long, involved story about an article he'd come across in the *National Geographic*, something about Egyptian pyramids and how the members of a pharaoh's funeral procession were either blinded on the spot or entombed with their leaders—something along those lines. I didn't know what to make of it. So I put on my meditative look, and when he finished I flashed him a smile that would have melted ice.

Ike smiled back.

By now, of course, I'm sure you've guessed just what my special duties were to consist of—I was to be the president's liaison with Mrs. Khrushchev, a go-between, a pillow smoother and excuse maker: I was to be Ike's panderer. Looking back on it, I can say in all honesty that I did not then, nor do I now, feel any qualms whatever regarding my role in the affair. No, I feel privileged to have witnessed one of the grand passions of our time, a love both tender and profane, a love that smoldered beneath the watchful eyes of two embattled nations and erupted in an explosion of passionate embraces and hungry kisses.

Ike, as I was later to learn, had first fallen under the spell of Madame K. in 1945, during his triumphal visit to Moscow after the fall of the Third Reich. It was the final day of his visit, a momentous day, the day Japan had thrown in the towel and the great war was at long last ended. Ambassador Harriman arranged a reception and buffet supper at the U.S. embassy by way of celebration, and to honor Ike and his comrade-in-arms, Marshal Zhukov. In addition to Ike's small party, a number of high-ranking Russian military men and politicos turned out for what evolved into an uproarious evening of singing, dancing, and congratulatory back-slapping. Corks popped, vodka flowed, the exuberant clamor of voices filled the room. And then Nina Khrushcheva stepped through the door.

Ike was stunned. Suddenly nothing existed for him—not Zhukov, not Moscow, not Harriman, the armistice, or "The Song of the Volga Boatmen," which an instant before had been ringing in his ears—there was only this vision in the doorway, simple, unadorned, elegant, this true princess of the earth. He didn't know what to say, didn't know who she was; the only words of Russian he could command—*zdrav'st* and *spasibo**—flew to his lips like an unanswered prayer. He begged Harriman for an introduction, and then spent the rest of the evening at her side, the affable Ike, gazing into the quiet depths of her rich mud-brown eyes, entranced. He didn't need an interpreter.

It would be ten long years before their next meeting, years that would see the death of Stalin, the ascendancy of Khrushchev, and Ike's own meteoric rise to political prominence as the thirty-fourth president of the United States. Through all that time, through all the growing enmity between their countries, Ike and Nina cherished that briefest memory of one another. For his part, Ike felt he had seen a vision, sipped from the cup of perfection, and that no other woman could hope to match it—not Mamie, not Ann Whitman, nor even his old flame, the lovely and adept Kay Summersby. He plowed through CIA dossiers on this captivating spirit, Nina Petrovna, wife of the Soviet premier, maintained a scrapbook crammed with photos of her and news clippings detailing her husband's movements; twice, at the risk of everything, he was able to communicate with her through the offices of a discreet and devoted agent of the CIA. In July of 1955, he flew to Geneva, hungering for peaceful coexistence.

At the Geneva Conference, the two came together once again, and what had begun ten years earlier as a riveting infatuation blossomed into the mature and passionate love that would haunt them the rest of their days. Ike was sixty-five, in his prime, the erect warrior, the canny leader, a man who could shake off a stroke as if it were a head cold; Nina, ten years his junior, was in the flush of womanly maturity, lovely, solid, a soft inscrutable smile playing on her elfin lips. With a subterfuge that would have tied the intelligence networks of their respective countries in knots, the two managed to steal ten minutes here, half an hour there—they managed, despite the talks, the dinners, the receptions, and the interminable, stultifying rounds of speechmaking, to appease their desire and sanctify their love forever. "Without personal contact," Ike said at a dinner for the Russian delegation, his boyish blue eyes fixed on Mrs. Khrushchev, "you might imagine someone was fourteen feet high, with horns and a tail." Russians and Americans alike burst into spontaneous laughter and applause. Nina Petrovna, first lady of the Soviet Union, stared down at her chicken Kiev and blushed.

*"Hello" and "thank you."

■ ■ ■

And so, when the gargantuan Soviet TU 114 shrieked into Andrews Air Force Base in September of 1959, I stood by my president with a lump in my throat: I alone knew just how much the Soviet visit meant to him, I alone knew by how tenuous a thread hung the balance of world peace. What could the president have been thinking as the great sleek jet touched down? I can only conjecture. Perhaps he was thinking that she'd forgotten him, or that the scrutiny of the press would make it impossible for them to steal their precious few moments together, or that her husband—that torpedo-headed bully boy—would discover them and tear the world to pieces with his rage. Consider Ike at that moment, consider the all-but-insurmountable barriers thrown in his way, and you can appreciate my calling him one of the truly impassioned lovers of all time. Romeo had nothing on him, nor Douglas Fairbanks either—even the starry-eyed Edward Windsor pales by comparison. At any rate, he leaped at his opportunity like a desert nomad delivered to the oasis: there would be an assignation that very night, and I was to be instrumental in arranging it.

After the greeting ceremonies at Andrews, during which Ike could do no more than exchange smiles and handshakes with the premier and premiersha, there was a formal state dinner at the White House. Ambassador Menshikov was there, Khrushchev and his party, Ike and Mamie, Christian Herter, Dick Nixon, and others; afterward, the ladies retired to the Red Room for coffee. I sat at Ike's side throughout dinner, and lingered in the hallway outside the Red Room directly thereafter. At dinner, Ike had kissed Madame K.'s hand and chatted animatedly with her for a few minutes, but they covered their emotions so well that no one would have guessed they were anything other than amenable strangers wearing their social faces. Only I knew better.

I caught the premiersha as she and Mamie emerged from the Red Room in a burst of photographers' flashbulbs. As instructed, I took her arm and escorted her to the East Room, for the program of American songs that would highlight the evening. I spoke to her in Russian, though to my surprise she seemed to have a rudimentary grasp of conversational English (did she recall it from her schoolteaching days, or had she boned up for Ike?). Like a Cyrano, I told her that the president yearned for her tragically, that he'd thought of nothing else in the four years since Geneva, and then I recited a love poem he'd written her in English— I can't recall the sense of it now, but it boiled with Elizabethan conceits and the imagery of war, with torn hearts, manned bastions, and references to heavy ordnance, pillboxes, and scaling the heights of love. Finally, just before we entered the East Room, I pressed a slip of paper into her hand. It read, simply: *3:00 A.M., back door, Blair House.*

At five of three, in a rented, unmarked limousine, the president and I pulled up at the curb just down the street from Blair House, where the Khrushchev party had been installed for the night. I was driving. The rear panel slid back and the president's voice leaped at me out of the darkness: "Okay, Paderewski, do your stuff—and good luck."

I eased out of the car and started up the walk. The night was warm and damp, the darkness a cloak, street lights dulled as if they'd been shaded for the occasion. Every shadow was of course teeming with Secret Service agents— there were enough of them ringing the house to fill Memorial Stadium twice over—but they gave way for me. (Ike had arranged it thus: one person was to be allowed to enter the rear of Blair House at the stroke of three; two would be leaving an instant thereafter.)

She was waiting for me at the back door, dressed in pants and a man's over-coat and hat. "Madame Khrushcheva?" I whispered. *"Da,"* came the reply, soft as a kiss. We hurried across the yard and I handed her into the car, admiring Ike's cleverness: if anyone—including the legion of Secret Service, CIA, and FBI men—had seen us, they would have mistaken the madame for her husband and concluded that Ike had set up a private, ultrasecret conference. I slid into the driver's seat and Ike's voice, shaken with emotion, came at me again: "Drive, Paderewski," he said. "Drive us to the stars." And then the panel shot to with a passionate click.

For two hours I circled the capitol, and then, as prearranged, I returned to Blair House and parked just down the street. I could hear them—Ike and Nina, whispering, embracing, rustling clothing—as I cut the engine. She giggled. Ike was whistling. She giggled again, a lovely windchime of a sound, musical and coltish—if I hadn't known better I would have thought Ike was back there with a coed. I was thinking with some satisfaction that we'd just about pulled it off when the panel slid back and Ike said: "Okay, Paderewski—let's hit it." There was the sound of a protracted kiss, a sound we all recognize not so much through experience—who's listening, after all?—but thanks to the attention Hollywood sound men have given it. Then Ike's final words to her, delivered in a passionate susurrus, words etched in my memory as if in stone; "Till we meet again," he whispered.

Something odd happened just then, just as I swung back the door for Mrs. Khrushchev: a car was moving along the street in the opposite direction, a for-eign car, and it slowed as she stepped from the limousine. Just that—it slowed— and nothing more. I hardly remarked it at the time, but that instant was to reverberate in history. The engine ticked up the street, crickets chirruped. With all dispatch, I got Mrs. Khrushchev round back of Blair House, saw her in the door, and returned to the limousine.

"Well done, Paderewski, well done," Ike said as I put the car in drive and headed up the street, and then he did something he hadn't done in years—lit a cigarette. I watched the glow of the match in the rearview mirror, and then he was exhaling with rich satisfaction, as if he'd just come back from swimming the Potomac or taming a mustang in one of those televised cigarette ads. "The White House," he said. "Chop-chop."

■ ■ ■

Six hours later, Madame K. appeared with her husband on the front steps of Blair House and fielded questions from reporters. She wore a modest gray silk chemise and a splash of lipstick. One of the reporters asked her what she was most interested in seeing while touring the U.S., and she glanced over at her husband before replying (he was grinning to show off his pointed teeth, as impervious to English as he might have been to Venusian). "Whatever is of biggest interest to Mr. Khrushchev," she said. The reporters lapped it up: flashbulbs popped, a flurry of stories went out over the wire. Who would have guessed?

From there, the Khrushchevs took a special VIP train to New York, where Madame K. attended a luncheon at the Waldorf and her husband harangued a group of business magnates in Averell Harriman's living room. "The Moscow Cha-Cha" and Jimmy Driftwood's "The Bear Flew Over the Ocean" blared from every radio in town, and a special squad of NYPD's finest—six-footers, experts in jujitsu and marksmanship—formed a human wall around the premier and his wife as they took in the sights of the Big Apple. New York rolled out the red carpet, and the Khrushchevs trod it with a stately satisfaction that rapidly gave way to finger-snapping, heel-kicking glee. As the premier boarded the plane for Los Angeles, Nina at his side, he mugged for cameras, kissed babies, and shook hands so assiduously he might have been running for office.

And then the bottom fell out.

In Los Angeles, ostensibly because he was nettled at Mayor Paulson's hard-line speech and because he discovered that Disneyland would not be on his itinerary, the raging, tabletop-pounding, Magyar-cowing Khrushchev came to the fore: he threw a tantrum. The people of the United States were inhospitable boors—they'd invited him to fly halfway round the world simply to abuse him. He'd had enough. He was curtailing the trip and heading back to Moscow.

I was with Ike when the first reports of the premier's explosion flashed across the TV screen. Big-bellied and truculent, Khrushchev was lecturing the nation on points of etiquette, jowls atremble, fists beating the air, while Nina, her head bowed, stood meekly at his side. Ike's voice was so pinched it could have come from a ventriloquist's dummy: "My God," he whispered, "he knows." (I suddenly remembered the car slowing, the flash of a pale face behind the darkened glass, and thought of Alger Hiss, the Rosenbergs, the vast network of Soviet spies operating unchecked in the land of the free: they'd seen her after all.) Shaking his head, Ike got up, crossed the room, and lit another verboten cigarette. He looked weary, immeasurably old, Rip Van Winkle waking beside his rusted gun. "Well, Paderewski," he sighed, a blue haze playing round the wisps of silver hair at his temples, "I guess now the shit's really going to hit the fan."

He was right, but only partially. To his credit, Khrushchev covered himself like a trouper—after all, how could he reveal so shocking and outrageous a business as this without losing face himself, without transforming himself in that instant from the virile, bellicose, iron-fisted ruler of the Soviet masses to a pudgy, pathetic cuckold? He allowed himself to be mollified by apologies from Paulson and Cabot Lodge over the supposed insult, posed for a photograph with Shirley MacLaine at Twentieth Century–Fox, and then flew on to San Francisco for a tense visit. He made a dilatory stop in Iowa on his way back to Washington and the inevitable confrontation with the man who had suddenly emerged as his rival in love as well as ideology. (I'm sure you recall the celebrated photographs in *Life*, *Look*, and *Newsweek*—Khrushchev leering at a phallic ear of corn, patting the belly of a crewcut interloper at the Garst farm in Iowa, hefting a piglet by the scruff of its neck. Study them today—especially in contrast to the pre–Los Angeles photos—and you'll be struck by the mixture of jealous rage and incomprehension playing across the premier's features, and the soft, tragic, downcast look in his wife's eyes.)

I sat beside the president on the way out to Camp David for the talks that would culminate the Khrushchev visit. He was subdued, desolated, the animation gone out of his voice. He'd planned for these talks as he'd planned for the European Campaign, devising stratagems and feints, studying floorplans, mapping the territory, confident he could spirit away his inamorata for an idyllic hour or two beneath the pines. Now there was no chance of it. No chance, in fact, that he'd ever see her again. He was slumped in his seat, his head thrown back against the bullet-proof glass as if he no longer had the will to hold it up. And then—I've never seen anything so moving, so emotionally ravaging, in my life— he began to cry. I offered him my handkerchief but he motioned me away, great wet heaving sobs tearing at his lungs, the riveting blue eyes that had gazed with equanimity on the most heinous scenes of devastation known to civilized man reddened with a sorrow beyond despair. "Nina," he choked, and buried his face in his hands.

You know the rest. The "tough" talks at Camp David (ostensibly over the question of the Berlin Wall), the Soviet premier's postponement of Ike's reciprocal visit till the spring, "when things are in bloom," the eventual rescinding of the invitation altogether, and the virulent anti-Eisenhower speech Khrushchev delivered in the wake of the U-2 incident. Then there was Ike's final year in office, his loss of animation, his heart troubles (*heart troubles*—could anything be more ironic?), the way in which he so rapidly and visibly aged, as if each moment of each day weighed on him like an eternity. And finally, our last picture of him: the affable, slightly foggy old duffer chasing a white ball across the links as if it were some part of himself he'd misplaced.

As for myself, I was rapidly demoted after the Khrushchev visit—it almost seemed as if I were an embarrassment to Ike, and in a way I guess I was, having seen him with his defenses down and his soul laid bare. I left the government a few months later and have pursued a rewarding academic career ever since, and am in fact looking forward to qualifying for tenure in the upcoming year. It has been a rich and satisfying life, one that has had its ups and downs, its years of quotidian existence and its few breathless moments at the summit of human history. Through it all, through all the myriad events I've witnessed, the loves I've known, the emotions stirred in my breast by the tragic events of our times, I can say with a sense of reverent gratitude and the deepest sincerity that nothing has so moved and tenderly astonished me as the joy, the sorrow, the epic sweep of the star-crossed love of Ike and Nina. I think of the Cold War, of nuclear proliferation, of Hungary, Korea, and the U-2 incident, and it all finally pales beside this: he loved her, and she loved him.

(1981)

SORRY FUGU

"Limp radicchio."

"Sorry fugu."

"A blasphemy of baby lamb's lettuce, frisée, endive."

"A coulibiac made in hell."

For six months he knew her only by her by-line—Willa Frank—and by the sting of her adjectives, the derisive thrust of her metaphors, the cold precision of her substantives. Regardless of the dish, despite the sincerity and ingenuity of the chef and the freshness or rarity of the ingredients, she seemed always to find it wanting. "The duck had been reduced to the state of the residue one might expect to find in the nether depths of a funerary urn"; "For all its rather testy piquancy, the orange sauce might just as well have been citron preserved in pickling brine"; "Paste and pasta. Are they synonymous? Hardly. But one wouldn't have known the difference at Udolpho's. The 'fresh' angel hair had all the taste and consistency of mucilage."

Albert quailed before those caustic pronouncements, he shuddered and blanched and felt his stomach drop like a croquette into a vat of hot grease. On the morning she skewered Udolpho's, he was sitting over a cup of reheated espresso and nibbling at a wedge of hazelnut dacquoise that had survived the previous night's crush. As was his habit on Fridays, he'd retrieved the paper from the mat, got himself a bite, and then, with the reckless abandon of a diver plunging into an icy lake, turned to the "Dining Out" column. On alternate weeks, Willa Frank yielded to the paper's other regular reviewer, a bighearted, appreciative woman by the name of Leonora Merganser, who approached every restaurant like a mother of eight feted by her children on Mother's Day, and whose praise gushed forth in a breathless salivating stream that washed the reader out of his chair and up against the telephone stand, where he would dial frantically for a reservation. But this was Willa Frank's week. And Willa Frank never liked anything.

With trembling fingers—it was only a matter of time before she slipped like a spy, like a murderess, into D'Angelo's and filleted him like all the others—he smoothed out the paper and focused on the bold black letters of the headline:

UDOLPHO'S: TROGLODYTIC CUISINE IN A CAVELIKE ATMOSPHERE

He read on, heart in mouth. She'd visited the restaurant on three occasions, once in the company of an abstract artist from Detroit, and twice with her regular companion, a young man so discerning she referred to him only as "The Palate." On all three occasions, she'd been—sniff—disappointed. The turn-of-the-century gas lamps Udolpho's grandfather had brought over from Naples hadn't appealed to her ("so dark we joked that it was like dining among Neanderthals in the sub-basement of their cave"), nor had the open fire in the massive stone fireplace that dominated the room ("smoky, and stinking of incinerated chestnuts"). And then there was the food. When Albert got to the line about the pasta, he couldn't go on. He folded the paper as carefully as he might have folded the winding sheet over Udolpho's broken body and set it aside.

It was then that Marie stepped through the swinging doors to the kitchen, the wet cloth napkin she'd been using as a dishrag clutched in her hand. "Albert?" she gasped, darting an uneasy glance from his stricken face to the newspaper. "Is anything wrong? Did she—? Today?"

She assumed the worst, and now he corrected her in a drawl so lugubrious it might have been his expiring breath: "Udolpho's."

"Udolpho's?" Relief flooded her voice, but almost immediately it gave way to disbelief and outrage. "Udolpho's?" she repeated.

He shook his head sadly. For thirty years Udolpho's had reigned supreme among West Side restaurants, a place impervious to fads and trends, never chic but steady—classy in a way no nouvelle *mangerie* with its pastel walls and Breuer chairs could ever hope to be. Cagney had eaten here, Durante, Roy Rogers, Anna Maria Alberghetti. It was a shrine, an institution.

Albert himself, a pudgy sorrowful boy of twelve, ridiculed for his flab and the great insatiable fist of his appetite, had experienced the grand epiphany of his life in one of Udolpho's dark, smoky, and—for him, at least—forever exotic banquettes. Sampling the vermicelli with oil, garlic, olives, and forest mushrooms, the osso buco with the little twists of bow-tie pasta that drank up its buttery juices, he knew just as certainly as Alexander must have known he was born to conquer, that he, Albert D'Angelo, was born to eat. And that far from being something to be ashamed of, it was glorious, avocation and vocation both, the highest pinnacle to which he could aspire. Other boys had their Snider, their

Mays, their Reese and Mantle, but for Albert the magical names were Pellaprat, Escoffier, Udolpho Melanzane.

Yes. And now Udolpho was nothing. Willa Frank had seen to that.

Marie was bent over the table now, reading, her piping girlish voice hot with indignation.

"Where does she come off, anyway?" Albert shrugged. Since he'd opened D'Angelo's eighteen months ago the press had all but ignored him. Yes, he'd had a little paragraph in *Barbed Wire*, the alternative press weekly handed out on street corners by greasy characters with straight pins through their noses, but you could hardly count that. There was only one paper that really mattered— Willa Frank's paper—and while word of mouth was all right, without a review in *the* paper, you were dead. Problem was, if Willa Frank wrote you up, you were dead anyway.

"Maybe you'll get the other one," Marie said suddenly. "What's her name— the good one."

Albert's lips barely moved. "Leonora Merganser."

"Well, you could."

"I want Willa Frank," he growled.

Marie's brow lifted. She closed the paper and came to him, rocked back from his belly, and pecked a kiss to his beard. "You can't be serious?"

Albert glanced bitterly around the restaurant, the simple pine tables, white-washed walls, potted palms soft in the filtered morning light. "Leonora Merganser would faint over the Hamburger Hamlet on the corner, Long John Silver's, anything. Where's the challenge in that?"

"Challenge? But we don't want a challenge, honey—we want business. Don't we? I mean if we're going to get married and all—"

Albert sat heavily, took a miserable sip of his stone-cold espresso. "I'm a great chef, aren't I?" There was something in his tone that told her it wasn't ex-actly a rhetorical question.

"Honey, baby," she was in his lap now, fluffing his hair, peering into his ear, "of course you are. The best. The very best. But—"

"Willa Frank," he rumbled. "Willa Frank. I want her."

There are nights when it all comes together, when the monkfish is so fresh it flakes on the grill, when the pesto tastes like the wind through the pines and the party of eight gets their seven appetizers and six entrées in palettes of rising steam and delicate colors so perfect they might have been a single diner sitting down to a single dish. This night, however, was not such a night. This was a night when everything went wrong.

First of all, there was the aggravating fact that Eduardo—the Chilean waiter who'd learned, à la Chico Marx, to sprinkle superfluous "ahs" through his speech and thus pass for Italian—was late. This put Marie off her pace vis-à-vis the desserts, for which she was solely responsible, since she had to seat and serve the first half-dozen customers. Next, in rapid succession, Albert found that he was out of mesquite for the grill, sun-dried tomatoes for the fusilli with funghi, capers, black olives, and, yes, sun-dried tomatoes, and that the fresh cream for the frittata piemontese had mysteriously gone sour. And then, just when he'd managed to recover his equilibrium and was working in that translated state where mind and body are one, Roque went berserk.

Of the restaurant's five employees—Marie, Eduardo, Torrey, who did day cleanup, Albert himself, and Roque—Roque operated on perhaps the most elemental level. He was the dishwasher. The Yucateco dishwasher. Whose responsibility it was to see that D'Angelo's pink and gray sets of heavy Syracuse china were kept in constant circulation through the mid-evening dinner rush. On this particular night, however, Roque was slow to accept the challenge of that responsibility, scraping plates and wielding the nozzle of his supersprayer as if in a dream. And not only was he moving slowly, the dishes, with their spatters of red and white sauce and dribbles of grease piling up beside him like the Watts Towers, but he was muttering to himself. Darkly. In a dialect so arcane even Eduardo couldn't fathom it.

When Albert questioned him—a bit too sharply, perhaps: he was overwrought himself—Roque exploded. All Albert had said was, "Roque—you all right?" But he might just as well have reviled his mother, his fourteen sisters, and his birthplace. Cursing, Roque danced back from the stainless-steel sink, tore the apron from his chest, and began scaling dishes against the wall. It took all of Albert's two hundred twenty pounds, together with Eduardo's one-eighty, to get Roque, who couldn't have weighed more than one-twenty in hip boots, out the door and into the alley. Together they slammed the door on him—the door on which he continued to beat with a shoe for half an hour or more—while Marie took up the dishrag with a sigh.

A disaster. Pure, unalloyed, unmitigated. The night was a disaster.

Albert had just begun to catch up when Torrey slouched through the alley door and into the kitchen, her bony hand raised in greeting. Torrey was pale and shrunken, a nineteen-year-old with a red butch cut who spoke with the rising inflection and oblate vowels of the Valley Girl, born and bred. She wanted an advance on her salary.

"Momento, momento," Albert said, flashing past her with a pan of béarnaise in one hand, a mayonnaise jar of vivid orange sea-urchin roe in the other. He liked to use his rudimentary Italian when he was cooking. It made him feel impregnable.

Meanwhile, Torrey shuffled halfheartedly across the floor and positioned herself behind the porthole in the "out" door, where, for lack of anything better to do, she could watch the customers eat, drink, smoke, and finger their pastry. The béarnaise was puddling up beautifully on a plate of grilled baby summer squash, the roe dolloped on a fillet of monkfish nestled snug in its cruet, and Albert was thinking of offering Torrey battle pay if she'd stay and wash dishes, when she let out a low whistle. This was no cab or encore whistle, but the sort of whistle that expresses surprise or shock—a "Holy cow!" sort of whistle. It stopped Albert cold. Something bad was about to happen, he knew it, just as surely as he knew that the tiny hairs rimming his bald spot had suddenly stiffened up like hackles.

"What?" he demanded. "What is it?"

Torrey turned to him, slow as an executioner. "I see you got Willa Frank out there tonight—everything going okay?"

The monkfish burst into flame, the béarnaise turned to water, Marie dropped two cups of coffee and a plate of homemade millefoglie.

No matter. In an instant, all three of them were pressed up against the little round window, as intent as torpedoers peering through a periscope. "Which one?" Albert hissed, his heart doing paradiddles.

"Over there?" Torrey said, making it a question. "With Jock—Jock Mc-Namee? The one with the blond wig?"

Albert looked, but he couldn't see. "Where? Where?" he cried.

"There? In the corner?"

In the corner, in the corner. Albert was looking at a young woman, a girl, a blonde in a black cocktail dress and no brassiere, seated across from a hulking giant with a peroxide-streaked flattop. "Where?" he repeated.

Torrey pointed.

"The blonde?" He could feel Marie go slack beside him. "But that can't be—" Words failed him. *This* was Willa Frank, doyenne of taste, grande dame of haute cuisine, ferreter out of the incorrect, the underachieved, and the unfortunate? And this clod beside her, with the great smooth-working jaw and forearms like pillars, *this* was the possessor of the fussiest, pickiest, most sophisticated and fastidious palate in town? No, it was impossible.

"Like I know him, you know?" Torrey was saying. "Jock? Like from the Anti-Club and all that scene?"

But Albert wasn't listening. He was watching her—Willa Frank—as transfixed as the tailorbird that dares look into the cobra's eye. She was slim, pretty, eyes dark as a houri's, a lot of jewelry—not at all what he'd expected. He'd pictured a veiny elegant woman in her fifties, starchy, patrician, from Boston or Newport or some such place. But wait, wait: Eduardo was just setting the plates down—she was the Florentine tripe, of course—a good dish, a dish he'd stand by any day, even a bad one like . . . but the Palate, what was he having? Albert strained forward, and he could feel Marie's lost and limp hand feebly pressing his own. There: the veal piccata, yes, a very good dish, an outstanding dish. Yes. Yes.

Eduardo bowed gracefully away. The big man in the punk hairdo bent to his plate and sniffed. Willa Frank—blond, delicious, lethal—cut into the tripe, and raised the fork to her lips.

■ ■ ■

"She hated it. I know it. I know it." Albert rocked back and forth in his chair, his face buried in his hands, the toque clinging to his brow like a carrion bird. It was past midnight, the restaurant was closed. He sat amidst the wreckage of the kitchen, the waste, the slop, the smell of congealed grease and dead spices, and his breath came in ragged sobbing gasps.

Marie got up to rub the back of his neck. Sweet, honey-complected Marie with her firm heavy arms and graceful wrists, the spill and generosity of her flesh—his consolation in a world of Willa Franks. "It's okay," she kept saying, over and over, her voice a soothing murmur, "it's okay, it was good, it was."

He'd failed and he knew it. Of all nights, why this one? Why couldn't she have come when the structure was there, when he was on, when the dishwasher was sober, the cream fresh, and the mesquite knots piled high against the wall, when he could concentrate, for christ's sake? "She didn't finish her tripe," he said, disconsolate. "Or the grilled vegetables. I saw the plate."

"She'll be back," Marie said. "Three visits minimum, right?"

Albert fished out a handkerchief and sorrowfully blew his nose. "Yeah," he said, "three strikes and you're out." He twisted his neck to look up at her. "The Palate, Jock, whatever the jerk's name is, he didn't touch the veal. One bite maybe. Same with the pasta. Eduardo said the only thing he ate was the bread. And a bottle of beer."

"What does he know," Marie said. "Or her either."

Albert shrugged. He pushed himself up wearily, impaled on the stake of his defeat, and helped himself to a glass of Orvieto and a plate of leftover sweet-breads. "Everything," he said miserably, the meat like butter in his mouth, fragrant, nutty, inexpressibly right. He shrugged again. "Or nothing. What does it matter? Either way we get screwed."

"And 'Frank'? What kind of name is that, anyhow? German? Is that it?" Marie was on the attack now, pacing the linoleum like a field marshal probing for a weakness in the enemy lines, looking for a way in. "The Franks—weren't they those barbarians in high school that sacked Rome? Or was it Paris?"

Willa Frank. The name was bitter on his tongue. Willa, Willa, Willa. It was a bony name, scant and lean, stripped of sensuality, the antithesis of the round, full-bodied Leonora. It spoke of a knotty Puritan toughness, a denying of the flesh, no compromise in the face of temptation. Willa. How could he ever hope to seduce a Willa? And Frank. That was even worse. A man's name. Cold, forbidding, German, French. It was the name of a woman who wouldn't complicate her task with notions of charity or the sparing of feelings. No, it was the name of a woman who would wield her adjectives like a club.

Stewing in these sour reflections, eating and no longer tasting, Albert was suddenly startled by a noise outside the alley door. He picked up a saucepan and stalked across the room—What next? Were they planning to rob him now too, was that it?—and flung open the door.

In the dim light of the alleyway stood two small dark men, the smaller of whom looked so much like Roque he might have been a clone. "Hello," said the larger man, swiping a greasy Dodgers cap from his head. "I am called Raul, and this"—indicating his companion—"is called Fulgencio, cousin of Roque." At the mention of his name, Fulgencio smiled. "Roque is gone to Albuquerque," Raul continued, "and he is sorry. But he sends you his cousin, Fulgencio, to wash for you."

Albert stood back from the door, and Fulgencio, grinning and nodding, mimed the motion of washing a plate as he stepped into the kitchen. Still grinning, still miming, he sambaed across the floor, lifted the supersprayer from its receptacle as he might have drawn a rapier from its scabbard, and started in on the dishes with a vigor that would have prostrated his mercurial cousin.

For a long moment Albert merely stood there watching, barely conscious of Marie at his back and Raul's parting gesture as he gently shut the door. All of a sudden he felt redeemed, reborn, capable of anything. There was Fulgencio, a total stranger not two minutes ago, washing dishes as if he were born to it. And there was Marie, who'd stand by him if he had to cook cactus and lizard for the saints in the desert. And here he was himself, in all the vigor of his manhood, accomplished, knowledgeable, inspired, potentially one of the great culinary artists of his time. What was the matter with him? What was he crying about?

He'd wanted Willa Frank. All right: he'd gotten her. But on an off-night, the kind of night anyone could have. Out of mesquite. The cream gone sour, the dishwasher mad. Even Puck, even Soltner, couldn't have contended with that.

She'd be back. Twice more. And he would be ready for her.

All that week, a cloud of anticipation hung over the restaurant. Albert outdid himself, redefining the bounds of his nouvelle Northern Italian cuisine with a dozen new creations, including a very nice black pasta with grilled shrimp, a pungent jugged hare, and an absolutely devastating meadowlark marinated in shallots, white wine, and mint. He worked like a man possessed, a man inspired. Each night he offered seven appetizers and six entrées, and each night they were different. He outdid himself, and outdid himself again.

Friday came and went. The morning paper found Leonora Merganser puffing some Greek place in North Hollywood, heralding spanakopita as if it had been invented yesterday and discovering evidence of divine intervention in the folds of a grape leaf. Fulgencio scrubbed dishes with a passion, Eduardo worked on his accent and threw out his chest, Marie's desserts positively floated on air. And day by day, Albert rose to new heights.

It was on Tuesday of the following week—a quiet Tuesday, one of the quietest

Albert could remember—that Willa Frank appeared again. There were only two other parties in the restaurant, a skeletal septuagenarian with a professorial air and his granddaughter—at least Albert hoped she was his granddaughter—and a Beverly Hills couple who'd been coming in once a week since the place opened.

Her presence was announced by Eduardo, who slammed into the kitchen with a drawn face and a shakily scrawled cocktail order. "She's here," he whispered, and the kitchen fell silent. Fulgencio paused, sprayer in hand. Marie looked up from a plate of tortes. Albert, who'd been putting the finishing touches to a dish of sautéed scallops al pesto for the professor and a breast of duck with wild mushrooms for his granddaughter, staggered back from the table as if he'd been shot. Dropping everything, he rushed to the porthole for a glimpse of her.

It was his moment of truth, the moment in which his courage very nearly failed him. She was stunning. Glowing. As perfect and unapproachable as the plucked and haughty girls who looked out at him from the covers of magazines at the supermarket, icily elegant in a clingy silk chemise the color of béchamel. How could he, Albert D'Angelo, for all his talent and greatness of heart, ever hope to touch her, to move such perfection, to pique such jaded taste buds?

Wounded, he looked to her companions. Beside her, grinning hugely, as hearty, handsome, and bland as ever, was the Palate—he could expect no help from that quarter. And then he turned his eyes on the couple they'd brought with them, looking for signs of sympathy. He looked in vain. They were middle-aged, silver-haired, dressed to the nines, thin and stringy in the way of those who exercise inflexible control over their appetites, about as sympathetic as vigilantes. Albert understood then that it was going to be an uphill battle. He turned back to the grill, girded himself in a clean apron, and awaited the worst.

Marie fixed the drinks—two martinis, a Glenlivet neat for Willa, and a beer for the Palate. For appetizers they ordered mozzarella di buffala marinara, the caponata D'Angelo, the octopus salad, and the veal medallions with onion marmalade. Albert put his soul into each dish, arranged and garnished the plates with all the patient care and shimmering inspiration of a Toulouse-Lautrec bent over a canvas, and watched, defeated, as each came back to the kitchen half eaten. And then came the entrées. They ordered a selection—five different dishes—and Albert, after delivering them up to Eduardo with a face of stone, pressed himself to the porthole like a voyeur.

Riveted, he watched as they sat back so that Eduardo could present the dishes. He waited, but nothing happened. They barely glanced at the food. And then, as if by signal, they began passing the plates around the table. He was stunned: what did they think this was—the Imperial Dinner at Chow Foo Luck's? But then he understood: each dish had to suffer the scrutiny of the big man with the brutal jaw before they would deign to touch it. No one ate, no one spoke, no one lifted a glass of the Château Bellegrave, 1966, to his lips, until

Jock had sniffed, finger-licked, and then gingerly tasted each of Albert's creations. Willa sat rigid, her black eyes open wide, as the great-jawed, brush-headed giant leaned intently over the plate and rolled a bit of scallop or duck over his tongue. Finally, when all the dishes had circulated, the écrevisses Alberto came to rest, like a roulette ball, in front of the Palate. But he'd already snuffed it, already dirtied his fork in it. And now, with a grand gesture, he pushed the plate aside and called out in a hoarse voice for beer.

The next day was the blackest of Albert's life. There were two strikes against him, and the third was coming down the pike. He didn't know what to do. His dreams had been feverish, a nightmare of mincing truffles and reanimated pigs' feet, and he awoke with the wildest combinations on his lips—chopped pickles and shad roe, an onion-cinnamon mousse, black-eyed peas vinaigrette. He even, half-seriously, drew up a fantasy menu, a list of dishes no one had ever tasted, not sheiks or presidents. La Cuisine des Espèces en Danger, he would call it. Breast of California condor aux chanterelles; snail darter à la meunière; medallions of panda alla campagnola. Marie laughed out loud when he presented her with the menu that afternoon—"I've invented a new cuisine!" he shouted—and for a moment, the pall lifted.

But just as quickly, it descended again. He knew what he had to do. He had to speak to her, his severest critic, through the medium of his food. He had to translate for her, awaken her with a kiss. But how? How could he even begin to rouse her from her slumber when that clod stood between them like a watchdog?

As it turned out, the answer was closer at hand than he could have imagined.

It was late the next afternoon—Thursday, the day before Willa Frank's next hatchet job was due to appear in the paper—and Albert sat at a table in the back of the darkened restaurant, brooding over his menu. He was almost certain she'd be in for her final visit that night, and yet he still hadn't a clue as to how he was going to redeem himself. For a long while he sat there in his misery, absently watching Torrey as she probed beneath the front tables with the wand of her vacuum. Behind him, in the kitchen, sauces were simmering, a veal loin roasting; Marie was baking bread and Fulgencio stacking wood. He must have watched Torrey for a full five minutes before he called out to her. "Torrey!" he shouted over the roar of the vacuum. "Torrey, shut that thing off a minute, will you?"

The roar died to a wheeze, then silence. Torrey looked up.

"This guy, what's his name, Jock—what do you know about him?" He glanced down at the scrawled-over menu and then up again. "I mean, you don't know what he likes to eat, by any chance, do you?"

Torrey shambled across the floor, scratching the stubble of her head. She was wearing a torn flannel shirt three sizes too big for her. There was a smear of grease under her left eye. It took her a moment, tongue caught in the corner of her mouth, her brow furrowed in deliberation. "Plain stuff, I guess," she said finally, with a shrug of her shoulders. "Burned steak, potatoes with the skins on, boiled peas, and that—the kind of stuff his mother used to make. You know, like shanty Irish?"

Albert was busy that night—terrifically busy, the place packed—and when Willa Frank and her Palate sauntered in at nine-fifteen, he was ready for them. They had reservations (under an assumed name, of course—M. Cavil, party of two), and Eduardo was able to seat them immediately. In he came, breathless, the familiar phrase like a tocsin on his lips—"She's here!"—and out he fluttered again, with the drinks: one Glenlivet neat, one beer. Albert never glanced up.

On the stove, however, was a smallish pot. And in the pot were three tough scarred potatoes, eyes and dirt-flecked skin intact, boiling furiously; in and amongst them, dancing in the roiling water, were the contents of a sixteen-ounce can of Mother Hubbard's discount peas. Albert hummed to himself as he worked, searing chunks of grouper with shrimp, crab, and scallops in a big pan, chopping garlic and leeks, patting a scoop of foie gras into place atop a tournedos of beef. When, some twenty minutes later, a still-breathless Eduardo rocked through the door with their order, Albert took the yellow slip from him and tore it in two without giving it a second glance. Zero hour had arrived.

"Marie!" he called, "Marie, quick!" He put on his most frantic face for her, the face of a man clutching at a wisp of grass at the very edge of a precipice.

Marie went numb. She set down her cocktail shaker and wiped her hands on her apron. There was catastrophe in the air. "What is it?" she gasped.

He was out of sea-urchin roe. And fish fumet. And Willa Frank had ordered the fillet of grouper oursinade. There wasn't a moment to lose—she had to rush over to the Edo Sushi House and borrow enough from Greg Takesue to last out the night. Albert had called ahead. It was okay. "Go, go," he said, wringing his big pale hands.

For the briefest moment, she hesitated. "But that's all the way across town—if it takes me an hour, I'll be lucky."

And now the matter-of-life-and-death look came into his eyes. "Go," he said. "I'll stall her."

No sooner had the door slammed behind Marie, than Albert took Fulgencio by the arm. "I want you to take a break," he shouted over the hiss of the sprayer. "Forty-five minutes. No, an hour."

Fulgencio looked up at him out of the dark Aztecan slashes of his eyes. Then he broke into a broad grin. "No entiendo," he said.

Albert mimed it for him. Then he pointed at the clock, and after a flurry of nodding back and forth, Fulgencio was gone. Whistling ("Core 'ngrato," one of his late mother's favorites), Albert glided to the meat locker and extracted the hard-frozen lump of gray gristle and fat he'd purchased that afternoon at the local Safeway. Round steak, they called it, $2.39 a pound. He tore the thing from its plastic wrapping, selected his largest skillet, turned the heat up high beneath it, and unceremoniously dropped the frozen lump into the searing black depths of the pan.

Eduardo hustled in and out, no time to question the twin absences of Marie and Fulgencio. Out went the tournedos Rossini, the fillet of grouper oursinade, the veal loin rubbed with sage and coriander, the anguille alla veneziana, and the zuppa di datteri Alberto; in came the dirty plates, the congested forks, the wineglasses smeared with butter and lipstick. A great plume of smoke rose from the pan on the front burner. Albert went on whistling.

And then, on one of Eduardo's mad dashes through the kitchen, Albert caught him by the arm. "Here," he said, shoving a plate into his hand. "For the gentleman with Miss Frank."

Eduardo stared bewildered at the plate in his hand. On it, arranged with all the finesse of a blue-plate special, lay three boiled potatoes, a splatter of reduced peas, and what could only be described as a plank of meat, stiff and flat as the chopping block, black as the bottom of the pan.

"Trust me," Albert said, guiding the stunned waiter toward the door. "Oh, and here," thrusting a bottle of ketchup into his hand, "serve it with this."

Still, Albert didn't yield to the temptation to go to the porthole. Instead, he turned the flame down low beneath his saucepans, smoothed back the hair at his temples, and began counting—as slowly as in a schoolyard game—to fifty.

He hadn't reached twenty when Willa Frank, scintillating in a tomato-red Italian knit, burst through the door. Eduardo was right behind her, a martyred look on his face, his hands spread in supplication. Albert lifted his head, swelled his chest, and adjusted the great ball of his gut beneath the pristine field of his apron. He dismissed Eduardo with a flick of his hand, and turned to Willa Frank with the tight composed smile of a man running for office. "Excuse me," she was saying, her voice toneless and shrill, as Eduardo ducked out the door, "but are you the chef here?"

He was still counting: twenty-eight, twenty-nine.

"Because I just wanted to tell you"—she was so wrought up she could barely go on—"I never, never in my life . . ."

"Shhhhh," he said, pressing a finger to his lips. "It's all right," he murmured, his voice as soothing and deep as a backrub. Then he took her gently by the elbow and led her to a table he'd set up between the stove and chopping block. The table was draped with a snowy cloth, set with fine crystal, china, and sterling inherited from his mother. There was a single chair, a single napkin. "Sit," he said.

She tore away from him. "I don't want to sit," she protested, her black eyes lit with suspicion. The knit dress clung to her like a leotard. Her heels clicked on the linoleum. "You know, don't you?" she said, backing away from him. "You know who I am."

Huge, ursine, serene, Albert moved with her as if they were dancing. He nodded.

"But why—?" He could see the appalling vision of that desecrated steak dancing before her eyes. "It's, it's like suicide."

A saucepan had appeared in his hand. He was so close to her he could feel the grid of her dress through the thin yielding cloth of his apron. "Hush," he purred, "don't think about it. Don't think at all. Here," he said, lifting the cover from the pan, "smell this."

She looked at him as if she didn't know where she was. She gazed down into the steaming pan and then looked back up into his eyes. He saw the gentle, involuntary movement of her throat.

"Squid rings in aioli sauce," he whispered. "Try one."

Gently, never taking his eyes from her, he set the pan down on the table, plucked a ring from the sauce, and held it up before her face. Her lips—full, sensuous lips, he saw now, not at all the thin stingy flaps of skin he'd imagined—began to tremble. Then she tilted her chin ever so slightly, and her mouth dropped open. He fed her like a nestling.

First the squid: one, two, three pieces. Then a pan of lobster tortellini in a thick, buttery saffron sauce. She practically licked the sauce from his fingers. This time, when he asked her to sit, when he put his big hand on her elbow and guided her forward, she obeyed.

He glanced through the porthole and out into the dining room as he removed from the oven the little toast rounds with sun-dried tomatoes and baked Atascadero goat cheese. Jock's head was down over his plate, the beer half gone, a great wedge of incinerated meat impaled on the tines of his fork. His massive jaw was working, his cheek distended as if with a plug of tobacco. "Here," Albert murmured, turning to Willa Frank and laying his warm, redolent hand over her eyes, "a surprise."

It was after she'd finished the taglierini alla pizzaiola, with its homemade fennel sausage and chopped tomatoes, and was experiencing the first rush of his glacé of grapefruit and Meyer lemon, that he asked about Jock. "Why him?" he said.

She scooped ice with a tiny silver spoon, licked a dollop of it from the corner of her mouth. "I don't know," she said, shrugging. "I guess I don't trust my own taste, that's all."

He lifted his eyebrows. He was leaning over her, solicitous, warm, the pan of Russian coulibiac of salmon, en brioche, with its rich sturgeon marrow and egg, held out in offering.

She watched his hands as he whisked the ice away and replaced it with the gleaming coulibiac. "I mean," she said, pausing as he broke off a morsel and fed it into her mouth, "half the time I just can't seem to taste anything, really," chewing now, her lovely throat dipping and rising as she swallowed, "and Jock—well, he hates *everything*. At least I know he'll be consistent." She took another bite, paused, considered. "Besides, to like something, to really like it and come out and say so, is taking a terrible risk. I mean, what if I'm wrong? What if it's really no good?"

Albert hovered over her. Outside it had begun to rain. He could hear it sizzling like grease in the alley. "Try this," he said, setting a plate of spiedino before her.

She was warm. He was warm. The oven glowed, the grill hissed, the scents of his creations rose about them, ambrosia and manna. "Um, good," she said, unconsciously nibbling at prosciutto and mozzarella. "I don't know," she said after a moment, her fingers dark with anchovy sauce, "I guess that's why I like fugu."

"Fugu?" Albert had heard of it somewhere. "Japanese, isn't it?"

She nodded. "It's a blowfish. They do it sushi or in little fried strips. But it's the liver you want. It's illegal here, did you know that?"

Albert didn't know.

"It can kill you. Paralyze you. But if you just nibble, just a little bit, it numbs your lips, your teeth, your whole mouth."

"What do you mean—like at the dentist's?" Albert was horrified. Numbs your lips, your mouth? It was sacrilege. "That's awful," he said.

She looked sheepish, looked chastised.

He swung to the stove and then back again, yet another pan in his hand. "Just a bite more," he coaxed.

She patted her stomach and gave him a great, wide, blooming smile. "Oh, no, no, Albert—can I call you Albert?—no, no, I couldn't."

"Here," he said, "here," his voice soft as a lover's. "Open up."

(1986)

WITHOUT A HERO

In the end, through luck and perseverance and an unwavering commitment to the spirit of glasnost, she did finally manage to get what she wanted. It was amazing. With two weeks to go on her six-month visa, she fell head-over-heels in love, got swept up in a whirlwind romance and found herself married—and to an American, no less. His name was Yusef Ozizmir, he was a naturalized citizen from a small town outside of Ankara, and he was production manager for a prosthetics firm based in Culver City. She called me late one night to give me the news and gloat a bit over her honeymoon in Las Vegas and her new apartment in Manhattan Beach that featured three bedrooms, vast closets and a sweet clean smell of the sea. Her voice was just as I'd remembered it: tiny, heavily accented and with the throaty arrhythmic scratch of sensuality that had awakened me in every fiber when I first heard it—the way she said "wodka" still aroused me even after all that had happened.

"I'm happy for you, Irina," I said.

"Oh," she gasped in her tiny voice that was made tinier by the uncertain connection, "that is very kind of you; I am very grateful. Yusef has made me very happy too, yes? He has given me a ring of twenty-four karats gold and a Lincoln automobile."

There was a pause. I glanced across my apartment at the sagging bookshelves, the TV tuned to a dim romantic comedy from the black-and-white era, the darkened window beyond. Her voice became tinier still, contracting till it was barely audible, a hesitant little squeak of passion. "You know . . . I miss you, Casey," she breathed. "I will always miss you too much."

"Listen, Irina, I have to go . . ." I was trying to think of an excuse—the kitchen was on fire, my mother had been stricken with ptomaine and rushed to the hospital, my knives needed sharpening—but she cut me off.

"Yes, Casey, I know. You have to go. You must go. Always you go."

"Listen," I began, and then I caught myself. "See you," I said.

"For a moment there was nothing. I listened to the cracks and pops of static. Finally her voice came back at me, the smallest voice in the world. "Yes," she said. "See you."

When I first saw her—when I laid eyes on her for the first time, that is—it was by prearrangement. She was in the baggage-claim area of the Tom Bradley International Terminal at LAX, and I was there to pick her up. I was late—a failing of mine, I admit it—and anxious on several counts: about meeting her, missing her, about sleeping arrangements and dinner and a hundred other things, ranging from my total deficiency in Russian to my passing acquaintance with the greats of Russian literature and the fear that she would offer to buy my jeans with a fistful of rubles. I was jogging through the corridors, dodging bleary-eyed Sikhs, hearty Brits and circumspect salesmen from Japan and Korea, the big names—Solzhenitsyn, Chekhov, Dostoevsky and Tolstoy—running through my head like an incantation, when I spotted her.

There was no mistaking her. I had Rob Peterman's description to go by—twenty-eight, blond, with a figure right out of the Bolshoi and a face that could kill—but I didn't need it. She was the center of a vortex of activity, a cigarette in one hand, a plastic cup of vodka in the other, her things scattered about her in cyclonic disarray—newspapers, luggage, makeup, paper towels and tissues, a sweater, several purses, half-a-dozen stuffed animals and a Dodgers cap occupying the two rows of seats behind her. She was engaged in an animated discussion of perestroika, Lithuanian independence, the threat of nuclear war and the relative merits of the Jaguar XJS as opposed to the Mercedes 560 SEC with three well-lubricated businessmen in rumpled suits. The cigarette—"A Gauloise, of course; what else is there?"—described an arc in the air, the hopelessly out-of-date go-go boots did a mazurka on the carpet, the fringe of the baby-blue patent-leather jacket trembled and shook. I didn't know what to do. I was sweating from my dash through the airport and I must have had that crazed, trapped-in-a-burning-barn look in my eyes.

"And do you know what I give you for that Mercedes?" she demanded of the shortest and most rumpled of the businessmen. "Eh?"

No response. All three men just stared at her, their mouths slightly agape, as if she'd just touched down from the far reaches of space.

"Nichevo." A little laugh escaped her. "This is what means 'nothing' in Russia. Nichevo."

I edged into her line of sight and made an extenuating gesture, describing a little circle of apology and lament with my hands and shirtsleeve arms. "Irina?" I asked.

She looked at me then, stopped dead in the middle of her next phrase and focused her milky blue—and ever so slightly exophthalmic—eyes on me. And then she smiled, allowing me my first take of her slim, sharp-toothed grin, and I felt a rush of warmth as the blood shot through me—a Russian smile, I thought, my first Russian smile. "Casey," she said, and there was no interrogatory lift to it, no doubt. "Casey." And then she turned away from her three interlocutors, dismissing them as if they'd never existed, and fell into my arms.

There was no shame in wanting things, and Irina wanted plenty. "Where I come from," she would say in her tiny halting breathy voice, "we do not have."

She revealed this to me for the first time in the car on the way back from the airport. Her eyes were shining, the Dodgers cap (a gift from one of the businessmen) rode the crown of her head like a victory wreath, and she gaily sang out the names and citations of the cars we passed on the freeway: "Corvette! Z-car! BMW 750!" I tried to keep my eyes on the road, but couldn't help stealing a glance at her from time to time.

Rob Peterman had been generous in his description, I could see that now. In the rush of excitement at the airport I saw only the exotic Irina, Rob Peterman's ideal made flesh, but as I began to study her I saw that she was no beauty—interesting, certainly, and pretty to a degree, but a far cry from the hyperborean goddess I'd been led to expect. But isn't that the way it always is?

"Is that not I. Magnin?" she cried as we pulled off the freeway. And then she turned to me and gave me that smile again, purring, cooing. "Oh, Casey, this is so—how do I say it?—so very much exciting to me."

There was the bulge of her eyes, too much forehead, the drawn mouth and sharp little teeth, but she fit her jeans as if they'd been tailored for her, and there was her hair, and her smile too. To a man three months divorced, as I then was, she looked good—better than good: I forgot the ideal and tumbled into the actual. "I'll take you there tomorrow," I said, "and you can run wild through the store." She was beaming at me, worshiping me with her eyes. "Tonight," I said, letting my voice trail off a bit so as not to betray my eagerness, "tonight I thought we'd just have a quiet dinner—I mean, that is, if you're not too tired—"

Two weeks earlier Rob Peterman had called me from Georgetown, where he was one of the principal buttresses of the International Relations Department at the university. He'd just come back from a six-week lecture tour of Russia and he had some good news for me—better, even: he'd brought back a little gift for me.

I'd known Rob since college. We were fraternity brothers, and we'd had some wild times. We'd kept in touch ever since. "Gift?"

"Let me put it to you this way, Case," he said. "There are a lot of university students in Moscow, thousands upon thousands of them, and a high percentage of them are young women from the provinces who'll do anything to stay in the big city. Or to travel, for that matter."

He had my attention, I had to admit it.

"You'd be surprised how many of them tend to gather round the Intourist bars and hotels, and how polished and intelligent they are, not to mention beautiful—you know, the Ukrainian princess, the Georgian fleshpot, the exotic long-limbed Slav . . ."

"Yes? And so?"

"Her name's Irina, Case," he said, "and she'll be in L.A. next week, TWA flight number eight nine five, arriving from Paris, where she connects from Moscow. Irina Sudeikina. I, uh, met her while I was over there, and she needs attachments." He lowered his voice. "If Sarah found out about her she'd take me to the vet and have me fixed, know what I mean?"

"What does she look like?"

"Who, Irina?" And then he gave me his generous description, which ran to twelve paragraphs and fanned the flames of my anticipation until I was a fireball of need, greed, hope and lust.

"Okay," I said finally, "okay, I hear you. What flight did you say she was on?"

And so there we were, in the car, driving up Pico to my apartment, my question about dinner, with all its loaded implications, hanging in the air between us. I'd pulled out the sofa bed in the back bedroom, stuck a pole lamp in the corner, tidied up a bit. She hadn't said anything about a hotel, and I hadn't asked. I glanced at the road ahead, and then back at her. "You're tired, aren't you?" I said.

"Do you not live in Beverly Hills, Casey?" she asked.

"Century City," I said. "It borders on Beverly Hills."

"In a mansion?"

"An apartment. It's nice. Plenty of room."

She shifted the Dodgers cap so that the brim fell over the crown of her sun-struck hair. "Oh, I have slept on the airplane," she said, turning her smile up a notch. "I am not tired. I am not tired at all."

As it turned out, Irina was to be my houseguest for the next two months. She settled into the back room like a Bedouin settling into a desert outpost, and within a week her things were everywhere, ubiquitous, from the stuffed panda perched atop the TV to the sweat socks beneath the kitchen table and the Harlequin romances sprouting up from the carpet like toadstools. She took a free, communistic approach to my things as well, thinking nothing of scattering my classic Coltrane albums across the couch or breezing down to the Beverly Center on my eight-hundred-dollar Bianchi all-terrain bike, without reference to lock or chain (where it was promptly stolen), not to mention using the telephone as if it had been provided by the state for the convenience of apartment dwellers and their guests. Slovenly, indolent, nearly inert, she was the end product of three generations of the workers' paradise, that vast dark crumbling empire in which ambition and initiative counted for nothing. Do I sound bitter? I am bitter. But I didn't know all this back then, and if I had known, I wouldn't have cared. All I knew was Irina's smile and her hair and the proximity of her flesh; all I knew was that she was in the bedroom, unpacking and dressing for dinner.

I took her to a sushi place on Wilshire, thinking to impress her with my savoir-faire and internationalism, but she surprised me not only in being an adept at *ebi, unagi* and *katsuo,* but by ordering in flawless Japanese to boot. She was wearing a low-cut minidress made of some shiny brittle material, she'd drawn her hair back severely and knotted it up over her head in a big puffy bun, and she'd put some effort into her makeup. The sushi chef was all over her, chattering away in Japanese, fashioning whimsical creations of radish and carrot for her, rolling out his rare stock of *fugu,* the Japanese blowfish. I'd been a regular at the restaurant for two years at least, and he'd never looked at me twice. "Uh, Irina," I said, as the chef slouched reluctantly off to make a scallop roll for the couple beside me, "where did you learn your Japanese? I mean, I'm impressed."

She paused, a sliver of Norwegian salmon tucked neatly between her lips, patted her mouth and gasped, "Oh, this is nothing. I have spent six months in Japan in 1986."

I was surprised. "They—the government, I mean, the Russian government— they let you travel then?"

She gave me a wink. "I am at that time a student of languages at Moscow State University, Casey . . . am I not then to learn these languages by visiting the countries in which they are spoken?" She turned back to her plate, plucked a morsel from some creation the chef had set before us. "Besides," she said, speaking to the plate in her tiny voice, "there is a man I know in Moscow and he is able to arrange things—even difficult things."

I had a hundred questions for her—about life behind the iron curtain, about Japan, about her girlhood and college and the mysterious benefactor in Moscow—but I focused instead on my sake and a slippery bit of *maguro* that kept eluding my chopsticks, and thought only of getting in the car and driving home with her.

I was a little tense on the way back—the first-date jitters, the sort of thing every male goes through from adolescence to the grave: will she or won't she?— and I couldn't think of much to say. It didn't really matter. Irina was oblivious, lit with sake and three big pint-and-a-half bottles of Asahi, waving her cigarette, crossing and uncrossing her legs and rolling the exotic Anglo-Saxon and Latinate phrases over her tongue with real relish. How nice it was here in America, she thought, how sympathetic, and what a nice car I had, but wouldn't I prefer a sportier model? I made a lot of money, didn't I?—she could tell because I was so generous—and wasn't it nice to have Japanese food, something you could find in one place only in Moscow, and then only if you were an apparatchik?

At home we had an after-dinner drink in the living room—Grand Marnier, twenty-six dollars the fifth; she filled the snifter to the top—while Coltrane serenaded us with "All or Nothing at All." We talked about little things, inconsequential things, and she became progressively more animated as the level fell in her glass. And then, without a word of explanation—hello, goodbye, good night and thank you for dinner, nothing—she stood, refilled her glass and disappeared into the bedroom.

I was devastated. So this is it, I thought bitterly, this is my passionate Russian experience—a hundred and twenty bucks for sushi, half a bottle of Grand Marnier and a rush-hour schlep to the airport and back. I sat there, a little sick in the stomach, and listened to the sad expiring click of the turntable as the record ended and the machine shut itself down.

With all she'd had to drink, with the time change and the long flight from Moscow, I figured she'd probably hit the bed in a cold faint, but I was wrong. Just as I was about to give it up, heave myself out of the chair and tumble into my own comfortless bed, she appeared in the doorway. "Casey," she murmured, her voice rich and low, and in the muted light I could see that she was wearing something silky and diaphanous—a teddy, a Russian teddy. "Casey," she crooned, "I cannot seem to sleep."

It was about a week later that she first asked me if I knew Akhmatova. I did know her, but not personally. She was dimmer to me even than Pushkin or Lermontov, a fading memory out of a drowsy classroom.

"We studied her in college," I said lamely. "After she died—in the sixties, right? It was a survey course in Russian literature. In translation, I mean."

Irina was sitting cross-legged on the couch in a litter of newspapers and magazines. She was wearing only a T-shirt and a pair of panties, and I'd just watched in fascination as she applied a glistening coat of neon-pink polish to her toenails. She looked up at me a moment and narrowed her pale-blue eyes. Then she closed them and began to recite:

"FROM THE YEAR NINETEEN-FORTY
AS FROM A HIGH TOWER I LEAN,
ONCE MORE BIDDING GOODBYE
TO WHAT I LONG AGO FORSOOK,
AS THOUGH I HAVE CROSSED MYSELF
AND AM GOING DOWN UNDER DARK
VAULTS.

"It is from Akhmatova's great work, 'Poem Without a Hero.' Is it not sad and beautiful?"

I looked at her toenails shimmering in the light of the morning; I looked at her bare legs, her face, her eyes. We'd been out every night—I'd taken her to

Chinatown, Disneyland, the Music Center and Malibu pier—and the glow of it was on me. "Yes," I said.

"This is a great work about dying for love, Casey, about a poet who kills himself because his lover will not have him." She shut her eyes again. " 'For one moment of peace I would give the peace of the tomb.' " She let the moment hang, mesmeric, motes of dust floating in a shaft of light through the window, the bird-of-paradise gilded with sun, the traffic quiet on the street. And then she was looking at me, soft and shrewd at once. "Tell me, Casey, where does one find such a hero today? Where does one find a man who will die for love?"

The next day was the day she took my bike to the Beverly Center and we had our first falling-out.

I'd come home late from work—there was a problem with the new person we'd hired, the usual semiliteracy and incompetence—and the place was a mess. No: actually, "mess" didn't do it justice. The apartment looked as if a troop of baboons had been locked inside it for a week. Every record I owned was out of its jacket and collecting dust; my books were scattered throughout the living room, spread open flat like crippled things; there were clothes and sheets and pillows wadded about; and every horizontal surface was inundated with a farrago of take-out food and crumpled wrappers: Colonel Sanders, Chow Foo Luck, McDonald's, Arby's, Taco Bell. She was on the phone in the back room—long-distance to Russia—and she hadn't changed out of the T-shirt she'd been wearing the previous morning. She said something in Russian, and then I heard her say, "Yes, and my American boyfriend he is so very wealthy—"

"Irina?"

"I must go now. *Do svidaniya.*"

I stepped into the bedroom and she flew across the room to fling herself into my arms, already sobbing, sobbing in midair. I was disconcerted. "What's the matter?" I said, clutching her hopelessly. I had a sudden intimation that she was leaving me, that she was going on to visit Chicago and New Orleans and New York, and I felt a sinkhole of loss open up inside me. "Are you—is everything all right?"

Her breath was hot on my throat. She began to kiss me there, over and over, till I took hold of her shoulders and forced her to look me in the eye. "Irina, tell me: what is it?"

"Oh, Casey," she gasped, and her voice was so diminished I could barely hear her. "I have been so stupid. Even in Russia we must lock up our things, I know, but I have never dreamed that here, where you have so much—"

And so I discovered that my eight-hundred-dollar bicycle was no more, just as I was to learn that she'd sheared the blades off the Cuisinart attempting to dice a whole pineapple and that half my records had gouges in them and that my new white Ci Siamo jacket was stained with lipstick or cranberry juice or what might have been blood for all I knew.

I lost my sense of humor, my forbearance, my graciousness, my cool. We had a scene. Accusations flew. I didn't care about her, she shrieked; things meant more to me than she did. "Things!" I snorted. "And who spends half her time at Robinson's and Saks and the May Company? Who calls Russia as if God Himself would come down from heaven and pay the bills? Who hasn't offered to pay a penny of anything, not even once?"

Her hair hung wild in her face. Strands of it adhered to the sudden moisture that glistened on her cheekbones. "You do not care for me," she said in her tiniest voice. "I am only for you a momentary pleasure."

I had nothing more to say. I stood there fuming as she fussed round the room, drawing on her jeans and boots, shrugging into the baby-blue patent-leather jacket and tamping out a cigarette in an abandoned coffee mug. She gave me a look—a look of contempt, anger, sorrow—and then she snatched up her purse and slammed out the door.

I didn't sleep well that night. I kept listening for her key in the lock, kept picturing her shouldering her way through the punks and beggars on the boulevard and wondering if she had friends to go to. She had some money, I knew that, but she hoarded it like a capitalist, and though she knew all the brand names, she bought nothing. I saw the absurd go-go boots, the fringed jacket, the keen sexy spring in her walk that belied her phlegmatic Russian nature, and half-a-dozen times I got up to look for her and then thought better of it. In the morning, when I got up for work, the apartment was desolate.

I called home sporadically throughout the day, but there was no answer. I was angry, hurt, sick with worry. Finally, around four, she picked up the phone. "It is Irina," she said, her voice tired and small.

"It's me, Casey."

No response.

"Irina? Are you all right?"

A pause. "I am very well, thank you."

I wanted to ask where she'd spent the night, wanted to know and possess her and make demands, but I faltered in the presence of that quavering whispery voice. "Irina, listen, about last night . . . I just want to say I'm sorry."

"That is no problem," she said. And then, after a pause, "I leave you fifty dollars, Casey, on the table in the kitchen."

"What do you mean?"

"I am going now, Casey. I know when I am not wanted."

"No, no—I didn't mean . . . I mean I was mad, I was angry, that was all. You're wanted. You are." I was pleading with her and even as I pleaded I could hear that I'd subconsciously picked up something of her diction, clipping my phrases in a too-formal way, a Russian way. "Listen, just wait there a minute, will you? I'm on my way home from work. I'll take you wherever you want to go— you want to go to the airport? The bus? Whatever you want."

Nothing.

"Irina?"

The smallest voice: "I will wait."

I took her out to Harry's that night for Italian food, and she was radiant, beaming, almost giddy—she couldn't stop grinning at me, and everything I said was the funniest thing she'd ever heard. She cut her veal into neat little strips, chattered at the waiter in a breathy fluid Italian, tossed off one glass of Chianti after another, all the while pecking kisses at me and entwining her fingers with mine as if we were sixteen-year-olds at the mall. I didn't mind. This was our reconciliation, and the smoke of sensuality hung over the table.

She leaned toward me over dessert—millefoglie with a cappuccino and Grand Marnier—and gave me the full benefit of her swollen eyes. The lights were low. Her voice was a whisper. I expected her to say, "Do you not want to take me home to bed now?" but she surprised me. With a randy look, she cleared her throat and said, "Casey, I have been wondering"—pause—"do you think I should put my money in CD or mutual fund?"

I couldn't have been more stunned if she'd asked me who played third base for the Dodgers. "What?"

"The Magellan has performed best, has it not?" she whispered, and the talk of money seemed to make her voice sultrier still. "But then the founder is retiring, is this not so?"

A sudden anger came over me. Was she hustling me, was that it? She had money to invest and yet accepted her room and meals and all the rest from me as if it were her divine right? I stared down into my cappuccino and muttered, "Hell, I don't know. What are you asking me for?"

She patted my hand and then said in her fading slip of a voice, "Perhaps this is not the time." Her mouth made a little moue of contrition. And then, almost immediately, she brightened again. "It is early yet, Casey," she said, quaffing her Grand Marnier and rising. "Do you not want to take me to the Odessa?"

The Odessa was a club in the Fairfax district where Russian émigrés of all ages would gather to sit at long cafeteria-style tables and listen to schmaltzy singers and third-rate comedians. They drank water glasses of warm Coke and vodka—the Coke in the left hand, vodka in the right, alternating swigs—and they sang along with and got up from the table and careened round the room to the frenetic Tatar strains of the orchestra. We stayed past closing, danced till we were soaked in sweat and drank enough vodka to fuel a 747. In the course of the evening we toasted Gorbachev, Misha Baryshnikov, the girls of Tbilisi, Leningrad and Murmansk, and drank the health of everyone in the room, individually, at least three times. Irina passed out in the car on the way home, and the night ended after she vomited gloriously in the potted ficus and I helped her to bed as if she were an invalid.

I felt queasy myself the next morning and called in sick at the office. When I finally got out of bed, around noon, Irina's door was still closed. I was brewing coffee when she slumped through the kitchen door and fell into a chair. She was wearing a rumpled housecoat and she looked as if she'd been buried and dug up again.

"Me too," I said, and I put both hands to my temples.

She said nothing, but accepted the coffee I poured for her. After a moment she pointed out the window to where one of my neighbors was letting her dog nose about in the shrubs that rimmed our little patch of lawn. "Do you see that dog, Casey?" she asked.

I nodded.

"It is a very lucky dog."

"Lucky?"

"Yes," she said, slow and lethargic, drawing it out. "It is a dog that has never tasted wodka."

I laughed, but my eyes felt as if they were being sucked into my head and the coffee set my insides churning.

And then she took me by surprise again. Outside, the dog had disappeared, jerked rudely away at the end of a leash. The coffee machine dripped coffee. Someone gunned an engine two blocks away. "Casey," she said, utterly composed, utterly serious, and she looked deep into my eyes. "Do you not want to marry me?"

The second blowup came at the end of the month, when the phone bill arrived. Four hundred twenty-seven dollars and sixty-two cents. I recognized a few calls—my lawyer's number, Rob Peterman's, a drunken cri de coeur I'd made to an old flame (now married) in Santa Barbara. But the rest were long-distance overseas—to Moscow, Novgorod, London, Paris, Milan. I was outraged. I was in shock. Why should I be responsible for her bills? I did not want to marry her, as I'd explained to her the morning after the Odessa. I told her I'd just been divorced and was leery of new attachments, which was true. I told her I still had feelings for my wife, which was also true (of course, those feelings were exclusively antipathetic, but I didn't mention that). Irina had only stared at me, and then she got up from the kitchen table and went into her room, shutting the door firmly behind her.

But now, now she was out somewhere—no doubt looking at popcorn makers or water-purifying systems at some department store—the house was in a shambles, I hadn't even loosened my tie yet and the phone bill was sending shock waves through me. I'd just poured a drink when I heard her key in the door; she came in beaming, oblivious, in a rustle of shopping bags and cheap trinkets, and I was all over her. "Don't you know what this means?" I shouted. "Don't you know that the telephone isn't free in this society, that somebody has to pay for it? That *I* have to pay for it?"

She gave me a hard cold look. Her eyes narrowed; her chin trembled. "I will pay it," she said, "if that is how you feel."

"How I feel?" I shouted. "How I feel? Everybody pays their way in life, that's how I feel. That's the way society works, like it or not. Maybe it's different in the workers' paradise, I don't know, but over here you play by the rules."

She had nothing to say to that—she just held me with her contemptuous look, as if I were the one being unreasonable, and in that moment she reminded me of Julie, my ex-wife, as if she were in league with her, as if she were her double, and I felt bitter and disgusted to the core. I dropped the bill on the coffee table and stalked out the door.

When I got home from work the next day, the phone bill was still there, but there were five pristine one-hundred-dollar bills laid out beside it like a poker hand. Irina was in the kitchen. I didn't know what to say to her. Suddenly I felt ashamed of myself.

I drifted into the room and draped my sportcoat over the back of one of the chairs and went to the refrigerator for a glass of orange juice. "Hello, Casey," she said, glancing up from her magazine. It was one of those women's magazines, thick as a phone book.

"Hi," I said. And then, after an interval during which the level of the orange juice mounted in the glass and I gazed numbly out the window on a blur of green, I turned to her. "Irina," I murmured, and my voice seemed to be caught in my throat, "I want to say thanks for the phone bill—the money, I mean."

She looked up at me and shrugged. "It is nothing," she said. "I have a job now."

"A job?"

And there was her smile, the sharp little teeth. *"Da,"* she said. "I have met a man at the Odessa when I go for tea last Thursday? Do you remember I told you? His name is Zhenya and he has offered me a job."

"Great," I said. "Terrific. We should celebrate." I lifted my glass as if it contained Perrier-Jouët. "What kind of work?"

She looked down at her magazine and then back up again, holding my eyes. "Escort service."

I thought I hadn't heard her right. "What? What are you saying?"

"It is an escort service, Casey. Zhenya says the men who come here for important business—in the movies, banking, real estate—they will like me. He says I am very beautiful."

I was stunned. I felt as if I'd had the wind knocked out of me. "You can't be serious?" My voice was pitched high, a yelp. "Irina, this is"—I couldn't find the words—"this is not right, it's not legitimate. It's, it's prostitution, don't you know that?"

She was studying me, her shrewd eyes, the little nugget of her face. She sighed, closed the magazine and rose from her seat. "It is not a problem," she said finally. "If I do not like them I will not sleep with them."

And what about me? I wanted to say. *What about Disneyland and Zuma Beach and all the rest of it?* Instead I turned on her. "You're crazy," I spat. "Nuts. Don't you know what you're getting into?"

Her eyes hadn't left mine, not for a second. She was a foot away from me. I could smell her perfume—French, four hundred dollars the ounce. She shrugged and then stretched her arms so that her breasts rose tight against her chest. "What am I to do," she said in her smallest voice, so languid and sad. "I have nothing, and you will not marry me."

That was the end for us, and we both knew it.

I took her out to dinner that night, but it was a requiem, an interment. She stared off into vacancy. Neither of us had much to say. When we got home I saw her face illuminated for an instant as she bent to switch on the lamp, and I felt something stir in me, but I killed it. We went to our separate rooms and to our separate beds.

In the morning, I sat over a cup of lukewarm coffee and watched her pack. She looked sweet and sad, and she moved as if she were fighting an invisible current, her hair streaming, imaginary fish hanging in the rafters. I didn't know if the escort-service business was a bluff or not, didn't know how naive—or how calculating—she was, but I felt that a burden had been lifted from my shoulders. Now that it was over, I began to see her in a different light, a softer light, and a sliver of guilt began to stab at me. "Look, Irina," I said as she struggled to force her suitcase shut, "I'm sorry. I really am."

She threw her hair back with a jerk of her chin, shrugged into the baby-blue patent-leather jacket.

"Irina, look at me—"

She wouldn't look. She leaned over to snap the latches on her suitcase.

"This is no poem, Irina," I said. "This is life."

She swung round so suddenly I flinched. "I am the one, Casey," she said, and her eyes leapt at me. "I am the one who can die for love."

All the bitterness came back to me in that instant, all the hurt and guilt. Zhenya, Japan, the mysterious benefactor in Moscow, Rob Peterman and how many others? This was free enterprise, this was trade and barter and buying and selling—and where was the love in that? Worse yet: where was the love in me?

I was hard, a rock, granite. "Then die for it," I said.

The phrase hung between us like a curtain. A car moved up the street. I could hear the steady drip-drip-drip of the kitchen tap. And then she bowed her head, as if accepting a blow, and bent for her suitcases. I was paralyzed. I was dead. I watched her struggle with her things, watched her fight the door, and then, as the sudden light gave way to darkness, I watched the door swing shut.

(1990)

HEART OF A CHAMPION

We scan the cornfields and the wheatfields winking gold and goldbrown and yellowbrown in the midday sun, on up the grassy slope to the barn redder than red against the sky bluer than blue, across the smooth stretch of the barnyard with its pecking chickens, and then right on up to the screen door at the back of the house. The door swings open, a black hole in the sun, and Timmy emerges with his corn-silk hair, corn-fed face. He is dressed in crisp overalls, striped T-shirt, stubby blue Keds. There'd have to be a breeze—and we're not disappointed—his clean fine cup-cut hair waves and settles as he scuffs across the barnyard and out to the edge of the field. The boy stops there to gaze out over the nodding wheat, eyes unsquinted despite the sun, and blue as tinted lenses. Then he brings three fingers to his lips in a neat triangle and whistles long and low, sloping up sharp to cut off at the peak. A moment passes: he whistles again. And then we see it—way out there at the far corner of the field—the ripple, the dashing furrow, the blur of the streaking dog, white chest, flashing feet.

They're in the woods now. The boy whistling, hands in pockets, kicking along with his short baby-fat strides; the dog beside him wagging the white tip of her tail like an all-clear flag. They pass beneath an arching old black-barked oak. It creaks. And suddenly begins to fling itself down on them: immense, brutal: a panzer strike. The boy's eyes startle and then there's a blur, a smart snout clutching his pantleg, the thunderblast of the trunk, the dust and spinning leaves. "Golly, Lassie . . . I didn't even see it," says the boy sitting safe in a mound of moss. The collie looks up at him (the svelte snout, the deep gold logician's eyes), and laps at his face.

And now they're down by the river. The water is brown with angry suppurations, spiked with branches, fence posts, tires and logs. It rushes like the sides of boxcars—and chews deep and insidious at the bank under Timmy's feet. The roar is like a jetport: little wonder he can't hear the dog's warning bark. We watch the crack appear, widen to a ditch; then the halves separating (snatch of red earth, writhe of worm), the poise and pitch, and Timmy crashing down with it. Just a flash—but already he's way downstream, his head like a plastic jug, dashed and bobbed, spinning toward the nasty mouth of the falls. But there's the dog—fast as a struck match—bursting along the bank all white and gold melded in motion, hair sleeked with the wind of it, legs beating time to the panting score . . . Yet what can she hope to do?—the current surges on, lengths ahead, sure bet to win the race to the falls. Timmy sweeps closer, sweeps closer, the falls loud now as a hundred timpani, the war drums of the Sioux, Africa gone bloodlust mad! The dog strains, lashing over the wet earth like a whipcrack; strains every last ganglion and dendrite until finally she draws abreast of him. Then she's in the air, the foaming yellow water. Her paws churning like pistons, whiskers chuffing with the exertion—oh the roar!—and there, she's got him, her sure jaws clamping down on the shirt collar, her eyes fixed on the slip of rock at the falls' edge. Our blood races, organs palpitate. The black brink of the falls, the white paws digging at the rock—and then they're safe. The collie sniffs at Timmy's inert little form, nudges his side until she manages to roll him over. Then clears his tongue and begins mouth-to-mouth.

Night: the barnyard still, a bulb burning over the screen door. Inside, the family sit at dinner, the table heaped with pork chops, mashed potatoes, applesauce and peas, a pitcher of clean white milk. Home-baked bread. Mom and Dad, their faces sexless, bland, perpetually good-humored and sympathetic, poise stiff-backed, forks in midswoop, while Timmy tells his story: "So then Lassie grabbed me by the collar and golly I musta blanked out cause I don't remember anything more till I woke up on the rock—"

"Well I'll be," says Mom.

"You're lucky you've got such a good dog, son," says Dad, gazing down at the collie where she lies patiently, snout over paw, tail wapping the floor. She is combed and washed and fluffed, her lashes mascaraed and curled, her chest and paws white as dishsoap. She looks up humbly. But then her ears leap, her neck jerks round—and she's up at the door, head cocked, alert. A high yipping yowl like a stuttering fire whistle shudders through the room. And then another. The dog whines.

"Darn," says Dad. "I thought we were rid of those coyotes—next thing they'll be after the chickens again."

■ ■ ■

The moon blanches the yard, leans black shadows on the trees, the barn. Upstairs in the house, Timmy lies sleeping in the pale light, his hair fastidiously mussed, his breathing gentle. The collie lies on the throw rug beside the bed. We see that her eyes are open. Suddenly she rises and slips to the window, silent as a shadow. And looks down the long elegant snout to the barnyard below, where the coyote slinks from shade to shade, a limp pullet dangling from his jaws. He is stunted, scabious, syphilitic, his forepaw trap-twisted, his eyes running. The collie whimpers softly from behind the window. And the coyote stops in mid-trot, frozen in a cold shard of light, ears high on his head. Then drops the chicken at his feet, leers up at the window and begins a soft, crooning, sad-faced song.

The screen door slaps behind Timmy as he bolts from the house, Lassie at his heels. Mom's head emerges on the rebound. "Timmy!" (He stops as if jerked by a rope, turns to face her.) "You be home before lunch, hear?"

"Sure, Mom," he says, already spinning off, the dog by his side. We get a close-up of Mom's face: she is smiling a benevolent boys-will-be-boys smile. Her teeth are perfect.

In the woods Timmy steps on a rattler and the dog bites its head off. "Gosh," he says. "Good girl, Lassie." Then he stumbles and slips over an embankment, rolls down the brushy incline and over a sudden precipice, whirling out into the breathtaking blue space like a sky diver. He thumps down on a narrow ledge twenty feet below. And immediately scrambles to his feet, peering timorously down the sheer wall to the heap of bleached bone at its base. Small stones break loose, shoot out like asteroids. Dirt-slides begin. But Lassie yarps reassuringly from above, sprints back to the barn for a winch and cable, hoists the boy to safety.

On their way back for lunch Timmy leads them through a still and leaf-darkened copse. We remark how odd it is that the birds and crickets have left off their cheeping, how puzzling that the background music has begun to rumble so. Suddenly, round a bend in the path before them, the coyote appears. Nose to the ground, intent, unaware of them. But all at once he jerks to a halt, shudders like an epileptic, the hackles rising, tail dipping between his legs. The collie too stops short, just yards away, her chest proud and shaggy and white. The coyote cowers, bunches like a cat, glares at them. Timmy's face sags with alarm. The coyote lifts his lip. But then, instead of leaping at her adversary's throat, the collie prances up and stretches her nose out to him, her eyes soft as a leading lady's, round as a doe's. She's balsamed and perfumed; her full chest tapers a lovely S to her sleek haunches and sculpted legs. He is puny, runted, half her size, his coat like a discarded doormat. She circles him now, sniffing. She whimpers, he growls: throaty and tough, the bad guy. And stands stiff while she licks at his whiskers, noses at his rear, the bald black scrotum. Timmy is horror-struck.

Then, the music sweeping off in birdtrills of flute and harpstring, the coyote slips round behind, throat thrown back, black lips tight with anticipation.

"What was she doing, Dad?" Timmy asks over his milk and sandwich.

"The sky was blue today, son," he says.

"But she had him trapped, Dad—they were stuck together end to end and I thought we had that wicked old coyote but then she went and let him go— what's got into her, Dad?"

"The barn was red today, son," he says.

Late afternoon: the sun mellow, more orange than white. Purpling clots of shadow hang from the branches, ravel out from the tree trunks. Bees and wasps and flies saw away at the wet full-bellied air. Timmy and the dog are far out beyond the north pasture, out by the old Indian burial mound, where the boy stoops now to search for arrowheads. Oddly, the collie is not watching him: instead she's pacing the crest above, whimpering softly, pausing from time to time to stare out across the forest, her eyes distant and moonstruck. Behind her, storm clouds squat on the horizon like dark kidneys or brains.

We observe the wind kicking up: leaves flapping like wash, saplings quivering, weeds whipping. It darkens quickly now, the clouds scudding low and smoky over the treetops, blotting the sun from view. Lassie's white is whiter than ever, highlighted against the dark horizon, the wind-whipped hair foaming around her. Still she doesn't look down at the boy: he digs, dirty-kneed, stoop-backed, oblivious. Then the first fat random drops, a flash, the volcanic blast of thunder. Timmy glances over his shoulder at the noise: he's just in time to watch the scorched pine plummeting toward the constellated freckles in the center of his forehead. Now the collie turns—too late!—the *swoosh-whack!* of the tree, the trembling needles. She's there in an instant, tearing at the green welter, struggling through to his side. He lies unconscious in the muddying earth, hair artistically arranged, a thin scratch painted on his cheek. The trunk lies across the small of his back like the tail of a brontosaurus. The rain falls.

Lassie tugs doggedly at a knob in the trunk, her pretty paws slipping in the wet—but it's no use—it would take a block and tackle, a crane, an army of Bunyans to shift that stubborn bulk. She falters, licks at his ear, whimpers. We observe the troubled look in her eye as she hesitates, uncertain, priorities warring: should she stand guard, or dash for help? The decision is sure and swift—her eyes firm with purpose and she is off like a shard of shrapnel, already up the hill, shooting past the dripping trees, over the river, already cleaving through the high wet banks of wheat.

A moment later she's dashing through the puddled and rain-screened barnyard, barking right on up to the back door, where she pauses to scratch daintily, her voice high-pitched and insistent. Mom swings open the door and the collie pads in, claws clacking on the shiny linoleum. "What is it, girl? What's the matter? Where's Timmy?"

"Yarf! Yarfata-yarf-yarf!"

"Oh my! Dad! Dad, come quickly!"

Dad rushes in, his face stolid and reassuring as the Lincoln Memorial. "What is it, dear? . . . Why, Lassie?"

"Oh Dad, Timmy's trapped under a pine tree out by the old Indian burial ground—"

"Arpit-arp."

"—a mile and a half past the north pasture."

Dad is quick, firm, decisive. "Lassie—you get back up there and stand watch over Timmy . . . Mom and I'll go for Doc Walker. Hurry now!"

The collie hesitates at the door: "Rarf-arrar-ra!"

"Right," says Dad. "Mom, fetch the chainsaw."

We're back in the woods now. A shot of the mud-running burial mound locates us—yes, there's the fallen pine, and there: Timmy. He lies in a puddle, eyes closed, breathing slow. The hiss of the rain is loud as static. We see it at work: scattering leaves, digging trenches, inciting streams to swallow their banks. It lies deep now in the low areas, and in the mid areas, and in the high areas. Then a shot of the dam, some indeterminate (but short we presume) distance off, the yellow water churning over its lip like urine, the ugly earthen belly distended, blistered with the pressure. Raindrops pock the surface like a plague.

Suddenly the music plunges to those thunderous crouching chords—we're back at the pine now—what is it? There: the coyote. Sniffing, furtive, the malicious eyes, the crouch and slink. He stiffens when he spots the boy—but then slouches closer, a rubbery dangle drooling from between his mismeshed teeth. Closer. Right over the prone figure now, those ominous chords setting up ominous vibrations in our bowels. He stoops, head dipping between his shoulders, irises caught in the corners of his eyes: wary, sly, predatory: the vulture slavering over the fallen fawn.

But wait!—here comes the collie, sprinting out of the wheatfield, bounding rock to rock across the crazed river, her limbs contourless with sheer speed and purpose, the music racing in a mad heroic prestissimo!

The jolting front seat of a Ford. Dad, Mom and the Doctor, all dressed in rain slickers and flap-brimmed rain hats, sitting shoulder to shoulder behind the clapping wipers. Their jaws set with determination, eyes aflicker with pioneer gumption.

■ ■ ■

The coyote's jaws, serrated grinders, work at the tough bone and cartilage of Timmy's left hand. The boy's eyelids flutter with the pain, and he lifts his head feebly—but almost immediately it slaps down again, flat and volitionless, in the mud. At that instant Lassie blazes over the hill like a cavalry charge, show-dog indignation aflame in her eyes. The scrag of a coyote looks up at her, drooling blood, choking down frantic bits of flesh. Looks up at her from eyes that go back thirty million years, savage and bloodlustful and free. Looks up unmoved, uncringing, the bloody snout and steady yellow eyes less a physical challenge than philosophical. We watch the collie's expression alter in midbound—the look of offended AKC morality giving way, dissolving. She skids to a halt, drops her tail and approaches him, a buttery gaze in her golden eyes. She licks the blood from his lips.

The dam. Impossibly swollen, rain festering the yellow surface, a hundred new streams a minute rampaging in, the pressure of those millions of gallons hard-punching those millions more. There! the first gap, the water spewing out, a burst bubo. And now the dam shudders, splinters, falls to pieces like so much cheap pottery. The roar is devastating.

The two animals start at that terrible rumbling, and, still working their gummy jaws, they dash up the far side of the hill. We watch the white-tipped tail retreating side by side with the hacked and tick-blistered gray one—wagging like raggled banners as they disappear into the trees at the top of the rise. We're left with a tableau: the rain, the fallen pine in the crotch of the valley's V, the spot of the boy's head. And that chilling roar in our ears. Suddenly the wall of water appears at the far end of the V, smashing through the little declivity like a god-sized fist, prickling with shattered trunks and boulders, grinding along like a quick-melted glacier, like planets in collision. We cut to Timmy: eyes closed, hair plastered, his left arm looking as though it should be wrapped in butcher's paper. How? we wonder. How will they ever get him out of this? But then we see them—Mom, Dad and the Doctor—struggling up that same rise, rushing with the frenetic music now, the torrent seething closer, booming and howling. Dad launches himself in full charge down the hillside—but the water is already sweeping over the fallen pine, lifting it like paper—there's a blur, a quick clip of a typhoon at sea (is that a flash of blond hair?), and it's over. The valley is filled to the top of the rise, the water ribbed and rushing like the Colorado in adolescence. Dad's pants are wet to the crotch.

Mom's face, the Doctor's. Rain. And then the opening strains of the theme song, one violin at first, swelling in mournful mid-American triumph as the full orchestra comes in, tearful, beautiful, heroic, sweeping us up and out of the dismal rain, back to the golden wheatfields in the midday sun. The boy cups his hands to his mouth and pipes: "Laahh-sie! Laahh-sie!" And then we see it—way out there at the end of the field—the ripple, the dashing furrow, the blur of the streaking dog, white chest, flashing feet.

(1974)

CARNAL KNOWLEDGE

I'd never really thought much about meat. It was there in the supermarket in a plastic wrapper; it came between slices of bread with mayo and mustard and a dill pickle on the side; it sputtered and smoked on the grill till somebody flipped it over, and then it appeared on the plate, between the baked potato and the julienne carrots, neatly cross-hatched and floating in a puddle of red juice. Beef, mutton, pork, venison, dripping burgers and greasy ribs—it was all the same to me, food, the body's fuel, something to savor a moment on the tongue before the digestive system went to work on it. Which is not to say I was totally unconscious of the deeper implications. Every once in a while I'd eat at home, a quartered chicken, a package of Shake 'n Bake, Stove Top stuffing and frozen peas, and as I hacked away at the stippled yellow skin and pink flesh of the sanitized bird I'd wonder at the darkish bits of organ clinging to the ribs—what was that, liver? kidney?—but in the end it didn't make me any less fond of Kentucky Fried or Chicken McNuggets. I saw those ads in the magazines, too, the ones that showed the veal calves penned up in their own waste, their limbs atrophied and their veins so pumped full of antibiotics they couldn't control their bowels, but when I took a date to Anna Maria's, I could never resist the veal scallopini.

And then I met Alena Jorgensen.

It was a year ago, two weeks before Thanksgiving—I remember the date because it was my birthday, my thirtieth, and I'd called in sick and gone to the beach to warm my face, read a book and feel a little sorry for myself. The Santa Anas were blowing and it was clear all the way to Catalina, but there was an edge to the air, a scent of winter hanging over Utah, and as far as I could see in either direction I had the beach pretty much to myself. I found a sheltered spot in a tumble of boulders, spread a blanket and settled down to attack the pastrami on rye I'd brought along for nourishment. Then I turned to my book—a comfortingly apocalyptic tract about the demise of the planet—and let the sun warm me as I read about the denuding of the rain forest, the poisoning of the atmosphere and the swift silent eradication of species. Gulls coasted by overhead. I saw the distant glint of jetliners.

I must have dozed, my head thrown back, the book spread open in my lap, because the next thing I remember, a strange dog was hovering over me and the sun had dipped behind the rocks. The dog was big, wild-haired, with one staring blue eye, and it just looked at me, ears slightly cocked, as if it expected a Milk-Bone or something. I was startled—not that I don't like dogs, but here was this woolly thing poking its snout in my face—and I guess I must have made some sort of defensive gesture, because the dog staggered back a step and froze. Even in the confusion of the moment I could see that there was something wrong with this dog, an unsteadiness, a gimp, a wobble to its legs. I felt a mixture of pity and revulsion—had it been hit by a car, was that it?—when all at once I became aware of a wetness on the breast of my windbreaker, and an unmistakable odor rose to my nostrils: I'd been pissed on.

Pissed on. As I lay there unsuspecting, enjoying the sun, the beach, the solitude, this stupid beast had lifted its leg and used me as a pissoir—and now it was poised there on the edge of the blanket as if it expected a reward. A sudden rage seized me. I came up off the blanket with a curse, and it was only then that a dim apprehension seemed to seep into the dog's other eye, the brown one, and it lurched back and fell on its face, just out of reach. And then it lurched and fell again, bobbing and weaving across the sand like a seal out of water. I was on my feet now, murderous, glad to see that the thing was hobbled—it would simplify the task of running it down and beating it to death.

"Alf!" a voice called, and as the dog floundered in the sand, I turned and saw Alena Jorgensen poised on the boulder behind me. I don't want to make too much of the moment, don't want to mythologize it or clutter the scene with allusions to Aphrodite rising from the waves or accepting the golden apple from Paris, but she was a pretty impressive sight. Bare-legged, fluid, as tall and uncompromising as her Nordic ancestors and dressed in a Gore-Tex bikini and hooded sweatshirt unzipped to the waist, she blew me away, in any event. Piss-spattered and stupefied, I could only gape up at her.

"You bad boy," she said, scolding, "you get out of there." She glanced from the dog to me and back again. "Oh, you bad boy, what have you done?" she demanded, and I was ready to admit to anything, but it was the dog she was addressing, and the dog flopped over in the sand as if it had been shot. Alena skipped lightly down from the rock, and in the next moment, before I could protest, she was rubbing at the stain on my windbreaker with the wadded-up hem of her sweatshirt.

I tried to stop her—"It's all right," I said, "it's nothing," as if dogs routinely pissed on my wardrobe—but she wouldn't hear of it.

"No," she said, rubbing, her hair flying in my face, the naked skin of her thigh pressed unconsciously to my own, "no, this is terrible, I'm so embarrassed—Alf, you bad boy—I'll clean it for you, I will, it's the least—oh, look at that, it's stained right through to your T-shirt—"

I could smell her, the mousse she used in her hair, a lilac soap or perfume, the salt-sweet odor of her sweat—she'd been jogging, that was it. I murmured something about taking it to the cleaner's myself.

She stopped rubbing and straightened up. She was my height, maybe even a fraction taller, and her eyes were ever so slightly mismatched, like the dog's: a deep earnest blue in the right iris, shading to sea-green and turquoise in the left. We were so close we might have been dancing. "Tell you what," she said, and her face lit with a smile, "since you're so nice about the whole thing, and most people wouldn't be, even if they knew what poor Alf has been through, why don't you let me wash it for you—and the T-shirt too?"

I was a little disconcerted at this point—I was the one who'd been pissed on, after all—but my anger was gone. I felt weightless, adrift, like a piece of fluff floating on the breeze. "Listen," I said, and for the moment I couldn't look her in the eye, "I don't want to put you to any trouble. . . ."

"I'm ten minutes up the beach, and I've got a washer and dryer. Come on, it's no trouble at all. Or do you have plans? I mean, I could just pay for the cleaner's if you want. . . ."

I was between relationships—the person I'd been seeing off and on for the past year wouldn't even return my calls—and my plans consisted of taking in a solitary late-afternoon movie as a birthday treat, then heading over to my mother's for dinner and the cake with the candles. My aunt Irene would be there, and so would my grandmother. They would exclaim over how big I was and how handsome and then they would begin to contrast my present self with my previous, more diminutive incarnations, and finally work themselves up to a spate of reminiscence that would continue unabated till my mother drove them home. And then, if I was lucky, I'd go out to a singles bar and make the acquaintance of a divorced computer programmer in her mid-thirties with three kids and bad breath.

I shrugged. "Plans? No, not really. I mean, nothing in particular."

Alena was housesitting a one-room bungalow that rose stump-like from the sand, no more than fifty feet from the tide line. There were trees in the yard behind it and the place was sandwiched between glass fortresses with crenellated decks, whipping flags and great hulking concrete pylons. Sitting on the couch inside, you could feel the dull reverberation of each wave hitting the shore, a slow steady pulse that forever defined the place for me. Alena gave me a faded UC Davis sweatshirt that nearly fit, sprayed a stain remover on my T-shirt and windbreaker, and in a single fluid motion flipped down the lid of the washer and extracted two beers from the refrigerator beside it.

There was an awkward moment as she settled into the chair opposite me and we concentrated on our beers. I didn't know what to say. I was disoriented, giddy, still struggling to grasp what had happened. Fifteen minutes earlier I'd been dozing on the beach, alone on my birthday and feeling sorry for myself, and now I was ensconced in a cozy beach house, in the presence of Alena Jorgensen and her naked spill of leg, drinking a beer. "So what do you do?" she said, setting her beer down on the coffee table.

I was grateful for the question, too grateful maybe. I described to her at length how dull my job was, nearly ten years with the same agency, writing ad copy, my brain gone numb with disuse. I was somewhere in the middle of a blow-by-blow account of our current campaign for a Ghanian vodka distilled from calabash husks when she said, "I know what you mean," and told me she'd dropped out of veterinary school herself. "After I saw what they did to the animals. I mean, can you see neutering a dog just for our convenience, just because it's easier for us if they don't have a sex life?" Her voice grew hot. "It's the same old story, species fascism at its worst."

Alf was lying at my feet, grunting softly and looking up mournfully out of his staring blue eye, as blameless a creature as ever lived. I made a small noise of agreement and then focused on Alf. "And your dog," I said, "he's arthritic? Or is it hip dysplasia or what?" I was pleased with myself for the question—aside from "tapeworm," "hip dysplasia" was the only veterinary term I could dredge up from the memory bank, and I could see that Alf's problems ran deeper than worms.

Alena looked angry suddenly. "Don't I wish," she said. She paused to draw a bitter breath. "There's nothing wrong with Alf that wasn't inflicted on him. They tortured him, maimed him, mutilated him."

"Tortured him?" I echoed, feeling the indignation rise in me—this beautiful girl, this innocent beast. "Who?"

Alena leaned forward and there was real hate in her eyes. She mentioned a prominent shoe company—spat out the name, actually. It was an ordinary name, a familiar one, and it hung in the air between us, suddenly sinister. Alf had been part of an experiment to market booties for dogs—suede, cordovan, patent leather, the works. The dogs were made to pace a treadmill in their booties, to assess wear; Alf was part of the control group.

"Control group?" I could feel the hackles rising on the back of my neck.

"They used eighty-grit sandpaper on the treads, to accelerate the process." Alena shot a glance out the window to where the surf pounded the shore; she bit her lip. "Alf was one of the dogs without booties."

I was stunned. I wanted to get up and comfort her, but I might as well have been grafted to the chair. "I don't believe it," I said. "How could anybody—"

"Believe it," she said. She studied me a moment, then set down her beer and crossed the room to dig through a cardboard box in the corner. If I was moved by the emotion she'd called up, I was moved even more by the sight of her bending over the box in her Gore-Tex bikini; I clung to the edge of the chair as if it were a plunging roller coaster. A moment later she dropped a dozen file folders in my lap. The uppermost bore the name of the shoe company, and it was crammed with news clippings, several pages of a diary relating to plant operations and workers' shifts at the Grand Rapids facility and a floor plan of the laboratories. The folders beneath it were inscribed with the names of cosmetics firms, biomedical research centers, furriers, tanners, meatpackers. Alena perched on the edge of the coffee table and watched as I shuffled through them.

"You know the Draize test?"

I gave her a blank look.

"They inject chemicals into rabbits' eyes to see how much it'll take before they go blind. The rabbits are in cages, thousands of them, and they take a needle and jab it into their eyes—and you know why, you know in the name of what great humanitarian cause this is going on, even as we speak?"

I didn't know. The surf pounded at my feet. I glanced at Alf and then back into her angry eyes.

"Mascara, that's what. Mascara. They torture countless thousands of rabbits so women can look like sluts."

I thought the characterization a bit harsh, but when I studied her pale lashes and tight lipstickless mouth, I saw that she meant it. At any rate, the notion set her off, and she launched into a two-hour lecture, gesturing with her flawless hands, quoting figures, digging through her files for the odd photo of legless mice or morphine-addicted gerbils. She told me how she'd rescued Alf herself, raiding the laboratory with six other members of the Animal Liberation Front, the militant group in honor of which Alf had been named. At first, she'd been content to write letters and carry placards, but now, with the lives of so many animals at stake, she'd turned to more direct action: harassment, vandalism, sabotage. She described how she'd spiked trees with Earth-First!-ers in Oregon, cut miles of barbed-wire fence on cattle ranches in Nevada, destroyed records in biomedical research labs up and down the coast and insinuated herself between the hunters and the bighorn sheep in the mountains of Arizona. I could only nod and exclaim, smile ruefully and whistle in a low "holy cow!" sort of way. Finally, she paused to level her unsettling eyes on me. "You know what Isaac Bashevis Singer said?"

We were on our third beer. The sun was gone. I didn't have a clue.

Alena leaned forward. " 'Every day is Auschwitz for the animals.' "

I looked down into the amber aperture of my beer bottle and nodded my head sadly. The dryer had stopped an hour and a half ago. I wondered if she'd go out to dinner with me, and what she could eat if she did. "Uh, I was wondering," I said, "if . . . if you might want to go out for something to eat—"

Alf chose that moment to heave himself up from the floor and urinate on the wall behind me. My dinner proposal hung in the balance as Alena shot up off the edge of the table to scold him and then gently usher him out the door. "Poor Alf," she sighed, turning back to me with a shrug. "But listen, I'm sorry if I talked your head off—I didn't mean to, but it's rare to find somebody on your own wavelength."

She smiled. *On your own wavelength:* the words illuminated me, excited me, sent up a tremor I could feel all the way down in the deepest nodes of my reproductive tract. "So how about dinner?" I persisted. Restaurants were running through my head—would it have to be veggie? Could there be even a whiff of grilled flesh on the air? Curdled goat's milk and tabbouleh, tofu, lentil soup, sprouts: *Every day is Auschwitz for animals.* "No place with meat, of course."

She just looked at me.

"I mean, I don't eat meat myself," I lied, "or actually, not anymore"—since the pastrami sandwich, that is—"but I don't really know any place that . . ." I trailed off lamely.

"I'm a Vegan," she said.

After two hours of blind bunnies, butchered calves and mutilated pups, I couldn't resist the joke. "I'm from Venus myself."

She laughed, but I could see she didn't find it all that funny. Vegans didn't eat meat or fish, she explained, or milk or cheese or eggs, and they didn't wear wool or leather—or fur, of course.

"Of course," I said. We were both standing there, hovering over the coffee table. I was beginning to feel a little foolish.

"Why don't we just eat here," she said.

The deep throb of the ocean seemed to settle in my bones as we lay there in bed that night, Alena and I, and I learned all about the fluency of her limbs and the sweetness of her vegetable tongue. Alf sprawled on the floor beneath us, wheezing and groaning in his sleep, and I blessed him for his incontinence and his doggy stupidity. Something was happening to me—I could feel it in the way the boards shifted under me, feel it with each beat of the surf—and I was ready to go along with it. In the morning, I called in sick again.

Alena was watching me from bed as I dialed the office and described how the flu had migrated from my head to my gut and beyond, and there was a look in her eye that told me I would spend the rest of the day right there beside her, peeling grapes and dropping them one by one between her parted and expectant lips. I was wrong. Half an hour later, after a breakfast of brewer's yeast and what appeared to be some sort of bark marinated in yogurt, I found myself marching up and down the sidewalk in front of a fur emporium in Beverly Hills, waving a placard that read HOW DOES IT FEEL TO WEAR A CORPSE? in letters that dripped like blood.

It was a shock. I'd seen protest marches on TV, antiwar rallies and civil-rights demonstrations and all that, but I'd never warmed my heels on the pavement or chanted slogans or felt the naked stick in my hand. There were maybe forty of us in all, mostly women, and we waved our placards at passing cars and blocked traffic on the sidewalk. One woman had smeared her face and hands with cold cream steeped in red dye, and Alena had found a ratty mink stole somewhere— the kind that features whole animals sewed together, snout to tail, their minia-ture limbs dangling—and she'd taken a can of crimson spray paint to their muzzles so that they looked freshly killed. She brandished this grisly banner on a stick high above her head, whooping like a savage and chanting, "Fur is death, fur is death," over and over again till it became a mantra for the crowd. The day was unseasonably warm, the Jaguars glinted in the sun and the palms nodded in the breeze, and no one, but for a single tight-lipped salesman glowering from be-hind the store's immaculate windows, paid the slightest bit of attention to us.

I marched out there on the street, feeling exposed and conspicuous, but marching nonetheless—for Alena's sake and for the sake of the foxes and mar-tens and all the rest, and for my own sake too: with each step I took I could feel my consciousness expanding like a balloon, the breath of saintliness seeping steadily into me. Up to this point I'd worn suede and leather like anybody else, ankle boots and Air Jordans, a bombardier jacket I'd had since high school. If I'd drawn the line with fur, it was only because I'd never had any use for it. If I lived in the Yukon—and sometimes, drowsing through a meeting at work, I found my-self fantasizing about it—I would have worn fur, no compunction, no second thoughts.

But not anymore. Now I was a protestor, a placard waver, now I was fighting for the right of every last weasel and lynx to grow old and die gracefully, now I was Alena Jorgensen's lover and a force to be reckoned with. Of course, my feet hurt and I was running sweat and praying that no one from work would drive by and see me there on the sidewalk with my crazy cohorts and denunciatory sign.

We marched for hours, back and forth, till I thought we'd wear a groove in the pavement. We chanted and jeered and nobody so much as looked at us twice. We could have been Hare Krishnas, bums, antiabortionists or lepers, what did it matter? To the rest of the world, to the uninitiated masses to whose sorry num-ber I'd belonged just twenty-four hours earlier, we were invisible. I was hungry, tired, discouraged. Alena was ignoring me. Even the woman in red-face was slowing down, her chant a hoarse whisper that was sucked up and obliterated in the roar of traffic. And then, as the afternoon faded toward rush hour, a wizened silvery old woman who might have been an aging star or a star's mother or even the first dimly remembered wife of a studio exec got out of a long white car at the curb and strode fearlessly toward us. Despite the heat—it must have been eighty degrees at this point—she was wearing an ankle-length silver fox coat, a bristling shouldery wafting mass of peltry that must have decimated every burrow on the tundra. It was the moment we'd been waiting for.

A cry went up, shrill and ululating, and we converged on the lone old woman like a Cheyenne war party scouring the plains. The man beside me went down on all fours and howled like a dog, Alena slashed the air with her limp mink and the blood sang in my ears. "Murderer!" I screamed, getting into it. "Torturer! Nazi!" The strings in my neck were tight. I didn't know what I was saying. The crowd gibbered. The placards danced. I was so close to the old woman I could smell her—her perfume, a whiff of mothballs from the coat—and it intoxicated me, maddened me, and I stepped in front of her and blocked her path with all the seething militant bulk of my one hundred eighty-five pounds of sinew and muscle.

I never saw the chauffeur. Alena told me afterward that he was a former kickboxing champion who'd been banned from the sport for excessive brutality. The first blow seemed to drop down from above, a shell lobbed from deep within enemy territory; the others came at me like a windmill churning in a storm. Someone screamed. I remember focusing on the flawless rigid pleats of the chauffeur's trousers, and then things got a bit hazy.

I woke to the dull thump of the surf slamming at the shore and the touch of Alena's lips on my own. I felt as if I'd been broken on the wheel, dismembered and put back together again. "Lie still," she said, and her tongue moved against my swollen cheek. Stricken, I could only drag my head across the pillow and gaze into the depths of her parti-colored eyes. "You're one of us now," she whispered.

Next morning I didn't even bother to call in sick.

By the end of the week I'd recovered enough to crave meat, for which I felt deeply ashamed, and to wear out a pair of vinyl huaraches on the picket line. Together, and with various coalitions of antivivisectionists, militant Vegans and cat lovers, Alena and I tramped a hundred miles of sidewalk, spray-painted inflammatory slogans across the windows of supermarkets and burger stands, denounced tanners, farriers, poulterers and sausage makers, and somehow found time to break up a cockfight in Pacoima. It was exhilarating, heady, dangerous. If I'd been disconnected in the past, I was plugged in now. I felt righteous—for the first time in my life I had a cause—and I had Alena, Alena above all. She fascinated me, fixated me, made me feel like a tomcat leaping in and out of second-story windows, oblivious to the free-fall and the picket fence below. There was her beauty, of course, a triumph of evolution and the happy interchange of genes going all the way back to the cavemen, but it was more than that—it was her commitment to animals, to the righting of wrongs, to morality that made her irresistible. Was it love? The term is something I've always had difficulty with, but I suppose it was. Sure it was. Love, pure and simple. I had it, it had me.

"You know what?" Alena said one night as she stood over the miniature stove, searing tofu in oil and garlic. We'd spent the afternoon demonstrating out front of a tortilla factory that used rendered animal fat as a congealing agent, after which we'd been chased three blocks by an overweight assistant manager at Von's who objected to Alena's spray-painting MEAT IS DEATH over the specials in the front window. I was giddy with the adolescent joy of it. I sank into the couch with a beer and watched Alf limp across the floor to fling himself down and lick at a suspicious spot on the floor. The surf boomed like thunder.

"What?" I said.

"Thanksgiving's coming."

I let it ride a moment, wondering if I should invite Alena to my mother's for the big basted bird stuffed with canned oysters and buttered bread crumbs, and then realized it probably wouldn't be such a great idea. I said nothing.

She glanced over her shoulder. "The animals don't have a whole lot to be thankful for, that's for sure. It's just an excuse for the meat industry to butcher a couple million turkeys, is all it is." She paused; hot safflower oil popped in the pan. "I think it's time for a little road trip," she said. "Can we take your car?"

"Sure, but where are we going?"

She gave me her Gioconda smile. "To liberate some turkeys."

In the morning I called my boss to tell him I had pancreatic cancer and wouldn't be in for a while, then we threw some things in the car, helped Alf scrabble into the back seat, and headed up Route 5 for the San Joaquin Valley. We drove for three hours through a fog so dense the windows might as well have been packed with cotton. Alena was secretive, but I could see she was excited. I knew only that we were on our way to rendezvous with a certain "Rolfe," a longtime friend of hers and a big name in the world of ecotage and animal rights, after which we would commit some desperate and illegal act, for which the turkeys would be eternally grateful.

There was a truck stalled in front of the sign for our exit at Calpurnia Springs, and I had to brake hard and jerk the wheel around twice to keep the tires on the pavement. Alena came up out of her seat and Alf slammed into the armrest like a sack of meal, but we made it. A few minutes later we were gliding through the ghostly vacancy of the town itself, lights drifting past in a nimbus of fog, glowing pink, yellow and white, and then there was only the blacktop road and the pale void that engulfed it. We'd gone ten miles or so when Alena instructed me to slow down and began to study the right-hand shoulder with a keen, unwavering eye.

The earth breathed in and out. I squinted hard into the soft drifting glow of the headlights. "There, there!" she cried and I swung the wheel to the right, and suddenly we were lurching along a pitted dirt road that rose up from the blacktop like a goat path worn into the side of a mountain. Five minutes later Alf sat up in the back seat and began to whine, and then a crude unpainted shack began to detach itself from the vagueness around us.

Rolfe met us on the porch. He was tall and leathery, in his fifties, I guessed, with a shock of hair and rutted features that brought Samuel Beckett to mind. He was wearing gumboots and jeans and a faded lumberjack shirt that looked as if it had been washed a hundred times. Alf took a quick pee against the side of the house, then fumbled up the steps to roll over and fawn at his feet.

"Rolfe!" Alena called, and there was too much animation in her voice, too much familiarity, for my taste. She took the steps in a bound and threw herself in his arms. I watched them kiss, and it wasn't a fatherly-daughterly sort of kiss, not at all. It was a kiss with some meaning behind it, and I didn't like it. Rolfe, I thought: What kind of name is that?

"Rolfe," Alena gasped, still a little breathless from bouncing up the steps like a cheerleader, "I'd like you to meet Jim."

This was my signal. I ascended the porch steps and held out my hand. Rolfe gave me a look out of the hooded depths of his eyes and then took my hand in a hard callused grip, the grip of the wood splitter, the fence mender, the liberator of hothouse turkeys and laboratory mice. "A pleasure," he said, and his voice rasped like sandpaper.

There was a fire going inside, and Alena and I sat before it and warmed our hands while Alf whined and sniffed and Rolfe served Red Zinger tea in Japanese cups the size of thimbles. Alena hadn't stopped chattering since we stepped through the door, and Rolfe came right back at her in his woodsy rasp, the two of them exchanging names and news and gossip as if they were talking in code. I studied the reproductions of teal and widgeon that hung from the peeling walls, noted the case of Heinz vegetarian beans in the corner and the half-gallon of Jack Daniel's on the mantel. Finally, after the third cup of tea, Alena settled back in her chair—a huge old Salvation Army sort of thing with a soiled antimacassar—and said, "So what's the plan?"

Rolfe gave me another look, a quick predatory darting of the eyes, as if he weren't sure I could be trusted, and then turned back to Alena. "Hedda Gabler's Range-Fed Turkey Ranch," he said. "And no, I don't find the name cute, not at all." He looked at me now, a long steady assay. "They grind up the heads for cat food, and the neck, the organs and the rest, that they wrap up in paper and stuff back in the body cavity like it was a war atrocity or something. Whatever did a turkey go and do to us to deserve a fate like that?"

The question was rhetorical, even if it seemed to have been aimed at me, and I made no response other than to compose my face in a look that wedded grief, outrage and resolve. I was thinking of all the turkeys I'd sent to their doom, of the plucked wishbones, the pope's noses and the crisp browned skin I used to relish as a kid. It brought a lump to my throat, and something more: I realized I was hungry.

"Ben Franklin wanted to make them our national symbol," Alena chimed in, "did you know that? But the meat eaters won out."

"Fifty thousand birds," Rolfe said, glancing at Alena and bringing his incendiary gaze back to rest on me. "I have information they're going to start slaughtering them tomorrow, for the fresh-not-frozen market."

"Yuppie poultry." Alena's voice was drenched in disgust.

For a moment, no one spoke. I became aware of the crackling of the fire. The fog pressed at the windows. It was getting dark.

"You can see the place from the highway," Rolfe said finally, "but the only access is through Calpurnia Springs. It's about twenty miles—twenty-two point three, to be exact."

Alena's eyes were bright. She was gazing on Rolfe as if he'd just dropped down from heaven. I felt something heave in my stomach.

"We strike tonight."

Rolfe insisted that we take my car—"Everybody around here knows my pickup, and I can't take any chances on a little operation like this"—but we did mask the plates, front and back, with an inch-thick smear of mud. We blackened our faces like commandos and collected our tools from the shed out back—tin snips, a crowbar and two five-gallon cans of gasoline. "Gasoline?" I said, trying the heft of the can. Rolfe gave me a craggy look. "To create a diversion," he said. Alf, for obvious reasons, stayed behind in the shack.

If the fog had been thick in daylight, it was impermeable now, the sky collapsed upon the earth. It took hold of the headlights and threw them back at me till my eyes began to water from the effort of keeping the car on the road. But for the ruts and bumps we might have been floating in space. Alena sat up front between Rolfe and me, curiously silent. Rolfe didn't have much to say either, save for the occasional grunted command: "Hang a right here"; "Hard left"; "Easy, easy." I thought about meat and jail and the heroic proportions to which I was about to swell in Alena's eyes and what I intended to do to her when we finally got to bed. It was 2:00 A.M. by the dashboard clock.

"Okay," Rolfe said, and his voice came at me so suddenly it startled me, "pull over here—and kill the lights."

We stepped out into the hush of night and eased the doors shut behind us. I couldn't see a thing, but I could hear the not-so-distant hiss of traffic on the highway, and another sound, too, muffled and indistinct, the gentle unconscious suspiration of thousands upon thousands of my fellow creatures. And I could smell them, a seething rancid odor of feces and feathers and naked scaly feet that crawled down my throat and burned my nostrils. "Whew," I said in a whisper, "I can smell them."

Rolfe and Alena were vague presences at my side. Rolfe flipped open the trunk and in the next moment I felt the heft of a crowbar and a pair of tin snips in my hand. "Listen, you, Jim," Rolfe whispered, taking me by the wrist in his iron grip and leading me half-a-dozen steps forward. "Feel this?"

I felt a grid of wire, which he promptly cut: *snip, snip, snip.*

"This is their enclosure—they're out there in the day, scratching around in the dirt. You get lost, you follow this wire. Now, you're going to take a section out of this side, Alena's got the west side and I've got the south. Once that's done I signal with the flashlight and we bust open the doors to the turkey houses—they're these big low white buildings, you'll see them when you get close—and flush the birds out. Don't worry about me or Alena. Just worry about getting as many birds out as you can."

I was worried. Worried about everything, from some half-crazed farmer with a shotgun or AK-47 or whatever they carried these days, to losing Alena in the fog, to the turkeys themselves: How big were they? Were they violent? They had claws and beaks, didn't they? And how were they going to feel about me bursting into their bedroom in the middle of the night?

"And when the gas cans go up, you hightail it back to the car, got it?"

I could hear the turkeys tossing in their sleep. A truck shifted gears out on the highway. "I think so," I whispered.

"And one more thing—be sure to leave the keys in the ignition."

This gave me pause. "But—"

"The getaway." Alena was so close I could feel her breath on my ear. "I mean, we don't want to be fumbling around for the keys when all hell is breaking loose out there, do we?"

I eased open the door and reinserted the keys in the ignition, even though the automatic buzzer warned me against it. "Okay," I murmured, but they were already gone, soaked up in the shadows and the mist. At this point my heart was hammering so loudly I could barely hear the rustling of the turkeys—this is crazy, I told myself, it's hurtful and wrong, not to mention illegal. Spray-painting slogans was one thing, but this was something else altogether. I thought of the turkey farmer asleep in his bed, an entrepreneur working to make America strong, a man with a wife and kids and a mortgage . . . but then I thought of all those innocent turkeys consigned to death, and finally I thought of Alena, long-legged and loving, and the way she came to me out of the darkness of the bathroom and the boom of the surf. I took the tin snips to the wire.

I must have been at it half an hour, forty-five minutes, gradually working my way toward the big white sheds that had begun to emerge from the gloom up ahead, when I saw Rolfe's flashlight blinking off to my left. This was my signal to head to the nearest shed, snap off the padlock with my crowbar, fling open the doors and herd a bunch of cranky suspicious gobblers out into the night. It was now or never. I looked twice round me and then broke for the near shed in an awkward crouching gait. The turkeys must have sensed that something was up—from behind the long white windowless wall there arose a watchful gabbling, a soughing of feathers that fanned up like a breeze in the treetops. *Hold on, you toms and hens,* I thought, *freedom is at hand.* A jerk of the wrist, and the padlock fell to the ground. Blood pounding in my ears, I took hold of the sliding door and jerked it open with a great dull booming reverberation—and suddenly, there they were, turkeys, thousands upon thousands of them, cloaked in white feathers under a string of dim yellow bulbs. The light glinted in their reptilian eyes. Somewhere a dog began to bark.

I steeled myself and sprang through the door with a shout, whirling the crowbar over my head. "All right!" I boomed, and the echo gave it back to me a hundred times over, "this is it! Turkeys, on your feet!" Nothing. No response. But for the whisper of rustling feathers and the alertly cocked heads, they might have been sculptures, throw pillows, they might as well have been dead and butchered and served up with yams and onions and all the trimmings. The barking of the dog went up a notch. I thought I heard voices.

The turkeys crouched on the concrete floor, wave upon wave of them, stupid and immovable; they perched in the rafters, on shelves and platforms, huddled in wooden stalls. Desperate, I rushed into the front rank of them, swinging my crowbar, stamping my feet and howling like the wishbone plucker I once was. That did it. There was a shriek from the nearest bird and the others took it up till an unholy racket filled the place, and now they were moving, tumbling down from their perches, flapping their wings in a storm of dried excrement and pecked-over grain, pouring across the concrete floor till it vanished beneath them. Encouraged, I screamed again—"Yeeee-ha-ha-ha-ha!"—and beat at the aluminum walls with the crowbar as the turkeys shot through the doorway and out into the night.

It was then that the black mouth of the doorway erupted with light and the *ka-boom!* of the gas cans sent a tremor through the earth. *Run!* a voice screamed in my head, and the adrenaline kicked in and all of a sudden I was scrambling for the door in a hurricane of turkeys. They were everywhere, flapping their wings, gobbling and screeching, loosing their bowels in panic. Something hit the back of my legs and all at once I was down amongst them, on the floor, in the dirt and feathers and wet turkey shit. I was a roadbed, a turkey expressway. Their claws dug at my back, my shoulders, the crown of my head. Panicked now, choking on feathers and dust and worse, I fought to my feet as the big screeching birds launched themselves round me, and staggered out into the barnyard. "There! Who's that there?" a voice roared, and I was off and running.

What can I say? I vaulted turkeys, kicked them aside like so many footballs, slashed and tore at them as they sailed through the air. I ran till my lungs felt as if they were burning right through my chest, disoriented, bewildered, terrified of the shotgun blast I was sure would cut me down at any moment. Behind me the fire raged and lit the fog till it glowed blood-red and hellish. But where was the fence? And where the car?

I got control of my feet then and stood stock-still in a flurry of turkeys, squinting into the wall of fog. Was that it? Was that the car over there? At that moment I heard an engine start up somewhere behind me—a familiar engine with a familiar coughing gurgle in the throat of the carburetor—and then the lights blinked on briefly three hundred yards away. I heard the engine race and listened, helpless, as the car roared off in the opposite direction. I stood there a moment longer, forlorn and forsaken, and then I ran blindly off into the night, putting the fire and the shouts and the barking and the incessant mindless squawking of the turkeys as far behind me as I could.

When dawn finally broke, it was only just perceptibly, so thick was the fog. I'd made my way to a blacktop road—which road and where it led I didn't know— and sat crouched and shivering in a clump of weed just off the shoulder. Alena wouldn't desert me, I was sure of that—she loved me, as I loved her; needed me, as I needed her—and I was sure she'd be cruising along the back roads looking for me. My pride was wounded, of course, and if I never laid eyes on Rolfe again I felt I wouldn't be missing much, but at least I hadn't been drilled full of shot, savaged by farm dogs or pecked to death by irate turkeys. I was sore all over, my shin throbbed where I'd slammed into something substantial while vaulting through the night, there were feathers in my hair and my face and arms were a mosaic of cuts and scratches and long trailing fissures of dirt. I'd been sitting there for what seemed like hours, cursing Rolfe, developing suspicions about Alena and unflattering theories about environmentalists in general, when finally I heard the familiar slurp and roar of my Chevy Citation cutting through the mist ahead of me.

Rolfe was driving, his face impassive. I flung myself into the road like a tattered beggar, waving my arms over my head and giving vent to my joy, and he very nearly ran me down. Alena was out of the car before it stopped, wrapping me up in her arms, and then she was bundling me into the rear seat with Alf and we were on our way back to the hideaway. "What happened?" she cried, as if she couldn't have guessed. "Where were you? We waited as long as we could."

I was feeling sulky, betrayed, feeling as if I was owed a whole lot more than a perfunctory hug and a string of insipid questions. Still, as I told my tale I began to warm to it—they'd got away in the car with the heater going, and I'd stayed behind to fight the turkeys, the farmers and the elements, too, and if that wasn't heroic, I'd like to know what was. I looked into Alena's admiring eyes and pictured Rolfe's shack, a nip or two from the bottle of Jack Daniel's, maybe a peanut-butter-and-tofu sandwich and then the bed, with Alena in it. Rolfe said nothing.

Back at Rolfe's, I took a shower and scrubbed the turkey droppings from my pores, then helped myself to the bourbon. It was ten in the morning and the house was dark—if the world had ever been without fog, there was no sign of it here. When Rolfe stepped out on the porch to fetch an armload of firewood, I pulled Alena down into my lap. "Hey," she murmured, "I thought you were an invalid."

She was wearing a pair of too-tight jeans and an oversize sweater with nothing underneath it. I slipped my hand inside the sweater and found something to hold on to. "Invalid?" I said, nuzzling at her sleeve. "Hell, I'm a turkey liberator, an ecoguerrilla, a friend of the animals and the environment, too."

She laughed, but she pushed herself up and crossed the room to stare out the occluded window. "Listen, Jim," she said, "what we did last night was great, really great, but it's just the beginning." Alf looked up at her expectantly. I heard Rolfe fumbling around on the porch, the thump of wood on wood. She turned round to face me now. "What I mean is, Rolfe wants me to go up to Wyoming for a little bit, just outside of Yellowstone—"

Me? Rolfe wants me? There was no invitation in that, no plurality, no acknowledgment of all we'd done and meant to each other. "For what?" I said. "What do you mean?"

"There's this grizzly—a pair of them, actually—and they've been raiding places outside the park. One of them made off with the mayor's Doberman the other night and the people are up in arms. We—I mean Rolfe and me and some other people from the old Bolt Weevils in Minnesota?—we're going to go up there and make sure the Park Service—or the local yahoos—don't eliminate them. The bears, I mean."

My tone was corrosive. "You and Rolfe?"

"There's nothing between us, if that's what you're thinking. This has to do with animals, that's all."

"Like us?"

She shook her head slowly. "Not like us, no. We're the plague on this planet, don't you know that?"

Suddenly I was angry. Seething. Here I'd crouched in the bushes all night, covered in turkey crap, and now I was part of a plague. I was on my feet. "No, I don't know that."

She gave me a look that let me know it didn't matter, that she was already gone, that her agenda, at least for the moment, didn't include me and there was no use arguing about it. "Look," she said, her voice dropping as Rolfe slammed back through the door with a load of wood, "I'll see you in L.A. in a month or so, okay?" She gave me an apologetic smile. "Water the plants for me?"

An hour later I was on the road again. I'd helped Rolfe stack the wood beside the fireplace, allowed Alena to brush my lips with a goodbye kiss, and then stood there on the porch while Rolfe locked up, lifted Alf into the bed of his pickup and rumbled down the rutted dirt road with Alena at his side. I watched till their brake lights dissolved in the drifting gray mist, then fired up the Citation and lurched down the road behind them. *A month or so:* I felt hollow inside. I pictured her with Rolfe, eating soy yogurt and wheat germ, stopping at motels, wrestling grizzlies and spiking trees. The hollowness opened up, cored me out till I felt as if I'd been plucked and gutted and served up on a platter myself.

I found my way back through Calpurnia Springs without incident—there were no roadblocks, no flashing lights and grim-looking troopers searching trunks and back seats for a tallish thirty-year-old ecoterrorist with turkey tracks down his back—but after I turned onto the highway for Los Angeles, I had a shock. Ten miles up the road my nightmare materialized out of the gloom: red lights everywhere, signal flares and police cars lined up on the shoulder. I was on the very edge of panicking, a beat away from cutting across the meridian and giving them a run for it, when I saw the truck jackknifed up ahead. I slowed to forty, thirty, and then hit the brakes again. In a moment I was stalled in a line of cars and there was something all over the road, ghostly and white in the fog. At first I thought it must have been flung from the truck, rolls of toilet paper or crates of soap powder ruptured on the pavement. It was neither. As I inched closer, the tires creeping now, the pulse of the lights in my face, I saw that the road was coated in feathers, turkey feathers. A storm of them. A blizzard. And more: there was flesh there too, slick and greasy, a red pulp ground into the surface of the road, thrown up like slush from the tires of the car ahead of me, ground beneath the massive wheels of the truck. Turkeys. Turkeys everywhere.

The car crept forward. I flicked on the windshield wipers, hit the washer button, and for a moment a scrim of diluted blood obscured the windows and the hollowness opened up inside of me till I thought it would suck me inside out. Behind me, someone was leaning on his horn. A trooper loomed up out of the gloom, waving me on with the dead yellow eye of his flashlight. I thought of Alena and felt sick. All there was between us had come to this, expectations gone sour, a smear on the road. I wanted to get out and shoot myself, turn myself in, close my eyes and wake up in jail, in a hair shirt, in a straitjacket, anything. It went on. Time passed. Nothing moved. And then, miraculously, a vision began to emerge from behind the smeared glass and the gray belly of the fog, lights glowing golden in the waste. I saw the sign, Gas/Food/Lodging, and my hand was on the blinker.

It took me a moment, picturing the place, the generic tile, the false cheer of the lights, the odor of charred flesh hanging heavy on the air, Big Mac, three-piece dark meat, carne asada, cheeseburger. The engine coughed. The lights glowed. I didn't think of Alena then, didn't think of Rolfe or grizzlies or the doomed bleating flocks and herds, or of the blind bunnies and cancerous mice— I thought only of the cavern opening inside me and how to fill it. "Meat," and I spoke the word aloud, talking to calm myself as if I'd awakened from a bad dream, "it's only meat."

(1990)

ACTS OF GOD

He'd been married before, and now he was married again. The last wife, Dixie, had taken the house, the car, the dog, the blender and his collection of Glenn Miller and Tommy Dorsey records. The wife before that, Margot, had been his first, and he'd known her since he'd worn shoulder pads and spikes and she cried out his name from the sidelines, her big chocolate eyes wide with excitement and the black bobbed hair cutting a Spanish fringe across her brow; she'd taken the first house, the children and his self-respect. Muriel was different. She was a force upon the earth, an act of God, demanding, unshakable, born a queen, an empress, born to dictate and command. She took everything that was left.

And there wasn't a whole lot of that. Willis was seventy-five years old— seventy-six, come October—he had some money in CDs and an undeveloped lot or two, he owned a pair of classic 1972 Ford Fairlanes—"classic" being a code word for junk—and he was so weak in the hips he had to work on his feet for fear he wouldn't be able to get up again once he sat down. And work he did. He was a builder, a master builder, and he'd been in the trade for sixty years, working with the pride and compulsion his mother had instilled in him in a bygone era. No retirement villages for him, no putting greens or clubhouses. If you're not working you might as well be dead, that's how he saw it. And it wasn't as if he had a choice—Muriel would never let him retire, or rest even. She worked him like a mule and he bowed his head and did what was expected of him.

For her part, Muriel had been married four times, counting the present arrangement. She'd pretty well forgotten the middle two husbands—tired men, tired under the eyes, in the blood, in bed—but the first had been a saint. Handsome, a saxophone player with wavy dark hair and a perfect little Ronald

Colman mustache—and rich, too. His father owned a whole constellation of rental properties and a resort in the Catskills, with a lake and a casino and quaint little bungalows that looked as if they'd been lifted off their foundations in the English countryside and transported, lock, stock and barrel, to Gaudinet Lake. The shoulders on that man, Lester Gaudinet . . . she didn't know why she'd ever divorced him. Of course, she had Willis now, and he was all right—if she kept after him. Still, as she sat through the long afternoons with a bottle of Petit-Sirah, clipping things from the newspaper, baking roasts and hams and pies enough for an army though she wouldn't eat two bites herself and Willis, even with his appetite, couldn't begin to make a dent in them, she couldn't help pining, just a bit, for Lester Gaudinet and the lilting breathy rhapsody of his saxophone, and she couldn't help feeling that at sixty-eight, life had begun to pass her by.

It was a close brooding morning in late September, and Willis was up at six, as usual, washing last night's dishes, sweeping up, sneaking a half-eaten leg of lamb coated with a greenish fluorescent fuzz into the trash. He fetched the newspaper from the front lawn and was about to sit down over a cup of coffee and a slice of toast when he discovered that they were out of Vita-Health Oat Bran Nutri-Nugget bread. Each morning for her breakfast, which Willis prepared with care and trepidation before hurrying off to the job site, Muriel had two slices, lightly toasted and dry, of Vita-Health Oat Bran Nutri-Nugget bread with a two-minute, twenty-seven-second egg, six ounces of fresh-squeezed Florida orange juice and three thimble-sized cups of espresso. If she was difficult in the evening, when all he wanted was to collapse in front of the TV with a tall scotch and water, she was impossible in the morning, crawling out of the blood-red cave of her insomniac's sleep like a lioness poked with a stick, and he'd long since learned the survival value of presenting her with the placebo of a flawless breakfast. Willis squinted in vain into the cavernous depths of the breadbox and understood that he had a full-blown crisis on his hands.

A sunless dawn was breaking beyond the windows and it filled the kitchen with a sick hopeless light. For a moment Willis stood there at the counter, gaping round him as if he didn't recognize the place, and then he got hold of himself and fastened on the thought of the twenty-four-hour Quick-Stop on the corner. Would they have it? Not a chance, he decided, mentally browsing the bright but niggardly shelves—beer they had, yes, cigarettes, pornographic magazines, candy, videotape, gum—but who needed bread? He could already picture the six stale loaves of Wonder bread stiffening in their wrappers, but he fished his Mets cap out of the closet, stepped out the front door and crossed the dewy lawn to the car, figuring he had nothing to lose.

Outside, as he stood fumbling with the keys at the door of Muriel's car—they called it Muriel's car because she'd insisted on buying the thing though she'd

been raised in the city and had never been behind the wheel of a car in her life—
he was struck by something in the air. What was it? There was a raw smell of the
ocean, much stronger than usual, and the atmosphere seemed to brood over
him, heavy, damp, the pull and tug of a thousand tiny fingers. And the birds—
where were the birds? There was no sound except for the rattle of a truck out on
the highway . . . but then he really didn't have time to dawdle and smell the
breeze and linger over the little mysteries of life like some loopy-eyed kid on his
way to school, and he ducked into the car, fired up the mufflerless engine with a
roar and shriek that set every dog in the neighborhood howling—and there was
noise now, noise to spare—and rumbled up the road for the Quick-Stop.

The man behind the counter gave a violent start when Willis stepped through
the door but relaxed almost immediately—the store had been robbed once or
twice a week for as long as Willis could remember, and he supposed they had a
right to be nervous. He shuffled up to the counter, patting his pockets unconsciously to locate his wallet, keys and checkbook, and said, "Bread?," making a
question of it. The clerk was small, slight, dark-skinned, and he peered up at
Willis in mute incomprehension, as if he'd been speaking another language,
which in fact he had: Willis didn't know what the man was—Pakistani, Puerto
Rican or Pathan—but it was apparent that English was not his first language.
"Pan?" Willis tried, tossing out a nugget of the Spanish he'd picked up in Texas
during the war. The man stared at him out of deep-set eyes. He must have been
twenty-one—he'd have to be to work here—but to Willis, from the perspective
of his accumulating years, the man was a boy, absurdly young, twelve, ten years
old, a baby. The boy/man raised a languid arm and pointed, and Willis moved off
in the direction indicated. Pasta, kitty litter, nachos . . . and there it was, sure
enough—bread, sandwiched between the suntan oil and disposable diapers. A
sad little collection of hot-dog buns, pita bread, tortillas and a single fortified nut
loaf greeted him: there was no Vita-Health Oat Bran Nutri-Nugget bread. What
did he expect, miracles?

When he shuffled back into the kitchen, running late now, the fortified nut
loaf tucked like a football under his arm, he had a shock: Muriel was up. There
were telltale traces of her on the counter, at the door of the refrigerator and on
the base of the coffeemaker. He saw where yesterday's grounds had been flung at
the trash can and dribbled down the wall behind it, saw where she'd set her cup
down on the stove and where she'd torn through the cabinet in search of her
pills and artificial sweetener; in the same moment the muted rumble of the TV
came to him from the next room. He was fumbling with the espresso machine,
hurrying, the framers due at seven-thirty and the plumber at eight, when she appeared in the doorway.

Muriel's face composed itself around the point of her Scotch-Irish nose and
the tight little pout of her stingy lips. She was short and busty, and the tips of her
toes peeked out from beneath the hem of her nightgown. "Where the hell have
you been?" she demanded.

He turned to the stove. A jolt of pain shot through his hips—there was weather coming, he could feel it. "We were out of bread, sweetie," he said, presenting the side of his face to her as he spooned the eggs from their shells. "I had to go down to the Quick-Stop."

This seemed to placate her, and she subsided into the living room and huddled over her coffee mug in front of the TV screen. Willis could see the TV from the kitchen, where he popped the toast, brewed the espresso and squeezed the oranges. A chirpy woman with a broad blond face and hair that might have been spun sugar was chirping something about weight loss and a new brand of cracker made from seaweed. Willis arranged Muriel's things on a tray and brought them in to her.

She gave him a hard look as he set the tray down on the coffee table, but then she smiled and grabbed his arm to pull his face down, peck him a kiss and tell him how much he spoiled her. "Got to go, sweetie," he murmured, already backing away, already thinking of the car, the road, the house by the ocean that was rising before his eyes like a dream made concrete.

"You'll be home for lunch?"

"Yes, sweetie," he murmured, and then he made a fatal miscalculation: he lingered there before the glowing ball of the TV. The weatherman, in a silly suit and bow tie and mugging like a shill, had replaced the chirping confection of a woman, and Willis lingered—he'd smelled the weather on the air and felt it in his hips, and he was briefly curious. After all, he was going to be out in it all day long.

It was at that moment that Muriel's cry rose up out of the depths of the couch as from the ringside seats at a boxing match—harsh, querulous, the voice of disbelief and betrayal. "And what do you call *this?*" she boomed, nullifying the weatherman, his maps and pointers and satellite photos, the TV itself.

"What, sweetie?" Willis managed, his voice a small scuttling thing receding into its hole. The windows were gray. The weatherman blathered about wind velocity and temperature readings.

"This, this *toast.*"

"They didn't have your bread, sweetie, and Waldbaum's won't be open for another hour yet—"

"You son of a bitch." Suddenly she was on her feet, red-faced and panting for breath. "Didn't I tell you I wanted to go shopping last night? Didn't I tell you I needed things?"

They'd been together for two years now, and Willis knew there was no reasoning with her, not at this hour, not before she'd had her eggs and toast, not before she'd been sedated by the parade of game shows and soap operas that marched relentlessly through her mornings. All he could do was slump his shoulders penitently and edge toward the door.

But she anticipated him, darting furiously at him and crying, "That's right, leave me, go on off to work and leave me here, you son of a bitch!" She was in a mood, she could do anything, he knew it, and he shrank away from her as she changed course suddenly, jerked back from him and snatched up the breakfast tray in an explosion of crockery, cutlery and searing black liquid. "Toast!" she shrieked. "You call this toast!?" And then, as he watched in horror, the tray itself sailed across the room like a heat-seeking missile, sure and swift, dodging the lamp and coasting over the crest of the couch to discover its inevitable target in the grinning, winking, pointer-wielding image of the weatherman.

Later, after Willis had gone off to work and Muriel had had a chance to calm herself and reflect on the annihilation of the TV and the espresso stains on the rug, she felt ashamed and repentant. She'd let her nerves get the better of her and she was wrong, she'd be the first to admit it. And not only that, but who had she hurt but herself—it was like murdering her only friend, cutting herself off from the world like a nun in a convent—worse: at least a nun had her prayers. The repairman—in her grief and confusion she very nearly dialed 911, and she was so distraught when she finally got through to him that he was there before a paramedic would even have got his jacket on—the repairman told her it was hopeless. The picture tube was shot and the best thing to do was just go out to Caldor and buy herself a new set, and then he named half-a-dozen Japanese brands and she lost control all over again. She'd be goddamned and roasted three times over in hell before she'd ever buy anything from a Jap after what they did to her brother in the war and what was he, the repairman, an American or what? Didn't he know how they laughed at us, the Japs? He hit his van on the run and didn't look back.

It was 10:00 A.M. Willis was at work, the weather was rotten and she was missing "Hollywood Squares" and couldn't even salve her hurt with the consolation of shopping—not till Willis came home, anyway. God, he was such a baby, she thought as she sat there at the kitchen table over a black and bitter cup of espresso. He'd been a real mess when she'd met him—the last wife had squeezed him like a dishrag and hung him out to dry. His clothes were filthy, he was drunk from morning till night, he'd been fired from his last three jobs and the car he was driving was like a coffin on wheels. She'd made a project of him. She'd rescued him, given him a home and clean underwear and hankies, and if he thanked her a hundred times a day it wouldn't be enough. If she kept the reins tight, it was because she had to. Let him go—even for an hour—and he'd come home three days later stinking of gin and vomit.

The house was silent as a tomb. She gazed out the window; the clouds hung low and roiled over the roof, strung out like sausage, like entrails, black with blood and bile. There was a storm watch on, she'd heard that much on the "Morning" show, and again she felt a tug of regret over the TV. She wanted to get up that minute and turn on the news channel, but the news channel was no more—not for her, at any rate. There was the radio—and she experienced a sudden sharp stab of nostalgia for her girlhood and the nights when the whole family would crowd around the big Emerson console and listen to one program after another—but these days she never listened; it just gave her a headache. And with Willis around, who needed another headache?

She thought of the newspaper then and pushed herself up from the table to poke through the living room for it—if there was anything serious, a hurricane or something, they'd have a story on the front page. She was thinking about that, fixating on the newspaper, and she forgot all about the TV, so that when she stepped through the door, the sight of it gave her a shock. She'd swept up the broken glass, feeling chastened and heartbroken, but now the shattered screen accused her all over again. Guiltily, she shuffled through the heap of papers and magazines stuffed under the coffee table, then poked through the bedroom and finally went outside to comb the front lawn. No newspaper. Of all days, Willis must have taken it to work with him. And suddenly, standing there on the hushed and gray lawn in her housecoat and slippers, she was furious again. The son of a bitch. He never thought of her, never. Now she had the whole drizzling black miserable day ahead of her—TV-less, friendless, joyless—and she didn't even have the consolation of the newspaper.

While she was standing there out front of the house, poking halfheartedly under the bushes and noticing how shabby a job the gardener had done—and he'd hear from her, by god he would—a big brown UPS van glided into the driveway with a gentle sigh of the brakes. The driver was a young man, handsome, broad-shouldered, and for a minute she had a vision of Lester Gaudinet as he was all those many years ago. Lester Gaudinet. And where was he now? God knew if he was even alive still . . . but how she'd like to see him, wouldn't that be something?

"Mrs. Willis Blythe?" The man had crossed the lawn and he stood at her elbow now, a parcel tucked under his arm.

"Yes," she said, and the wind came up and took her hair out of its bun.

The man held out a clipboard to her, pages flapping. "Sign here," he said, handing her a pen, and she saw a list of names and signatures and the big red X he'd scrawled beside the space for her name.

She took the clipboard from him and smiled up into his sea-green eyes, into Lester's eyes, and she couldn't help trying to hold on to the moment. "Rotten day," she said.

He looked tense, anxious, looked as if he were about to lunge out of the blocks and disappear down a cinder track. "Hurricane weather," he said. "Supposed to miss us except for some rain later on—that's what the radio says, anyway."

She held the clipboard in her hand still and she bent forward to sign the form, but then a thought occurred to her and she straightened up again. "Hurricanes," she said with a little snort of contempt. "And I suppose it's called Bill or Fred or something like that—not like in the old days, when they had the sense to name them after women. It's a shame, isn't it?"

The UPS man was shuffling his feet on the spongy carpet of the lawn. "Yeah," he said, "sure—but would you sign, please, ma'am? I've got—"

She held up her hand to forestall him. God, he was handsome—the image of Lester. Of course, Lester had the mustache and he was taller and his eyes were prettier, brighter somehow . . . "I know, I know—you've got a million deliveries to make." She gave him a bright steady look. "It's women that're like hurricanes, they used to understand that"—was she flirting with him? Yes, of course she was—"but now it's Hurricane Tom, Dick or Harry. It just makes you sick, doesn't it?"

"Yeah," he said, "I know, but—"

"Okay, okay already, I'm signing." She inscribed his delivery sheet for him in the neat geometric script she'd mastered in parochial school in another age and then turned her coquette's smile on him—why not, was she so old it was impossible? Not in this world, not with the things that went on on TV these days. She touched his arm and held it a moment as he handed her the package. "Thank you," she murmured. "You're so handsome, do you know that?"

And then he stood there like an oaf, like a schoolboy, and he actually blushed. "Yes, yes," he stammered, "I mean no, I mean thank you," and then he was darting across the lawn with his clipboard flapping and the wind took her hair again. "Have a nice day!" she called, but he didn't hear her.

Inside, she examined the package briefly—*The Frinstell Corporation,* the label read—and then she went into the sewing room to fetch her scissors. The Frinstell Corporation, she thought, running it over in her mind, and what was this all about? She was forever clipping things out of magazines and sending away for them—once-in-a-lifetime offers and that sort of thing—but Frinstell didn't ring a bell. It took her a moment, the scissors gleaming dully in the crepuscular light of the kitchen, and then she had the tape slit up the seam and she was digging through the welter of tissue paper stuffed inside. And there—oh yes, of course—there was her genuine U.S.-Weather-Service-Approved Home Weather Center mounted on a genuine polished-walnut veneer plaque—thermometer, barometer and humidity gauge all in one—with a lifetime guarantee.

It was a pretty sort of thing, she thought, holding it up to admire it. Polished brass, good bold figures and hash marks you didn't need binoculars to read, made in the U.S. of A. It would look nice up on the wall over the fireplace—or maybe in the dining room; the walnut would match the color of the dining set, wouldn't it? She was on her way into the dining room, the genuine Home Weather Center in hand, when she noticed that the barometer needle was stuck all the way down in the left-hand corner. Pinned. She shook it, patted the glass lens. Nothing. It was stuck fast.

Suddenly she couldn't help herself—she could feel the rage coming up on her, a rage as inevitable and relentless as the smashing of the sea on the rocks—and how many pills had she swallowed and how many doctors, not to mention husbands, had tried to quell it? The Frinstell Corporation. Cheats and con artists, that's what they were. You couldn't get anything anymore that wasn't a piece of junk and no wonder America was the laughingstock of the world. Not ten seconds out of the box and it was garbage already. She was seething. It was all she could do to keep from smashing it against the wall, stamping it underfoot—dope addicts, hopheads, the factories were full of them—but then she remembered the TV and she held on till the first hot wave of fury passed over her.

All right, she would be rational about it, she would. It had a lifetime guarantee, didn't it? But what a joke, she thought bitterly, and again she had to restrain herself from flinging the thing into the wall—a glass of wine, that's what she needed. Yes. To calm her. And then she'd wrap the thing up in the box and send it right back to the bastards—they'd see how fast their own shit came sailing back to them, they'd see whether they could put anything over on her . . . she'd have Willis down at the post office the minute he came in the door. And she'd be damned if she'd pay postage on it either. *Return to Sender,* that's how she'd mark it. *Damaged in Transit, Take Your Garbage and—*

But then she glanced up at the clock. It was quarter to twelve already and he'd be home any minute now. Suddenly all the rage she'd generated over the Frinstell Corporation was gone, extinguished as quickly as it had arisen, and she felt a wild rush of affection for her man, her husband, for Willis—the poor guy, out there in all kinds of weather, working like a man half his age, providing for her and protecting her . . . and she'd been hard on him at breakfast, she had. What he needed was a nice lunch, she decided, a nice hot lunch. She set the Home Weather Center back in the box as gently as if she were lowering a baby into its crib, and then she wrapped the package up again, retaped the seams, and went to the cupboard. She poured herself a glass of wine from the jug and then fastened on a can of split-pea-and-ham soup—she'd heat that for Willis, and she'd make him a nice egg salad on toast. . . .

Toast. But they were out of bread, weren't they? There was nothing but that sawdust-and-nut crap he'd tried to pawn off on her for breakfast. She thought about that for a moment and a black cloud seemed to rise up before her. And then, before she knew it, the fury of the morning swept over her again, the tragedy of the TV and the cheat of the Home Weather Center doubling it and redoubling it, and by the time she heard Willis's key turn in the lock, she was smoldering like Vesuvius.

If she was testy in the morning, if she lashed into him for no reason and jumped down his throat at the slightest provocation, by lunchtime she was inevitably transformed, so that an all-embracing cloud of maternal sweetness wrapped him up as he stepped through the door, and then ushered him out again, half an hour later, with a series of tender lingering hugs, squeezes and back pats. That was the usual scenario, but today was different. Willis sensed it even before he shambled down the hallway to discover her in the kitchen fussing over a can of soup and a box of saltines. He saw that she was still in her nightdress and housecoat, a bad sign, and he recognized the stunned, hurt, put-upon look in her eyes. He just stood there at the kitchen door and waited.

"Willis, oh, Willis," she sighed—or no, moaned, bleated, wailed as if all the trials of Job had been visited on her in the five hours since he'd seen her last. He knew the tone and knew it was trouble—anything could have set her off, from a stopped-up drain to the war in Bosnia or teary memories of her first husband, the saint. "Honey," she cried, crossing the room to catch him up in an embrace so fierce it nearly ruptured his kidneys, "you've got to help me out—just a little favor, a tiny little one." Her voice hardened almost imperceptibly as she clung to him and swayed back and forth in a kind of dance of grief: "Everything is just so, so *rotten*."

He was seventy-five years old and he'd been working since the day he climbed out of the cradle. Most men his age were dead. He was tired. His hips felt as if an army of mad acupuncturists had been driving hot needles into them. All he wanted was to sit down.

"Honey, here," she said, cooing now, nothing but concern, and she led him awkwardly to the table, still half-clinging to him. "Sit down and eat; poor man, you're probably starved. And exhausted, too. Is it raining out there?"

It was a question that didn't require an answer, a variant on her luncheon monologue, a diversion to distract him from the true subject at hand, the crisis, whatever it was—the shattered TV screen, was that it?—the crisis which required his immediate attention and expertise. And no, it wasn't raining, not yet, but it was blowing like holy hell out there and his morning had been an unmitigated disaster, a total waste of time. The framers hadn't showed—or the damn plumber, either—and he'd spent the whole morning in the skeleton of the house, which was already behind schedule, watching the wind whip the waves to a froth and batter the seawall as if it were made of cardboard instead of concrete. He'd called the sons of bitches five or six times from the pay phone out front of the bank, but they weren't answering. Pups, that's what they were, afraid of a little weather. He glanced up and the soup appeared on the table before him, along with a platter of sardines, six neat squares of cheddar, saltines, and a glass of apple juice. Muriel hovered over him.

He took a sip of the juice, fingered his spoon and set it down again. Why forestall the inevitable? "What's the trouble, sweetie?" he asked.

"I know you're not going to like this, but you're going to have to go to the post office for me."

"The post office?" He didn't want to go to the post office—he wanted to get back to the torn earth and wooden vertebrae of the rising house, to the mounds of rubble and refuse and the hot sudden smell of roofing tar. He thought of the doctor and his wife who'd hired him, a young couple in their forties, building their dream house by the sea. He'd promised them fifty-five hundred square feet with balconies, sundeck and wraparound view in six months' time—and here two months had gone by already and the damn frame wasn't even up yet. And Muriel wanted him to go to the post office.

"It's the Home Weather Center," she said. "It's got to go back. And I mean to-day, immediately, right now." Her voice threatened to ignite. "I won't have it here in the house another minute . . . if those bastards think they can—"

She was working herself up, her ire directed for the moment at the Home Weather Center, whatever that was, and the unnamed bastards, whoever they were, but he knew that if he didn't watch himself, if he didn't look sharp, the full weight of her outrage would shift to him with the sudden killing swiftness of an avalanche. He heard himself saying, "I'll take care of it, sweetie, don't you worry."

But when he glanced up to gauge her reaction, he found he was talking to himself: she'd left the room. Now what? There were sounds from the dining room—a fierce rending of tape and an impatient rustle of tissue paper, followed by the sharp tattoo of her approaching footsteps—and before he could lift the spoon to his lips she was back with a cardboard box the size of an ottoman. She swept across the room and dropped it on the table with a percussive thump that jarred the soup bowl and sent the juice swirling round the rim of the glass. Outside, the wind howled at the windows.

"Just look at this, will you?" she was saying, her elbows leaping as she tore the package open and extracted a long slim wooden plaque with three gleaming gauges affixed to it. He had a moment of enlightenment: the weather center. "Did you ever see such junk in your life?"

It looked all right to him. He wanted soup, he wanted sleep, he wanted the doctor's house to rise up out of the dunes and bravely confront the sea, perfect in every detail. "What's wrong with it, sweetie?"

"What's wrong with it?" Her voice jumped an octave. "Are you blind? Look at this"—a blunt chewed fingernail stabbed at the middle gauge—"that's what's wrong. Junk. Nothing but junk."

He frowned over the thing while his soup got cold and then he fished his glasses out of his shirt pocket and studied it. The barometer needle was pinned all the way down at twenty-eight inches—he'd never seen anything like it. He lifted the plaque from the table and shook it. He inverted it. He tapped the glass. Nothing.

Muriel was seething. She went off into a tirade about con men, cheats, the Japanese and what they'd done to her brother, not to mention the American economy, and all he could do to calm her was agree with everything she said and croon "sweetie" over and over again till his soup turned gelid and he pushed himself up from the table, tucked the package under his arm, and headed out the door for the post office.

The wind was up, whipping the treetops like rags, and the smell of the ocean was stronger now, rank and enveloping, as if the bottom of the sea had turned over and littered the shore with its dead. A trash can skittered down the street and a shopping bag shot across the lawn to cling briefly to his ankles. As he settled into the car, the package beside him, the wind jerked the door out of his hand and he began to realize that there would be no more work today. At this rate he'd be lucky if what they'd put up so far was still there in the morning. No wonder the framers hadn't showed: this was a real blow.

He dodged trash-can lids and branches that glided magically across the road, the car pulling him along to the post office as faithfully as an old horse. The streets were deserted. He encountered exactly three other cars, all with their lights on and all going like hell. By the time he got to the traffic light outside the post office and sat there for an eternity watching the stoplight heave on its wires, it was so dark it might have been dusk. Maybe it was a hurricane after all, he thought, maybe that was it. He would have turned on the radio, but the damn thing had never worked to begin with, and then, two months ago, some jerk had smashed out the window on the driver's side and made off with it.

Sitting there watching the stoplight leap and sway over the deserted pavement, he felt a sudden sense of foreboding, a quick hot jolt of fear that made him gun the engine impatiently and inch forward into the intersection. He was thinking he'd better get home and see to the windows, see to Muriel—he'd been caught in a hurricane in Corpus Christi once and they'd been without lights or water for six days. He remembered an old woman sitting in the middle of a flooded street with a bloody strip of somebody's parlor curtains knotted round her head. That was an image. And he and his buddies with two cases of tequila they'd fished out of the wreckage of a liquor store. He'd better get home. He'd better.

But then the light changed and he figured he was here already and might as well take care of business—there'd be hell to pay at home if he didn't, hurricane or no—and he pulled into the lot, parked the car and reached for the package. Five minutes, that's all it would take. Then he'd be home.

As he came up the walk—and it was blowing now, Jesus, dirt or sand or something in his eyes—he saw the postmaster and a bearded guy with a ponytail scurrying around with a sheet of plywood big enough to seal off a shopping mall. The postmaster had a hammer in his hand and he was shouting something to the other one, but then a gust took hold of the plywood and sent them both sprawling into the bushes. Willis hunched himself over and snatched at the Mets cap, but it was too late: it shot from his head and sailed up over the trees like a clay pigeon. Hurrying now, he fought his way through the heavy double doors and into the post office.

There was no one at the counter, no one waiting in line, no one in the building at all as far as he could see. The lights were all up full and the polished floor ran on down the corridor as usual, but the place was eerily silent. Outside, the sky raged at the plate-glass windows, a wild spatter of rain driving before it now. Willis hit the handbell, just to be sure no one was back there in the sorting room or on the toilet or something, and then he turned to go. Muriel would have to understand, that was all: they were closed down. There was a hurricane coming. He'd done all he could.

He'd just pulled back the inner door when the big plate-glass window in the lobby gave way with a pop like a champagne cork, followed by the splash of shattering glass. *Leave the damn package,* his brain told him, *drop it and get on home and lock yourself up in the basement with Muriel and the cat and a case of pork and beans,* but his legs failed him. He just stood there as a window shattered somewhere in the back and the lights faltered and then blew. "Hey, you, old man!" a voice was shouting, and there was the postmaster, right beside him, his face drawn and white, hair disheveled. The bearded man was with him and their eyes were jumping with excitement. In the next moment they had Willis by the arms, wind screaming in his ears; a flurry of white envelopes lifted suddenly into the air, and he was moving, moving fast, down a hallway and into the darkness and the quiet.

He could smell the postmaster and the other one, could smell the wet and the fear on them. Their breath came in quick greedy pants. Outside, way in the distance, he could hear the muted keening of the wind.

"Anybody got a match?" It was the postmaster's voice, a voice he knew from the roped-off line and the window and the gleaming tiled expanse of the lobby.

"Here," came another voice and a match flared to reveal the pockmarked face of the bearded man and a cement-block storage room of some kind, mailbags, cardboard boxes, heaps of paper.

The postmaster fumbled through a cabinet behind him and came up with a flashlight, one of those big boxy jobs with a lighthouse beam at one end and a little red emergency light at the other. He played it round the room, then set the flashlight down on a carton and cut the beam. The room glowed with an eerie reddish light. "Holy shit," he said, "did you see the way that window blew? You didn't get cut, did you, Bob?"

Bob answered in the negative.

"Man, we were lucky." The postmaster was a big bearish man in his fifties who'd worn a beard for years but now had the pasty stubbly look of a man newly acquainted with a razor. He paused. The wind screamed in the distance. "God, I wonder if Becky's okay—she was supposed to take Jimmy to the dentist, to the orthodontist, I mean—"

Bob said nothing, but then both of them turned to Willis, as if they'd just realized he was there.

"You okay?" the postmaster asked him.

"I'm all right," Willis said. He was, wasn't he? But what about the car? What about Muriel? "But listen, I've got to get home—"

The postmaster let out a little bark of a laugh. "Home? Don't you get it? That's Hurricane Leroy out there—you'll be lucky if you got a home left to go to—and whatever possessed you to come out in this mess? I mean, don't you listen to the TV? Christ," he said, as if that summed it all up.

There was a silence, and then, with a sigh, Bob eased himself back into a cradle of folded cardboard boxes. "Well," he said, and the faint red light glinted off the face of the pint bottle he extracted from his shirt, "we might as well enjoy ourselves—looks like we're going to be here a while."

Willis must have dozed. They'd passed the bottle and he'd got a good deep burning taste of whiskey—a taste Muriel denied him; she was worse than the Schick Center when it came to that, though she sipped wine all day herself—and then Bob had begun to drone on in a stopped-up, back-of-the-throat sort of voice, complaining about his marriage, his bad back, his sister on welfare and the way the cat sprayed the bedposts and the legs of the kitchen table, and Willis had found it increasingly difficult to focus on the glowing red beacon of the light. He was slouched over in a folding chair the postmaster had dragged in from one of the offices, and when awareness gripped him, Bob was enumerating the tragic flaws of the auto-insurance industry, his face ghastly in the hellish light. For a moment Willis didn't know where he was, but then he heard the wind in the distance and it all came back to him.

"With only two accidents, Bob? I can't believe it," the postmaster said.

"Hell," Bob countered, "I'll show you the damn bill."

Willis tried to get up but his hips wouldn't allow it. "Muriel," he said.

The two faces turned to him then, the bearded one and the one that should have been bearded, and they looked strange and menacing in that unnatural light. "You all right, old-timer?" the postmaster asked.

Willis felt like Rip Van Winkle, like Methuselah; he felt tired and hopeless, felt as if everything he'd known and done in his life had been wasted. "I've got to"—he caught himself; he'd been about to say *I've got to go home,* but they'd probably try to stop him and he didn't want any arguments. "I've got to take a leak," he said.

The postmaster studied him a moment. "It's still blowing out there," he said, "but the radio says the worst of it's past." Willis heard the faint whisper of the radio then—one of those little transistors the kids all wear; it was tucked into the postmaster's breast pocket. "Give it another hour," the postmaster said, "and we'll make sure you get home all right. And your car's okay, if that's what's worrying you. Nothing worse than maybe a branch on the roof."

Willis said nothing.

"Down the hall and to your left," the postmaster said.

It took him a moment to fight the inertia of his hips, and then he was emerging from the shadows of the storage room and into the somber gray twilight of the hallway. Nuggets of glass crunched and skittered underfoot and everything was wet. It was raining hard outside and there was that rank smell in the air still, but the wind seemed to have tapered off. He found the toilet and he kept on going.

The lobby was a mess of wet clinging paper and leaves, but the doors swung open without a hitch, and in the next moment Willis was out on the front steps and the rain was driving down with a vengeance on his bare bald head. He reached automatically for the Mets cap, but then he remembered it was gone, and he hunched his shoulders and started off across the parking lot. He moved cautiously, wary of the slick green welter of leaves and windblown debris underfoot, and he was wet through by the time he reached the car. A single crippled branch was draped over the windshield, but there was no damage; he swept it to the ground and ducked into the driver's seat.

His mind wasn't working well at this point—perhaps it was the shock of the storm or the effects of the whiskey and his nap in the folding chair. The keys. He fumbled twice through his pants and jacket before he finally found them, and then he flooded the engine and had to hold his foot to the floor while the starter whined and the rain smeared the windshield. Finally he got the thing going with a roar and jerked it into gear; it was then that he discovered the tree blocking the exit. And now what? The specter of Muriel rose before him, pale and trembling, and then he glanced up to see the postmaster and Bob planted on the steps and gawking at him as if he'd just dropped down from another planet. What the hell, he thought, and he gave them a jaunty wave, revved the engine and shot up over the curb and into the street.

But here the world was truly transformed. It was as if a big hand had swept the street, slapping down trees and telephone poles, obliterating windows, stripping shingles from the roofs. The road that led out to the highway was impassable, churning with shit-brown water and one of those little Japanese cars awash in it, overturned on its roof. Willis tried Meridian Street and then Seaboard, but both were blocked. An oak tree that must have been five hundred years old had taken the veranda out of the house where Joe Diggs had lived before he passed on, and there were live wires thrashing the shattered shaft of a telephone pole out front. Even through the tattoo of the rain on the roof Willis could hear the sirens, a continuous, drawn-out wail of grief.

He was worried now—this was as bad as Corpus Christi, worse—and his hands trembled on the wheel when he turned into his own street and found the entrance buried in rubble and vegetation. The house on the corner—the Needlemans'—was untouched, but across the street, on his side, the Stovers' place had lost its roof. And the street itself, the placid tree-lined street that had attracted Muriel in the first place, was unrecognizable, a double row of maples laid down flat like a deck of cards. Willis backed out of the street, water running up to his hubcaps, and made a left on Susan and then another left on Massapequa, trying to make it around the block and come up on the house from the far side.

He was in luck. Neither street seemed to have suffered much damage, and he was able to make his way round a fallen telephone pole at the entrance to Massapequa by climbing up over the curb as he'd done at the post office. And then he was turning into Laurel, his own street, dodging refuse and swinging wide to avoid the clogged storm drain at the corner. People were out on their lawns now, assessing the damage—he saw Mrs. Tilden or Tillotson or whatever her name was trying to brace up a cypress that clung to her front porch like a wet mustache. It was almost comical, that little woman and that big limp tree, and he began to relax—everything was going to be okay, it was, there was hardly any damage on this end—and there was the fat guy—what was his name?—holding his head and dancing round the carcass of his crushed Cadillac. Yes, he said aloud, everything's going to be all right, and he repeated it to himself, making a little prayer of it.

He was more afraid of Muriel now than of the storm—he could hear her already: how could he leave her in the middle of a hurricane? Where had he been? Was that liquor on his breath? The damage he could take care of—he was a builder, wasn't he? It was just a matter of materials, that was all—bricks, lumber, drywall, shingles. And glass. The glaziers would be busy, that was for sure. As he eased past a lawn mower standing forlornly in the middle of the street and crept round the big sweeping curve that gave him his first view of the house, he was expecting the worst—shutters gone, a hole in the roof, the elm lying atop the garage like a crippled beast—but the reality made his heart seize.

There was nothing there. Nothing. Where the house had stood not two hours ago, the elm towering over it, the two-car garage in back with his tools and workbench and all the rest, there was now a vacant lot. The yard had been swept clean but for the torn and crenellated foundation, filled with rubble like some ancient ruin. Panic seized him, shock, and he hit the brake instinctively, sending the car into a fishtail that carried him across the street and slammed him into the curb with a jolt.

Trembling, he pried his fingers from the wheel. There was a throb of pain above his right eye where he'd hit the rearview mirror. His hands were shaking. But no, he thought, looking up again, it couldn't be. He was on the wrong street, that was it—he'd got turned around and fetched up in front of somebody else's place. It took him a moment, but then he swung the door open and stepped tentatively into the litter of the street, and there was the number on the curb to refute him, there the mailbox with his name stenciled across it in neat white letters, untouched, the red flag still standing tall. And that was the Novaks' place next door, no doubt about it, a sick lime green with pink trim. . . .

Then he thought of Muriel. Muriel. She was, she was . . . he couldn't form the thought, and he staggered across the lawn like a drunk to stand gaping into that terrible hole in the ground. "Muriel," he bleated, "Muriel!" and the rain drove down at him.

He stood there a long while, head bowed, feeling as old as the stones themselves, as old as the gashed earth and the dead gray sky. And then, the car still rumbling and stuttering behind him, he had the very first intimation of a thought that sparked and swelled till it glowed like a torch in his brain: *Dewar's and water.* He saw himself as he was when Muriel first found him, wedded to the leatherette stool at the Dew Drop Inn, and his lips formed the words involuntarily: "Make mine a Dewar's and water." The house was gone, but he'd lost houses before—mainly to wives, which were a sort of natural disaster anyway; that he could live with—and he'd lost wives, too, but never like this.

It hit him then, a wave of grief that started in his hips and crested in his throat: Muriel. He saw her vividly, the lunchtime Muriel who rubbed his shoulders and fussed over him, making those little crackers with anchovy paste and avocado . . . he saw her turning down the sheets on the bed at night, saw her frowning over a crossword puzzle, the glasses perched on the end of her nose—little things, homey things. With a pang he remembered the way she'd kid him over the TV programs or a football game and how she'd dance round the kitchen with a bottle of wine and a beef brisket studded with cloves of garlic . . . and now it was over. He was seventy-five—seventy-six, come October—and he stared into that pit and felt the icy breath of eternity on his face.

His jacket was wet through and his arms hung limp at his sides by the time he turned away and limped back over the sodden lawn, a soldier returning from the wars. He dragged himself across the street to the car, and all he could think of was Ted Casselman, down at the Dew Drop—he would know what to do—and he actually had the door open, one foot poised on the rocker panel, when he glanced up for a final bewildered look, and a movement on the Novaks' porch caught his eye. All at once the storm door swung back with a dull flash of light and there she was, Muriel, rescued from oblivion. She was in her housecoat still and it was bedraggled and wet, and her long white hair hung tangled round her shoulders so that she was like some old woman of the woods in a children's tale. Anna Novak hovered behind her, a tragic look pressed into the immobile Slavic folds of her eyes. Muriel just stood there, gazing across the street to where he hovered at the door of the car, half a beat from release.

The wind came up then and rattled the branches of the trees that were still standing. Someone was calling a dog up the street: "Hermie, Hermie! Here, baby!" The rain slackened. "Willis!" Muriel suddenly cried, "Willis!" and the spell was broken. She was coming down the steps, grand and invincible, her arms spread wide.

What could he do? He dropped his foot to the pavement, ignoring the pain that shot through his hip, and opened his arms to receive her.

(1989)

HOPES RISE

I took my aching back to my brother-in-law, the doctor, and he examined me, ran some X-rays, and then sat me down in his office. Gazing out the window on the early manifestations of spring—inchoate buds crowning the trees, pussy willows at the edge of the marsh, the solitary robin probing the stiff yellow grass—I felt luxurious and philosophical. So what if my back felt as if it had been injected with a mixture of battery acid and Louisiana hot sauce? There was life out there, foliate and rich, a whole planet seething with possibility. It was spring, time to wake up and dance to the music of life.

My brother-in-law had finished fiddling with his unfashionable beard and pushing his reading glasses up and down the bridge of his nose. He cleared his throat. "Listen, Peter," he said in his mellifluous healing tones, "we've known each other a long time, haven't we?"

A hundred corny jokes flew to my lips, but I just smiled and nodded.

"We're close, right?"

I reminded him that he was married to my sister and had fathered my niece and nephew.

"Well, all right," he said. "Now that that's been established, I think I can reveal to you the first suppressed axiom of the medical cabal."

I leaned forward, a fierce pain gripping the base of my spine, like a dog shaking a rat in its teeth. Out on the lawn, the robin beat its shabby wings and was sucked away on the breeze.

My brother-in-law held the moment, and then, enunciating with elaborate care, he said, "Any injury you sustain up to the age of twenty-one, give or take a year, is better the next day; after twenty-one, any injury you sustain will haunt you to the grave."

I gave a hoot of laughter that made the imaginary dog dig his claws in, and then, wincing with the pain, I said, "And what's the second?"

He was grinning at me, showing off the white, even, orthodontically assisted marvel of his teeth. "Second what?"

"Axiom. Of the medical cabal."

He waved his hand. It was nothing. "Oh, that," he said, pushing at his glasses. "Well, that's not suppressed really, not anymore. I mean, medical men of the past have told their wives, children, brother-in-laws—or is it brothers-in-law? Anyway, it's 'Get plenty of rest and drink plenty of fluids.' "

This time my laugh was truncated, cut off like the drop of a guillotine. "And my back?"

"Get plenty of rest," he said, "and drink plenty of fluids."

The pain was there, dulling a bit as the dog relaxed its grip, but there all the same. "Can we get serious a minute?"

But he wouldn't allow it. He never got serious. If he got serious he'd have to admit that half the world was crippled, arthritic, suffering from dysplasia and osteoporosis; he'd have to admit that there were dwarves and freaks and glandular monsters, not to mention the legions of bandy-legged children starving in the streets even as we spoke. If he got serious he'd have to acknowledge his yawning impotence in the face of the rot and chaos that were engulfing the world. He got up from his desk and led me to the door with a brother-in-lawly touch at the elbow.

I stood at the open door, the waiting room gaping behind me. I was astonished: he wasn't going to do anything. Not a thing. "But, but," I stammered, "aren't you going to give me some pills at least?"

He held his flawless grin—not so much as a quiver of his bearded lip—and I had to love him for it: his back didn't hurt; his knees were fine. "Peter," he said, his voice rich with playful admonition, "there's no magic pill—you should know that."

I didn't know it. I wanted codeine, morphine, heroin; I wanted the pain to go away. "Physician," I hooted, "heal thyself!" And I swung round on my heels, surfeited with repartee, and nearly ran down a tiny wizened woman suspended like a spider in a gleaming web of aluminum struts and wheels and ratchets.

"You still seeing Adrian?" he called as I dodged toward the outer door. My coat—a jab of pain; my scarf—a forearm shiver. Then the gloves, the door, the wind, the naked cheat of spring. "Because I was thinking," the man of healing called, "I was thinking we could do some doubles at my place"—thunderous crash of door, voice pinched with distance and the interposition of a plane of impermeable oak—"Saturday, maybe?"

At home, easing into my chair with a heating pad, I pushed the playback button on my answering machine. Adrian's voice leapt out at me, breathless, wound up, shot through with existential angst and the low-threshold hum of day-to-day worry. "The frogs are disappearing. All over the world. Frogs. Can you believe it?" There was a pause. "They say they're like the canary in the coal mine—it's the first warning, the first sign. The apocalypse is here, it's now, we're doomed. Call me."

Adrian and I had been seeing each other steadily for eleven years. We shopped together, went to movies, concerts, museums, had dinner three or four nights a week and talked for hours on the phone. In the early years, consumed by passion, we often spent the night together, but now, as our relationship had matured, we'd come increasingly to respect each other's space. There'd been talk of marriage, too, in the early years—talk for the most part generated by parents, relatives and friends tied to mortgages and diaper services—but we felt we didn't want to rush into anything, especially in a world hurtling toward ecological, fiscal and microbial disaster. The concept was still on hold.

I dialed her number and got her machine. I waited through three choruses of "Onward, Christian Soldiers"—her joke of the week—before I could leave my message, which was, basically, "I called; call me." I was trying to think of a witty tag line when she picked up the phone. "Peter?"

"No, it's Liberace risen from the dead."

"Did you hear about the frogs?"

"I heard about the frogs. Did you hear about my back?"

"What did Jerry say?"

" 'Get plenty of rest and drink plenty of fluids.' "

She was laughing on the other end of the line, a gurgle and snort that sounded like the expiring gasps of an emphysemic horse, a laugh that was all her own. Two days earlier I'd been carrying a box of old college books down to the basement when I tore everything there is to tear in the human back and began to wonder how much longer I'd need to hold on to my pristine copy of *Agrarian Corsica, 900 B.C. to the Present.* "I guess it must not be so bad, then," she said, and the snorting and chuffing rose a notch and then fell off abruptly.

"Not so bad for you," I said. "Or for Jerry. I'm the one who can't even bend down to tie his shoes."

"I'll get you a pair of loafers."

"You spoil me. You really do. Can you find them in frog skin?"

There was a silence on the other end of the line. "It's not funny," she said. "Frogs, toads and salamanders are vital to the food chain—and no jokes about frogs' legs, please—and no one knows what's happening to them. They're just disappearing. Poof."

I considered that a moment, disappearing frogs, especially as they related to my throbbing and ruined back. I pictured them—squat, long of leg, with extruded eyes and slick mucus-covered skin. I remembered stalking them as a boy with my laxly strung bow and blunt arrows, recalled the sound of the spring peepers and their clumsy attempts at escape, their limbs bound up in ropy strings of eggs. Frogs. Suddenly I was nostalgic: what kind of world would it be without them?

"I hope you're not busy this weekend," Adrian said.

"Busy?" My tone was guarded; a pulse of warning stabbed at my spine through its thin tegument of muscle fiber and skin. "Why?"

"I've already reserved the tickets."

The sound of my breathing rattled in my ear. I wasn't about to ask. I took a stoic breath and held it, awaiting the denouement.

"We're going to a conference at NYU—the Sixth Annual International Herpetology and Batrachiology Conference. . . ."

I shouldn't have asked, but I did. "The what?"

"Snakes and frogs," she said.

On Saturday morning we took the train into Manhattan. I brought along a book to thumb through on the way down—a tattered ancient tome called *The Frog Book*, which I'd found wedged in a corner of one of the denuded shelves of the Frog and Toad section at the local library. I wondered at all that empty space on the shelves and what it portended for the genuses and species involved. Apparently Adrian wasn't the only one concerned with their headlong rush to extinction—either that, or the sixth grade had been assigned a report on amphibians. I wasn't convinced, but I checked the book out anyway.

My back had eased up a bit—there was a low tightness and an upper constriction, but nothing like the knifing pain I'd been subjected to a few days earlier. As a precautionary measure I'd brought along a Naugahyde pillow to cushion my abused vertebrae against the jolts and lurches of the commuter train. Adrian slouched beside me, long legs askew, head bent in concentration over *Mansfield Park*, which she was rereading, by her own calculation, for the twenty-third time. She taught a course in the novels of Jane Austen at Bard, and I never really understood how she could tolerate reading the same books over and over again, semester after semester, year after year. It was like a prison sentence.

"Is that really your twenty-third time?"

She looked up. Her eyes were bright with the nuances of an extinguished world. "Twenty-fourth."

"I thought you said twenty-third?"

"Reread. The first time doesn't count as a reread—that's your original read. Like your birthday—you live a year before you're one."

Her logic was irrefutable. I gazed out on the vast gray reaches of the frogless Hudson and turned to my own book: *The explosive note of the Green Frog proceeds from the shallow water; the purring trill of "the Tree Toad" comes from some spot impossible to locate. But listen! The toad's lullaby note comes from the far margin, sweeter than all the others if we except the two notes in the chickadee's spring call. We could never have believed it to be the voice of a toad if we had not seen and heard on that first May Day.* I read about the love life of toads until we plunged into the darkness at Ninety-seventh Street, and then gave my eyes a rest. In the early days, Adrian and I would have traded witticisms and cutting portraits of our fellow passengers all the way down, but now we didn't need to talk, not really. We were beyond talk.

It might have been one of those golden, delicately lit spring mornings invested with all the warmth and urgency of the season, bees hovering, buds unfolding, the air soft and triumphant, but it wasn't. We took a cab down Park Avenue in a driving wintry rain and shivered our way up two flights of steps and into a drafty lecture hall where a balding man in a turtleneck sweater was holding forth on the molting habits of the giant Sumatran toad. I was feeling lighthearted—frogs and toads: I could hold this one over her head for a month; two, maybe—and I poked Adrian in the ribs at regular intervals over the course of the next two stultifyingly dull hours. We heard a monograph on the diet and anatomy of *Discoglossus nigriventer,* the Israeli painted frog, and another on the chemical composition of the toxin secreted by the poison-arrow frog of Costa Rica, but nothing on their chances of surviving into the next decade. Adrian pulled her green beret down over her eyebrows. I caught her stifling a yawn. After a while, my eyes began to grow heavy.

There was a dry little spatter of applause as the poison-arrow man stepped down from the podium, and it roused me from a morass of murky dreams. I rose and clapped feebly. I was just leaning into Adrian with the words "dim sum" on my lips, words that were certain to provoke her into action—it was past one, after all, and we hadn't eaten—when a wild-looking character in blond dreadlocks and tinted glasses took hold of the microphone. "Greetings," he said, his hoarse timbreless voice rustling through the speakers and an odd smile drifting across his lips. He was wearing a rumpled raincoat over a T-shirt that featured an enormous crouching toad in the act of flicking an insect into its mouth. The program identified him as B. Reid, of UC Berkeley. For a long moment he merely stood there, poised over the microphone, holding us with the blank gaze of his blue-tinted lenses.

Someone coughed. The room was so still I could hear the distant hiss of the rain.

"We've been privileged to hear some provocative and stimulating papers here this morning," B. Reid began, and he hadn't moved a muscle, save for his lips, "papers that have focused brilliantly on the minute and painstaking research crucial to our science and our way of knowledge, and I want to thank Professors Abercrombie and Wouzatslav for a job well done, but at the same time I want to ask you this: will there be a Seventh Annual International Herpetology and Batrachiology Conference? Will there be an eighth? Will there be a discipline, will there be batrachiologists? Ladies and gentlemen, why play out a charade here: will there be frogs?"

A murmur went up. The woman beside me, huge and amphibious-looking herself, shifted uneasily in her seat. My lower back announced itself with a distant buzz of pain and I felt the hackles rise on the back of my neck: this was what we'd come for.

"Cameroon," B. Reid was saying, his voice rasping like dead leaves, "Ecuador, Borneo, the Andes and the Alps: everywhere you look the frogs and toads are disappearing, extinction like a plague, the planet a poorer and shabbier place. And what is it? What have we done? Acid rain? The ozone layer? Some poison we haven't yet named? Ladies and gentlemen," he rasped, "it's the frogs today and tomorrow the biologists . . . before we know it the malls will stand empty, the freeways deserted, the creeks and ponds and marshes forever silent. We're committing suicide!" he cried, and he gave his dreadlocks a Medusan swirl so that they beat like snakes round his head. "We're doomed, can't you see that?"

The audience sat riveted in their seats. No one breathed a word. I didn't dare look at Adrian.

His voice dropped again. *"Bufo canorus,"* he said, and the name was like a prayer, a valediction, an obituary. "You all know my study in Yosemite. Six years I put into it, six years of crouching in the mud and breathing marsh gas and fighting leeches and ticks and all the rest of it, and what did it get me? What did it get the Yosemite toad? Extinction, that's what. They're gone. Wiped from the face of the earth." He paused as if to gather his strength. "And what of Richard Wassersug's albino leopard frogs in Nova Scotia? White tadpoles. Exclusively. What kind of mutation is that?" His voice clawed its way through the speakers, harsh with passion and the clangorous knelling of doom. "I'll tell you what kind: a fatal one. A year later they were gone."

My face was hot. Suddenly my back felt as if it were crawling with fire ants, seared by molten rain, drawn tight in a burning lariat. I looked at Adrian and her eyes were wild, panicky, a field of white in a thin net of veins. We'd come on a lark, and now here was the naked truth of our own mortality staring us in the face. I wanted to cry out for the frogs, the toads, the salamanders, for my own disconnected and rootless self.

But it wasn't over yet. B. Reid contorted his features and threw back his head, and then he plunged a hand into the deep pocket of his coat; in the next instant his clenched fist shot into the air. I caught a glimpse of something dark and leathery, a strip of jerky, tissue with the life drained from it. "The Costa Rican golden toad," he cried in his wild burnished declamatory tones, "R.I.P.!"

The woman beside me gasped. A cry went up from the back of the room. There was a shriek of chairs as people leapt to their feet.

B. Reid dug into his breast pocket and brandished another corpse. *"Atelopus zeteki,* the Peruvian variegated toad, R.I.P.!"

Cries of woe and lamentation.

"Rana marinus, R.I.P.! The Gambian reed frog, R.I.P.!"

B. Reid held the lifeless things up before him as if he were exorcising demons. His voice sank to nothing. Slowly, painfully, he shook his head so that the coils of his hair drew a shroud over his face. "Don't bother making the trip to Costa Rica, to Peru or Gambia," he said finally, the shouts rising and dying round him. "These"—and his voice broke—"these are the last of them."

The following day was my sister's birthday, and I'd invited her, Jerry and the children to my place for dinner, though I didn't feel much like going through with it after B. Reid's presentation. The lecture hall had echoed like a chamber of doom with the dying rasp of his voice and I couldn't get it out of my head. Stunned silent, our deepest fears made concrete in those grisly pennants of frog flesh, Adrian and I had left as soon as he stepped down from the podium, fighting our way through the press of stricken scientists and heartsick toad lovers and out into the rain. The world smelled of petroleum, acid, sulfur, the trees were bent and crippled, and the streets teemed with ugly and oblivious humanity. We took a cab directly to Grand Central. Neither of us had the stomach for lunch after what we'd been through, and we sat in silence all the way back, Adrian clutching Jane Austen to her breast and I turning *The Frog Book* over and over again in my hands. Each bump and rattle of the Hudson Line drove a burning stake into the small of my back.

The next morning I debated calling Charlene and telling her I was sick, but I felt guilty about it: why ruin my sister's birthday simply because the entire planet was going to hell in a handbasket? When Adrian showed up at ten with three bags of groceries and acting as if nothing had happened, I took two aspirin, cinched an apron round my waist and began pulverizing garbanzo beans.

All in all, it was a pleasant afternoon. The rain drove down outside and we built a fire in the dining room and left the door to the kitchen open while we cooked. Adrian found some chamber music on the radio and we shared a bottle of wine while she kneaded dough for the pita bread and I folded tahini into the garbanzo mash, sliced tomatoes and chopped onions. We chatted about little things—Frank Sinatra's hair, whether puree was preferable to whole stewed tomatoes, our friends' divorces, lint in the wash—steering clear of the fateful issue burning in both our minds. It was very nice. Tranquil. Domestic. The wine conspired with the aspirin, and after a while the knot in my back began to loosen.

Jerry, Charlene and the kids were early, and I served the hummus and pita bread while Adrian braised chunks of goat in a big black cast-iron pan she'd brought with her from her apartment. We were on our second drink and Jay and Nayeli, my nephew and niece, were out on the porch catching the icy rainwater as it drooled from the eaves, when Adrian threw herself down in the chair opposite Jerry and informed him in a clarion voice that the frogs were dying out.

The statement seemed to take him by surprise. He and Charlene had been giving me a seriocomic history of their yacht, which had thus far cost them something like $16,000 per hour at sea and which had been rammed, by Jerry, into a much bigger yacht on its maiden voyage out of the marina. Now they both paused to stare at Adrian. Jerry began to formulate his smile. "What did you say?"

Adrian smelled of goat and garlic. She was lanky and wide-eyed, with long beautifully articulated feet and limbs that belonged on a statue. She drew herself up at the edge of the chair and tried out a tentative smile. "Frogs," she said. "And toads. Something is killing them off all over the world, from Alaska to Africa. We went to a conference yesterday. Peter and I."

"Frogs?" Jerry repeated, stroking the bridge of his nose. His smile, in full efflorescence now, was something to behold. My sister, who favored my late mother around the eyes and nose, emitted a little chirp of amusement.

Adrian looked uncertain. She gave out with an abbreviated version of her horsey laugh and turned to me for encouragement.

"It's not a joke," I said. "We're talking extinction here."

"There was this man," Adrian said, the words coming in a rush, "a biologist at the conference, B. Reid—from Berkeley—and he had all these dried frogs in his pockets . . . it was horrible. . . ."

I could hear the rain on the roof, cold and unseasonal. Nayeli shouted something from the porch. The fire crackled in the hearth. I could see that we weren't getting it right, that my brother-in-law, the doctor, was making a little notation of our mental state on the prescription pad of his mind. Why were we telling him all this? Was he, the perennial jokester who couldn't even salvage my lower back, about to take on loss of habitat, eternal death and the transfiguration of life as we know it?

No, he wasn't.

"You're serious, aren't you?" he said after a moment. "You really believe in all this environmental hysteria." He let the grin fade and gave us his stern off-at-the-knee look. "Peter, Adrian," he said, drawing out the syllables in a profound and pedagogical way, "species conflict is the way of the world, has been from the beginning of time. Extinction is natural, expected: no species can hope to last forever. Even man. Conditions change." He waved his hand and then laughed, making a joke of it. "If this weather doesn't let up I think we're in for a new ice age, and then where will your frogs be?"

"That's not the point," I said.

"What about the dinosaurs, Peter?" Charlene interjected. "And the woolly mammoth?"

"Not to mention snake oil and bloodletting." Jerry's smile was back. He was in control. All was right with the world. "Things move on, things advance and change—why cry over something you can't affect, a kind of fairy-tale Garden of Eden half these environmentalists never knew? Which is not to say I don't agree with you—"

"My god!" Adrian cried, springing from her seat as if she'd been hot-wired. "The goat!"

Late that night, after everyone had gone home—even Adrian, though she'd gotten amorous at the door and would, I think, have spent the night but for my lack of enthusiasm—I eased into my armchair with the newspaper and tried to wipe my mind clean, a total abstersion, tabula rasa. I felt drained, desolate, a mass of meat, organ and bone slipping inexorably toward the grave along with my distant cousins the frogs and the toads. The rain continued. A chill fell over the room and I saw that the fire had burned down. There was a twinge in my back as I shifted my buttocks to adjust the heating pad, and then I began to read. I didn't feel up to war in the Middle East, AIDS and the homeless or the obituaries, so I stuck to the movie reviews and personal-interest stories.

It was getting late, my mind had gone gratifyingly numb and I was just about to switch off the light and throw myself into bed, when I turned to the science section. A headline caught my eye:

HOPES RISE AS NEW SPECIES MOVE INTO SLUDGE OFF COAST

And what was this? I read on and discovered that these rising hopes were the result of the sudden appearance of tubeworms, solemya clams and bacteria in a formerly dead stretch of water in the Hudson Canyon, used from time immemorial as a repository for the city's sewage and refuse. Down there, deep in the ancient layers of sludge, beneath the lapping fishless waves, there was life, burgeoning and thriving in a new medium. What hope. What terrific uplifting news.

Tubeworms. They had to be joking.

After a while I folded up the newspaper, found my slippers and took this great and rising hope to bed with me.

The week that followed was as grim and unrelenting as the week that had given rise to it. Work was deadening (I shifted numbers on a screen for a living and the numbers had never seemed more meaningless), my back went through half a dozen daily cycles of searing agony and utter absence of feeling, and the weather never broke, not even for an hour. The skies were close and bruised, and the cold rain fell. I went directly home after work and didn't answer the phone at night, though I knew it was Adrian calling. All week I thought of frogs and death.

And then, on Saturday, I woke to an outpouring of light and a sudden sharp apprehension of the world that was as palpable as a taste. I sat up. My feet found the floor. Naked and trembling, I crossed the room and stood at the window, the cord to the glowing blinds caught up in my hand, the stirrings of barometric change tugging at the long muscles of my lower back. Then I pulled the cord and the light spilled into the room, and in the next moment I was shoving the blinds aside and throwing open the window.

The air was pregnant, rich, thick with the scent of renewal and the perspicacious hum of the bees. All that moping, all those fears, the named dread and the nameless void: it all evaporated in the face of that hosanna of a morning. I felt like Ebenezer Scrooge roused on Christmas Day, Lazarus reanimated, Alexander the Great heading into Thrace. I opened every window in the house; I ate a muffin, read the paper, matched the glorious J. S. Bach to the triumph of the morning. It was heady, but I couldn't sustain it. Ultimately, inevitably, like a sickness, the frogs and toads crept back into my head, and by 10:00 A.M. I was just another mortal with a bad back sinking into oblivion.

It was then, at the bottom of that trough, that I had an inspiration. The coffee was cold in the cup, the newsprint rumpled, Bach silenced by the tyranny of a mechanical arm, and suddenly a notion hit me and I was up and out of the kitchen chair as if I'd been launched. The force of it carried me to the bedroom closet, where I dug around for my hiking boots, a sweatshirt, my Yankees cap and a denim jacket, and then to the medicine cabinet, where I unearthed the tick repellant and an old aerosol can of Off! Then I dialed Adrian.

"Adrian," I gasped, "my heart, my love—"

Her voice was thick with sleep. "Is this an obscene phone call?"

"I've been gloomy lately, I know it—"

"Not to mention not answering the phone."

"I admit it, I admit it. But have you seen the day out there?"

She hadn't. She was still in bed.

"What I'm thinking is this: how can we take B. Reid's word for it? How can we take anybody's?"

I didn't know where to begin looking for the elusive toad, *Bufo americanus,* let alone the spring peeper or the leopard frog, but I was seized with a desire to know them, touch them, observe their gouty limbs and clumsy rituals, partake once more of the seething life of pond, puddle and ditch, and at least temporarily lay to rest the nagging memory of B. Reid and his diminutive corpses. It was irrational, I knew it, but I felt that if I could see them, just this once, and know they were occupying their humble niche in the hierarchy of being, everything would be all right.

We parked along the highway and poked desultorily through the ditch alongside it, but there was nothing animate in sight. The old cane was sharp and brittle, and there was Styrofoam, glass and aluminum everywhere. Trucks stole the air from our lungs, teenagers jeered. Adrian suggested a promising-looking puddle on the far verge of the rutted commuter lot at the Garrison station, but we found nothing there except submerged gum wrappers and potato-chip bags ground into the muck by the numbing impress of steel-belted radials. "We can't give up," she said, and there was just the faintest catch of desperation in her voice. "What about the woods off the Appalachian Trail? You know, where it crosses the road down by K mart?"

"All right," I said, and the fever was on me, "we'll give it a try."

Twenty minutes later we were in the woods, sun glazing bole and branch, tender new yellow-green leaves unfolding overhead, birds shooting up from the path as if jerked on a string. There was a smell here I'd forgotten, the dark wet odor of process, of things breaking down and springing up again, of spore and pollen and seed and mulch. Bugs hovered round my face. I was sweating. And yet I felt good, strong in back and leg, already liberated from the cloud that had hung over me all week, and as I followed Adrian up the long slow incline of the path, I thought I'd never seen such a miracle as the way the muscles of her thighs and buttocks flexed and relaxed in the grip of her jeans. This was nature.

We'd gone a mile or so when she suddenly stopped dead in the middle of the path. "What's the matter?" I said, but she waved her hand to shush me. I edged forward till I stood beside her, my pulse quickening, breath caught high in my throat. "What?" I whispered. "What is it?"

"Listen."

At first I couldn't hear it, my ears attuned to civilization, the chatter of the TV, high fidelity, the blast of the internal-combustion engine, but then the woods began to speak to me. The sound was indistinct at first, but after a while it began to separate into its individual voices, the smallest rustlings and crepitations, the high-pitched disputations of the birds, the trickle of running water—and something else, something at once strange and familiar, a chirping fluid trill that rose strong and multivoiced in the near distance. Adrian turned to me and smiled.

All at once we were in a hurry, breathless, charging through the frost-burned undergrowth and sharp stinging branches, off the path and down the throat of a dark and sodden ravine. I thought nothing. B. Reid, Jerry, herniated discs, compound fractures, the soft green glow of the computer monitor: nothing. We moved together, with a fluid balletic grace, the most natural thing in the world, hunched over, darting right, then left, ducking this obstruction, vaulting the next, shoving through the tangle as easily as we might have parted the bead curtains in a Chinese restaurant. And as we drew closer, that sound, that trill, that raucous joyous paean to life swelled round us till it seemed to vibrate in our every cell and fiber. "There!" Adrian cried suddenly. "Over there!"

I saw it in that moment, a shallow little scoop of a pond caught in the web of the branches. The water gave nothing back, dead black under the buttery sun, and it was choked with the refuse of the trees. I saw movement there, and the ululating chorus rang out to the treetops, every new leaf shuddering on every branch. The smell came at me then, the working odor, rank and sweet and ripe. I took Adrian's hand and we moved toward the water in a kind of trance.

We were up to our ankles, our boots soaked through, when the pond fell silent—it happened in a single stroke, on the beat, as if a conductor had dropped his baton. And then we saw that there was no surface to that pond, that it was a field of flesh, a grand and vast congress of toads. They materialized before our eyes, stumpy limbs and foreshortened bodies clambering over one another, bobbing like apples in a barrel. There they were—toads, toads uncountable— humping in a frenzy of webbed feet and seething snouts, humping blindly, stacked up three and four high. Their eggs were everywhere, beaded and wet with the mucus of life, and all their thousands of eyes glittered with lust. We could hear them clawing at one another, grunting, and we didn't know what to do. And then a single toad at the edge of the pond started in with his thin piping trill and in an instant we were forgotten and the whole pullulating mass of them took it up and it was excruciating, beautiful, wild to the core.

Adrian looked at me and I couldn't help myself: I moved into her arms. I was beyond reason or thought, and what did it matter? She pushed away from me then, for just a moment, and stepped back, water swirling, toads thrilling, to strip off her shirt and the black lace brassiere beneath it. Holding me with her eyes, she moved back another step and dropped them there, in the wet at the edge of the pond, and eased herself down as if into a nest. I'd never seen any- thing like it. I shrugged out of my denim jacket, tore off my shirt, sailed the Yan- kees cap into oblivion. And when I came for her, the toads leapt for their lives.

(1990)

DESCENT OF MAN

I was living with a woman who suddenly began to stink. It was very difficult. The first time I confronted her she merely smiled. "Occupational hazard," she said. The next time she curled her lip. There were other problems too. Hairs, for instance. Hairs that began to appear on her clothing, sharp and black and brutal. Invariably I would awake to find these hairs in my mouth, or I would glance into the mirror to see them slashing like razor edges across the collars of my white shirts. Then too there was the fruit. I began to discover moldering bits of it about the house—apple and banana most characteristically—but plum and tangelo or even passion fruit and yim-yim were not at all anomalous. These fruit fragments occurred principally in the bedroom, on the pillow, surrounded by darkening spots. It was not long before I located their source: they lay hidden like gems in the long wild hanks of her hair. Another occupational hazard.

Jane was in the habit of sitting before the air conditioner when she came home from work, fingering out her hair, drying the sweat from her face and neck in the cool hum of the machine, fruit bits sifting silently to the carpet, black hairs drifting like feathers. On these occasions the room would fill with the stink of her, bestial and fetid. And I would find my eyes watering, my mind imaging the dark rotting trunks of the rain forest, stained sienna and mandalay and Hooker's green with the excrements dropped from above. My ears would keen with the whistling and crawking of the jungle birds, the screechings of the snot-nosed apes in the branches. And then, slack-faced and tight-boweled, I would step into the bathroom and retch, the sweetness of my own intestinal secrets a balm against the potent hairy stench of her.

One evening, just after her bath (the faintest odor lingered, yet still it was so trenchant I had to fight the impulse to get up and urinate on a tree or a post or something), I laid my hand casually across her belly and was suddenly startled to see an insect flit from its cover, skate up the swell of her abdomen, and bury itself in her navel. "Good Christ," I said.

"Hm?" she returned, peering over the cover of her Yerkish reader.

"That," I said. "That bug, that insect, that vermin."

She sat up, plucked the thing from its cachette, raised it to her lips and popped it between her front teeth. "Louse," she said, sucking. "Went down to the old age home on Thirteenth Street to pick them up."

I anticipated her. "Not for—?"

"Why certainly, potpie—so Konrad can experience a tangible gratification of his social impulses during the grooming ritual. You know: you scratch my back, I scratch yours."

I lay in bed that night sweating, thinking about Jane and those slippery-fingered monkeys poking away at her, and listening for the lice crawling across her scalp or nestling their bloody little siphons in the tufts under her arms. Finally, about four, I got up and took three Doriden. I woke at two in the afternoon, an insect in my ear. It was only an earwig. I had missed my train, failed to call in at the office. There was a note from Jane: Pick me up at four. Konrad sends love.

The Primate Center stood in the midst of a macadamized acre or two, looking very much like a school building: faded brick, fluted columns, high mesh fences. Finger paintings and mobiles hung in the windows, misshapen ceramics crouched along the sills. A flag raggled at the top of a whitewashed flagpole. I found myself bending to examine the cornerstone: Asa Priff Grammar School, 1939. Inside it was dark and cool, the halls were lined with lockers and curling watercolors, the linoleum gleamed like a shy smile. I stepped into the BOYS' ROOM. The urinals were a foot and a half from the floor. Designed for little people, I mused. Youngsters. Hardly big enough to hold their little peters without the teacher's help. I smiled, and situated myself over one of the toy urinals, the strong honest scent of Pine-Sol in my nostrils. At that moment the door wheezed open and a chimpanzee shuffled in. He was dressed in shorts, shirt and bow tie. He nodded to me, it seemed, and made a few odd gestures with his hands as he moved up to the urinal beside mine. Then he opened his fly and pulled out an enormous slick red organ like a peeled banana. I looked away, embarrassed, but could hear him urinating mightily. The stream hissed against the porcelain like a thunderstorm, rattled the drain as it went down. My own water wouldn't come. I began to feel foolish. The chimp shook himself daintily, zippered up, pulled the plunger, crossed to the sink, washed and dried his hands, and left. I found I no longer had to go.

Out in the hallway the janitor was leaning on his flathead broom. The chimp stood before him gesticulating with manic dexterity: brushing his forehead and tugging his chin, slapping his hands under his armpits, tapping his wrists, his tongue, his ear, his lip. The janitor watched intently. Suddenly—after a particularly virulent flurry—the man burst into laughter, rich braying globes of it. The chimp folded his lip and joined in, adding his weird nasal snickering to the janitor's barrel-laugh. I stood by the door to the BOYS' ROOM in a quandary. I began to feel that it might be wiser to wait in the car—but then I didn't want to call attention to myself, darting in and out like that. The janitor might think I was stealing paper towels or something. So I stood there, thinking to have a word with him after the chimp moved on—with the expectation that he could give me some grassroots insight into the nature of Jane's job. But the chimp didn't move on. The two continued laughing, now harder than ever. The janitor's face was tear-streaked. Each time he looked up the chimp produced a gesticular flurry that would stagger him again. Finally the janitor wound down a bit, and still chuckling, held out his hands, palms up. The chimp flung his arms up over his head and then heaved them down again, rhythmically slapping the big palms with his own. "Right on! Mastuh Konrad," the janitor said. "Right on!" The chimp grinned, then hitched up his shorts and sauntered off down the hall. The janitor turned back to his broom, still chuckling.

I cleared my throat. The broom began a geometrically precise course up the hall toward me. It stopped at my toes, the ridge of detritus flush with the pinions of my wingtips. The janitor looked up. The pupil of his right eye was fixed in the corner, beneath the lid, and the white was red. There was an ironic gap between his front teeth. "Kin ah do sumfin fo yo, mah good man?" he said.

"I'm waiting for Miss Good."

"Ohhh, Miz *Good*," he said, nodding his head. "Fust ah tought yo was thievin paypuh tow-els outen de Boys' Room but den when ah sees yo standin dere rigid as de Venus de Milo ah thinks to mahsef: he is some kinda new sculpture de stoodents done made is what he is." He was squinting up at me and grinning like we'd just come back from sailing around the world together.

"That's a nice broom," I said.

He looked at me steadily, grinning still. "Yo's wonderin what me and Mastuh Konrad was jivin bout up dere, isn't yo? Well, ah tells yo: he was relatin a hoomerous anecdote, de punch line ob which has deep cosmic implications in dat it establishes a common groun between monks and Ho-mo sapiens despite dere divergent ancestries." He shook his head, chortled. "Yes, in-deed, dat Mastuh Konrad is quite de wit."

"You mean to tell me you actually understand all that lip-pulling and finger-waving?" I was beginning to feel a nameless sense of outrage.

"Oh sartinly, mah good man. Dat ASL."

"What?"

"ASL is what we was talkin. A-merican Sign Language. Developed for de deef n dumb. Yo sees, Mastuh Konrad is sumfin ob a genius round here. He can commoonicate de mos esoteric i-deas in bof ASL and Yerkish, re-spond to and translate English, French, German and Chinese. Fack, it was Miz Good was tellin me dat Konrad is workin right now on a Yerkish translation ob Darwin's *De-scent o Man*. He is mainly into anthro-pology, yo knows, but he has culti-vated a in-teress in udder fields too. Dis lass fall he done undertook a Yerkish translation ob Chomsky's *Language and Mind* and Nietzsche's *Jenseits von Gut und Böse*. And dat's some pretty heavy shit, Jackson."

I was hot with outrage, "Stuff," I said. "Stuff and nonsense."

"No sense in feelin personally treatened by Mastuh Konrad's chievements, mah good fellow—yo's got to ree-lize dat he is a genius."

A word came to me: "Bullhonk," I said. And turned to leave.

The janitor caught me by the shirtsleeve. "He is now scorin his turd opera," he whispered. I tore away from him and stamped out of the building.

Jane was waiting in the car. I climbed in, cranked down the sunroof and opened the air vents.

At home I poured a water glass of gin, held it to my nostrils and inhaled. Jane sat before the air conditioner, her hair like a urinal mop, stinking. Black hairs cut the atmosphere, fruit bits whispered to the carpet. Occasionally the tip of my tongue entered the gin. I sniffed and tasted, thinking of plastic factories and tur-pentine distilleries and rich sulfurous smoke. On my way to the bedroom I poured a second glass.

In the bedroom I sniffed gin and dressed for dinner. "Jane?" I called, "shouldn't you be getting ready?" She appeared in the doorway. She was dressed in her work clothes: jeans and sweatshirt. The sweatshirt was gray and hooded. There were yellow stains on the sleeves. I thought of the lower depths of animal cages, beneath the floor meshing. "I figured I'd go like this," she said. I was knot-ting my tie. "And I wish you'd stop insisting on baths every night—I'm getting tired of smelling like a coupon in a detergent box. It's unnatural. Unhealthy."

In the car on the way to the restaurant I lit a cigar, a cheap twisted black thing like half a pepperoni. Jane sat hunched against the door, unwashed. I had never before smoked a cigar. I tried to start a conversation but Jane said she didn't feel like talking: talk seemed so useless, such an anachronism. We drove on in silence. And I reflected that this was not the Jane I knew and loved. Where, I wondered, was the girl who changed wigs three or four times a day and sported nails like a Chinese emperor's?—and where was the girl who dressed like an Arabian bazaar and smelled like the trade winds?

She was committed. The project, the study, grants. I could read the signs: she was growing away from me.

■   ■   ■

The restaurant was dark, a maze of rocky gardens, pancake-leafed vegetation, black fountains. We stood squinting just inside the door. Birds whistled, carp hissed through the pools. Somewhere a monkey screeched. Jane put her hand on my shoulder and whispered in my ear. "Siamang," she said. At that moment the leaves parted beside us: a rubbery little fellow emerged and motioned us to sit on a bench beneath a wicker birdcage. He was wearing a soiled loincloth and eight or ten necklaces of yellowed teeth. His hair flamed out like a brushfire. In the dim light from the braziers I noticed his nostrils—both shrunken and pinched, as if once pierced straight through. His face was of course inscrutable. As soon as we were seated he removed my socks and shoes, Jane's sneakers, and wrapped our feet in what I later learned were plantain leaves. I started to object—I bitterly resent anyone looking at my feet—but Jane shushed me. We had waited three months for reservations.

The maître d' signed for us to follow, and led us through a dripping stone-walled tunnel to an outdoor garden where the flagstones gave way to dirt and we found ourselves on a narrow plant-choked path. He licked along like an iguana and we hurried to keep up. Wet fronds slapped back in my face, creepers snatched at my ankles, mud sucked at the plantain leaves on my feet. The scents of mold and damp and long-lying urine hung in the air, and I thought of the men's room at the subway station. It was dark as a womb. I offered Jane my hand, but she refused it. Her breathing was fast. The monkey chatter was loud as a zoo afire. "Far out," she said. I slapped a mosquito on my neck.

A moment later we found ourselves seated at a bamboo table overhung with branch and vine. Across from us sat Dr. and Mrs. U-Hwak-Lo, director of the Primate Center and wife. A candle guttered between them. I cleared my throat, and then began idly tracing my finger around the circular hole cut in the table's center. The Doctor's ears were the size of peanuts. "Glad you two could make it," he said. "I've long been urging Jane to sample some of our humble island fare." I smiled, crushed a spider against the back of my chair. The Doctor's English was perfect, pure Martha's Vineyard—he sounded like Ted Kennedy's insurance salesman. His wife's was weak: "Yes," she said, "nussing cook here, all roar." "How exciting!" said Jane. And then the conversation turned to primates, and the Center.

Mrs. U-Hwak-Lo and I smiled at one another. Jane and the Doctor were already deeply absorbed in a dialogue concerning the incidence of anal retention in chimps deprived of Frisbee coordination during the sensorimotor period. I gestured toward them with my head and arched my eyebrows wittily. Mrs. U-Hwak-Lo giggled. It was then that Jane's proximity began to affect me. The close wet air seemed to concentrate her essence, distill its potency. The U-Hwak-Los seemed unaffected. I began to feel queasy. I reached for the fingerbowl and drank down its contents. Mrs. U-Hwak-Lo smiled. It was coconut oil. Just then the waiter appeared carrying a wooden bowl the size of a truck tire. A single string of teeth slapped against his breastbone as he set the bowl down and slipped off into the shadows. The Doctor and Jane were oblivious—they were talking excitedly, occasionally lapsing into what I took to be ASL, ear- and nose- and lip-picking like a manager and his third-base coach. I peered into the bowl: it was filled to the rim with clean-picked chicken bones. Mrs. U-Hwak-Lo nodded, grinning: "No ontray," she said. "Appeticer." At that moment a simian screamed somewhere close, screamed like death itself. Jane looked up. "Rhesus," she said.

On my return from the men's room I had some difficulty locating the table in the dark. I had already waded through two murky fountains and was preparing to plunge through my third when I heard Mrs. U-Hwak-Lo's voice behind me. "Here," she said. "Make quick, repass now serve." She took my hand and led me back to the table. "Oh, they're enormously resourceful," the Doctor was saying as I stumbled into my chair, pants wet to the knees. "They first employ a general anesthetic—distillation of the chu-bok root—and then the chef (who logically doubles as village surgeon) makes a circular incision about the macaque's cranium, carefully peeling back the already-shaven scalp, and stanching the blood flow quite effectively with maura-ro, a highly absorbent powder derived from the tamana leaf. He then removes both the frontal and parietal plates to expose the brain . . ." I looked at Jane: she was rapt. I wasn't really listening. My attention was directed toward what I took to be the main course, which had appeared in my absence. An unsteady pinkish mound now occupied the center of the table, completely obscuring the circular hole—it looked like cherry vanilla yogurt, a carton and a half, perhaps two. On closer inspection I noticed several black hairs peeping out from around its flaccid edges. And thought immediately of the bush-headed maître d'. I pointed to one of the hairs, remarking to Mrs. U-Hwak-Lo that the rudiments of culinary hygiene could be a little more rigorously observed among the staff. She smiled. Encouraged, I asked her what exactly the dish was. "Much delicacy," she said. "Very rare find in land of Lincoln." At that moment the waiter appeared and handed each of us a bamboo stick beaten flat and sharpened at one end.

". . . then the tribal elders or visiting dignitaries are seated around the table," the Doctor was saying. "The chef has previously of course located the macaque beneath the table, the exposed part of the creature's brain protruding from the hole in its center. After the feast, the lower ranks of the village population divide up the remnants. It's really quite efficient."

"How fascinating!" said Jane. "Shall we try some?"

"By all means . . . but tell me, how has Konrad been coming with that Yerkish epic he's been working up?"

Jane turned to answer, bamboo stick poised: "Oh I'm so glad you asked—I'd almost forgotten. He's finished his tenth book and tells me he'll be doing two more—out of deference to the Miltonic tradition. Isn't that a groove?"

"Yes," said the Doctor, gesturing toward the rosy lump in the center of the table. "Yes it is. He's certainly—and I hope you won't mind the pun—a brainy fellow. Ho-ho."

"Oh Doctor," Jane laughed, and plunged her stick into the pink. Beneath the table, in the dark, a tiny fist clutched at my pantleg.

I missed work again the following day. This time it took five Doriden to put me under. I had lain in bed sweating and tossing, listening to Jane's quiet breathing, inhaling her fumes. At dawn I dozed off, dreamed briefly of elementary school cafeterias swarming with knickered chimps and weltered with trays of cherry vanilla yogurt, and woke stale-mouthed. Then I took the pills. It was three-thirty when I woke again. There was a note from Jane: Bringing Konrad home for dinner. Vacuum rug and clean toilet.

Konrad was impeccably dressed—long pants, platform wedgies, cufflinks. He smelled of eau de cologne, Jane of used litter. They arrived during the seven o'clock news. I opened the door for them. "Hello, Jane," I said. We stood at the door, awkward, silent. "Well?" she said. "Aren't you going to greet our guest?" "Hello, Konrad," I said. And then: "I believe we met in the boys' room at the Center the other day?" He bowed deeply, straight-faced, his upper lip like a halved cantaloupe. Then he broke into a snicker, turned to Jane and juggled out an impossible series of gestures. Jane laughed. Something caught in my throat. "Is he trying to say something?" I asked. "Oh potpie," she said, "it was nothing—just a little quote from Yeats."

"Yeats?"

"Yes, you know: 'An aged man is but a paltry thing.' "

Jane served watercress sandwiches and animal crackers as hors d'oeuvres. She brought them into the living room on a cut-glass serving tray and set them down before Konrad and me, where we sat on the sofa, watching the news. Then she returned to the kitchen. Konrad plucked up a tiny sandwich and swallowed it like a communion wafer, sucking the tips of his fingers. Then he lifted the tray and offered it to me. I declined. "No thank you," I said. Konrad shrugged, set the plate down in his lap and carefully stacked all the sandwiches in its center. I pretended to be absorbed with the news: actually I studied him, half-face. He was filling the gaps in his sandwich-construction with animal crackers. His lower lip protruded, his ears were rubbery, he was balding. With both hands he crushed the heap of crackers and sandwiches together and began kneading it until it took on the consistency of raw dough. Then he lifted the whole thing to his mouth and swallowed it without chewing. There were no whites to his eyes.

Konrad's only reaction to the newscast was a burst of excitement over a war story—the reporter stood against a wasteland of treadless tanks and recoilless guns in Thailand or Syria or Chile; huts were burning, old women weeping. "Wow-wow! Eeeeeeee! Er-er-er-er," Konrad said. Jane appeared in the kitchen doorway, hands dripping. "What is it, Konrad?" she said. He made a series of violent gestures. "Well?" I asked. She translated: "Konrad says that 'the pig oppressors' genocidal tactics will lead to their mutual extermination and usher in a new golden age . . .' "—here she hesitated, looked up at him to continue (he was springing up and down on the couch, flailing his fists as though they held whips and scourges)—" '. . . of freedom and equality for all, regardless of race, creed, color—or genus.' I wouldn't worry," she added, "it's just his daily slice of revolutionary rhetoric. He'll calm down in a minute—he likes to play Che, but he's basically nonviolent."

Ten minutes later Jane served dinner. Konrad, with remarkable speed and coordination, consumed four cans of fruit cocktail, thirty-two spareribs, half a dozen each of oranges, apples and pomegranates, two cheeseburgers and three quarts of chocolate malted. In the kitchen, clearing up, I commented to Jane about our guest's prodigious appetite. He was sitting in the other room, listening to *Don Giovanni*, sipping brandy. Jane said that he was a big, active male and that she could attest to his need for so many calories. "How much does he weigh?" I asked. "Stripped," she said, "one eighty-one. When he stands up straight he's four-eight and three quarters." I mulled over this information while I scraped away at the dishes, filed them in the dishwasher, neat ranks of blue china. A few moments later I stepped into the living room to observe Jane stroking Konrad's ears, his head in her lap. I stand five-seven, one forty-three.

When I returned from work the following day, Jane was gone. Her dresser drawers were bare, the closet empty. There were white rectangles on the wall where her Rousseau reproductions had hung. The top plank of the bookcase was ribbed with the dust-prints of her Edgar Rice Burroughs collection. Her girls' softball trophy, her natural foods cookbook, her oaken cudgel, her moog, her wok: all gone. There were no notes. A pain jabbed at my sternum, tears started in my eyes. I was alone, deserted, friendless. I began to long even for the stink of her. On the pillow in the bedroom I found a fermenting chunk of pineapple. And sobbed.

By the time I thought of the Primate Center the sun was already on the wane. It was dark when I got there. Loose gravel grated beneath my shoes in the parking lot; the flag snapped at the top of its pole; the lights grinned lickerishly from the Center's windows. Inside the lighting was subdued, the building hushed. I began searching through the rooms, opening and slamming doors. The linoleum glowed all the way up the long corridor. At the far end I heard someone whistling "My Old Kentucky Home." It was the janitor. "Howdedo," he said. "Wut kin ah do fo yo at such a inauspicious hour ob de night?"

I was candid with him. "I'm looking for Miss Good."

"Ohhh, she leave bout fo-turdy evy day—sartinly yo should be well apprised ob dat fack."

"I thought she might be working late tonight."

"Noooo, no chance ob dat." He was staring at the floor.

"Mind if I look for myself?"

"Mah good man, ah trusts yo is not intimatin dat ah would dis-kise de troof . . . far be it fum me to pre-varicate jus to proteck a young lady wut run off fum a man dat doan unnerstan her needs nor 'low her to spress de natchrul inclination ob her soul."

At that moment a girlish giggle sounded from down the hall. Jane's girlish giggle. The janitor's right hand spread itself across my chest. "Ah wooden insinooate mahsef in de middle ob a highly sinificant speriment if ah was yo, Jackson," he said, hissing through the gap in his teeth. I pushed by him and started down the corridor. Jane's laugh leaped out again. From the last door on my left. I hurried. Suddenly the Doctor and his wife stepped from the shadows to block the doorway. "Mr. Horne," said the Doctor, arms folded against his chest, "take hold of yourself. We are conducting a series of experiments here that I simply cannot allow you to—"

"A fig for your experiments," I shouted. "I want to speak to my, my— roommate." I could hear the janitor's footsteps behind me. "Get out of my way, Doctor," I said. Mrs. U-Hwak-Lo smiled. I felt panicky. "Is dey a problem here, Doc?" the janitor said, his breath hot on the back of my neck. I broke. Grabbed the Doctor by his elbows, wheeled around and shoved him into the janitor. They went down on the linoleum like spastic skaters. I applied my shoulder to the door and battered my way in, Mrs. U-Hwak-Lo's shrill in my ear: "You make big missake, Misser!" Inside I found Jane, legs and arms bare, pinching a lab smock across her chest. She looked puzzled at first, then annoyed. She stepped up to me, made some rude gestures in my face. I could hear scrambling in the hallway behind me. Then I saw Konrad—in a pair of baggy BVDs. I grabbed Jane. But Konrad was there in an instant—he hit me like the grille of a Cadillac and I spun across the room, tumbling desks and chairs as I went. I slumped against the chalkboard. The door slammed: Jane was gone. Konrad swelled his chest, swayed toward me, the fluorescent lights hissing overhead, the chalkboard cold against the back of my neck. And I looked up into the black eyes, teeth, fur, rock-ribbed arms.

(1974)

CAVIAR

I ought to tell you right off I didn't go to college. I was on the wrong run of the socioeconomic ladder, if you know what I mean. My father was a commercial fisherman on the Hudson, till the PCBs got to him, my mother did typing and filing down at the lumberyard, and my grandmother crocheted doilies and comforters for sale to rich people. Me, I took over my father's trade. I inherited the shack at the end of the pier, the leaky fourteen-foot runabout with the thirty-five-horse Evinrude motor and the seine that's been in the family for three generations. Also, I got to move into the old man's house when he passed on, and he left me his stamp collection and the keys to his '62 Rambler, rusted through till it looked like a gill net hung out to dry.

Anyway, it's a living. Almost. And if I didn't go to college I do read a lot, magazines mostly, but books on ecology and science too. Maybe it was the science part that did me in. You see, I'm the first one around here—I mean, me and Marie are the first ones—to have a baby this new way, where you can't have it on your own. Dr. Ziss said not to worry about it, a little experiment, think of it as a gift from heaven.

Some gift.

But don't get me wrong, I'm not complaining. What happens happens, and I'm as guilty as anybody, I admit it. It's just that when the guys at the Flounder Inn are sniggering in their beer and Marie starts looking at me like I'm a toad or something, you've got to put things in perspective, you've got to realize that it was her all along, she's the one that started it.

"I want a baby," was how she put it.

It was April, raw and wet. Crocuses and dead man's fingers were poking through the dirt along the walk, and the stripers were running. I'd just stepped in the door, beat, chilled to the teeth, when she made her announcement. I went straight for the coffeepot. "Can't afford it," I said.

She didn't plead or try to reason with me. All she did was repeat herself in a matter-of-fact tone, as if she were telling me about some new drapes or a yard sale, and then she marched through the kitchen and out the back door. I sipped at my coffee and watched her through the window. She had a shovel. She was burying something. Deep. When she came back in, her nose was running a bit and her eyes were crosshatched with tiny red lines.

"What were you doing out there?" I asked.

Her chin was crumpled, her hair was wild. "Burying something."

I waited while she fussed with the teapot, my eyebrows arched like question marks. Ten seconds ticked by. "Well, what?"

"My diaphragm."

I've known Marie since high school. We were engaged for five years while she worked for *Reader's Digest* and we'd been married for three and a half when she decided she wanted some offspring. At first I wasn't too keen on the idea, but then I had to admit she was right: the time had come. Our lovemaking had always been lusty and joyful, but after she buried the diaphragm it became tender, intense, purposeful. We tried. For months we tried. I'd come in off the river, reeking of the creamy milt and silver roe that floated two inches deep in the bottom of the boat while fifty- and sixty-pound stripers gasped their last, come in like a wild bull or something, and Marie would be waiting for me upstairs in her nightie and we'd do it before dinner, and then again after. Nothing happened.

Somewhere around July or August, the sweet blueclaw crabs crawling up the riverbed like an army on maneuvers and the humid heat lying over the valley like a cupped hand, Marie went to Sister Eleazar of the Coptic Brotherhood of Ethiop. Sister Eleazar was a black woman, six feet tall at least, in a professor's gown and a fez with a red tassel. Leroy Lent's wife swore by her. Six years Leroy and his wife had been going at it, and then they went to Sister Eleazar and had a pair of twins. Marie thought it was worth a try, so I drove her down there.

The Coptic Brotherhood of Ethiop occupied a lime-green building the size of a two-car garage with a steeple and cross pinned to the roof. Sister Eleazar answered our knock scowling, a little crescent of egg yolk on her chin. "What you want?" she said.

Standing there in the street, a runny-eyed Chihuahua sniffing at my heels, I listened to Marie explain our problem and watched the crescent of egg on Sister Eleazar's face fracture with her smile. "Ohhh," she said, "well, why didn't you say so? Come own in, come own in."

There was one big room inside, poorly lit. Old bottom-burnished pews stretched along three of the four walls and there was a big shiny green table in the center of the floor. The table was heaped with religious paraphernalia—silver salvers and chalices and tinted miniatures of a black man with a crown dwarfing his head. A cot and an icebox huddled against the back wall, which was decorated with magazine clippings of Africa. "Right here, sugar," Sister Eleazar said, leading Marie up to the table. "Now, you take off your coat and your dress, and less ex-amine them wombs."

Marie handed me her coat, and then her tight blue dress with the little white clocks on it, while Sister Eleazar cleared the chalices and whatnot off the table. The Chihuahua had followed us in, and now it sprang up onto the cot with a sigh and buried its nose in its paws. The room stank of dog.

"All right," Sister Eleazar said, turning back to Marie, "you climb up own the table now and stretch yourself out so Sister 'Leazar can listen to your insides and say a prayer over them barren wombs." Marie complied with a nervous smile, and the black woman leaned forward to press an ear to her abdomen. I watched the tassel of Sister Eleazar's fez splay out over Marie's rib cage and I began to get excited: the place dark and exotic, Marie in brassiere and panties, laid out on the table like a sacrificial virgin. Then the sister was mumbling something—a prayer, I guess—in a language I'd never heard before. Marie looked embarrassed. "Don't you worry about nothin'," Sister Eleazar said, looking up at me and winking. "I got just the thing."

She fumbled around underneath the cot for a minute, then came back to the table with a piece of blue chalk—the same as they use in geography class to draw rivers and lakes on the blackboard—and a big yellow can of Colman's dry mustard. She bent over Marie like a heart surgeon, and then, after a few seconds of deliberation, made a blue X on Marie's lower abdomen and said, "Okay, honey, you can get up now."

I watched Marie shrug into her dress, thinking the whole thing was just a lot of superstitious mumbo jumbo and pisantry, when I felt Sister Eleazar's fingers on my arm; she dipped her head and led me out the front door. The sky was overcast. I could smell rain in the air. "Listen," the black woman whispered, handing me the can of mustard, "the problem ain't with her, it's with you. Must be you ain't penetratin' deep enough." I looked into her eyes, trying to keep my face expressionless. Her voice dropped. "What you do is this: make a plaster of this here mustard and rub it on your parts before you go into her, and it'll force out that 'jaculation like a torpedo coming out a submarine—know what I mean?" Then she winked. Marie was at the door. A man with a hoe was digging at his garden in the next yard over. "Oh yeah," the sister said, holding out her hand, "you want to make a donation to the Brotherhood, that'll be eleven dollars and fifty cent."

I never told Marie about the mustard—it was too crazy. All I said was that the sister had told me to give her a mustard plaster on the stomach an hour after we had intercourse—to help the seeds take. It didn't work, of course. Nothing worked. But the years at _Reader's Digest_ had made Marie a superstitious woman, and I was willing to go along with just about anything as long as it made her feel better. One night I came to bed and she was perched naked on the edge of the footstool, wound round three times with a string of garlic. "I thought that was for vampires?" I said. She just parted her lips and held out her arms.

In the next few weeks she must have tried every quack remedy in the book. She kept a toad in a clay pot under the bed, ate soup composed of fish eyes and roe, drank goat's milk and cod-liver oil, and filled the medicine chest with elixirs made from nimble weed and rhinoceros horn. Once I caught her down in the basement, dancing in the nude round a live rooster. I was eating meat three meals a day to keep my strength up. Then one night I came across an article about test-tube babies in _Science Digest_. I studied the pictures for a long while, especially the one at the end of the article that showed this English couple, him with a bald dome and her fat as a sow, with their little test-tube son. Then I called Marie.

Dr. Ziss took us right away. He sympathized with our plight, he said, and would do all he could to help us. First he would have to run some tests to see just what the problem was and whether it could be corrected surgically. He led us into the examining room and looked into our eyes and ears, tapped our knees, measured our blood pressure. He drew blood, squinted at my sperm under a microscope, took X rays, did a complete pelvic exam on Marie. His nurse was Irene Goddard, lived up the street from us. She was a sour, square-headed woman in her fifties with little vertical lines etched around her lips. She prodded and poked and pricked us and then had us fill out twenty or thirty pages of forms that asked about everything from bowel movements to whether my grandmother had any facial hair. Two weeks later I got a phone call. The doctor wanted to see us.

We'd hardly got our jackets off when Mrs. Goddard, with a look on her face like she was about to pull the switch at Sing Sing, showed us into the doctor's office. I should tell you that Dr. Ziss is a young man—about my age, I guess—with narrow shoulders, a little clipped mustache, and a woman's head of hair that he keeps brushing back with his hand. Anyway, he was sitting behind his desk sifting through a pile of charts and lab reports when we walked in. "Sit down," he said. "I'm afraid I have some bad news for you." Marie went pale, like she did the time the state troopers called about her mother's accident; her ankles swayed over her high heels and she fell back into the chair as if she'd been shoved. I thought she was going to cry, but the doctor forestalled her. He smiled, showing off all those flossed and fluoridated teeth: "I've got some good news too."

The bad news was that Marie's ovaries were shot. She was suffering from the Stein-Leventhal syndrome, he said, and was unable to produce viable ova. He put it to us straight: "She's infertile, and there's nothing we can do about it. Even if we had the facilities and the know-how, test-tube reproduction would be out of the question."

Marie was stunned. I stared down at the linoleum for a second and listened to her sniffling, then took her hand.

Dr. Ziss leaned across the desk and pushed back a stray lock of hair. "But there is an alternative."

We both looked at him.

"Have you considered a surrogate mother? A young woman who'd be willing to impregnate herself artificially with the husband's semen—for a fee, of course—and then deliver the baby to the wife at the end of the term." He was smoothing his mustache. "It's being done all over the country. And if Mrs. Trimpie pads herself during her 'pregnancy' and 'delivers' in the city, none of your neighbors need ever know that the child isn't wholly and naturally yours."

My mind was racing. I was bombarded with selfish and acquisitive thoughts, seething with scorn for Marie—*she* was the one, *she* was defective, not me—bursting to exercise my God-given right to a child and heir. It's true, it really is—you never want something so much as when somebody tells you you can't have it. I found myself thinking aloud: "So it would really be half ours, and . . . and half—"

"That's right, Mr. Trimpie. And I have already contacted a young woman on your behalf, should you be interested."

I looked at Marie. Her eyes were watering. She gave me a weak smile and pressed my hand.

"She's Caucasian, of course, attractive, fit, very bright: a first-year medical student in need of funds to continue her education."

"Um, uh," I fumbled for the words, "how much; I mean, if we decide to go along with it, how much would it cost?"

The doctor was ready for this one. "Ten thousand dollars," he said without hesitation, "plus hospital costs."

Two days later there was a knock at the door. A girl in peacoat and blue jeans stood there, flanked by a pair of scuffed aquamarine suitcases held shut with masking tape. She looked to be about sixteen, stunted and bony and pale, cheap mother-of-pearl stars for earrings, her red hair short and spiky, as if she were letting a crewcut grow out. I couldn't help thinking of those World War II movies where they shave the actresses' heads for consorting with the Germans; I couldn't help thinking of waifs and wanderers and runaway teen-agers. Dr. Ziss's gunmetal Mercedes sat at the curb, clouds of exhaust tugging at the tail-pipe in the chill morning air; he waved, and then ground away with a crunch of gravel. "Hi," the girl said, extending her hand, "I'm Wendy."

It had all been arranged. Dr. Ziss thought it would be a good idea if the mother-to-be came to stay with us two weeks or so before the "procedure," to give us a chance to get to know one another, and then maybe stay on with us through the first couple of months so we could experience the pregnancy first-hand; when she began to show she'd move into an apartment on the other side of town, so as not to arouse any suspicion among the neighbors. He was delicate about the question of money, figuring a commercial fisherman and a part-time secretary, with no college and driving a beat-up Rambler, might not exactly be rolling in surplus capital. But the money wasn't a problem really. There was the insurance payoff from Marie's mother—she'd been blindsided by a semi coming off the ramp on the thruway—and the thirty-five hundred I'd got for delivering spawning stripers to Con Ed so they could hatch fish to replace the ones sucked into the screens at the nuclear plant. It was sitting in the County Trust, collecting five and a quarter percent, against the day some emergency came up. Well, this was it. I closed out the account.

The doctor took his fee and explained that the girl would get five thousand dollars on confirmation of pregnancy, and the balance when she delivered. Hospital costs would run about fifteen hundred dollars, barring complications. We shook hands on it, and Marie and I signed a form. I figured I could work nights at the bottling plant if I was strapped.

Now, with the girl standing there before me, I couldn't help feeling a stab of disappointment—she was pretty enough, I guess, but I'd expected something a little more, well, substantial. And red hair. It was a letdown. Deep down I'd been hoping for a blonde, one of those Scandinavian types you see in the cigarette ads. Anyway, I told her I was glad to meet her, and then showed her up to the spare room, which I'd cleaned up and outfitted with a chest of drawers, a bed and a Salvation Army desk, and some cheery knickknacks. I asked her if I could get her a bite to eat, Marie being at work and me waiting around for the tide to go out. She was sitting on the bed, looking tired; she hadn't even bothered to glance out the window at the view of Croton Bay. "Oh yeah," she said after a minute, as if she'd been asleep or day-dreaming. "Yeah, that would be nice." Her eyes were gray, the color of drift ice on the river. She called me Nathaniel, soft and formal, like a breathless young schoolteacher taking attendance. Marie never called me anything but Nat, and the guys at the marina settled for Ace. "Have you got a sandwich, maybe? And a cup of hot Nestlé's? I'd really like that, Nathaniel."

I went down and fixed her a BLT, her soft syllables tingling in my ears like a kiss. Dr. Ziss had called her an "oh pear" girl, which I guess referred to her shape. When she'd slipped out of her coat I saw that there was more to her than I'd thought—not much across the top, maybe, but sturdy in the hips and thighs. I couldn't help thinking it was a good sign, but then I had to check myself: I was looking at her like a horse breeder or something.

She was asleep when I stepped in with the sandwich and hot chocolate. I shook her gently and she started up with a gasp, her eyes darting round the room as if she'd forgotten where she was. "Oh yes, yes, thanks," she said, in that maddening, out-of-breath, little girl's voice. I sat on the edge of the desk and watched her eat, gratified to see that her teeth were strong and even, and her nose just about right. "So you're a medical student, Dr. Ziss tells me."

"Hm-hmm," she murmured, chewing. "First-year. I'm going to take the spring semester off, I mean for the baby and all—"

This was the first mention of our contract, and it fell over the conversation like a lead balloon. She hesitated, and I turned red. Here I was, alone in the house with a stranger, a pretty girl, and she was going to have my baby.

She went on, skirting the embarrassment, trying to brighten her voice. "I mean, I love it and all—med school—but it's a grind already and I really don't see how I can afford the tuition, without, without"—she looked up at me—"without your help."

I didn't know what to say. I stared into her eyes for a minute and felt strangely excited, powerful, like a pasha interviewing a new candidate for the harem. Then I picked up the china sturgeon on the desk and turned it over in my hands. "I didn't go to college," I said. And then, as if I were apologizing, "I'm a fisherman."

A cold rain was falling the day the three of us drove down to Dr. Ziss's for the "procedure." The maples were turning, the streets splashed with red and gold, slick, glistening, the whole world a cathedral. I felt humbled somehow, respectful in the face of life and the progress of the generations of man: My seed is going to take hold, I kept thinking. In half an hour I'll be a father. Marie and Wendy, on the other hand, seemed oblivious to the whole thing, chattering away like a sewing circle, talking about shoes and needlepoint and some actor's divorce. They'd hit it off pretty well, the two of them, sitting in the kitchen over coffee at night, going to movies and thrift shops together, trading gossip, looking up at me and giggling when I stepped into the room. Though Wendy didn't do much around the house—didn't do much more than lie in bed and stare at textbooks—I don't think Marie really minded. She was glad for the company, and there was something more too, of course: Wendy was making a big sacrifice for us. Both of us were deeply grateful.

Dr. Ziss was all smiles that afternoon, pumping my hand, kissing the girls, ushering us into his office like an impresario on opening night. Mrs. Goddard was more restrained. She shot me an icy look, as if I was conspiring to overthrow the Pope or corrupt Girl Scouts or something. Meanwhile, the doctor leaned toward Marie and Wendy and said something I didn't quite catch, and suddenly they were all three of them laughing like Canada geese. Were they laughing at me, I wondered, all at once feeling self-conscious and vulnerable, the odd man out. Dr. Ziss, I noticed, had his arm around Wendy's waist.

If I felt left out, I didn't have time to brood over it. Because Mrs. Goddard had me by the elbow and she was marching me down the hallway to the men's room, where she handed me a condom sealed in tinfoil and a couple of tattered girlie magazines. I didn't need the magazines. Just the thought of what was going to happen in the next room—Marie had asked the doctor if she could do the in-

semination herself—gave me an erection like a tire iron. I pictured Wendy leaning back on the examining table in a little white smock, nothing underneath, and
Marie, my big loving wife, with this syringelike thing . . . that's all it took. I was
out of the bathroom in sixty seconds, the wet condom tucked safely away in a
sterilized jar.

Afterward, we shared a bottle of pink champagne and a lasagna dinner at
Mama's Pasta House. My treat.

One morning, about a month later, I was lying in bed next to Marie and I heard
Wendy pad down the hallway to the bathroom. The house was still, and a soft
gray light clung to the window sill like a blanket. I was thinking of nothing, or
maybe I was thinking of striped bass, sleek and silver, how they ride up out of
the deep like pieces of a dream. Next thing I heard was the sound of gagging.
Morning sickness, I thought, picking up on a phrase from one of the countless
baby books scattered round the house, and suddenly, inexplicably, I was doubled
over myself. "Aaaaargh," Wendy gasped, the sound echoing through the house,
"aaaargh," and it felt like somebody was pulling my stomach inside out.

At breakfast, she was pale and haggard, her hair greasy and her eyes puffed
out. She tried to eat a piece of dry toast, but wound up spitting it into her hand.
I couldn't eat, either. Same thing the next day, and the next: she was sick, I was
sick. I'd pull the cord on the outboard and the first whiff of exhaust would turn
my stomach and I'd have to lean over and puke in the river. Or I'd haul the gill
nets up off the bottom and the exertion would nearly kill me. I called the doctor.

"Sympathetic pregnancy," he said, his voice cracking at the far end of a bad
connection. "Perfectly normal. The husband identifies with the wife's symptoms."

"But I'm not her husband."

"Husband, father: what difference does it make. You're it."

I thought about that. Thought about it when Wendy and I began to eat like
the New York Jets at the training table, thought about it nights at the bottling
plant, thought about it when Wendy came into the living room in her underwear
one evening and showed us the hard white bulge that was already beginning to
open her navel up like a flower. Marie was watching some sappy hospital show
on TV; I was reading about the dead water between Manhattan and Staten
Island—nothing living there, not even eels. "Look," Wendy said, an angels-in-
heaven smile on her face, "it's starting to show." Marie got up and embraced her.
I grinned like an idiot, thrilled at the way the panties grabbed her thighs—white
nylon with dancing pink flowers—and how her little pointed breasts were beginning to strain at the brassiere. I wanted to put my tongue in her navel.

Next day, while Marie was at work, I tapped on Wendy's door. "Come on in,"
she said. She was wearing a housecoat, Japanese-y, with dragons and pagodas on
it, propped up against the pillows reading an anatomy text. I told her I didn't feel
like going down to the river and wondered if she wanted anything. She put the

book down and looked at me like a pat of butter sinking into a halibut steak. "Yes," she said, stretching it to two syllables, "as a matter of fact I do." Then she unbuttoned the robe. Later she smiled at me and said: "So what did we need the doctor for, anyway?"

If Marie suspected anything, she didn't show it. I think she was too caught up in the whole thing to have an evil thought about either one of us. I mean, she doted on Wendy, hung on her every word, came home from work each night and shut herself up in Wendy's room for an hour or more. I could hear them giggling. When I asked her what the deal was, Marie just shrugged. "You know," she said, "the usual—girls' talk and such." The shared experience had made them close, closer than sisters, and sometimes I would think of us as one big happy family. But I stopped short of telling Marie what was going on when she was out of the house. Once, years ago, I'd had a fling with a girl we'd known in high school—an arrow-faced little fox with starched hair and raccoon eyes. It had been brief and strictly biological, and then the girl had moved to Ohio. Marie never forgot it. Just the mention of Ohio—even so small a thing as the TV weatherman describing a storm over the Midwest—would set her off.

I'd like to say I was torn, but I wasn't. I didn't want to hurt Marie—she was my wife, my best friend, I loved and respected her—and yet there was Wendy, with her breathy voice and gray eyes, bearing my child. The thought of it, of my son floating around in his own little sea just behind the sweet bulge of her belly . . . well, it inflamed me, got me mad with lust and passion and spiritual love too. Wasn't Wendy as much my wife as Marie? Wasn't marriage, at bottom, simply a tool for procreating the species? Hadn't Sarah told Abraham to go in unto Hagar? Looking back on it, I guess Wendy let me make love to her because maybe she was bored and a little horny, lying around in a negligee day and night and studying all that anatomy. She sure didn't feel the way I did—if I know anything, I know that now. But at the time I didn't think of it that way, I didn't think at all. Surrogate mother, surrogate wife. I couldn't get enough of her.

Everything changed when Marie taped a feather bolster around her waist and our "boarder" had to move over to Depew Street. ("Don't know what happened," I told the guys down at the Flounder, "she just up and moved out. Low on bucks, I guess." Nobody so much as looked up from their beer until one of the guys mentioned the Knicks game and Alex DeFazio turned to me and said, "So you got a bun in the oven, is what I hear.") I was at a loss. What with Marie working full-time now, I found myself stuck in the house, alone, with nothing much to do except wear a path in the carpet and eat my heart out. I could walk down to the river, but it was February and nothing was happening, so I'd wind up at the Flounder Inn with my elbows on the bar, watching the mollies and swordtails bump into the sides of the aquarium, hoping somebody would give me a lift across town. Of course Marie and I would drive over to Wendy's after dinner every couple of days or so, and I could talk to her on the telephone till my throat went dry—but it wasn't the same. Even the few times I did get over there in the day, I could feel it. We'd make love, but she seemed shy and reluctant, as if she were performing a duty or something. "What's wrong?" I asked her. "Nothing," she said. It was as if someone had cut a neat little hole in the center of my life.

One time, a stiff windy day in early March, I couldn't stand the sight of four walls anymore and I walked the six miles across town and all the way out to Depew Street. It was an ugly day. Clouds like steel wool, a dirty crust of ice underfoot, dog turds preserved like icons in the receding snowbanks. The whole way over there I kept thinking up various scenarios: Wendy and I would take the bus for California, then write Marie to come join us; we'd fly to the Virgin Islands and raise the kid on the beach; Marie would have an accident. When I got there, Dr. Ziss's Mercedes was parked out front. I thought that was pretty funny, him being there in the middle of the day, but then I told myself he was her doctor after all. I turned around and walked home.

Nathaniel Jr. was born in New York City at the end of June, nine pounds, one ounce, with a fluff of orange hair and milky gray eyes. Wendy never looked so beautiful. The hospital bed was cranked up, her hair, grown out now, was freshwashed and brushed, she was wearing the turquoise earrings I'd given her. Marie, meanwhile, was experiencing the raptures of the saints. She gave me a look of pride and fulfillment, rocking the baby in her arms, cooing and beaming. I stole a glance at Wendy. There were two wet circles where her nipples touched the front of her gown. When she put Nathaniel to her breast I thought I was going to faint from the beauty of it, and from something else too: jealousy. I wanted her, then and there.

Dr. Ziss was on the scene, of course, all smiles, as if he'd been responsible for the whole thing. He pecked Marie's cheek, patted the baby's head, shook my hand, and bent low to kiss Wendy on the lips. I handed him a cigar. Three days later Wendy had her five thousand dollars, the doctor and the hospital had been paid off, and Marie and I were back in Westchester with our son. Wendy had been dressed in a loose summer gown and sandals when I gave her the check. I remember she was sitting there on a lacquered bench, cradling the baby, the hospital corridor lit up like a clerestory with sunbeams. There were tears—mainly Marie's—and promises to keep in touch. She handed over Nathaniel as if he was a piece of meat or a sack of potatoes, no regrets. She and Marie embraced, she rubbed her cheek against mine and made a perfunctory little kissing noise, and then she was gone.

I held out for a week. Changing diapers, heating formula, snuggling up with Marie and little Nathaniel, trying to feel whole again. But I couldn't. Every time I looked at my son I saw Wendy, the curl of the lips, the hair, the eyes, the pout—in my distraction, I even thought I heard something of her voice in his gasping howls. Marie was asleep, the baby in her arms. I backed the car out and headed for Depew Street.

The first thing I saw when I rounded the corner onto Depew was the doctor's

Mercedes, unmistakable, gunmetal gray, gleaming at the curb like a slap in the face. I was so startled to see it there I almost ran into it. What was this, some kind of postpartum emergency or something? It was 10:00 A.M. Wendy's curtains were drawn. As I stamped across the lawn my fingers began to tremble like they do when I'm tugging at the net and I can feel something tugging back.

The door was open. Ziss was sitting there in T-shirt and jeans, watching cartoons on TV and sipping at a glass of milk. He pushed the hair back from his brow and gave me a sheepish grin. "David?" Wendy called from the back room. "David? Are you going out?" I must have looked like the big loser on a quiz show or something, because Ziss, for once, didn't have anything to say. He just shrugged his shoulders. Wendy's voice, breathy as a flute, came at us again: "Because if you are, get me some sweetcakes and yogurt, and maybe a couple of corn muffins, okay? I'm hungry as a bear."

Ziss got up and walked to the bedroom door, mumbled something I couldn't hear, strode past me without a glance and went on out the back door. I watched him bend for a basketball, dribble around in the dirt, and then cock his arm for a shot at an imaginary basket. On the TV, Sylvester the cat reached into a trash can and pulled out a fish stripped to the bones. Wendy was standing in the doorway. She had nothing to say.

"Look, Wendy," I began. I felt betrayed, cheated, felt as if I was the brunt of a joke between this girl in the housecoat and the curly-headed hotshot fooling around on the lawn. What was his angle, I wondered, heart pounding at my chest, what was hers? "I suppose you two had a good laugh over me, huh?"

She was pouting, the spoiled child. "I fulfilled my part of the bargain."

She had. I got what I'd paid for. But all that had changed, couldn't she see that? I didn't want a son, I didn't want Marie; I wanted her. I told her so. She said nothing. "You've got something going with Ziss, right?" I said, my voice rising. "All along, right?"

She looked tired, looked as if she'd been up for a hundred nights running. I watched her shuffle across the room into the kitchenette, glance into the refrigerator, and come up with a jar of jam. She made herself a sandwich, licking the goo from her fingers, and then she told me I stank of fish. She said she couldn't have a lasting relationship with me because of Marie.

"That's a lot of crap, and you know it." I was shouting. Ziss, fifty feet away, turned to look through the open door.

"All right. It's because we're—" She put the sandwich down, wiped a smear of jelly from her lip. "Because we move in different circles."

"You mean because I'm not some fancy-ass doctor, because I didn't go to college."

She nodded. Slow and deliberate, no room for argument, she held my eyes and nodded.

I couldn't help it. Something just came loose in my head, and the next second I was out the door, knocking Ziss into the dirt. He kicked and scratched, tried to bite me on the wrist, but I just took hold of his hair and laid into his face while Wendy ran around in her Japanese housecoat, screeching like a cat in heat. By the time the police got there I'd pretty well closed up both his eyes and re-arranged his dental work. Wendy was bending over him with a bottle of rubbing alcohol when they put the cuffs on me.

Next morning there was a story in the paper. Marie sent Alex DeFazio down with the bail money, and then she wouldn't let me in the house. I banged on the door halfheartedly, then tried one of the windows, only to find she'd nailed it shut. When I saw that, I was just about ready to explode, but then I figured what the hell and fired up the Rambler in a cloud of blue smoke. Cops, dogs, kids, and pedestrians be damned, I ran it like a stock car eight blocks down to the dock and left it steaming in the parking lot. Five minutes later I was planing across the river, a wide brown furrow fanning out behind me.

This was my element, sun, wind, water, life pared down to the basics. Gulls hung in the air like puppets on a wire, spray flew up in my face, the shore sank back into my wake until docks and pleasure boats and clapboard houses were swallowed up and I was alone on the broad gray back of the river. After a while I eased up on the throttle and began scanning the surface for the buoys that marked my gill nets, working by rote, the tight-wound spool in my chest finally beginning to pay out. Then I spotted them, white and red, jogged by the waves. I cut the engine, coasted in and caught hold of the nearest float.

Wendy, I thought, as I hauled at the ropes, ten years, twenty-five, a lifetime: every time I look at my son I'll see your face. Hand over hand, Wendy, Wendy, Wendy, the net heaving up out of the swirling brown depths with its pounds of flesh. But then I wasn't thinking about Wendy anymore, or Marie or Nathaniel Jr.—I was thinking about the bottom of the river, I was thinking about fins and scales and cold lidless eyes. The instant I touched the lead rope I knew I was on to something. This time of year it would be sturgeon, big as logs, long-nosed and barbeled, coasting up the riverbed out of some dim watery past, anadromous, preprogrammed, homing in on their spawning grounds like guided missiles. Just then I felt a pulsing in the soles of my sneakers and turned to glance up at the Day Liner, steaming by on its way to Bear Mountain, hundreds of people with picnic baskets and coolers, waving. I jerked at the net like a penitent.

There was a single sturgeon in the net, tangled up like a ball of string. It was dead. I strained to haul the thing aboard, six feet long, two hundred pounds. Cold from the depths, still supple, it hadn't been dead more than an hour—while I banged at my own front door, locked out, it had been thrashing in the dark, locked in. The gulls swooped low, mocking me. I had to cut it out of the net.

Back at the dock I got one of the beer drinkers to give me a hand and we dragged the fish over to the skinning pole. With sturgeon, we hang them by the gills from the top of a ten-foot pole, and then we peel back the scutes like you'd peel a banana. Four or five of the guys stood there watching me, nobody saying anything. I cut all the way round the skin just below the big stiff gill plates and then made five vertical slits the length of the fish. Flies settled on the blade of the knife. The sun beat at the back of my head. I remember there was a guy standing there, somebody I'd never seen before, a guy in a white shirt with a kid about eight or so. The kid was holding a fishing pole. They stepped back, both of them, when I tore the first strip of skin from the fish.

Sturgeon peels back with a raspy, nails-on-the-blackboard sort of sound, reminds me of tearing up sheets or ripping bark from a tree. I tossed the curling strips of leather in a pile, flies sawing away at the air, the big glistening pink carcass hanging there like a skinned deer, blood and flesh. Somebody handed me a beer: it stuck to my hand and I drained it in a gulp. Then I turned to gut the fish, me a doctor, the knife a scalpel, and suddenly I was digging into the vent like Jack the Ripper, slitting it all the way up to the gills in a single violent motion.

"How do you like that?" the man in the white shirt said. "She's got eggs in her."

I glanced down. There they were, wet, beaded and gray, millions of them, the big clusters tearing free and dropping to the ground like ripe fruit. I cupped my hands and held the trembling mass of it there against the gashed belly, fifty or sixty pounds of the stuff, slippery roe running through my fingers like the silver coins from a slot machine, like a jackpot.

(1981)

ALL SHOOK UP

About a week after the FOR RENT sign disappeared from the window of the place next door, a van the color of cough syrup swung off the blacktop road and into the driveway. The color didn't do much for me, nor the oversize tires with the raised white letters, but the side panel was a real eye-catcher. It featured a life-size portrait of a man with high-piled hair and a guitar, beneath which appeared the legend *Young Elvis, The Boy Who Dared To Rock.* When the van pulled in I was sitting in the kitchen, rereading the newspaper and blowing into my eighth cup of coffee. I was on vacation. My wife was on vacation too. Only she was in Mill Valley, California, with a guy named Fred, and I was in Shrub Oak, New York.

The door of the van eased open and a kid about nineteen stepped out. He was wearing a black leather jacket with the collar turned up, even though it must have been ninety, and his hair was a glistening, blue-black construction of grease and hair spray that rose from the crown of his head like a bird's nest perched atop a cliff. The girl got out on the far side and then ducked round the van to stand gaping at the paint-blistered Cape Cod as if it were Graceland itself. She was small-boned and tentative, her big black-rimmed eyes like puncture wounds. In her arms, as slack and yielding as a bag of oranges, was a baby. It couldn't have been more than six months old.

I fished three beers out of the refrigerator, slapped through the screen door, and crossed the lawn to where they stood huddled in the driveway, looking lost. "Welcome to the neighborhood," I said, proffering the beers.

The kid was wearing black ankle boots. He ground the toe of the right one into the pavement as if stubbing out a cigarette, then glanced up and said, "I don't drink."

"How about you?" I said, grinning at the girl.

"Sure, thanks," she said, reaching out a slim, veiny hand bright with lacquered nails. She gave the kid a glance, then took the beer, saluted me with a wink, and raised it to her lips. The baby never stirred.

I felt awkward with the two open bottles, so I gingerly set one down on the grass, then straightened up and took a hit from the other. "Patrick," I said, extending my free hand.

The kid took my hand and nodded, a bright wet spit curl swaying loose over his forehead. "Joey Greco," he said. "Glad to meet you. This here is Cindy."

There was something peculiar about his voice—tone and accent both. For one thing, it was surprisingly deep, as if he were throwing his voice or doing an impersonation. Then too, I couldn't quite place the accent. I gave Cindy a big welcoming smile and turned back to him. "You from down South?" I said.

The toe began to grind again and the hint of a smile tugged at the corner of his mouth, but he suppressed it. When he looked up at me his eyes were alive. "No," he said. "Not really."

A jay flew screaming out of the maple in back of the house, wheeled overhead, and disappeared in the hedge. I took another sip of beer. My face was beginning to ache from grinning so much and I could feel the sweat leaching out of my armpit and into my last clean T-shirt.

"No," he said again, and his voice was pitched a shade higher. "I'm from Brooklyn."

Two days later I was out back in the hammock, reading a thriller about a double agent who turns triple agent for a while, is discovered, pursued, captured, and finally persuaded under torture to become a quadruple agent, at which point his wife leaves him and his children change their surname. I was also drinking my way through a bottle of Chivas Regal Fred had given my wife for Christmas, and contemplatively rubbing tanning butter into my navel. The doorbell took me by surprise. I sat up, plucked a leaf from the maple for a bookmark, and padded round the house in bare feet and paint-stained cutoffs.

Cindy was standing at the front door, her back to me, peering through the screen. At first I didn't recognize her: she looked waifish, lost, a Girl Scout peddling cookies in a strange neighborhood. Just as I was about to say something, she pushed the doorbell again. "Hello," she called, cupping her hands and leaning into the screen.

The chimes tinnily reproduced the first seven notes of "Camptown Races," an effect my wife had found endearing; I made a mental note to disconnect them first thing in the morning. "Anybody home?" Cindy called.

"Hello," I said, and watched her jump. "Looking for me?"

"Oh," she gasped, swinging round with a laugh. "Hi." She was wearing a halter top and gym shorts, her hair was pinned up, and her perfect little toes looked freshly painted. "Patrick, right?" she said.

"That's right," I said. "And you're Cindy."

She nodded, and gave me the sort of look you get from a haberdasher when you go in to buy a suit. "Nice tan."

I glanced down at my feet, rubbed a slick hand across my chest. "I'm on vacation."

"That's great," she said. "From what?"

"I work up at the high school? I'm in Guidance."

"Oh, wow," she said, "that's really great." She stepped down off the porch. "I really mean it—that's something." And then: "Aren't you kind of young to be a guidance counselor?"

"I'm twenty-nine."

"You're kidding, right? You don't look it. Really. I would've thought you were twenty-five, maybe, or something." She patted her hair tentatively, once around, as if to make sure it was all still there. "Anyway, what I came over to ask is if you'd like to come to dinner over at our place tonight."

I was half drunk, the thriller wasn't all that thrilling, and I hadn't been out of the yard in four days. "What time?" I said.

"About six."

There was a silence, during which the birds could be heard cursing one another in the trees. Down the block someone fired up a rotary mower. "Well, listen, I got to go put the meat up," she said, turning to leave. But then she swung round with an afterthought. "I forgot to ask: are you married?"

She must have seen the hesitation on my face.

"Because if you are, I mean, we want to invite her too." She stood there watching me. Her eyes were gray, and there was a violet clock in the right one. The hands pointed to three-thirty.

"Yes," I said finally, "I am." There was the sound of a stinging ricochet and a heartfelt guttural curse as the unseen mower hit a stone. "But my wife's away. On vacation."

I'd been in the house only once before, nearly eight years back. The McCareys had lived there then, and Judy and I had just graduated from the state teachers' college. We'd been married two weeks, the world had been freshly created from out of the void, and we were moving into our new house. I was standing in the driveway, unloading boxes of wedding loot from the trunk of the car, when Henry McCarey ambled across the lawn to introduce himself. He must have been around seventy-five. His pale, bald brow swept up and back from his eyes like a helmet, square and imposing, but the flesh had fallen in on itself from the cheekbones down, giving his face a mismatched look. He wore wire-rim glasses. "If you've got a minute there," he said, "we'd like to show you and your wife some-thing." I looked up. Henry's wife, Irma, stood framed in the doorway behind him. Her hair was pulled back in a bun and she wore a print dress that fell to the tops of her white sweat socks.

I called Judy. She smiled, I smiled, Henry smiled; Irma, smiling, held the door for us, and we found ourselves in the dark, cluttered living room with its excess furniture, its framed photographs of eras gone by, and its bric-a-brac. Irma asked us if we'd like a cup of tea. "Over here," Henry said, gesturing from the far cor-ner of the room.

We edged forward, smiling but ill at ease. We were twenty-two, besotted with passion and confidence, and these people made our grandparents look young. I didn't know what to say to them, didn't know how to act: I wanted to get back to the car and the boxes piled on the lawn.

Henry was standing before a glass case that stood atop a mound of doilies on a rickety-looking corner table. He fumbled behind it for a moment, and then a little white Christmas bulb flickered on inside the case. I saw a silver trowellike thing with an inscription on it and a rippled, petrified chunk of something that looked as if it might once have been organic. It was a moment before I realized it was a piece of wedding cake.

"It's from our golden anniversary," Henry said, "six years ago. And that there is the cake knife—can you read what it says?"

I felt numb, felt as if I'd been poking around in the dirt and unearthed the traces of a forgotten civilization. I stole a look at Judy. She was transfixed, her face drawn up as if she were about to cry: she was so beautiful, so rapt, so moved by the moment and its auguries, that I began to feel choked up myself. She took my hand.

"It says 'Henry and Irma, 1926–1976, Semper Fidelis.' That last bit, that's Latin," Henry added, and then he translated for us.

Things were different now.

I rapped at the flimsy aluminum storm door and Joey bobbed into view through the dark mesh of the screen. He was wearing a tight black sportcoat with the collar turned up, a pink shirt, and black pants with jagged pink light-ning bolts ascending the outer seam. At first he didn't seem to recognize me, and for an instant, standing there in my cutoffs and T-shirt with half a bottle of Chivas in my hand, I felt more like an interloper than an honored guest—she *had* said tonight, hadn't she?—but then he was ducking his head in greeting and swinging back the door to admit me.

"Glad you could make it," he said without enthusiasm.

"Yeah, me too," I breathed, wondering if I was making a mistake.

I followed him into the living room, where spavined boxes and green plastic trash bags stuffed with underwear and sweaters gave testimony to an ongoing adventure in moving. The place was as close and dark as I'd remembered, but where before there'd been doilies, bric-a-brac, and end tables with carved feet, now there was a plaid sofa, an exercycle, and a dirty off-white beanbag lounger. Gone was the shrine to marital fidelity, replaced by a Fender amp, a microphone stand, and an acoustic guitar with capo and pickup. (Henry was gone too, dead of emphysema, and Irma was in a nursing home on the other side of town.) There was a stereo with great black monolithic speakers, and the walls were hung with posters of Elvis. I looked at Joey. He was posed beside a sneering young Elvis, rocking back and forth on the heels of his boots. "Pretty slick," I said, indicating his get-up.

"Oh this?" he said, as if surprised I'd noticed. "I've been rehearsing—trying on outfits, you know."

I'd figured he was some sort of Elvis impersonator, judging from the van, the clothes, and the achieved accent, but aside from the hair I couldn't really see much resemblance between him and the King. "You, uh—you do an Elvis act?"

He looked at me as if I'd just asked if the thing above our heads was the ceiling. Finally he just said, "Yeah."

It was then that Cindy emerged from the kitchen. She was wearing a white peasant dress and sandals, and she was holding a glass of wine in one hand and a zucchini the size of a souvenir baseball bat in the other. "Patrick," she said, crossing the room to brush my cheek with a kiss. I embraced her ritualistically— you might have thought we'd known each other for a decade—and held her a moment while Joey and Elvis looked on. When she stepped back, I caught a whiff of perfume and alcohol. "You like zucchini?" she said.

"Uh-huh, sure." I was wondering what to do with my hands. Suddenly I remembered the bottle and held it up like a turkey I'd shot in the woods. "I brought you this."

Cindy made a gracious noise or two, I shrugged in deprecation—"It's only half full," I said—and Joey ground his toe into the carpet. I might have been imagining it, but he seemed agitated, worked up over something.

"How long till dinner?" he said, a reedy, adolescent whine snaking through the Nashville basso.

Cindy's eyes were unsteady. She drained her wine in a gulp and held out the glass for me to refill. With Scotch. "I don't know," she said, watching the glass. "Half an hour."

"Because I think I want to work on a couple numbers, you know?"

She gave him a look. I didn't know either of them well enough to know what it meant. That look could have said, "Go screw yourself," or "I'm just wild about you and Elvis"—I couldn't tell.

"No problem," she said finally, sipping at her drink, the zucchini tucked under her arm. "Patrick was going to help me in the kitchen, anyway—right, Patrick?"

"Sure," I said.

■ ■ ■

At dinner, Joey cut into his *braciola,* lifted a forkful of tomatoes, peppers, and zucchini to his lips, and talked about Elvis. "He was the most photographed man in the history of the world. He had sixty-two cars and over a hundred guitars." Fork, knife, meat, vegetable. "He was the greatest there ever was."

I didn't know about that. By the time I gave up pellet guns and minibikes and began listening to rock and roll, it was the Doors, Stones, and Hendrix, and Elvis was already degenerating into a caricature of himself. I remembered him as a bloated old has-been in a white jumpsuit, crooning corny ballads and slobbering on middle-aged women. Besides, between the Chivas and the bottle of red Cindy had opened for dinner, I was pretty far gone. "Hmph," was about all I could manage.

For forty-five minutes, while I'd sat on a cracked vinyl barstool at the kitchen counter, helping slice vegetables and trading stories with Cindy, I'd heard Joey's rendition of half a dozen Elvis classics. He was in the living room, thundering; I was in the kitchen, drinking. Every once in a while he'd give the guitar a rest or step back from the microphone, and I would hear the real Elvis moaning faintly in the background: *Don't be cruel / To a heart that's true* or *You ain't nothin' but a hound dog.*

"He's pretty good," I said to Cindy after a particularly thunderous rendition of "Jailhouse Rock." I was making conversation.

She shrugged. "Yeah, I guess so," she said. The baby lay in a portable cradle by the window, giving off subtle emanations of feces and urine. It was asleep, I supposed. If it weren't for the smell, I would have guessed it was dead. "You know, we had to get married," she said.

I made a gesture of dismissal, tried for a surprised expression. Of course they'd had to get married. I'd seen a hundred girls just like her—they passed through the guidance office like flocks of unfledged birds flying in the wrong direction, north in the winter, south in the summer. Slumped over, bony, eyes sunk into their heads, and made up like showgirls or whores, they slouched in the easy chair in my office and told me their stories. They thought they were hip and depraved, thought they were nihilists and libertines, thought they'd invented sex. Two years later they were housewives with preschoolers and station wagons. Two years after that they were divorced.

"First time I heard Elvis, first time I remember, anyway," Joey was saying now, "was in December of '68 when he did that TV concert—the Singer Special? It blew me away. I just couldn't believe it."

"Sixty-eight?" I echoed. "What were you, four?"

Cindy giggled. I turned to look at her, a sloppy grin on my face. I was drunk.

Joey didn't bat an eye. "I was seven," he said. And then: "That was the day I stopped being a kid." He'd tucked a napkin under his collar to protect his pink shirt, and strands of hair hung loose over his forehead. "Next day my mom picked up a copy of *Elvis's Greatest Hits, Volume One*, and a week later she got me my first guitar. I've been at it ever since."

Joey was looking hard at me. He was trying to impress me; that much was clear. That's why he'd worn the suit, dabbed his lids with green eye shadow, greased his hair, and hammered out his repertoire from the next room so I couldn't help but catch every lick. Somehow, though, I wasn't impressed. Whether it was the booze, my indifference to Elvis, or the fear and loathing that had gripped me since Judy's defection, I couldn't say. All I knew was that I didn't give a shit. For Elvis, for Joey, for Fred, Judy, Little Richard, or Leonard Bernstein. For anybody. I sipped my wine in silence.

"My agent's trying to book me into the Catskills—some of the resorts and all, you know? He says my act's really hot." Joey patted his napkin, raised a glass of milk to his lips, and took a quick swallow. "I'll be auditioning up there at Brown's in about a week. Meanwhile, Friday night I got this warm-up gig—no big deal, just some dump out in the sticks. It's over in Brewster—you ever heard of it?"

"The sticks, or Brewster?" I said.

"No, really, why not drop by?"

Cindy was watching me. Earlier, over the chopping board, she'd given me the rundown on this and other matters. She was twenty, Joey was twenty-one. Her father owned a contracting company in Putnam Valley and had set them up with the house. She'd met Joey in Brooklyn the summer before, when she was staying with her cousin. He was in a band then. Now he did Elvis. Nothing but. He'd had gigs in the City and out on the Island, but he wasn't making anything and he refused to take a day job: nobody but hacks did that. So they'd come to the hinterlands, where her father could see they didn't starve to death and Cindy could work as a secretary in his office. They were hoping the Brewster thing would catch on—nobody was doing much with Elvis up here.

I chewed, swallowed, washed it down with a swig of wine. "Sounds good, I said. I'll be there."

Later, after Joey had gone to bed, Cindy and I sat side by side on the plaid sofa and listened to a tape of *Swan Lake* I'd gone next door to fetch ("Something soft," she'd said. "Have you got something soft?"). We were drinking coffee, and a sweet yellowish cordial she'd dug out of one of the boxes of kitchen things. We'd been talking. I'd told her about Judy. And Fred. Told her I'd been feeling pretty rotten and that I was glad she'd moved in. "Really," I said, "I mean it. And I really appreciate you inviting me over too."

She was right beside me, her arms bare in the peasant dress, legs folded under her yoga-style. "No problem," she said, looking me in the eye.

I glanced away and saw Elvis. Crouching, dipping, leering, humping the microphone, and spraying musk over the first three rows, Elvis in full rut. "So how do you feel about all this"—I waved my arm to take in the posters, the guitar and amp, the undefined space above us where Joey lay sleeping—"I mean, living with the King?" I laughed and held my cupped hand under her chin. "Go ahead, dear—speak right into the mike."

She surprised me then. Her expression was dead serious, no time for levity. Slowly, deliberately, she set down her coffee cup and leaned forward to swing round so that she was kneeling beside me on the couch; then she kicked her leg out as if mounting a horse and brought her knee softly down between my legs until I could feel the pressure lighting up my groin. From the stereo, I could hear the swan maidens bursting into flight. "It's like being married to a clone," she whispered.

When I got home, the phone was ringing. I slammed through the front door, stumbled over something in the dark, and took the stairs to the bedroom two at a time. "Yeah?" I said breathlessly as I snatched up the receiver.

"Pat?"

It was Judy. Before I could react, her voice was coming at me, soft and passionate, syllables kneading me like fingers. "Pat, listen," she said. "I want to explain something—"

I hung up.

The club was called Delvecchio's, and it sat amid an expanse of blacktop like a cruise ship on a flat, dark sea. It was a big place, with two separate stages, a disco, three bars, and a game room. I recognized it instantly: teen nirvana. Neon pulsed, raked Chevys rumbled out front, guys in Hawaiian shirts and girls in spike heels stood outside the door, smoking joints and cigarettes and examining one another with frozen eyes. The parking lot was already beginning to fill up when Cindy and I pulled in around nine.

"Big on the sixteen-year-old crowd tonight," I said. "Want me to gun the engine?"

Cindy was wearing a sleeveless blouse, pedal pushers, and heels. She'd made herself up to look like a cover girl for *Slash* magazine, and she smelled like a candy store. "Come on, Pat," she said in a hoarse whisper. "Don't be that way."

"What way?" I said, but I knew what she meant. We were out to have a good time, to hear Joey on his big night, and there was no reason to kill it with cynicism.

Joey had gone on ahead in the van to set up his equipment and do a sound check. Earlier, he'd made a special trip over to my place to ask if I'd mind taking Cindy to the club. He stood just inside the door, working the toe of his patent-leather boot and gazing beyond me to the wreckage wrought by Judy's absence: the cardboard containers of takeout Chinese stacked atop the TV, the beer bottles and Devil Dog wrappers on the coffee table, the clothes scattered about like the leavings of a river in flood. I looked him in the eye, wondering just how much he knew of the passionate groping Cindy and I had engaged in while he was getting his beauty rest the other night, wondering if he had even the faintest notion that I felt evil and betrayed and wanted his wife because I had wounds to salve and because she was there, wanted her like forbidden fruit, wanted her like I'd wanted half the knocked-up, washed-out, defiant little twits who paraded through my office each year. He held my gaze until I looked away. "Sure," I murmured, playing Tristan to his Mark. "Be happy to."

And so, come eight o'clock, I'd showered and shaved, slicked back my hair, turned up the collar of my favorite gigolo shirt, and strolled across the lawn to pick her up. The baby (her name was Gladys, after Elvis's mother) was left in the care of one of the legions of pubescent girls I knew from school, Cindy emerged from the bedroom on brisk heels to peck my cheek with a kiss, and we strolled back across the lawn to my car.

There was an awkward silence. Though we'd talked two or three times since the night of the *braciola* and the couch, neither of us had referred to it. We'd done some pretty heavy petting and fondling, we'd got the feel of each other's dentition and a taste of abandon. I was the one who backed off. I had a vision of Joey standing in the doorway in his pajamas, head bowed under the weight of his pompadour. "What about Joey," I whispered, and we both swiveled our heads to gaze up at the flat, unrevealing surface of the ceiling. Then I got up and went home to bed.

Now, as we reached the car and I swung back the door for her, I found something to say. "I can't believe it"—I laughed, hearty, jocular, all my teeth showing—"but I feel like I'm out on a date or something."

Cindy just cocked her head and gave me a little smirk. "You are," she said.

They'd booked Joey into the Troubadour Room, a place that seated sixty or seventy and had the atmosphere of a small club. Comedians played there once in a while, and the occasional folk singer or balladeer—acts that might be expected to draw a slightly older, more contemplative crowd. Most of the action, obviously, centered on the rock bands that played the main stage, or the pounding fantasia of the disco. We didn't exactly have to fight for a seat.

Cindy ordered a Black Russian. I stuck with Scotch. We talked about Elvis, Joey, rock and roll. We talked about Gladys and how precocious she was and how her baby raptures alternated with baby traumas. We talked about the watercolors Cindy had done in high school and how she'd like to get back to them. We talked about Judy. About Fred. About guidance counseling. We were on our third drink—or maybe it was the fourth—when the stage lights went up and the emcee announced Joey.

"Excited?" I said.

She shrugged, scanning the stage a moment as the drummer, bass player, and guitarist took their places. Then she found my hand under the table and gave it a squeeze.

At that moment Joey whirled out of the wings and pounced on the mike as if it were alive. He was dressed in a mustard-colored suit spangled with gold glitter, a sheeny gold tie, and white patent-leather loafers. For a moment he just stood there, trying his best to radiate the kind of outlaw sensuality that was Elvis's signature, but managing instead to look merely awkward, like a kid dressed up for a costume party. Still, he knew the moves. Suddenly his right fist shot up over his head and the musicians froze; he gave us his best sneer, then the fist came crashing down across the face of his guitar, the band lurched into "Heartbreak Hotel," and Joey threw back his head and let loose.

Nothing happened.

The band rumbled on confusedly for a bar or two, then cut out as Joey stood there tapping at the microphone and looking foolish.

"AC/DC!" someone shouted from the darkness to my left.

"Def Leppard!"

The emcee, a balding character in a flowered shirt, scurried out onstage and crouched over the pedestal of the antiquated mike Joey had insisted on for authenticity. Someone shouted an obscenity, and Joey turned his back. There were more calls for heavy-metal bands, quips and laughter. The other band members—older guys with beards and expressionless faces—looked about as concerned as sleepwalkers. I stole a look at Cindy; she was biting her lip.

Finally the mike came to life, the emcee vanished, and Joey breathed "Testing, testing," through the PA system. "Ah'm sorry 'bout the de-lay, folks," he murmured in his deepest, backwoodsiest basso, "but we're 'bout ready to give it another shot. A-one, two, three!" he shouted, and "Heartbreak Hotel," take two, thumped lamely through the speakers:

> Well, since my baby left me,
> I found a new place to dwell,
> It's down at the end of Lonely Street,
> That's Heartbreak Hotel.

Something was wrong, that much was clear from the start. It wasn't just that he was bad, that he looked nervous and maybe a bit effeminate and out of control, or that he forgot the words to the third verse and went flat on the choruses, or that the half-assed pickup band couldn't have played together if they'd rehearsed eight hours a day since Elvis was laid in his grave—no, it went deeper than that. The key to the whole thing was in creating an illusion—Joey had to convince his audience, for even an instant, that the real flesh-and-blood Elvis, the boy who dared to rock, stood before them. Unfortunately, he just couldn't cut it. Musically or visually. No matter if you stopped your ears and squinted till the lights blurred, this awkward, greasy-haired kid in the green eye shadow didn't come close, not even for a second. And the audience let him know it.

Hoots and catcalls drowned out the last chord of "Heartbreak Hotel," as Joey segued into one of those trembly, heavy-breathing ballads that were the bane of the King's middle years. I don't remember the tune or the lyrics—but it was sappy and out of key. Joey was sweating now, and the hair hung down in his eyes. He leaned into the microphone, picked a woman out of the audience, and attempted a seductive leer that wound up looking more like indigestion than passion. Midway through the song a female voice shouted "Faggot!" from the back of the room, and two guys in fraternity jackets began to howl like hound dogs in heat.

Joey faltered, missed his entrance after the guitar break, and had to stand there strumming over nothing for a whole verse and chorus till it came round again. People were openly derisive now, and the fraternity guys, encouraged, began to intersperse their howls with yips and yodels. Joey bowed his head, as if in defeat, and let the guitar dangle loose as the band closed out the number. He picked up the tempo a bit on the next one—"Teddy Bear," I think it was—but he never got anywhere with the audience. I watched Cindy out of the corner of my eye. Her face was white. She sat through the first four numbers wordlessly, then leaned across the table and took hold of my arm. "Take me home," she said.

We sat in the driveway awhile, listening to the radio. It was warm, and with the windows rolled down we could hear the crickets and whatnot going at it in the bushes. Cindy hadn't said much on the way back—the scene at the club had been pretty devastating—and I'd tried to distract her with a line of happy chatter. Now she reached forward and snapped off the radio. "He really stinks, doesn't he?" she said.

I wasn't biting. I wanted her, yes, but I wasn't about to run anybody down to get her. "I don't know," I said. "I mean, with that band Elvis himself would've stunk."

She considered this a moment, then fished around in her purse for a cigarette, lit it, and expelled the smoke with a sigh. The sigh seemed to say: "Okay, and what now?" We both knew that the babysitter was hunkered down obliviously in front of the TV next door and that Joey still had another set to get through. We had hours. If we wanted them.

The light from her place fell across the lawn and caught in her hair; her face was in shadow. "You want to go inside a minute?" I said, remembering the way she'd moved against me on the couch. "Have a drink or something?"

When she said "Sure," I felt my knees go weak. This was it: counselor, counsel thyself. I followed her into the house and led her up the dark stairs to the bedroom. We didn't bother with the drink. Or lights. She felt good, and a little strange: she wasn't Judy.

I got us a drink afterward, and then another. Then I brought the bottle to bed with me and we made love again—a slow, easeful, rhythmic love, the crickets keeping time from beyond the windows. I was ecstatic. I was drunk. I was in love. We moved together and I was tonguing her ear and serenading her in a passionate whisper, mimicking Elvis, mimicking Joey. "Well-a bless-a my soul, what's-a wrong with me," I murmured, "I'm itchin' like a ma-han on a fuzzy tree . . . oh-oh-oh, oh, oh yeah." She laughed, and then she got serious. We shared a cigarette and a shot of sticky liqueur afterward; then I must have drifted off.

I don't know what time it was when I heard the van pull in next door. Downstairs the door slammed and I went to the window to watch Cindy's dark form hurrying across the lawn. Then I saw Joey standing in the doorway, the babysitter behind him. There was a curse, a shout, the sound of a blow, and then Joey and the babysitter were in the van, the brake lights flashed, and they were gone.

I felt bad. I felt like a dog, a sinner, a homewrecker, and a Lothario. I felt like Fred must have felt. Naked, in the dark, I poured myself another drink and watched Cindy's house for movement. There was none. A minute later I was asleep.

I woke early. My throat was dry and my head throbbed. I slipped into a pair of running shorts I found in the clutter on the floor, brushed my teeth, rinsed my face, and contemplated the toilet for a long while, trying to gauge whether or not I was going to vomit.

Half a dozen aspirin and three glasses of water later, I stepped gingerly down the stairs. I was thinking poached eggs and dry toast—and maybe, if I could take it, half a cup of coffee—when I drifted into the living room and saw her huddled there on the couch. Her eyes were red, her makeup smeared, and she was wearing the same clothes she'd had on the night before. Beside her, wrapped in a pink blanket the size of a bath towel, was the baby.

"Cindy?"

She shoved the hair back from her face and narrowed her eyes, studying me. "I didn't know where else to go," she murmured.

"You mean, he—?"

I should have held her, I guess, should have probed deep in my counselor's lexicon for words of comfort and assurance, but I couldn't. Conflicting thoughts were running through my head, acid rose in my throat, and the baby, conscious for the first time since I'd laid eyes on it, was fixing me with a steady, unblinking gaze of accusation. This wasn't what I'd wanted, not at all.

"Listen," I said, "can I get you anything—a cup of coffee or some cereal or something? Milk for the baby?"

She shook her head and began to make small sounds of grief and anguish. She bit her lip and averted her face.

I felt like a criminal. "God," I said, "I'm sorry. I didn't—" I started for her, hoping she'd raise her tear-stained face to me, tell me it wasn't my fault, rise bravely from the couch, and trudge off across the lawn and out of my life.

At that moment there was a knock at the door. We both froze. It came again, louder, booming, the sound of rage and impatience. I crossed the room, swung open the door, and found Joey on the doorstep. He was pale, and his hair was in disarray. When the door pulled back, his eyes locked on mine with a look of hatred and contempt. I made no move to open the storm door that separated us.

"You want her?" he said, and he ground the toe of his boot into the welcome mat like a ram pawing the earth before it charges.

I had six inches and forty pounds on him; I could have shoved through the door and drowned my guilt in blood. But it wasn't Joey I wanted to hurt, it was Fred. Or, no, deep down, at the root of it all, it was Judy I wanted to hurt. I glanced into his eyes through the flimsy mesh of the screen and then looked away.

" 'Cause you can have her," he went on, dropping the Nashville twang and reverting to pure Brooklynese. "She's a whore. I don't need no whore. Shit," he spat, looking beyond me to where she sat huddled on the couch with the baby. "Elvis went through a hundred just like her. A thousand."

Cindy was staring at the floor. I had nothing to say.

"Fuck you both," he said finally, then turned and marched across the lawn. I watched him slam into the van, fire up the engine, and back out of the driveway. Then the boy who dared to rock was gone.

I looked at Cindy. Her knees were drawn up under her chin and she was crying softly. I knew I should comfort her, tell her it would be all right and that everything would work out fine. But I didn't. This was no pregnant fifteen-year-old who hated her mother or a kid who skipped cheerleading practice to smoke pot and hang out at the video arcade—this wasn't a problem that would walk out of my office and go home by itself. No, the problem was at my doorstep, here on my couch: I was involved—I was responsible—and I wanted no part of it.

"Patrick," she stammered finally. "I-I don't know what to say. I mean"—and here she was on the verge of tears again—"I feel as if . . . as if—"

I didn't get to hear how she felt. Not then, anyway. Because at that moment the phone began to ring. From upstairs, in the bedroom. Cindy paused in midphrase; I froze. The phone rang twice, three times. We looked at each other. On the fourth ring I turned and bounded up the stairs.

"Hello?"

"Pat, listen to me." It was Judy. She sounded breathless, as if she'd been running. "Now don't hang up. Please."

The blood was beating in my head. The receiver weighed six tons. I struggled to hold it to my ear.

"I made a mistake," she said. "I know it. Fred's a jerk. I left him three days ago in some winery in St. Helena." There was a pause. "I'm down in Monterey now and I'm lonely. I miss you."

I held my breath.

"Pat?"

"Yeah?"

"I'm coming home, okay?"

I thought of Joey, of Cindy downstairs with her baby. I glanced out the window at the place next door, vacant once again, and thought of Henry and Irma and the progress of the years. And then I felt something give way, as if a spell had been broken.

"Okay," I said.

(1983)

I DATED JANE AUSTEN

Her hands were cold. She held them out for me as I stepped into the parlor. "Mr. Boyle," announced the maid, and Jane was rising to greet me, her cold white hands like an offering. I took them, said my good evenings, and nodded at each of the pairs of eyes ranged round the room. There were brothers, small-ish and large of head, whose names I didn't quite catch; there was her father, the Reverend, and her sister, the spinster. They stared at me like sharks on the verge of a feeding frenzy. I was wearing my pink boots, my "Great Disasters" T-shirt and my Tiki medallion. My shoulders slumped under the scrutiny. My wit evaporated.

"Have a seat, son," said the Reverend, and I backed onto a settee between two brothers. Jane retreated to an armchair on the far side of the room. Cassandra, the spinster, plucked up her knitting. One of the brothers sighed. I could see it coming, with the certainty and illogic of an aboriginal courtship rite: a round of polite chit-chat.

The Reverend cleared his throat. "So what do you think of Mrs. Radcliffe's new book?"

I balanced a glass of sherry on my knee. The Reverend, Cassandra and the broth-ers revolved tiny spoons around the rims of teacups. Jane nibbled at a croissant and focused her huge unblinking eyes on the side of my face. One of the brothers had just made a devastating witticism at the expense of the *Lyrical Ballads* and was still tittering over it. Somewhere cats were purring and clocks ticking. I glanced at my watch: only seventeen minutes since I'd stepped in the door.

I stood. "Well, Reverend," I said, "I think it's time Jane and I hit the road."

He looked up at the doomed Hindenburg blazing across my chest and smacked his lips. "But you've only just arrived."

There really wasn't much room for Cassandra in the Alfa Romeo, but the Reverend and his troop of sons insisted that she come along. She hefted her skirts, wedged herself into the rear compartment and flared her parasol, while Jane pulled a white cap down over her curls and attempted a joke about Phaetons and the winds of Aeolus. The Reverend stood at the curb and watched my fingers as I helped Jane fasten her seat belt, and then we were off with a crunch of gravel and a billow of exhaust.

The film was Italian, in black and white, full of social acuity and steamy sex. I sat between the two sisters with a bucket of buttered popcorn. Jane's lips were parted and her eyes glowed. I offered her some popcorn. "I do not think that I care for any just now, thank you," she said. Cassandra sat stiff and erect, tireless and silent, like a mileage marker beside a country lane. She was not interested in popcorn either.

The story concerned the seduction of a long-legged village girl by a mustachioed adventurer who afterward refuses to marry her on the grounds that she is impure. The girl, swollen with child, bursts in upon the nuptials of her seducer and the daughter of a wealthy merchant, and demands her due. She is turned out into the street. But late that night, as the newlyweds thrash about in the bridal bed—

It was at this point that Jane took hold of my arm and whispered that she wanted to leave. What could I do? I fumbled for her wrap, people hissed at us, great nude thighs slashed across the screen, and we headed for the glowing EXIT sign.

I proposed a club. "Oh do let's walk!" Jane said. "The air is so frightfully delicious after that close, odious theatre—don't you think?" Pigeons flapped and cooed. A panhandler leaned against the fender of a car and drooled into the gutter. I took Jane's arm. Cassandra took mine.

At the Mooncalf we had our wrists stamped with luminescent ink and then found a table near the dance floor. The waitress's fingernails were green daggers. She wore a butch haircut and three-inch heels. Jane wanted punch, Cassandra tea. I ordered three margaritas.

The band was re-creating the fall of the Third Reich amid clouds of green smoke and flashing lights. We gazed out at the dancers in their jumpsuits and platform shoes as they bumped bums, heads and genitals in time to the music. I thought of Catherine Morland at Bath and decided to ask Jane for a dance. I leaned across the table. "Want to dance?" I shouted.

"Beg your pardon?" Jane said, leaning over her margarita.

"Dance," I shouted, miming the actions of holding her in my arms.

"No, I'm very sorry," she said. "I'm afraid not."

Cassandra tapped my arm. "I'd love to," she giggled.

Jane removed her cap and fingered out her curls as Cassandra and I got up from the table. She grinned and waved as we receded into the crowd. Over the heads of the dancers I watched her sniff suspiciously at her drink and then sit back to ogle the crowd with her black satiric eyes.

Then I turned to Cassandra. She curtsied, grabbed me in a fox-trot sort of way and began to promenade round the floor. For so small a woman (her nose kept poking at the moribund *Titanic* listing across my lower rib cage), she had amazing energy. We pranced through the hustlers and bumpers like kiddies round a Maypole. I was even beginning to enjoy myself when I glanced over at our table and saw that a man in fierce black sideburns and mustache had joined Jane. He was dressed in a ruffled shirt, antique tie and coattails that hung to the floor as he sat. At that moment a fellow terpsichorean flung his partner into the air, caught her by wrist and ankle and twirled her like a toreador's cape. When I looked up again Jane was sitting alone, her eyes fixed on mine through the welter of heads.

The band concluded with a crunching metallic shriek and Cassandra and I made our way back to the table. "Who was that?" I asked Jane.

"Who was who?"

"That mustachioed murderer's apprentice you were sitting with."

"Oh," she said. "Him."

I realized that Cassandra was still clutching my hand.

"Just an acquaintance."

As we pulled in to the drive at Steventon, I observed a horse tethered to one of the palings. The horse lifted its tail, then dropped it. Jane seemed suddenly animated. She made a clucking sound and called to the horse by name. The horse flicked its ears. I asked her if she liked horses. "Hm?" she said, already looking off toward the silhouettes that played across the parlor curtains. "Oh yes, yes. Very much so," she said, and then she released the seat belt, flung back the door and tripped up the stairs into the house. I killed the engine and stepped out into the dark drive. Crickets sawed their legs together in the bushes. Cassandra held out her hand.

■ ■ ■

Cassandra led me into the parlor, where I was startled to see the mustachioed ne'er-do-well from the Mooncalf. He held a teacup in his hand. His boots shone as if they'd been razor-stropped. He was talking quietly with Jane.

"Well, well," said the Reverend, stepping out of the shadows. "Enjoy yourselves?"

"Oh, immensely, Father," said Cassandra.

Jane was grinning at me again. "Mr. Boyle," she said. "Have you met Mr. Crawford?" The brothers, with their fine bones and disproportionate heads, gathered round. Crawford's sideburns reached nearly to the line of his jaw. His mustache was smooth and black. I held out my hand. He shifted the teacup and gave me a firm handshake. "Delighted," he said.

We found seats (Crawford shoved in next to Jane on the love seat; I wound up on the settee between Cassandra and a brother in naval uniform), and the maid served tea and cakes. Something was wrong—of that I was sure. The brothers were not their usual witty selves, the Reverend floundered in the midst of a critique of Coleridge's cult of artifice, Cassandra dropped a stitch. In the corner, Crawford was holding a whispered colloquy with Jane. Her cheeks, which tended toward the flaccid, were now positively bloated, and flushed with color. It was then that it came to me. "Crawford," I said, getting to my feet. "*Henry* Crawford?"

He sprang up like a gunfighter summoned to the O.K. Corral. "That's right," he leered. His eyes were deep and cold as crevasses. He looked pretty formidable—until I realized that he couldn't have been more than five-three or -four, give or take an inch for his heels.

Suddenly I had hold of his elbow. The Tiki medallion trembled at my throat. "I'd like a word with you outside," I said. "In the garden."

The brothers were on their feet. The Reverend spilled his tea. Crawford jerked his arm out of my grasp and stalked through the door that gave onto the garden. Nightsounds grated in my ears, the brothers murmured at my back, and Jane, as I pulled the door closed, grinned at me as if I'd just told the joke of the century.

Crawford was waiting for me in the ragged shadows of the trees, turned to face me like a bayed animal. I felt a surge of power. I wanted to call him a son of a bitch, but, in keeping with the times, I settled for "cad." "You cad," I said, shoving him back a step, "how dare you come sniffing around here after what you did to Maria Bertram in *Mansfield Park*? It's people like you—corrupt, arbitrary, egocentric—that foment all the lust and heartbreak of the world and challenge the very possibility of happy endings."

"Hah!" he said. Then he stepped forward and the moon fell across his face.

His eyes were like the birth of evil. In his hand, a riding glove. He slapped my face with it. "Tomorrow morning, at dawn," he hissed. "Beneath the bridge."

"Okay, wiseguy," I said, "okay," but I could feel the *Titanic* sinking into my belt.

A moment later the night was filled with the clatter of hoofs.

I was greeted by silence in the parlor. They stared at me, sated, as I stepped through the door. Except for Cassandra, who mooned from behind her knitting, and Jane, who was bent over a notebook, scribbling away like a court reporter. The Reverend cleared his throat and Jane looked up. She scratched off another line or two and then rose to show me out. She led me through the parlor and down the hall to the front entrance. We paused at the door.

"I've had a memorable evening," she said, and then glanced back to where Cassandra had appeared at the parlor door. "Do come again." And then she held out her hands.

Her hands were cold.

(1977)

CAYE

O mother Ida, harken ere I die.

—Tennyson, *Oenone*

Orlando's uncle fathered thirty-two children. Fifteen by the first wife, five by the second, twelve by the third. Now he lives with a Canadian woman, post-menopausal. You can hear them after the generator shuts down. When the island is still and dark as a dreamless sleep, and the stone crabs crawl out of their holes.

The ground here is pocked with dark craters, burrows, veins in the earth. They are beginnings and endings. Some small as coins, others big enough to swallow a softball. The crabs creep down these orifices like the functions of the body.

Fran has a gas stove, a bed, some shelves, a battery-run tape player. She cooks. People who weren't born here can sit on the edge of the bed and eat, sip rum with her. Then unwrinkle some bills. Fran cooks lobster, or conch, sometimes she cooks stone crab. She was not born here either, her bed is narrow, and the batteries in the tape player are getting weak.

Orlando sets and checks lobster traps. All the men on the island set and check lobster traps. The traps are made of wooden strips, shaped like Quonset huts, a conical entranceway at one end. Bait is unnecessary. The lobster, scouting the margins of the reef, the sea chanting over him, will prowl around this trap until he finds the conical entranceway. He will scrabble into the trap, delighted, secure from attack. The lobster psyche takes solace in holes. When the traps are hauled the law requires the fishermen to release any lobster whose tail is smaller than three inches, a seeding measure. The fishermen do not release lobsters whose tails are smaller than three inches—nor do they take them to market. Instead they twist off the heads, make a welter of the sweet curled tails, black against the frayed and blanched floorboards of their boats, carry the bloodless white meat home to their pots. Orlando tells me that the lobster catch is smaller this season than it was a year ago, and that a year ago it was smaller than the preceding season. I nod my head. Like the point of a cone I say.

There are no roads, sidewalks, automobiles, bicycles or shoes on the island.

Tito is a grandson of Orlando's uncle. Orlando's uncle does not know it. The island's population is just over three hundred. It is not surprising that a good number of the island's inhabitants should be related to Orlando's uncle, considering his energy. Tito does not live in the village, but in a shack in the jungle on the far side of the island. He lives alone, his eyes blue, his mother (now dead) English. Tito roams the forest with his .22, putting holes in birds and lizards. Their carcasses fertilize the soil. When he is hungry he lifts a lobster trap, spears fish, dives for conch. Or splits coconut.

The sun here is mellow as an orange. One day it will flare up and turn the solar system to cinders. Then it will fall into itself, suck in the ribbons of flame like a pale ember, gather its last breath and explode, driving particles eternally through the universe, cosmic wind.

Fran is forty, paints her toenails, wears her hair in short curls. The muscles of her abdomen are lax. She dresses in saris, halters, things of the tropics. Fifteen years ago Fran came to the island and set up residence in a ten-by-twenty-foot shack. For the first six months she had money. Afterward she cooked. Now she drinks rum beneath the bulb in her shack, finds coins for the island's children, cooks meals for visitors and occasionally for islanders. No man, tourist or islander, has been known to satisfy more than a single appetite in Fran's shack. Though not from lack of trying.

Coconut palms grow here, without (scrutable) design. The coconuts, elaborate seeds, fall to the sand like blows in the stomach. Wet from the rain, they lie cradled in the sand until one day they split. Coconut palms grow from the split coconuts, without (scrutable) design.

■ ■ ■

Tito and Ida have been observed walking hand in hand along the path to the far end of the island, the uninhabited crescent of bird and bush. In Tito's right hand, Ida's fingers; in his left, the .22. Ida's face is wide, Indian, her eyes black. Black as caverns.

Conch fritters hiss on the griddle in Fran's shack. Four lots away Orlando's uncle sits in his yard, conch shells piled high, the wedge-headed hammer and thin knife at his side, a wet conch in his lap. He presses the spiral shell to his knee and taps at it with the beak of his hammer. Twice, three times, and he's tapped a thin rectangular hole just below the point of the spiral. The knife eases in, the conch out, the shell in his hand spewing up its secrets. *Konk* he calls it.

I am sitting on the edge of Fran's bed, sipping rum, chewing lobster. There is another man in the shack, a West German. He speaks neither English nor Spanish. We eat in silence. Fran wears a halter, her belly slack, at the stove. When we finish our meal the man stands, pays, leaves. I pour another drink of rum. Fran's back is turned. I lay my hand on her flank. She tells me to leave.

In 1962 Hurricane Hilda stirred up waves thirty-five feet tall and churned them across the Caribbean in the direction of the island. The sky was smoky, dark as iron, the wind bent the trees, hurtled coconut and leaf. Tito and Ida were children, Fran was in her prime, Orlando's uncle had never heard of Canada and was yet to father four more children. The reef broke the biggest waves. All the traps were lost, the boats staved in, the shacks collapsed. Eight feet of salt water (home to lobster, conch, brine shrimp) washed over the island. Five drowned. The wind screamed blood and teeth.

The Canadian woman takes the biweekly boat to the mainland and Orlando's uncle is alone. I see him in the yard, feeding chickens and turkeys. His face is like a mud pond dried in the sun. But his hair is rich and black, he walks straight as a hoe and his arms and chest are solid. He no longer checks traps. Instead he cleans conch. Soaks the white meat in lime, sprinkles it with pepper, and exercises his aging teeth. The protein does him good.

There is no law on the island. No JP, no police, no jail.

■ ■ ■

At night I lie in my hammock, listening to the rattle of the crabs as they emerge from their burrows (dark to dark) and prowl through the scrub. I watch the sky: fronds like scissors, stars like frost. There are meteors, planets, spaces between the stars, black holes. The black holes are not visible, but there nonetheless. Stars bigger than the sun, collapsed in on themselves, with a gravitational pull that sucks in light like water down a drain. Black holes, black as the moments before birth and after death.

Ida's toes in the sand, sea wrack, the shells of conch, heads of lobster. She strolls past the boats, past the trembling docks with the outhouses perched over them, past the crude gate and the chickens and the turkeys, on up to the door of Orlando's uncle's house. Her mother is Orlando's uncle's granddaughter. She knows it, and Orlando's uncle knows it. Neither cares.

Between the shore and the reef is a stretch of about half a mile. The water is twenty or thirty feet deep, there are nests of rock, plains of sweeping thick-bladed grass, rolling like wheat in a deep wind. Among the blades, conch. The handsome flame-orange and pink shells turned to the dark bottom, the spiral peaks indicating the sky. You dive, snatch at the peaks, turn them over—they are ghostly and gray, a hole, black hole, tapped in the roof. The vacant shells frighten off the living conch, Orlando tells me, like a graveyard after dark.

Still in the afternoon heat, dogs chickens children asleep, the generator like the hum of an organ, there are cries in the air, sudden as ice, cries of passion and rhythm, the pressure of groin and groin, cries that squeeze between the planks of Orlando's uncle's shack like air escaping a brown paper bag.

Tito's shack is difficult to find in the dark. For one thing, the island is washed in night after the generator shuts down. For another, the path is narrow, not much used. If you step off the path you run the risk of snapping an ankle in the ruts dug by the stone crabs or of touching down on the carcass of a bird or lizard, sharp plumage, wet meat.

The Canadian woman was not hurt, but Orlando's uncle is dead. She'd been back two days, it was dark, she stepped out to squat and urinate. I'd heard them celebrating her return: I swung in my hammock, thinking prurient thoughts, listening. I heard the door slam, I heard the five shots. The man who came out by boat from the mainland dug a bullet from the headboard of the bed. It was a small caliber, .22 he said. He asked the islanders if any of them owned a .22. And he asked me. We knew of no one who owned a .22, we told him, and he returned to the mainland the following day. Dark and sudden, these events have adumbrated change. Fran and the Canadian woman live together now. I visit them two times a day, eat, sip rum, pay. Orlando's uncle's shack stood empty for a few weeks. Then I moved in.

Deep in the shadows I spread a towel across the ground. It is too dark to see them, but I know the holes are there, beneath the cloth, the island pocked with them like a sickness. She stretches her back there, drops her shorts. Her knees fall apart. The breeze drifts in from the sea, bare night sky above. The sand fleas are asleep. I kneel, work myself into her, poke at her mouth with my tongue. Ida, I whisper, burrowing into her, dark blood beating, rooting, thrusting, digging, deep as I can go. I want to dig deeper.

(1975)

LITTLE FUR PEOPLE

They wanted to take her babies away. Wanted to seize them by court order and deny her access to them as if she were some welfare mother smoking crack in the ghetto, as if she couldn't nurse and doctor them herself though she'd been doing it all these years and when had there ever been a complaint? Even the rumor of a complaint? She was furious, but she was scared too, scared in a way that tugged at her bowels and made the roots of her hair ache as if she'd been suspended by her ponytail in some hellish high-wire act. Even her babies couldn't comfort her, not at first, not after the door slammed behind the officer and all the gloom of the uncaring world rushed in to fill the house with the dismal fog of defeat.

And the day had begun so promisingly—that's what made it all the worse. After two days of overcast, Grace had woken to a kitchen suffused with a sun so ripe and mellow it was as if she were standing inside an orange and looking out, and she just knew that Rudolfo would take his medication without a fuss and that Birgitta's temperature would have come down during the night. And she was right, she was right! Even Phil seemed better, looking bright-eyed and bushy-tailed at breakfast and nodding his cunning little head in time to the music on the radio as she cleaned up the dishes. And then the UPS man came—and that was a blessing too, because the copy of *Sciuridae in History* she'd ordered from a mail-order house in Connecticut had finally arrived, and she was just sitting down to leaf through it, already fascinated by the pictures of mummified squirrels dug out of the ruins at Pompeii, when the bell rang again.

She opened the door on a nervous-looking young man with a pale clean-shaven expanse of upper lip and a puff of tawny beard clinging like plumage to the very tip of his chin. He was wearing a beige uniform with some sort of piping on the left shoulder and a circular patch over the breast pocket. His eyes—a dull, watery blue—stared out of his head in two different directions and his feet seemed to be working out the steps of some intricate dance routine on the door- mat. "Mrs. Gargano?" he said, lifting his eyebrows and tightening the flesh round his mouth so that the flag of his beard seemed to stand at attention.

"Yes?" Grace said, with just the right blend of caution and hospitality—no matter how rude and venal the world might have become, she was always pre- pared to be gracious. The young man seemed to be looking beyond her at the knickknack shelf and her collection of ceramic figurines, though it was hard to say with those roving eyes. Suddenly she was overcome by a wave of pity—what must his mother have thought when she pressed him to her breast for the first time?—and she saw herself offering him a cup of tea and a slice of the banana nut bread she'd baked for her daughter, Jet.

"I'm Officer Kraybill," he said, "of Fish and Game? We've had a complaint."

It was then that she saw the curtains stir in the front window of the house across the street—Gladys Tranh's house—and she had her first intimation of what was coming. "A complaint?"

"Yes," the young man said, and his eyes had pulled into focus now, both of them locked on her face with a sudden intensity that made her wilt. "We under- stand you're harboring wild animals on the premises."

"Wild—?" For a moment, that was all she could manage to say, but she looked at him again, looked at him harder, and recovered herself. "Well, no. Not at all. There's just my babies—"

"Babies?"

"My squirrels—my sick ones, the ones in need. People have been bringing them to me for years. . . ."

Officer Kraybill's jaw sagged and then composed itself again. His eyes were all over the place. He smiled—or tried to. "Mind if I have a look? I mean, if it's not too much trouble, would you show them to me?"

Everything hung in the balance, but she didn't know, didn't suspect—she was too much an innocent, too trusting, too willing to judge a stranger by his poor homely walleyed face. "Well, I don't know," she said, but her tone was the tone of a woman who wants to be persuaded, "—I have a beauty parlor appointment at eleven. . . ."

"It wouldn't take a minute," he said, coming right back at her. "I'd just like a look, to see what you're doing—with the sick ones, I mean."

And that was it, that was what got her: how could she resist anyone who spoke of her sick ones, her poor ailing babies? She opened the door wide and Officer Kraybill, with his misaligned eyes and insinuating beard, was in the house.

He lingered a moment over the ceramic squirrels—"Aren't they pre- cious?" she said. "They're from Surrey, England, the 'Squirrels of the World' collection?"—and then she invited him into the living room. Misty and Bruno were there, stretched out on the sofa watching a "Lassie" rerun, a show that never failed to excite them. Whenever the collie barked out a message to his master, Bruno would stand up on his hind legs and chitter at the screen while Misty spun cartwheels across the rug. It was quite a sight, cute as pie, but as Grace stepped into the room with Officer Kraybill, both squirrels were lounging on their bellies contemplating a revolutionary new cheese slicer from Sweden. "That's Misty," Grace said, "the little Douglas's? And the gray squirrel is Bruno. They're inseparable. Like brother and sister."

"Are they sick?" Officer Kraybill wanted to know.

"Sick?" she echoed, freezing him with a look of astonishment even as the image of the cheese slicer was replaced by that of a collie vaulting a white picket fence. "Why, they wouldn't last ten minutes if I let them out the door."

Still playing dumb, still stringing her along, Officer Kraybill lifted his eyebrows and let his wet eyes settle on her. "What's wrong with them?"

Jet had warned her not to lecture people, but Grace couldn't help herself, she just couldn't—this was her life. "Misty's been with me three years now—or almost three years; let's see, it'll be three in April. She was partially eviscerated by a Cadillac in Rancho Park and she'd gone into a coma before she was brought here—for the first week it was touch and go. Dr. Diaz got her patched up, but then we discovered she was diabetic—oh, yes, squirrels contract diabetes, just like people—and she requires two shots of insulin a day. Without it she'd go into shock and die."

The officer had moved closer to the couch and he was peering down at Misty, his expression noncommittal.

"And Bruno," she said, rushing on—and so what if Jet thought she put people off, that didn't matter a whit, not where her babies were concerned— "Bruno's been with me over six years now. He's my favorite, except for Phil, of course, and I don't mind admitting it." She pinched her voice in a soft crooning falsetto: "Here, Bruno, come on, baby, come on." Bruno twisted his neck to fasten his black glittering eyes on her and then, though you could see he was racked with pain, he hauled himself up the slope of the couch and made a feeble leap into her arms. "That's right," she crooned, bending to peck him a kiss.

Officer Kraybill cleared his throat.

"Oh, I'm sorry," she said, "I didn't mean to get carried away—it's just that they're so lovable, they are. . . . Well Bruno, Bruno suffers from arthritis and lumbago, and when he first came to me—here, you can see it here, along the base of his spine?—he'd lost the better part of his tail in an accident involving a Weber charcoal grill. And while that may not sound like much to you, you have to understand what something like that will do to a squirrel's self-respect. I mean, his tail is everything—his blanket and pillow, his napkin, his new suit of clothes—and he flags every female in the forest with it. Bruno was devastated. Mr. Kraybill, you never saw such a depressed squirrel."

But Officer Kraybill didn't seem to be focusing on Bruno. He was scribbling something in a little leatherbound notebook. "And how many others do you have?" he asked, his voice flat and mechanical.

"You're taking notes?" she said, and for the first time the gravity of the situation began to dawn on her.

"Just a formality," he told her, but his wild eye betrayed him. "We've had a complaint. I've got to check it out. Now, how many do you have in all?"

"Thirty-two," Grace said, tight-lipped. She cradled Bruno in her arms, afraid suddenly. "But why do you need to know? What sort of complaint was it?" She tried out a nervous laugh. "You don't—I mean, I'm not doing anything wrong, am I?"

"And where do you keep them?" he said, ignoring the question. "Besides these two?"

Grace tried to compose herself. There'd been a complaint, that was all, nothing to get excited about. "I've got cages in the garage—but at any given time of the day, the squirrels have the run of the house. They're litter-trained, you know, each and every one of them, even the pair that just came to me last week. Don't think I keep them cooped up—I'd never do that. And I clean the cages daily, without fail—"

"I'd like to see the cages." He was facing her, pen poised over the notebook, and he was no longer asking.

There was a silence. From the TV came the sound of a dog barking and Grace prayed that Misty and Bruno wouldn't go into their routine—it just wouldn't be appropriate right now, even she could see that. She thought for just a second of asking if he had a search warrant, like they do on the police shows, but that wouldn't be courteous, and instead she heard herself saying, "Yes, of course."

It was then that the door from the garage pushed open ever so slightly and Phil crawled in. There he was, tacked to the rug and looking up inquisitively at the visitor, not a trace of fear in him, while the sounds of the others—a contented mid-morning chatter—drifted through the doorway. And the smell. The smell too. Grace felt she had to offer an explanation. "Don't mind that musty odor," she said, "that's natural. I could scrub the cages and change the wood shavings a hundred times a day and it'd still be there—think of it as their natural perfume. And this"—indicating the big yellow and chocolate Douglas's squirrel at their feet—"this is Phil."

"And he's sick too, right?"

She gave the man a look. Was he trying to be rude? Her voice turned cold. "Phil was mauled by a pit bull. He required sixty-seven stitches to close his wounds and he will never have the use of his rear legs again. I'll have you know, what with his various ailments, that I've taken him to Dr. Diaz over seventy times in the past two years."

But Officer Kraybill wasn't interested in Phil's problems. He stepped over him and strode into the garage, where all the caged squirrels set up an expectant chittering. Molly went up and down the mesh of her cage like a monkey—she thought it was treat time—and Rudolfo sat up and clicked his teeth like a pair of castanets. In the time it took Grace to scoop Phil from the floor and step into the garage, a squirrel under each arm, Officer Kraybill had made up his mind. "You are in illegal possession of wildlife," he announced, turning to her, "and unless these creatures are released back into the wild, we will have to confiscate them."

Grace was stunned. "Confiscate? But they need me, can't you see that? They'd die if I set them loose."

"These squirrels—and all wildlife—are the property of the State of California, and it is against the law to keep, traffic in or domesticate them."

Grace felt her heart stop, just like that, as if she was stretched out on the operating table, as if her pacemaker had gone dead in her chest. And then she caught her breath and her heart started up again and she was fierce with the sudden hammering of it. They weren't going to take her babies away, no one was. Never. She came right back at him and she felt no obligation to be polite now that he'd shown his colors. "But I can kill them, though, can't I? I can stalk them with a gun, innocent things that wouldn't hurt a fly, isn't that right?"

The eyes were back in their orbits. The beard stabbed at her. "If you have a valid hunting license, in season; there's no bag limit on ground squirrels."

"That's crazy."

He shrugged.

"But they're people," Grace said, and she could hear the break in her own voice, "little fur people."

When the phone rang, Jet was coloring her hair. She was only twenty-eight, but she'd had gray in her hair since she was in her teens, and now she had to touch up her roots every other week if she didn't want to look like the Bride of Frankenstein. It didn't really bother her—haircolor was one of the grim necessities of life, like lipstick, eyeliner and makeup—but lately she'd begun to notice some gray down below—or white, actually, coiled white hairs of amazing length—and that really upset her. She'd spent nearly an hour the other night with the tweezers and a mirror, her legs propped up against the bathtub, the whole thing feeling vaguely obscene and not a little ridiculous, but she kept wondering what Vincent would think if he saw her turning white before his eyes. They'd only been dating a month, but he was two years younger than her and she'd told him she was twenty-five. Gray hairs. Little folds under her eyes. Some sort of scale on the back of her hands. And now she had the black paste all over her scalp, wondering if she should try it down there too—not this time, but maybe next—and the phone started ringing. She wriggled out of the plastic gloves and held the receiver gingerly to her wet ear.

Her mother's voice was there suddenly, gasping out her name over the wire, and it was the gasp of a drowning woman, a woman asphyxiating on her own sobs. "My babies! They want to take my babies!"

When Jet got to the house, her hair still damp and black now with the sheer glistening chemical glow of the dye that would take two or three good shampooings to mellow into something that could pass for natural, she found the front door locked. "Ma," she called, "you in there?" and she was about to go round back when a movement across the street caught her attention. It was her mother, dressed in an oversize green sweater that hid the flare of her hips, and she was rattling the wrought-iron gate out front of Mrs. Tranh's house. This struck Jet as odd on a number of counts, not the least of which was that her mother and Mrs. Tranh had never been particularly friendly—or even neighborly, for that matter. But then nothing her mother did lately would have surprised Jet. People called Grace eccentric, but to Jet's mind the term didn't begin to describe the gulf of abstraction her mother seemed to be floundering in. That was what it meant to get old and have your husband die and your heart go bad. Eccentricity. It was like gray hairs.

Jet crossed the street, watching her mother's shoulders as Grace fumbled with the latch, bewildered by the simple mechanism. Maybe it was one of the squirrels, Jet was thinking, maybe that was it. One of them escaped or something and she was canvassing the neighborhood. From the sound of her voice on the phone you would have thought they'd dropped a bomb on the house or something.

"Gladys!" Grace cried out suddenly in a high, oddly fluty voice, as if she were locked in an echo chamber. "Gladys Tranh! You open this gate!" A car that was badly in need of a muffler sputtered up the street. The starlings nesting in the twin palms out front of the Tranh house began to squabble and a few shot out from beneath the protection of the fronds as if they'd been expelled. "Gladys! I want to talk to you!"

Mrs. Tranh had cautiously cracked open her front door and extruded the nearly bald bulb of her head by the time Jet had reached her mother. Mrs. Tranh had a tight smile frozen on her face. She was so old she'd begun to look like a Chihuahua, and when was the last time Jet had seen her? "Go 'way," she said.

"Ma?" Jet reached out to touch her mother's arm. "Ma, what's wrong—is it the squirrels?"

Her mother turned to fix her with a tragic look and Jet felt something tighten inside her. "Jet," was all her mother could say, and she forced out the single syllable of her only daughter's name as if with her expiring breath. There were tears in her eyes. Her hands shook as they tried to make sense of the latch. But then she swung back round on Mrs. Tranh, who was gazing defiantly at her from across the expanse of the front walk, and lifted her voice: "You made that complaint, didn't you? I know it was you. You just can't stand to see anybody doing any good in this world, can you?"

"Ma," Jet said, taking hold of her mother's arm, but Grace shook her off.

"They want to take my babies!" she cried suddenly, and half a dozen starlings flew shrieking from the palms.

Mrs. Tranh's eyes glittered, two fragments of volcanic glass buried in the worn hide of her face. "They stink, your baby," Mrs. Tranh said in a gritty, dried-out voice. "Dirty animal."

Jet had begun to feel conspicuous. At least two cars had passed and slowed as if this were some sort of spectacle, a sideshow, and a woman three doors down—was that Mrs. Mahon?—had stepped out onto her porch. Jet's scalp tingled under the lingering assault of the chemical, and she looked away for a moment, distracted. That was when her mother threw one sneaker-clad foot atop the spikes of the wrought-iron fence and attempted to boost herself over, muttering under her breath. "Ma," Jet snapped, and she couldn't help herself, everyone was looking, "have you gone crazy or what? Come down off there, come on," and she was tugging at her mother's sweater and fighting the rigid pole of her mother's leg when Violet Tranh appeared in the doorway behind her own mother. "What's going on here?" she demanded. And then: "Jet? Mrs. Gargano?"

At this point, Jet had succeeded in extricating her mother's foot from the spikes of the railing, but perversely Grace had seized two of the palings and refused to let go. *"Damn it, Ma, what's wrong?"* Jet hissed as Violet Tranh came down the walk and stationed herself on the far side of the gate, an expression that might be interpreted as satiric pressed into the smooth flesh at the corners of her eyes and mouth. Violet was the youngest of the Tranhs and she and Jet had gone to high school together. Jet was thinking about that as the faces seemed to multiply up and down the block and the cars slowed and Violet smirked. They'd both had a crush on the same guy once—Derek Kubota—and Violet was the one he'd finally asked out.

"What's the problem?" Violet said.

"It's nothing," Jet assured her. "My mom's just a little upset, is all." Jet wanted to sink right on down through the sidewalk and become one with the grubs, beetles and worms.

"I'm not upset," Grace insisted, turning a furious face on her. "It's your mother," she said, coming back to Violet. "She"—and here her voice broke again—"she put in a complaint about my, my *babies*."

Mrs. Tranh spoke up then, her voice leaping and pitching through a morass of Vietnamese that sounded like the recipe for a six-course meal. Violet looked straight into Jet's eyes as she translated. "My mother says this is a residential neighborhood, zoned for houses, not animals."

"Animals?" Jet echoed, and though she knew the whole thing was ridiculous, she could feel the anger rising in her. "We're talking squirrels here, aren't we? Are we on the same page or what? Look up in the trees, why don't you?—the squirrels were here before we were."

Violet never took her eyes off her. It was like a staring contest, a stripping away of the flesh to probe at the vitals beneath. "Yeah," she said, and her voice had a real edge to it, "and so were the dinosaurs."

Grace knew what was coming. She knew the Officer Kraybills of the world didn't care a fig about mercy or tenderness or what was right and good—no, all they cared about was the law, the stupid law that allowed you to blast your fellow creatures out of the trees but made you into a criminal if you dared to try and ease their suffering. And they would be back, she was sure of that.

All that week she was up before dawn, up and dressed, brooding over her coffee while her babies played at her feet. She'd released Florio (as if that would satisfy them) because he didn't need her care anymore—Dr. Diaz had removed the splint and pronounced him fit. The only thing was, Florio refused to go. Every time she looked up, there he was, staring in at the window, and it didn't matter what part of the house she went to—living room, basement, kitchen, bedroom—there he was, chittering at the glass. Finally, last night, when the temperature dipped down into the thirties, she'd broken down and let him back in. He was under the table now, wrestling with Rudolfo. They'd become best friends, nothing short of that, and how could she justify separating them?

Still, she was no fool, and she knew they'd be back—Officer Kraybill and probably some other officious puff-bearded servant of the law—to badger and bully her into giving up her babies. They'd have a subpoena or search warrant or something and they'd tramp through her house like the Gestapo, hauling away her sick ones even as she barred the door with her body. The image appealed to her—barring the door with her body—and she was holding it there in the steam that rose from her second cup of coffee when the doorbell rang and all her worst fears were realized.

It was Officer Kraybill—she recognized him through the receding lens of the peephole in the front door—and he had two others with him, a man and a woman dressed in uniforms identical to his. Three of them, and she couldn't help thinking that was the way it always was in the movies and on TV when they had to evict widows or tear children from their mothers' breasts, safety in numbers, don't get your hands dirty. But oh, boy, her heart was going. She crouched there behind the door and she didn't know what to do. The bell rang again and then again. She heard them conferring in a blur of voices and then a shadow flitted past the curtains in the living room and she heard the doorknob rattle in the kitchen. She was one step ahead of them: it was locked, locked and bolted.

"Mrs. Gargano? Are you in there?"

It was his voice, Officer Kraybill's, and she could picture his fish eyes going crazy in his head. She held her breath, crouched lower. And that might have been the end of it, at least for then, but just at that moment Misty came shooting across the rug with Florio on her heels and the two of them made a leap for the clothestree and the clothestree slammed into the wall with a thump you could have heard all the way to Sherman Oaks and back.

"Mrs. Gargano? I can hear you in there. Now will you open up or do I have to use force? It's in our power, you know—you are harboring wild animals in there and as agents of the Fish and Game Department we have the right of search and seizure. Do you hear me? Mrs. Gargano?"

She had to speak up then, because she was afraid and because the germ of an idea had begun to take hold in her brain. "I'm, I'm not feeling well," she called, trying to distort her clear natural soprano into something feeble and stricken.

There was a moment's silence. The rumble of voices: more conferring. Then a new voice, a woman's: "This is Officer Soto, Mrs. Gargano. We're very sorry to hear that you're ill, but you stand in violation of the law and this is no small matter. If you refuse to cooperate we'll have no recourse but to obtain a warrant, do you understand me?"

"Yes," she bleated, putting everything she had into the subterfuge of her voice. "I don't want any trouble—I just want the best for my . . . my babies. But I'm not dressed yet, I'm not, really. If you come back later I'll let you in—"

Officer Kraybill: "Promise?"

She'd never let them in. She'd die first. Set the house afire and take her babies with her. "Yes," she called. "I promise."

Another silence. Then the voices, consulting. "All right," Officer Soto said finally, "you've got twenty-four hours. We'll be back here tomorrow morning at eight A.M. sharp, and there'll be no more of this business, do you hear? We'll have a warrant with us."

Grace watched them leave through a crack in the curtains. There was a cockiness to their gait that irritated her—even the woman walked like a football player. She watched them climb into the cab of a truck big enough to take away all her babies at once and haul them off to some Fish and Game compound, some concentration camp somewhere. It made her heart pound even to think about it.

But she wasn't finished yet, not by a long shot. This wasn't Nazi Germany, this was America, and if they thought they were going to just walk in and trample all over her rights, they had another think coming. Before they'd turned the corner, Grace had Jet on the phone.

Jet didn't know the first thing about U-Haul trucks and she was afraid to drive anything that big anyway, so she called up Vincent at work—he was bartending till closing—and asked him if he'd meet her at her place when he got off. She'd managed to get the thing as far as her apartment, but that was only six blocks from the rental office, in light traffic and with no turns or stoplights—getting it all the way over to her mother's was something else altogether. Vincent didn't sound too happy about the whole proposition—she wasn't exactly overjoyed herself—but there it was.

It was past eleven when he came up the walk to her apartment—business had been slow and he'd closed up early—and she was out the door in a hooded sweatshirt before he could ring the bell. She fell into his arms and groped at him a bit while they kissed, and then she held up the keys to the truck. Vincent was tall and bone-thin, with a high-stacked pompadour and long sideburns and a fading green tattoo on the left side of his neck. The tattoo was homemade and it was so old and shapeless you couldn't really tell what it was—Vincent said he'd done it with a couple of friends one night when he was fifteen or sixteen, he couldn't remember exactly. "And what's it supposed to be?" she'd asked him when they first met. He'd shrugged. "It didn't really come out," he said. "Yeah," she said. "And so?" He shrugged again. "It's supposed to be Donatello—you know, the Ninja Turtles?"

Tonight, he just climbed into the truck, shaking his head. "Nobody would believe me if I told them what we were doing here," he said, "—I mean, safehouses for squirrels? Or maybe we should call them safeholes or something." The truck started up then with a rumbling clatter, as if there were nothing under the hood but iron filings and cheap aluminum fans. Vincent jerked at the gearshift, and the lights of a passing car isolated his look of bemusement, a look Jet found irresistible. They kissed again, a long lingering kiss, and she assured him he'd have his reward—later.

Grace blinked the porchlight twice when they pulled up in front of the house, then all the lights went out. A moment later she joined them in the driveway, a tiny figure dressed all in black. "Shh," she warned as they stepped down from the truck, "they could be watching—you never know."

Vincent hunched his shoulders in his leather jacket and lit a cigarette. Jet had brought him to the house to meet her mother two weeks ago, and after making him what she called a highball with some of the V.S.O.P. bourbon she'd inherited from Jet's father, Grace had taken him out to the garage and introduced him to each and every one of her thirty-odd squirrels—and of course there was a story behind each of them, a long and detailed story. Vincent had taken it pretty well—at least nothing showed on his face as far as Jet could see—but now he said, "Who? Who'd be watching at this hour?"

"Shhhh!" Grace clamped a hand round Vincent's arm and pressed a finger to her lips. "You don't want to know," she whispered, and then they were following her into the garage, where the squirrels greeted them with a vigorous whirring of their exercise wheels and the usual rising odor of dank fermentation that Jet could only liken to the smell of the shower room in high school.

They worked by the ghostly glimmer of two nightlights, all the illumination her mother would risk, and as Jet and Vincent hauled the big awkward wire cages out the door and stacked them in the back of the truck, Grace hovered at their elbows, urging them to be extra careful with this one and to set that one down easy and not to disturb Molly or Lucretius or whoever. The last three cages contained her favorites, the squirrels that seemed to mean more to her than Jet or her father or anyone ever had—Phil, Misty and Bruno. These were the ones she gave the run of the house to and they were destined for Jet's apartment, an arrangement that Jet had decidedly mixed feelings about, even though her mother assured her that it would only be for a week or so and that she'd be there every day to look after them herself. "Careful! Careful!" Grace cried as they bobbled the last cage, their fingers numb with the cold and the impress of the wire. "Oh, Philly, you poor baby, mamakins is going to look after you, yes she is—"

When they'd loaded him in and shut the door, Grace broke down. "Ma," Jet pleaded, but her mother began to sob and she had to wrap her arms round her and rock her back and forth while Vincent lit an impatient cigarette and fiddled with the collar of his jacket.

"Did you know that Phil is nearly twelve years old, Vincent—did you know that?" Grace said, struggling for control. She was rocking in Jet's arms, the light of the streetlamp making a glistening doughy ball of her face. "That's what Dr. Diaz estimates, anyway—and that's ancient for a squirrel, almost like Methuselah, though they can live to be fifteen, so they say—" And then she did the unforgivable, her mind gone loose with age and anxiety or whatever, but she somehow made the connection between the squirrel's birthday and Jet's and before Jet could stop her she said, "But haven't you got a birthday coming up?"

"We've got to be going, Ma," Jet said. "We've got to deliver your, your"—she couldn't bring herself to use the term "babies," not in front of Vincent—"these squirrels to six different addresses, one of them all the way out in Simi Valley."

But her mother wouldn't quit. "You do have a birthday coming up, don't you? December fifth. God," she went on, "I can hardly believe you're going to be twenty-nine—or is it thirty?"

"Ma—" Jet said.

Vincent said nothing, but Jet could feel him looking at her.

The sound of a car engine half a block away inserted itself into the silence. Overhead, a jet scrawled its graffiti in the sky. Grace sighed. "We're none of us getting any younger, I guess."

Vincent climbed back into the truck and Jet gave her mother a hug and told her not to worry, they'd take care of everything. And that would have been that, but for the fact that when Vincent swung wide out of the driveway he let the wheel slip out of his hands for an instant and the right front bumper of the truck cut a long screeching furrow into the side of Mrs. Tranh's brand-new white Honda Accord, which was pulled up at the curb in front of her house. Instantly, the porchlight at the Tranhs' went on and Mrs. Tranh and Violet stood there at the door, their necks craning into the light. It was amazing. You would have thought they'd been sleeping on the doormat or something. But that was nothing compared to Grace's reaction. She let out with a long withering cry of despair that would have waked the dead, and the squirrels, jostled in their cages, responded with such a cacophony of yips, squeals and screeches you would have thought they'd been set afire—and in that moment Jet couldn't help wishing they had.

The truck was stalled in the middle of the street, emergency lights flashing, the incontrovertible evidence of Vincent's miscalculation planted in the side of the Accord. Jet's mother emitted a series of short piping screeches as she skittered across the road and began to claw at the rear door of the truck, which only provoked the squirrels all the more. By this time Vincent was standing on the pavement in the glare of the headlights, scratching his head and puzzling over the rent Accord as if it had dropped down from outer space, and the Tranhs, mother and daughter, were right there too, their voices clamoring in excitement and outrage. Jet climbed down out of the truck and attempted to calm her mother. "Ma," she said, "Ma, the squirrels are all right, it's nothing, just a fender bender, that's all—"

Unfortunately, Mrs. Tranh overheard this last and cried, "Fender bender, that all, huh? Nothing to you, huh? Huh?" She was dressed in a faded pink housecoat and her voice was high and unholy in the night. "I pay good money!" she screeched. And there was Violet, in shorts and bare feet, with a black leather jacket hastily thrown over a little black top, trying to calm her mother too. A long moment ticked by, the timpanic thump of the squirrels throwing themselves against the mesh of their cages punctuating Grace's sobs, Vincent's protestations of innocence and Mrs. Tranh's angry outbursts, and then Violet leveled a look on Jet and said, "We'll need to see your insurance and we're going to have to call the police."

That was all Grace needed to hear. "No, no police!" she sobbed.

Mrs. Tranh perked up suddenly. "Your squirrel baby," she said, "that's what this is about, yes?" The flashing lights played off her face, shot sparks from her eyes. "In Bien-hoa we eat squirrel. Monkey too." She was looking at Jet now, her mouth twisted tight with the effort of the words. "Tell your mother save people, not squirrel."

Grace said something then that Jet would never believe had come from the lips of her mother, and she had to hold her back, the older woman's arms straining against her as when their roles were reversed and Jet was the child. That was when her mother turned on her with a hiss: "One simple thing I ask from you, one simple thing, and look what happens—"

It was a mess, a real mess. Mrs. Tranh wouldn't let Vincent pull the truck away from the car until the police came and wrote up their report, and though there wasn't much traffic, Jet had to stand out in the middle of the street, shivering in her hooded sweatshirt, and wave the cars by with a flashlight. Her mother wanted to unload the squirrels and hide them back in the garage before the police came, but Jet talked her out of it, and finally Grace staggered across the street like a woman twice her age and hid herself in the darkened house.

After a while it began to rain, a soft breathing mist of a rain that took the curl out of Jet's hair but didn't seem to discourage the Tranhs, who sat grimly at the curb waiting for the law to arrive. It must have been nearly half past one when the police finally showed up, two gray-haired men in their forties, one Mexican, one white. They were half-asleep, rolling out of the car like the jelly doughnuts that sustained them, until Mrs. Tranh woke them up. "All right," the white cop said in the chop of the lights and the swirl of mist that hung round him like a curtain, "who was driving here?"

The Tranhs looked to Jet and Jet looked to Vincent. It seemed to her he had a pleading sort of look in his eyes, the sort of look that was meant to convey a complex message about love and commitment, about guilt and responsibility and maybe even lapsed insurance payments. "He was," she said finally, and she couldn't help lifting her finger to point him out.

Grace never drank, not more than once or twice a year anyway, but as she sat in the darkened house and watched the lights clench and unclench the belly of the curtains while the Tranhs and her daughter and Vincent and half a dozen or so of the curious or bored moved back and forth in silhouette across the scene of the accident, she groped in the liquor cabinet for one of Bill's bottles of liquor—any one—screwed off the cap and took a swallow. It was like drinking acid. Instantly her stomach was on fire and she wanted to spit the stuff back into the bottle, but it was too late. After a minute, though, she took another sip, and then another, and before long her heart stopped hammering at her rib cage. She had to be careful. She did. She could have another episode and that was the last thing she wanted—that wouldn't do her babies any good, no, no good at all.

She peeked through the curtains, waiting now, waiting for the police to ask what was in the truck, as if they couldn't hear—and smell—for themselves. And if they didn't ask, Gladys Tranh would tell them, you could count on that. "Squirrels?" the policeman would say, and then: "Do you have a permit for these animals?" And if that happened it was just a matter of time before Officer Kraybill showed up to have the last laugh. But maybe she should go out there, maybe she could distract them—or maybe, if she pleaded and begged and threatened to kill herself, they'd at least let her have Phil; Phil, that's all she wanted—

But nothing happened. The rain fell. The odd car drove round the truck. Gladys Tranh went back into the house and one of the policemen wrote out his report while Jet, Vincent and Violet looked on. Then the police were gone and the Tranh house was dark and Jet was knocking at the door. "Ma? Are you in there?" Jet called. "Listen, Ma, is it okay if we call it off for tonight? Vincent's tired. Ma? He says he doesn't want to do it."

Grace just stood there, the door between her and her daughter, the pacemaker keeping its rock-steady beat in her chest, and she didn't say a word.

(1994)

JOHN BARLEYCORN LIVES

There were three men came out of the West,
Their fortunes for to try.
And these three men made a solemn vow:
John Barleycorn must die.

—"John Barleycorn" (traditional)

I was just lifting the glass to my lips when she stormed through the swinging doors and slapped the drink out of my hand. "Step back," she roared, "or suffer hellfire and eternal damnation," and then she pulled a hatchet out from under her skirts and started to splinter up Doge's new cherrywood bar. I ducked out of the way, ten-cent whiskey darkening the crotch of my pants, and watched her light into the glassware. It was like a typhoon in a distillery—nuggets of glass raining down like hail, the sweet bouquet of that Scots whisky and rum and rye going up in a mist till it teared your eyes. Then Doge came charging out of the back room like a fresh-gelded bull, rage and bewilderment tugging at the corners of his mustache, just in time to watch her annihilate the big four-by-six mirror in the teakwood frame he'd had shipped up from New Orleans. BOOM! it went, shards of light washing out over the floor. Doge grabbed her arm as she raised the hatchet to put another cleft in the portrait of Vivian DeLorbe, but the madwoman swung round and caught him with a left hook. Down he went—and Vivian DeLorbe followed him.

The only other soul in the barroom was Cal Hoon, the artist. He was passed out at one of the tables, a bottle of whiskey and a shot glass at his elbow. I was up against the back wall, ready to snatch up a chair and defend myself if necessary. The wild woman strode over to Cal's table and shattered the bottle with a hammering blow that jarred the derby from his head and left the hatchet quivering in the tabletop. And then the place was still. Cal raised his head from the table, slow as an old tortoise. His eyes were like smashed tomatoes and something dangled from the corner of his mouth. The madwoman stared down at him, hands on her hips. "Who hath woe? who hath sorrow? who hath babbling? who hath wounds without cause? who hath redness of eyes?" she demanded. Cal goggled up at her, stupefied. She pointed a finger at his nose and concluded: "He who tarries long at the wine." She must have been six feet tall. "Down on your knees!" she snarled, "and pray forgiveness of the Lord." Suddenly she kicked the chair out from under him and he toppled to the floor. A few taps from the toe of her boot persuaded him to clamber to his knees. Then she turned to me. I was Editor in Chief of *The Topeka Sun*, a freethinker, one of the intellectual lights of the town. But my knees cracked all the same as I went down and clasped my hands together. We sang "Art thou weary, art thou languid?," Cal's voice like a saw grinding through knotty pine, and then she was gone.

Two days later I was sitting at a table in the Copper Dollar Saloon over on Warsaw Street waiting for a steak and some fried eggs. John McGurk, my typesetter, was with me. It couldn't have been more than nine-thirty in the morning. We'd been up all night getting out a special edition on McKinley's chances for a second term and we were drooping like thirsty violets. McGurk no sooner called for whiskey and soda water than there she was, the madwoman, shoulders like a lumberjack's, black soutane from her chin to the floor. A file of women in black bonnets and skirts whispered in behind her. "Look here!" guffawed one of the bad characters at the bar. "It's recess time at the con-vent." His cronies cackled like jays. McGurk laughed out loud. I grinned, watchful and wary.

Her left eye was swollen closed, maroon and black; the other leered and goggled in a frightening, deranged way. She fixed the bad character with a look that would freeze a bowl of chili, and then she raised her arm and the women burst into song, their voices pitched high and fanatical, the rush of adrenaline and moral fervor swelling their bosoms and raking the rafters:

> *Praise ye the Lord.*
> *Praise ye the Lord from the heavens:*
> *Praise ye Him in the heights.*
> *Praise ye Him, all ye angels:*
> *Praise ye Him, all His hosts.*
> *Praise ye Him, sun and moon.*
> *Praise ye Him, all ye stars of light.*

We were defeated, instantly and utterly. The bad character hung his head, the barkeep wrung his bar rag, two of the cronies actually joined in the singing. McGurk cursed under his breath while I fought the impulse to harmonize, a childhood of choir rehearsals and gleaming organ pipes welling up in my eyes. Then she brandished the hatchet, waving it high over her head like a Blackfoot brave, the other women following suit, drawing their weapons from the folds of their gowns. They laid waste to the barroom, splinter by splinter, howling hosannas all the while, and no one lifted a finger to stop them.

   I watched my beer foam out over the pitted counter, and somewhere, from the depths of the building, I recognized the odor of beefsteak burned to the bottom of an iron fry pan.

We decided to strike back. The ruins of the Copper Dollar Saloon lay strewn about us: splinters and sawdust, the scalloped curls of broken glass, puddles of froth. I reached across the table and grabbed hold of McGurk's wrist. "We'll do an exposé, front page," I said, "and back it up with an editorial on civil liberties." McGurk grinned like a weasel in a chicken coop. I told him to get on the wire and dig up something on Mrs. Mad that would take some of the teeth out of her bite. Then I trundled off home to get some sleep.

   An hour later he was knocking at my door. I threw on a robe and opened up, and he burst into the parlor, his eyes shrunk back and feverish. I offered him a chair and a brandy. He waved them away. "Name's Carry Gloyd Nation," he said. "Born in '46 in Kentucky. Married Charles Gloyd, M.D., in '67—and get this— she left him after two months because he was a rummy. She married Nation ten years later and he divorced her just a few months back on the grounds of desertion."

   "Desertion?"

   "Yep. She's been running around tearing up saloons and tobacco shops and Elks and Moose lodges all over the Midwest. Arrested in Fort Dodge for setting fire to a tobacco shop, in Lawrence for tearing the dress off a woman in the street because she was wearing a corset. Spent three days in jail in St. Louis for assaulting the owner of a Chinese restaurant. She claims Chinese food is immoral."

   I held up my palm. "All right. Fine. Go home and get some sleep and then work this thing up for tomorrow's paper. Especially the arrest record. We'll take some of the edge off that hatchet, all right."

We ran the story next day. Two-inch headlines, front page. On the inside, just under a thought-provoking piece on the virtues of the motorcar as the waste-free vehicle of the future, I ran a crisp editorial on First and Fourth Amendment guarantees and the tyranny of the majority. It was a mistake.

   By 8 A.M. there were two hundred women outside the office singing "We Shall Overcome" and chaining themselves to the railing. Banners waved over the throng, DEMON ALCOHOL and JOHN BARLEYCORN MUST DIE, and one grim woman held up a caricature of me with a bottle in my hand and the sun sinking into its neck. The legend beneath it read: THE TOPEKA SUN SETS.

None of my employees showed up for work—even McGurk deserted me. At eight-fifteen his son Jimmy slipped into the front office. He'd come to tell me his father was sick. Well so was I. I bolted the door after him and dodged into the back room to consult a bottle of Kentucky bourbon I kept on hand for emergencies. I took a long swallow while snatches of song, speechifying, cheers and shouts sifted in from the street. Then there was a crash in the front office. I peered through the doorway and saw that the window had been shattered—on the floor beneath it lay the gleaming blade, tough oaken handle of a hatchet.

Someone was pounding on the front door. I crept to the window and peeped out. The crows now filled the street. Reverend Thorpe was there, a group of Mennonites in beards and black, another hundred women. I thought I saw McGurk's wife Lucy in the press, obscured by the slow helix of smoke that rose from a heap of still-folded newspapers. I wondered where the Sheriff was.

The door had now begun to heave on its hinges with each successive blow. It was at this point that I altered my line of perspective and saw that it was Mrs. Mad herself at the door, hammering away with the mallet head of her hatchet. "Open up!" she bellowed. "I demand a retraction of those Satan-serving lies! Open up I say!" On hands and knees, like an Indian fighter or a scout for Teddy Roosevelt, I made my way to the back room, took another pull at the bung and then ducked out the loading entrance. I tugged the hat down over my brow and headed for Doge's Place to regroup.

Doge had replaced the swinging doors with a three-inch-thick oak slab, which was kept bolted at all times. I tapped at the door and a metal flap opened at eye level. "It's me, Doge," I said, and the bolt shot back. Inside, two workmen were busy with hammer and saw, and Cal sat at a table with canvas, palette and a bottle of whisky, shakily reproducing the portrait of Vivian DeLorbe from the defaced original. Beside him, hanging his head like a skunked coonhound, was McGurk.

I stepped up to the improvised bar (a pair of sawhorses and a splintery plank) and threw down two quick whiskeys. Then I sauntered over to join Cal and McGurk. McGurk muttered an apology for leaving me to face the music alone. "Forget it, John," I said.

"They got Lucy, you know," he said.

"I know."

Doge pulled up a chair and for a long moment we sat there silent, watching Cal trace the quivering perimeter of Vivian DeLorbe's bust. Then Doge asked me if I was going to retract the story. I told him hell would freeze over first. McGurk pointed out that we'd be out of business in a week if I didn't. Doge cursed Mrs. Mad. McGurk cursed Temperance. We had a drink on it.

Cal laid down his brush and gave me a watery-eyed stare. "Know how you git yerself rid of 'er?"

"I'd give a hundred silver dollars to know that, friend," Doge said.

"Simple," Cal croaked, choking off to clear his throat and expectorate on the floor. "Git hold on that first husband of hers—Doc Gloyd. Sight of him and she'll scare out of town like a horse with his ass-hairs afire."

The three of us came alive, hope springing eternal, et cetera, and we pressed him for details. Did he know Gloyd? Could he find him? Would Gloyd consent to it? Cal lifted the derby to smooth back his hair and then launched a windy narrative that jumped around like a palsied frog. Seems he'd been on a three-week drunk with "the Doc" in St. Louis's skid row six months earlier. The Doc had come into some money—a twenty-dollar gold piece—and the two of them had lain out in a field behind a distillery until they'd gone through it. "Fresh-corked bottles of the smoothest, fifty cent," said Cal, his eyes gone the color of butter. When he'd asked Gloyd about the twenty, Gloyd told him it was a token of gratitude from the thirsty citizens of Manhattan, Kansas. They'd paid his trainfare and soaked him full of hooch to come out and rid the town of a plague.

"Mrs. Mad?" I said.

"You guessed it," said Cal, a rasping snicker working its way up his throat. "All she got to do is see him. It's liken to holdin a cross up front of a vampire."

Two hours later Cal and I were leaning back in the club car of the Atchison, Topeka and Santa Fe line, trying out their sipping whiskey, savoring a cigar, heading east. For St. Louis.

We were feeling pretty ripe by the time we stepped down at the St. Louis station. I was a bit disoriented, what with the railway yard alone half the size of Topeka proper, and what with the rush of men in derby hats and short coats and women with their backsides hefted up all out of proportion. Cal, on the other hand, was right at home. He stooped to pluck up a cigar butt and then swaggered through the crowd to where a man, all tatters and ribs, sat propped against a bench like a discarded parasol. The man sat on the pavement, his elbows splayed on the bench behind him, head hanging as if his neck had been broken. Cal plunked down beside him like a wornout drayhorse, oblivious to the suspicious-looking puddle the fellow was sitting in. The man's eyelids drooped open as Cal produced a bottle and handed it to him. The man drank, held the bottle up for Cal. Cal drank, handed it back. They conferred, sniggering, for five or ten minutes, then Cal rose with a crack of knee and beckoned to me. "He's in town, all right, the salty dog. Redfearns here seen him yestiddy." I glanced down at Redfearns. He looked as if he hadn't seen anything in a long while. "Is he sure?"

"Down by the docks," Cal croaked, already whistling for a hackney cab.

We left our things—my things, Cal had nothing but the hat on his head and a pair of suspenders—at Potter's Saloon, Beds Five Cents, corner of Wharf St. and Albermarle Ave. Potter sold us two bottles of local whiskey for research purposes and we strolled out to explore the underworld of the docks and environs. Each time we passed a supine figure in the street Cal stopped to make an identity check, and if expedient, to revive it with a slug or two of Potter's poison. Then followed a period of bottle passing and sniggering colloquy that twinned the Redfearns encounter as if they'd rehearsed it:

After a while I found myself heaving down beside Cal and these reeking winesoaks, the sun building a campfire under my hat, trousers soiled, taking my turn when the bottle was passed. There I sat, Editor in Chief of *The Topeka Sun*, a freethinker and one of the intellectual lights of the town, on the blackened cobblestones of St. Louis's most disreputable streets, my judgment and balance eroded, vision going, while lazy bluebottles floated between the sweat-beaded tip of my nose and the mounds of horseshit that lay round us like a series of primitive sculptures. All in the cause of humanity.

As the day wore on I began to lose touch with my surroundings. I rose when Cal touched my arm, collapsed like a rump-shot dog when he stopped to interrogate another souse. We walked, talked and drank endlessly. I remember a warehouse full of straw boaters and whalebone corsets, a bowl of chili and a cup of black coffee in a walk-up kitchen, a succession of filthy quays, garbage bins, toothless faces and runny eyes. But no Gloyd. When the sun finally lurched into the hills, Cal took me by the elbow and steered us back to Potter's.

I was discouraged, disheartened, and thanks to Potter's home brew, nearly disemboweled. After puking against the side of a carriage and down the front of my shirt, there was only one thing I wanted from life: a bed. Potter (the only thing I remember about him is that he had the most flaccid, pendulous jowls I'd ever seen on man or beast—they looked like nothing so much as buttocks grafted onto his face) led me up the stairs to the dormitory and gave me a gentle shove into the darkened room. "Number Nine," he said. When my eyes became accustomed to the light I saw that the ranks of wooden bedsteads were painted with white numbers. I started down the row, reeling and reeking, fighting for balance, until I drew up to Number Nine. As I clutched at the bedpost with my left hand and fought to unbutton my shirt with my right, I became aware of a form beneath the horsehair blanket spread across my bunk. Someone was in my bed. This was too much. I began to shake him. "Hey, wake up there, pardner. That's my bunk you got there. Hey." It was then that I lost my footing and tumbled atop him.

He came alive like a whorehouse fire, screeching and writhing. "Buggery!" he shrieked. "Murder and sodomy!" The other occupants of the dormitory, jolted awake, began spitting threats and epithets into the darkness. I tried to extract myself but the madman had my head in a vise-grip. His voice was high-pitched and spasmodic, a sow scenting the butcher's block. "Pederasty!" he bawled.

Suddenly the room blazed with light. It was Potter, wagging his inhuman jowls, a lantern in his hand. Cal stood at his elbow, squinting into the glare. I turned my head. The man who had hold of me was hoary as a goat, yellow-toothed, his eyes like the eggs of some aquatic insect. "Doc!" shouted Cal.

The madman loosened his grip. "Cal?" he said.

■ ■ ■

McGurk met us at the Topeka station and gave us the lay of the land. A group of them—women in black bonnets, teetotalers and Holy Rollers—were still picketing the office, and in the absence of *The Sun* had begun an alternative press in the basement of the Baptist church. McGurk showed me a broadside they'd printed. It described me as "a crapulous anarchist," "a human viper," and "a lackey of the immoral and illicit business enterprises which prey on the emotionally feeble for the purpose of fiduciary gain." But a syntactical lashing wasn't the worst of it. Mrs. Mad had bought off the Sheriff and she and her vigilantes were scouring the town in the name of Jesus Christ, sobriety and abstinence from tobacco, fraternity and Texicano food. She'd evacuated the Moose Lodge and Charlie Trumbull's Tobacco Emporium, and then her disciples had boarded up the doors. And she'd closed down Pedro Páramo's eatery because he served fresh-pounded tortillas and refried beans with an order of eggs. It was high time for a showdown.

We threw open the massive oaken door at Doge's Place, took the boards down from the new plate-glass windows, lit the oil lamps, and hired a one-legged banjo strummer from Arkansas to cook us up some knee-slapping music. Before Cal had finished tracing the big winged *D* for DOGE'S PLACE on the front window, the saloon was shoulder-deep in drinking men, including a healthy salting of bad characters. That banjo rang and thrilled through the streets like the sweet song of the Sirens. Somebody even fired off a big horse pistol once or twice.

Our secret weapon sat at the bar. His fee was fifty dollars and all he could drink. Doge had donated a bottle of his finest, and I took up a collection for the rest, beginning with a greenback ten out of my own pocket. Gloyd was pretty far gone. He stared into his empty shot glass, mooing her name over and over like a heifer coming into heat. "Carry. Ohhh, Carry."

It took her half an hour. On the nose. Up the street she came, grim and foreboding, her jackals and henchwomen in tow. I lounged against the doorframe, picking my teeth. The banjo rang in my ears. I could see their heads thrown back as they shrieked out the lyrics of some spiritual or other, and I felt the tremor as their glossy black boots descended on the pavement in unison, tramp, tramp, tramp. Up the street, arms locked, teeth flashing, uvulas aquiver. "He is my refuge and my fortress!" they howled. Tramp, tramp, tramp. She led them up the porch, shoved me aside, and bulled her way in.

Suddenly the place fell silent. The banjo choked off, yahoos and yip-hays were swallowed, chatter died. She raised her arm and the chorus swept up the scale to finish on a raging high C, pious and combative. Then she went into her act, snorting and stamping round the room till her wire-rimmed spectacles began to mist up with emotion. "Awake, ye drunkards, and weep!" she roared. "Howl, all ye drinkers of wine, for strong drink shall be bitter to them that drink it." She was towering, swollen, red-faced, awesome as a twister roaring up out of the southwest. We were stunned silent—Cal, Doge, McGurk, Pedro—all of us. But then, from the rear of the crowd, all the long way down the far end of the bar, came the low moan of ungulate distress. "Carrrrry, ohhhh baby, what have I done to you?"

The look on her face at that moment could have constituted a criminal act in itself. She was hideous. There was a scuffle of chairs and feet as we cleared out of her way, every man for himself. Doge ducked down behind the bar, Cal and McGurk sought refuge back of an overturned table, the bad characters made themselves scarce, and suddenly there were just the two of them—Mrs. Mad and Gloyd—staring into each other's eyes across the vacant expanse of the bar-room. Gloyd got down off the bar stool and started toward her, his gait shuffling and unsteady, his arms spread in a vague empty embrace. Suddenly the hatchet appeared in her hand, legerdemain, her knuckles clenched white round the handle. She was breathing like a locomotive, he was calm as comatose. She started toward him.

When they got within two yards of one another they stopped. Gloyd tottered, swaying on his feet, a lock of yellowed hair catching in his eye socket. "Carry," he said, his voice rough and guttural. "Honey, peachblossom, come back to me, come back to your old Doc." And then he winked at her.

She flushed red, but then got hold of herself and came back at him with the Big Book: "At the last it biteth like a serpent, and stingeth like an adder."

He looked deep into her eyes, randy as an old coyote. "I am like a drunken man, and like a man whom wine hath overcome." He was grinning. He raised his arms to embrace her and suddenly she lashed out at him with the hatchet, the arc and the savage swish of it as it sliced the air, missing him by a clean two feet or more. "Carry," he said, his voice sad and admonishing. "Let bygones be bygones, honey, and come on back to your old Doc." Her arm fell, the hatchet dropped to the floor. She hung her head. And then, just a whisper at first, he began crooning in a rusty old voice, soft and sad, quavering like a broken heart:

> *The huntsman he can't hunt the fox,*
> *Nor so loudly to blow his horn,*
> *And the tinker he can't mend kettle nor pot,*
> *Without a little barleycorn.*

When he finished we stood there silent—the women in black, the bad characters, Doge, Cal, McGurk and me—as though we'd just watched the big brocaded curtain fall across the stage of Tyler's Playhouse in Kansas City. And then suddenly she fell to her knees sobbing—wailing and clucking in the back of her throat till I couldn't tell if it was laughing or crying. Her sobs, like her fulminations, were thunderous—they filled the room, shook the rafters. I began to feel embarrassed. But the Doc, he just stood over her, hands on his hips, grinning, until one of the women—it was Lucy McGurk—helped her from the room.

The faces of her retinue were pale as death against their black bonnets and choirboy collars. No longer the core of a moral cyclone, they were just towns-women, teetotalers and pansies. We jeered like the bad characters we were, and they turned tail and ran.

A month later a wagon rumbled up Warsaw Street from the station with Doge's new mahogany bar counter in back. McGurk and I took the afternoon off to sit in the cool dusk of Doge's Place and watch Doge and Cal nail it down and put the first coat of wax on it. The new Vivian DeLorbe, a bit rippled, but right in the right spots, hung proudly, and a sort of mosaic mirror—made up of pieces salvaged from the original and set in plaster—cast its submarine reflections round the room. We had a couple of whiskeys, and then Doge mentioned he'd heard Mrs. Mad was back at it again, parching all the good citizens down in Wichita. Cal and I laughed, but poor John didn't take it so well, seeing that Lucy had left him to go off with her and join the movement.

Cal shook his head. "These women," he said. "There's no stoppin 'em. Next thing you know they'll be wantin the vote."

(1977)

THE HAT

They sent a hit squad after the bear. Three guys in white parkas with National Forestry Service patches on the shoulders. It was late Friday afternoon, about a week before Christmas, the snow was coming down so fast it seemed as if the sky and earth were glued together, and Jill had just opened up the lodge for drinks and dinner when they stamped in through the door. The tall one—he ordered shots of Jim Beam and beers for all of them—could have been a bear himself, hunched under the weight of his shoulders in the big quilted parka, his face lost in a bristle of black beard, something feral and challenging in the clash of his blue eyes. "Hello, pretty lady," he said, looking Jill full in the face as he swung a leg over the barstool and pressed his forearms to the gleaming copper rail. "I hear you got a bear problem."

I was sitting in the shadows at the end of the bar, nursing a beer and watching the snow. Jill hadn't turned up the lights yet and I was glad—the place had a soothing underwater look to it, snow like a sheet stretched tight over the window, the fire in the corner gentle as a backrub. I was alive and moving—lighting a cigarette, lifting the glass to my lips—but I felt so peaceful I could have been dozing.

"That's right," Jill said, still flushing from the "pretty lady" remark. Two weeks earlier, in bed, she'd told me she hadn't felt pretty in years. What are you talking about? I'd said. She dropped her lower lip and looked away. I gained twenty pounds, she said. I reached out to touch her, smiling, as if to say twenty pounds—what's twenty pounds? Little Ball of Suet, I said, referring to one of the Maupassant stories in the book she'd given me. It's not funny, she said, but then she'd rolled over and touched me back.

"Name's Boo," the big man said, pausing to throw back his bourbon and take a sip of beer. "This is Scott," nodding at the guy on his left, also in beard and watchcap, "and Josh." Josh, who couldn't have been more than nineteen, appeared on his right like a jack-in-the-box. Boo unzipped the parka to expose a thermal shirt the color of dried blood.

"Is this all together?" Jill asked.

Boo nodded, and I noticed the scar along the ridge of his cheekbone, thinking of churchkey openers, paring knives, the long hooked ivory claws of bears. Then he turned to me. "What you drinking, friend?"

I'd begun to hear sounds from the kitchen—the faint kiss of cup and saucer, the rattle of cutlery—and my stomach suddenly dropped like an elevator out of control. I hadn't eaten all day. It was the middle of the month, I'd read all the paperbacks in the house, listened to all the records, and I was waiting for my check to come. There was no mail service up here of course—the road was closed half the time in winter anyway—but Marshall, the lodgeowner and unofficial kingpin of the community, had gone down the mountain to lay in provisions against the holiday onslaught of tourists, ski-mobilers and the like, and he'd promised to pick it up for me. If it was there. If it was, and he made it back through the storm, I was going to have three or four shots of Wild Turkey, then check out the family dinner and sip coffee and Kahlúa till Jill got off work. "Beer," I said.

"Would you get this man a beer, pretty lady?" said Boo in his backwoods basso, and when she'd opened me one and come back for his money, he started in on the bear. Had she seen him? How much damage had he done? What about his tracks—anything unusual? His scat? He was reddish in color, right? Almost cinnamon? And with one folded ear?

She'd seen him. But not when he'd battered his way into the back storeroom, punctured a case of twelve-and-a-half-ounce cans of tuna, lapped up a couple of gallons of mountain red burgundy and shards of glass, and left a bloody trail that wound off through the ponderosa pines like a pink ribbon. Not then. No, she'd seen him under more intimate circumstances—in her own bedroom, in fact. She'd been asleep in the rear bedroom with her eight-year-old son, Adrian (they slept in the same room to conserve heat, shutting down the thermostat and tossing a handful of coal into the stove in the corner), when suddenly the back window went to pieces. The air came in at them like a spearthrust, there was the dull booming thump of the bear's big body against the outer wall, and an explosion of bottles, cans, and whatnot as he tore into the garbage on the back porch. She and Adrian had jolted awake in time to see the bear's puzzled shaggy face appear in the empty windowframe, and then they were up like Goldilocks and out the front door, where they locked themselves in the car. They came to me in their pajamas, trembling like refugees. By the time I got there with my Weatherby, the bear was gone.

"I've seen him," Jill said. "He broke the damn window out of my back bedroom and now I've got it all boarded up." Josh, the younger guy, seemed to find this funny, and he began a low snickering suck and blow of air like an old dog with something caught in his throat.

"Hell," Jill said, lighting up, centerstage, "I was in my nightie and barefoot too and I didn't hesitate a second—zoom, I grabbed my son by the hand and out the door we went."

"Your nightie, huh?" Boo said, a big appreciative grin transforming his face so that for a minute, in the dim light, he could have been a leering, hairy-hocked satyr come in from the cold.

"Maybe it wasn't just the leftovers he wanted," I offered, and everyone cracked up. Just then Marshall stepped through the door, arms laden, stamping the snow from his boots. I got up to help him, and when he began fumbling in his breast pocket, I felt a surge of relief: he'd remembered my check. I was on my way out the door to help with the supplies when I heard Boo's rumbling bass like distant thunder: "Don't you worry, pretty lady," he was saying, "we'll get him."

Regina showed up three days later. For the past few years she'd rented a room up here over the holidays, ostensibly for her health, the cross-country skiing, and the change of scene, but actually so she could display her backend in stretch pants to the sex-crazed hermits who lived year-round amidst the big pines and sequoias. She was from Los Angeles, where she worked as a dental hygienist. Her teeth were perfect, she smiled nonstop and with the serenity of the Mona Lisa, and she wore the kind of bra that was popular in the fifties—the kind that thrust the breasts out of her ski sweater like nuclear warheads. She'd been known to give the tumble to the occasional tourist or one of the lucky locals when the mood took her, but she really had it for Marshall. For two weeks every Christmas and another week at Easter, she became a fixture at the bar, as much a part of the decor as the moosehead or the stuffed bear, perched on a barstool in Norwegian sweater, red ski pants, and mukluks, sipping a champagne cocktail and waiting for him to get off work. Sometimes she couldn't hold out and someone else would walk off with her while Marshall scowled from behind the grill, but usually she just waited there for him like a flower about to drop its petals.

She came into the white world that afternoon like a foretaste of the good times to come—city women, weekend cowboys, grandmas, children, dogs, and lawyers were on their way, trees and decorations going up, the big festival of the goose-eating Christians about to commence—rolling into the snowbound parking lot in her Honda with the neat little chain-wrapped tires that always remind me of Tonka toys. It was about 4:00 P.M., the sky was a sorrowful gray, and a loose flurry was dusting the huge logs piled up on the veranda. In she came, stamping and shaking, the knit cap pulled down to her eyebrows, already on the lookout for Marshall.

I was sitting in my usual place, working on my fifth beer, a third of the way through the check Marshall had brought me three days previous and calculating gloomily that I'd be out of money by Christmas at this rate. Scooter was bartending, and his daughter-in-law Mae-Mae, who happened to be a widow, was hunched morosely over a Tom Collins three stools up from me. Mae-Mae had lost her husband to the mountain two years earlier (or, rather, to the tortuous road that connected us to civilization and snaked up 7300 feet from the floor of the San Joaquin Valley in a mere twenty-six miles, treacherous as a goat trail in the Himalayas), and hadn't spoken or smiled since. She was a Thai. Scooter's son, a Vietnam hero, had brought her back from Southeast Asia with him. When Jill was off, or the holiday crowd bearing down on the place, Scooter would drive up the mountain from his cabin at Little Creek, elevation 5500 feet, hang his ski parka on a hook in back, and shake, stir, and blend cocktails. He brought Mae-Mae with him to get her out of the house.

Scooter and I had been discussing some of the finer points of the prevent defense with respect to the coming pro-football playoffs when Regina's Honda rolled into the lot, and now we gave it up to gape at her as she shook herself like a go-go dancer, opened her jacket to expose the jutting armaments of her breasts, and slid onto a barstool. Scooter slicked back his white hair and gave her a big grin. "Well," he said, fumbling for her name, "um, uh, good to see you again."

She flashed him her fluoridated smile, glanced past the absorbed Mae-Mae to where I sat grinning like an overworked dog, then turned back to him. "Marshall around?"

Scooter informed her that Marshall had gone down the mountain on a supply run and should be back by dinnertime. And what would she like?

She sighed, crossed her legs, lit a cigarette. The hat she was wearing was part of a set—hand-knit, imported from Scandinavia, woven from ram's whiskers by the trolls themselves, two hundred bucks at I. Magnin. Or something like that. It was gray, like her eyes. She swept it from her head with a flourish, fluffed out her short black hair and ordered a champagne cocktail. I looked at my watch.

I'd read somewhere that nine out of ten adults in Alaska had a drinking problem. I could believe it. Snow, ice, sleet, wind, the dark night of the soul: what else were you supposed to do? It was the same way up on the mountain. Big Timber was a collection of maybe a hundred widely scattered cabins atop a broad-beamed peak in the southern Sierras. The cabins belonged to summer people from L.A. and San Diego, to cross-country skiers, gynecologists, talent agents, ad men, drunks, and nature lovers, for the most part, and to twenty-seven hard-core antisocial types who called the place home year-round. I was one of this latter group. So was Jill. Of the remaining twenty-five xenophobes and rustics, three were women, and two of them were married and post-menopausal to boot. The sole remaining female was an alcoholic poet with a walleye who lived in her parents' cabin on the outer verge of the development and hated men. TV reception was spotty, radio nonexistent, and the nearest library a one-room affair at the base of the mountain that boasted three copies of *The Thorn Birds* and the complete works of Irving Wallace.

And so we drank.

Social life, such as it was, revolved around Marshall's lodge, which dispensed all the amenities in a single huge room, from burgers and chili omelets to antacid pills, cold remedies, cans of pickled beets, and toilet paper, as well as spirits, human fraternity, and a chance to fight off alien invaders at the controls of the video game in the corner. Marshall organized his Friday-night family dinners, did a turkey thing on Thanksgiving and Christmas, threw a New Year's party, and kept the bar open on weekends through the long solitary winter, thinking not so much of profit, but of our sanity. The lodge also boasted eight woodsy hotel rooms, usually empty, but now—with the arrival of Boo and his fellow hit men, Regina, and a couple other tourists—beginning to fill up.

On the day Regina rolled in, Jill had taken advantage of the break in the weather to schuss down the mountain in her station wagon and do some Christmas shopping. I was supposed to have gone with her, but we'd had a fight. Over Boo. I'd come in the night before from my late-afternoon stroll to see Jill half spread across the bar with a blank bovine look on her face while Boo mumbled his baritone blandishments into her eyes from about six inches away. I saw that, and then I saw that she'd locked fingers with him, as if they'd been arm wrestling or something. Marshall was out in the kitchen, Josh was sticking it to the video game, and Scott must have been up in his room. "Hey," Boo said, casually turning his head, "what's happening?" Jill gave me a defiant look before extricating herself and turning her back to fool around with the cash register. I stood there in the doorway, saying nothing. *Bishzz, bishzz* went the video game, *zoot-zoot-zoot.* Marshall dropped something out in the kitchen. "Buy this man a drink, honey," Boo said. I turned and walked out the door.

"Christ, I can't believe you," Jill had said when I came round to pick her up after work. "It's my job, you know? What am I supposed to do, hang a sign around my neck that says 'Property of M. Koerner'?"

I told her I thought that was a pretty good idea.

"Forget the ride," she said. "I'm walking."

"And what about the bear?" I said, knowing how the specter of it terrified her, knowing that she dreaded walking those dark snowlit roads for fear of chancing across him—knowing it and wanting for her to admit it, to tell me she needed me.

But all she said was "Screw the bear," and then she was gone.

Now I ordered another beer, sauntered along the bar, and sat down one stool up from Regina. "Hi," I said, "remember me? Michael Koerner? I live up back of Malloy's place?"

She narrowed her eyes and gave me a smile I could feel all the way down in the remotest nodes of my reproductive tract. She no more knew me than she would have known a Chinese peasant plucked at random from the faceless hordes. "Sure," she said.

We made small talk. How slippery the roads were—worse than last year. A renegade bear? Really? Marshall grew a beard?

I'd bought her two champagne cocktails and was working on yet another beer, when Jill catapulted through the door, arms festooned with foil-wrapped packages and eyes ablaze with goodwill and holiday cheer; Adrian tagged along at her side, looking as if he'd just sprung down from the back of a flying reindeer. If Jill felt put out by the spectacle of Regina—or more particularly by my proximity to and involvement in that spectacle—she didn't miss a beat. The packages hit the bar with a thump, Scooter and Mae-Mae were treated to joyous salutatory squeals, Regina was embraced and I was ignored. Adrian went straight for the video game, pausing only to scoop up the six quarters I held out to him like an offering. Jill ordered herself a cocktail and started in on Regina, bantering away about hairstyles, nails, shoes, blouses, and the like as if she were glad to see her. "I just love that hat!" she shouted at one point, reaching out to finger the material. I swung round on my stool and stared out the window.

It was then that Boo came into sight. Distant, snow-softened, trudging across the barren white expanse of the lot as if in a dream. He was wearing his white parka, hood up, a rifle was slung over his shoulder, and he was dragging something behind him. Something heavy and dark, a long low-slung form that raveled out from his heels like a shadow. When he paused to straighten up and catch his streaming breath, I saw with a shock that the carcass of an animal lay at his feet, red and raw like a gash in the snow. "Hey!" I shouted. "Boo got the bear!" And the next minute we were all out in the windblown parking lot, hemmed in by the forbidding ranks of the trees and the belly of the gray deflated sky, as Boo looked up puzzled from the carcass of a gutted deer. "What happened, the bar catch fire?" he said, his sharp blue eyes parrying briefly with mine, swooping past Scooter, Adrian, and Mae-Mae to pause a moment over Jill and finally lock on Regina's wide-eyed stare. He was grinning.

The deer's black lip was pulled back from ratty yellowed teeth; its eyes were opaque in death. Boo had slit it from chest to crotch, and a half-frozen bulb of grayish intestine poked from the lower end of the ragged incision. I felt foolish.

"Bait," Boo said in explanation, his eyes roving over us again. "I'm leaving a blood smear you could follow with your eyes closed and your nose stopped up. Then I'm going to hang the meat up a tree and wait for Mr. Bear."

Jill turned away, a bit theatrically I thought, and made small noises of protest and disgust on the order of "the poor animal," then took Adrian by the hand and pulled him back in the direction of the lodge. Mae-Mae stared through us all, this carnage like that other that had claimed her husband's life, end over end in the bubble of their car, blood on the slope. Regina looked at Boo. He stood over the fallen buck, grinning like a troglodyte with his prey, then bent to catch the thing by its antlers and drag it off across the lot as if it were an old rug for the church rummage sale.

That night the lodge was hopping. Tourists had begun to trickle in and there were ten or twelve fresh faces at the bar. I ate a chicken pot pie and a can of cold beets in the solitude of my cabin, wrapped a tacky black-and-gold scarf round my neck, and ambled through the dark featureless forest to the lodge. As I stepped through the door I smelled perfume, sweet drinks, body heat, and caught the sensuous click of the pool balls as they punctuated the swell of riotous voices churning up around me. Holiday cheer, oh, yes, indeed.

Jill was tending bar. Everyone in the development was there, including the old wives and the walleyed poetess. An array of roaring strangers and those recognized vaguely from previous seasons stood, slouched, and stamped round the bar or huddled over steaks in the booths to the rear. Marshall was behind the grill. I eased up to the bar between a bearded stranger in a gray felt cowboy hat and a familiar-looking character who shot me a glance of mortal dislike and then turned away. I was absently wondering what I could possibly have done to offend this guy (winter people—I could hardly remember what I'd said and done last week, let alone last year), when I spotted Regina. And Boo. They were sitting at a booth, the table before them littered with empty glasses and beer bottles. Good, I said to myself, an insidious little smile of satisfaction creeping across my lips, and I glanced toward Jill.

I could see that she was watching them out of the corner of her eye, though an impartial observer might have guessed she was giving her full attention to Alf Cornwall, the old gas bag who sat across the bar from her and toyed with a glass of peppermint schnapps while he went on ad nauseam about the only subject dear to him—i.e., the lamentable state of his health. "Jill," I barked with malicious joy, "how about some service down here?"

She gave me a look that would have corroded metal, then heaved back from the bar and poured me a long slow shot of Wild Turkey and an even slower glass of beer. I winked at her as she set the drinks down and scraped my money from the bar. "Not tonight, Michael," she said, "I don't feel up to it," and her tone was so dragged down and lugubrious she could have been a professional mourner. It was then that I began to realize just how much Boo had affected her (and by extension, how little I had), and I glanced over my shoulder to focus a quick look of jealous hatred on him. When Jill set down my change I grabbed her wrist. "What the hell do you mean 'not tonight,' " I hissed. "Now I can't even talk to you, or what?"

She looked at me like a martyr, like a twenty-eight-year-old woman deserted by her husband in the backend of nowhere and saddled with an unhappy kid and a deadbeat sometime beau to whom the prospect of marriage was about as appealing as a lobotomy, she looked at me like a woman who's given up on romance. Then she jerked her arm away and slouched off to hear all the fascinating circumstances attending Alf Cornwall's most recent bowel movement.

The crowd began to thin out about eleven, and Marshall came out from behind the grill to saunter up to the bar for a Rémy-Martin. He too seemed preternaturally interested in Alf Cornwall's digestive tract, and sniffed meditatively at his cognac for five minutes or so before he picked up the glass and strolled over to join Boo and Regina. He slid in next to Regina, nodding and smiling, but he didn't look too pleased.

Like Boo, Marshall was big. Big-hearted, big-bellied, with grizzled hair and a beard flecked with white. He was in his mid-forties, twice divorced, and he had a casual folksy way about him that women found appealing, or unique—or whatever. Women who came up the mountain, that is. Jill had had a thing with him the year before I moved in, he was one of the chief reasons the walleyed poetess hated men, and any number of cross-country ski bunnies, doctors' wives, and day trippers had taken some extracurricular exercise in the oak-framed waterbed that dominated his room in the back of the lodge. Boo didn't stand a chance. Ten minutes after Marshall had sat down Boo was back up at the bar, a little unsteady from all he'd had to drink, and looking Jill up and down like he had one thing on his mind.

I was on my third shot and fifth beer, the lights were low, the fire going strong, and the twenty-foot Christmas tree lit up like a satellite. Alf Cornwall had taken his bullshit home with him; the poetess, the wives, and two-thirds of the new people had cleared out. I was discussing beach erosion with the guy in the cowboy hat, who as it turned out was from San Diego, and keeping an eye on Boo and Jill at the far end of the bar. "Well, Christ," San Diego roared as if I was half a mile away, "you put up them godforsaken useless damn seawalls and what have you got, I ask you? Huh?"

I wasn't listening. Boo was stroking Jill's hand like a glove salesman, Marshall and Regina were grappling in the booth, and I was feeling sore and hurt and left out. A log burned through and tumbled into the coals with a thud. Marshall got up to poke it, and all of a sudden I was seething. Turning my back on San Diego, I pushed off of my stool and strode to the end of the bar.

Jill saw the look on my face and drew back. I put my hand on Boo's shoulder and watched him turn to me in slow motion, his face huge, the scar glistening over his eyebrow. "You can't do that," I said.

He just looked at me.

"Michael," Jill said.

"Huh?" he said. "Do what?" Then he turned his head to look at Jill, and when he swung back round he knew.

I shoved him, hard, as he was coming up off the barstool, and he went down on one knee before he caught himself and lunged at me. He would have destroyed me if Marshall hadn't caught hold of him, but I didn't care. As it was, he gave me one terrific shot to the breastbone that flattened me against the bar and sent a couple of glasses flying. Bang, bang, they shattered on the flagstone floor like lightbulbs dropped from a ladder.

"Goddamnit," Marshall was roaring, "that's about enough." His face was red to the roots of his whiskers. "Michael," he said—or blared, I should say—and then he waved his hand in disgust. Boo stood behind him, giving me a bad look. "I think you've had enough, Michael," Marshall said. "Go on home."

I wanted to throw it right back in his face, wanted to shout obscenities, take them both on, break up the furniture, and set the tree afire, but I didn't. I wasn't sixteen: I was thirty-one years old and I was reasonable. The lodge was the only bar in twenty-six miles and I'd be mighty thirsty and mighty lonely both if I was banished for good. "All right," I said. "All right." And then, as I shrugged into my jacket: "Sorry."

Boo was grinning, Jill looked like she had the night the bear broke in. Regina was studying me with either interest or amusement—I couldn't tell which—Scooter looked like he had to go to the bathroom, and San Diego just stepped aside. I pulled the door closed behind me. Softly.

Outside, it was snowing. Big, warm, healing flakes. It was the kind of snow my father used to hold his hands out to, murmuring, *God must be up there plucking chickens.* I wrapped the scarf round my throat and was about to start off across the lot when I saw something moving through the blur of falling flakes. The first thing I thought of was some late arrival from down below, some part-timer come to claim his cabin. The second thing I thought of was the bear.

I was wrong on both counts. The snow drove down against the dark branchless pillars of the treetrunks, chalk strokes on a blackboard, I counted off three breaths, and then Mae-Mae emerged from the gloom. "Michael?" she said, coming up to me.

I could see her face in the yellow light that seeped through the windows of the lodge and lay like a fungus on the surface of the snow. She gave me a rare smile, and then her face changed as she touched a finger to the corner of my mouth. "What happen you?" she said, and her finger glistened with blood.

I licked my lip. "Nothing. Bit my lip, I guess." The snow caught like confetti in the feathery puff of her hair and her eyes tugged at me from the darkness. "Hey," I said, surprised by inspiration, "you want to maybe come up to my place for a drink?"

Next day, at dusk, I was out in the woods with my axe. The temperature was about ten degrees above zero, I had a pint of Presidente to keep me warm, and I was looking for a nice round-bottomed silver fir about five feet tall. I listened to the snow groan under my boots, watched my breath hang in the air; I looked around me and saw ten thousand little green trees beneath the canopy of the giants, none of them right. By the time I found what I was looking for, the snow had drunk up the light and the trees had become shadows.

As I bent to clear the snow from the base of the tree I'd selected, something made me glance over my shoulder. Failing light, logs under the snow, branches, hummocks. At first I couldn't make him out, but I knew he was there. Sixth sense. But then, before the shaggy silhouette separated itself from the gloom, a more prosaic sense took over: I could smell him. Shit, piss, sweat, and hair, dead meat, bad breath, the primal stink. There he was, a shadow among shadows, big around as a fallen tree, the bear, watching me.

Nothing happened. I didn't grin him down, fling the axe at him, or climb a tree, and he didn't lumber off in a panic, throw himself on me with a bloody roar, or climb a tree either. Frozen like an ice sculpture, not even daring to come out of my crouch for fear of shattering the moment, I watched the bear. Communed with him. He was a renegade, a solitary, airlifted in a groggy stupor from Yosemite, where he'd become too familiar with people. Now he was familiar with me. I wondered if he'd studied my tracks as I'd studied his, wondered what he was doing out in the harsh snowbound woods instead of curled cozily in his den. Ten minutes passed. Fifteen. The woods went dark. I stood up. He was gone.

Christmas was a pretty sad affair. Talk of post-holiday depression, I had it before, during, and after. I was broke, Jill and I were on the outs, I'd begun to loathe the sight of three-hundred-foot trees and snow-capped mountains, and I liked the rest of humanity about as much as Gulliver liked the Yahoos. I did stop by Jill's place around six to share a miserable, tight-lipped meal with her and Adrian and exchange presents. I gave Adrian a two-foot-high neon-orange plastic dragon from Taiwan that spewed up puddles of reddish stuff that looked like vomit, and I gave Jill a cheap knit hat with a pink pom-pom on top. She gave me a pair of gloves. I didn't stay for coffee.

New Year's was different.

I gave a party, for one thing. For another, I'd passed from simple misanthropy to nihilism, death of the spirit, and beyond. It was 2:00 A.M., everybody in the lodge was wearing party hats, I'd kissed half the women in the place—including a reluctant Jill, pliant Regina, and sour-breathed poetess—and I felt empty and full, giddy, expansive, hopeful, despondent, drunk. "Party at my place," I shouted as Marshall announced last call and turned up the lights. "Everybody's invited."

Thirty bon vivants tramped through the snowy streets, blowing party horns and flicking paper ticklers at one another, fired up snowmobiles, Jeeps, and pickups, carried open bottles out of the bar, and hooted at the stars. They filled my little place like fish in a net, squirming against one another, grinning and shout-

ing, making out in the loft, vomiting in the toilet, sniggering around the fireplace. Boo was there, water under the bridge. Jill too. Marshall, Regina, Scooter,
Mae-Mae, Josh and Scott, the poetess, San Diego, and anybody else who happened to be standing under the moosehead in a glossy duncecap when I made
my announcement. Somebody put on a reggae album that sent seismic shudders
through the floor, and people began to dance. I was out in the kitchen fumbling
with the ice-cube tray when Regina banged through the door with a bar glass in
her hand. She gave me a crooked smile and held it out to me. "What're you
drinking?" she asked.

"Pink Boys," I said. "Vodka, crushed ice, and pink lemonade, slushed in the
blender."

"Pink Boys," Regina said, or tried to say. She was wearing her knit hat and
matching sweater, the hat pulled down to her eyebrows, the sweater unbuttoned
halfway to her navel. I took the glass from her and she moved into me, caught
hold of my biceps, and stuck her tongue in my mouth. A minute later I had her
pinned up against the stove, exploring her exemplary dentition with the tip of my
own tongue and dipping my hand into that fabulous sweater as if into the
mother lode itself.

I had no problems with any of this. I gave no thought to motives, mores, fidelity, or tomorrow: I was a creature of nature, responding to natural needs.
Besides which, Jill was locked in an embrace with Marshall in the front room,
the old satyr and king of the mountain reestablishing a prior claim, Boo was
hunched over the fire with Mae-Mae, giving her the full flash of his eyes and
murmuring about bear scat in a voice so deep it would have made Johnny Cash
turn pale, and Josh and the poetess were joyfully deflating Edna St. Vincent Mil-
lay while swaying their bodies awkwardly to Bob Marley's voodoo backbeat.
New Year's Eve. It was like something out of *La Ronde*.

By three-thirty, I'd been rejected by Regina, who'd obviously been using me
as a decoy, Marshall and Jill had disappeared and rematerialized twice, Regina
had tried unsuccessfully to lure Boo away from Mae-Mae (who was now secreted
with him in the bedroom), San Diego had fallen and smashed my coffee table to
splinters, one half-gallon of vodka was gone and we were well into the second,
and Josh and the poetess had exchanged addresses. Auld lang syne, I thought,
surveying the wreckage and moodily crunching taco chips while a drunken San
Diego raved in my ear about dune buggies, outboard engines, and tuna rigs.
Marshall and Jill were holding hands. Regina sat across the room, looking dangerous. She'd had four or five Pink Boys, on top of what she'd consumed at the
lodge, but who was counting? Suddenly she stood—or, rather, jumped to her
feet like a marine assaulting a beachhead—and began to gather her things.

What happened next still isn't clear. Somehow her hat had disappeared—that
was the start of it. At first she just bustled round the place, overturning piles of
scarves and down jackets, poking under the furniture, scooting people from the

couch and easy chair, but then she turned frantic. The hat was a keepsake, an heirloom. Brought over from Flekkefjord by her great-grandmother, who'd knitted it as a memento of Olaf the Third's coronation, or something like that. Anyway, it was irreplaceable. More precious than the Magna Carta, the Shroud of Turin, and the Hope Diamond combined. She grew shrill.

Someone cut the stereo. People began to shuffle their feet. One clown—a total stranger—made a show of looking behind the framed photograph of Dry Gulch, Wyoming, that hangs beside the fireplace. "It'll turn up," I said.

Regina had scattered a heap of newspapers over the floor and was frantically riffling through the box of kindling in the corner. She turned on me with a savage look. "The hell it will," she snarled. "Somebody stole it."

"Stole it?" I echoed.

"That's right," she said, the words coming fast now. She was looking at Jill. "Some bitch. Some fat-assed jealous bitch that just can't stand the idea of somebody showing her up. Some, some—"

She didn't get a chance to finish. Jill was up off the couch like something coming out of the gate at Pamplona and suddenly the two of them were locked in combat, pulling hair and raking at one another like Harpies. Regina was cursing and screeching at the same time; Jill went for the vitals. I didn't know what to do. San Diego made the mistake of trying to separate them, and got his cheek raked for the effort. Finally, when they careened into the pole lamp and sent it crashing to the floor with a climactic shriek of broken glass, Marshall took hold of Regina from behind and wrestled her out the door, while I did my best to restrain Jill.

The door slammed. Jill shrugged loose, heaving for breath, and turned her back on me. There were twenty pale astonished faces strung round the room like Japanese lanterns. A few of the men looked sheepish, as if they'd stolen a glimpse of something they shouldn't have. No one said a word. Just then Boo emerged from the bedroom, Mae-Mae in tow. "What's all the commotion?" he said.

I glanced around the room. All of a sudden I felt indescribably weary. "Party's over," I said.

I woke at noon with a hangover. I drank from the tap, threw some water in my face, and shambled down to the lodge for breakfast. Marshall was there, behind the grill, looking as if he was made of mashed potatoes. He barely noticed as I shuffled in and took a window seat among a throng of chipper, alert, and well-fed tourists.

I was leafing through the *Chronicle* and puffing away at my third cup of coffee when I saw Regina's car sail past the window, negotiate the turn at the end of the lot, and swing onto the road that led down the mountain. I couldn't be sure—it was a gloomy day, the sky like smoke—but as near as I could tell she was hatless. No more queen of the mountain for her, I thought. No more champagne cocktails and the tight thrilling clasp of spandex across the bottom—from here on out it was stinking mouths and receding gums. I turned back to the newspaper.

When I looked up again, Boo, Josh, and Scott were stepping out of a Jeep Cherokee, a knot of gawkers and Sunday skiers gathered round them. Draped over the hood of the thing, still red at the edges with raw meat and blood, was a bearskin, head intact. The fur was reddish, almost cinnamon-colored, and one ear was folded down. I watched as Boo ambled up to the door, stepped aside for a pair of sixteen-year-old ski bunnies with layered hair, and then pushed his way into the lodge.

He took off his shades and stood there a moment in the doorway, carefully wiping them on his parka before slipping them into his breast pocket. Then he started toward the cash register, already easing back to reach for his wallet. "Hey," he said when he saw me, and he stopped to lean over the table for a moment. "We got him," he said, scraping bottom with his baritone and indicating the truck beyond the window with a jerk of his head. There was a discoloration across the breast of his white parka, a brownish spatter. I swiveled my head to glance out the window, then turned back to him, feeling as if I'd had the wind punched out of me. "Yeah," I said.

There was a silence. He looked at me, I looked at him. "Well," he said after a moment, "you take care," and then he strode up to the cash register to pay his bill and check out.

Jill came in about one. She was wearing shades too, and when she slipped behind the bar and removed them, I saw the black-and-blue crescent under her right eye. As for Marshall, she didn't even give him a glance. Later, after I'd been through the paper twice and figured it was time for a Bloody Mary or two and some Bowl games, I took a seat at the bar. "Hi, Michael," she said, "what'll you have?," and her tone was so soft, so contrite, so sweet and friendly and conciliatory, that I could actually feel the great big heaving plates of the world shifting back into alignment beneath my feet.

Oh, yes, the hat. A week later, when the soot and dust and woodchips around the cabin got too much for me, I dragged out the vacuum cleaner for my semi-annual sweep around the place. I scooted over the rug, raked the drapes, and got the cobwebs in the corners. When I turned over the cushions on the couch, the wand still probing, I found the hat. There was a label inside. *JCPenney*, it read, $7.95. For a long moment I just stood there, turning the thing over in my hand. Then I tossed it in the fire.

(1984)

WHALES WEEP

*They say the sea is cold, but the sea contains
the hottest blood of all. . .*

—D. H. Lawrence, "Whales Weep Not"

I don't know what it was exactly—the impulse toward preservation in the face of flux, some natal fascination with girth—who can say? But suddenly, in the winter of my thirty-first year, I was seized with an overmastering desire to seek out the company of whales. That's right: whales. Flukes and blowholes. Leviathan. Moby Dick.

People talked about the Japanese, the Russians. Factory ships, they said. Dwindling numbers and a depleted breeding stock, whales on the wane. I wanted desperately to see them before they sang their swan song, before they became a mere matter of record, cards in an index, skeletal remains strung out on coat hangers and suspended from the high concave ceilings of the Smithsonian like blueprints of the past. More: I wanted to know them, smell them, touch them. I wanted to mount their slippery backs in the high seas, swim amongst them, come to understand their expansive gestures, sweeping rituals, their great whal- ish ecstasies and stupendous sorrows.

This cetaceamania was not something that came on gradually, a predilection that developed over a period of months into interest, awareness, and finally absorption—not at all. No: it took me by storm. Of course I'd been at least mar- ginally aware of the plight of whales and dolphins for years, blitzed as I was by pleas from the Sierra Club, the National Wildlife Federation, and the Save the Whales people. I gave up tuna fish. Wrote a letter to my congressman. Still, I'd never actually seen a whale and can't say that I was any more concerned about cetaceans than I was about the mountain gorilla, inflation, or the chemicals in processed foods. Then I met Harry Macey.

It was at a party, somewhere in the East Fifties. One of those seasonal affairs: Dom Pérignon, cut crystal, three black girls whining over a prerecorded disco track. Furs were in. Jog togs. The hustle. Health. I was with Stephanie King, a fashion model. She was six feet tall, irises like well water, the *de rigueur* mole at the corner of her mouth. Like most of the haute couture models around town, she'd developed a persona midway between Girl Scout and vampire. I did not find it at all unpalatable.

Stephanie introduced me to a man in beard, blazer, and bifocals. He was rebuking an elderly woman for the silver-fox boa dangling from her neck. "Disgusting," he snarled, working himself into a froth. "Savage and vestigial. What do you think we've developed synthetics for?" His hair was like the hair of Kennedys, boyish, massed over his brow, every strand shouting for attention; his eyes were cold and messianic. He rattled off a list of endangered species, from snail darter to three-toed sloth, his voice sucking mournfully at each syllable as if he were a rabbi uttering the secret names of God. Then he started on whales.

I cleared my throat and held out my hand. "Call me Roger," I said.

He didn't even crack a smile. Just widened his sphere of influence to include Stephanie and me. "The blue whale," he was saying, flicking the ash from his cigarette into the ashtray he held supine in his palm, "is a prime example. One hundred feet long, better than a quarter of a million pounds. By far and away the largest creature ever to inhabit the earth. His tongue alone weighs three tons, and his penis, nine and a half feet long, would dwarf a Kodiak bear. And how do we reward this exemplar of evolutionary impetus?" He paused and looked at me like a quiz-show host. Stephanie, who had handed her lynx maxicoat to the hostess when we arrived, bowed twice, muttered something unintelligible, and wandered off with a man in dreadlocks. The old woman was asleep. I shrugged my shoulders.

"We hunt him to the brink of extinction, that's how. We boil him down and convert him into margarine, pet food, shoe polish, lipstick."

This was Harry Macey. He was a marine biologist connected with NYU and, as I thought at the time, something of an ass. But he did have a point. Never mind his bad breath and egomania; his message struck a chord. As he talked on, lecturing now, his voice modulating between anger, conviction, and a sort of evangelical fervor, I began to develop a powerful visceral sympathy with him. Whales, I thought, sipping at my champagne. Magnificent, irreplaceable creatures, symbols of the wild and all that, brains the size of ottomans, courting, making love, chirping to one another in the fathomless dark—just as they'd been doing for sixty million years. And all this was threatened by the greed of the Japanese and the cynicism of the Russians. Here was something you could throw yourself into, an issue that required no soul-searching, good guys and bad as clearly delineated as rabbits and hyenas.

Macey's voice lit the deeps, illuminated the ages, fired my enthusiasm. He talked of the subtle intelligence of these peaceful, lumbering mammals, of their courage and loyalty to one another in the face of adversity, of their courtship and foreplay and the monumental suboceanic sex act itself. I drained my glass, shut my eyes, and watched an underwater *pas de deux:* great shifting bulks pressed to one another like trains in collision, awesome, staggering, drums and bass pounding through the speakers until all I could feel through every cell of my body was that fearful, seismic humping in the depths.

Two weeks later I found myself bobbing about in a rubber raft somewhere off the coast of British Columbia. It was raining. The water temperature was thirty-four degrees. A man unlucky enough to find himself immersed in such water would be dead of exposure inside of five minutes. Or so I was told.

I was given this morsel of information by either Nick, Gary, or Ernie, my companions in the raft. All three were in their mid-twenties, wild-eyed and bearded, dressed in Norwegian sweaters, rain slickers, and knit skullcaps. They were aficionados of rock and roll, drugs, airplanes, and speedboats. They were also dangerous lunatics dedicated to thrusting themselves between the warheads of six-foot, quadri-barbed, explosive harpoons and the colossal rushing backs of panic-stricken whales.

At the moment, however, there were no whales to be seen. Living whales, at any rate. The carcasses of three sei whales trailed behind the rictus of a Russian factory ship, awaiting processing. A low cloud cover, purple-gray, raveled out from horizon to horizon like entrails on a butcher's block, while the Russian ship loomed above us, its endless rust-streaked bows high as the Jersey palisades, the stony Slavic faces of the Russian seamen ranged along the rail like a string of peas. There were swells eight feet high. All around us the sea was pink with the blood of whales and sliced by the great black dorsal fins of what I at first took to be sharks. A moment later I watched a big grinning killer whale rush up out of the depths and tear a chunk of meat the size of a Holstein from one of the carcasses.

Nick was lighting his pipe. "Uh," I said, "shouldn't we be getting back to the ship?"

If he heard me, he gave no sign of it. He was muttering under his breath and jerking angrily at his knuckles. He took a long, slow hit from a tarnished flask, then glared up at the stoic Russian faces and collectively gave them the finger. "Murderers!" he shouted. "Cossack faggots!"

I was on assignment for one of the news magazines, and I'd managed to come up with some expense money from *Audubon* as well. The news magazine wanted action shots of the confrontation between the whalers and Nick, Gary, and Ernie; *Audubon* wanted some wide-angles of spouting whales for an article by some cetologist studying the lung capacity of the minke. I'd talked them into the assignment. Like a fool. For the past few years I'd been doing pretty well on the fashion circuit (I'd done some Junior Miss things for Sears and Bloomingdale's and freelanced for some of the women's magazines), but had begun to feel that I was missing something. Call it malaise, call it boredom. I was making a living, but what was I doing for the generations of mankind? Saving the whales—or at least doing my part in it—seemed a notch or two higher on the ethical scale than inflaming the lust of pubescent girls for snakeskin boots and fur collars. And what's more, I was well equipped to do it, having begun my career as a naturalist.

That's right: I too had my youthful illusions. I was just six months out of college when I did my study of the bearded tit for the *National Geographic*, and I was flush with success and enthusiasm. The following year *Wildlife* sent me up the Xingu to record the intimate life of the capybara. I waded through swamps, wet to my waist, crouched behind blinds for days on end, my skin black with mosquitoes though I didn't dare slap them for fear of spooking my quarry. I was bitten by three different species of arachnids. I contracted bilharziasis. It was then that I decided to trade in my telephoto lens and devote myself to photographing beautiful women with haunted eyes in clean, airy studios.

Nick was on his feet now, fighting for balance as the waves tossed our raft. "Up Brezhnev!" he shrieked, the cords in his neck tight as hawsers.

Suddenly one of the Russians reared back and threw something at us, something round and small. I watched its trajectory as it shot out over the high bow of the ship and arced gracefully for us. It landed with a rush of air and a violent elastic hiss like a dozen rubber bands snapping simultaneously. The missile turned out to be a grapefruit, frozen hard as a brick. It tore a hole through the floor of the raft.

After the rescue, I spent a few days in a hospital in Vancouver, then flew back to New York. Gary—or was it Ernie?—lost two toes. I took a nasty crack over the eyebrow that required nineteen stitches and made me look either rakish or depraved, depending on your point of view. The photos, for which I'd been given an advance, were still in the camera—about thirty fathoms down. Still, things wouldn't have been so bad if it weren't for the headaches. Headaches that began with a quick stab at something beneath the surface of the eye and then built with a steadily mounting pressure until the entire left side of my head felt like a helium balloon and I began to understand that I was no longer passionate on the subject of whales. After all, the only whales I'd managed to catch sight of were either dead, dying, or sprinting for their lives in a rush of foam. Where was the worth and beauty in that? And where, I wondered, was the affirmation these diluvian and mystical beasts were supposed to inject into my own depleted life?

The night I got in, Stephanie showed up at my apartment with a bottle of Appleton's rum. We made piña coladas and love. There was affirmation in that. In the morning, 7:00 A.M., Harry Macey was at the door in a warm-up suit. He whistled at the stitching over my eye, compared me unfavorably with Franken-stein's monster, offered me a dried lemon peel, and sat down at the kitchen table. "All right," he barked, "let's have it—all the details. Currents, sightings, the Russian take—everything." I reconstructed the trip for him over Red Zinger and granola, while he nodded and spooned, spooned and nodded, filing mental notes. But before I'd even got halfway he cut me off, jumped up from the table, and told me there was someone I just had to meet, right away, no arguments, a person I could really relate to.

I looked up from my granola, head throbbing. He was standing over me, shot through with energy, tugging at his ear, blowing the steam from his teacup, all but dancing. "I know you're going to love him," he said. "The man knows whales inside and out."

Eyolf Holluson lived in a two-room apartment on East Twenty-sixth Street. He was eighty-six years old. We mounted the steps two at a time—all five flights—and stood outside the door while Harry counted his heartbeats. "Forty-four a minute," he said, matter-of-factly. "Nothing when you consider the lungfish, but not bad for a man of thirty-nine." In the process, my own heart seemed to have migrated to my head, where it was pounding like a letterpress over my left eye.

A voice, high and nasal, shaken with vibrato, echoed from behind the door. "Harry?"

Harry answered in the affirmative, the voice indicated that the door was open, and we stepped into a darkened room lit only by flashing Christmas bulbs and smelling of corned beef and peppermint. On the far side of the room, lost in the folds of a massive, dun-colored armchair draped with layers of doily and an-timacassar, sat Eyolf. Before him was a TV tray, and beyond that a color TV, pictures flashing, sound turned off.

"Eyolf," Harry said, "I'd like you to meet a friend of mine—he's come to talk about whales."

The old man turned and squinted up at me over the top of his steel-rimmed spectacles, then turned back to the tray. "Oh yah," he said. "Yust finishing up my breakfast." He was eating corned beef, plum tomatoes from the can, dinner mints.

Harry prompted him. "Eyolf fished whales for fifty-seven years—first with the Norwegian fleet, and then, when they packed it in, with the Portuguese off the Canary Islands."

"The old way," Eyolf said, his mouth a stew of mint and tomato. "Oars and harpoons."

We crossed the room and settled into a spongy loveseat that smelled of cat urine. Harry produced a pocket-sized tape recorder, flicked it on, and placed it on the TV tray beside the old man's plate. Then he sank back into the loveseat, crossed his legs at the knee, and said, "Tell us about it, Eyolf."

The old man was wearing a plaid bathrobe and slippers. His frame was big, flesh wasted, his skin the color and texture of beef jerky. He talked for two hours, the strange nasal voice creaking like oars in their locks, rising and falling like the tide. He told us of a sperm whale that had overturned a chase boat in the Sea of Japan, of shipmates towed out of sight and lost in the Antarctic, of a big Swede who lost his leg in a fight with flensing knives. With a crack of his knees he rose up out of the chair and took a harpoon down from the wall, cocked his arm, and told us how he'd struck a thousand whales, hot blood spurting in his face over the icy spume, how it tasted and how his heart rushed with the chase. "You stick him," he said, "and it's like sticking a woman. Better."

There was a copy of the *Norsk Hvalfangst-Tildende* on the table. Behind me, mounted on hooks, was a scrimshaw pipe, and beside it a huge blackened sheet of leather, stiff with age. I ran my finger along its abrasive edge, wondering what it was—a bit of fluke, tongue?—and yet somehow, in a dim grope of intuition, knowing.

Eyolf was spinning a yarn about a sperm whale that had surfaced beneath him with an eighteen-foot squid clenched in its jaws when he turned to me. "I think maybe you are wondering what is this thing like a bullfighter's cape hanging from Eyolf's wall?" I nodded. "A present from the captain of the *Freya*, nearly forty years back, it was. In token of my take of finback and bowhead over a period of two, three hectic weeks. Hectic, oh yah. Blood up to my knees—hot first, then cold. There was blood in my shoes at night."

"The leather, Eyolf," Harry said. "Tell Roger about it."

"Oh yah," he said, looking at me now as if I were made of plastic. "This here is off of the biggest creater on God's earth. The sulfur-bottom, what you call the blue. I keep it here for vigor and long life."

The old man gingerly lifted it from the wall and handed it to me. It was the size of a shower curtain, rigid as tree bark. Eyolf was smiling and nodding. "Solid, no?" He stood there, looking down at me, trembling a bit with one of his multiple infirmities.

"So what is it?" I said, beginning to lose patience.

"You don't know?" He was picking his ear. "This here is his foreskin."

Out on the street Harry said he had a proposition for me. A colleague of his was manning a whale watch off the Península Valdés on the Patagonian coast. He was studying the right whale on its breeding grounds and needed some high-quality photographs to accompany the text of a book he was planning. Would I take the assignment for a flat fee?

My head throbbed at the thought of it. "Will you come along with me?"

Harry looked surprised. "Me?" Then he laughed. "Hell no, are you kidding? I've got classes to teach, I'm sitting on a committee to fund estuarine research, I'm committed for six lectures on the West Coast."

"I just thought—"

"Look, Roger—whales are fascinating and they're in a lot of trouble. I'm hoping to do a monograph on the reproductive system of the rorquals, in fact, but I'm no field man. Actually, pelagic mammals are almost as foreign to my specialty area as elephants."

I was puzzled. "Your specialty area?"

"I study holothurians. My dissertation was on the sea cucumber." He looked a little abashed. "But I think big."

The Patagonian coast of Argentina is a desolate, godforsaken place, swept by perpetual winds, parched for want of rain, home to such strange and hardy creatures as the rhea, crested tinamou, and Patagonian fox. Darwin anchored with the *Beagle* here in 1832, rowed ashore and described a dozen new species. Wildlife abounded. The rocks were crowded with birds—kelp and dolphin gulls, cormorants in the thousands, the southern lapwing, red-backed hawk, tawny-throated dotterel. Penguins and sea lions lolled among the massed black boulders and bobbed in the green swells, fish swarmed offshore, and copepods—ten billion for each star in the sky—thickened the Falkland current until it took on the consistency of porridge. Whales gathered for the feast. Rights, finbacks, minkes—Darwin watched them spouting and lobtailing, sounding and surfacing, courting, mating, calving.

Nothing has changed here—but for the fact that there are fewer whales now. The cormorants and penguins and seals are still there, numbers uncountable, still battening on the rich *potage* that washes the littoral. And still undisturbed by man—with one small exception. The Tsunamis. Shuhei, Grace, and their three daughters. For five months out of the year the Tsunamis occupy the Península Valdés, living in a concrete bunker, eating pots of rice, beans, and fish, battling the wind and the loneliness, watching whales.

Stephanie and I landed with the supply plane, not two hundred feet from the Tsunami bunker. It was August, and the right whales were mating. During the intervening months I'd nursed my split head, drained pitchers of piña coladas, and gone back to the Junior Miss circuit. But I kept in touch with Harry Macey, read ravenously on the subject of whales, joined Greenpeace, and flew to Tokyo for the trial of six members of a cetacean terrorist group accused of harpooning a Japanese industrialist at the Narita airport. I attended lectures, looked at slides, visited Nantucket. At night, after a long day in the studio, I closed my eyes and whales slipped through the Stygian sea of my dreams. There was no denying them.

Grace was waiting for us as the Cessna touched down: hooded sweatshirt, blue jeans, eyes like polished walnut. The girls were there too—Gail, Amy, and Melia—bouncing, craning their necks, rabid with excitement at the prospect of seeing two new faces in the trackless waste. Shuhei was off in the dunes somewhere, in a welter of sonar dishes, listening for whales.

I shook hands with Grace; Stephanie, in a blast of perfume and windswept hair, pecked her cheek. Stephanie was wearing sealskin boots, her lynx coat, and a "Let Them Live" T-shirt featuring the flukes of a sounding whale. She had called me two days before I was scheduled to leave and said that she needed a vacation. Okay, I told her, glad to have you. She found a battery-operated hair dryer and a pith helmet at the Abercrombie & Fitch closeout sale, a wolf-lined parka at Max Bogen, tents, alcohol stoves, and freeze-dried Stroganoff at Paragon; she mail-ordered a pair of khaki puttees and sheepskin mukluks from L. L. Bean, packed up her spare underwear, eyeshadow, three gothic romances, and six pounds of dried apricots, and here she was, in breezy Patagonia, ready for anything.

"Christ!" she shouted, over the roar of the wind. "Does it always blow like this?" It was howling in off the sea, a steady fifty knots.

Grace was grinning, hood up, hair in her face. With her oblate eyes and round face and the suggestion of the hood, she looked like an Eskimo. "I was just going to say," she shouted, "this is calm for the Península Valdés."

That night we sat around the Franklin stove, eating game pie and talking whale. Grace was brisk and efficient, cooking, serving, clearing up, joking, padding round the little room in shorts and white sweat socks. Articulated calves, a gap between the thighs: earth mother, I thought. Shuhei was brooding and hesitant, born in Osaka (Grace was from L.A.). He talked at length about his project, of chance and probability, of graphs, permutations, and species-replacement theory. He was dull. When he attempted a witticism—a play on "flukes," I think it was—it caught us unaware and he turned red.

Outside the wind shrieked and gibbered. The girls giggled in their bunks. We burned our throats on Shuhei's sake and watched the flames play over the logs. Stephanie was six feet long, braless and luxuriant. She yawned and stretched. Shuhei was looking at her the way an indigent looks at a veal cutlet.

"Well," I said, yawning myself. "Guess we better turn in."

We'd pitched our tent just before dark, and it had blown down three times since. Now, as we made for the door, Shuhei became insistent. "No, no," he said, all but blocking our way. "Stay in here tonight—with us."

Grace looked up from her sake. "Yes," she said. "We insist."

I woke to the sound of whales. A deep, resonant huffing and groaning I could feel in my bones, a sound like trombones and English horns. It was light. I glanced round and saw that the Tsunamis were gone, hurriedly pulled on my clothes, grabbed my camera, and slipped out the door. There was no need to wake Stephanie.

The sky was overcast and the wind was still blowing a steady gale—it threw sand in my face as I made my way down to the cove where the Tsunamis kept their inflatable raft. There were birds everywhere—gulls whitening the sky, cormorants diving for fish, penguins loitering among the rocks as if they'd been carved of wood. Elephant seals and their pups sprawled on the beach; right whales spouted in the bay. It was like a *National Geographic Special.* I took a few shots of the seals, then worked my way down the shoreline until I found Grace and Melia perched atop a sand dune with a pair of binoculars and a notepad. Grace was wearing a windbreaker, white shorts, and a scarf; Melia was six years old.

Grace waved. "Want to go out in the boat?" she called.

I stood in water up to my knees, bracing the raft, while Grace pulled the starter cord and Melia held my Bronica. As we lurched off into the persistent swells I found myself thinking of Nick, Gary, and Ernie, but my initial fears proved unfounded: Grace was a faultless and assured pilot. We cut diagonally across the bay toward a distant sand spit. Gulls keened overhead, seals barked, spray flew, and then, before I could even get my camera focused, a big right pounded the water with his massive flukes, not thirty feet from us. "That was Bob Tail," Grace said, laughing.

I was wiping the spray from my lens. "How could you tell?"

"Easy. There's a piece missing from his left fluke."

We cruised the bay, and I was introduced to thirty whales or so, some recognized by name, others anonymous. I saw Gray Spot, Cyclops, Farrah Fawcett, and Domino, and actually got close enough to touch one of them. He was skimming the surface, black as a barge and crusted over with barnacles and lice, the huge yellowed mesh of his baleen exposed like the insides of a piano. Grace wheeled the raft round on him, throttle cranked down to idle, and as we came up alongside him I reached out and patted his cool, smooth hide. It was like patting a very wet horse the size of a house. I laid my open palm against the immensity of the whale's flank and for one mad moment thought I could feel the blood coursing through him, the colossal heart beating time with the roll of the tides and the crash of distant oceans; I felt I was reaching out and touching the great steaming heart of the planet itself. And then, in a rush of foam, he was gone.

For the next two weeks I spent mornings, afternoons—and when the light was good—evenings out on the bay. Stephanie came out with us once or twice, but preferred beachcombing with the girls; Shuhei was busy with the other boat, running up to Punta Tombo and back—something to do with his sonar dishes. He was gathering data on the above-water sounds of the right whale, while

Grace was busy surveying the local population for size, color, distinguishing characteristics. She was also intent on observing their breeding behavior.

One afternoon we came upon a female floating belly up. Two males—one an adolescent no more than two-thirds her size—were nudging her, shoving at her great inert form with their callused snouts like a pair of beavers trying to maneuver a log. Grace cut the engine and pulled out her notepad. "Is she dead?" I asked.

Grace laughed. The sun was climbing, and she held up a hand to shade her eyes as she looked at me. "They're mating," she said. "Or about to."

"A *ménage à trois?*"

She explained it, patiently. The female was rejecting her suitors, heaving her working parts from the water to avoid being taken forcibly. The reason for the cold flipper was anybody's guess. Perhaps she was tired, or suffering from a cold, or simply discriminating. She did have a problem, though. Since she couldn't breathe while inverted, she'd have to right herself every fifteen minutes or so to take a quick breath. And then they'd be on her.

The first time she rolled over we recognized her as Domino, so named for the symmetrical arrangement of callosities on her forehead. She was an adept coquette: rolling, spouting, filling her lungs, and turning belly up again before her suitors had a chance. I made some sort of joke about the prom and the back seat of a Studebaker. Grace giggled, the raft bobbed, we had peanut butter sandwiches—and waited.

Grace told me about growing up over her father's sushi bar in Little Tokyo, about dropping out of veterinary school to study oceanography at Miami, about Osaka and Shuhei. I told her about the crested tit and the capybara, and was in the middle of a devastatingly witty aperçu of the Junior Miss world when suddenly the raft was rammed from behind and tossed into the air like a bit of driftwood. A third male, big as an express train, had come charging past us in the heat of his passion, intent on Domino. We were shaken, but unhurt. The raft was right side up, the camera round my neck, the notepad in Grace's lap.

Meanwhile, it became clear that the interloper was not about to stand on ceremony. He chased off his rivals, pounded the water to a froth with his tail, forced Domino over, and ravished her. It was frightening, appalling, fascinating— like nothing I'd ever imagined. They re-enacted the birth of Surtsey, the consolidation of the moon, the eruption of Vesuvius. He slid beneath her, belly to belly, locked his flippers in hers and pitched into her. Leviathan indeed.

I was swollen with emotion, transported, ticking with excitement. So awestruck I hadn't taken a single photograph. Grace's hand was on my knee. The raft rose and settled, rose and settled, as if keeping time with each monumental thrust and heave. Somehow—I have no clear recollection of how it happened— we were naked. And then we were on the floor of the raft, gently undulating rubber, the cries of gulls, salt sea spray, locked in a mystery and a rhythm that defied the drift of continents and the receding of the waters.

■ ■ ■

A month later, in New York, I ran into Harry Macey at a bar. "So what gives with Grace and Shuhei?" he said.

"What do you mean?"

I hadn't heard? There'd been some sort of blowup between them. A vicious temper. Stormy. Hadn't I noticed? Well, he'd really taken it to her: black eye, scratched cornea, right arm in a sling. She was in San Francisco with the children. He was in Miami, brooding. The project was dead.

Harry ground out his cigarette in the ashtray he held in his palm. "Did you notice any strain between them when you were down there?"

"None."

He grinned. "Cabin fever, I guess, huh? I mean, I take it it's pretty bleak down there." He ordered me another drink. "So listen," he said. "You interested in flying out to the Azores? There's a big broil going on over that little local whaling operation—the Portuguese thing."

I downed my drink in a gulp. I felt like a saboteur, a killer, the harpoonist crouched in the bow of the rushing boat. "If you want to know the truth," I said, holding his eyes, "I'm just a little bit tired of whales right now."

(1979)

A WOMEN'S RESTAURANT

. . . the monomaniac incarnation of all those malicious
agencies which some deep men feel eating in them, till
they are left living on with half a heart and half a lung.

—Melville, *Moby Dick*

I

It is a women's restaurant. Men are not permitted. Women go there to be in the company of other women, to sit in the tasteful rooms beneath the ancient revolving fans and the cool green of spilling plants, to cross or uncross their legs as they like, to chat, sip liqueurs, eat. At the door, the first time they enter, they are asked to donate twenty-five cents and they are issued a lifetime membership card. Thus the women's restaurant has the legal appearance of a private club, and its proprietors, Grace and Rubie, avoid running afoul of the antidiscrimination laws. A women's restaurant. What goes on there, precisely, no man knows. I am a man. I am burning to find out.

This I do know: they drink wine. I have been out back, at night, walking my dog, and I have seen the discarded bottles: chablis, liebfraumilch, claret, mountain burgundy, Bristol Cream. They eat well too. The garbage is rich with dark exotic coffee grounds and spiced teas, the heads of sole, leaves of artichoke, shells of oyster. There is correspondence in the trash as well. Business things for the most part, but once there was a letter from Grace's mother in Moscow, Iowa. Some of the women smoke cigars. Others—perhaps the same ones—drive motorcycles. I watched two of them stutter up on a Triumph 750. In leathers. They walked like meatpackers, heavy, shoulders back, hips tight. Up the steps of the front porch, through the curtained double doors, and in. The doors closed like eyes in mascara.

There is more. Grace, for instance. I know Grace. She is tall, six three or four I would guess, thin and slightly stooped, her shoulders rounded like a question mark. Midthirties. Not married. She walks her square-headed cat on a leash, an advocate of women's rights. Rubie I have spoken with. If Grace is austere, a cactus tall and thorny, Rubie is lush, a spreading peony. She is a dancer. Five feet tall, ninety pounds, twenty-four years old. Facts. She told me one afternoon, months ago, in a bar. I was sitting at a table, alone, reading, a glass of beer sizzling in the sunlight through the window. Her arms and shoulders were bare, the thin straps of her dancer's tights, blue jeans. She was twirling, on point, between groups of people, her laughter like a honky-tonk piano. She came up from behind, ran her finger along the length of my nose, called it elegant. Her own nose was a pug nose. We talked. She struck poses, spoke of her body and the rigors of dancing, showed me the hard muscle of her arms. The sun slanted through the high windows and lit her hair. She did not ask about my life, about the book I was reading, about how I make a living. She did not sit down. When she swept away in a series of glissades, her arms poised, I ordered another beer. She wouldn't know me on the street.

The women's restaurant fronts a street that must have been a main thoroughfare fifty years ago. It comprises the whole of an old mansion, newly painted and shuttered. There is a fence, a gate, a tree, a patch of lawn. Gargoyles. The mayor may once have lived there. On either side blocks of two-story brick buildings stretch to the street corners like ridges of glacial detritus. Apartments above, storefronts below: a used clothing store, an organic merchant, a candle shop. Across the street, incongruous, is a bar that features a picture window and topless dancers. From behind this window, washed in shadow, I reconnoiter the women's restaurant.

I have watched women of every stripe pass through those curtained front doors: washerwomen, schoolmarms, gymnasts, waitresses, Avon ladies, Scout leaders, meter maids, grandmothers, great-grandmothers, spinsters, widows, dykes, gay divorcées, the fat, the lean, the wrinkled, the bald, the sagging, the firm, women in uniform, women in scarves and bib overalls, women in stockings, skirts, and furs, the towering Grace, the flowing Rubie, a nun, a girl with a plastic leg—and yes, even the topless dancers. There is something disturbing about this gathering of women, this classless convocation, this gynecomorphous melting pot. I think of Lysistrata, Gertrude Stein, Carry Nation.

My eyes and ears are open. Still, what I have come to know of Grace & Rubie's is what any interested observer might know. I hunger for an initiate's knowledge.

II

I have made my first attempt to crack the women's restaurant.

The attempt was repulsed.

I was sitting at the picture window of the topless bar, chain-drinking tequila and tonic, watching the front porch of Grace & Rubie's, the bloom of potted flowers, the promise of the curtained doors, and women, schools of them, electric with color, slamming car doors, dismounting from bicycles, motorcycles, trotting up the steps, in and out, tropical fish behind a spotted pane of glass. The sun was drifting toward the horizon, dipping behind the twin chimneys, spooning honey over the roof, the soft light blurring edges and corners, smoothing back the sneers of the gargoyles. It was then that I spotted Rubie. Her walk fluid and unperturbed as a drifting skater. There was another girl with her, an oriental girl. Black hair like a coat. I watched the door gape and then swallow them. Then I stood, put some money in my pocket, left some on the table, and stepped out into the street.

It was warm. The tree was budding. The sun had dropped a notch and the house flooded the street with shadow. I swam toward it, blood beating quick, stopped at the gate to look both ways, pushed through and mounted the steps. Then made my first mistake. I knocked. Knocked. Who knocks at the door of a restaurant? No one answered. I could hear music through the door. Electric jazz. I peered through the oval windows set in the door and saw that the curtains were very thick indeed. I felt uneasy. Knocked again.

After an interval Grace opened the door. Her expression was puzzled. "Yes?" she said.

I was looking beyond her, feeling the pulse of the music, aware of a certain indistinct movement in the background, concentrating on the colors, plants, polished woodwork. Underwater. Chagall.

"Can I help you?"

"Yes, you can," I said. "I'd like—ah—a cup of coffee for starters, and I'd like to see the menu. And your wine list."

"I'm very sorry," Grace said. "But this is a women's restaurant."

III

A women's restaurant. The concept inflames me. There are times, at home, fish poached, pots scrubbed, my mind gone blank, when suddenly it begins to rise in my consciousness, a sunken log heaving to the surface. A women's restaurant. The injustice of it, the snobbery, the savory dark mothering mystery: what do they *do* in there?

I picture them, Rubie, Grace, the oriental girl, the nun, the girl with one leg, all of them—picture them sipping, slouching, dandling sandals from their great toes (a mental peep beneath the skirts). I see them dropping the coils of their hair, unfastening their brassieres, rubbing the makeup from their faces. They are soft, heavy, glowing with muliebrity. The pregnant ones remove their tentish blouses, pinching shoes, slacks, underwear, and begin a slow primitive shuffle to the African beat of the drums and the cold moon music of the electric piano. The others watch, chanting, an arcane language, a formula, locked in a rhythm and a mystery that soar grinning above all things male, dark and fertile as the earth.

Or perhaps they're shooting pool in the paneled back room, cigars smoking, brandy in snifters, eyes intense, their breasts pulled toward the earth, the slick cue sticks easing through the dark arches of their fingers, stuffed birds on the walls, the glossy balls clacking, riding down the black pockets like burrowing things darting for holes in the ground . . .

IV

Last night there was a fog, milk in an atomizer. The streets steamed. Turner, I thought. Fellini. Jack the Ripper. The dog led me to the fence outside the women's restaurant, where he paused to sniff and balance on three legs. The house was a bank of shadow, dark in a negligee of moonlit mist. Fascinating, enigmatic, compelling as a white whale. Grace's VW hunched at the curb behind me, the moon sat over the peaked roof cold as a stone, my finger was on the gate. The gate was latched. I walked on, then walked back. Tied the dog to one of the pickets, reached through to unlatch the gate, and stepped into the front yard at Grace & Rubie's for the second time.

This time I did not knock.

Instead I slipped up to a window and peered through a crack in the curtains. It was black as the inside of a closet. On an impulse I tried the window. It was locked. At that moment a car turned into the street, tires chirping, engine revving, the headlights like hounds of heaven. Rubie's Fiat.

I lost my head. Ran for the gate, tripped, scrambled back toward the house, frantic, ashamed, mortified. Trapped. The car hissed to a stop, the engine sang a hysterical chorus, the headlights died. I heard voices, the swat of car doors. Keys rattling. I crouched. Then crept into the shrubbery beneath the porch. Out by the fence the dog began to whimper.

Heels. Muffled voices. Then Rubie: "Aww, a puppy. And what's he doing out here, huh?" This apparently addressed to the dog, whose whimpering cut a new octave. I could hear his tail slapping the fence. Then a man's voice, impatient. The gate creaked, slapped shut. Footsteps came up the walk. Stopped at the porch. Rubie giggled. Then there was silence. My hand was bleeding. I was stretched out prone, staring at the ground. They were kissing. "Hey," said Rubie, soft as fur, "I like your nose—did I tell you that?"

"How about letting me in tonight," he whispered. "Just this once."

Silence again. The rustle of clothing. I could have reached out and shined their shoes. The dog whimpered.

"The poor pup," Rubie breathed.

"Come on," the guy said. I hated him.

And then, so low I could barely catch it, like a sleeping breath or the hum of a moth's wing: "Okay." Okay? I was outraged. This faceless cicisbeo, this panting lover, schmuck, male—this shithead was going to walk into Grace & Rubie's just like that? A kiss and a promise? I wanted to shout out, call the police, stop this unthinkable sacrilege.

Rubie's key turned in the lock. I could hear the shithead's anticipatory breathing. A wave of disillusion deadened me. And then suddenly the porch light was blazing, bright as a cafeteria. I shrank. Grace's voice was angry. "What is this?" she hissed. I held my breath.

"Look—" said Rubie.

"No men allowed," said Grace. "None. Ever. Not now, not tomorrow—you know how I feel about this sort of thing."

"—Look, I pay rent here too—"

I could hear the shithead shuffling his feet on the dry planks of the porch. Then Grace: "I'm sorry. You'll have to leave." In the shadows, the ground damp, my hand bleeding, I began to smile.

The door slammed. Someone had gone in. Then I heard Grace's voice swelling to hurricane pitch, and Rubie raging back at her like a typhoon. Inside. Muffled by the double doors, oval windows, thick taffeta curtains. The shithead's feet continued to shuffle on the porch. A moment ticked by, the voices storming inside, and then the light cut out. Dead. Black. Night.

My ears followed the solitary footsteps down the walk, through the gate and into the street.

V

I shadowed Rubie for eight blocks this morning. There were packages in her arms. Her walk was the walk of a slow-haunching beast. As she passed the dark windows of the shops she turned to watch her reflection, gliding, flashing in the sun, her bare arms, clogs, the tips of her painted toenails peeping from beneath the wide-bottomed jeans. Her hair loose, undulating across her back like a wheatfield in the wind. She stopped under the candy-striped pole outside Red's Barber Shop.

I crossed the street, sat on a bench and opened a book. Then I saw Grace: slouching, wide-striding, awkward. Her sharp nose, the bulb of frizzed hair. She walked up to Rubie, unsmiling. They exchanged cheek-pecks and stepped into the barbershop.

When they emerged I dropped my book: Rubie was desecrated. Her head shaven, the wild lanks of hair hacked to stubble. Charlie Manson, I thought. Auschwitz. Nuns and neophytes. Grace was smiling. Rubie's ears stuck out from her head, the color of butchered chicken. Her neck and temples were white as flour, blue-veined and vulnerable. I was appalled.

They walked quickly, stiffly, Rubie hurrying to match Grace's long strides. Grace a sunflower, Rubie a stripped dandelion. I followed them to the women's restaurant. Rubie did not turn to glance at her reflection in the shop windows.

VI

I have made my second attempt to crack the women's restaurant.

The attempt was repulsed.

This time I was not drunk: I was angry. Rubie's desecration had been rankling me all day. While I could approve of Grace's firmness with the faceless cicisbeo, I could not countenance her severity toward Rubie. She is like a stroke of winter, I thought, folding up Rubie's petals, traumatizing her roots. An early frost, a blight. But then I am neither poet nor psychologist. My metaphors are primitive, my actions impulsive.

I kicked the gate open, stamped up the front steps, twisted the doorknob and stepped into the women's restaurant. My intentions were not clear. I thought vaguely of rescuing Rubie, of entering that bastion of womanhood, of sex and mystery and rigor, and of walking out with her on my arm. But I was stunned. Frozen. Suddenly, and after all those weeks, I had done it. I was inside.

The entrance hall was narrow and dark, candlelit, overheated, the walls shaggy with fern and wandering Jew. Music throbbed like blood. I felt squeezed, pinched, confined, Buster Crabbe in the shrinking room. My heart left me. I was slouching. Ahead, at the far end of the hallway, a large room flowered in darkness and lights glowed red. Drum, drum, drum, the music like footsteps. That dim and deep central chamber drawing me: a women's restaurant, a women's restaurant: the phrase chanted in my head.

And then the door opened behind me. I turned. Two of the biker girls stepped through the doorway, crowding the hall. One of them was wearing a studded denim jacket, the collar turned up. Both were tall. Short-haired. Their shoulders congested the narrow hallway. I wheeled and started for the darkened room ahead. But stopped in midstride. Grace was there, a tray in her hand, her face looking freshly slapped. "You!" she hissed. The tray fell, glasses shattered, I was grabbed from behind. Rabbit-punched. One of the biker girls began emitting fierce gasping Ninja sounds as her white fists and sneakered feet lashed out at me. I went down, thought I saw Rubie standing behind Grace, a soft flush of alarm suffusing her cheeks. A rhythm developed. The biker girls kicked, I huddled. Then they had me by belt and collar, the door was flung open and they rocked me, one, two, three, the bum's rush, down the front steps and onto the walk. The door slammed.

I lay there for a moment, hurting. Then I became aware of the clack of heels on the pavement. A woman was coming up the walk: skirt, stockings, platforms.

She hesitated when she saw me there. And then, a look of disgust creasing her makeup, she stepped over me as if she were stepping over a worm or a fat greasy slug washed up in a storm. Her perfume was devastating.

VII

I have been meditating on the essential differences between men and women, isolating distinguishing traits. The meditation began with points of dissimilarity. Women, I reasoned, do not have beards, while they do have breasts. And yet I have seen women with beards and men with breasts—in fact, I came to realize, all men have breasts. Nipples too. Ah, but women have long hair, I thought. Narrow shoulders, expansive hips. Five toes on each foot. Pairs of eyes, legs, arms, ears. But ditto men. They are soft, yielding, dainty, their sensibilities refined—they like shopping. I ran through all the stereotypes, dismissed them one after another. There was only one distinguishing sexual characteristic, I concluded. A hole. A hole as dark and strange, as fascinating and forbidding, as that interdicted entrance to Grace and Rubie's. Birth and motherhood, I thought. The maw of mystery.

I have also been perusing a letter from Rubie, addressed to a person named Jack. The letter is a reconstruction of thirty-two fragments unearthed in the trash behind the women's restaurant. "I miss you and I love you, Jack," the letter said in part, "but I cannot continue seeing you. My responsibilities are here. Yes I remember the night on the beach, the night in the park, the night at the cabin, the night on the train, the night in Saint Patrick's Cathedral—memories I will always cherish. But it's over. I am here. A gulf separates us. I owe it to Grace. Take care of yourself and your knockout nose. Love, R." The letter disturbs me. In the same way that the women's restaurant disturbs me. Secrets, stifling secrets. I want admission to them all.

VIII

The girl in the department store asked me what size my wife took. I hesitated. "She's a big one," I said. "About the same size as me." The girl helped me pick out a pink polyester pantsuit, matching brassiere, tall-girl panty hose. Before leaving the store I also visited the ladies' shoe department and the cosmetic counter. At the cosmetic counter I read from a list: glosser, blusher, hi-lighter, eyeshadow (crème, cake and stick), mascara, eyeliner, translucent powder, nail polish (frosted pink), spike eyelashes, luscious tangerine lipstick, tweezers, a bottle of My Sin and the current issue of *Be Beautiful*. At the shoe department I asked for Queen Size.

IX

After two weeks of laying foundation, brushing on, rubbing in, tissuing off, my face was passable. Crude, yes—like the slick masks of the topless dancers—but passable nonetheless. And my hair, set in rollers and combed out in a shoulder-length flip, struck close on the heels of fashion. I was no beauty, but neither was I a dog.

I eased through the gate, sashayed up the walk, getting into the rhythm of it. Bracelets chimed at my wrists, rings shot light from my fingers. Up the steps, through the front door and into that claustrophobic hallway. My movement fluid, silky, the T-strap flats gliding under my feet like wind on water. I was on-stage, opening night, and fired for the performance. But then I had a shock. One of the biker girls slouched at the end of the hallway lighting a cigar. I tossed my chin and strutted by. Our shoulders brushed. She grinned. "Hi," she breathed. I stepped past her, and into the forbidden room.

It was dark. Candlelit. There were tables, booths, sofas and lounge chairs. Plants, hangings, carpets, woodwork. Women. I held back. Then felt a hand on my elbow. It was the biker. "Can I buy you a drink?" she said.

I shook my head, wondering what to do with my voice. Falsetto? A husky whisper?

"Come on," she said. "Get loose. You're new here, right?—you need some-body to show you around." She pinched my elbow and ushered me to a booth across the room—wooden benches like church pews. I slid in, she eased down beside me. I could feel her thigh against mine. "Listen," I said, opting for the husky whisper, "I'd really rather be alone—"

Suddenly Rubie was standing over us. "Would you like something?" she said.

The biker ordered a Jack Daniel's on the rocks. I wanted a beer, asked for a sunrise. "Menu?" said Rubie. She was wearing a leather apron, and she seemed slimmer, her shoulders rounded. Whipped, I thought. Her ears protruded and her brushcut bristled. She looked like a Cub Scout. An Oliver Twist.

"Please," I said, huskily.

She looked at me. "Is this your first time?"

I nodded.

She dug something—a lavender card—from an apron pocket. "This is our membership card. It's twenty-five cents for a lifetime membership. Shall I put it on the bill?"

I nodded. And followed her with my eyes as she padded off.

The biker turned to me. "Ann Jenks," she said, holding out her hand.

I froze. A name, a name, a name. This part I hadn't considered. I pretended to study the menu. The biker's hand hung in the air. "Ann Jenks," she repeated.

"Valerie," I whispered, and nearly shook hands. Instead I held out two fin-gers, ladylike. She pinched them, rubbed her thumb over the knuckles and looked into my eyes.

Then Rubie appeared with our drinks. "Cheers," said Ann Jenks. I downed the libation like honey and water.

An hour and a half later I was two sheets to the wind and getting cocky. Here I was, embosomed in the very nave, the very omphalos of furtive femininity—a prize patron of the women's restaurant, a member, privy to its innermost secrets. I sipped at my drink, taking it all in. There they were—women—chewing, drinking, digesting, chatting, giggling, crossing and uncrossing their legs. Shoes off, feet up. Smoking cigarettes, flashing silverware, tapping time to the music. Women among women. I bathed in their soft chatter, birdsong, the laughter like falling coils of hair. I lit a cigarette, and grinned. No more fairybook-hero thoughts of rescuing Rubie—oh no, this was paradise.

Below the table, in the dark, Ann Jenks's fingertips massaged my knee.

I studied her face as she talked (she was droning on about awakened consciousness, liberation from the mores of straight society, feminist terrorism). Her cheekbones were set high and cratered the cheeks below, the hair lay flat across her crown and rushed straight back over her ears, like duck's wings. Her eyes were black, the mouth small and raw. I snubbed out the cigarette, slipped my hand under the jacket and squeezed her breast. Then I put my tongue in her mouth.

"Hey," she said, "want to go?"

I asked her to get me one more drink. When she got up I slid out and looked for the restroom. It was a minor emergency: six tequila sunrises and a carafe of dinner wine tearing at my vitals. I fought an impulse to squeeze my organ.

There were plants everywhere. And behind the plants, women. I passed the oriental girl and two housewives/divorcées in a booth, a nun on a divan, a white-haired woman and her daughter. Then I spotted the one-legged girl, bump and grind, passing through a door adjacent to the kitchen. I followed.

The restroom was pink, carpeted: imitation marble countertops, floodlit mirrors, three stalls. Grace was emerging from the middle one as I stepped through the door. She smiled at me. I smiled back, sweetly, my bladder aflame. Then rushed into the stall, fought down the side zipper, tore at the silky panties, and forgot to sit down. I pissed, long and hard. Drunk. Studying the graffiti—women's graffiti. I laughed, flushed, turned to leave. But there was a problem: a head suspended over the door to the stall. Angry eyes. The towering Grace.

I shrugged my shoulders and held out my palms. Grace's face was the face of an Aztec executioner. This time there would be no quarter. I felt sick. And then suddenly my shoulder hit the door like a wrecker's ball, Grace sat in the sink, and the one-legged girl began gibbering from the adjoining compartment. Out the door and into the kitchen, rushing down an aisle lined with ovens, the stink of cooking food, scraps, greased-over plates, a screen door at the far end, slipping in the T-straps, my brassiere working round, Grace's murderous rasping shriek at my back, STOP HIM! STOP HIM!, and Rubie, pixie Rubie, sack of garbage in her hand at the door.

Time stopped. I looked into Rubie's eyes, imploring, my breath cut in gasps, five feet from her. She let the garbage fall. Then dropped her head and right shoulder, and hit my knees like a linebacker. I went down. My face in coffee grounds and eggshells. Rubie's white white arms shackles on my legs and on my will.

X

I have penetrated the women's restaurant, yes, but in actuality it was little more than a rape. There was no sympathy, I did not belong: why kid myself? True, I do have a lifetime membership card, and I was—for a few hours at any rate—an un-exceptionable patron of the women's restaurant. But that's not enough. I am not satisfied. The obsession grows in me, pregnant, swelling, insatiable with the first taste of fulfillment. Before I am through I will drink it to satiety. I have plans.

Currently, however, I am unable to make bail. Criminal trespass (Rubie testified that I was there to rob them, which, in its way, is true, I suppose), and assault (Grace showed the bruises on her shins and voice box where the stall door had hit her). Probation I figure. A fine perhaps. Maybe even psychiatric evaluation.

The police have been uncooperative, antagonistic even. Malicious jokes, pranks, taunts, their sweating red faces fastened to the bars night and day. There has even been brutality. Oddly enough—perhaps as a reaction to their gibes—I have come to feel secure in these clothes. I was offered shirt, pants, socks, shoes, and I refused them. Of course, these things are getting somewhat gritty, my makeup is a fright, and my hair has lost its curl. And yet I defy them.

In drag. I like the sound of it. I like the feel. And, as I say, I have plans. The next time I walk through those curtained doors at Grace & Rubie's there will be no dissimulation. I will stroll in and I will belong, an initiate, and I will sit back and absorb the mystery of it, feed on honeydew and drink the milk of paradise. There are surgeons who can assure it.

After all, it is a women's restaurant.

(1976)

THAWING OUT

They were feet that he loved, feet that belonged in high heels, calfskin, furry slippers with button eyes and rabbit ears, and here they were, naked to the snow. He was hunched in his denim jacket, collar up, scarf wound tight round his throat, and his fingers were so numb he could barely get a cigarette lit. She stood beside him in her robe, barely shivering, the wild ivy of her hair gone white with a dusting of snow. He watched her lift her arms, watched her breasts rise gently as she fought back her hair and pulled the bathing cap tight to her skull. He took a quick drag on the cigarette and looked away.

There were maybe twenty cars in the lot: station wagons, Volvos, VW Bugs, big steel-blue Buicks with their crushproof bumpers and nautical vents. An inch of new snow softened the frozen ruts and the strips of yellowed ice that lay like sores beneath it. Beyond the lot, a short slope, the white rails of the dock, and the black lapping waters of the Hudson. It was five of two—he checked his watch—but the belly of the sky hung so low it might have been dusk.

A moment earlier, when Naina had stepped from her car, a chain reaction had begun, and now the car doors were flung open one by one and the others began to emerge. They were old, all of them, as far as he could see. A few middle-aged, maybe. Some in robes, some not. The men were ghosts in baggy trunks, bowlegged, splay-footed and bald, with fallen bellies and dead gray hair fringing their nipples. He thought of Buster Keaton, in his antiquated swimsuit and straw boater. The women were heavier, their excrescences forced like sausage stuffing into the black spandex casings of their one-piece suits. Their feet were bloated and red, their thighs mottled with disuse, their upper arms heavy, bulbous, the color of suet. They called out to one another gaily, like schoolgirls at a picnic, in accents thick with another time and place.

"Jesus, Naina," he whispered, turning to her, "this is crazy. It's like something out of Fellini. Look at them."

Naina gave him a soft tight-lipped smile—a tolerant smile, understated, serene, a smile that stirred his groin and made him go weak with something like hunger—and then her mother's car schussed into the lot. The whole group turned as one to watch as the ancient, rust-eaten Pontiac heaved over the ruts toward them. He could see the grin on Mama Vyshensky's broad, faintly mustachioed face as she fought the wheel and rode the bumps. He froze for an instant, certain her final, veering skid would send her careening into the side of his Camaro, but the big splotched bumper jerked to a halt six feet short of him. "Naina!" she cried, lumbering from the car to embrace her daughter as if she hadn't seen her in twenty years. "And Marty," turning to envelop him in a quick bear hug. "Nice weather, no?"

The breath streamed from her nostrils. She was a big woman with dimples and irrepressible eyes, a dead ringer for Nina Khrushchev. Her feet—as swollen and red as any of the others'—were squeezed into a pair of cheap plastic thongs and she wore a tentlike swimsuit in a shade of yellow that made the Camaro look dull. "Sonia!" she shouted, turning away and flagging her hand. "Marfa!" A gabble of Ukrainian, and then the group began to gather.

Marty felt the wind on his exposed hand and he took a final drag on his cigarette, flicked the butt away, and plunged his hand deep in his pocket. This was really something. Crazy. He felt like a visitor to another planet. One old bird was rubbing snow into the hair of his bare chest, another skidding down the slope on his backside. "A toast!" someone shouted, and they all gathered round a bottle of Stolichnaya, thimble-sized glasses materializing in their hands. And when one old man with reddened ears asked him where his swim trunks were, Marty said it wasn't cold enough for him, not by half.

They drank. One round, then another, and then they shouted something he didn't catch and flung the glasses over their shoulders. Two ponderous old women began fighting playfully over a towel while Naina's mother shouted encouragement and the others laughed like wizened children. And Naina? Naina stood out among them like a virgin queen, the youngest by thirty years. At least. That's what it was, he suddenly realized—an ancient rite, sacrifice of the virgin. But they were a little late in this case, he thought, and felt his groin stir again. He squeezed her hand, gazed off into the curtain of falling snow, and saw the mountains fade and reappear in the distance.

Then he heard the first splash and turned to see a flushed bald head bobbing in the water and the old man with reddened ears suspended in the air, knees clutched tightly to his chest. There was a second splash—a real wallop—and then another, and then they were all in, frolicking like seals. Naina was one of the last to go, tucking her chin, planting her feet, her thighs flexing as she floated out into the tumult of the storm and cut the flat black surface in perfect grace and harmony.

The whole thing left him cold.

They'd been going together a month when she first took him to meet her mother. It was mid-October, chilly, a persistent rain beating the leaves from the trees. He didn't want to meet her mother. He wanted to stay in bed and touch every part of her. He was twenty-three and he'd had enough of mothers.

"Don't expect anything fancy," Naina said, sitting close as he drove. "It's the house I grew up in. Mama's no housekeeper."

He glanced at her, her face as open as a doll's, high forehead, thick eyebrows, eyes pale as ice, and that hair. That's what caught him the first time he saw her. That and her voice, as hushed and placid as the voice talking inside his head. "How long do we have to stay?" he said.

The house was in Cold Spring, two stories, white with green trim, in need of paint. It was an old house, raked back from the steep hill that dropped through town to the foot of the river. Naina's mother was waiting for them at the door. "This is Marty," she pronounced, as if he could have been anyone else, and to his horror, she embraced him. "In," she said, "in," sweeping them before her and slamming the door with a boom. "Such nasty day."

Inside, it was close and hot, the air heavy with the odor of cooking. He was no gourmet, and he couldn't identify the aroma, but it brought him back to high school and the fat-armed women who stood guard over the big simmering pots in the cafeteria. It wasn't a good sign.

"Sit," said Naina's mother, gesturing toward a swaybacked sofa draped with an afghan and three overfed cats. "Shoo," she said, addressing the cats, and he sat. He looked around him. There were doilies everywhere, lamps with stained shades, mounds of newspapers and magazines. On the wall above the radiator, the framed portrait of a blue-eyed Christ.

Naina sat beside him while her mother trundled back and forth, rearranging the furniture, fussing with things, and all the while watching him out of the corner of her eye. He was sleeping with her daughter, and she knew it. "A peppermint," she said, whirling round on him with a box the size of a photo album, "maybe you want? Beer maybe? A nice glass of buttermilk?"

He didn't want anything. "No thanks," he managed, the voice stuck in his throat. Naina took a peppermint.

Finally the old woman settled into the sofa beside him—beside him, when there were six other chairs in the room—and he felt himself sinking into the cushions as into a morass. Something was boiling over in the kitchen: he could smell it, hear it hissing. Sitting, she towered over him. "You like my Naina?" she asked.

The question stunned him. She'd tossed him a medicine ball and he was too weak to toss it back. Like? Did he like her Naina? He lingered over her for hours at a time, hours that became days, and he did things to her in the dark and with the lights on too. Did he like her? He wanted to jump through the roof.

"You call me Mama," she said, patting his hand. "None of this Mrs. business." She was peering into his eyes like an ophthalmologist. "So. You like her?" she repeated.

Miserable, squirming, glancing at Naina—that smile, tight-lipped and serene, her eyes dancing—and then back to her mother, he couldn't seem to find anything to focus on but his shoes. "Yeah," he whispered.

"Um," the old woman grunted, narrowing her eyes as if she were deciding something. Then she rose heavily to her feet, and as he looked up in surprise and mortification, she spread her arms above him in a grand gesture. "All this," she said, "one days is yours."

"So what do you mean, like love and marriage and all that crap?"

Marty was staring down into his Harvey Wallbanger. It was November. Naina was at art class and he was sitting in the bar of the Bum Steer, talking about her. With Terry. Terry was just back from San Francisco and he was wearing a cowboy hat and an earring. "No," Marty protested, "I mean she's hot, that's all. And she's a great person. You're going to like her. Really. She's—"

"What's her mother look like?"

Mama Vyshensky rose up before his eyes, her face dark with a five o'clock shadow, her legs like pylons, the square of her shoulders and the drift of her collapsed bosom. "What do you mean?"

Terry was drinking a mug of beer with a shot of tomato juice on the side. He took a swallow of beer, then upended the tomato juice in the mug. The stain spread like blood. "I mean, they all wind up looking like their mother. And they all want something from you." Terry stirred the tomato beer with his forefinger and then sucked it thoughtfully. "Before you know it you got six slobbering kids, a little pink house, and you're married to her mother."

The thought of it made him sick. "Not me," he said. "No way."

Terry tilted the hat back on his head and fiddled briefly with the earring. "You living together yet?"

Marty felt his face flush. He lifted his drink and put it down again. "We talked about it," he said finally, "like why pay rent on two places, you know? She's living in an apartment in Yorktown and I'm still in the bungalow. But I don't know."

Terry was grinning at him. He leaned over and gave him a cuff on the shoulder. "You're gone, man," he said. "It's all over. Birdies singing in the trees."

Marty shrugged. He was fighting back a grin. He wanted to talk about her— he was full of her—but he was toeing a fine line here. He and Terry were both men of the world, and men of the world didn't moon over their women. "There's one rule," he said, "they've got to love you first. And most. Right?"

"Amen," Terry said.

They were quiet a moment, mulling over this nugget of wisdom. Marty drained his glass and ordered another. "What the hell," Terry said, "give me another one too."

The drinks came. They sipped meditatively. "Shit," Terry said, "you know what? I saw your mother. At La Guardia. It was weird. I mean I'm coming in after six months out there and I get off the plane and there's your mother."

"Who was she with?"

"I don't know. Some skinny old white-haired dude with a string tie and a suit. She said hello to me and I shook the guy's hand. They were going to Bermuda, I think she said."

Marty said nothing. He sipped at his drink. "She's a bitch," he said finally.

"Yeah," Terry said, reprising the ceremony of the beer and the tomato juice, "whatever. But listen," turning to him now, his face lit beneath the brim of his ten-gallon hat, "let me tell you about San Francisco—I mean that's where it's really happening."

In January, a month after he'd watched her part the frigid waters of the Hudson, the subject of living arrangements came up again. She'd cooked for him, a tomato-and-noodle dish she called spaghetti but that was pure Kiev in flavor, texture, and appearance—which is not to say it was bad, just that it wasn't spaghetti as he knew it. He had three helpings, then he built a fire and they lay on the sofa together. "You know, this is crazy," she said in her softest voice, the one with the slight catch to it.

It had been a long day—he was in his first year of teaching, Special Ed, and the kids had been wild. They'd sawed the oak handles off the tools in shop class and chucked stones at the schoolbus during lunch break. He was drowsy. "Hm?" was all the response he could manage.

Her voice purred in his ear. "Spending all my time here; I mean, half my clothes here and half at my place. It's crazy."

He said nothing, but his eyes were open.

She was silent too. A log shifted in the fireplace. "It's just such a waste, is all," she said finally. "The rent alone, not to mention gas and wear and tear on my car . . ."

He got up to poke the fire, his back to her. "Terry's going back to the West Coast this summer. He wants me to go along. For a vacation. I mean, I've never seen it."

"So what does that mean?" she said.

He poked the fire.

"You know I can't go," she said after a moment. "I've got courses to take at New Paltz. You know that, right?"

He felt guilty. He looked guilty. He shrugged.

Later, he made Irish coffee, heavy on sugar, cream, and whiskey. She was curled up in the corner of the sofa, her legs bare, feet tucked under her. She was spending the night.

The wind had come up and sleet began to rattle the windows. He brought the coffee to her, sat beside her and took her hand. It was then that the picture of her perched at the edge of the snowy dock came back to him. "Tell me again," he said, "about the water, how it felt."

"Hm?"

"You know, with the Polar Bear Club?"

He watched her slow smile, watched the snowy afternoon seep back into her eyes. "Oh, that—I've been doing it since I was three. It's nothing. I don't even think about it." She looked past him, staring into the flames. "You won't believe this, but it's not that cold—almost the opposite."

"You're right," he said. "I won't."

"No, really," she insisted, looking him full in the face now. She paused, shrugged, took a sip of her coffee. "It depends on your frame of mind, I guess."

At the end of June, just before he left for San Francisco, they took a trip together. He'd heard about a fishing camp in northern Quebec, a place called Chibouga-mau, where pike and walleye attacked you in the boat. There were Eskimos there, or near there, anyway. And the last four hours of driving was on dirt roads.

She had no affection for pike, or walleye either, but this was their vacation, their last chance to be together for a while. She smiled her quiet smile and packed her bag. They spent one night in Montreal and then drove the rest of the way the following day. When they got there—low hills, a scattering of crude cabins, and a river as raw and hard as metal—Marty was so excited his hands trembled on the wheel. "I want to fish," he said to the guide who greeted them.

The guide was in his forties, hard-looking, with a scar that ran in a white ridge from his ear to his Adam's apple. He was dressed in rubber knee boots, jeans, and a lumberjack shirt. "Hi" and "thank you" was about all the English he could manage. He gestured toward the near cabin.

"Ours?" Marty said, pointing first to Naina and then himself.

The guide nodded.

Marty looked up at the sun; it squatted on the horizon, bloated and misshapen.

"Listen, Naina," he said, "honey, would you mind if . . . I mean, I'm dying to wet my line and since we're paying for today and all—"

"Sure," she said. "I'll unpack. Have fun." She grinned at the guide. The guide grinned back.

A moment later, Marty was out on the river, experimentally manning the oars while the guide stood in the bow, discoursing on technique. Marty tried to listen, but French had never been his strong suit; in the next instant the guide cast a lure ahead of them and immediately connected with a fish that bent the rod double. Marty pulled at the oars, and the guide, fighting his fish, said something over his shoulder. This time, though, the guide's face was alive with urgency and the something came in an angry rush, as if he were cursing. Pull harder? Marty thought. Is that what he wants?

He dug in a bit harder, his eyes on the line and the distant explosion where the fish—it was a walleye—cut the surface. But now the guide was raving at him, nonstop, harsh and guttural, and all the while looking desperately from Marty to the bent rod and back again. Marty looked round him. The river was loud as a freight train. "What?" he shouted. "What's the matter?" And then all at once, his eyes wild, the guide heaved the pole into the water, knocked Marty aside, and took up the oars in a frenzy. Then Marty saw it, the precipice yawning before them, the crash and flow of the water, spray in his face, the shore looming up, and the guide snatching frantically at the brush shooting past them. With ten feet to spare, the guide caught a low-hanging branch, the boat jerked back, and all of a sudden Marty was in the water.

But what water! The shock of it beat the breath from him and he went under. He grasped at the air and then he was swept over the falls like a bit of fluff, pounded on the rocks, and flung ashore with the flotsam below. He was lucky. Nothing broken. The guide, muttering under his breath and shooting him murderous looks, sewed up the gash in his thumb with fishing line while Marty gritted his teeth and drank off a glass of whiskey like the wounded sheriff in an old western. It took him two hours to stop shivering.

In bed that night they heard the howling of wolves, a sound that opened up the darkness like a surgeon's blade. "It was a communication problem," Marty insisted, "that's all." Naina pressed her lips to his bruises, kneaded his back, nursed him with a sad, tender, tireless grace.

He woke at dawn, aching. She lay stiff beside him, her eyes open wide. "Will you miss me?" she said.

At first, he'd written her every day—postcards, mainly—from Des Moines, Albuquerque, the Grand Canyon. But then he got to San Francisco, found a job bartending, and drifted into another life. For a while he and Terry stayed with a girl Terry knew from his last trip, then they found a room for sixty dollars a week in a tenement off Geary, but Terry got mugged one night and the two of them moved in with a cocktail waitress Marty knew from work. Things were loose. He stopped writing. And when September came around, he didn't write to the principal at school either.

December was half gone by the time he got back.

The Camaro had broken down on him just outside Chicago—a burnt valve— and the repairs ate up everything he had. He slept in the bus station for three nights while a Pakistani with mad black eyes worked over his car, and if it wasn't for the hitchhiker who split the cost of gas with him, he'd still be there. When he finally coasted into Yorktown and pulled up at the curb outside Naina's apartment, he was running on empty. For a long while, he stood there in the street looking up at her window. It had been a joyless trip back and he'd thought of her the whole way—her mouth, her eyes, the long tapering miracle of her body, especially her body—and twice he'd stopped to send her a card. Both times he changed his mind. Better to see her, try to explain himself. But now that he was here, outside her apartment, his courage failed him.

He stood there in the cold for fifteen minutes, then started up the driveway. There was ice on the steps and he lost his footing and fell against the door with a thump that shook the frame. Then he rang the bell and listened to the crashing in his chest. A stranger came to the door, a big fat-faced woman of thirty with a baby in her arms. No, Naina didn't live there anymore. She'd left in September. No, she didn't know where she was.

He sat in the car and tried to collect himself. Her mother's, he thought, she's probably at her mother's. He patted down his pockets and counted the money. Two dollars and sixty-seven cents. A dollar for gas, a pack of cigarettes, and two phone calls.

He called his landlord first. Mr. Weiner answered the phone himself, his breathing ravaged with emphysema. He was sorry, Mr. Weiner was, but when he hadn't heard from him he'd gone ahead and rented the place to someone else. His things were in the basement—and if he didn't pick them up within the week he'd have to put them out for the trash, was that understood?

The other call was to his mother. She sounded surprised to hear from him— surprised and defensive. But had he heard? Yes, she was remarried. And no, she didn't think Roger would like it if he spent the night. It was a real shame about his teaching job, but then he always was irresponsible. She punctuated each phrase with a sigh, as if the very act of speaking were torture. All right, she sighed finally, she'd loan him a hundred dollars till he got back on his feet.

It was getting dark when he pulled up in front of the house in Cold Spring. He didn't hesitate this time—he was too miserable. Get it over with, he told himself, one way or the other.

Naina's mother answered the door, peering myopically into the cold fading light. He could smell cabbage, cat, and vinegar, felt the warmth wafting out to him. "Marty?" she said.

He'd grown his hair long and the clipped mustache had become a patchy beard. His denim jacket was faded and it was torn across the shoulder where he'd fallen flat one afternoon in Golden Gate Park, laughing at the sky and the mescaline percolating inside his brain. He wore an earring like Terry's. He wondered that she recognized him, and somehow it made him feel sorrowful—sorrowful and guilty. "Yes," he said.

There was no embrace. She didn't usher him in the door. She just stood there, the support hose sagging round her ankles.

"I, uh . . . I was looking for Naina," he said, and then, attempting a smile, "I'm back."

The old woman's face was heavy, stern, hung with folds and pouches. She didn't respond. But she was watching him in her shrewd way, totting up the changes, deciding something. "All right," she said finally, "come," and she swung back the door for him.

Inside, it was as he remembered it, nothing changed but for an incremental swelling of the heaps of magazines in the corners. She gestured for him to sit on the swaybacked sofa and took the chair across from him. A cat sprang into his lap. It was so quiet he could hear the ticking of the kitchen clock. "So, is she," he faltered, "is she living here now?—I mean, I went out to Yorktown first thing. . . ."

Mama Vyshensky slowly shook her head. "College," she said. She shrugged her big shoulders and looked away, busying herself with the arrangement of the doily on the chair arm. "When she doesn't hear from you, she goes back to college. For the Master."

He didn't know what to say. She was accusing him, he knew it. And he had no defense. "I'm sorry," he said. He stood to go.

The old woman was studying him carefully, her chin propped on one hand, eyes reduced to slits. "Your house," she said, "the bungalow. Where do you sleep tonight?"

He didn't answer. He was going to sleep in the car, in a rubble of crumpled newspaper and fast-food containers, the greasy sleeping bag pulled up over his head.

"I have a cot," she said. "In the closet."

"I was going to go over to my mother's. . . ." he said, trailing off. He couldn't seem to keep his right foot still, the heel tapping nervously at the worn floorboards.

"Sit," she said.

He did as he was told. She brought him a cup of hot tea, a bowl of boiled cabbage and ham, and a plate of cold pirogen. Eating, he tried to explain himself. "About Naina," he began, "I—"

She waved her hand in dismissal. "Don't tell me," she said. "I'm not the one you should tell."

He set the cup down and looked at her—really looked at her—for the first time.

"Day after tomorrow," she said, "the solstice, shortest day of year. You come to dock on river." She held his eyes and he thought of the day she'd offered him the whole shabby pile of the house as if it were Hyde Park itself. "Same time as last year," she said.

■ ■ ■

The day was raw, cold, the wind gusting off the river. A dead crust of snow clung to the ground, used up and discolored, dirt showing through in streaks that were like wounds. Marty got there early. He pulled into the lot and parked the Camaro behind a Lincoln the size of a Rose Parade float. He didn't want her to see him right away. He let the car run, heater going full, and lit a cigarette. For a while he listened to the radio, but that didn't feel right, so he flicked it off.

The lot gradually filled. He recognized some of the cars from the previous year, watched the white-haired old masochists maneuver over the ruts as if they were bringing 747s in for a landing. Mama Vyshensky was late, as usual, and no one made a move till her battered Pontiac turned the corner and jolted into the lot. Then the doors began to open and bare feet gripped the snow.

Still, he waited. The driver's door of the Pontiac swung open, and then the passenger's door, and he felt something rising in him, a metallic compound of hope and despair that stuck in the back of his throat. And then Naina stepped out of the car. Her back was to him, her legs long and naked, a flash of her blood-red nails against the tarnished snow. He watched her toss her head and then gather her hair in a tight knot and force it under the bathing cap. He'd slept in the car the past two nights, he'd hunkered over cups of coffee at McDonald's like a bum. He saw her and he felt weak.

The crowd began to gather around Mama Vyshensky, ancient, all of them, spindly-legged, their robes like shrouds. He recognized the old man with red ears, bent double now and hunched over a cane. And a woman he'd seen last year, heaving along in a one-piece with a ballerina fringe round the hips. They drank a toast and shouted. Then another, and they flung their glasses. Naina stood silent among them.

He waited till they began to move down the slope to the dock and then he stepped noiselessly from the car, heart pounding in his chest. By the time they'd reached the dock, Naina and her mother at the head of the group, he was already passing the stragglers. "You bring a towel?" one old woman called out to him, and another tittered. He just gave her a blank stare, hurrying now, his eyes on Naina.

As he stepped onto the dock, Naina stood poised at the far end. She dropped her robe. Then she turned and saw him. She saw him—he could read it in her eyes—though she turned away as if she hadn't. He tried to get to her, wedging himself between two heavy-breasted women and a hearty-looking old man with a white goatee, but the dock was too crowded. And then came the first splash. Naina glanced back at him and the soft smile seemed to flicker across her lips. She held his eyes now, held them across the field of drooping flesh, the body hair, the toothless mouths. Then she turned and dove.

All right, he thought, his pulse racing, all right. And then he had a boot in his hand and he was hopping on one leg. Then the other boot. A confusion of splashes caromed around him, water flew, the wind cut across the dock. He tore off his jacket, sweater, T-shirt, dropped his faded jeans, and stood there in his briefs, scanning the black rollicking water. There she was, her head bobbing gently, arms flowing across her breast in an easy tread.

He never hesitated. His feet pounded against the rough planks of the dock, the wind caught his hair, and he was up and out over the churning water, hanging suspended for the briefest, maddest, most lucid instant of his life, and then he was in.

Funny. It was warm as a bath.

(1988)

BACK IN THE EOCENE

Abscissa, ordinate, isosceles, Carboniferous, Mesozoic, holothurian: the terms come to him in a rush of disinterred syllables, a forgotten language conjured by the sudden sharp smell of chalk dust and blackboards. It happens every time. All he has to do is glance at the bicycle rack out front or the flag snapping crisply atop the gleaming aluminum pole, and the memories begin to wash over him, a typhoon of faces and places and names, Ilona Sharrow and Richie Davidson, Manifest Destiny, Heddy Grieves, the Sea of Tranquillity and the three longest rivers in Russia. He takes his daughter's hand and shuffles toward the glowing auditorium, already choked up.

Inside, it's worse. There, under the pale yellow gaze of the overhead lights, recognition cuts at him like a knife. It's invested in the feel of the hard steel frames and cushionless planks of the seats, in the crackling PA system and the sad array of frosted cupcakes and chocolate-chip cookies presided over by a puffy matron from the PTA. And the smells—Pine Sol, floor wax, festering underarms and erupting feet, a faint lingering whiff of meat loaf and wax beans. *Wax beans:* he hasn't had a wax bean, hasn't inserted a wax bean in his mouth, in what—twenty years? The thought overwhelms him and he stands there awkwardly a moment, just inside the door, and then there's a tug at his hand and his daughter slips away, flitting through the crowd like a bird to chase after her friends. He finds a seat in back.

The big stark institutional clock shows five minutes of eight. Settling into the unforgiving grip of the chair, he concentrates on the faces of his fellow parents, vaguely familiar from previous incarnations, as they trudge up and down the aisles like automatons. Voices buzz round him in an expectant drone. High heels click on the linoleum. Chairs scrape. He's dreaming a scene from another auditorium an ice age ago, detention hall, the soporific text, shouts from beyond the windows and a sharp sweet taste of spring on the air, when Officer Rudman steps up to the microphone.

A hush falls over the auditorium, the gale of chatter dropping off to a breeze, a stir in the rafters, nothing. His daughter, ten years old and beautiful, her feet too big and her shoulders slumped, strides up the aisle and drops into the chair beside him as if her legs have been shot out from under her. "Dad," she whispers, "that's Officer Rudman."

He nods. Who else would it be, up there in his spit and polish, his close-cropped hair and custom-fit uniform? Who else, with his sunny smile and weight lifter's torso? Who else but Officer Rudman, coordinator of the school's antidrug program and heartthrob of all the fifth-grade girls?

A woman with frosted hair and remodeled hips ducks in late and settles noiselessly into the chair in front of him. "Good evening," Officer Rudman says, "I'm Officer Rudman." Someone coughs. Feedback hisses through the speakers.

In the next moment they're rising clumsily in a cacophony of rustling, stamping and nose blowing, as Officer Rudman leads them in the Pledge of Allegiance. Hands over hearts, a murmur of half-remembered words. He's conscious of his daughter's voice beside him, and of his own, and he shifts his eyes to steal a glimpse of her. Her face is serene, shining, hopeful, a recapitulation and refinement of her mother's, and suddenly it's too much for him and he has to look down at his feet: ". . . with liberty and justice for all." More coughing. The seats creak. They sit.

Officer Rudman gives the crowd a good long look, and then he begins. "Drugs are dangerous," he says, "we all know that," and he pauses while the principal, a thick-ankled woman with feathered hair and a dogged expression, translates in her halting Spanish: "Las drogas son peligrosas." The man sits there in back, his daughter at his side, tasting wax beans, rushing with weltschmerz and nostalgia.

Eocene: designating or of the earliest epoch of the Tertiary Period in the Cenozoic Era, during which mammals became the dominant animals.

Je romps; tu romps; il rompe; nous rompons; vous rompez; ils rompent.

They didn't have drugs when he was in elementary school, didn't have crack and crank, didn't have ice and heroin and AIDS to go with it. Not in elementary school. Not in the fifties. They didn't even have pot.

Mary Jane, that's what they called it in the high school health films, but no one ever called it that. Not on this planet, anyway. It was pot, pure and simple, and he smoked it, like anyone else. He's remembering his first joint, age seventeen, a walkup on Broome Street, holes in the walls, bottles, rats, padlocks on the doors, one puff and you're hooked, when Officer Rudman beckons a skinny dark-haired kid to the microphone. Big adult hands choke the neck of the stand and the mike drops a foot. Stretching till his ankles rise up out of his high-tops, the kid clutches at the microphone and recites his pledge to stay off drugs in a piping timbreless voice. "My name is Steven Taylor and I have good feelings of self-esteem about myself," he says, his superamplified breathing whistling through the interstices, "and I pledge never to take drugs or to put anything bad in my body. If somebody asks me if I want drugs I will just say no, turn my back, change the subject, walk away or just say no."

Brain-washing, that's what Linda called it when he phoned to break their date for tonight. Easy for her to say, but then she didn't have a daughter, didn't know, couldn't imagine what it was like to feel the net expand beneath you, high out over that chasm of crashing rock. *What good did it do you?* she said. *Or me?* She had a point. Hash, kif, LSD, cocaine, heroin. He'd heard all the warnings, watched all the movies, but how could you take anyone's word for it? Was it possible, even? He'd sat through driver's ed, sobering statistics, scare films and all, and then taken his mother's Ford out on the highway and burned the tires off it. Scotch, gin, whiskey, Boone's Farm, Night Train, Colt 45, Seconal, Tuinal, Quaalude. He'd heard all the warnings, yes, but when the time came he stuck the needle in his arm and drew back the plunger to watch the clear solution flush with his own smoldering blood. You remember to take your vitamins today?

"My name is Lucy Fadel and I pledge never to abuse drugs, alcohol or tobacco because I like myself and the world and my school and I can get high from just life."

"My name is Roberto Campos and I don't want to die from drugs. Peer pressure is what makes kids use drugs and I will just say no, I will walk away and I will change the subject."

"Voy a decir no—"

Officer Rudman adjusts the microphone, clasps his hands in front of him. The parents lean forward. He holds their eyes. "You've all just heard the fifth graders' pledges," he says, "and these kids mean it. I'm proud of them. Let's have a big hand for these kids."

And there it is, thunderous, all those parents in their suits and sportcoats and skirts, wearing sober, earnest, angry looks, pounding their hands together in relief, as if that could do it, as if the force of their acclamation could drive the gangs from the streets or nullify that infinitely seductive question to which "No" is never the answer. He claps along with them, not daring to glance down at his daughter, picturing the first boy, the skinny dark one, up against the wall with the handcuffs on him, dead in the street, wasting away in some charity ward. And the girl, mother of four, twice divorced, strung out on martinis and diet pills and wielding the Jeep Cherokee like a weapon. That's what it came down to: that's what the warnings meant. *Agon, agape, Ulysses S. Grant, parthenogenesis, the* Monitor *and the* Merrimack, *yond Cassius has a lean and hungry look.* His daughter takes his hand. "Now there's a movie," she whispers.

What happened to finger painting, hearts for Valentine's Day and bunnies for Easter? Fifth grade, for christ's sake. Where was *Treasure Island, Little Women,*

Lassie, Come Home? What had happened? Who was responsible? Where did it go wrong?

He's on the verge of raising his hand and demanding an answer of Officer Rudman, the nostalgia gone sour in his throat now, but the lights dim and the film begins. A flicker of movement on the screen, bars, a jail cell. He watches a junkie writhe and scream, a demonic sunken-eyed man beating his head against a wall, someone, somewhere, lights flashing, police, handcuffs, more screams. Smoke a joint and you're hooked: how they'd laughed over that one, he and Tony Gaetti, and laughed again to realize it was true, cooking the dope in a bottle cap, stealing disposable syringes, getting off in the rest room on the train and feeling they'd snowed the world. Things were different then. That was a long time ago.

Cro-Magnon, Neanderthal, Homo erectus: his daughter's hand is crushing him, prim and cool, lying across his palm like a demolished building, a cement truck, glacial moraine. Up on the screen, the junkies are gone, replaced by a sunny schoolyard and a clone of Officer Rudman, statistics now, grim but hopeful. Inspiring music, smiling faces, kids who Just Say No.

When it's over, he feels dazed, the lights flashing back on to transfix him like some animal startled along a darkened highway. All he wants is to be out of here, no more questions, no more tricks of memory, no more Officer Rudman or the vapid stares of his fellow parents. "Honey," he whispers, bringing his face down close to his daughter's, "we've got to go." Officer Rudman's chin is cocked back, his arms folded across his chest. "Any questions?" he asks.

"But Dad, the cake sale."

The cake sale.

"We'll have to miss it this time," he whispers, and suddenly he's on his feet, slumping his shoulders in the way people do when they duck out of meetings early or come late to the concert or theater, a gesture of submission and apology. His daughter hangs back—she wants to stay, wants cake, wants to see her friends—but he tugs at her hand and then they're fighting their way through the gauntlet of concerned parents at the door and out into the night. "Dad!" she cries, tugging back at him, and only then does he realize he's hurting her, clutching her hand like a lifeline in a swirl of darkening waters.

"I mean, have a cow, why don't you?" she says, and he drops her hand.

"Sorry. I wasn't thinking."

The flag is motionless, hanging limp now against the pole. He gazes up at the stars fixed in their tracks, cold and distant, and then the gravel crunches underfoot and they're in the parking lot. "I just wanted a piece of cake," his daughter says.

In the car, on the way home to her mother's house, she stares moodily out the window to let him feel the weight of her disappointment, but she can't sustain it. Before long she's chattering away about Officer Rudman and Officer Torres, who sometimes helps with the program, telling him how nice they are and how corrupt the world is. "We have gangs here," she says, "did you know that? Right here in our neighborhood."

He gazes out on half-million-dollar homes. Stone and stucco, mailboxes out front, basketball hoops over garage doors. The streets are deserted. He sees no gangs. "Here?"

"Uh-huh. Chrissie Mueller saw two guys in Raiders hats at the 7-Eleven the other day—"

"Maybe they were buying Ho-Ho's, maybe they just wanted a piece of cake."

"Come on, Dad," she says, but her tone tells him all is forgiven.

Her mother's house is lighted like an arena, porch light, security lights, even the windows poking bright gleaming holes in the fabric of the night. He leans over to kiss his daughter good night, the car vibrating beneath him.

"Dad?"

"Yes?"

"I just wanted to, you know, ask you: did you ever use drugs? Or Mom?"

The question catches him by surprise. He looks beyond her, looks at that glowing bright house a moment, curtains open wide, the wash of light on the lawn. *Abstersion, epopt, Eleusinian, the shortest distance between two points is a straight line.*

"No," he says finally. "No."

(1990)

SITTING ON TOP OF THE WORLD

People would ask her what it was like. She'd watch them from her tower as they weaved along the trail in their baseball caps and day packs, their shorts, hiking boots and sneakers. The brave ones would mount the hundred and fifty wooden steps hammered into the face of the mountain to stand at the high-flown railing of the little glass-walled shack she called home for seven months a year. Sweating, sucking at canteens and bota bags, heaving for breath in the undernourished air, they would ask her what it was like. "Beautiful," she would say. "Peaceful."

But that didn't begin to express it. It was like floating untethered, drifting with the clouds, like being cupped in the hands of God. Nine thousand feet up, she could see the distant hazy rim of the world, she could see Mount Whitney rising up above the crenellations of the Sierra, she could see stars that haven't been discovered yet. In the morning, she was the first to watch the sun emerge from the hills to the east, and in the evening, when it was dark beneath her, the valleys and ridges gripped by the insinuating fingers of the night, she was the last to see it set. There was the wind in the trees, the murmur of the infinite needles soughing in the uncountable branches of the pines, sequoias and cedars that stretched out below her like a carpet. There was daybreak. There was the stillness of 3:00 A.M. She couldn't explain it. She was sitting on top of the world.

Don't you get lonely up here? they'd ask. Don't you get a little stir-crazy?

And how to explain that? Yes, she did, of course she did, but it didn't matter. Todd was up here with her in the summer, one week on, one week off, and then the question was meaningless. But in September he went back to the valley, to his father, to school, and the world began to drag round its tired old axis. The hikers stopped coming then too. At the height of summer, on a weekend, she'd see as many as thirty or forty in the course of a day, but now, with the fall coming on, they left her to herself—sometimes she'd go for days without seeing a soul.

But that was the point, wasn't it?

She was making breakfast—a real breakfast for a change, ham and eggs from the propane refrigerator, fresh-dripped coffee and toast—when she spotted him working his way along one of the switchbacks below. She was immediately annoyed. It wasn't even seven yet and the sign at the trailhead quite plainly stated that visitors were welcome at the lookout between the hours of ten and five *only*. What was wrong with this guy—did he think he was exempt or sómething? She calmed herself: maybe he was only crossing the trail. Deer season had opened— she'd been hearing the distant muted pop of gunfire all week—and maybe he was only a hunter tracking a deer.

No such luck. When she glanced down again, flipping her eggs, peering across the face of the granite peak and the steep snaking trail that clung to it, she saw that he was coming up to the tower. Damn, she thought, and then the kettle began to hoot and her stomach clenched. Breakfast was ruined. Now there'd be some stranger gawking over her shoulder and making the usual banal comments as she ate. To them it might have been like Disneyland or something up here, but this was her home, she lived here. How would they like it if she showed up on their doorstep at seven o'clock in the morning?

She was eating, her back to the glass door, hoping he'd go away, slip over the lip of the precipice and disappear, vanish in a puff of smoke, when she felt his footfall on the trembling catwalk that ran round the outside of the tower. Still, she didn't turn or look up. She was reading—she went through a truckload of books in the course of a season—and she never lifted her eyes from the page. He could gawk round the catwalk, peer through the telescope and hustle himself back on down the steps for all she cared. She wasn't a tour guide. Her job was to watch for smoke, twenty-four hours a day, and to be cordial—if she was in the mood and had the time—to the hikers who made the sweaty panting trek in from the trailhead to join her for a brief moment atop the world. There was no law that said she had to let them in the shack or show them the radio and her plotting equipment and deliver the standard lecture on how it all worked. Especially at seven in the morning. To hell with him, she thought, and she forked up egg and tried to concentrate on her book.

The problem was, she'd trained herself to look up from what she was doing and scan the horizon every thirty seconds or so, day or night, except when she was asleep, and it had become a reflex. She glanced up, and there he was. It gave her a shock. He'd gone round the catwalk to the far side and he was standing right in front of her, grinning and holding something up to the window. Flowers, wildflowers, she registered that, but then his face came into focus and she felt something go slack in her: she knew him. He'd been here before.

"Lainie," he said, tapping the glass and brandishing the flowers, "I brought you something."

Her name. He knew her name.

She tried a smile and her face froze around it. The book on the table before her upset the saltshaker and flipped itself shut with a tiny expiring hiss. Should she thank him? Should she get up and latch the door? Should she put out an emergency call on the radio and snatch up the kitchen knife?

"Sorry to disturb you over breakfast—I didn't know the time," he said, and something happened to his grin, though his eyes—a hard metallic blue—held on to hers like pincers. He raised his voice to penetrate the glass: "I've been camping down on Long Meadow Creek and when I crossed the trail this morning I just thought you might be lonely and I'd surprise you"—he hesitated—"I mean, with some flowers."

Her whole body was frozen now. She'd had crazies up here before—it was an occupational hazard—but there was something unnerving about this one; this one she remembered. "It's too early," she said finally, miming it with her hands, as if the glass were impervious to sound, and then she got up from her untouched ham and half-eaten eggs and deliberately went to the radio. The radio was just under the window where he was standing, and when she picked up the mike and depressed the talk button she was two feet from him, the thin wall of glass all that separated them.

"Needles Lookout," she said, "this is Elaine. Zack, you there? Over."

Zack's voice came right back at her. He was a college student working on a degree in forestry, and he was her relief two days a week when she hiked out and went down the mountain to spend a day with her son, do her shopping and maybe hit a bar or movie with her best friend and soul mate, Cynthia Furman. "Elaine," he said, above the crackle of static, "what's up? See anything funny out there? Over."

She forced herself to look up then and locate the stranger's eyes—he was still grinning, but the grin was slack and unsteady and there was no joy in the deeps of those hard blue eyes—and she held the black plastic mike to her lips a moment longer than she had to before answering. "Nothing, Zack," she said, "just checking in."

His voice was tinny. "Okay," he said. "Talk to you. Over and out."

"Over and out," she said.

And now what? The guy wore a hunting knife strapped to his thigh. His cheeks were caved in as if he were sucking candy, and an old-fashioned mustache, thick and reddish, hid his upper lip. Instead of a baseball cap he wore a wide-brimmed felt hat. Wyatt Earp, she thought, and she was about to turn away from the window, prepared to ignore him till he took the hint, till he counted off the hundred and fifty wooden steps and vanished down the path and out of her life, when he rapped again on the glass and said, "You got something to put these in—the flowers, I mean?"

She didn't want his flowers. She didn't want him on her platform. She didn't want him in her thirteen-by-thirteen-foot sanctuary, touching her things, poking around, asking stupid questions, making small talk. "Look," she said finally, talking to the glass but looking through him, beyond him, scanning the infinite as she'd trained herself to do, no matter what the problem, "I've got a job to do up here and the fact is no one's allowed on the platform between the hours of five in the afternoon and ten in the morning"—now she came back to him and saw that his smile had collapsed—"you ought to know that. It says so in plain English right down there at the trailhead." She looked away; it was over, she was done with him.

She went back to her breakfast, forcing herself to stare at the page before her, though her heart was going and the words meant nothing. Todd had been with her the first time the man had come. Todd was fourteen, tall like his father, blond-headed and rangy. He was a good kid, her last and final hope, and he seemed to relish the time he spent with her up here. It was a Saturday, the middle of the afternoon, and they'd had a steady stream of visitors since the morning. Todd was in the storage room below, reading comics (in its wisdom, the Forestry Service had provided this second room, twenty-five steps down, not simply for storage but for respite too—it was a box, a womb, with only a single dull high-placed window to light it, antithesis and antidote to the naked glass box above). Elaine was at her post, chopping vegetables for soup and scanning the horizon.

She hadn't noticed him coming—there'd been so many visitors she wasn't attuned to them in the way she was in the quiet times. She was feeling hospitable, lighthearted, the hostess of an ongoing party. There'd been a professor up earlier, an ornithologist, and they'd had a long talk about the golden eagle and the red-tailed hawk. And then there was the young girl from Merced—she couldn't have been more than seventeen—with her baby strapped to her back, and two heavy-set women in their sixties who'd proudly made the two-and-a-half-mile trek in from the trailhead and were giddy with the thin air and the thrill of their own accomplishment. Elaine had offered them each a cup of tea, not wanting to spoil their fun and point out that it was still two and a half miles back out.

She'd felt his weight on the platform and turned to give him a smile. He was tall and powerful across the chest and shoulders and he'd tipped his hat to her and poked his head in the open door. "Enjoying the view?" he said.

There was something in his eyes that should have warned her off, but she was feeling sociable and buoyant and she saw the generosity in his shoulders and hands. "It's nothing compared to the Ventura Freeway," she deadpanned.

He laughed out loud at that, and he was leaning in the door now, both hands on the frame. "I see the monastic life hasn't hurt your sense of humor any—" and then he paused, as if he'd gone too far. "Or that's not the word I want, 'monastic'—is there a feminine version of that?"

Pretty presumptuous. Flirtatious, too. But she was in the mood, she didn't know what it was—maybe having Todd with her, maybe just the sheer bubbling joy of living on the crest of the sky—and at least he wasn't dragging her through the same old tired conversation about loneliness and beauty and smoke on the horizon she had to endure about a hundred times a week. "Come in," she said. "Take a load off your feet."

He sat on the edge of the bed and removed his hat. He wore his hair in a modified punk style—hard irregular spikes—and that surprised her: somehow it just didn't go with the cowboy hat. His jeans were stiff and new and his tooled boots looked as if they'd just been polished. He was studying her—she was wearing khaki shorts and a T-shirt, she'd washed her hair that morning in anticipation of the crowd, and her legs were good—she knew it—tanned and shaped by her treks up and down the trail. She felt something she hadn't felt in a long time, an ice age, and she knew her cheeks were flushed. "You probably had a whole slew of visitors today, huh?" he said, and there was something incongruous in the enforced folksiness of the phrase, something that didn't go with his accent, just as the haircut didn't go with the hat.

"I've counted twenty-six since this morning." She diced a carrot and tossed it into the pan to simmer with the onions and zucchini she'd chopped a moment earlier.

He was gazing out the window, working his hands on the brim of his hat. "Hope you don't mind my saying this, but you're the best thing about this view as far as I can see. You're pretty. Really pretty."

This one she'd heard before. About a thousand times. Probably seventy percent of the day-trippers who made the hike out to the lookout were male, and if they were alone or with other males, about ninety percent of those tried to hit on her in some way. She resented it, but she couldn't blame them really. There was probably something irresistible in the formula: young woman with blond hair and good legs in a glass tower in the middle of nowhere—and all alone. Rapunzel, let down your hair. Usually she deflected the compliment—or the moves—by turning officious, standing on her authority as Forest Service employee, government servant and the chief, queen and despot of the Needles Lookout. This time she said nothing. Just lifted her head for a quick scan of the horizon and then looked back down at the knife and the cutting board and began chopping green onion and cilantro.

He was still watching her. The bed was big, a double, one of the few creature comforts the Forestry Service provided up here. There was no headboard, of course—just a big flat hard slab of mattress attached to the wall at window level, so you could be lying in bed and still do your job. Presumably, it was designed for couples. When he spoke again, she knew what he was going to say before the words were out of his mouth. "Nice bed," he said.

What did she expect? He was no different from the rest—why would he be? All of a sudden he'd begun to get on her nerves, and when she turned her face to him her voice was cold. "Have you seen the telescope," she said, indicating the

Bushnell Televar mounted on the rail of the catwalk—beyond the window and out the door.

He ignored her. He rose to his feet. Thirteen by thirteen: two's a crowd. "You must get awfully lonely up here," he said, and his voice was different now too, no attempt at folksiness or jocularity, "a pretty woman like you. A beautiful woman. You've got sexy legs, you know that?"

She flushed—he could see that, she was sure of it—and the flush made her angry. She was about to tell him off, to tell him to get the hell out of her house and stay out, when Todd came rumbling up the steps, wild-eyed and excited. "Mom!" he shouted, and he was out of breath, his voice high-pitched and hoarse, "there's water leaking all over the place out there!"

Water. It took a moment to register. The water was precious up here, irreplaceable. Once a month two bearded men with Forestry Service patches on their sleeves brought her six twenty-gallon containers of it—in the old way, on the backs of mules. She husbanded that water as if she were in the middle of the Negev, every drop of it, rarely allowing herself the luxury of a quick shampoo and rinse, as she had that morning. In the next instant she was out the door and jolting down the steps behind her son. Down below, outside the storage room where the cartons were lined up in a straight standing row, she saw that the rock face was slick with a finely spread sheen of water. She bent to the near carton. It was leaking from a thin milky stress fracture in the plastic, an inch from the bottom. "Take hold of it, Todd," she said. "We've got to turn it over so the leak's on top."

Full, the carton weighed better than a hundred and sixty pounds, and this one was nearly full. She put her weight behind it, the power of her honed and muscular legs, but the best she could do, even with Todd's help, was to push the thing over on its side. She was breathing hard, sweating, she'd scraped her knee and there was a stipple of blood on the skin over the kneecap. It was then that she became aware of the stranger standing there behind her. She looked up at him framed against the vastness of the sky, the sun in his face, his big hands on his hips. "Need a hand there?" he asked.

Looking back on it, she didn't know why she'd refused—maybe it was the way Todd gaped at him in awe, maybe it was the old pretty-woman/lonely-up-here routine or the helpless-female syndrome—but before she could think she was saying "I don't need your help: I can do it myself."

And then his hands fell from his hips and he backed away a step, and suddenly he was apologetic, he was smooth and funny and winning and he was sorry for bothering her and he just wanted to help and he knew she was capable, he wasn't implying anything—and just as suddenly he caught himself, dropped his shoulders and slunk off down the steps without another word.

For a long moment she watched him receding down the trail, and then she turned back to the water container. By the time she and Todd got it upended it was half empty.

Yes. And now he was here when he had no right to be, now he was intruding and he knew it, now he was a crazy defining new levels of the affliction. She'd call in an emergency in a second—she wouldn't hesitate—and they'd have a helicopter here in less than five minutes, that's how quick these firefighters were, she'd seen them in action. Five minutes. She wouldn't hesitate. She kept her head down. She cut and chewed each piece of meat with slow deliberation and she read and reread the same paragraph until it lost all sense. When she looked up, he was gone.

After that, the day dragged on as if it would never end. He couldn't have been there more than ten minutes, slouching around with his mercenary grin and his pathetic flowers, but he'd managed to ruin her day. He'd upset her equilibrium and she found that she couldn't read, couldn't sketch or work on the sweater she was knitting for Todd. She caught herself staring at a fixed point on the horizon, drifting, her mind a blank. She ate too much. Lunch was a ceremony, dinner a ritual. There were no visitors, though for once she longed for them. Dusk lingered in the western sky and when night fell she didn't bother with her propane lantern but merely sat there on the corner of the bed, caught up in the wheeling immensity of the constellations and the dream of the Milky Way.

And then she couldn't sleep. She kept thinking of him, the stranger with the big hands and secretive eyes, kept scanning the catwalk for the sudden black shadow of him. If he came at seven in the morning, why not at three? What was to prevent him? There was no sound, nothing—the wind had died down and the night was clear and moonless. For the first time since she'd been here, for the first time in three long seasons, she felt naked and vulnerable, exposed in her glass house like a fish in a tank. The night was everything and it held her in its grip.

She thought about Mike then, about the house they'd had when he'd finished his degree and started as an assistant professor at a little state school out in the lost lush hills of Oregon. The house was an A-frame, a cabin with a loft, set down amidst the trees like a cottage in a fairy tale. It was all windows and everywhere you looked the trees bowed down and stepped into the house. The previous owner, an old widower with watery eyes and yellow hair climbing out of his ears, hadn't bothered with blinds or curtains, and Mike didn't like that—he was always after her to measure the windows and order blinds or buy the material for drapes. She'd balked. The openness, the light, the sense of connection and belonging: these were the things that had attracted her in the first place. They made love in the dark—Mike insisted on it—as if it were something to be ashamed of. After a while, it was.

Then she was thinking of a time before that, a time before Todd and graduate school, when Mike sat with her in the dormitory lounge, books spread out on the coffee table before them, the heat and murmur of a dozen other couples locking their mouths and bodies together. A study date. For hours she clung to him, the sofa like a boat pitching in a heavy sea, the tease of it, the fumbling innocence, the interminable foreplay that left her wet and itching while the wind screamed beyond the iced-over windows. That was something. The R.A. would flash the lights and it was quarter of one and they would fling themselves at each other, each step to the door drenched in hormones, sticky with them, desperate, until finally he was gone and she felt the loss like a war bride. Until the next night.

Finally—and it must have been two, three in the morning, the Big Dipper tugged down below the horizon, Orion looming overhead—she thought of the stranger who'd spoiled her breakfast. He'd sat there on the corner of the bed; he'd stood beyond the window with his sad bundle of flowers, devouring the sky. As she thought of him, in that very moment, there was a dull light thump on the steps, a faint rustle, movement, and she couldn't breathe, couldn't move. The seconds pounded in her head and the rustling—it was like the sweep of a broom—was gone, something in the night, a pack rat, the fleeting touch of an owl's wing. She thought of those hands, the eyes, the square of those shoulders, and she felt herself being drawn down into the night in relief, and finally, in gratitude.

She woke late, the sun slanting across the floor to touch her lips and mask her eyes. Zachary was on the radio with the news that Oakland had clinched the pennant and a hurricane was tearing up the East Coast. "You sound awful," he said. "I didn't wake you, did I?"

"I couldn't sleep."

"Stargazing again, huh?"

She tried out a laugh for him. "I guess," she said. There was a silence. "Jesus, you just relieved me. I've got four more days to put in before I come back down to the ground."

"Just don't get mystical on me. And leave me some granola this time, will you? And if you run out, call me. That's my breakfast we're talking about. And lunch. And sometimes, if I don't feel like cooking—"

She cut him off: "Dinner. I know. I will." She yawned. "Talk to you."

"Yeah. Over and out."

"Over and out."

When she set the kettle on the grill there was gas, but when she turned her back to dig the butter out of the refrigerator, the flame was gone. She tried another match, but there was nothing. That meant she had to switch propane tanks, a minor nuisance. The tanks, which were flown in once a year by helicopter, were located at the base of the stairway, one hundred and fifty steps down. There was a flat spot there, a gap cut into the teeth of the outcrop and overhung on one side by a sloping twenty-foot-high wall of rock. On the other side, the first step was a thousand feet down.

She shrugged into her shorts, and because it was cold despite the sun—she'd seen snow as early as the fifth of September, and the month was almost gone now—she pulled on an oversized sweater that had once belonged to Mike. After she'd moved out she'd found it in a pillowcase she'd stuffed full of clothes. He hadn't wanted it back. It was windy, and a blast knifed into her when she threw open the door and started down the steps. Big pristine tufts of cumulus hurried across the sky, swelling and attenuating and changing shape, but she didn't see anything dark enough—or big enough—to portend a storm. Still, you could never tell. The breeze was from the north and the radio had reported a storm front moving in off the Pacific—it really wouldn't surprise her to see snow on the ground by this time tomorrow. A good snowfall and the fire season would be over and she could go home. Early.

She thought about that—about the four walls of the little efficiency she rented on a dead street in a dead town to be near Todd during the winter—and hoped it wouldn't snow. Not now. Not yet. In a dry year—and this had been the third dry year in a row—she could stay through mid-November. She reached the bottom of the steps and crouched over the propane tanks, two three-hundred-gallon jobs painted Forest Service green, feeling depressed over the thought of those four dull walls and the cold in the air and the storm that might or might not develop. There was gooseflesh on her legs and her breath crowded the air round her. She watched a ground squirrel, its shoulders bulky with patches of bright gray fur, dart up over the face of the overhang, and then she unfastened the coupling on the empty tank and switched the hose to the full one.

"Gas problems?"

The voice came from above and behind her and she jumped as if she'd been stung. Even before she whirled round she knew whose voice it was.

"Hey, hey: didn't mean to startle you. Whoa. Sorry." There he was, the happy camper, knife lashed to his thigh, standing right behind her, two steps up. This time his eyes were hidden behind a pair of reflecting sunglasses. The brim of the Stetson was pulled down low and he wore a sheepskin coat, the fleecy collar turned up in back.

She couldn't answer. Couldn't smile. Couldn't humor him. He'd caught her out of her sanctuary, caught her out in the open, one hundred and fifty steep and unforgiving steps from the radio, the kitchen knife, the hard flat soaring bed. She was crouching. He towered above her, his shoulders cut out of the sky. Todd was in school. Mike—she didn't want to think about Mike. She was all alone.

He stood there, the mustache the only thing alive in his face. It lifted from his teeth in a grin. "Those things can be a pain," he said, the folksy tone creeping into his voice, "those tanks, I mean. Dangerous. I use electricity myself."

She lifted herself cautiously from her crouch, the hard muscles swelling in her legs. She would have risked a dash up the stairs, all hundred and fifty of them, would have put her confidence in her legs, but he was blocking the stairway—almost as if he'd anticipated her. She hadn't said a word yet. She looked scared, she knew it. "Still camping?" she said, fighting to open up her face and give him his smile back, insisting on banality, normalcy, the meaningless drift of meaningless conversation.

He looked away from her, light flashing from the slick convexity of the sunglasses, and kicked at the edge of the step with the silver-tipped toe of his boot. After a moment he turned back to her and removed the sunglasses. "Yeah," he said, shrugging. "I guess."

It wasn't an answer she expected. He guessed? What was that supposed to mean? He hadn't moved a muscle and he was watching her with that look in his eyes—she knew that look, knew that stance, that mustache and hat, but she didn't know his name. He knew hers but she didn't know his, not even his first name. "I'm sorry," she said, and when she put a hand up to her eyes to shade them from the sun, it was trembling, "but what was your name again? I mean, I remember you, of course, not just from yesterday but from that time a month or so ago, but . . ." She trailed off.

He didn't seem to have heard her. The wind sang in the trees. She just stood there, squinting into the sun—there was nothing else she could do. "I wasn't camping, not really," he said. "Not that I don't love the wilderness—and I do camp, backpack and all that—but I just—I thought that's what you'd want to hear."

What she'd want to hear? What was he talking about? She stole a glance at the tower, sun flashing the windows, clouds pricked on the peak of the roof, and it seemed as distant as the stars at night. If only she were up there she'd put out an emergency, she would, she'd have them here in five minutes. . . .

"Actually," and he looked away now, his shoulders slumping in that same hangdog way they had when she'd refused his help with the water carton, "actually I've got a cabin up on Cedar Slope. I just, I just thought you'd want to hear I was camping." He'd been staring down at the toes of his boots, but suddenly he looked up at her and grinned till his back fillings glinted in the light. "I think Elaine's a pretty name, did I tell you that?"

"Thank you," she said, almost against her will, and softly, so softly she could barely hear it herself. He could rape her here, he could kill her, anything. Was that what he wanted? Was that it? "Listen," she said, pushing it, she couldn't help herself, "listen, I've got to get back to work—"

"I know, I know," he said, holding up the big slab of his hand, "back to the nest, huh? I know I must be a pain in the—in the butt for you, and I'll bet I'm not the first one to say it, but you're just too good-looking a woman to be wasted out here on the squirrels and coyotes." He stepped down, stepped toward her, and she thought in that instant of trying to dart past him, a wild thought, instinctual and desperate, a thought that clawed its way into her brain and froze there before she could move. "Jesus," he said, and his voice was harsh with conviction, "don't you get lonely?"

And then she saw it, below and to the right, movement, two bobbing pink hunter's caps, coming up the trail. It was over. Just like that. She could walk away from him, mount the stairs, lock herself in the tower. But why was her heart still going, why did she feel as if it hadn't even begun? "Damn," she said, directing her gaze, "more visitors. Now I really have to get back."

He followed her eyes and looked down to where the hunters sank out of view and then bobbed back up again, working their way up the path. She could see their faces now—two men, middle-aged, wispy hair sticking out from beneath the fluorescent caps. No guns. Cameras. He studied them a moment and then looked into her eyes, looked deep, as if he'd lost something. Then he shrugged, turned his back and started down the path toward them.

She was in good shape, the best shape of her life. She'd been up the steps a thousand times, two thousand, but she'd never climbed them quicker than she did now. She flew up the stairs like something blown by the wind and she felt a kind of panic beating against her ribs and she smelled the storm coming and felt the cold to the marrow of her bones. And then she reached the door and slammed it shut behind her, fumbling for the latch. It was then, only then, that she noticed the flowers. They were in the center of the table, in a cut-glass vase, lupine, groundsel, forget-me-not.

It snowed in the night, monstrous swirling oversized flakes that clawed at the windows and filled her with despair. The lights would only have made her feel vulnerable and exposed, and for the second night running she did without them, sitting there in the dark, cradling the kitchen knife and listening for his footfall on the steps while the sky fell to pieces around her. But he wouldn't come, not in this weather, not at night—she was being foolish, childish, there was nothing to worry about. Except the snow. It meant that her season was over. And if her season was over, she had to go back down the mountain and into the real world, real time, into the smog and roar and clutter.

She thought of the four walls that awaited her, the hopeless job—waitressing or fast food or some such slow crucifixion of the spirit—and she thought of Mike before she left him, saw him there in the black glass of the window, sexless, pale, the little butterfly-wing bifocals perched on the tip of his nose, pecking at the typewriter, pecking, pecking, in love with Dryden, Swift, Pope, in love with dead poets, in love with death itself. She'd met a man at a party a month after she'd left him and he was just like Mike, only he was in love with arthropods. Arthropods. And then she came up to the tower.

She woke late again and the first thing she felt was relief. The sun was out and the snow—it was only a dusting, nothing really—had already begun to recede from the naked high crown of the rock. She put on the kettle and went to the radio. "Zack," she called, "Needle Rock. Do you copy?"

He was there, right at her fingertips. "Copy. Over."

"We had some snow up here—nothing much, just a dusting really. It's clear now."

"You're a little late—Lewis already checked in from Mule Peak with that information. Oversleep again?"

"Yeah, I guess so." She was watching the distant treetops shake off the patina of snow. A hawk sailed across the window. She held the microphone so close to her lips it could have been a part of her. "Zack—" She wanted to tell him about the crazy, about the man in the Stetson, about his hands, wanted to alert him just in case, but she hesitated. Her voice was tiny, detached, lost in the electronic crackle of time and space.

"Lainie?"

"Yes. Yes, I'm here."

"There's a cold front coming through, another storm behind it. They're saying it could drop some snow. The season's still on—Reichert says it will be until we get appreciable precipitation—but this one could be it. It's up to you. You want to come out or wait and see?"

Reichert was the boss, fifty, bald, soft as a clam. The mountains were parched—six inches of powdery duff covered the forest floor and half the creeks had run dry. The season could last till November. "Wait and see," she said.

"Okay, it's your choice. Lewis is staying too, if it makes you feel better. I'll keep in touch if anything develops on this end."

"Yeah. Thanks."

"Over and out."

"Over and out."

It clouded up late in the afternoon and the sky closed in on her again. The temperature began to drop. It looked bad. It was early for snow yet, but they could get snow any time of the year at this altitude. The average was twenty-five feet annually, and she'd seen storms drop four and five feet at a time. She talked to Zack at four and he told her it looked pretty grim—they were calling for a seventy-percent chance of snow, with the snow level dropping to three thousand feet. "I'll take my chances," she told him. There was a pair of snowshoes in the storage room if it came to that.

The snow started an hour later. She was cooking dinner—brown rice and vegetables—and she'd opened the bottle of wine she'd brought up to commemorate the last day of the season. The flakes were tiny, pellets that sifted down with a hiss, the sort of configuration that meant serious snow. The season was over. She could drink her wine and then think about packing up and cleaning the stove and refrigerator. She put another log on the woodstove and buttoned up her jacket.

The wine was half gone and she'd sat down to eat when she noticed the smoke. At first she thought it must be a trick of the wind, the smoke from her own stove twisting back on her. But no. Below her, no more than five hundred feet, just about where the trail would be, she could see the flames. The wind blew a screen of snow across the window. There hadn't been any lightning—but there was a fire down there, she was sure of it. She got up from the table, snatched her binoculars from the hook by the door and went out on the catwalk to investigate.

The wind took her breath away. All the universe had gone pale, white above and white beneath: she was perched on the clouds, living in them, diaphanous and ghostly. She could smell the smoke on the wind now. She lifted the binoculars to her eyes and the snow screened them; she tried again and her hair beat at the lenses. It took her a moment, but there, there it was: a fire leaping up out of the swirling grip of the snow. A campfire. But no, this was bigger, fallen trees stacked up in a pyramid—this was a bonfire, deliberate, this was a sign. The snow took it away from her. Her fingers were numb. When the fire came into focus again she saw movement there, a shadow leaping round the flames, feeding them, reveling in them, and she caught her breath. And then she saw the black stabbing peak of the Stetson and she understood.

He was camping.

Camping. He could die out there—he *was* crazy, he *was*—this thing could turn into a blizzard, it could snow for days. But he was camping. And then the thought came to her: he was camping for her.

Later, when the tower floated out over the storm and the coals glowed in the stove and the darkness settled in around her like a blanket, she disconnected the radio and put the knife away in the drawer where it belonged. Then she propped herself in the corner of the bed, way out over the edge of the abyss, and watched his fire raging in the cold heart of the night. He would be back, she knew that now, and she would be ready for him.

(1989)

IF THE RIVER WAS WHISKEY

The water was a heartbeat, a pulse, it stole the heat from his body and pumped it to his brain. Beneath the surface, magnified through the shimmering lens of his face mask, were silver shoals of fish, forests of weed, a silence broken only by the distant throbbing hum of an outboard. Above, there was the sun, the white flash of a faraway sailboat, the weatherbeaten dock with its weatherbeaten rowboat, his mother in her deck chair, and the vast depthless green of the world beyond.

He surfaced like a dolphin, spewing water from the vent of his snorkel, and sliced back to the dock. The lake came with him, two bony arms and the wedge of a foot, the great heaving splash of himself flat out on the dock like something thrown up in a storm. And then, without pausing even to snatch up a towel, he had the spinning rod in hand and the silver lure was sizzling out over the water, breaking the surface just above the shadowy arena he'd fixed in his mind. His mother looked up at the splash. "Tiller," she called, "come get a towel."

His shoulders quaked. He huddled and stamped his feet, but he never took his eyes off the tip of the rod. Twitching it suggestively, he reeled with the jerky, hesitant motion that would drive lunker fish to a frenzy. Or so he'd read, anyway.

"Tilden, do you hear me?"

"I saw a Northern," he said. "A big one. Two feet maybe." The lure was in. A flick of his wrist sent it back. Still reeling, he ducked his head to wipe his nose on his wet shoulder. He could feel the sun on his back now and he envisioned the skirted lure in the water, sinuous, sensual, irresistible, and he waited for the line to quicken with the strike.

* * *

The porch smelled of pine—old pine, dried up and dead—and it depressed him. In fact, everything depressed him—especially this vacation. Vacation. It was a joke. Vacation from what?

He poured himself a drink—vodka and soda, tall, from the plastic half-gallon jug. It wasn't noon yet, the breakfast dishes were in the sink, and Tiller and Caroline were down at the lake. He couldn't see them through the screen of trees, but he heard the murmur of their voices against the soughing of the branches and the sadness of the birds. He sat heavily in the creaking wicker chair and looked out on nothing. He didn't feel too hot. In fact, he felt as if he'd been cored and dried, as if somebody had taken a pipe cleaner and run it through his veins. His head ached too, but the vodka would take care of that. When he finished it, he'd have another, and then maybe a grilled swiss on rye. Then he'd start to feel good again.

* * *

His father was talking to the man and his mother was talking to the woman. They'd met at the bar about twenty drinks ago and his father was into his could-have-been, should-have-been, way-back-when mode, and the man, bald on top and with a ratty beard and long greasy hair like his father's, was trying to steer the conversation back to building supplies. The woman had whole galaxies of freckles on her chest, and she leaned forward in her sundress and told his mother scandalous stories about people she'd never heard of. Tiller had drunk all the Coke and eaten all the beer nuts he could hold. He watched the Pabst Blue Ribbon sign flash on and off above the bar and he watched the woman's freckles move in and out of the gap between her breasts. Outside it was dark and a cool clean scent came in off the lake.

"Uh huh, yeah," his father was saying, "the To the Bone Band. I played rhythm and switched off vocals with Dillie Richards. . . ."

The man had never heard of Dillie Richards.

"Black dude, used to play with Taj Mahal?"

The man had never heard of Taj Mahal.

"Anyway," his father said, "we used to do all this really outrageous stuff by people like Muddy, Howlin' Wolf, Luther Allison—"

"She didn't," his mother said.

The woman threw down her drink and nodded and the front of her dress went crazy. Tiller watched her and felt the skin go tight across his shoulders and the back of his neck, where he'd been burned the first day. He wasn't wearing any underwear, just shorts. He looked away. "Three abortions, two kids," the woman said. "And she never knew who the father of the second one was."

"Drywall isn't worth a damn," the man said. "But what're you going to do?"

"Paneling?" his father offered.

The man cut the air with the flat of his hand. He looked angry. "Don't talk to me about paneling," he said.

*   *   *

Mornings, when his parents were asleep and the lake was still, he would take the rowboat to the reedy cove on the far side of the lake where the big pike lurked. He didn't actually know if they lurked there, but if they lurked anywhere, this would be the place. It looked fishy, mysterious, sunken logs looming up dark from the shadows beneath the boat, mist rising like steam, as if the bottom were boiling with ravenous, cold-eyed, killer pike that could slice through monofilament with a snap of their jaws and bolt ducklings in a gulp. Besides, Joe Matochik, the old man who lived in the cabin next door and could charm frogs by stroking their bellies, had told him that this was where he'd find them.

It was cold at dawn and he'd wear a thick homeknit sweater over his T-shirt and shorts, sometimes pulling the stretched-out hem of it down like a skirt to warm his thighs. He'd take an apple with him or a slice of brown bread and peanut butter. And of course the orange lifejacket his mother insisted on.

When he left the dock he was always wearing the lifejacket—for form's sake and for the extra warmth it gave him against the raw morning air. But when he got there, when he stood in the swaying basin of the boat to cast his Hula Popper or Abu Reflex, it got in the way and he took it off. Later, when the sun ran through him and he didn't need the sweater, he balled it up on the seat beside him, and sometimes, if it was good and hot, he shrugged out of his T-shirt and shorts too. No one could see him in the cove, and it made his breath come quick to be naked like that under the morning sun.

*   *   *

"I heard you," he shouted, and he could feel the veins stand out in his neck, the rage come up in him like something killed and dead and brought back to life. "What kind of thing is that to tell a kid, huh? About his own father?"

She wasn't answering. She'd backed up in a corner of the kitchen and she wasn't answering. And what could she say, the bitch? He'd heard her. Dozing on the trundle bed under the stairs, wanting a drink but too weak to get up and make one, he'd heard voices from the kitchen, her voice and Tiller's. "Get used to it," she said, "he's a drunk, your father's a drunk," and then he was up off the bed as if something had exploded inside of him and he had her by the shoulders—always the shoulders and never the face, that much she'd taught him—and Tiller was gone, out the door and gone. Now, her voice low in her throat, a sick and guilty little smile on her lips, she whispered, "It's true."

"Who are you to talk?—you're shit-faced yourself." She shrank away from him, that sick smile on her lips, her shoulders hunched. He wanted to smash things, kick in the damn stove, make her hurt.

"At least I have a job," she said.

"I'll get another one, don't you worry."

"And what about Tiller? We've been here two weeks and you haven't done one damn thing with him, nothing, zero. You haven't even been down to the lake. Two hundred feet and you haven't even been down there once." She came up out of the corner now, feinting like a boxer, vicious, her sharp little fists balled up to drum on him. She spoke in a snarl. "What kind of father are you?"

He brushed past her, slammed open the cabinet, and grabbed the first bottle he found. It was whiskey, cheap whiskey, Four Roses, the shit she drank. He poured out half a water glass full and drank it down to spite her. "I hate the beach, boats, water, trees. I hate you."

She had her purse and she was halfway out the screen door. She hung there a second, looking as if she'd bitten into something rotten. "The feeling's mutual," she said, and the door banged shut behind her.

* * *

There were too many complications, too many things to get between him and the moment, and he tried not to think about them. He tried not to think about his father—or his mother either—in the same way that he tried not to think about the pictures of the bald-headed stick people in Africa or meat in its plastic wrapper and how it got there. But when he did think about his father he thought about the river-was-whiskey day.

It was a Tuesday or Wednesday, middle of the week, and when he came home from school the curtains were drawn and his father's car was in the driveway. At the door, he could hear him, the *chunk-chunk* of the chords and the rasping nasal whine that seemed as if it belonged to someone else. His father was sitting in the dark, hair in his face, bent low over the guitar. There was an open bottle of liquor on the coffee table and a clutter of beer bottles. The room stank of smoke.

It was strange, because his father hardly ever played his guitar anymore—he mainly just talked about it. In the past tense. And it was strange too—and bad—because his father wasn't at work. Tiller dropped his bookbag on the telephone stand. "Hi, Dad," he said.

His father didn't answer. Just bent over the guitar and played the same song, over and over, as if it were the only song he knew. Tiller sat on the sofa and listened. There was a verse—one verse—and his father repeated it three or four times before he broke off and slurred the words into a sort of chant or hum, and then he went back to the words again. After the fourth repetition, Tiller heard it:

If the river was whiskey,
And I was a divin' duck,
I'd swim to the bottom,
Drink myself back up.

For half an hour his father played that song, played it till anything else would have sounded strange. He reached for the bottle when he finally stopped, and that was when he noticed Tiller. He looked surprised. Looked as if he'd just woke up. "Hey, ladykiller Tiller," he said, and took a drink from the mouth of the bottle.

Tiller blushed. There'd been a Sadie Hawkins dance at school and Janet Rumery had picked him for her partner. Ever since, his father had called him ladykiller, and though he wasn't exactly sure what it meant, it made him blush anyway, just from the tone of it. Secretly, it pleased him. "I really liked the song, Dad," he said.

"Yeah?" His father lifted his eyebrows and made a face. "Well, come home to Mama, doggie-o. Here," he said, and he held out an open beer. "You ever have one of these, ladykiller Tiller?" He was grinning. The sleeve of his shirt was torn and his elbow was raw and there was a hard little clot of blood over his shirt pocket. "With your sixth-grade buddies out behind the handball court, maybe? No?"

Tiller shook his head.

"You want one? Go ahead, take a hit."

Tiller took the bottle and sipped tentatively. The taste wasn't much. He looked up at his father. "What does it mean?" he said. "The song, I mean—the one you were singing. About the whiskey and all."

His father gave him a long slow grin and took a drink from the big bottle of clear liquor. "I don't know," he said finally, grinning wider to show his tobacco-stained teeth. "I guess he just liked whiskey, that's all." He picked up a cigarette, made as if to light it, and then put it down again. "Hey," he said, "you want to sing it with me?"

*   *   *

All right, she'd hounded him and she'd threatened him and she was going to leave him, he could see that clear as day. But he was going to show her. And the kid too. He wasn't drinking. Not today. Not a drop.

He stood on the dock with his hands in his pockets while Tiller scrambled around with the fishing poles and oars and the rest of it. Birds were screeching in the trees and there was a smell of diesel fuel on the air. The sun cut into his head like a knife. He was sick already.

"I'm giving you the big pole, Dad, and you can row if you want."

He eased himself into the boat and it fell away beneath him like the mouth of a bottomless pit.

"I made us egg salad, Dad, your favorite. And I brought some birch beer."

He was rowing. The lake was churning underneath him, the wind was up and reeking of things washed up on the shore, and the damn oars kept slipping out of the oarlocks, and he was rowing. At the last minute he'd wanted to go back for a quick drink, but he didn't, and now he was rowing.

"We're going to catch a pike," Tiller said, hunched like a spider in the stern.

There was spray off the water. He was rowing. He felt sick. Sick and depressed.

"We're going to catch a pike, I can feel it. I know we are," Tiller said, "I know it. I just know it."

*   *   *

It was too much for him all at once—the sun, the breeze that was so sweet he could taste it, the novelty of his father rowing, pale arms and a dead cigarette clenched between his teeth, the boat rocking, and the birds whispering—and he closed his eyes a minute, just to keep from going dizzy with the joy of it. They were in deep water already. Tiller was trolling with a plastic worm and spinner, just in case, but he didn't have much faith in catching anything out here. He was taking his father to the cove with the submerged logs and beds of weed—that's where they'd connect, that's where they'd catch pike.

"Jesus," his father said when Tiller spelled him at the oars. Hands shaking, he crouched in the stern and tried to light a cigarette. His face was gray and the hair beat crazily around his face. He went through half a book of matches and then threw the cigarette in the water. "Where are you taking us, anyway," he said, "—the Indian Ocean?"

"The pike place," Tiller told him. "You'll like it, you'll see."

The sun was dropping behind the hills when they got there, and the water went from blue to gray. There was no wind in the cove. Tiller let the boat glide out across the still surface while his father finally got a cigarette lit, and then he dropped anchor. He was excited. Swallows dove at the surface, bullfrogs burped from the reeds. It was the perfect time to fish, the hour when the big lunker pike would cruise among the sunken logs, hunting.

"All right," his father said, "I'm going to catch the biggest damn fish in the lake," and he jerked back his arm and let fly with the heaviest sinker in the tackle box dangling from the end of the rod. The line hissed through the guys and there was a thunderous splash that probably terrified every pike within half a mile. Tiller looked over his shoulder as he reeled in his silver spoon. His father winked at him, but he looked grim.

It was getting dark, his father was out of cigarettes, and Tiller had cast the spoon so many times his arm was sore, when suddenly the big rod began to buck. "Dad! Dad!" Tiller shouted, and his father lurched up as if he'd been stabbed. He'd been dozing, the rod propped against the gunwale, and Tiller had been studying the long suffering-lines in his father's face, the grooves in his forehead, and the puffy discolored flesh beneath his eyes. With his beard and long hair and with the crumpled suffering look on his face, he was the picture of the crucified Christ Tiller had contemplated a hundred times at church. But now the rod was bucking and his father had hold of it and he was playing a fish, a big fish, the tip of the rod dipping all the way down to the surface.

"It's a pike, Dad, it's a pike!"

His father strained at the pole. His only response was a grunt, but Tiller saw something in his eyes he hardly recognized anymore, a connection, a charge, as if the fish were sending a current up the line, through the pole, and into his hands and body and brain. For a full three minutes he played the fish, his slack biceps gone rigid, the cigarette clamped in his mouth, while Tiller hovered over him with the landing net. There was a surge, a splash, and the thing was in the net, and Tiller had it over the side and into the boat. "It's a pike," his father said, "goddamnit, look at the thing, look at the size of it."

It wasn't a pike. Tiller had watched Joe Matochik catch one off the dock one night. Joe's pike had been dangerous, full of teeth, a long, lean, tapering strip of muscle and pounding life. This was no pike. It was a carp. A fat, pouty, stinking, ugly mud carp. Trash fish. They shot them with arrows and threw them up on the shore to rot. Tiller looked at his father and felt like crying.

"It's a pike," his father said, and already the thing in his eyes was gone, already it was over, "it's a pike. Isn't it?"

* * *

It was late—past two, anyway—and he was drunk. Or no, he was beyond drunk. He'd been drinking since morning, one tall vodka and soda after another, and he didn't feel a thing. He sat on the porch in the dark and he couldn't see the lake, couldn't hear it, couldn't even smell it. Caroline and Tiller were asleep. The house was dead silent.

Caroline was leaving him, which meant that Tiller was leaving him. He knew it. He could see it in her eyes and he heard it in her voice. She was soft once, his soft-eyed lover, and now she was hard, unyielding, now she was his worst enemy. They'd had the couple from the roadhouse in for drinks and burgers earlier that night and he'd leaned over the table to tell the guy something—Ed, his name was—joking really, nothing serious, just making conversation. "Vodka and soda," he said, "that's my drink. I used to drink vodka and grapefruit juice, but it tore the lining out of my stomach." And then Caroline, who wasn't even listening, stepped in and said, "Yeah, and that"—pointing to the glass—"tore the lining out of your brain." He looked up at her. She wasn't smiling.

All right. That was how it was. What did he care? He hadn't wanted to come up here anyway—it was her father's idea. Take the cabin for a month, the old man had said, pushing, pushing in that way he had, and get yourself turned around. Well, he wasn't turning around, and they could all go to hell.

After a while the chill got to him and he pushed himself up from the chair and went to bed. Caroline said something in her sleep and pulled away from him as he lifted the covers and slid in. He was awake for a minute or two, feeling depressed, so depressed he wished somebody would come in and shoot him, and then he was asleep.

In his dream, he was out in the boat with Tiller. The wind was blowing, his hands were shaking, he couldn't light a cigarette. Tiller was watching him. He pulled at the oars and nothing happened. Then all of a sudden they were going down, the boat sucked out from under them, the water icy and black, beating in on them as if it were alive. Tiller called out to him. He saw his son's face, saw him going down, and there was nothing he could do.

(1987)

JULIANA CLOTH

She was just sixteen, and still under her mother's wing, when William Wamala first came to town with his bright bolts of cloth. He was a trader from the North, and he'd come across the vast gray plane of the lake so early in the morning he was like a ghost rising from the mist. Picture him there, out on the lake, the cylinders of rich cotton batik hanging limp over the prow of the invisible boat as if suspended in ether, no movement discernible but for the distant dip and rise of his arms, and all the birds crying out, startled, while the naked statue of his torso levitated above the still and glassy surface. The fishermen were the first to see him coming. They were the eyes of the village, just as the dogs were its nose, and as they cast their nets for *dagaa* they raised their palms in silent greeting.

Miriam—she was the only child of Ann Namirimu and the late Joseph Namirimu, who had been struck by lightning and scorched out of this existence when she was an infant strapped to her mother's back—was at first unaware that the trader had arrived in town with a new season's patterns. She was asleep at such an hour, crushed under the weight of her sixteen years and the disco dance she'd attended the night before with her Aunt Abusaga and Uncle Milton Metembe. Uncle Milton's special friend, Gladys Makuma, had been there, and he danced with her all night while Aunt Abusaga danced with Miriam and a mural of boys and men painted themselves to the walls, alive only in their eyes. People were smoking and drinking beer and whiskey. The music thumped with a percussive bass, and the beat held steady except in those intervals when the electricity faltered and people fell laughing into each other's arms. It was like Heaven, a picture-book Heaven, and Miriam, asleep, lived only to go back there and dance till her feet got so heavy she couldn't lift them.

Coffee woke her. And griddle cakes. And the crowing of fugitive cocks. Her mother, richly draped in last year's *kanga* and exuding a smell of warm sheets and butter, was fixing breakfast preparatory to her departure to the government office where she worked as a secretary. Miriam got up, and her dog got up with her. She ate with her mother in silence, sitting at the polished wooden table as if she were chained to it.

When her mother had left for work, Miriam dug a pack of cigarettes from an innocent-looking fold of her bedclothes and stuck one experimentally in the corner of her mouth. They were Top Club cigarettes ("For Men Whose Decisions Are Final") and they'd been slipped into her hand at the disco dance, right there in the middle of the floor, while she was rolling her hips and cranking her shoulders in synch with the beat. And who had slipped them to her, unlooked for and unasked for, as a kind of tribute? A boy she'd known all her life, James Kariango, who was eighteen years old and as tall and wide-shouldered as any man. She felt a hand touch hers as everyone moved in a blur of limbs through sweat that was like a wall, the fumes of whiskey rose from the makeshift bar, and the shadowy blue clouds of smoke hung like curtains around imaginary windows, and there he was, dancing with a woman she'd never seen before and eclipsing his left eye in a sly wink.

She had never smoked a cigarette. Her mother wouldn't allow it. Cigarettes were for common people, and Ann Namirimu was no common person—educated in the capital and sister to one of the president's top advisers—and neither was her daughter. Her daughter was a lady, one of only eight girls in the village to go on to high school, and she would conduct herself like a lady at all times or suffer the rolling thunder and sudden strikes of her mother's wrath, and, while Aunt Abusaga and Uncle Milton Metembe might have thought a disco dance appropriate for a young lady, Ann Namirimu certainly did not, and it was against her better judgment that Miriam had been allowed to go at all. Still, once Miriam had stuck the cigarette in her mouth and studied herself in the mirror from various angles, she couldn't help putting a match to the tip of it and letting the sweet stinging smoke invade her mouth and swell out her cheeks until she exhaled like a veteran. She never took the smoke into her lungs, and she didn't really like the taste of it, but she smoked the cigarette down to a nub, watching herself in the mirror all the while, and then she went out into the yard and carefully buried the remnant where her mother wouldn't find it.

She fed her dog, swept the mats, and dressed for school in a dream oriented around the pulse of disco music and the movement of liberated bodies. Then she went off to school, barefoot, carrying her shoes in one hand and her satchel of books and papers in the other, thinking she might just have a peek at the market on her way.

It was early still, the sun long in the trees and all the striped and spotted dogs of the town stretching and yawning in the street, but it might as well have been noon in the marketplace. Everyone was there. Farmwives with their yams and tomatoes arranged in baskets and laid out on straw mats, a man selling smoked colobus monkey and *pangas* honed to a killing edge, the fishermen with their fresh-caught tilapia and tiger fish, the game and cattle butchers and the convocation of flies that had gathered to taste the wet sweetness of the carcasses dangling from metal hooks. And the crafts merchants, too—the women selling bright orange and yellow plastic bowls, pottery, mats and rugs and cloth. Cloth especially. And that was where Miriam found him, William Wamala, the smiling, handsome, persuasive young man and budding entrepreneur from the North, and his fine print cotton cloth, his Juliana cloth.

For that was what they christened it that morning, the crowd gathered around his stall that was nothing more than a rickety table set up at the far end of the marketplace where no one bothered about anything: Juliana cloth. William Wamala stood behind the table with his measuring tape and shears and the bolts of cloth in a blue so deep you fell into it, with slashes of pale papaya and bright arterial red for contrast. "How much for the Juliana cloth?" one woman asked, and they all knew the name was right as soon as she'd pronounced it. Because this print, unlike any they'd seen before, didn't feature flowers or birds or palm fronds or the geometric patterns that had become so popular in the last few years but a name—a name in English, a big, bold name spelled out in the aforementioned colors that ran in crazy zigzags all over the deep-blue field. "Juliana," it read. "Juliana, Juliana, Juliana."

Miriam wanted the cloth as soon as she saw it. Everyone wanted it. Everyone wanted to be the first to appear in the streets or at the disco dance in a *kanga* cut from this scintillating and enticing cloth. But it was expensive. Very expensive. And exclusive to William Wamala. Who proved ultimately to be a very understanding and affectionate young man, willing to barter and trade if shillings were unavailable, accepting pots of honey, dried *dagaa*, beer, whiskey, and cigarettes in payment, and especially, when it came to the beauties of the town, exchanging his Juliana cloth for what might be considered their most precious commodity, a commodity that cost them nothing but pleasure in the trading.

When Miriam stopped in the market two mornings later, he was there still, but the crowd around him was smaller and the bolts of cloth much depleted. He sat back now in a new cane chair, his splayed feet crossed at the ankles and looming large over the scrap-strewn table, his smile a bit haggard, a beer pressed like a jewel to his lips. "Hello, Little Miss," he crooned in a booming basso when he saw her standing there with her satchel between two fat-armed women wrapped in *kangas* that were as ancient as dust and not much prettier.

She looked him in the eye. There was nothing to be afraid of: Beryl Obote, fifteen and resplendent in Juliana cloth, had told her all about him, how he hummed and sang while removing a girl's clothes and how insatiable he was, as if that very day were his last on earth. "Hello," Miriam said, smiling widely. "I was just wondering how much the Juliana cloth is today?"

"For you?" He never even bothered to remove his feet from the table, and she could see the faintest glimmer of interest rising from the deeps of his eyes like a lonely fish, only to sink back down again into the murk. He was satiated, bloated with drink and drugs and rich food, rubbed so raw between his legs he could scarcely walk, and she was no beauty, she knew that. She made her eyes big. She held her breath. Finally, while the fat-armed women bickered over something in thin piping voices and the sun vaulted through the trees to take hold of her face, he quoted her a price. In shillings.

The first to fall ill was Gladys Makuma, Uncle Milton Metembe's special friend. It was during the long rains in April, and many people were sick with one thing or another, and no one thought much about it at first. "Let her rest," Miriam's mother insisted from her long slab of an aristocrat's face. "Give her tea with lemon and honey and an herbal broth in the evenings, and she'll soon be on her feet again." But Miriam's mother was wrong.

Miriam went with Aunt Abusaga and Uncle Milton to Gladys Makuma's neat mud-and-clapboard house to bring her beef tea and what comfort they could, and when they stepped into the yard there was Lucy Mawenzi, doyenne of the local healers, coming gray and shaken through the door. Inside was a wake, though Gladys Makuma wasn't dead yet. Surrounded by her children, her husband, and his stone-faced sisters, she had shrunk into herself like some artifact in the dirt. All you could see of her face was nostrils and teeth, no flesh but the flesh of a mummy, and her hands on the sheets like claws. There would be no more disco-dancing for her, no more sharing a pint of whiskey with Uncle Milton Metembe in a dark boat on the dark, pitching lake. Even an optimist could see that, and Miriam was an optimist—her mother insisted on it.

With Beryl Obote, it was even worse, because Beryl was her coeval, a girl with skinny legs and saucer eyes who wore her hair untamed and had a laugh so infectious she could bring chaos to a classroom merely by opening her mouth. Miriam was coming back from the market one afternoon, the streets a soup of mud and an army of beetles crawling over every fixed surface, when she spotted Beryl in the crowd ahead of her, the Juliana cloth like the ocean come to life and her hair a dark storm brooding over it. But something was wrong. She was lurching from side to side, taking little circumscribed steps, and people were making way for her as if she were drunk. She wasn't drunk, though when she fell to the ground, subsiding into the mud as if her legs had dissolved beneath her, Miriam saw that her eyes were as red as any drunkard's. Miriam tried to help her up—never mind the yellow tub of *matoke,* rice and beans her mother had sent her for—but Beryl couldn't find her feet, and there was a terrible smell about her. "I'm so embarrassed," she said, and if you couldn't smell it you could see it, the diarrhea and the blood seeping through the deep blue cloth into the fetid trodden mud.

After that everyone fell sick: the women who'd bought the Juliana cloth with their favors, their husbands, and their husbands' special friends, not to mention all the men who had consorted with a certain barmaid at the disco—the one who wore a *kanga* in the blue, red, and papaya of decay. It was a hex, that was what people believed at first, a spell put on them by William Wamala, who had come all the way across the lake from the homeland of their ancestral enemies—he was a sorcerer, a practitioner of the black arts, an evil spirit in the guise of a handsome and affectionate young man. But it soon became apparent that no hex, no matter how potent and far-reaching, could affect so many. No, this was a disease, one among a host of diseases in a region surfeited with them, and it seemed only natural that they call it Juliana's disease, after the cloth that had brought it to them.

Typically, it began with a headache and chills; then there was the loosening of the bowels and the progressive wasting. It could have been malaria or tuberculosis or marasmus, but it wasn't. It was something new. Something no one had ever seen before, and all who caught it—women and men in their prime, girls like Beryl Obote—were eventually wrapped up in bark cloth and sent to the grave before the breath of two months' time had been exhausted.

Uncle Milton Metembe and Aunt Abusaga contracted it at the same time, almost to the day, and Miriam moved into their house to tend them, afraid in her heart that the taint would spread to her. She cooked them soup and rice through the reek of their excrement, which flowed like stained water; she swept the house and changed their soiled sheets and read to them from the comic papers and the Bible. At night, the rats rustled in the thatch, and the things of the dark raised their voices in an unholy howl, and Miriam fell away deep into herself and listened to her aunt and uncle's tortured breathing.

The doctors came then from America, France, and England, white people in white coats, and a few who were almost white and even stranger for that, as if they'd been incompletely dipped into the milk of white life. They drew blood like vampires, vial after vial, till the sick and weary trembled at the sight of them, and still there was no cause or cure in sight, the corpses mounting, the orphans wailing; then one day the doctors went away and the government made an announcement over the radio and in the newspapers. Juliana's disease, the government said, was something new indeed, very virulent and always fatal, and it was transmitted not through cloth or hexes but through sexual contact. Distribution of condoms was being made possible by immediate implementation in every town and village, through the strenuous efforts of the government, and every man and woman, every wife and girl and special friend, should be sure of them every time sexual union was achieved. There was no other way and no other hope, short of monkhood, spinsterhood, or abstinence.

The news rocked the village. It was unthinkable. They were poor people who didn't have theaters or supermarkets or shiny big cars for diversion—they had only a plate of *dagaa*, a glass of beer, and sex, and every special friend had a special friend and there was no stopping it, even on pain of death. Besides which, the promised condoms never arrived, as if any true man or sensitive woman would allow a cold loop of latex rubber to come between them and pleasure in any event. People went on, almost defiantly, tempting fate, challenging it, unshakable in their conviction that though the whole world might wilt and die at their feet, they themselves would remain inviolate. The disco was as crowded as ever, the sales of beer and palm wine skyrocketed, and the corpses were shunted in a steady procession from sickbed to grave. Whatever else it might have been, it was a time of denial.

Miriam's mother was outraged. To her mind, the town's reaction was nothing short of suicidal. Through her position at the government office she had been put in charge of the local campaign for safe sex, and it was her job to disseminate the unwelcome news. Though the condoms remained forever only forthcoming because of logistical problems in the capital, Miriam's mother typed a sheet of warning and reproduced it a thousand times, and a facsimile of this original soon sagged damply from every tree and post and hoarding in town. "Love Carefully," it advised, and "Zero Grazing," a somewhat confusing command borrowed from one of the innumerable local agricultural campaigns. In fine print, it described the ravages of this very small and very dangerous thing, this virus (an entity for which there was no name in the local dialect), and what it was doing to the people of the village, the countryside, and even the capital. No one could have missed these ubiquitous sheets of warning and exhortation, and they would have had to be blind in any case to remain unaware of the plague in their midst. And deaf, too. Because the chorus of lament never ceased, day or night, and you could hear it from any corner of the village and even out in the mists of the lake—a thin, steady insectile wail broken only by the desperate beat of the disco.

"Suicide," Miriam's mother snarled over breakfast one morning, while Miriam, back now from her aunt and uncle's because there was no longer any reason to be there, tried to bury her eyes in her porridge. "Irresponsible, filthy behavior. You'd think everybody in town had gone mad." The day was still fresh, standing fully revealed in the lacy limbs of the yellow-bark acacia in the front yard. Miriam's dog looked up guiltily from the mat in the corner. Somewhere a cock crowed.

A long minute ticked by, punctuated by the scrape of spoon and bowl, and then her mother rose angrily from the table and slammed her cup into the wash-up tub. All her fury was directed at Miriam, as if fury alone could erect a wall between an adolescent girl and James Kariango of the nicotine-stained fingers. "No better than animals in the bush," she hissed, stamping across the floorboards with hunched shoulders and ricocheting eyes, talking to the walls, to the dense, mosquito-hung air, "and no shred of self-restraint or respect even."

Miriam wasn't listening. Her mother's rhetoric was as empty as a bucket in a dry well. What did *she* know? Sex to her mother was a memory. "That itch," she called it, as if it were something you caught from a poisonous leaf or a clump of nettles, but she never itched and as far as Miriam could see she'd as soon have a hyena in the house as a special friend. Miriam understood what her mother was telling her, she heard the fear seeping through the fierceness of that repetitive and concussive voice, and she knew how immortally lucky she was that William Wamala hadn't found her pretty enough to bother with. She understood all that and she was scared, the pleading eyes of Beryl Obote, Aunt Abusaga, Uncle Milton Metembe, and all the rest unsettling her dreams and quickening her pace through the market, but when James Kariango crept around back of the house fifteen minutes later and raised two yellowed fingers to his lips and whistled like an innocuous little bird, she was out the door before the sweat had time to sprout under her arms.

The first time he'd come around, indestructible with his new shoulders, jaunty and confident and fingering a thin silver chain at his throat, Miriam's mother had chased him down the front steps at the point of a paring knife, cursing into the trees till every head in the neighborhood was turned and every ear attuned. Tending Aunt Abusaga and Uncle Milton Metembe had in its way been Miriam's penance for attracting such a boy—any boy—and she'd been safe there among the walking dead and the weight of their sorrows. But now she was home and the months had gone by and James Kariango, that perfect specimen, was irresistible.

Her mother had gone off to work. Her dog was asleep. The eyes of the world were turned to the market and the laundry and a hundred other things. It was very, very early, and the taste of James Kariango's lips was like the taste of the sweetest fruit, mango and papaya and the sweet dripping syrup of fresh-cut pineapple. She kissed him there, behind the house, where the flowers grew thick and the lizards scuttered through the dirt and held their tails high in sign of some fleeting triumph. And then, after a long while, every pore of her body opening up like a desert plant at the first hint of rain, she led him inside.

He was very solemn. Very gentle. Every touch was electric, his fingers plugged into some internal socket, his face glowing like the ball at the disco. She let him strip off her clothes and she watched in fear and anticipation as he stepped out of his shorts and revealed himself to her. The fear was real. It was palpable. It meant the whole world and all of life. But then he laid her down in the familiar cradle of her bed and hovered over her in all of his glory, and, oh, it felt so good.

(1997)

· II ·

Death

BIG GAME

The way to hunt is for as long as you live against as long as there is such and such an animal.

—Ernest Hemingway, *Green Hills of Africa*

You could shoot anything you wanted, for a price, even the elephant, but Bernard tended to discourage the practice. It made an awful mess, for one thing, and when all was said and done it was the big animals—the elephant, the rhino, the water buff and giraffe—that gave the place its credibility, not to mention ambiance. They weren't exactly easy to come by, either. He still regretted the time he'd let the kid from the heavy-metal band pot one of the giraffes—even though he'd taken a cool twelve thousand dollars to the bank on that one. And then there was the idiot from MGM who opened up on a herd of zebra and managed to decapitate two ostriches and lame the Abyssinian ass in the process. Well, it came with the territory, he supposed, and it wasn't as if he didn't carry enough insurance on the big stuff to buy out half the L.A. Zoo if he had to. He was just lucky nobody had shot himself in the foot yet. Or the head. Of course, he was insured for that, too.

Bernard Puff pushed himself up from the big mahogany table and flung the dregs of his coffee down the drain. He wasn't exactly overwrought, but he was edgy, his stomach sour and clenched round the impermeable lump of his breakfast cruller, his hands afflicted with the little starts and tremors of the coffee shakes. He lit a cigarette to calm himself and gazed out the kitchen window on the dromedary pen, where one of the moth-eaten Arabians was methodically peeling the bark from an elm tree. He looked at the thing in amazement, as if he'd never seen it before—the flexible lip and stupid eyes, the dully working jaw—and made a mental note to offer a special on camels. The cigarette tasted like tin, like death. Somewhere a catbird began to call out in its harsh mewling tones.

The new people were due any minute now, and the prospect of new people always set him off—there were just too many things that could go wrong. Half of them didn't know one end of a rifle from the other, they expected brunch at noon and a massage an hour later, and they bitched about everything, from the heat to the flies to the roaring of the lions at night. Worse: they didn't seem to know what to make of him, the men regarding him as a subspecies of the blue-collar buddy, regaling him with a nonstop barrage of lickerish grins, dirty jokes and fractured grammar, and the women treating him like a cross between a maître d' and a water carrier. Dudes and greenhorns, all of them. Parvenus. Moneygrubbers. The kind of people who wouldn't know class if it bit them.

Savagely snubbing out the cigarette in the depths of the coffee mug, Bernard wheeled round on the balls of his feet and plunged through the swinging doors and out into the high dark hallway that gave onto the foyer. It was stifling already, the overhead fans chopping uselessly at the dead air round his ears and the sweat prickling at his new-shaven jowls as he stomped down the hall, a big man in desert boots and khaki shorts, with too much belly and something overeager and graceless in his stride. There was no one in the foyer and no one at the registration desk. (Espinoza was out feeding the animals—Bernard could hear the hyenas whooping in the distance—and the new girl—what was her name?—hadn't made it to work on time yet. Not once.) The place seemed deserted, though he knew Orbalina would be making up the beds and Roland sneaking a drink somewhere—probably out behind the lion cages.

For a long moment Bernard stood there in the foyer, framed against a bristling backdrop of kudu and oryx heads, as he checked the reservation card for the tenth time that morning:

Mike and Nicole Bender
BENDER REALTY
15125 Ventura Blvd.
Encino, California

Real estate people. Jesus. He'd always preferred the movie crowd—or even the rock-and-rollers, with their spiked wristbands and pouf hairdos. At least they were willing to buy into the illusion that Puff's African Game Ranch, situated on twenty-five hundred acres just outside Bakersfield, was the real thing—the Great Rift Valley, the Ngorongoro Crater, the Serengeti—but the real estate people saw every crack in the plaster. And all they wanted to know was how much he'd paid for the place and was the land subdividable.

He looked up into the yellow-toothed grin of the sable mounted on the wall behind him—the sable his father had taken in British East Africa back in the thirties—and let out a sigh. Business was business, and in the long run it didn't matter a whit who perforated his lions and gazelles—just as long as they paid. And they always paid, up front and in full. Bernard saw to that.

■ ■ ■

"What was it, Nik, six months ago when we went to Gino Parducci's for dinner? It was six months, wasn't it? And didn't I say we'd do the African thing in six months? Didn't I?"

Nicole Bender was curled up in the passenger seat of the white Jaguar XJS her husband had given her for Valentine's Day. A pile of knitting magazines lay scattered in her lap, atop a set of bamboo needles trailing an embryonic garment in a shade so pale it defied categorization. She was twenty-seven, blond, a former actress/model/poet/singer whose trainer had told her just two days earlier that she had perhaps the most perfectly sculpted physique of any woman he'd ever worked with. Of course, he was paid to say things like that, but in her heart she suspected they were true, and she needed to hear them. She turned to her husband. "Yes," she said. "You did. But I pictured us in Kenya or Tanzania, to tell the truth."

"Yeah, yeah," he fired back impatiently, "yeah, yeah, yeah," the words coming so fast they might have been bullets squeezed from one of the glistening new big-bore rifles in the trunk, "but you know I can't take six weeks off from work, not now when the new Beverly Hills office is about to open up and the Monte-moretto deal is all but in the bag . . . and besides, it's dangerous over there, what with the next revolution or war or whatever coming down every six minutes, and who do you think they're going to blame when the roof caves in? White people, right? And where do you think you'll want to be then?"

Mike Bender was a barely contained factory of energy, a steamroller of a man who had risen from receptionist to king and despot of his own real estate empire in the space of twelve short years. He was given to speechifying, the precious words dropping from his lips like coins from a slot machine, his fingertips alighting on his tongue, his hair, his ears, the crotch of his pants and his elbows as he spoke, writhing with the nervous energy that had made him rich. "And plus you've got your tsetse flies and black mambas and beriberi and the plague and god knows what all over there—I mean, picture Mexico, only a hundred times worse. No, listen, trust me—Gino swore this place is as close as it gets to the real thing, only without the hassles." He lowered his sunglasses to give her a look. "You're telling me you really want to get your ass chewed off in some lopsided tent in, in"—he couldn't seem to think of a place sufficiently grim, so he improvised—"Zambeziland?"

Nicole shrugged, giving him a glimpse of the pouty little half-smile she used to work up for the photographers when she was nineteen and doing the summerwear ads for JCPenney.

"You'll get your zebra-skin rug yet, you wait and see," Mike assured her, "and a couple lions' heads and gazelles or whatever for the wall in the den, okay?"

The Jaguar shot across the desert like a beam of light. Nicole lifted the knitted needles from her lap, thought better of it, and set them down again. "Okay," she said in a breathy little whisper, "but I just hope this place isn't too, you know, *tacky.*"

A sudden harsh laugh erupted from the back seat, where Mike Bender's twelve-year-old daughter, Jasmine Honeysuckle Rose Bender, was stretched out supine with the last ten issues of *Bop* and a sixpack of New York Seltzer. "Get real, will you? I mean like shooting lions in Bakersfield? Tacky city. Tacky, tacky, tacky."

Up front, behind the wheel, his buttocks caressed by the supple kid leather of the seat and visions of bontebok leaping before his eyes, Mike Bender was mildly annoyed. He'd had an itch to hunt lion and elephant and rhino since he was a kid and first read *Confessions of a White Hunter* and the Classic Comics version of *King Solomon's Mines.* And this was his chance. So maybe it wasn't Africa, but who had the time to go on safari? If he could spare three days he was lucky. And you couldn't shoot anything over there anyway. Not anymore. Everything was a preserve now, a game park, a conservancy. There was no more white hunters. Just photographers.

He wanted to say "Give me a break, will you?" in his most imperious voice, the voice that sent his sales force scurrying for cover and his competitors into shock, but he held his peace. Nothing was going to ruin this for him. Nothing.

It was midafternoon. The sun hung overhead like an egg shirred in a cup. The thermometer in the feed shed was pushing a hundred and fifteen degrees, nothing was moving but for the vultures aloft in the poor bleached expanse of the sky, and the whole world seemed to have gone to sleep. Except for Bernard. Bernard was beside himself—the Benders had been due at 10:00 A.M. and here it was quarter past two and still they hadn't arrived. He'd had Espinoza let the Tommies and eland out of their pens at nine, but he was afraid they'd all be lying up in the heat, and by noon he'd sent him out to round them up again. The giraffes were nowhere to be seen, and the elephant, tethered to a live oak Bernard had pruned to resemble an umbrella thorn, was looking as rumpled and dusty as a heap of Taiwanese luggage abandoned at the airport.

Bernard stood in the glare of the dried-up yard, squinting out on the screen of elephant grass and euphorbia he'd planted to hide the oil rig (if you knew it was there you could just detect the faintest motion of the big steel arm as it rose and fell and rose and fell again). He felt hopeless. For all the effort he'd put into it, the place looked like a circus camp, the bombed-out remains of a zoo, a dusty flat baking former almond ranch in the sun-blasted southeast corner of the San Joaquin Valley—which is exactly what it was. What would the Benders think? More important, what would they think at six hundred dollars a day, payable in advance, plus prices that ranged from a thousand a pop on the gazelles on up to twelve thousand for a lion and "priced as available" for the elephant? Real estate people had balked on him before, and business hadn't exactly been booming lately.

The vultures wheeled overhead. He was running sweat. The sun felt like a firm hand steering him toward the cool of the kitchen and a tall glass of quinine water (which he drank for effect rather than therapeutic value: there wasn't a malarial mosquito within a thousand miles). He was just about to pack it in when he caught the distant glint of sun on safety glass and saw the Benders' car throwing up dust clouds at the far end of the drive.

"Roland!" he bellowed, and every mortal ounce of him was in motion now. "Let the monkeys out into the trees! And the parrots!" Suddenly he was jogging across the dusty lot and up the path to where the elephant lay collapsed beneath the tree. He was working at the slip of the tether to set her loose and wondering if Roland would have the sense to stir up the lions and hyenas for the sake of sound effects, when suddenly she rose to her feet with a great blowing snort and gave a feeble trumpet.

Well. And that was a break—at least now he wouldn't have to use the ivory goad.

Bernard looked up at the old elephant in wonder—she still had a bit of showmanship in her, after all. Either that, or it was senile dementia. She was old—Bernard didn't know quite how old, though he did know she was a veteran of thirty-eight years with the Ringling Bros. and Barnum & Bailey Circus who'd performed under the name "Bessie Bee" and responded to "Shamba"—that is, if you happened to have the ivory goad in your hand. Bernard shot a glance up the drive, where a white Jaguar sedan was beginning to define itself against a billowing backdrop of dust, and then he heard the screech of the monkeys as they shot out of their cages and up into the trees, and he began to compose himself. He forced a smile, all red-cheeked and long-toothed, cinched the leopard-skin belt, squared his pith helmet and marched forward to greet his guests.

By the time the Benders rolled up to the veranda, the parrots were in the trees, the marabou stork was pecking at a spot of offal in the dirt, and the lions were roaring lustily from their hidden pens out back. Roland, decked out in his Masai toga and lion's-tooth necklace, bounded down the steps with alacrity to hold open the door for Bender, while Bessie Bee shambled around in the near distance, flapping her ears and blowing about in the dust. "Mr. Bender," Bernard cried, extending his hand to a fortyish man in sunglasses and polo shirt, "welcome to Africa."

Bender sprang out of the car like a child at the zoo. He was tall, lean, tanned—why did they all have to look like tennis pros? Bernard wondered—and stood there twitching a moment in the heat. He pumped Bernard's hand professionally and then launched into a lip-jerking, ear-tugging, foot-thumping apology: "Sorry we're late, Bernard, but my wife—have you met my wife?—my wife just had to get a couple rolls of film and we wound up buying out half of Reynoso's Camera in Bakersfield—you know it?—good prices. Real good prices. Hell, we needed a new video camera anyway, especially with"—he gestured to take in the house, the outbuildings, the elephant, the monkeys in the trees and the sun-blasted plains beyond—"all this."

Bernard was nodding, smiling, murmuring agreement, but he was on auto-pilot—his attention was fixed on the wife, whom Roland was fussing over now on the far side of the car. She raised her lovely white arms to fluff her hair and imprison her eyes behind a pair of sunglasses and Bernard called out a greeting in his best British-colonial accent (though he was British by ancestry only and had never in his life been east of Reno). The second wife, of course, he was thinking as she returned his greeting with a vague little pouting smile.

"Yes, yes, of course," Bernard said in response to some further idiocy from the husband's lips, his watery blue eyes shifting to the daughter now—as black-headed as an Indian, and nearly as dark—and he saw right away that she was trouble, the sort of child who cultivates ugliness as a weapon.

Nicole Bender gave him a long slow appraisal over the hood of the car, and in the next moment he was ducking round the grille to squeeze her hand as if he were trying on a glove for size. "Beastly day," he said, proud of the Britishism, and then he was leading her up the broad stone steps and into the house, while her husband fumbled with an armload of guns and the daughter slouched along behind, already complaining about something in a nagging querulous little whine of a voice.

"I'm not saying that, Mike—you're not listening to me. I *said* the gazelles are very nice and they'll be perfect for the office, but I wanted something, well, *bigger* for the front hall and at least three of the zebra—two for the den, I thought, and we're going to need one for the ski lodge . . . you know, to hide that ugly paneling behind the bar?"

Mike Bender was deep into his fourth gin and tonic. Already the elation he'd felt over his first kill had begun to dissipate, replaced now by a gnawing sense of frustration and anger—why couldn't Nikki shut her face, even for a second? No sooner had they changed clothes and got out there on the savannah or veldt or whatever you wanted to call it, than she'd started in. He'd squeezed off a clean shot at a Thomson's gazelle at two hundred yards and before the thing's head had hit the ground, she was running it down. *Oh,* she gasped, as if she'd been surprised on the toilet, *but it's so small, isn't it?* And then she struck a pose for Puff and the colored guy who carried the guns and skinned out the carcasses. *Almost like a rabbit with horns.*

And now the great white hunter was leaning across the table to reassure her, his gut drawn tight against the khaki safari shirt, his accent so phony it was like something out of a Monty Python routine. "Mrs. Bender, Nicole," he began, mopping his blood blister of a face with a big checked handkerchief, "we'll go out for zebra in the morning, when it's cool, and if it's three you want, we'll get them, there's no problem with that. Four, if you like. Five. If you've got the bullets, we've got the game."

Mike watched as the canny crewcut head swiveled toward him. "And Mike,"

Puff said, as amenable as any tour guide but with just the right hint of stagery in his voice, "in the evening, it's the big stuff, the man-maker, old Simba himself."

As if in response, there was a cough and roar from somewhere out beyond the darkened windows, and Mike Bender could feel the wildness of it on the thin night air—lion, the lion he'd dreamed about since his aunt had taken him to the Central Park Zoo as a boy and the roar of the great shaggy yellow-eyed things had shaken him to his primordial root. To be out there, in that African night that was haunted with predators, big-headed and thick-skinned, the pounce, the slash, the crack of sinew and bone—it was at once terrifying and wonderful. But what was that smell of oil?

"What do you say, old man? Are you game?" Puff was leering at him now, and behind Puff's blocky leonine figure, the faces of his wife and daughter, arrayed like tribal masks.

Nothing fazed Mike Bender, the King of Encino. No seller could hold out against him, no buyer hope for more. His contracts were vises, his promotions sledgehammers, his holdings as solid as a mountain of iron. "I'm game," he said, touching his lips, running his fingers through his hair, jabbing at his elbows and underarms in a rising plume of metabolic excess. "Just oil up my H&H Magnum and point me toward 'em; it's what I've wanted all my life—"

There was a silence and his words seemed to hang in the air, empty of conviction. His daughter crouched over her plate, looking as if she were sucking on something rotten; his wife had that alert, let's-go-shopping look in her glittering little eyes. "Really. I mean, ever since I was a kid, and—how many are out there, anyway? Or do you keep count?"

Puff stroked the graying stubble of his head. There was another roar, muted this time, followed by the stabbed-in-the-belly whoop of the hyena. "Oh, we've got a good-sized pride out there—twelve or fourteen, I'd say, and a few rogue males."

"Are there any big ones, with manes? That's what we want." He shifted his gaze to Nicole. "Maybe the whole thing, stuffed, standing up on its hind legs, what do you think, Nik? For maybe the reception room at the Beverly Hills office?" And then he made a joke of it: "Hey, if Prudential can get away with it—"

Nicole looked satisfied. So did Puff. But his daughter wasn't about to let him off so easily. She let out a snort of contempt, and the three of them turned toward her. "And so you go and kill some poor lion that isn't hurting anybody, and what's that supposed to prove?"

Puff exchanged a look with him, as if to say, *Now isn't that adorable?*

Jasmine Honeysuckle Rose pushed aside her salad plate. Her hair hung in her eyes in greasy black coils. She'd eaten nothing, having separated the tomatoes from the greens and the greens from the croutons and the croutons from the garbanzo beans. "Sting," she spat, "Brigitte Bardot, the New Kids, all of them say it's like animal death camps, like Hitler, and they're doing this special concert to save the animals in France, in Paris—"

"One lion more or less isn't going to hurt anybody," Nicole said, cutting the child off, and her mouth was drawn tight against the swell of her collagen-enhanced lips. "And I think your father's idea is super. An erect lion standing there as people come in the door—it's, it's symbolic is what it is."

Mike Bender couldn't tell if he was being ribbed or not. "Listen, Jasmine," he began, and his leg started to thump under the table as he tugged at his ear and fooled with his cutlery.

"Jasmine Honeysuckle Rose," she fired back.

Mike knew she'd always hated her name, an inspiration of her mother, the sort of crackbrained woman who saw spirits in the sunset and believed that he was the reincarnation of John D. Rockefeller. To throw it up to him, and to remind him of his ex-wife and all the mistakes he'd ever made or contemplated, his daughter insisted on her full name. Always.

"Okay: Jasmine Honeysuckle Rose," he said, "listen to me. All of this hippie-dippy save-the-environment crap might be all right if you're twelve, but you've got to realize hunting is as natural a part of man as, as—"

"Eating or drinking," Puff put in, rounding off the participle with a pseudo-Etonian ring.

"*Right!*" Jasmine cried, on her feet now, her eyes like sinkholes, her mouth twitching at the corners. "And so's shitting, farting and, and *fucking!*" And then she was gone, stamping down the trophy-hung hallway to her room, where she flung the door to with a thunderous crash.

A moment of silence descended on the table. Puff's eyes lingered on Nicole as she raised her arms to stretch and show off her breasts and the prim white pockets of shaved flesh under her arms. "Cute kid, huh?" he said. There was no mistaking the sarcasm this time.

"Real cute," Nicole said, and they were in league.

Turning to Mike as the colored guy came through the door with a platter of gazelle steaks and mesquite-roasted ears of corn, Puff let his voice grow warm and confidential. "Zebra in the morning, Mike," he said. "You'll like that." He leveled his watery gaze on him. "And then"—the gazelle steaks hitting the table, little dollops of blood-running flesh—"and then we load up for lion."

It wasn't that he bolted, actually—Bernard had seen worse, much worse—but he was on the verge of it. Either that or he was about to pass out. Any way you sliced it, it was a bad situation, the kind of encounter that made Bernard wish he'd never heard of Africa, lions, game parks or real estate people.

They'd come on the lion in the old almond grove. The trees there were like twisted antlers, leafless and dead, set out in rows as far as you could see, and the ground beneath them was littered with fallen branches. "Not too close now," Bernard had warned, but Bender wanted to be sure of the shot, and he got himself in a bind. In the next moment he was standing there knee-deep in the litter, jerking and shrugging like a spastic, the gun to his shoulder and nowhere to go, and the lion was coming at him with as much pure malice as Bernard had seen in his fourteen years as proprietor of Puff's African Game Ranch. And while Bernard didn't like to intervene—it always caused hard feelings after the fact—Mrs. Bender was a heartbeat away from being an aggrieved widow and his own insurance rates were about to go through the roof, never mind the lawsuits. It was a moment, no doubt about it.

The night before, after the Benders had gone off to bed, Bernard had had Espinoza go out and stir up the lions a bit and then set them loose—without their supper. That always put them in a mood, no matter how old, toothless and gimpy they might be. Let them go a night without horse meat and they were as savage as anything you'd encounter anywhere on earth. For Bernard, it was standard practice. Give the guests their money's worth, that was his motto. If they suspected that the lions were penned up ninety-nine percent of the time, none of them let on—for all they knew the beasts lived out there among the drought-ravaged almond trees and camouflaged oil rigs. And besides, it wasn't as if they had anywhere to go—the entire property was circumscribed by a twenty-foot-deep dry moat with a twelve-foot-high electrified fence rising up behind it. The ones the guests didn't put holes in would just wander back to their cages in a day or so, roaring their bellies out for horse meat and offal.

In the morning, after a breakfast of kippers and eggs and while the daughter slept in, Bernard had taken the Benders out after their zebra. They'd driven out to the water hole—an abandoned Olympic-sized swimming pool Bernard had planted up to look natural—and, after some discussion of price, the Benders—or, rather, the wife—decided on five. She was something, the wife. As good-looking a woman as Bernard had ever laid eyes on, and a better shot than her husband. She took two of the zebra at a hundred and fifty yards, barely a mark on the hides. "You can shoot, little lady," Bernard said as they sauntered up to the nearest of the fallen zebra.

The zebra lay there on its side beneath the knifing sun, and already the first flies had begun to gather. Bender was crouched over one of the carcasses in the near distance, inspecting it for bullet holes, and Roland was back in the Jeep, whetting his skinning knife. From the hills beyond, one of the starved lions let loose with an irascible roar.

Nicole smiled at him, pretty—awfully pretty—in her Banana Republic shorts and safari shirt. "I try," she said, unbuttoning her shirt to reveal a peach-colored halter top decorated with a gold pin in the shape of a rifle. He had to bend close to read the inscription: *Nicole Bender, Supermarksman Award, N.R.A., 1989.*

Then it was lunch and siesta, followed by gin and bitters and a few hands at canasta to while away the waning hours of the afternoon. Bernard did everything he could to amuse the lady, and not just in the interest of business—there was something there, something beating hot and hard beneath the mask of blusher and eyeliner and the puffed-up lips, and he couldn't help feeling the tug of it. It had been tough since Stella Rae had left him, and he took his tumbles where he could find them—after all, *that* came with the territory too.

At any rate, they took the Jeep Wrangler, a cooler of beer, Bender's .375 Holland & Holland, the lady's Winchester .458 Mag and his own stopper—the .600 Nitro—and headed out to where the twisted black branches of the orchard raked the flanks of the hills in the far corner of the ranch. It was where the lions always went when you set them loose. There was a little brook there—it was a torrent in season, but now it wasn't much more than a trickle. Still, they could lap up some water and roll in the grass and find a poor striped shade beneath the naked branches of the trees.

From the start, even when they were still on the gin and bitters and waiting out the heat, Bender had seemed edgy. The man couldn't sit still, rattling on about escrows and titles and whatnot, all the while tugging at his lips and ears and tongue like a third-base coach taking signals from the dugout. It was nerves, that's what it was: Bernard had taken enough dudes out there to recognize a fellow measuring out his own manhood against that big tawny thing stalking his imagination. One guy—he was a TV actor; maybe a fag, even—had got himself so worked up he'd overloaded on the gin and pissed his pants before they got the Jeep started. Bernard had seen him a hundred times since on the flickering tube, a hulking muscular character with a cleft chin and flashing eyes who was forever smashing crooks in the face and snaring women by the waist, but he could never forget the way the guy's eyes had vanished in his head as the piss stain spread from his crotch to his thighs and beyond. He took one look at Bender and knew there was trouble on the horizon.

They'd agreed on $11,500 for a big male with a mane, Bernard knocking off the odd five hundred because they'd taken the two extra zebra and he figured he'd give them a break. The only male he had of any size was Claude, who must have been something in his day but was now the leonine equivalent of a nonagenarian living on a diet of mush in a nursing home. Bernard had picked him up for a song at a flea-bitten circus in Guadalajara, and he must have been twenty-five years old if he was a day. He was half-blind, he stank like one of the walking dead and the molars on the lower left side of his jaw were so rotten he howled through his food when he ate. But he looked the part, especially at a distance, and he still carried some of the flesh he'd put on in his youth—and the pain in his jaw made him cranky; savage, even. He would do, Bernard had thought. He would do just fine.

But there was Bender, stuck in a morass of dead black branches, trembling all over like a man in an ice bath, and the lion coming at him. The first shot skipped in the dirt at two hundred feet and took Claude's left hind paw off at the joint, and he gave out with a roar of such pure raging claw-gutting bone-crunching nastiness that the idiot nearly dropped his rifle. Or so it seemed from where Bernard was standing with the Mrs. and Roland, fifteen yards back and with the angle to the right. Claude was a surprise. Instead of folding up into himself and skittering for the bushes, he came on, tearing up the dirt and roaring as if he'd been set afire—and Bender was jerking and twitching and twittering so much he couldn't have hit the side of a beer truck. Bernard could feel his own heart going as he lifted the Nitro to his shoulder, and then there was the head-thumping blast of the gun and old Claude suddenly looked like a balled-up carpet with a basket of ground meat spread on top of it.

Bender turned to him with a white face. "What the—?" he stammered, and he was jerking at his fingers and flailing his arms. "What do you think you're doing?"

It was Bernard's moment. A jetliner rode high overhead, bound for the northwest, a silver rivet in the sky. There was an absolute, unutterable silence. The wife held her peace, the remaining lions cowered somewhere in the grass and every bird on the ranch was holding its breath in the dying wake of that rolling cannonade. "Saving your bloody life," Bernard snarled, hot and disgusted and royally pissed off, but proud, as always, of the Britishism.

Mike Bender was angry—too angry to eat his kippered whatever and the deep-fried toast and runny eggs. And where was the coffee, for god's sake? They were in Bakersfield, after all, and not some canvas tent in Uganda. He barked at the colored guy—all tricked up to look like a native, but with an accent right out of Compton—and told him he wanted coffee, black and strong, even if he had to drive to Oildale for it. Nicole sat across the table and watched him with mocking eyes. *Her* zebra had been perfect, but he'd fouled up two of the three he'd shot: *But Mike,* she'd said, *we can't hang these—they'll look like colanders.* And then the business with the lion. He'd looked bad on that one, and what was worse, he was out eleven and a half thousand bucks and there was nothing to show for it. Not after Puff blew the thing away. It was just meat and bone, that's all. Shit, the thing didn't even *have* a head after the great white hunter got done with it.

"C'mon, Mike," Nicole said, and she reached out to pat his hand but he snatched it away in a rage. "C'mon, baby, it's not the end of the world." He looked at her in that moment, the triumph shining in her eyes, and he wanted to slap her, choke her, get up from the table, snatch a rifle from the rack and pump a couple slugs into her.

He was about to snap back at her when the swinging doors to the kitchen parted and the colored guy came in with a pot of coffee and set it on the table. Roland, that was his name. He was surprised they didn't call him Zulu or Jambo or something to go along with the silly skirts that were supposed to make him look like a native. Christ, he'd like to get up and drill him too, for that matter. About the only break he'd had on this trip was that Jasmine Honeysuckle Rose had taken to sleeping till noon.

"Mike," Nicole pleaded, but he wouldn't hear her. Brooding, burning, plotting his revenge on every lender, shopkeeper and homeowner from the San Fernando Valley to Hancock Park, Mike Bender sipped moodily at his tepid instant coffee and awaited the great white hunter.

Puff was late to breakfast, but he looked rejuvenated—had he dyed his hair, was that it?—beaming, a fountain of energy, as if he'd stolen the flame from the King of Encino himself. "Good morning," he boomed in his phony West End accent, practically inhaling his mustache, and then he gave Nicole a look that was unmistakable and Mike felt it all pouring out of him, like lava from a volcano.

"No more lions, right?" Mike said, his voice low and choked.

"Afraid not," Puff answered, sitting himself down at the head of the table and smearing a slab of toast with Marmite. "As I told you yesterday, we've got all the females you want, but the males are juveniles, no manes at all to speak of."

"That stinks."

Bernard regarded Bender for a long moment and saw the child who'd never grown up, the rich kid, the perennial hacker and duffer, the parvenu stifled. He looked from Bender to the wife and back again—what was she doing with a clown like that?—and had a fleeting but powerful vision of her stretched out beside him in bed, breasts, thighs, puffy lips and all. "Listen, Mike," he said, "forget it. It happens to everybody. I thought we'd go for eland today—"

"*Eland.* Shit on eland."

"All right, then—water buff. A lot of them say Mbogo is the most dangerous animal in Africa, bar none."

The sunny eyes went dark with rage. "This isn't Africa," Bender spat. "It's Bakersfield."

Bernard had tried hard, and he hated it when they did that, when they punctured the illusion he so carefully nurtured. It was the illusion he was selling, after all—close your eyes and you're in Africa—and in a way he'd wanted the place to *be* Africa, wanted to make the old stories come alive, wanted to bring back the thrill of the great days, if only for a moment at a time. But it was more than that, too: Puff's African Game Ranch stood as a testament and memorial to the towering figure of Bernard's father.

Bernard Puff, Sr., had been one of the last great white hunters of East Africa—friend and compatriot of Percival and Ionides, host to some of the biggest names of American cinema and European aristocracy. He married an American heiress and they built a place in the White Highlands, dined with Isak Dinesen, ate game the year round. And then the war turned the place on its head and he sought refuge in America, losing himself in the vastness of the Southwest and the pockets of his in-laws. As a boy, Bernard had thrilled to the stories of the old days, fingering the ragged white scar a bush pig's tusks had left on his father's forearm, cleaning and oiling the ancient weapons that had stopped rhino, elephant, leopard and lion, gazing for hours into the bright glass eyes of the trophies mounted on the wall in the den, the very names—sable, kudu, bushbuck, kongoni—playing like an incantation in his head. He'd tried to do it justice, had devoted his life to it, and now here was this sorehead, this condominium peddler, running it all down.

"All right," he said. "Granted. What do you want me to do? I've got more lions coming in at the end of the month, prime cats they've trapped and relocated from Tsavo East . . ." (He was fudging here: actually, he had an emaciated sack of bones lined up at the San Francisco Zoo, a cat so old the public was offended by it, and another that had broken its leg three times jumping through a hoop with a West German circus.) "Eland we have, water buff, oryx, gazelle, hyena—I've even got a couple ostrich for you. But unless you want a female, no lion. I'm sorry."

And then, a light shining up from the depths, the glitter came back into the dealmaker's eyes, the smile widened, the tennis pro and backyard swimmer climbed out from behind the mask of the petulant real estate wonder boy. Bender was grinning. He leaned forward. "What about the elephant?"

"What about it?" Bernard lifted the toast to his lips, then set it down carefully again on the edge of his plate. The wife was watching him now, and Roland, refilling the coffee mugs, paused to give him a look.

"I want it."

Bernard stared down at the plate and fussed a moment with the coffeepot, the sugar, the cream. He hated to part with her, though he was pretty sure he could replace her—and the feed bills were killing him. Even in her dotage, Bessie Bee could put away more in an afternoon than a herd of Guernseys would go through in a winter. He gave the wife a cool glance, then shot his eyes at Bender. "Eighteen grand," he said.

Bender looked uncertain, his eyes glittering still, but sunk in on themselves, as if in awe at the enormity of the deal. "I'll want the head," he said finally, "the whole thing, stuffed and mounted—and yes, I know it's big, but I can deal with that, I've got the space, believe me . . . and the feet, I want the feet, for those, uh, what do you call them, umbrella stands?"

They found her in a brushy ravine, just beyond the swimming-pool-cum-waterhole. She was having a dust bath, powdering her pitted hide with fine pale dirt till she looked like an enormous wad of dough rolled in flour. Bernard could see where she'd trampled the high grass that hid the blue lip of the pool and uprooted half a ton of water lily and cattail, which she'd mounded up in a festering heap on the coping. He cursed under his breath when he saw the stand of eucalyptus she'd reduced to splinters and the imported fever tree she'd stripped of bark. It was his policy to keep her tethered—precisely to avoid this sort of wholesale destruction—but when there were guests on the ranch, he let her roam. He was regretting it now, and thinking he'd have to remember to get Espinoza to call the landscaping company first thing in the morning, when Bender's voice brought him back to the moment. The voice was harsh, petulant, a rising squawk of protest: "But it's only got one tusk!"

Bernard sighed. It was true—she'd broken off half her left tusk somewhere along the line, but he'd gotten so used to her he hardly noticed. But there was Bender, sitting beside him in the Jeep, the wife in the back, the guns stacked up and the cooler full, and Bender was going to try to gouge him on the price, he could see it coming.

"When we said eighteen, I assumed we were talking a trophy animal," Bender said, and Bernard turned to him. "But now, I don't know."

Bernard just wanted it over with. Something told him he was making a mistake in going after Bessie Bee—the place wouldn't seem the same without her—but he was committed at this point, and he didn't want any arguments. "Okay," he sighed, shifting the weight of his paunch from left to right. "Seventeen."

"Sixteen."

"Sixteen-five, and that's as low as I'm going to go. You don't know what it's like to skin out something like this, let alone disposing of the carcass."

"You're on," Bender said, swiveling his head to give the wife a look, and then they were out of the Jeep and checking their weapons. Bender had a .470 Rigby elephant rifle and Bernard his Nitro—just in case the morning brought a reprise of the lion fiasco. The wife, who wasn't doing any shooting, had brought along a video camera. Roland was back at the house with a truck, a chain saw and a crew of Mexicans to clean up the mess once the deed was done.

It was still early, and the heat hadn't come up full yet—Bernard guessed it must have been eighty, eighty-five or so—but he was sweating already. He was always a little edgy on a hunt—especially with a clown like Bender twitching at his elbow, and most especially after what had happened with the lion. Bender was writhing and stamping up a storm, but his eyes were cool and focused as they strolled through the mesquite and tumbleweed and down into the ravine.

Bessie Bee was white with dust, flapping her ears and blowing up great clouds of it with her trunk. From a hundred yards you couldn't see much more than flying dirt, as if a tornado had touched down; at fifty, the rucked and seamed head of the old elephant began to take on shape. Though there was little more risk involved than in potting a cow in its stall, Bernard was habitually cautious, and he stopped Bender there, at fifty yards. A pair of vultures drifted overhead, attracted by the Jeep, which they knew as the purveyor of bleeding flesh and carrion. The elephant sneezed. A crow called out somewhere behind them. "This is as far as we go," Bernard said.

Bender gaped at him, popping his joints and bugging his eyes like a fraternity boy thwarted by the ID checker at the door of a bar full of sorority girls. "All I can see is dust," he said.

Bernard was deep inside himself now. He checked the bolt on the big gun and flipped back the safety. "Just wait," he said. "Find a spot—here, right here; you can use this rock to steady your aim—and just wait a minute, that's all. She'll tire of this in a minute or so, and when the dust settles you'll have your shot."

And so they crouched in the dirt, hunter and guide, and propped their guns up on a coarse red table of sandstone and waited for the dust to clear and the heat to rise and the vultures to sink down out of the sky in great ragged swoops.

For her part, Bessie Bee was more than a little suspicious. Though her eyes were poor, the Jeep was something she could see, and she could smell the hominids half a mile away. She should have been matriarch of a fine wild herd of elephants at Amboseli or Tsavo or the great Bahi swamp, but she'd lived all her fifty-two years on this strange and unnatural continent, amid the stink and confusion of man. She'd been goaded, beaten, tethered, taught to dance and stand on one leg and grasp the sorry wisp of a tail that hung from the sorry flanks of another sorry elephant like herself as they paraded before the teeming monkey masses in one forbidding arena after another. And then there was this, a place that stank of the oily secrets of the earth, and another tether and more men. She heard the thunder of the guns and she smelled the blood on the air and she knew they were killing. She knew, too, that the Jeep was there for her.

The dust settled round her, sifting down in a maelstrom of fine white motes. She flared her ears and trumpeted and lifted the standing timber of her right front foot from the ground and let it sway before her. She was tired of the goad, the tether, the brittle dry tasteless straw and cattle feed, tired of the sun and the air and the night and the morning: she charged.

She let her nose guide her till the guns crashed, once, twice, three times, and a new sort of goad tore into her, invasive and hot, but it just made her angry, made her come on all the harder, invincible, unstoppable, twelve feet at the shoulder and eight standing tons, no more circuses, no more palanquins, no more goads. And then she saw them, two pitiful sticklike figures springing up from behind a rock she could swallow and spit up three times over.

It wasn't panic exactly, not at first. Bender shot wide, and the heavy shock of the gun seemed to stun him. Bessie Bee came straight for them, homing in on them, and Bernard bit down on his mustache and shouted, "Shoot! Shoot, you idiot!"

He got his wish. Bender fired again, finally, but all he managed to do was blow some hair off the thing's back. Bernard stood then, the rifle to his shoulder, and though he remembered the lion and could already hear the nagging whining mealy-mouthed voice of Bender complaining over lunch of being denied *this* trophy too, the situation was critical; desperate, even—who would have thought it of Bessie Bee?—and he squeezed the trigger to the jerk and roar of the big gun.

Nothing. Had he missed? But then all at once he felt himself caught up in a landslide, the rush of air, the reek of elephant, and he was flying, actually flying, high out over the plain and into the blue.

When he landed, he sat up and found that his shoulder had come loose from the socket and that there was some sort of fluid—blood, his own blood—obscuring the vision in his right eye. He was in shock, he told himself, repeating it aloud, over and over: "I'm in shock, I'm in shock." Everything seemed hazy, and the arm didn't hurt much, though it should have, nor the gash in his scalp either. But didn't he have a gun? And where was it?

He looked up at the noise, a shriek of great conviction, and saw Bessie Bee rubbing her foot thoughtfully, almost tenderly, over Mike Bender's prostrate form. Bender seemed to be naked—or no, he didn't seem to be wearing any skin, either—and his head had been vastly transformed, so much more compact now. But there was something else going on too, something the insurance company wouldn't be able to rectify, of that he was sure, if only in a vague way—"I'm in shock," he repeated. This something was a shriek too, definitely human, but it rose and caught hold of the tail of the preceding shriek and climbed atop it, and before the vacuum of silence could close in there was another shriek, and another, until even the screams of the elephant were a whisper beside it.

It was Mrs. Bender, the wife, Nicole, one of the finest expressions of her species, and she was running from the Jeep and exercising her lungs. The Jeep seemed to be lying on its side—such an odd angle to see it from—and Mrs. Bender's reedy form was in that moment engulfed by a moving wall of flesh, the big flanks blotting the scene from view, all that movement and weight closing out the little aria of screams with a final elephantine roll of the drums.

It might have been seconds later, or an hour—Bernard didn't know. He sat there, an arm dangling from the shoulder, idly wiping the blood from his eye with his good hand while the naked black vultures drifted down on him with an air of professional interest. And then all at once, strange phenomenon, the sun was gone, and the vultures, and a great black shadow fell over him. He looked up dimly into the canvas of that colossal face framed in a riot of ears. "Bessie Bee?" he said. "Bessie Bee? Shamba?"

Half a mile away, fanned by the gentle breeze of the air conditioner, Jasmine Honeysuckle Rose Bender, two months short of her thirteenth birthday and sated with chocolate and dreams of lean spike-haired adolescents with guitars and leather jackets, shifted her head on the pillow and opened her eyes. She was, in that waking moment, sole inheritor of the Bender real estate empire, and all the monies and houses and stocks and bonds and properties that accrued to it, not to mention the beach house and the Ferrari Testarossa, but she wasn't yet aware of it. Something had awakened her, some ripple on the great pond of life. For just a moment there, over the drone of the air conditioner, she thought she'd heard a scream.

But no. It was probably just some peacock or baboon or whatever. Or that pitiful excuse for an elephant. She sat up, reached into her cooler for a root beer and shook her head. Tacky, she thought. Tacky, tacky, tacky.

                                                                    (1990)

GREASY LAKE

It's about a mile down on the dark side of Route 88.

—Bruce Springsteen

There was a time when courtesy and winning ways went out of style, when it was good to be bad, when you cultivated decadence like a taste. We were all dangerous characters then. We wore torn-up leather jackets, slouched around with toothpicks in our mouths, sniffed glue and ether and what somebody claimed was cocaine. When we wheeled our parents' whining station wagons out into the street we left a patch of rubber half a block long. We drank gin and grape juice, Tango, Thunderbird, and Bali Hai. We were nineteen. We were bad. We read André Gide and struck elaborate poses to show that we didn't give a shit about anything. At night, we went up to Greasy Lake.

Through the center of town, up the strip, past the housing developments and shopping malls, street lights giving way to the thin streaming illumination of the headlights, trees crowding the asphalt in a black unbroken wall: that was the way out to Greasy Lake. The Indians had called it Wakan, a reference to the clarity of its waters. Now it was fetid and murky, the mud banks glittering with broken glass and strewn with beer cans and the charred remains of bonfires. There was a single ravaged island a hundred yards from shore, so stripped of vegetation it looked as if the air force had strafed it. We went up to the lake because everyone went there, because we wanted to snuff the rich scent of possibility on the breeze, watch a girl take off her clothes and plunge into the festering murk, drink beer, smoke pot, howl at the stars, savor the incongruous full-throated roar of rock and roll against the primeval susurrus of frogs and crickets. This was nature.

I was there one night, late, in the company of two dangerous characters. Digby wore a gold star in his right ear and allowed his father to pay his tuition at Cornell; Jeff was thinking of quitting school to become a painter/musician/

headshop proprietor. They were both expert in the social graces, quick with a sneer, able to manage a Ford with lousy shocks over a rutted and gutted blacktop road at eighty-five while rolling a joint as compact as a Tootsie Roll Pop stick. They could lounge against a bank of booming speakers and trade "man"s with the best of them or roll out across the dance floor as if their joints worked on bearings. They were slick and quick and they wore their mirror shades at break-fast and dinner, in the shower, in closets and caves. In short, they were bad.

I drove, Digby pounded the dashboard and shouted along with Toots & the Maytals while Jeff hung his head out the window and streaked the side of my mother's Bel Air with vomit. It was early June, the air soft as a hand on your cheek, the third night of summer vacation. The first two nights we'd been out till dawn, looking for something we never found. On this, the third night, we'd cruised the strip sixty-seven times, been in and out of every bar and club we could think of in a twenty-mile radius, stopped twice for bucket chicken and forty-cent hamburgers, debated going to a party at the house of a girl Jeff's sister knew, and chucked two dozen raw eggs at mailboxes and hitchhikers. It was 2:00 A.M.; the bars were closing. There was nothing to do but take a bottle of lemon-flavored gin up to Greasy Lake.

The taillights of a single car winked at us as we swung into the dirt lot with its tufts of weed and washboard corrugations; '57 Chevy, mint, metallic blue. On the far side of the lot, like the exoskeleton of some gaunt chrome insect, a chop-per leaned against its kickstand. And that was it for excitement: some junkie half-wit biker and a car freak pumping his girlfriend. Whatever it was we were looking for, we weren't about to find it at Greasy Lake. Not that night.

But then all of a sudden Digby was fighting for the wheel.

"Hey, that's Tony Lovett's car! Hey!" he shouted, while I stabbed at the brake pedal and the Bel Air nosed up to the gleaming bumper of the parked Chevy. Digby leaned on the horn, laughing, and instructed me to put my brights on. I flicked on the brights. This was hilarious. A joke. Tony would experience prema-ture withdrawal and expect to be confronted by grim-looking state troopers with flashlights. We hit the horn, strobed the lights, and then jumped out of the car to press our witty faces to Tony's windows; for all we knew we might even catch a glimpse of some little fox's tit, and then we could slap backs with red-faced Tony, roughhouse a little, and go on to new heights of adventure and daring.

The first mistake, the one that opened the whole floodgate, was losing my grip on the keys. In the excitement, leaping from the car with the gin in one hand and a roach clip in the other, I spilled them in the grass—in the dark, rank, mys-terious nighttime grass of Greasy Lake. This was a tactical error, as damaging and irreversible in its way as Westmoreland's decision to dig in at Khe Sanh. I felt it like a jab of intuition, and I stopped there by the open door, peering vaguely into the night that puddled up round my feet.

The second mistake—and this was inextricably bound up with the first—was identifying the car as Tony Lovett's. Even before the very bad character in greasy jeans and engineer boots ripped out of the driver's door, I began to realize that this chrome blue was much lighter than the robin's-egg of Tony's car, and that Tony's car didn't have rear-mounted speakers. Judging from their expressions, Digby and Jeff were privately groping toward the same inevitable and unsettling conclusion as I was.

In any case, there was no reasoning with this bad greasy character—clearly he was a man of action. The first lusty Rockette's kick of his steel-toed boot caught me under the chin, chipped my favorite tooth, and left me sprawled in the dirt. Like a fool, I'd gone down on one knee to comb the stiff hacked grass for the keys, my mind making connections in the most dragged-out, testudineous way, knowing that things had gone wrong, that I was in a lot of trouble, and that the lost ignition key was my grail and my salvation. The three or four succeeding blows were mainly absorbed by my right buttock and the tough piece of bone at the base of my spine.

Meanwhile, Digby vaulted the kissing bumpers and delivered a savage kung-fu blow to the greasy character's collarbone. Digby had just finished a course in martial arts for phys-ed credit and had spent the better part of the past two nights telling us apocryphal tales of Bruce Lee types and of the raw power invested in lightning blows shot from coiled wrists, ankles and elbows. The greasy character was unimpressed. He merely backed off a step, his face like a Toltec mask, and laid Digby out with a single whistling roundhouse blow . . . but by now Jeff had got into the act, and I was beginning to extricate myself from the dirt, a tinny compound of shock, rage, and impotence wadded in my throat.

Jeff was on the guy's back, biting at his ear. Digby was on the ground, cursing. I went for the tire iron I kept under the driver's seat. I kept it there because bad characters always keep tire irons under the driver's seat, for just such an occasion as this. Never mind that I hadn't been involved in a fight since sixth grade, when a kid with a sleepy eye and two streams of mucus depending from his nostrils hit me in the knee with a Louisville slugger; never mind that I'd touched the tire iron exactly twice before, to change tires: it was there. And I went for it.

I was terrified. Blood was beating in my ears, my hands were shaking, my heart turning over like a dirtbike in the wrong gear. My antagonist was shirtless, and a single cord of muscle flashed across his chest as he bent forward to peel Jeff from his back like a wet overcoat. "Motherfucker," he spat, over and over, and I was aware in that instant that all four of us—Digby, Jeff, and myself included—were chanting "motherfucker, motherfucker," as if it were a battle cry. (What happened next? the detective asks the murderer from beneath the turned-down brim of his porkpie hat. I don't know, the murderer says, something came over me. Exactly.)

Digby poked the flat of his hand in the bad character's face and I came at him like a kamikaze, mindless, raging, stung with humiliation—the whole thing, from the initial boot in the chin to this murderous primal instant involving no more than sixty hyperventilating, gland-flooding seconds—and I came at him and brought the tire iron down across his ear. The effect was instantaneous, astonishing. He was a stunt man and this was Hollywood, he was a big grimacing toothy balloon and I was a man with a straight pin. He collapsed. Wet his pants. Went loose in his boots.

A single second, big as a zeppelin, floated by. We were standing over him in a circle, gritting our teeth, jerking our necks, our limbs and hands and feet twitching with glandular discharges. No one said anything. We just stared down at the guy, the car freak, the lover, the bad greasy character laid low. Digby looked at me; so did Jeff. I was still holding the tire iron, a tuft of hair clinging to the crook like dandelion fluff, like down. Rattled, I dropped it in the dirt, already envisioning the headlines, the pitted faces of the police inquisitors, the gleam of handcuffs, clank of bars, the big black shadows rising from the back of the cell . . . when suddenly a raw torn shriek cut through me like all the juice in all the electric chairs in the country.

It was the fox. She was short, barefoot, dressed in panties and a man's shirt. "Animals!" she screamed, running at us with her fists clenched and wisps of blow-dried hair in her face. There was a silver chain round her ankle, and her toenails flashed in the glare of the headlights. I think it was the toenails that did it. Sure, the gin and the cannabis and even the Kentucky Fried may have had a hand in it, but it was the sight of those flaming toes that set us off—the toad emerging from the loaf in *Virgin Spring*, lipstick smeared on a child: she was already tainted. We were on her like Bergman's deranged brothers—see no evil, hear none, speak none—panting, wheezing, tearing at her clothes, grabbing for flesh. We were bad characters, and we were scared and hot and three steps over the line—anything could have happened.

It didn't.

Before we could pin her to the hood of the car, our eyes masked with lust and greed and the purest primal badness, a pair of headlights swung into the lot. There we were, dirty, bloody, guilty, dissociated from humanity and civilization, the first of the Ur-crimes behind us, the second in progress, shreds of nylon panty and spandex brassiere dangling from our fingers, our flies open, lips licked—there we were, caught in the spotlight. Nailed.

We bolted. First for the car, and then, realizing we had no way of starting it, for the woods. I thought nothing. I thought escape. The headlights came at me like accusing fingers. I was gone.

Ram-bam-bam, across the parking lot, past the chopper and into the feculent undergrowth at the lake's edge, insects flying up in my face, weeds whipping, frogs and snakes and red-eyed turtles splashing off into the night: I was already ankle-deep in muck and tepid water and still going strong. Behind me, the girl's screams rose in intensity, disconsolate, incriminating, the screams of the Sabine women, the Christian martyrs, Anne Frank dragged from the garret. I kept going, pursued by those cries, imagining cops and bloodhounds. The water was up to my knees when I realized what I was doing: I was going to swim for it. Swim the breadth of Greasy Lake and hide myself in the thick clot of woods on the far side. They'd never find me there.

I was breathing in sobs, in gasps. The water lapped at my waist as I looked out over the moon-burnished ripples, the mats of algae that clung to the surface like scabs. Digby and Jeff had vanished. I paused. Listened. The girl was quieter now, screams tapering to sobs, but there were male voices, angry, excited, and the high-pitched ticking of the second car's engine. I waded deeper, stealthy, hunted, the ooze sucking at my sneakers. As I was about to take the plunge—at the very instant I dropped my shoulder for the first slashing stroke—I blundered into something. Something unspeakable, obscene, something soft, wet, moss-grown. A patch of weed? A log? When I reached out to touch it, it gave like a rubber duck, it gave like flesh.

In one of those nasty little epiphanies for which we are prepared by films and TV and childhood visits to the funeral home to ponder the shrunken painted forms of dead grandparents, I understood what it was that bobbed there so inadmissibly in the dark. Understood, and stumbled back in horror and revulsion, my mind yanked in six different directions (I was nineteen, a mere child, an infant, and here in the space of five minutes I'd struck down one greasy character and blundered into the waterlogged carcass of a second), thinking, The keys, the keys, why did I have to go and lose the keys? I stumbled back, but the muck took hold of my feet—a sneaker snagged, balance lost—and suddenly I was pitching face forward into the buoyant black mass, throwing out my hands in desperation while simultaneously conjuring the image of reeking frogs and muskrats revolving in slicks of their own deliquescing juices. AAAAArrrgh! I shot from the water like a torpedo, the dead man rotating to expose a mossy beard and eyes cold as the moon. I must have shouted out, thrashing around in the weeds, because the voices behind me suddenly became animated.

"What was that?"

"It's them, it's them: they tried to, tried to . . . *rape* me!" Sobs.

A man's voice, flat, Midwestern accent. "You sons a bitches, we'll kill you!"

Frogs, crickets.

Then another voice, harsh, *r*-less, Lower East Side: "Motherfucker!" I recognized the verbal virtuosity of the bad greasy character in the engineer boots. Tooth chipped, sneakers gone, coated in mud and slime and worse, crouching breathless in the weeds waiting to have my ass thoroughly and definitively kicked and fresh from the hideous stinking embrace of a three-days-dead-corpse, I suddenly felt a rush of joy and vindication: the son of a bitch was alive! Just as quickly, my bowels turned to ice. "Come on out of there, you pansy motherfuckers!" the bad greasy character was screaming. He shouted curses till he was out of breath.

The crickets started up again, then the frogs. I held my breath. All at once there was a sound in the reeds, a swishing, a splash: thunk-a-thunk. They were throwing rocks. The frogs fell silent. I cradled my head. Swish, swish, thunk-a-thunk. A wedge of feldspar the size of a cue ball glanced off my knee. I bit my finger.

It was then that they turned to the car. I heard a door slam, a curse, and then the sound of the headlights shattering—almost a good-natured sound, celebratory, like corks popping from the necks of bottles. This was succeeded by the dull booming of the fenders, metal on metal, and then the icy crash of the windshield. I inched forward, elbows and knees, my belly pressed to the muck, thinking of guerrillas and commandos and *The Naked and the Dead*. I parted the weeds and squinted the length of the parking lot.

The second car—it was a Trans-Am—was still running, its high beams washing the scene in a lurid stagy light. Tire iron flailing, the greasy bad character was laying into the side of my mother's Bel Air like an avenging demon, his shadow riding up the trunks of the trees. Whomp. Whomp. Whomp-whomp. The other two guys—blond types, in fraternity jackets—were helping out with tree branches and skull-sized boulders. One of them was gathering up bottles, rocks, muck, candy wrappers, used condoms, poptops, and other refuse and pitching it through the window on the driver's side. I could see the fox, a white bulb behind the windshield of the '57 Chevy. "Bobbie," she whined over the thumping, "come *on*." The greasy character paused a moment, took one good swipe at the left taillight, and then heaved the tire iron halfway across the lake. Then he fired up the '57 and was gone.

Blond head nodded at blond head. One said something to the other, too low for me to catch. They were no doubt thinking that in helping to annihilate my mother's car they'd committed a fairly rash act, and thinking too that there were three bad characters connected with that very car watching them from the woods. Perhaps other possibilities occurred to them as well—police, jail cells, justices of the peace, reparations, lawyers, irate parents, fraternal censure. Whatever they were thinking, they suddenly dropped branches, bottles, and rocks and sprang for their car in unison, as if they'd choreographed it. Five seconds. That's all it took. The engine shrieked, the tires squealed, a cloud of dust rose from the rutted lot and then settled back on darkness.

I don't know how long I lay there, the bad breath of decay all around me, my jacket heavy as a bear, the primordial ooze subtly reconstituting itself to accommodate my upper thighs and testicles. My jaws ached, my knee throbbed, my coccyx was on fire. I contemplated suicide, wondered if I'd need bridgework, scraped the recesses of my brain for some sort of excuse to give my parents—a tree had fallen on the car, I was blindsided by a bread truck, hit and run, vandals had got to it while we were playing chess at Digby's. Then I thought of the dead man. He was probably the only person on the planet worse off than I was: I thought about him, fog on the lake, insects chirring eerily, and felt the tug of fear, felt the darkness opening up inside me like a set of jaws. Who was he, I wondered, this victim of time and circumstance bobbing sorrowfully in the lake at my back. The owner of the chopper, no doubt, a bad older character come to this. Shot during a murky drug deal, drowned while drunkenly frolicking in the lake. Another headline. My car was wrecked; he was dead.

When the eastern half of the sky went from black to cobalt and the trees began to separate themselves from the shadows, I pushed myself up from the mud and stepped out into the open. By now the birds had begun to take over for the crickets, and dew lay slick on the leaves. There was a smell in the air, raw and sweet at the same time, the smell of the sun firing buds and opening blossoms. I contemplated the car. It lay there like a wreck along the highway, like a steel sculpture left over from a vanished civilization. Everything was still. This was nature.

I was circling the car, as dazed and bedraggled as the sole survivor of an air blitz, when Digby and Jeff emerged from the trees behind me. Digby's face was crosshatched with smears of dirt; Jeff's jacket was gone and his shirt was torn across the shoulder. They slouched across the lot, looking sheepish, and silently came up beside me to gape at the ravaged automobile. No one said a word. After a while Jeff swung open the driver's door and began to scoop the broken glass and garbage off the seat. I looked at Digby. He shrugged. "At least they didn't slash the tires," he said.

It was true: the tires were intact. There was no windshield, the headlights were staved in, and the body looked as if it had been sledge-hammered for a quarter a shot at the county fair, but the tires were inflated to regulation pressure. The car was drivable. In silence, all three of us bent to scrape the mud and shattered glass from the interior. I said nothing about the biker. When we were finished, I reached in my pocket for the keys, experienced a nasty stab of recollection, cursed myself, and turned to search the grass. I spotted them almost immediately, no more than five feet from the open door, glinting like jewels in the first tapering shaft of sunlight. There was no reason to get philosophical about it: I eased into the seat and turned the engine over.

It was at that precise moment that the silver Mustang with the flame decals rumbled into the lot. All three of us froze; then Digby and Jeff slid into the car and slammed the door. We watched as the Mustang rocked and bobbed across the ruts and finally jerked to a halt beside the forlorn chopper at the far end of the lot. "Let's go," Digby said. I hesitated, the Bel Air wheezing beneath me.

Two girls emerged from the Mustang. Tight jeans, stiletto heels, hair like frozen fur. They bent over the motorcycle, paced back and forth aimlessly, glanced once or twice at us, and then ambled over to where the reeds sprang up in a green fence round the perimeter of the lake. One of them cupped her hands to her mouth. "Al," she called. "Hey, Al!"

"Come on," Digby hissed. "Let's get out of here."

But it was too late. The second girl was picking her way across the lot, unsteady on her heels, looking up at us and then away. She was older—twenty-five or -six—and as she came closer we could see there was something wrong with her: she was stoned or drunk, lurching now and waving her arms for balance. I gripped the steering wheel as if it were the ejection lever of a flaming jet, and Digby spat out my name, twice, terse and impatient.

"Hi," the girl said.

We looked at her like zombies, like war veterans, like deaf-and-dumb pencil peddlers.

She smiled, her lips cracked and dry. "Listen," she said, bending from the waist to look in the window, "you guys seen Al?" Her pupils were pinpoints, her eyes glass. She jerked her neck. "That's his bike over there—Al's. You seen him?"

Al. I didn't know what to say. I wanted to get out of the car and retch, I wanted to go home to my parents' house and crawl into bed. Digby poked me in the ribs. "We haven't seen anybody," I said.

The girl seemed to consider this, reaching out a slim veiny arm to brace herself against the car. "No matter," she said, slurring the *t*'s, "he'll turn up." And then, as if she'd just taken stock of the whole scene—the ravaged car and our battered faces, the desolation of the place—she said: "Hey, you guys look like some pretty bad characters—been fightin', huh?" We stared straight ahead, rigid as catatonics. She was fumbling in her pocket and muttering something. Finally she held out a handful of tablets in glassine wrappers: "Hey, you want to party, you want to do some of these with me and Sarah?"

I just looked at her. I thought I was going to cry. Digby broke the silence. "No thanks," he said, leaning over me. "Some other time."

I put the car in gear and it inched forward with a groan, shaking off pellets of glass like an old dog shedding water after a bath, heaving over the ruts on its worn springs, creeping toward the highway. There was a sheen of sun on the lake. I looked back. The girl was still standing there, watching us, her shoulders slumped, hand outstretched.

(1981)

PEACE OF MIND

First she told them the story of the family surprised over their corn muffins by the masked intruder. "He was a black man," she said, dropping her voice and at the same time allowing a hint of tremolo to creep into it, "and he was wearing a lifelike mask of President Reagan. He just jimmied the lock and waltzed in the front door with the morning paper as if he was delivering flowers or something. . . . They thought it was a joke at first." Giselle's voice became hushed now, confidential, as she described how he'd brutalized the children, humiliated the wife—"Sexually, if you know what I mean"—and bound them all to the kitchen chair with twists of sheer pantyhose. Worse, she said, he drug a scratchy old copy of Sam and Dave's "Soul Man" out of the record collection and made them listen to it over and over as he looted the house. They knew he was finished when Sam and Dave choked off, the stereo rudely torn from the socket and thrown in with the rest of their things—she paused here to draw a calculated breath—"And at seven-thirty A.M., no less."

She had them, she could see it in the way the pretty little wife's eyes went dark with hate and the balding husband clutched fitfully at his pockets—she had them, but she poured it on anyway, flexing her verbal muscles, not yet noon and a sale, a big sale, already in the bag. So she gave them an abbreviated version of the story of the elderly lady and the overworked Mexican from the knife-sharpening service and wrung some hideous new truths from the tale of the housewife who came home to find a strange car in her garage. "A strange car?" the husband prompted, after she'd paused to level a doleful, frightened look on the wife. Giselle sighed. "Two white men met her at the door. They were in their early forties, nicely dressed, polite—she thought they were real-estate people or something. They escorted her into the house, bundled up the rugs, the paintings, the Camcorder and VCR and then took turns desecrating"—that was the term she used, it got them every time—"desecrating her naked body with the cigarette lighter from her very own car."

The husband and wife exchanged a glance, then signed on for the whole shmeer—five thousand and some-odd dollars for the alarm system—every window, door, keyhole, and crevice wired—and sixty bucks a month for a pair of "Armed Response" signs to stick in the lawn. Giselle slid into the front seat of the Mercedes and cranked up the salsa music that made her feel as if every day was a fiesta, and then let out a long slow breath. She checked her watch and drew a circle around the next name on her list. It was a few minutes past twelve, crime was rampant, and she was feeling lucky. She tapped her foot and whistled along with the sour, jostling trumpets—no doubt about it, she'd have another sale before lunch.

The balding husband stood at the window and watched the Mercedes back out of the driveway, drift into gear, and glide soundlessly up the street. It took him a moment to realize he was still clutching his checkbook. "God, Hil," he said (or, rather, croaked—something seemed to be wrong with his throat), "it's a lot of money."

The pretty little wife, Hilary, crouched frozen on the couch, legs drawn up to her chest, feet bare, toenails glistening. "They stuff your underwear in your mouth," she whispered, "that's the worst thing. Can you imagine that, I mean the taste of it—your own underwear?"

Ellis didn't answer. He was thinking of the masked intruder—the maniac disguised as the President—and of his own children, whose heedless squeals of joy came to him like hosannas from the swingset out back. He'd been a fool, he saw that now. How could he have thought, even for a minute, that they'd be safe out here in the suburbs? The world was violent, rotten, corrupt, seething with hatred and perversion, and there was no escaping it. Everything you worked for, everything you loved, had to be locked up as if you were in a castle under siege.

"I wonder what they did to her," Hilary said.

"Who?"

"The woman—the one with the cigarette lighter. I heard they burn their initials into you."

Yes, of course they did, he thought—why wouldn't they? They sold crack in the elementary schools, pissed in the alleys, battered old women for their Social Security checks. They'd cleaned out Denny Davidson while he was in the Bahamas and ripped the stereo out of Phyllis Steubig's Peugeot. And just last week they'd stolen two brand-new Ironcast aluminum garbage cans from the curb in front of the neighbors' house—just dumped the trash in the street and drove off with them. "What do you think, Hil?" he said. "We can still get out of it."

"I don't care what it costs," she murmured, her voice drained of emotion. "I won't be able to sleep till it's in."

Ellis crossed the room to gaze out on the sun-dappled backyard. Mifty and Corinne were on the swings, pumping hard, lifting up into the sky and falling back again with a pure rhythmic grace that was suddenly so poignant he could feel a sob rising in his throat. "I won't either," he said, turning to his wife and spreading his hands as if in supplication. "We've got to have it."

"Yes," she said.

"If only for our peace of mind."

Giselle was pretty good with directions—she had to be, in her business—but still she had to pull over three times to consult her Thomas' Guide before she found the next address on her list. The house was in a seedy, run-down neighborhood of blasted trees, gutted cars, and tacky little houses, the kind of neighborhood that just made her blood boil—how could people live like that? she wondered, flicking off the tape in disgust. Didn't they have any self-respect? She hit the accelerator, scattering a pack of snarling, hyenalike dogs, dodged a stained mattress and a pair of overturned trash cans and swung into the driveway of a house that looked as if it had been bombed, partially reconstructed, and then bombed again. There has to be some mistake, she thought. She glanced up and caught the eye of the man sitting on the porch next door. He was fat and shirtless, his chest and arms emblazoned with lurid tattoos, and he was in the act of lifting a beer can to his lips when he saw that she was peering at him from behind the frosted window of her car. Slowly, as if it cost him an enormous effort, he lowered the beer can and raised the middle finger of his free hand.

She rechecked her list. 7718 Picador Drive. There was no number on the house in front of her, but the house to the left was 7716 and the one to the right 7720. This was it, all right. She stepped out of the car with her briefcase, squared her shoulders, and slammed the door, all the while wondering what in god's name the owner of a place like this would want with an alarm system. These were the sort of people who broke into houses—and here she turned to give the fat man an icy glare—not the ones who had anything to protect. But then what did she care?—a sale was a sale. She set the car alarm with a fierce snap of her wrist, waited for the reassuring bleat of response from the bowels of the car, and marched up the walk.

The man who answered the door was tall and stooped—mid-fifties, she guessed—and he looked like a scholar in his wire-rims and the dingy cardigan with the leather elbow patches. His hair was the color of freshly turned dirt and his eyes, slightly distorted and swimming behind the thick lenses, were as blue as the skies over Oklahoma. "Mr. Coles?" she said.

He looked her up and down, taking his time. "And what're you supposed to be," he breathed in a wheezy humorless drawl, "the Avon Lady or something?" It was then that she noticed the nervous little woman frozen in the shadows of the hallway behind him. "Everett," the woman said in a soft, pleading tone, but the man took no notice of her. "Or don't tell me," he said, "you're selling Girl Scout cookies, right?"

When it came to sales, Giselle was unshakable. She saw her opening and thrust out her hand. "Giselle Nyerges," she said, "I'm from SecureCo? You contacted us about a home security system?"

The woman vanished. The fat man next door blew into his fist and produced a rude noise and Everett Coles, with a grin that showed too much gum, took her hand and led her into the house.

Inside, the place wasn't as bad as she'd expected. Kmart taste, of course, furniture made of particle board, hopelessly tacky bric-a-brac, needlepoint homilies on the walls, but at least it was spare. And clean. The man led her through the living room to the open-beam kitchen and threw himself down in a chair at the Formica table. A sliding glass door gave onto the dusty expanse of the backyard. "So," he said. "Let's hear it."

"First I want to tell you how happy I am that you're considering a SecureCo home security system, Mr. Coles," she said, sitting opposite him and throwing the latches on her briefcase with a professional snap. "I don't know if you heard about it," she said, the conspiratorial whisper creeping into her voice, "but just last week they found a couple—both retirees, on a fixed income—bludgeoned to death in their home not three blocks from here. And they'd been security-conscious too—deadbolts on the doors and safety locks on the windows. The killer was this black man—a Negro—and he was wearing a lifelike mask of President Reagan . . . Well, he found this croquet mallet . . ."

She faltered. The man was looking at her in the oddest way. Really, he was. He was grinning still—grinning as if she were telling a joke—and there was something wrong with his eyes. They seemed to be jerking back and forth in the sockets, jittering like the shiny little balls in a pinball machine. "I know it's not a pleasant story, Mr. Coles," she said, "but I like my customers to know that, that . . ." Those eyes were driving her crazy. She looked down, shuffling through the papers in her briefcase.

"They crowd you," he said.

"Pardon?" Looking up again.

"Sons of bitches," he growled, "they crowd you."

She found herself gazing over his shoulder at the neat little needlepoint display on the kitchen wall: SEMPER FIDELIS; HOME SWEET HOME; BURN, BABY, BURN.

"You like?" he said.

Burn, Baby, Burn?

"Did them myself." He dropped the grin and gazed out on nothing. "Got a lot of time on my hands."

She felt herself slipping. This wasn't the way it was supposed to go at all. She was wondering if she should hit him with another horror story or get down to inspecting the house and writing up an estimate, when he asked if she wanted a drink.

"Thank you, no," she said. And then, with a smile, "It's a bit early in the day for me."

He said nothing, just looked at her with those jumpy blue eyes till she had to turn away. "Shit," he spat suddenly, "come down off your high horse, lady, let your hair down, loosen up."

She cleared her throat. "Yes, well, shouldn't we have a look around so I can assess your needs?"

"Gin," he said, and his voice was flat and calm again, "it's the elixir of life." He made no move to get up from the table. "You're a good-looking woman, you know that?"

"Thank you," she said in her smallest voice. "Shouldn't we—?"

"Got them high heels and pretty little ankles, nice earrings, hair all done up, and that smart little tweed suit—of course you know you're a good-looking woman. Bet it don't hurt the sales a bit, huh?"

She couldn't help herself now. All she wanted was to get up from the table and away from those jittery eyes, sale or no sale. "Listen," she said, "listen to me. There was this woman and she came home and there was this strange car in her garage—"

"No," he said, "you listen to me."

" 'Panty Rapist Escapes,' " Hilary read aloud in a clear declamatory tone, setting down her coffee mug and spreading out the "Metro" section as if it were a sacred text. " 'Norbert Baptiste, twenty-seven, of Silverlake, dubbed the Panty Rapist because he gagged his victims with their own underthings . . .' " She broke off to give her husband a look of muted triumph. "You see," she said, lifting the coffee mug to her lips, "I told you. *With their own underthings.*"

Ellis Hunsicker was puzzling over the box scores of the previous night's ballgames, secure as a snail in its shell. It was early Saturday morning, Mifty and Corinne were in the den watching cartoons, and the house alarm was still set from the previous night. In a while, after he'd finished his muesli and his second cup of coffee, he'd punch in the code and disarm the thing and then maybe do a little gardening and afterward take the girls to the park. He wasn't really listening, and he murmured a halfhearted reply.

"And can you imagine Tina Carfarct trying to tell me we were just wasting our money on the alarm system?" She pinched her voice in mockery: " 'I hate to tell you, Hil, but this is the safest neighborhood in L.A.' Jesus, she's like a Pollyanna or something, but you know what it is, don't you?"

Ellis looked up from the paper.

"They're too cheap, that's what—her and Sid both. They're going to take their chances, hope it happens to the next guy, and all to save a few thousand dollars. It's sick. It really is."

Night before last they'd had the Carfarcts and their twelve-year-old boy, Brewster, over for dinner—a nice sole amandine and scalloped potatoes Ellis had whipped up himself—and the chief object of conversation was, of course, the alarm system. "I don't know," Sid had said (Sid was forty, handsome as a prince, an investment counselor who'd once taught high-school social studies), "it's kind of like being a prisoner in your own home."

"All that money," Tina chimed in, sucking at the cherry of her second Manhattan, "I mean I don't think I could stand it. Like Sid says, I'd feel like I was a prisoner or something, afraid to step out into my own yard because some phantom mugger might be lurking in the marigolds."

"The guy in the Reagan mask was no phantom," Hilary said, leaning across the table to slash the air with the flat of her hand, bracelets ajangle. "Or those two men—*white* men—who accosted that woman in her own garage—" She was so wrought up she couldn't go on. She turned to her husband, tears welling in her eyes. "Go on," she'd said, "tell them."

It was then that Tina had made her "safest neighborhood in L.A." remark and Sid, draining his glass and setting it down carefully on the table, had said in a phlegmy, ruminative voice, "I don't know, it's like you've got no faith in your fellow man," to which Ellis had snapped, "Don't be naive, Sid."

Even Tina scored him for that one. "Oh, come off it, Sid," she said, giving him a sour look.

"Let's face it," Ellis said, "it's a society of haves and have-nots, and like it or not, we're the haves."

"I don't deny there's a lot of crazies out there and all," Tina went on, swiveling to face Ellis, "it's just that the whole idea of having an alarm on everything— I mean you can't park your car at the mall without it—is just, well, it's a sad thing. I mean next thing you know people'll be wearing these body alarms to work, rub up against them in a crowd and—bingo!—lights flash and sirens go off." She sat back, pleased with herself, a tiny, elegant blonde in a low-cut cocktail dress and a smug grin, untouched, unafraid, a woman without a care in the world.

But then Sid wanted to see the thing and all four of them were at the front door, gathered round the glowing black plastic panel as if it were some rare jewel, some treasure built into the wall. Ellis was opening the closet to show them the big metal box that contained the system's "brain," as the SecureCo woman had called it, when Sid, taken by the allure of the thing, lightly touched the tip of his index finger to the neat glowing red strip at the bottom that read EMERGENCY.

Instantly, the scene was transformed. Whereas a moment earlier they'd been calm, civilized people having a drink before a calm, civilized meal, they were suddenly transformed into hand-wringing zombies, helpless in the face of the technology that assaulted them. For Sid had activated the alarm and no one, least of all Ellis, knew what to do about it. The EMERGENCY strip was flashing wildly, the alarm beep-beep-beeping, the girls and the Carfarcts' boy fleeing the TV room in confusion, four pairs of hands fluttering helplessly over the box, and Ellis trying to dredge up the disarm code from the uncertain pocket of memory in which it was stored. "One-two-two-one!" Hilary shouted. Tina was holding her ears and making a face. Sid looked abashed.

When at last—after two false starts—Ellis had succeeded in disarming the thing and they'd settled back with their drinks and exclamations of "Jesus!" and "I thought I was going to die," there was a knock at the door. It was a man in a SecureCo uniform, with nightstick and gun. He was tall and he had a mustache. He invited himself in. "There a problem?" he asked.

"No, no," Ellis said, standing in the entranceway, heart pounding, acutely aware of his guests' eyes on him, "it's a new system and we, uh—it was a mistake."

"Name?" the man said.

"Hunsicker. Ellis."

"Code word?"

Here Ellis faltered. The code word, to be used for purposes of positive identification in just such a situation as this, was Hilary's inspiration. Pick something easy to remember, the SecureCo woman had said, and Hilary had chosen the name of the kids' pet rabbit, Honey Bunny. Ellis couldn't say the words. Not in front of this humorless man in the mustache, not with Sid and Tina watching him with those tight mocking smiles on their lips . . .

"Code word?" the man repeated.

Hilary was sunk into the couch at the far end of the coffee table. She leaned forward and raised her hand like a child in class, waving it to catch the guard's attention. "Honey Bunny," she said in a gasp that made the hair prickle at the back of Ellis' neck, "it's Honey Bunny."

That had been two nights ago.

But now, in the clear light of Saturday morning, after sleeping the sleep of the just—and prudent (Panty Rapist—all the Panty Rapists in the world could escape and it was nothing to him)—feeling self-satisfied and content right on down to the felt lining of his slippers, Ellis sat back, stretched, and gave his wife a rich little smile. "I guess it's a matter of priorities, honey," he said. "Sid and Tina can think what they want, but you know what I say—better safe than sorry."

When she talked about it afterward—with her husband at Gennaro's that night (she was too upset to cook), with her sister, with Betty Berger on the telephone— Giselle said she'd never been so scared in all her life. She meant it too. This was no horror story clipped from the newspaper, this was real. And it happened to her.

The guy was crazy. Creepy. Sick. He'd kept her there over four hours, and he had no intention of buying anything—she could see that in the first fifteen minutes. He just wanted an audience. Somebody to rant at, to threaten, to pin down with those jittery blue eyes. Richard had wanted her to go to the police, but she balked. What had he done, really? Scared her, yes. Bruised her arm. But what could the police do—she'd gone there of her own free will.

Her own free will. He'd said that. Those were his exact words.

Indignant, maybe a little shaken, she'd got up from the kitchen table to stuff her papers back into the briefcase. He was cursing under his breath, muttering darkly about the idiots on the freeway in their big-ass Mercedeses, crowding him, about spics and niggers and junior-high kids cutting through his yard— "Free country, my ass!" he'd shouted suddenly. "Free for every punk and weirdo and greaser to crap all over what little bit I got left, but let me get up from this table and put a couple holes in one of the little peckerheads and we'll see how it is. And I suppose you're going to protect me, huh, Miss Mercedes Benz with your heels and stockings and your big high-tech alarm system, huh?"

When she snapped the briefcase closed—no sale, nothing, just get me out of here, she was thinking—that was when he grabbed her arm. "Sit down," he snarled, and she tried to shake free but couldn't, he was strong with the rage of the psychopath, the lion in its den, the loony up against the wall.

"You're hurting me," she said as he forced her back down. "Mr. . . . Coles!" and she heard her own voice jump with anger, fright, pain.

"Yeah, that's right," he said, tightening his grip, "but you came here of your own free will, didn't you? Thought you were going to sucker me, huh? Run me a song and dance and lay your high-tech crap and your big bad SecureCo guards on me—oh, I've seen them, bunch of titsuckers and college wimps, who they going to stop? Huh?" He dropped her arm and challenged her with his jumpy mad tight-jawed glare.

She tried to get up but he roared, "Sit down! We got business here, goddamnit!" And then he was calling for his wife: "Glenys! Woman! Get your ass in here."

If she'd expected anything from the wife, any help or melioration, Giselle could see at a glance just how hopeless it was. The woman wouldn't look at her. She appeared in the doorway, pale as death, her hands trembling, staring at the carpet like a whipped dog. "Two G&T's," Coles said, sucking in his breath as if he were on the very edge of something, at the very beginning, "tall with a wedge of lime."

"But—" Giselle began to protest, looking from Coles to the woman.

"You'll drink with me, all right." Coles' voice came at her like a blade of ice. "Get friendly, huh? Show me what you got." And then he turned away, his face violent with disgust. "SecureCo," he spat. He looked up, staring past her. "You going to keep the sons of bitches away from me, you going to keep them off my

back, you going to give me any guarantees?" His voice rose. "I got a gun collection worth twelve thousand dollars in there—you going to answer for that? For
my color TV? The goddamned trash can even?"

Giselle sat rigid, wondering if she could make a break for the back door and
wondering if he was the type to keep it locked.

"Sell me," he demanded, looking at her now.

The woman set down the gin-and tonics and then faded back into the shadows of the hallway. Giselle said nothing.

"Tell me about the man in the mask," he said, grinning again, grinning wide,
too wide, "tell me about those poor old retired people. Come on," he said, his
eyes taunting her, "sell me. I want it. I do. I mean I really need you people and
your high-tech bullshit. . . ."

He held her eyes, gulped half his drink, and set the glass down again. "I mean
really," he said. "For my peace of mind."

It wasn't the fender-bender on the freeway the night before or the two hundred
illegals lined up and looking for work on Canoga Avenue at dawn, and it wasn't
the heart-clenching hate he still felt after being forced into early retirement two
years ago or the fact that he'd sat up all night drinking gin while Glenys slept
and the police and insurance companies filed their reports—it wasn't any of that
that finally drove Everett Coles over the line. Not that he'd admit, anyway. It
wasn't that little whore from SecureCo either (that's what she was, a whore, selling her tits and her lips and her ankles and all the rest of it too) or the veiny old
hag from Westec or even the self-satisfied, smirking son of a bitch from Metro-
politan Life, though he'd felt himself slipping on that one ("Death and dismemberment!" he'd hooted in the man's face, so thoroughly irritated, rubbed wrong,
and just plain pissed he could think of nothing but the big glistening Mannlicher
on the wall in the den) . . . No, it was Rance Ruby's stupid, fat-faced, shit-licking
excuse of a kid.

Picture him sitting there in the first faint glow of early morning, the bottle
mostly gone now and the fire in his guts over that moron with the barking face
who'd run into him on the freeway just about put out, and then he looks up from
the kitchen table and what does he see but this sorry lardassed spawn of a sorry
tattooed beer-swilling lardass of a father cutting through the yard with his black
death's-head T-shirt and his looseleaf and book jackets, and that's it. There's no
more thinking, no more reason, no insurance or hope. He's up out of the chair
like a shot and into the den, and then he's punching the barrel of the Mannlicher
right through the glass of the den window. The fat little fuck, he's out there under the grapefruit tree, shirttail hanging out, turning at the sound, and then *ka-
boom*, there's about half of him left.

Next minute Everett Coles is in his car, fender rubbing against the tire in back where that sorry sack of shit ran into him, and slamming out of the drive-way. He's got the Mannlicher on the seat beside him and a couple fistfuls of am-munition and he's peppering the side of Ruby's turd-colored house with a blast from his Weatherby pump-action shotgun. He grazes a parked camper on his way up the block, slams over a couple of garbage cans, and leans out the window to take the head off somebody's yapping poodle as he careens out onto the boule-vard, every wire gone loose in his head.

Ellis Hunsicker woke early. He'd dreamt he was a little cloud—the little cloud of the bedtime story he'd read Mifty and Corinne the night before—scudding along in the vast blue sky, free and untethered, the sun smiling on him as it does in pic-turebooks, when all at once he'd felt himself swept irresistibly forward, moving faster and faster, caught up in a huge, darkening, malevolent thunderhead that rose up faceless from the far side of the day . . . and then he woke. It was just first light. Hilary was breathing gently beside him. The alarm panel glowed soothingly in the shadow of the half-open door.

It was funny how quickly he'd got used to the thing, he reflected, yawning and scratching himself there in the muted light. A week ago he'd made a fool of himself over it in front of Sid and Tina, and now it was just another appliance, no more threatening or unusual—and no less vital—than the microwave, the Cuisinart, or the clock radio. The last two mornings, in fact, he'd been awakened not by the clock radio but by the insistent beeping of the house alarm—Mifty had set it off going out the back door to cuddle her rabbit. He thought now of getting up to shut the thing off—it was an hour yet before he'd have to be up for work—but he didn't. The bed was warm, the birds had begun to whisper out-side, and he shut his eyes, drifting off like a little cloud.

When he woke again it was to the beep-beep-beep of the house alarm and to the hazy apprehension of some godawful crash—a jet breaking the sound bar-rier, the first rumbling clap of the quake he lived in constant fear of—an appre-hension that something was amiss, that this beep-beep-beeping, familiar though it seemed, was somehow different, more high-pitched and admonitory than the beep-beep-beeping occasioned by a child going out to cuddle a bunny. He sat up. Hilary rose to her elbows beside him, looking bewildered, and in that instant the alarm was silenced forever by the unmistakable roar of gunblast. Ellis' heart froze. Hilary cried out, there was the heavy thump of footsteps below, a faint choked whimper as of little girls startled in their sleep and then a strange voice—high, hoarse, and raging—that chewed up the morning like a set of jaws. "Armed response!" the voice howled. "Armed response, goddamnit! Armed response!"

The couple strained forward like mourners at a funeral. Giselle had them, she knew that. They'd looked scared when she came to the door, a pair of timid rabbity faces peering out at her from behind the matching frames of their prescription glasses, and they seated themselves on the edge of the couch as if they were afraid of their own furniture. She had them wringing their hands and darting uneasy glances out the window as she described the perpetrator—"A white man, dressed like a schoolteacher, but with these wicked, jittery eyes that just sent a shiver through you." She focused on the woman as she described the victims. There was a boy, just fourteen years old, on his way to school, and a woman in a Mercedes driving down to the corner store for coffee filters. And then the family—they must have read about it—all of them, not three blocks from where they were now sitting. "He was thirty-five years old," she said in a husky voice, "an engineer at Rocketdyne, his whole life ahead of him . . . and she, she was one of these supernice people who . . . and the children . . ." She couldn't go on. The man—Mr. Dunsinane, wasn't that the name?—leaned forward and handed her a Kleenex. Oh, she had them, all right. She could have sold them the super-deluxe laser alert system, stock in the company, mikes for every flower in the garden, but the old charge just wasn't there.

"I'm sorry," she whispered, fighting back a sob.

It was weird, she thought, pressing the Kleenex to her face, but the masked intruder had never affected her like this, or the knife-sharpening Mexican either. It was Coles, of course, and those sick jumpy eyes of his, but it was the signs too. She couldn't stop thinking about those signs—if they hadn't been there, that is, stuck in the lawn like a red flag in front of a bull . . . But there was no future in that. No, she told the story anyway, told it despite the chill that came over her and the thickening in her throat.

She had to. If only for her peace of mind.

(1987)

KING BEE

In the mail that morning there were two solicitations for life insurance, a coupon from the local car wash promising a "100% Brushless Wash," four bills, three advertising flyers, and a death threat from his ex-son, Anthony. Anthony had used green ink, the cyclonic scrawl of his longhand lifting off into the loops, lassos, and curlicues of heavy weather aloft, and his message was the same as usual: *I eat the royal jelly. I sting and you die. Bzzzzzzzz. Pat too, the bitch.* He hadn't bothered to sign it.

"Ken? What is it?"

Pat was right beside him now, peering over his elbow at the sheaf of ads and bills clutched in his hand. She'd been pruning the roses and she was still wearing her work gloves. They stood there out front of the house in the sunshine, hunched forward protectively, the mailbox rising up like a tombstone between them. "It's Anthony," she said, "isn't it?"

He handed her the letter.

"My god," she said, sucking in a whistle of breath like a wounded animal. "How'd he get the address?"

It was a good question. They'd known he was to be released from Juvenile Hall on his eighteenth birthday, and they'd taken precautions. Like changing their phone number, their address, their places of employment, and the city and state in which they lived. For a while, they'd even toyed with the idea of changing their name, but then Ken's father came for a visit from Wisconsin and sobbed over the family coat of arms till they gave it up. Over the years, they'd received dozens of Anthony's death threats—all of them bee-oriented; bees were his obsession—but nothing since they'd moved. This was bad. Worse than bad.

"You'd better call the police," he said. "And take Skippy to the kennel."

■ ■ ■

Nine years earlier, the Mallows had been childless. There was something wrong with Pat's fallopian tubes—some congenital defect that reduced her odds of conception to 222,000 to one—and to compound the problem, Ken's sperm count was inordinately low, though he ate plenty of red meat and worked out every other day on the racquetball court. Adoption had seemed the way to go, though Pat was distressed by the fact that so many of the babies available were—well, she didn't like to say it, but they weren't white. There were Thai babies, Guianese babies, Herero babies, babies from Haiti, Kuala Lumpur, and Kashmir, but Caucasian babies were at a premium. You could have a nonwhite baby in six days—for a price, of course—but there was an eleven-year waiting list for white babies—twelve for blonds, fourteen for blue-eyed blonds—and neither Ken nor Pat was used to being denied. "How about an older child?" the man from the adoption agency had suggested.

They were in one of the plush, paneled conference rooms of Adopt-A-Kid, and Mr. Denteen, a handsome, bold-faced man in a suit woven of some exotic material, leaned forward with a fatherly smile. He bore an uncanny resemblance to Robert Young of "Father Knows Best," and on the wall behind him was a photomontage of plump and cooing babies. Pat was mesmerized. "What?" she said, as if she hadn't heard him.

"An older child," Denteen repeated, his voice rich with insinuation. It was the voice of a seducer, a shrink, a black-marketeer.

"No," Ken said, "I don't think so."

"How old?" Pat said.

Denteen leaned forward on his leather elbow patches. "I just happen to have a child—a boy—whose file just came to us this morning. Little Anthony Cademartori. Tony. He's nine years old. Just. Actually, his birthday was only last week."

The photo Denteen handed them showed a sunny, smiling, towheaded boy, a generic boy, archetypal, the sort of boy you envision when you close your eyes and think "boy." If they'd looked closer, they would have seen that his eyes were like two poked holes and that there was something unstable about his smile and the set of his jaw, but they were in the grip of a conceit and they didn't look that closely. Ken asked if there was anything wrong with him. "Physically, I mean," he said.

Denteen let a good-humored little laugh escape him. "This is your average nine-year-old boy, Mr. Mallow," he said. "Average height, weight, build, average—or above average—intelligence. He's a boy, and he's one heck of a lot fitter than I am." Denteen cast a look to the heavens—or, rather, to the ceiling tiles. "To be nine years old again," he sighed.

"Does he behave?" Pat asked.

"Does he behave?" Denteen echoed, and he looked offended, hurt almost.

"Does the President live in the White House? Does the sun come up in the morning?" He straightened up, shot his cuffs, then leaned forward again—so far forward his hands dangled over the edge of the conference table. "Look at him," he said, holding up the picture again. "Mr. and Mrs. Mallow—Ken, Pat—let me tell you that this child has seen more heartbreak than you and I'll know in a lifetime. His birth parents were killed at a railway crossing when he was two, and then, the irony of it, his adoptive parents—they were your age, by the way—just dropped dead one day while he was at school. One minute they're alive and well and the next"—he snapped his finger—"they're gone." His voice faltered. "And then poor little Tony . . . poor little Tony comes home . . ."

Pat looked stunned. Ken reached out to squeeze her hand.

"He needs love, Pat," Denteen said. "He has love to give. A lot of love."

Ken looked at Pat. Pat looked at Ken.

"So," Denteen said, "when would you like to meet him?"

They met him the following afternoon, and he seemed fine. A little shy, maybe, but fine. Super-polite, that's what Pat thought. May I this and may I that, please, thank you, and it's a pleasure to meet you. He was adorable. Big for his age—that was a surprise. They'd expected a lovable little urchin, the kind of kid Norman Rockwell might have portrayed in the barber's chair atop a stack of phone books, but Anthony was big, already the size of a teenager—big-headed, big in the shoulders, and big in the rear. Tall too. At nine, he was already as tall as Pat and probably outweighed her. What won them over, though, was his smile. He turned his smile on them that first day in Denteen's office—a blooming angelic smile that showed off his dimples and the perfection of his tiny white glistening teeth—and Pat felt something give way inside her. At the end of the meeting she hugged him to her breast.

The smile was a regular feature of those first few months—the months of the trial period. Anthony smiled at breakfast, at dinner, smiled when he helped Ken rake the leaves from the gutters or tidy up the yard, smiled in his sleep. He stopped smiling when the trial period was over, as if he'd suddenly lost control of his facial muscles. It was uncanny. Almost to the day the adoption became formal—the day that he was theirs and they were his—Anthony's smile vanished. The change was abrupt and it came without warning.

"Scooter," Ken called to him one afternoon, "you want to help me take those old newspapers to the recycling center and then maybe stop in at Baskin and Robbins?"

Anthony was upstairs in his room, the room they'd decorated with posters of ballplayers and airplanes. He didn't answer.

"Scooter?"

Silence.

Puzzled, Ken ascended the stairs. As he reached the landing, he became aware of an odd sound emanating from Anthony's room—a low hum, as of an appliance kicking in. He paused to knock at the door and the sound began to take on resonance, to swell and shrink again, a thousand muted voices speaking in unison. "Anthony?" he called, pushing open the door.

Anthony was seated naked in the middle of his bed, wearing a set of headphones Ken had never seen before. The headphones were attached to a tape player the size of a suitcase. Ken had never seen the tape player before either. And the walls—gone were the dazzling sunstruck posters of Fernando Valenzuela, P-38s, and Mitsubishi Zeroes, replaced now by black-and-white photos of insects—torn, he saw, from library books. The books lay scattered across the floor, gutted, their spines broken.

For a long moment, Ken merely stood there in the doorway, the sizzling pulse of that many-voiced hum leaking out of Anthony's headphones to throb in his gut, his chest, his bones. It was as if he'd stumbled upon some ancient rite in the Australian Outback, as if he'd stepped out of his real life in the real world and into some cheap horror movie about demonic possession and people whose eyes lit up like Christmas-tree ornaments. Anthony was seated in the lotus position, his own eyes tightly closed. He didn't seem to be aware of Ken. The buzzing was excruciating. After a moment, Ken backed out of the room and gently shut the door.

At dinner that evening, Anthony gave them their first taste of his why-don't-you-get-off-my-back look, a look that was to become habitual. His hair stood up jaggedly, drawn up into needlelike points—he must have greased it, Ken realized—and he slouched as if there were an invisible piano strapped to his shoulders. Ken didn't know where to begin—with the scowl, the nudity, the desecration of library books, the tape player and its mysterious origins (had he borrowed it—perhaps from school? a friend?). Pat knew nothing. She served chicken croquettes, biscuits with honey, and baked beans, Anthony's favorite meal. She was at the stove, her back to them, when Ken cleared his throat.

"Anthony," he said, "is there anything wrong? Anything you want to tell us?"

Anthony shot him a contemptuous look. He said nothing. Pat glanced over her shoulder.

"About the library books . . ."

"You were spying on me," Anthony snarled.

Pat turned away from the stove, stirring spoon in hand. "What do you mean? Ken? What's this all about?"

"I wasn't spying, I—" Ken faltered. He felt the anger rising in him. "All right," he said, "where'd you get the tape player?"

Anthony wiped his mouth with the back of his hand, then looked past Ken to his adoptive mother. "I stole it," he said.

Suddenly Ken was on his feet. "Stole it?" he roared. "Don't you know what that means, library books and now, now stealing?"

Anthony was a statue, big-headed and serene. "Bzzzzzzzz," he said.

■ ■ ■

The scene at the library was humiliating. Clearly, the books had been willfully destroyed. Mrs. Tutwillow was outraged. And no matter how hard Ken squeezed his arm, Anthony remained pokerfaced and unrepentant. "I won't say I'm sorry," he sneered, "because I'm not." Ken gave her a check for $112.32, to cover the cost of replacing the books, plus shipping and handling. At Steve's Stereo Shoppe, the man behind the counter—Steve, presumably—agreed not to press charges, but he had a real problem with offering the returned unit to the public as new goods, if Ken knew what he meant. Since he'd have to sell it used now, he wondered if Ken had the $87.50 it was going to cost him to mark it down. Of course, if Ken didn't want to cooperate, he'd have no recourse but to report the incident to the police. Ken cooperated.

At home, after he'd ripped the offending photos from the walls and sent Anthony to his room, he phoned Denteen. "Ken, listen. I know you're upset," Denteen crooned, his voice as soothing as a shot of whiskey, "but the kid's life has been real hell, believe me, and you've got to realize that he's going to need some time to adjust." He paused. "Why don't you get him a dog or something?"

"A dog?"

"Yeah. Something for him to be responsible for for a change. He's been a ward—I mean, an adoptee—all this time, with people caring for him, and maybe it's that he feels like a burden or something. With a dog or a cat he could do the giving."

A dog. The idea of it sprang to sudden life and Ken was a boy himself again, roaming the hills and stubble fields of Wisconsin, Skippy at his side. A dog. Yes. Of course.

"And listen," Denteen was saying, "if you think you're going to need professional help with this, the man to go to is Maurice Barebaum. He's one of the top child psychologists in the state, if not the country." There was a hiss of shuffling papers, the flap of Rolodex cards. "I've got his number right here."

"I don't want a dog," Anthony insisted, and he gave them a strained, histrionic look.

We're onstage, Ken was thinking, that's what it is. He looked at Pat, seated on the couch, her legs tucked under her, and then at his son, this stranger with the staved-in eyes and tallowy arms who'd somehow won the role.

"But it would be so nice," Pat said, drawing a picture in the air, "you'd have a little friend."

Anthony was wearing a black T-shirt emblazoned with red and blue letters that spelled out MEGADETH. On the reverse was the full-color representation of a stupendous bumblebee. "Oh, come off it, Pat," he sang, a keening edge to his voice, "that's so stupid. Dogs are so slobbery and shitty."

"Don't use that language," Ken said automatically.

"A little one, maybe," Pat said, "a cocker or a sheltie."

"I don't want a dog. I want a hive. A beehive. That's what I want." He was balancing like a tightrope walker on the edge of the fireplace apron.

"Bees?" Ken demanded. "What kind of pet is that?" He was angry. It seemed he was always angry lately.

Pat forestalled him, her tone soft as a caress. "Bees, darling?" she said. "Can you tell us what you like about them? Is it because they're so useful, because of the honey, I mean?"

Anthony was up on one foot. He tipped over twice before he answered. "Because they have no mercy."

"Mercy?" Pat repeated.

"Three weeks, that's how long a worker lasts in the summer," Anthony said. "They kick the drones out to die. The spent workers too." He looked at Ken. "You fit in or you die."

"And what the hell is that supposed to mean?" Ken was shouting; he couldn't help himself.

Anthony's face crumpled up. His cheeks were corrugated, the spikes of his hair stood out like thorns. "You hate me," he whined. "You fuck, you dickhead—you hate me, don't you, don't you?"

"Ken!" Pat cried, but Ken already had him by the arm. "Don't you ever—" he said.

"Ever what? Ever what? Say 'fuck'? You do it, you do it, you do it!" Anthony was in a rage, jerking away, tears on his face, shouting. "Upstairs, at night. I hear you. Fucking. That's what you do. Grunting and fucking just like, like, like *dogs!*"

"I'll need to see him three days a week," Dr. Barebaum said. He was breathing heavily, as if he'd just climbed several flights of stairs.

Anthony was out in the car with Pat. He'd spent the past forty-five minutes sequestered with Barebaum. "Is he—is he all right?" Ken asked. "I mean, is he normal?"

Barebaum leaned back in his chair and made a little pyramid of his fingers. "Adjustment problems," he breathed. "He's got a lot of hostility. He's had a difficult life."

Ken stared down at the carpet.

"He tells me," Barebaum dredged up the words as if from some inner fortress, "he tells me he wants a dog."

Ken sat rigid in the chair. This must be what it feels like before they switch on the current at Sing Sing, he thought. "No, you've got it wrong. *We* wanted to get *him* a dog, but he said no. In fact, he went schizoid on us."

Barebaum's nose wrinkled up at the term "schizoid." Ken regretted it instantly. "Yes," the doctor drawled, "hmmph. But the fact is the boy quite distinctly told me the whole blow-up was because he does indeed want a dog. You know, Mr., ah—"

"Mallow."

"—Mallow, we often say exactly the opposite of what we mean; you are aware of that, aren't you?"

Ken said nothing. He studied the weave of the carpet.

After a moment, the doctor cleared his throat. "You do have health insurance?" he said.

In all, Anthony was with them just over three years. The dog—a sheltie pup Ken called "Skippy" and Anthony referred to alternately as "Ken" and "Turd"—was a mistake, they could see that now. For the first few months or so, Anthony had ignored it, except to run squealing through the house, the puppy's warm excreta cupped in his palms, shouting, "It shit! It shit! The dog shit!" Ken, though, got to like the feel of the pup's wet nose on his wrist as he skimmed the morning paper or sat watching TV in the evening. The pup was alive, it was high-spirited and joyful, and it brought him back to his own childhood in a way that Anthony, with his gloom and his sneer, never could have. "I want a hive," Anthony said, over and over again. "My very own hive."

Ken ignored him—bees were dangerous, after all, and this was a residential neighborhood—until the day Anthony finally did take an interest in Skippy. It was one of those rare days when Pat's car was at the garage, so Ken picked her up at work and they arrived home together. The house was quiet. Skippy, who usually greeted them at the door in a paroxysm of licking, rolling, leaping, and tail-thumping, was nowhere to be seen. And Anthony, judging from the low-threshold hum washing over the house, was up in his room listening to the bee tapes Pat had given him for Christmas. "Skippy," Ken called, "here, boy!" No Skippy. Pat checked the yard, the basement, the back room. Finally, together, they mounted the stairs to Anthony's room.

Anthony was in the center of the bed, clad only in his underwear, reprising the ritual Ken had long since grown to accept (Dr. Barebaum claimed it was nothing to worry about—"It's his way of meditating, that's all, and if it calms him down, why fight it?"). Huge color photographs of bees obliterated the walls, but these were legitimate photos, clipped from the pages of *The Apiarian's Monthly*, another gift from Pat. Anthony looked bloated, fatter than ever, pale and white as a grub. When he became aware of them, he slipped the headphones from his ears. "Honey," Pat said, reaching down to ruffle his hair, "have you seen Skippy?"

It took him a moment to answer. He looked bewildered, as if she'd asked him to solve an equation or name the twenty biggest cities in Russia. "I put him in his cell," he said finally.

"Cell?" Ken echoed.

"In the hive," Anthony said. "The big hive."

It was Ken who noticed the broomstick wedged against the oven door, and it was Ken who buried Skippy's poor singed carcass and arranged to have the oven replaced—Pat wouldn't, couldn't cook in it, ever again. It was Ken too who lost control of himself that night and slapped Anthony's sick pale swollen face till Pat pulled him off. In the end, Anthony got his hive, thirty thousand honeybees in a big white wooden box with fifteen frames inside, and Barebaum got to see Anthony two more days a week.

At first, the bees seemed to exert a soothing influence on the boy. He stopped muttering to himself, used his utensils at the table, and didn't seem quite as vulnerable to mood swings as he had. After school and his daily sessions with Barebaum, he'd spend hours tending the hive, watching the bees at their compulsive work, humming softly to himself as if in a trance. Ken was worried he'd be stung and bought him a gauze bonnet and gloves, but he rarely wore them. And when he was stung—daily, it seemed—he displayed the contusions proudly, as if they were battle scars. For Ken and Pat, it was a time of accommodation, and they were quietly optimistic. Gone was the smiling boy they'd taken into their home, but at least now he wasn't so—there was no other word for it—so odd, and he seemed less agitated, less ready to fly off the handle.

The suicide attempt took them by surprise.

Ken found him, at dusk, crouched beneath the hive and quietly bleeding from both wrists. Pat's X-ACTO knife lay in the grass beside him, black with blood. In the hospital the next day, Anthony looked lost and vulnerable, looked like a little boy again. Barebaum was there with them. "It's a phase," he said, puffing for breath. "He's been very depressed lately."

"Why?" Pat asked, sweeping Anthony's hair back from his forehead, stroking his swollen hands. "Your bees," she choked. "What would your bees do without you?"

Anthony let his eyes fall shut. After a moment he lifted his lids again. His voice was faint. "Bzzzzzzzz," he said.

They kept him at the Hart Mental Health Center for nine months, and then they let him come home again. Ken was against it. He'd contacted a lawyer about voiding the adoption papers—Anthony was just too much to handle; he was emotionally unstable, disturbed, dangerous; the psychiatric bills alone were killing them—but Pat overruled him. "He needs us," she said. "He has no one else to turn to." They were in the living room. She bent forward to light a cigarette. "Nobody said it would be easy," she said.

"Easy?" he retorted. "You talk like it's a war or something. I didn't adopt a kid to go to war—or to save the world either."

"Why did you adopt him then?"

The question took him by surprise. He looked past Pat to the kitchen, where one of Anthony's crayon drawings—of a lopsided bee—clung to the refrigerator door, and then past the refrigerator to the window, and the lush still yard beyond. He shrugged. "For love, I guess."

As it turned out, the question was moot—Anthony didn't last six months this time. When they picked him up at the hospital—"Hospital," Ken growled, "nut hatch is more like it"—they barely recognized him. He was taller and he'd put on weight. Pat couldn't call it baby fat anymore—this was true fat, adult fat, fat that sank his eyes and strained at the seams of his pants. And his hair, his rich fine white-blond hair, was gone, shaved to a transparent stubble over a scalp the color of boiled ham. Pat chattered at him, but he got into the car without a word. Halfway home he spoke for the first time. "You know what they eat in there," he said, "in the hospital?"

Ken felt like the straightman in a comedy routine. "What do they eat?" he said, his eyes fixed on the road.

"Shit," Anthony said. "They eat shit. Their own shit. That's what they eat."

"Do you have to use that language?"

Anthony didn't bother to respond.

At home, they discovered that the bees had managed to survive on their own, a fact that somehow seemed to depress Anthony, and after shuffling halfheartedly through the trays and getting stung six or seven times, he went up to bed.

The trouble—the final trouble, the trouble that was to take Anthony out of their hands for good—started at school. Anthony was almost twelve now, but because of his various problems, he was still in fifth grade. He was in a special program, of course, but he took lunch and recess with the other fifth-graders. On the playground, he towered over them, plainly visible a hundred yards away, like some great unmoving statue of the Buddha. The other children shied away from him instinctively, as if they knew he was beyond taunting, beyond simple joys and simple sorrows. But he was aware of them, aware in a new way, aware of the girls especially. Something had happened inside him while he was away— "Puberty," Barebaum said, "he has urges like any other boy"—and he didn't know how to express it.

One afternoon, he and Oliver Monteiros, another boy from the special program, cornered a fifth-grade girl behind one of the temporary classrooms. There they "stretched" her, as Anthony later told it—Oliver had her hands, Anthony her feet—stretched her till something snapped in her shoulder and Anthony felt his pants go wet. He tried to tell the principal about it, about the wetness in his pants, but the principal wouldn't listen. Dr. Conarroe was a gray-bearded black man who believed in dispensing instant justice. He was angry, gesturing in their faces, his beard jabbing at them like a weapon. When Anthony unzipped his fly to show him what had happened, Dr. Conarroe suspended him on the spot.

Pat spoke with Anthony, and they both—she and Ken—went in to meet with Dr. Conarroe and the members of the school board. They brought Barebaum with them. Together, they were able to overcome the principal's resistance, and Anthony, after a week's suspension, was readmitted. "One more incident," Conarroe said, his eyes aflame behind the discs of his wire-framed glasses, "and I don't care how small it is, and he's out. Is that understood?"

At least Anthony didn't keep them in suspense. On his first day back he tracked down the girl he'd stretched, chased her into the girls' room, and as he told it, put his "stinger" in her. The girl's parents sued the school district, Anthony was taken into custody and remanded to Juvenile Hall following another nine-month stay at Hart, and Ken and Pat finally threw in the towel. They were exhausted, physically and emotionally, and they were in debt to Barebaum for some thirty thousand dollars above what their insurance would cover. They felt cheated, bitter, worn down to nothing. Anthony was gone, adoption a sick joke. But they had each other, and after a while—and with the help of Skippy II—they began to pick up the pieces.

And now, six years later, Anthony had come back to haunt them. Ken was enraged. He, for one, wasn't about to be chased out of this house and this job— they'd moved once, and that was enough. If he'd found them, he'd found them—so much the worse. But this was America, and they had their rights too. While Pat took Skippy to the kennel for safekeeping, Ken phoned the police and explained the situation to an Officer Ocksler, a man whose voice was so lacking in inflection he might as well have been dead. Ken was describing the incident with Skippy the First when Officer Ocksler interrupted him. "I'm sorry," he said, and there was a faint animation to his voice now, as if he were fighting down a belch or passing gas, "but there's nothing we can do."

"Nothing you can do?" Ken couldn't help himself: he was practically yelping. "But he broiled a harmless puppy in the oven, raped a fifth-grade girl, sent us thirty-two death threats, and tracked us down even though we quit our jobs, packed up and moved, and left no forwarding address." He took a deep breath. "He thinks he's a bee, for christsake."

Officer Ocksler inserted his voice into the howling silence that succeeded this outburst. "He commits a crime," he said, the words stuck fast in his throat, "you call us."

The next day's mail brought the second threat. It came in the form of a picture postcard, addressed to Pat, and postmarked locally. The picture—a Japanese print—showed a pale fleshy couple engaged in the act of love. The message, which took some deciphering, read as follows:

> Dear Mother Pat,
>
> I'm a King Bee,
> Gonna buzz round your hive,
> Together we can make honey
> Let me come inside.
>
> Your son, Anthony

Ken tore it to pieces. He was red in the face, trembling. White babies, he thought bitterly. An older child. They would have been better off with a seven-foot Bantu, an Eskimo, anything. "I'll kill him," he said. "He comes here, I'll kill him."

It was early the next morning—Pat was in the kitchen, Ken upstairs shaving—when a face appeared in the kitchen window. It was a large and familiar face, transformed somewhat by the passage of the years and the accumulation of flesh, but unmistakable nonetheless. Pat, who was leaning over the sink to rinse her coffee cup, gave a little gasp of recognition.

Anthony was smiling, beaming at her like the towheaded boy in the photograph she'd kept in her wallet all these years. He was smiling, and suddenly that was all that mattered to her. The sweetness of those first few months came back in a rush—he was her boy, her own, and the rest of it was nothing—and before she knew what she was doing she had the back door open. It was a mistake. The moment the door swung open, she heard them. Bees. A swarm that blackened the side of the house, the angry hiss of their wings like grease in a fryer. They were right there, right beside the door. First one bee, then another, shot past her head. "Mom," Anthony said, stepping up onto the porch, "I'm home."

She was stunned. It wasn't just the bees, but Anthony. He was huge, six feet tall at least, and so heavy. His pants—they were pajamas, hospital-issue—were big as a tent, and it looked as if he'd rolled up a carpet beneath his shirt. She could barely make out his eyes, sunk in their pockets of flesh. She didn't know what to say.

He took hold of the door. "I want a hug," he said, "give me a hug."

She backed away from him instinctively. "Ken!" she called, and the catch in her throat turned it into a mournful, drawnout bleat. "Ken!"

Anthony was poised on the threshold. His smile faded. Then, like a magician, he reached out his hand and plunged it into the mass of bees. She saw him wince as he was stung, heard the harsh sizzle of the insects rise in crescendo, and then he drew back his hand, ever so slowly, and the bees came with him. They moved so fast—glutinous, like meringue clinging to a spoon—that she nearly missed it. There was something in his hand, a tiny box, some sort of mesh, and then his hand was gone, his arm, the right side of his body, his face and head and the left side too. Suddenly he was alive with bees, wearing them, a humming, pulsating ball of them.

She felt a sharp pain in her ankle, then another at her throat. She backed up a step.

"You sent me away," Anthony scolded, and the bees clung to his lips. "You never loved me. Nobody ever loved me."

She heard Ken behind her—"What is this?" he said, and then a weak curse escaped him—but she couldn't turn. The hum of the bees mesmerized her. They clung to Anthony, one mind, thirty thousand bodies.

And then the blazing ball of Anthony's hand separated itself from his body and his bee-thick fingers opened to reveal the briefest glimpse of the gauze-covered box. "The queen," Anthony said. "I throw her down and you're"—she could barely hear him, the bees raging, Ken shouting out her name—"you're history. Both of you."

For a long moment Anthony stood there motionless, afloat in bees. Huge as he was, he seemed to hover over the linoleum, derealized in the mass of them. And then she knew what was going to happen, knew that she was barren then and now and forever and that it was meant to be, and that this, her only child, was beyond human help or understanding.

"Go away," Anthony said, the swarm thrilling louder, "go . . . into the . . . next room . . . before, before—" and then Ken had her by the arm and they were moving. She thought she heard Anthony sigh, and as she darted a glance back over her shoulder he crushed the box with a snap loud as the crack of a limb. There was an answering roar from the bees, and in her last glimpse of him he was falling, borne down by the terrible animate weight of them.

"I'll kill him," Ken spat, his shoulder pressed to the parlor door. Bees rattled against the panels like hailstones.

She couldn't catch her breath. She felt a sudden stab under her collar, and then another. Ken's words didn't make sense—Anthony was gone from them now, gone forever—didn't he understand that? She listened to the bees raging round her kitchen, stinging blindly, dying for their queen. And then she thought of Anthony, poor Anthony, in his foster homes, in the hospital, in prison, thought of his flesh scored a thousand, ten thousand times, wound in his cerement of bees.

He was wrong, she thought, leaning into the door as if bracing herself against a storm, they do have mercy. They do.

(1988)

SINKING HOUSE

When Monty's last breath caught somewhere in the back of his throat with a sound like the tired wheeze of an old screen door, the first thing she did was turn on the water. She leaned over him a minute to make sure, then she wiped her hands on her dress and shuffled into the kitchen. Her fingers trembled as she jerked at the lever and felt the water surge against the porcelain. Steam rose in her face; a glitter of liquid leapt for the drain. Croak, that's what they called it. Now she knew why. She left the faucet running in the kitchen and crossed the gloomy expanse of the living room, swung down the hallway to the guest bedroom, and turned on both taps in the bathroom there. It was almost as an afterthought that she decided to fill the tub too.

For a long while she sat in the leather armchair in the living room. The sound of running water—pure, baptismal, as uncomplicated as the murmur of a brook in Vermont or a toilet at the Waldorf—soothed her. It trickled and trilled, burbling from either side of the house and driving down the terrible silence that crouched in the bedroom over the lifeless form of her husband.

The afternoon was gone and the sun plunging into the canopy of the big eucalyptus behind the Finkelsteins' when she finally pushed herself up from the chair. Head down, arms moving stiffly at her sides, she scuffed out the back door, crossed the patio, and bent to turn on the sprinklers. They sputtered and spat—not enough pressure, that much she understood—but finally came to life in halfhearted umbrellas of mist. She left the hose trickling in the rose garden, then went back into the house, passed through the living room, the kitchen, the master bedroom—not even a glance for Monty, no: she wouldn't look at him, not yet—and on into the master bath. The taps were weak, barely a trickle, but she left them on anyway, then flushed the toilet and pinned down the float with the brick Monty had used as a doorstop. And then finally, so weary she could barely lift her arms, she leaned into the stall and flipped on the shower.

Two weeks after the ambulance came for the old man next door, Meg Terwilliger was doing her stretching exercises on the prayer rug in the sunroom, a menthol cigarette glowing in the ashtray on the floor beside her, the new CD by Sandee and the Sharks thumping out of the big speakers in the corners. Meg was twenty-three, with the fine bones and haunted eyes of a poster child. She wore her black hair cut close at the temples, long in front, and she used a sheeny black eye-shadow to bring out the hunger in her eyes. In half an hour she'd have to pick up Tiffany at nursery school, drop off the dog at the veterinarian's, take Sonny's shirts to the cleaner's, buy a pound and a half of thresher shark, cilantro, and flour tortillas at the market, and start the burritos for supper. But now, she was stretching.

She took a deep drag on the cigarette, tugged at her right foot, and brought it up snug against her buttocks. After a moment she released it and drew back her left foot in its place. One palm flat on the floor, her head bobbing vaguely to the beat of the music, she did half a dozen repetitions, then paused to relight her cigarette. It wasn't until she turned over to do her straight-leg lifts that she noticed the dampness in the rug.

Puzzled, she rose to her knees and reached behind her to rub at the twin wet spots on the seat of her sweats. She lifted the corner of the rug, suspecting the dog, but there was no odor of urine. Looking closer, she saw that the concrete floor was a shade darker beneath the rug, as if it were bleeding moisture as it sometimes did in the winter. But this wasn't winter, this was high summer in Los Angeles and it hadn't rained for months. Cursing Sonny—he'd promised her ceramic tile and though she'd run all over town to get the best price on a nice Italian floral pattern, he still hadn't found the time to go look at it—she shot back the sliding door and stepped into the yard to investigate.

Immediately, she felt the Bermuda grass squelch beneath the soles of her aerobic shoes. She hadn't taken three strides—the sun in her face, Queenie yapping frantically from the fenced-in pool area—and her feet were wet. Had Sonny left the hose running? Or Tiffany? She slogged across the lawn, the pastel Reeboks spattered with wet, and checked the hose. It was innocently coiled on its tender, the tap firmly shut. Queenie's yapping went up an octave. The heat—it must have been ninety-five, a hundred—made her feel faint. She gazed up into the cloudless sky, then bent to check each of the sprinklers in succession.

She was poking around in the welter of bushes along the fence, looking for an errant sprinkler, when she thought of the old lady next door—Muriel, wasn't that her name? What with her husband dying and all, maybe she'd left the hose running and forgotten all about it. Meg rose on her tiptoes to peer over the redwood fence that separated her yard from the neighbors' and found herself looking into a glistening, sunstruck garden, with banks of Impatiens, bird of paradise, oleander, and loquat, roses in half a dozen shades. The sprinklers were on and the hose was running. For a long moment Meg stood there, mesmerized by the play of light through the drifting fans of water; she was wondering what it would be like to be old, thinking of how it would be if Sonny died and Tiffany were grown up and gone. She'd probably forget to turn off the sprinklers too.

The moment passed. The heat was deadening, the dog hysterical. Meg knew she would have to do something about the sodden yard and wet floor in the sunroom, but she dreaded facing the old woman. What would she say—I'm sorry your husband died but could you turn off the sprinklers? She was thinking maybe she'd phone—or wait till Sonny got home and let him handle it—when she stepped back from the fence and sank to her ankles in mud.

When the doorbell rang, Muriel was staring absently at the cover of an old *National Geographic* which lay beneath a patina of dust on the coffee table. The cover photo showed the beige and yellow sands of some distant desert, rippled to the horizon with corrugations that might have been waves on a barren sea. Monty was dead and buried. She wasn't eating much. Or sleeping much either. The sympathy cards sat unopened on the table in the kitchen, where the tap overflowed the sink and water plunged to the floor with a pertinacity that was like a redemption. When it was quiet—in the early morning or late at night—she could distinguish the separate taps, each with its own voice and rhythm, as they dripped and trickled from the far corners of the house. In those suspended hours she could make out the comforting gurgle of the toilet in the guest room, the musical wash of the tub as water cascaded over the lip of its porcelain dam, the quickening rush of the stream in the hallway as it shot like a miniature Niagara down the chasm of the floor vent . . . she could hear the drip in the master bedroom, the distant hiss of a shower, and the sweet external sizzle of the sprinklers on the back lawn.

But now she heard the doorbell.

Wearily, gritting her teeth against the pain in her lower legs and the damp lingering ache of her feet, she pushed herself up from the chair and sloshed her way to the door. The carpet was black with water, soaked through like a sponge—and in a tidy corner of her mind she regretted it—but most of the runoff was finding its way to the heating vents and the gaps in the corners where Monty had miscalculated the angle of the baseboard. She heard it dripping somewhere beneath the house and for a moment pictured the water lying dark and still in a shadowy lagoon that held the leaking ship of the house poised on its trembling surface. The doorbell sounded again. "All right, all right," she muttered, "I'm coming."

A girl with dark circles round her eyes stood on the doorstep. She looked vaguely familiar, and for a moment Muriel thought she recognized her from a TV program about a streetwalker who rises up to kill her pimp and liberate all the other leather-clad, black-eyed streetwalkers of the neighborhood, but then the girl spoke and Muriel realized her mistake. "Hi," the girl said, and Muriel saw that her shoes were black with mud, "I'm your neighbor? Meg Terwilliger?"

Muriel was listening to the bathroom sink. She said nothing. The girl looked down at her muddy shoes. "I, uh, just wanted to tell you that we're, uh—Sonny and I, I mean—he's my husband?—we're sorry about your trouble and all, but I wondered if you knew your sprinklers were on out back?"

Muriel attempted a smile—surely a smile was appropriate at this juncture, wasn't it?—but managed only to lift her upper lip back from her teeth in a sort of wince or grimace.

The girl was noticing the rug now, and Muriel's sodden slippers. She looked baffled, perhaps even a little frightened. And young. So young. Muriel had had a young friend once, a girl from the community college who used to come to the house before Monty got sick. She had a tape recorder, and she would ask them questions about their childhood, about the days when the San Fernando Valley was dirt roads and orange groves. Oral history, she called it. "It's all right," Muriel said, trying to reassure her.

"I just—is it a plumbing problem?" the girl said, backing away from the door. "Sonny . . ." she said, but didn't finish the thought. She ducked her head and re-treated down the steps, but when she reached the walk she wheeled around. "I mean you really ought to see about the sprinklers," she blurted, "the whole place is soaked, my sunroom and everything—"

"It's all right," Muriel repeated, and then the girl was gone and she shut the door.

"She's nuts, she is. Really. I mean she's out of her gourd."

Meg was searing chunks of thresher shark in a pan with green chilies, sweet red pepper, onion, and cilantro. Sonny, who was twenty-eight and so intoxicated by real estate he had to forgo the morning paper till he got home at night, was slumped in the breakfast nook with a vodka tonic and the sports pages. His white-blond hair was cut fashionably, in what might once have been called a flat-top, though it was thinning, and his open, appealing face, with its boyish look, had begun to show sings of wear, particularly around the eyes, where years of es-crow had taken their toll. Tiffany was in her room, playing quietly with a pair of six-inch dolls that had cost sixty-five dollars each.

"Who?" Sonny murmured, tugging unconsciously at the gold chain he wore around his neck.

"Muriel. The old lady next door. Haven't you heard a thing I've been saying?"

With an angry snap of her wrist, Meg cut the heat beneath the saucepan and clapped a lid over it. "The floor in the sunroom is flooded, for god's sake," she said, stalking across the kitchen in her bare feet till she stood poised over him. "The rug is ruined. Or almost is. And the yard—"

Sonny slapped the paper down on the table. "All right! Just let me relax a minute, will you?"

She put on her pleading look. It was a look compounded of pouty lips, tousled hair, and those inevitable eyes, and it always had its effect on him. "One minute," she murmured. "That's all it'll take. I just want you to see the backyard."

She took him by the hand and led him through the living room to the sunroom, where he stood a moment contemplating the damp spot on the concrete floor. She was surprised herself at how the spot had grown—it was three times what it had been this afternoon, and it seemed to have sprouted wings and legs like an enormous Rorschach. She pictured a butterfly. Or no, a hovering crow or bat. She wondered what Muriel would have made of it.

Outside, she let out a little yelp of disgust—all the earthworms in the yard had crawled up on the step to die. And the lawn wasn't merely spongy now, it was soaked through, puddled like a swamp. "Jesus Christ," Sonny muttered, sinking in his wingtips. He cakewalked across the yard to where the fence had begun to sag, the post leaning·drunkenly, the slats bowed. "Will you look at this?" he shouted over his shoulder. Squeamish about the worms, Meg stood at the door to the sunroom. "The goddam fence is falling down!"

He stood there a moment, water seeping into his shoes, a look of stupefaction on his face. Meg recognized the look. It stole over his features in moments of extremity, as when he tore open the phone bill to discover mysterious twenty-dollar calls to Billings, Montana, and Greenleaf, Mississippi, or when his buyer called on the day escrow was to close to tell him he'd assaulted the seller and wondered if Sonny had five hundred dollars for bail. These occasions always took him by surprise. He was shocked anew each time the crisply surveyed, neatly kept world he so cherished rose up to confront him with all its essential sloppiness, irrationality, and bad business sense. Meg watched the look of disbelief turn to one of injured rage. She followed him through the house, up the walk, and into Muriel's yard, where he stalked up to the front door and pounded like the Gestapo.

There was no response.

"Son of a bitch," he spat, turning to glare over his shoulder at her as if it were her fault or something. From inside they could hear the drama of running water, a drip and gurgle, a sough and hiss. Sonny turned back to the door, hammering his fist against it till Meg swore she could see the panels jump.

It frightened her, this sudden rage. Sure, there was a problem here and she was glad he was taking care of it, but did he have to get violent, did he have to get crazy? "You don't have to beat her door down," she called, focusing on the swell of his shoulder and the hammer of his fist as it rose and fell in savage rhythm. "Sonny, come on. It's only water, for god's sake."

"Only?" he snarled, spinning round to face her. "You saw the fence—next thing you know the foundation'll shift on us. The whole damn house—" He never finished. The look on her face told him that Muriel had opened the door.

Muriel was wearing the same faded blue housecoat she'd had on earlier, and the same wet slippers. Short, heavyset, so big in front it seemed as if she were about to topple over, she clung to the doorframe and peered up at Sonny out of a stony face. Meg watched as Sonny jerked round to confront her and then stopped cold when he got a look at the interior of the house. The plaster walls were stained now, drinking up the wet in long jagged fingers that clawed toward the ceiling, and a dribble of coffee-colored liquid began to seep across the door-step and puddle at Sonny's feet. The sound of rushing water was unmistakable, even from where Meg was standing. "Yes?" Muriel said, the voice withered in her throat. "Can I help you?"

It took Sonny a minute—Meg could see it in his eyes: this was more than he could handle, willful destruction of a domicile, every tap in the place on full, the floors warped, plaster ruined—but then he recovered himself. "The water," he said. "You—our fence—I mean you can't, you've got to stop this—"

The old woman drew herself up, clutching the belt of her housedress till her knuckles bulged with the tension. She looked first at Meg, still planted in the corner of the yard, and then turned to Sonny. "Water?" she said. "What water?"

The young man at the door reminded her, in a way, of Monty. Something about the eyes or the set of the ears—or maybe it was the crisp high cut of the side-burns . . . Of course, most young men reminded her of Monty. The Monty of fifty years ago, that is. The Monty who'd opened up the world to her over the shift lever of his Model-A Ford, not the crabbed and abrasive old man who called her bonehead and dildo and cuffed her like a dog. Monty. She saw him pinned be-neath his tubes in the hospital and something stirred in her; she brought him home and changed his bedpan, peered into the vaults of his eyes, fed him Ger-ber's like the baby she'd never had, and she knew it was over. Fifty years. No more drunken rages, no more pans flung against the wall, never again his sour flesh pressed to hers. She was on top now.

The second young man—he was a Mexican, short, stocky, with a mustache so thin it could have been penciled on and wicked little red-flecked eyes—also re-minded her of Monty. Not so much in the way he looked as in the way he held himself, the way he swaggered and puffed out his chest. And the uniform too, of course. Monty had worn a uniform during the war.

"Mrs. Burgess?" the Mexican asked.

Muriel stood at the open door. It was dusk, the heat cut as if there were a thermostat in the sky. She'd been sitting in the dark. The electricity had gone out on her—something to do with the water and the wires. She nodded her head in response to the policeman's question.

"We've had a complaint," he said.

Little piggy eyes. A complaint. *We've had a complaint.* He wasn't fooling her, not for a minute. She knew what they wanted, the police, the girl next door, and the boy she was married to—they wanted to bring Monty back. Prop him up against the bedframe, stick his legs back under him, put the bellow back in his voice. Oh, no, they weren't fooling her.

She followed the policeman around the darkened house as he went from faucet to faucet, sink to tub to shower. He firmly twisted each of the taps closed and drained the basins, then crossed the patio to kill the sprinklers and the hose too. "Are you all right?" he kept asking. "Are you all right?"

She had to hold her chin in her palm to keep her lips from trembling. "If you mean am I in possession of my faculties, yes, I am, thank you. I am all right."

They were back at the front door now. He leaned nonchalantly against the doorframe and dropped his voice to a confidential whisper. "So what's this with the water then?"

She wouldn't answer him. She knew her rights. What business was it of his, or anybody's, what she did with her own taps and her own sprinklers? She could pay the water bill. Had paid it, in fact. Eleven hundred dollars' worth. She watched his eyes and shrugged.

"Next of kin?" he asked. "Daughter? Son? Anybody we can call?"

Now her lips held. She shook her head.

He gave it a moment, then let out a sigh. "Okay," he said, speaking slowly and with exaggerated emphasis, as if he were talking to a child, "I'm going now. You leave the water alone—wash your face, brush your teeth, do the dishes. But no more of this." He swaggered back from her, fingering his belt, his holster, the dead weight of his nightstick. "One more complaint and we'll have to take you into custody for your own good. You're endangering yourself and the neighbors too. Understand?"

Smile, she told herself, smile. "Oh, yes," she said softly. "Yes, I understand."

He held her eyes a moment, threatening her—just like Monty used to do, just like Monty—and then he was gone.

She stood there on the doorstep a long while, the night deepening around her. She listened to the cowbirds, the wild parakeets that nested in the Murtaughs' palm, the whoosh of traffic from the distant freeway. After a while, she sat on the step. Behind her, the house was silent: no faucet dripped, no sprinkler hissed, no toilet gurgled. It was horrible. Insupportable. In the pit of that dry silence she could hear him, Monty, treading the buckled floors, pouring himself another vodka, cursing her in a voice like sandpaper.

She couldn't go back in there. Not tonight. The place was deadly, contaminated, sick as the grave—after all was said and done, it just wasn't clean enough.

If the rest of it was a mystery—oral history, fifty years of Monty, the girl with the blackened eyes—that much she understood.

Meg was watering the cane plant in the living room when the police cruiser came for the old lady next door. The police had been there the night before and Sonny had stood out front with arms folded while the officer shut down Muriel's taps and sprinklers. "I guess that's that," he said, coming up the walk in the oversized Hawaiian shirt she'd given him for Father's Day. But in the morning, the sprinklers were on again and Sonny called the local substation three times before he left for work. She's crazy, he'd hollered into the phone, irresponsible, a threat to herself and the community. He had a four-year-old daughter to worry about, for christ's sake. A dog. A wife. His fence was falling down. Did they have any idea what that amount of water was going to do to the substrata beneath the house?

Now the police were back. The patrol car stretched across the window and slid silently into the driveway next door. Meg set down the watering can. She was wearing her Fila sweats and a new pair of Nikes and her hair was tied back in a red scarf. She'd dropped Tiffany off at nursery school, but she had the watering and her stretching exercises to do and a pasta salad to make before she picked up Queenie at the vet's. Still, she went directly to the front door and then out onto the walk.

The police—it took her a minute to realize that the shorter of the two was a woman—were on Muriel's front porch, looking stiff and uncertain in their razor-creased uniforms. The man knocked first—once, twice, three times. Nothing happened. Then the woman knocked. Still nothing. Meg folded her arms and waited. After a minute, the man went around to the side gate and let himself into the yard. Meg heard the sprinklers die with a wheeze, and then the officer was back, his shoes heavy with mud.

Again he thumped at the door, much more violently now, and Meg thought of Sonny. "Open up," the woman called in a breathy contralto she tried unsuccessfully to deepen, "police."

It was then that Meg saw her, Muriel, at the bay window on the near side of the door. "Look," she shouted before she knew what she was saying, "she's there, there in the window!"

The male officer—he had a mustache and pale, fine hair like Sonny's—leaned out over the railing and gestured impatiently at the figure behind the window. "Police," he growled. "Open the door." Muriel never moved. "All right," he grunted, cursing under his breath, "all right," and he put his shoulder to the door. There was nothing to it. The frame splintered, water dribbled out, and both officers disappeared into the house.

Meg waited. She had things to do, yes, but she waited anyway, bending to pull the odd dandelion the gardener had missed, trying to look busy. The police were in there an awful long time—twenty minutes, half an hour—and then the woman appeared in the doorway with Muriel.

Muriel seemed heavier than ever, her face pouchy, arms swollen. She was wearing white sandals on her old splayed feet, a shapeless print dress, and a white straw hat that looked as if it had been dug out of a box in the attic. The woman had her by the arm; the man loomed behind her with a suitcase. Down the steps and up the walk, she never turned her head. But then, just as the policewoman was helping her into the backseat of the patrol car, Muriel swung round as if to take one last look at her house. But it wasn't the house she was looking at: it was Meg.

The morning gave way to the heat of afternoon. Meg finished the watering, made the pasta salad—bow-tie twists, fresh salmon, black olives, and pine nuts—ran her errands, picked up Tiffany, and put her down for a nap. Somehow, though, she just couldn't get Muriel out of her head. The old lady had stared at her for five seconds maybe, and then the policewoman was coaxing her into the car. Meg had felt like sinking into the ground. But then she realized that Muriel's look wasn't vengeful at all—it was just sad. It was a look that said this is what it comes to. Fifty years and this is what it comes to.

The backyard was an inferno, the sun poised directly overhead. Queenie, de-fleaed, shampooed, and with her toenails clipped, was stretched out asleep in the shade beside the pool. It was quiet. Even the birds were still. Meg took off her Nikes and walked barefoot through the sopping grass to the fence, or what was left of it. The post had buckled overnight, canting the whole business into Muriel's yard. Meg never hesitated. She sprang up onto the plane of the slats and dropped to the grass on the other side.

Her feet sank in the mud, the earth like pudding, like chocolate pudding, and as she lifted her feet to move toward the house the tracks she left behind her slowly filled with water. The patio was an island. She crossed it, dodging potted plants and wicker furniture, and tried the back door; finding it locked, she moved to the window, shaded her face with her hands, and peered in. The sight made her catch her breath. The plaster was crumbling, wallpaper peeling, the rug and floors ruined: she knew it was bad, but this was crazy, this was suicide.

Grief, that's what it was. Or was it? And then she was thinking of Sonny again—what if he was dead and she was old like Muriel? She wouldn't be so fat, of course, but maybe like one of those thin and elegant old ladies in Palm Springs, the ones who'd done their stretching all their lives. Or what if she wasn't an old lady at all—the thought swooped down on her like a bird out of the sky—what if Sonny was in a car wreck or something? It could happen.

She stood there gazing in on the mess through her own wavering reflection. One moment she saw the wreckage of the old lady's life, the next the fine mouth and expressive eyes everyone commented on. After a while, she turned away from the window and looked out on the yard as Muriel must have seen it. There were the roses, gorged with water and flowering madly, the Impatiens, rigid as sticks, oleander drowning in their own yellowed leaves—and there, poking innocuously from the bushes at the far corner of the patio, was the steel wand that controlled the sprinklers. Handle, neck, prongs: it was just like theirs.

And then it came to her. She'd turn them on—the sprinklers—just for a minute, to see what it felt like. She wouldn't leave them on long—it could threaten the whole foundation of her house.

That much she understood.

(1987)

THE DEVIL AND IRV CHERNISKE

Just outside the sleepy little commuter village of Irvington, New York, there stands a subdivision of half-million-dollar homes, each riding its own sculpted acre like a ship at sea and separated from its neighbors by patches of scrub and the forlorn-looking beeches that lend a certain pricey and vestigial air to the place. The stockbrokers, lawyers, doctors and software salesmen who live here with their families know their community as Beechwood, in deference to the legend hammered into the slab of pink marble at the entrance of Beechwood Drive. This slab was erected by the developer, Sal Maggio, in the late nineteen-sixties, though there are few here now who can remember that far back. For better or worse, Beechwood is the sort of community in which the neighbors don't know one another and don't really care to, though they do survey each other's gardeners and automobiles with all the perspicacity of appraisers, and while the proper names of the people next door may escape them, they are quick to invent such colorful sobriquets as the Geeks, the Hackers, the Volvos, and the Chinks by way of compensation.

For the most part, the handsome sweeping macadam streets go untrodden but for the occasional backward jogger, and the patches of wood are ignored to the point at which they've begun to revert to the condition of the distant past, to the time before Maggio's bulldozer, when the trees stretched unbroken all the way to Ardsley. Fieldmice make their home in these woods, moths, spiders, sparrows, and squirrels. In the late afternoon, garter snakes silently thread the high rank thick-stemmed morass of bluegrass gone wild, and toads thump from one fetid puddle to another. An unpropitious place, these woods. A forgotten place. But it was here, in one of these primordial pockets, beneath a wind-ravaged maple and within earshot of the chit-chit-chit of the gray squirrel, that Irv Cherniske made the deal of his life.

Irv was one of the senior residents of Beechwood, having moved into his buff-and-chocolate Tudor with the imitation flagstone façade some three years earlier. He was a hard-nosed cynic in his early forties, a big-headed, heavy-paunched, irascible stock trader who'd seen it all—and then some. The characteristic tone of his voice was an unmodulated roar, but this was only the daintiest of counterpoint to the stentorian bellow of his wife, Tish. The two fought so often and at such a pitch that their young sons, Shane and Morgan, often took refuge in the basement game room while the battle raged over their heads and out across the placid rolling lawns of Beechwood Estates. To the neighbors, these battles were a source of rueful amusement: separately, yet unanimously, they had devised their own pet nickname for the Cherniskes. A torn, ragged cry would cut the air around dinnertime each evening, and someone would lift a watery gimlet to his lips and remark, with a sigh, that the Screechers were at it again.

One evening, after a particularly bracing confrontation with his wife over the question of who had last emptied the trash receptacle in the guest room, Irv was out in the twilit backyard, practicing his chip shot and swatting mosquitoes. It was the tail end of a long Fourth of July weekend, and an unearthly stillness had settled over Beechwood, punctuated now and again by the distant muffled pop of leftover fireworks. The air was muggy and hot, a fiery breath of the tropics more suitable to Rangoon than New York. Irv bent in the fading light to address a neon-orange Titleist. Behind him, in the house which seemed almost to sink under the weight of its mortgage, Tish and his sons were watching TV, the muted sounds of conflict and sorrow carrying fitfully to where he stood in the damp grass, awash in birdsong. He raised the nine-iron, dropped it in a fluid rush, and watched the ball rise mightily into the darkening belly of the sky. Unfortunately, he overshot the makeshift flag he'd set up at the foot of the lawn and carried on into the ragged clump of trees beyond it.

With a curse, Irv trundled down the hill and pushed his way through the mounds of cuttings the gardener had piled up like breastworks at the edge of the woods and a moment later found himself in the hushed and shadowy stand of beeches. An odor of slow rot assaulted his nostrils. Crickets chirruped. There was no sign of the ball. He was kicking aimlessly through the leaves, all but certain it was gone for good—two and a half bucks down the drain—when he was startled by a noise from the gloom up ahead.

Something—or someone—was coming toward him, a presence announced by the crush of brittle leaves and the hiss of uncut grass. "Who is it?" he demanded, and the crickets fell silent. "Is someone there?"

The shape of a man began to emerge gradually from the shadows—head and shoulders first, then a torso that kept getting bigger. And bigger. His skin was dark—so dark Irv at first took him to be a Negro—and a wild feral shock of hair stood up jaggedly from his crown like the mane of a hyena. The man said nothing.

Irv was not easily daunted. He believed in the Darwinian struggle, believed, against all signs to the contrary, that he'd risen to the top of the pack and that the choicest morsels of the feast of life were his for the taking. And though he wasn't nearly the bruiser he'd been when he started at nose tackle for Fox Lane High, he was used to wielding his paunch like a weapon and blustering his way through practically anything, from a potential mugging right on down to putting a snooty maître d' in his place. For all that, though, when he saw the size of the man, when he factored in his complexion and considered the oddness of the circumstances, he felt uncertain of himself. Felt as if the parameters of the world as he knew it had suddenly shifted. Felt, unaccountably, that he was in deep trouble. Characteristically, he fell back on bluster. "Who in hell are you?" he demanded.

The stranger, he now saw, wasn't black at all. Or, rather, he wasn't a Negro, as he'd first supposed, but something else altogether. Swarthy, that's what he was. Like a Sicilian or a Greek. Or maybe an Arab. He saw too that the man was dressed almost identically to himself, in a Lacoste shirt, plaid slacks, and white Adidas. But this was no golf club dangling from the stranger's fingertips—it was a chainsaw. "Hell?" the big man echoed, his voice starting down low and then rising in mockery. "I don't believe it. Did you actually say 'Who in hell are you?'?" He began to laugh in a shallow, breathy, and decidedly unsettling way.

It was getting darker by the minute, the trunks of the trees receding into the shadows, stars dimly visible now in the dome of the sky. There was a distant sound of fireworks and a sharp sudden smell of gunpowder on the air. "Are you . . . are you somebody's gardener or something?" Irv asked, glancing uncomfortably at the chainsaw.

This got the stranger laughing so hard he had to pound his breastbone and wipe the tears from his eyes. "Gardener?" he hooted, stamping around in the undergrowth and clutching his sides with the sheer hilarity of it. "You've got to be kidding. Come on, tell me you're kidding."

Irv felt himself growing annoyed. "I mean, because if you're not," he said, struggling to control his voice, "then I want to know what you're doing back here with that saw. This is private property, you know."

Abruptly, the big man stopped laughing. When he spoke, all trace of amusement had faded from his voice. "Oh?" he growled. "And just who does it belong to, then—it wouldn't be yours, by any chance, would it?"

It wasn't. As Irv well knew. In fact, he'd done a little title-searching six months back, when Tish had wanted to mow down the beeches and put in an ornamental koi pond with little pink bridges and mechanical waterfalls. The property, useless as it was, belonged to the old bird next door—"the Geek" was the only name Irv knew him by. Irv thought of bluffing, but the look in the stranger's eye made him think better of it. "It belongs to the old guy next door—Beltzer, I think his name is. Bitzer. Something like that."

The stranger was smiling now, but the smile wasn't a comforting one. "I see," he said. "So I guess you're trespassing too."

Irv had had enough. "We'll let the police decide that," he snapped, turning to stalk back up the lawn.

"Hey, Irv," the stranger said suddenly, "don't get huffy—old man Belcher won't be needing this plot anymore. You can hide all the golf balls you want down here."

The gloom thickened. Somewhere a dog began to howl. Irv felt the tight hairs at the base of his neck begin to stiffen. "How do you know my name?" he said, whirling around. "And how do you know what Belcher needs or doesn't need?" All of a sudden, Irv had the odd feeling that he'd seen this stranger somewhere before—real estate, wasn't it?

"Because he'll be dead five minutes from now, that's how." The big man let out a disgusted sigh. "Let's quit pissing around here—you know damn well who I am, Irv." He paused. "October twenty-two, 1955, Our Lady of the Immaculate Heart Church in Mount Kisco. Monsignor O'Kane. The topic is the transubstantiation of the flesh and you're screwing around with Alfred LaFarga in the back pew, talking 'Saturday Night Creature Features.' 'Did you see it when the mummy pulled that guy's eyes out?' you whispered. Alfred was this ratty little clown, looked like his shoulders were going to fall through his chest—now making a killing in grain futures in Des Moines, by the way—and he says, 'That wasn't his eye, shit-for-brains, it was his tongue.' "

Irv was stunned. Shocked silent for maybe the first time in his life. He'd seen it all, yes—but not this. It was incredible, it really was. He'd given up on all that God and Devil business the minute he left parochial school—no percentage in it—and now here it was, staring him in the face. It took him about thirty seconds to reinvent the world, and then he was thinking there might just be something in it for him. "All right," he said, "all right, yeah, I know who you are. Question is, what do you want with me?"

The stranger's face was consumed in shadow now, but Irv could sense that he was grinning. "Smart, Irv," the big man said, all the persuasion of a born closer creeping into his voice. "What's in it for me, right? Let's make a deal, right? The wife isn't working, the kids need designer jeans, PCs, and dirt bikes, and the mortgage has you on the run, am I right?"

He was right—of course he was right. How many times, bullying some loser over the phone or wheedling a few extra bucks out of some grasping old hag's retirement account, had Irv wondered if it was all worth it? How many times had he shoved his way through a knot of pink-haired punks on the subway only to get home all the sooner to his wife's nagging and his sons' pale, frightened faces? How many times had he told himself he deserved more, much more—ease and elegance, regular visits to the track and the Caribbean, his own firm, the two or maybe three million he needed to bail himself out for good? He folded his arms. The stranger, suddenly, was no more disturbing than sweet-faced Ben Franklin gazing up benevolently from a mountain of C-notes. "Talk to me," Irv said.

The big man took him by the arm and leaned forward to whisper in his ear. He wanted the usual deal, nothing less, and he held out to Irv the twin temptations of preternatural business success and filthy lucre. The lucre was buried right there in that shabby patch of woods, a hoard of Krugerrands, bullion, and silver candlesticks socked away by old man Belcher as a hedge against runaway inflation. The business success would result from the collusion of his silent partner—who was leaning into him now and giving off an odor oddly like that of a Szechuan kitchen—and it would take that initial stake and double and redouble it till it grew beyond counting. "What do you say, Irv?" the stranger crooned.

Irv said nothing. He was no fool. Poker face, he told himself. Never look eager. "I got to think about it," he said. He was wondering vaguely if he could rent a metal detector or something and kiss the creep off. "Give me twenty-four hours."

The big man drew away from him. "Hmph," he grunted contemptuously. "You think I come around every day? This is the deal of a lifetime I'm talking here, Irv." He paused a moment to let this sink in. "You don't want it, I can always go to Joe Luck across the street over there."

Irv was horrified. "You mean the Chinks?"

At that moment the porch light winked on in the house behind him. The yellowish light caught the big man's face, bronzing it like a statue. He nodded. "Import/export. Joe's got connections with the big boys in Taiwan—and believe me, it isn't just backscratchers he's bringing in in those crates. But I happen to know he's hard up for capital right now, and I think he'd jump at the chance—"

Irv cut him off. "Okay, okay," he said. "But how do I know you're the real thing? I mean, what proof do I have? Anybody could've talked to Alfred LaFarga."

The big man snorted. Then, with a flick of his wrist, he fired up the chainsaw. *Rrrrrrrrrow,* it sang as he turned to the nearest tree and sent it home. Chips and sawdust flew off into the darkness as he guided the saw up and down, back and across, carving something in the bark, some message. Irv edged forward. Though the light was bad, he could just make out the jagged uppercase *B,* and then the *E* that followed it. When the big man reached the *L,* Irv anticipated him, but waited, arms folded, for the sequel. The stranger spelled out BELCHER, then sliced into the base of the tree; in the next moment the tree was toppling into the gloom with a shriek of clawing branches.

Irv waited till the growl of the saw died to a sputter. "Yeah?" he said. "So what does that prove?"

The big man merely grinned, his face hideous in the yellow light. Then he reached out and pressed his thumb to Irv's forehead and Irv could hear the sizzle and feel the sting of his own flesh burning. "There's my mark," the stranger said.

"Tomorrow night, seven o'clock. Don't be late." And then he strode off into the shadows, the great hulk of him halved in an instant, and then halved again, as if he were sinking down into the earth itself.

The first thing Tish said to him as he stepped in the door was "Where the hell have you been? I've been shouting myself hoarse. There's an ambulance out front of the neighbor's place."

Irv shoved past her and parted the living-room curtains. Sure enough, there it was, red lights revolving and casting an infernal glow over the scene. There were voices, shouts, a flurry of people clustered round a stretcher and a pair of quick-legged men in hospital whites. "It's nothing," he said, a savage joy rising in his chest—it was true, true after all, and he was going to be rich—"just the old fart next door kicking off."

Tish gave him a hard look. She was a year younger than he—his college sweetheart, in fact—but she'd let herself go. She wasn't so much obese as muscular, big, broad-beamed—every inch her husband's match. "What's that on your forehead?" she asked, her voice pinched with suspicion.

He lifted his hand absently to the spot. The flesh seemed rough and abraded, raised in an annealed disc the size of a quarter. "Oh, this?" he said, feigning nonchalance. "Hit my head on the barbecue."

She was having none of it. With a move so sudden it would have surprised a cat, she shot forward and seized his arm. "And what's that I smell—Chinese food?" Her eyes leapt at him; her jaw clenched. "I suppose the enchiladas weren't good enough for you, huh?"

He jerked his arm away. "Oh, yeah, I know—you really slaved over those enchiladas, didn't you? Christ, you might have chipped a nail or something tearing the package open and shoving them in the microwave."

"Don't give me that shit," she snarled, snatching his arm back and digging her nails in for emphasis. "The mark on your head, the Chinese food, that stupid grin on your face when you saw the ambulance—I know you. Something's up, isn't it?" She clung to his arm like some inescapable force of nature, like the tar in the La Brea pits or the undertow at Rockaway Beach. "Isn't it?"

Irv Cherniske was not a man to confide in his wife. He regarded marriage as an arbitrary and essentially adversarial relationship, akin to the yoking of prisoners on the chain gang. But this once, because the circumstances were so arresting and the stranger's proposal so unique (not to mention final), he relented and let her in on his secret.

At first, she wouldn't believe it. It was another of his lies, he was covering something up—*devils:* did he think she was born yesterday? But when she saw how solemn he was, how shaken, how feverish with lust over the prospect of laying his hands on the loot, she began to come around. By midnight she was urging him to go back and seal the bargain. "You fool. You idiot. What do you need twenty-four hours for? Go. Go now."

Though Irv had every intention of doing just that—in his own time, of course—he wasn't about to let her push him into anything. "You think I'm going to damn myself forever just to please you?" he sneered.

Tish took it for half a beat, then she sprang up from the sofa as if it were electrified. "All right," she snapped. "I'll find the son of a bitch myself and we'll both roast—but I tell you I want those Krugerrands and all the rest of it too. And I want it now."

A moment later, she was gone—out the back door and into the soft suburban night. Let her go, Irv thought in disgust, but despite himself he sat back to wait for her. For better than an hour he sat there in his mortgaged living room, dreaming of crushing his enemies and ascending the high-flown corridors of power, envisioning the cut-glass decanter in the bar of the Rolls and breakfast on the yacht, but at last he found himself nodding and decided to call it a day. He rose, stretched, and then padded through the dining room and kitchen to the back porch. He swung open the door and halfheartedly called his wife's name. There was no answer. He shrugged, retraced his steps, and wearily mounted the stairs to the bedroom: devil or no devil, he had a train to catch in the morning.

Tish was sullen at breakfast. She looked sorrowful and haggard and there were bits of twig and leaf caught in her hair. The boys bent silently over their caramel crunchies, waiflike in the khaki jerseys and oversized shorts they wore to camp. Irv studied his watch while gulping coffee. "Well," he said, addressing his stone-faced wife, "any luck?"

At first she wouldn't answer him. And when she did, it was in a voice so constricted with rage she sounded as if she were being throttled. Yes, she'd found the sorry son of a bitch, all right—after traipsing all over hell and back for half the night—and after all that he'd had the gall to turn his back on her. He wasn't in the mood, he said. But if she were to come back at noon with a peace offering—something worth talking about, something to show she was serious—he'd see what he could do for her. That's how he'd put it.

For a moment Irv was seized with jealousy and resentment—was she trying to cut him out, was that it?—but then he remembered how the stranger had singled him out, had come to him, and he relaxed. He had nothing to worry about. It was Tish. She just didn't know how to bargain, that was all. Her idea of a give and take was to reiterate her demands, over and over, each time in a shriller tone than the last. She'd probably pushed and pushed till even the devil wouldn't have her. "I'll be home early," he said, and then he was driving through a soft misting rain to the station.

It was past seven when finally he did get home. He pulled into the driveway and was surprised to see his sons sitting glumly on the front stoop, their legs drawn up under them, rain drooling steadily from the eaves. "Where's your mother?" he asked, hurrying up the steps in alarm. The elder, Shane, a pudgy, startled-looking boy of eight, whose misfortune it was to favor Tish about the nose and eyes, began to whimper. "She, she never came back," he blubbered, smearing snot across his lip.

Filled with apprehension—and a strange, airy exhilaration too: maybe she was gone, gone for good!—Irv dialed his mother. "Ma?" he shouted into the phone. "Can you come over and watch the kids? It's Tish. She's missing." He'd no sooner set the phone down than he noticed the blank space on the wall above the sideboard. The painting was gone. He'd always hated the thing—a gloomy dark swirl of howling faces with the legend "Cancer Dreams" scrawled in red across the bottom, a small monstrosity Tish had insisted on buying when he could barely make the car payments—but it was worth a bundle, that much he knew. And the moment he saw that empty space on the wall he knew she'd taken it to the big man in the woods—but what else had she taken? While the boys sat listlessly before the TV with a bag of taco chips, he tore through the house. Her jewelry would have been the first thing to go, and he wasn't surprised to see that it had disappeared, teak box and all. But in growing consternation he discovered that his coin collection was gone too, as were his fly rod and his hip waders and the bottle of V.S.O.P. he'd been saving for the World Series. The whole business had apparently been bundled up in the Irish-linen cloth that had shrouded the dining-room table for as long as he could remember.

Irv stood there a moment over the denuded table, overcome with grief and rage. She *was* cutting him out, the bitch. She and the big man were probably down there right now, dancing round a gaping black hole in the earth. Or worse, she was on the train to New York with every last Krugerrand of Belcher's hoard, heading for the Caymans in a chartered yacht, hurtling out of Kennedy in a big 747, two huge, bursting, indescribably heavy trunks nestled safely in the baggage compartment beneath her. Irv rushed to the window. There were the woods: still, silent, slick with wet. He saw nothing but trees.

In the next instant, he was out the back door, down the grassy slope, and into the damp fastness of the woods. He'd forgotten all about the kids, his mother, the house at his back—all he knew was that he had to find Tish. He kicked through dead leaves and rotting branches, tore at the welter of grapevine and sumac that seemed to rise up like a barrier before him. "Tish!" he bawled.

The drizzle had turned to a steady, pelting rain. Irv's face and hands were scratched and insect-bitten and the hair clung to his scalp like some strange species of mold. His suit—all four hundred bucks' worth—was ruined. He was staggering through a stubborn tangle of briars, his mind veering sharply toward the homicidal end of the spectrum, when a movement up ahead made him catch his breath. Stumbling forward, he flushed a great black carrion bird from the bushes; as it rose silently into the darkening sky, he spotted the tablecloth. Still laden, it hung from the lower branches of a pocked and leprous oak. Irv looked round him cautiously. All was still, no sound but for the hiss of the rain in the leaves. He straightened up and lumbered toward the pale damp sack, thinking at least to recover his property.

No such luck. When he lifted the bundle down, he was disappointed by its weight; when he opened it, he was shocked to the roots of his hair. The table-cloth contained two things only: a bloody heart and a bloody liver. His own heart was beating so hard he thought his temples would burst; in horror he flung the thing to the ground. Only then did he notice that the undergrowth round the base of the tree was beaten down and trampled, as if a scuffle had taken place beneath it. There was a fandango of footprints in the mud and clumps of stiff black hair were scattered about like confetti—and wasn't that blood on the bark of the tree?

"Irv," murmured a voice at his back, and he whirled round in a panic. There he was, the big man, his swarthy features hooded in shadow. This time he was wearing a business suit in a muted gray check, a power-yellow tie, and an im-maculate trenchcoat. In place of the chainsaw, he carried a shovel, which he'd flung carelessly over one shoulder. "Whoa," he said, holding up a massive palm, "I didn't mean to startle you." He took a step forward and Irv could see that he was grinning. "All's I want to know is do we have a deal or not?"

"Where's Tish?" Irv demanded, his voice quavering. But even as he spoke he saw the angry red welt running the length of the big man's jaw and disappearing into the hair at his temple, and he knew.

The big man shrugged. "What do you care? She's gone, that's all that mat-ters. Hey, no more of that nagging whiny voice, no more money down the drain on face cream and high heels—just think, you'll never have to wake up again to that bitchy pout and those nasty red little eyes. You're free, Irv. I did you a favor."

Irv regarded the stranger with awe. Tish was no mean adversary, and judging from the look of the poor devil's face, she'd gone down fighting.

The big man dropped his shovel to the ground and there was a clink of metal on metal. "Right here, Irv," he whispered. "Half a million easy. Cash. Tax-free. And with my help you'll watch it grow to fifty times that."

Irv glanced down at the bloody tablecloth and then back up at the big man in the trenchcoat. A slow grin spread across his lips.

Coming to terms wasn't so easy, however, and it was past dark before they'd concluded their bargain. At first the stranger had insisted on Irv's going into one of the big Hollywood talent agencies, but when Irv balked, he said he figured the legal profession was just as good—but you needed a degree for that, and begging Irv's pardon, he was a bit old to be going back to school, wasn't he? "Why can't I stay where I am," Irv countered, "—in stocks and bonds? With all this cash I could quit Tiller Ponzi and set up my own office."

The big man scratched his chin and laid a thoughtful finger alongside his nose. "Yeah," he murmured after a moment, "yeah, I hadn't thought of that. But I like it. You could promise them thirty percent and then play the futures market and gouge them till they bleed."

Irv came alive at the prospect. "Bleed 'em dry," he hooted. "I'll scalp and bucket and buy off the CFTC investigators, and then I'll set up an offshore company to hide the profits." He paused, overcome with the beauty of it. "I'll screw them right and left."

"Deal?" the devil said.

Irv took the big callused hand in his own. "Deal."

Ten years later, Irv Cherniske was one of the wealthiest men in New York. He talked widows into giving him their retirement funds to invest in ironclad securities and sure bets, lost them four or five hundred thousand, and charged half that again in commissions. With preternatural luck his own investments paid off time and again and he eventually set up an inside-trading scheme that made guesswork superfluous. The police, of course, had been curious about Tish's disappearance, but Irv showed them the grisly tablecloth and the crude hole in which the killer had no doubt tried to bury her, and they launched an intensive manhunt that dragged on for months but produced neither corpse nor perpetrator. The boys he shunted off to his mother's, and when they were old enough, to a military school in Tangiers. Two months after his wife's disappearance, the newspapers uncovered a series of ritual beheadings in Connecticut and dropped all mention of the "suburban ghoul," as they'd dubbed Tish's killer; a week after that, Tish was forgotten and Beechwood went back to sleep.

It was in the flush of his success, when he had everything he'd ever wanted—the yacht, the sweet and compliant young mistress, the pair of Rolls Corniches, and the houses in the Bahamas and Aspen, not to mention the new wing he'd added to the old homestead in Beechwood—that Irv began to have second thoughts about the deal he'd made. Eternity was a long time, yes, but when he'd met the stranger in the woods that night it had seemed a long way off too. Now he was in his fifties, heavier than ever, with soaring blood pressure and flat feet, and the end of his career in this vale of profits was drawing uncomfortably near. It was only natural that he should begin to cast about for a loophole.

And so it was that he returned to the church—not the Roman church, to which he'd belonged as a boy, but the Church of the Open Palm, Reverend Jimmy, Pastor. He came to Reverend Jimmy one rainy winter night with a fire in his gut and an immortal longing in his heart. He sat through a three-hour sermon in which Reverend Jimmy spat fire, spoke in tongues, healed the lame, and lectured on the sanctity of the one and only God—profit—and then distributed copies of the *Reverend Jimmy Church-Sponsored Investment Guide* with the chili and barbecue recipes on the back page.

After the service, Irv found his way to Reverend Jimmy's office at the back of the church. He waited his turn among the other supplicants with growing impatience, but he reminded himself that the way to salvation lay through humility and forbearance. At long last he was ushered into the presence of the Reverend himself. "What can I do for you, brother?" Reverend Jimmy asked. Though he was from Staten Island, Reverend Jimmy spoke in the Alabama hog-farmer's dialect peculiar to his tribe.

"I need help, Reverend," Irv confessed, flinging himself down on a leather sofa worn smooth by the buttocks of the faithful.

Reverend Jimmy made a small pyramid of his fingers and leaned back in his adjustable chair. He was a youngish man—no older than thirty-five or so, Irv guessed—and he was dressed in a flannel shirt, penny loafers, and a plaid fishing hat that masked his glassy blue eyes. "Speak to me, brother," he said.

Irv looked down at the floor, then shot a quick glance round the office—an office uncannily like his own, right down to the computer terminal, mahogany desk, and potted palms—and then whispered, "You're probably not going to believe this."

Reverend Jimmy lit himself a cigarette and shook out the match with a snap of his wrist. "Try me," he drawled.

When Irv had finished pouring out his heart, Reverend Jimmy leaned forward with a beatific smile on his face. "Brother," he said, "believe me, your story's nothin' new—I handle just as bad and sometimes worser ever day. Cheer up, brother: salvation is on the way!"

Then Reverend Jimmy made a number of pointed inquiries into Irv's financial status and fixed the dollar amount of his tithe—to be paid weekly in small bills, no checks please. Next, with a practiced flourish, he produced a copy of Adam Smith's *Wealth of Nations*, the text of which was interspersed with biblical quotes in support of its guiding theses, and pronounced Irv saved. "You got your holy book," the Reverend Jimmy boomed as Irv ducked gratefully out the door, "—y'all keep it with you ever day, through sleet and snow and dark of night, and old Satan he'll be paarless against you."

And so it was. Irv gained in years and gained in wealth. He tithed the Church of the Open Palm, and he kept the holy book with him at all times. One day, just after his sixtieth birthday, his son Shane came to the house to see him. It was a Sunday and the market was closed, but after an early-morning dalliance with Sushoo, his adept and oracular mistress, he'd placed a half dozen calls to Hong Kong, betting on an impending monsoon in Burma to drive the price of rice through the ceiling. He was in the Blue Room, as he liked to call the salon in the west wing, eating a bit of poached salmon and looking over a coded letter from Butram, his deep man in the SEC. The holy book lay on the desk beside him.

Shane was a bloated young lout in his late twenties, a sorrowful, shameless leech who'd flunked out of half a dozen schools and had never held a job in his life—unlike Morgan, who'd parlayed the small stake his father had given him into the biggest used-car dealership in the country. Unwashed, unshaven, the gut he'd inherited from his father peeping out from beneath a Hawaiian shirt so lurid it looked as if it had been used to stanch wounds at the emergency ward, Shane loomed over his father's desk. "I need twenty big ones," he grunted, giving his father a look of beery disdain. "Bad week at the track."

Irv looked up from his salmon and saw Tish's nose, Tish's eyes, saw the greedy, worthless, contemptible slob his son had become. In a sudden rage he shot from the chair and hammered the desk so hard the plate jumped six inches. "I'll be damned if I give you another cent," he roared.

Just then there was a knock at the door. His face contorted with rage, Irv shoved past his son and stormed across the room, a curse on his lips for Magdalena, the maid, who should have known better than to bother him at a time like this. He tore open the door only to find that it wasn't Magdalena at all, but his acquaintance of long ago, the big black man with the wild mane of hair and the vague odor of stir-fry on his clothes. "Time's up, Irv," the big man said gruffly. In vain did Irv look over his shoulder to where the Reverend Jimmy's holy book sat forlorn on the desk beside the plate of salmon that was already growing cold. The big man took his arm in a grip of steel and whisked him through the hallway, down the stairs, and out across the lawn to where a black BMW with smoked windows sat running at the curb. Irv turned his pale fleshy face to the house and saw his son staring down at him from above, and then the big man laid an implacable hand on his shoulder and shoved him into the car.

The following day, of course, as is usual in these cases, all of Irv's liquid assets—his stocks and bonds, his Swiss and Bahamian bankbooks, even the wads of new-minted hundred-dollar bills he kept stashed in safe-deposit boxes all over the country—turned to cinders. Almost simultaneously, the house was gutted by a fire of mysterious origin, and both Rolls-Royces were destroyed. Joe Luck, who shuffled out on his lawn in a silk dressing gown at the height of the blaze, claimed to have seen a great black bird emerge from the patch of woods behind the house and mount into the sky high above the roiling billows of steam and smoke, but for some reason, no one else seemed to have shared his vision.

The big refurbished house on Beechwood Drive has a new resident now, a corporate lawyer by the name of O'Faolain. If he's bothered by the unfortunate history of the place—or even, for that matter, aware of it—no one can say. He knows his immediate neighbors as the Chinks, the Fat Family, and the Turf Builders. They know him as the Shyster.

(1987)

THE HUMAN FLY

Just try to explain to anyone the art of fasting!

—Franz Kafka, "A Hunger Artist"

In the early days, before the press took him up, his outfit was pretty basic: tights and cape, plastic swim goggles and a bathing cap in the brightest shade of red he could find. The tights were red too, though they'd faded to pink in the thighs and calves and had begun to sag around the knees. He wore a pair of scuffed hightops—red, of course—and the cape, which looked as if it had last been used to line a trash can, was the color of poached salmon. He seemed to be in his thirties, though I never did find out how old he was, and he was thin, skinny, emaciated—so wasted you worried about his limbs dropping off. When he limped into the office that first afternoon, I didn't know what to think. If he brought an insect to mind, it was something spindly and frail—a daddy longlegs or one of those spidery things that scoot across the surface of the pool no matter how much chlorine the pool man dumps in.

"A gentleman here to see you," Crystal sang through the intercom.

My guard was down. I was vulnerable. I admit it. Basking in the glow of my first success (ten percent of a walk-on for Bettina Buttons, a nasally inflected twelve-year-old with pushy parents, in a picture called *Tyrannosaurus II*—no lines, but she did manage a memorable screech) and bloated with a celebratory lunch, I was feeling magnanimous, large-spirited, and saintly. Of course, the two splits of Sangre de Cristo, 1978, might have had something to do with it. I hit the button on the intercom. "Who is it?"

"Your name, sir?" I heard Crystal ask, and then, through the crackle of static, I heard him respond in the peculiar unmodulated rumble he associated with speech.

"Pardon?" Crystal said.

"La Mosca Humana," he rumbled.

Crystal leaned into the intercom. "Uh, I think he's Mexican or something."

At that stage in my career, I had exactly three clients, all inherited from my predecessor: the aforementioned Bettina; a comic with a harelip who did harelip jokes only; and a soft-rock band called Mu, who believed they were reincarnated court musicians from the lost continent of Atlantis. The phone hadn't rung all morning and my next (and only) appointment, with Bettina's mother, grandmother, acting coach, and dietician, was at seven. "Show him in," I said grandly.

The door pushed open, and there he was. He drew himself up with as much dignity as you could expect from a grown man in a red bathing cap and pink tights, and hobbled into the office. I took in the cap, the cape, the hightops and tights, the slumped shoulders and fleshless limbs. He wore a blond mustache, droopy and unkempt, the left side of his face was badly bruised, and his nose looked as if it had been broken repeatedly—and recently. The fluorescent light glared off his goggles.

My first impulse was to call security—he looked like one of those panhandling freaks out on Hollywood Boulevard—but I resisted it. As I said, I was full of wine and feeling generous. Besides, I was so bored I'd spent the last half-hour crumpling up sheets of high-fiber bond and shooting three-pointers into the wastebasket. I nodded. He nodded back. "So," I said, "what can I do for you, Mr., ah—?"

"Mosca," he rumbled, the syllables thick and muffled, as if he were trying to speak and clear his throat at the same time. "La Mosca Humana."

"The Human Fly, right?" I said, dredging up my high-school Spanish.

He looked down at the desk and then fixed his eyes on mine. "I want to be famous," he said.

How he found his way to my office, I'll never know. I've often wondered if it wasn't somebody's idea of a joke. In those days, I was nothing—I had less seniority than the guy who ran the Xerox machine—and my office was the smallest and farthest from the door of any in the agency. I was expected to get by with two phone lines, one secretary, and a workspace not much bigger than a couple of good-sized refrigerator boxes. There were no Utrillos or Demuths on my walls. I didn't even have a window.

I understood that the man hovering over my desk was a nut case, but there was more to it than that. I could see that he had something—a dignity, a sad elemental presence—that gave the lie to his silly outfit. I felt uneasy under his gaze. "Don't we all," I said.

"No, no," he insisted, "you don't understand," and he pulled a battered manila envelope from the folds of his cape. "Here," he said, "look."

The envelope contained his press clippings, a good handful of them, yellowed and crumbling, bleached of print. All but one were in Spanish. I adjusted the desk lamp, squinted hard. The datelines were from places like Chetumal, Tuxtla,

Hidalgo, Tehuantepec. As best I could make out, he'd been part of a Mexican circus. The sole clipping in English was from the "Metro" section of the *Los Angeles Times:* MAN ARRESTED FOR SCALING ARCO TOWER.

I read the first line—"A man known only as 'The Human Fly' "—and I was hooked. What a concept: *a man known only as the Human Fly!* It was priceless. Reading on, I began to see him in a new light: the costume, the limp, the bruises. This was a man who'd climbed twenty stories with nothing more than a couple pieces of rope and his fingernails. A man who defied the authorities, defied death—my mind was doing backflips; we could run with this one, oh, yes, indeed. Forget your Rambos and Conans, this guy was the real thing.

"Five billion of us monkey on the planet," he said in his choked, moribund tones, "I want to make my mark."

I looked up in awe. I saw him on Carson, Letterman, grappling his way to the top of the Bonaventure Hotel, hurtling Niagara in a barrel, starring in his own series. I tried to calm myself. "Uh, your face," I said, and I made a broad gesture that took in the peach-colored bruise, the ravaged nose and stiffened leg, "what happened?"

For the first time, he smiled. His teeth were stained and ragged; his eyes flared behind the cracked plastic lenses of the goggles. "An accident," he said.

As it turned out, he wasn't Mexican at all—he was Hungarian. I saw my mistake when he peeled back the goggles and bathing cap. A fine band of skin as blanched and waxen as the cap of a mushroom outlined his ears, his hairline, the back of his neck, dead-white against the sun-burnished oval of his face. His eyes were a pale watery blue and the hair beneath the cap was as wispy and colorless as the strands of his mustache. His name was Zoltan Mindszenty, and he'd come to Los Angeles to live with his uncle when the Russian tanks rolled through Budapest in 1956. He'd learned English, Spanish and baseball, practiced fire-eating and tightrope-walking in his spare time, graduated at the top of his high-school class, and operated a forklift in a cannery that produced refried beans and cactus salad. At the age of nineteen he joined the Quesadilla Brothers' Circus and saw the world. Or at least that part of it bounded by California, Arizona, New Mexico, and Texas to the north and Belize and Guatemala to the south. Now he wanted to be famous.

He moved fast. Two days after I'd agreed to represent him he made the eyewitness news on all three major networks when he suspended himself in a mesh bag from the twenty-second floor of the Sumitomo Building and refused to come down.

Terrific. The only problem was that he didn't bother to tell me about it. I was choking down a quick salad lunch—avocado and sprouts on a garlic-cheese croissant—already running late for an audition I'd set up for my harelipped comedian—when the phone rang. It was a Lieutenant Peachtree of the LAPD.

"Listen," the lieutenant hissed, "if this is a publicity stunt . . ." and he trailed off, leaving the threat—heavy ire, the violation of penal codes, the arcane and merciless measures taken to deal with accessories—unspoken.

"Pardon?"

"The nutball up on the Sumitomo Building. Your client."

Comprehension washed over me. My first thought was to deny the connection, but instead I found myself stammering, "But, but how did you get my name?"

Terse and efficient, a living police report, Peachtree gave me the details. One of his men, hanging out of a window on the twenty-first floor, had pleaded with Zoltan to come down. "I am the Human Fly," Zoltan rumbled in response as the wind snapped and the traffic sizzled below, "you want to talk to me, call my agent."

"Twenty minutes," Peachtree added, and his tone was as flat and unforgiving as the drop of a guillotine, "I want you down here. Five minutes after that I want this clown in the back of the nearest patrol car—is that understood?"

It was. Perfectly. And twenty minutes later, with the help of an Officer Dientes, a screaming siren, and several hundred alert motorists who fell away from us on the freeway like swatted flies, I was taking the breeze on the twenty-first floor of the Sumitomo Building. Two of Peachtree's men gripped my legs and eased my torso out onto the slick grassy plane of the building's façade.

I was sick with fear. Before me lay the immensity of the city, its jaws and molars exposed. Above was the murky sky, half a dozen pigeons on a ledge, and Zoltan, bundled up like a sack of grapefruit and calmly perusing a paperback thriller. I choked back the remains of the croissant and cleared my throat. "Zoltan!" I shouted, the wind snatching the words from my lips and flinging them away. "Zoltan, what are you doing up there?"

There was a movement from the bag above me, Zoltan stirring himself like a great leathery fruit bat unfolding its wings, and then his skinny legs and outsized feet emerged from their confinement as the bag swayed gently in the breeze. He peered down at me, the goggles aflame with the sun, and gave me a sour look. "You're supposed to be my agent, and you have to ask me that?"

"It's a stunt, then—is that it?" I shouted.

He turned his face away, and the glare of the goggles died. He wouldn't answer me. Behind me, I could hear Peachtree's crisp, efficient tones: "Tell him he's going to jail."

"They're going to lock you up. They're not kidding."

For a long moment, he didn't respond. Then the goggles caught the sun again and he turned to me. "I want the TV people, Tricia Toyota, 'Action News,' the works."

I began to feel dizzy. The pavement below, with its toy cars and its clots of tiny people, seemed to rush up at me and recede again in a pulsing wave. I felt Peachtree's men relax their grip. "They won't come!" I gasped, clutching the windowframe so desperately my fingers went numb. "They can't. It's network policy." It was true, as far as I knew. Every flake in the country would be out on that ledge if they thought they could get a ten-second clip on the evening news.

Zoltan was unimpressed. "TV," he rumbled into the wind, "or I stay here till you see the white of my bone."

I believed him.

As it turned out, he stayed there, aloft, for two weeks. And for some reason—because he was intractable, absurd, mad beyond hope or redemption—the press couldn't get enough of it. TV included. How he passed the time, what he ate, how he relieved himself, no one knew. He was just a presence, a distant speck in a mesh sack, the faintest intrusion of reality on the clear smooth towering face of the Sumitomo Building. Peachtree tried to get him down, of course—harassing him with helicopters, sending a squad of window cleaners, firemen, and lederhosen up after him—but nothing worked. If anyone got close to him, Zoltan would emerge from his cocoon, cling to the seamless face of the building, and float—float like a big red fly—to a new position.

Finally, after the two weeks were up—two weeks during which my phone never stopped ringing, by the way—he decided to come down. Did he climb in the nearest window and take the elevator? No, not Zoltan. He backed down, inch by inch, uncannily turning up finger- and toe-holds where none existed. He sprang the last fifteen feet to the ground, tumbled like a sky diver, and came up in the grip of a dozen policemen. There was a barricade up, streets were blocked, hundreds of spectators had gathered. As they were hustling him to a patrol car, the media people converged on him. Was it a protest? they wanted to know. A hunger strike? What did it mean?

He turned to them, the goggles steamed over, pigeon feathers and flecks of airborne debris clinging to his cape. His legs were like sticks, his face nearly black with sun and soot. "I want to be famous," he said.

"A DC-10?"

Zoltan nodded. "The bigger, the better," he rumbled.

It was the day after he'd decamped from the face of the Sumitomo Building and we were in my office, discussing the next project. (I'd bailed him out myself, though the figure was right up there with what you'd expect for a serial killer. There were fourteen charges against him, ranging from trespassing to creating a public nuisance and refusing the reasonable request of a police officer to indecent exposure. I had to call in every favor that was ever owed to me and go down on my knees to Sol Bankoff, the head of the agency, to raise the cash.) Zoltan was wearing the outfit I'd had specially made for him: new tights, a black silk cape without a wrinkle in it, a pair of Air Jordan basketball shoes in red and black, and most important of all, a red leather aviator's cap and goggles. Now he looked less like a geriatric at a health spa and more like the sort of fearless dare-devil/superhero the public could relate to.

"But Zoltan," I pleaded, "those things go five hundred miles an hour. You'd be ripped to pieces. Climbing buildings is one thing, but this is insane. It's suicidal."

He was slouched in the chair, one skinny leg thrown over the other. "The Human Fly can survive anything," he droned in his lifeless voice. He was staring at the floor, and now he lifted his head. "Besides, you think the public have any respect for me if I don't lay it all on line?"

He had a point. But strapping yourself to the wing of a DC-10 made about as much sense as taking lunch at a sidewalk café in Beirut. "Okay," I said, "you're right. But you've got to draw the line somewhere. What good's it going to do you to be famous if you're dead?"

Zoltan shrugged.

"I mean already, just with the Sumitomo thing, I can book you on half the talk shows in the country. . . ."

He rose shakily to his feet, lifted his hand, and let it drop. Two weeks on the face of the Sumitomo Building with no apparent source of nourishment hadn't done him any good. If he was skinny before, he was nothing now—a shadow, a ghost, a pair of tights stuffed with straw. "Set it up," he rumbled, the words riding up out of the depths of his sunken abdomen, "I talk when I got something to talk about."

It took me a week. I called every airline in the directory, listened to a lifetime's worth of holding jingles, and talked to everyone from the forklift operator at KLM to the president and CEO of Texas Air. I was met by scorn, hostility, disbelief, and naked contempt. Finally I got hold of the schedules manager of Aero Masoquisto, the Ecuadorian national airline. It was going to cost me, he said, but he could hold up the regular weekly flight to Quito for a few hours while Zoltan strapped himself to the wing and took a couple passes round the airport. He suggested an airstrip outside Tijuana, where the officials would look the other way. For a price, of course.

Of course.

I went to Sol again. I was prepared to press my forehead to the floor, shine his shoes, anything—but he surprised me. "I'll front the money," he rasped, his voice ruined from forty years of whispering into the telephone, "no problem." Sol was seventy, looked fifty, and he'd had his own table in the Polo Lounge since before I was born. "If he bags it," he said, his voice as dry as a husk, "we got the rights to his life story and we'll do a paperback/miniseries/action-figure tie-in. Just get him to sign this, that's all." He slid a contract across the table. "And if he makes it, which I doubt—I mean I've seen some crazies in my time, but this guy is something else—if he makes it, we'll have a million and a half offers for him. Either way, we make out, right?"

"Right," I said, but I was thinking of Zoltan, his brittle limbs pressed to the unyielding metal, the terrible pull of the G-forces, and the cyclonic blast of the wind. What chance did he have?

Sol cleared his throat, shook a few lozenges into his fist, and rattled them like dice. "Your job," he said, "is to make sure the press shows up. No sense in this nimrod bagging it for nothing, right?"

I felt something clench in my gut.

Sol repeated himself, "Right?"

"Right," I said.

Zoltan was in full regalia as we boarded the plane at LAX, along with a handful of reporters and photographers and a hundred grim-looking Ecuadorians with plastic bags full of disposable diapers, cosmetics, and penlight batteries. The plan was for the pilot to announce a minor problem—a clogged air-conditioning vent or a broken handle in the flush toilet; we didn't want to panic anybody— and an unscheduled stop to repair it. Once on the ground, the passengers would be asked to disembark and we'd offer them free drinks in the spacious terminal while the plane taxied out of sight and Zoltan did his thing.

Problem was, there was no terminal. The landing strip looked as if it had been bombed during the Mexican Revolution, it was a hundred degrees inside the airplane and 120 out on the asphalt, and all I could see was heat haze and prickly-pear cactus. "What do you want to do?" I asked Zoltan.

Zoltan turned to me, already fumbling with his chin strap. "It's perfect," he whispered, and then he was out in the aisle, waving his arms and whistling for the passengers' attention. When they quieted down, he spoke to them in Spanish, the words coming so fast you might have thought he was a Mexican disc jockey, his voice riding on a current of emotion he never approached in English. I don't know what he said—he could have been exhorting them to hijack the plane, for all I knew—but the effect was dramatic. When he finished, they rose to their feet and cheered.

With a flourish, Zoltan threw open the emergency exit over the wing and began his preparations. Flashbulbs popped, reporters hung out the door and shouted questions at him—Had this ever been attempted before? Did he have his will made out? How high was he planning to go?—and the passengers pressed their faces to the windows. I'd brought along a TV crew to capture the death-defying feat for syndication, and they set up one camera on the ground while the other shot through the window.

Zoltan didn't waste any time. He buckled what looked like a huge leather truss around the girth of the wing, strapped himself into the pouch attached to it, tightened his chin strap a final time, and then gave me the thumbs-up sign. My heart was hammering. A dry wind breathed through the open window. The heat was like a fist in my face. "You're sure you want to go through with this?" I yelled.

"One hundred percent, A-OK," Zoltan shouted, grinning as the reporters crowded round me in the narrow passageway. Then the pilot said something in Spanish and the flight attendants pulled the window shut, fastened the bolts, and told us to take our seats. A moment later the big engines roared to life and we were hurtling down the runway. I could barely stand to look. At best, I consider flying an unavoidable necessity, a time to resurrect forgotten prayers and contemplate the end of all joy in a twisted howling heap of machinery; at worst, I rank it right up there with psychotic episodes and torture at the hands of malevolent strangers. I felt the wheels lift off, heard a shout from the passengers, and there he was—Zoltan—clinging to the trembling thunderous wing like a second coat of paint.

It was a heady moment, transcendent, the camera whirring, the passengers cheering, Zoltan's greatness a part of us all. This was an event, a once-in-a-lifetime thing, like watching Hank Aaron stroke his seven hundred fifteenth homer or Neil Armstrong step out onto the surface of the moon. We forgot the heat, forgot the roar of the engines, forgot ourselves. He's doing it, I thought, he's actually doing it. And I truly think he would have pulled it off, if—well, it was one of those things no one could have foreseen. Bad luck, that's all.

What happened was this: just as the pilot was coming in for his final approach, a big black bird—a buzzard, somebody said—loomed up out of nowhere and slammed into Zoltan with a thump that reverberated throughout the plane. The whole thing took maybe half a second. This black bundle appears, there's a thump, and next thing Zoltan's goggles are gone and he's covered from head to toe in raw meat and feathers.

A gasp went through the cabin. Babies began to mewl, grown men burst into tears, a nun fainted. My eyes were riveted on Zoltan. He lay limp in his truss while the hot air sliced over the wing, and the jagged yellow mountains, the prickly pear, and the pocked landing strip rushed past him like the backdrop of an old movie. The plane was still rolling when we threw open the emergency exit and staggered out onto the wing. The copilot was ahead of me, a reporter on my heels. "Zoltan!" I cried, scared and sick and trembling. "Zoltan, are you all right?"

There was no answer. Zoltan's head lolled against the flat hard surface of the wing and his eyes were closed, sunk deep behind the wrinkled flaps of his lids. There was blood everywhere. I bent to tear at the straps of the aviator's cap, my mind racing, thinking alternately of mouth-to-mouth and the medical team I should have thought to bring along, when an urgent voice spoke at my back. "Perdóneme, perdóneme, I yam a doaktor."

One of the passengers, a wizened little man in Mickey Mouse T-shirt and Bermudas, knelt over Zoltan, shoving back his eyelids and feeling for his pulse.

There were shouts behind me. The wing was as hot as the surface of a frying pan. "Jes, I yam getting a pulse," the doctor announced and then Zoltan winked open an eye. "Hey," he rumbled, "am I famous yet?"

Zoltan was right: the airplane stunt fired the imagination of the country. The wire services picked it up, the news magazines ran stories—there was even a bit on the CBS evening news. A week later the *National Enquirer* was calling him the reincarnation of Houdini and the *Star* was speculating about his love life. I booked him on the talk-show circuit, and while he might not have had much to say, he just about oozed charisma. He appeared on the Carson show in his trademark outfit, goggles and all, limping and with his arm in a sling (he'd suffered a minor concussion, a shoulder separation, and a fractured kneecap when the bird hit him). Johnny asked him what it was like out there on the wing and Zoltan said: "Loud." And what was it like spending two weeks on the face of the Sumitomo Building? "Boring," Zoltan rumbled. But Carson segued into a couple of airline jokes ("Have you heard the new slogan for China Airlines?" Pause. "You've seen us drive, now watch us fly") and the audience ate it up. Offers poured in from promoters, producers, book editors, and toy manufacturers. I was able to book David Mugillo, my hare-lipped comedian, on Zoltan's coattails, and when we did the Carson show we got Bettina Buttons on for three minutes of nasal simpering about *Tyrannosaurus II* and how educational an experience it was for her to work with such a sensitive and caring director as so-and-so.

Zoltan had arrived.

A week after his triumph on "The Tonight Show" he hobbled into the office, the cape stained and torn, tights gone in the knees. He brought a distinctive smell with him—the smell of pissed-over gutters and fermenting dumpsters—and for the first time I began to understand why he'd never given me an address or a phone number. ("You want me," he said, "leave a message with Ramón at Jiffy Cleaners.") All at once I had a vision of him slinging his grapefruit sack from the nearest drainpipe and curling up for the night. "Zoltan," I said, "are you okay? You need some cash? A place to stay?"

He sat heavily in the chair across from me. Behind him, on the wall, was an oil painting of an open window, a gift from Mu's bass player. Zoltan waved me off. Then, with a weary gesture, he reached up and removed the cap and goggles. I was shocked. His hair was practically gone and his face was as seamed and scarred as an old hockey puck. He looked about a hundred and twelve. He said nothing.

"Well," I said, to break the silence, "you got your wish. You made it." I lifted a stack of correspondence from the desk and waved it at him. "You're famous."

Zoltan turned his head and spat on the floor. "Famous," he mocked. "Fidel Castro is famous. Irving Berlin. Evel Knievel." His rumble had turned bitter. "Peterbilt," he said suddenly.

This last took me by surprise. I'd been thinking of consolatory platitudes, and all I could do was echo him weakly: "Peterbilt?"

"I want the biggest rig going. The loudest, the dirtiest."

I wasn't following him.

"Maine to L.A.," he rumbled.

"You're going to drive it?"

He stood shakily, fought his way back into the cap, and lowered the goggles. "Shit," he spat, "I ride the axle."

I tried to talk him out of it. "Think of the fumes," I said, "the road hazards. Potholes, dead dogs, mufflers. You'll be two feet off the pavement, going seventy-five, eighty miles an hour. Christ, a cardboard box'll tear you apart."

He wouldn't listen. Not only was he going through with it, but he wanted to coordinate it so that he ended up in Pasadena, for the swap meet at the Rose Bowl. There he would emerge from beneath the truck, wheel a motorcycle out of the back, roar up a ramp, and sail over twenty-six big rigs lined up fender to fender in the middle of the parking lot.

I asked Sol about it. Advance contracts had already made back the money he'd laid out for the airplane thing ten times over. And now we could line up backers. "Get him to wear a Pirelli patch on his cape," Sol rasped, "it's money in the bank."

Easy for Sol to say, but I was having problems with the whole business. This wasn't a plastic dinosaur on a movie lot or a stinko audience at the Improv, this was flesh and blood we were talking about here, a human life. Zoltan wasn't healthy—in mind or body. The risks he took weren't healthy. His ambition wasn't healthy. And if I went along with him, I was no better than Sol, a mercenary, a huckster who'd watch a man die for ten percent of the action. For a day or two I stayed away from the office, brooding around the kitchen in my slippers. In the end, though, I talked myself into it—Zoltan was going to do it with or without me. And who knew what kind of bloodsucker he'd wind up with next?

I hired a PR firm, got a major trucking company to carry him for the goodwill and free publicity, and told myself it was for the best. I'd ride in the cab with the driver, keep him awake, watch over Zoltan personally. And of course I didn't know how it was going to turn out—Zoltan *was* amazing, and if anyone could pull it off, he could—and I thought of the Sumitomo Building and Aero Masoquisto and hoped for the best.

We left Bangor in a cold drizzle on a morning that could have served as the backdrop for a low-budget horror picture: full-bellied clouds, gloom, mist, nose-running cold. By the time we reached Portland the drizzle had begun to crust on the windshield wipers; before we reached New Hampshire it was sleet. The driver was an American Indian by the name of Mink—no middle name, no surname, just Mink. He weighed close to five hundred pounds and he wore his hair in a single braided coil that hung to his belt loops in back. The other driver, whose name was Steve, was asleep in the compartment behind the cab. "Listen, Mink," I said, the windshield wipers beating methodically at the crust, tires hissing beneath us, "maybe you should pull over so we can check on Zoltan."

Mink shifted his enormous bulk in the seat. "What, the Fly?" he said. "No sweat. That guy is like amazing. I seen that thing with the airplane. He can survive that, he's got no problem with this rig—long's I don't hit nothin'."

The words were barely out of his mouth when an animal—a huge brown thing like a cow on stilts—materialized out of the mist. Startled, Mink jerked the wheel, the truck went into a skid, there was a jolt like an earthquake, and the cow on stilts was gone, sucked under the front bumper like a scrap of food sucked down a drain. When we finally came to a stop a hundred yards up the road, the trailer was perpendicular to the cab and Mink's hands were locked to the wheel.

"What happened?" I said.

"Moose," Mink breathed, adding a soft breathless curse. "We hit a fuckin' moose."

In the next instant I was down and out of the cab, racing the length of the trailer, and shouting Zoltan's name. Earlier, in the cold dawn of Bangor, I'd watched him stretch out his mesh bag and suspend it like a trampoline from the trailer's undercarriage, just ahead of the rear wheels. He'd waved to the reporters gathered in the drizzle, ducked beneath the trailer, and climbed into the bag. Now, my heart banging, I wondered what a moose might have done to so tenuous an arrangement. "Zoltan!" I shouted, going down on my knees to peer into the gloom beneath the trailer.

There was no moose. Zoltan's cocoon was still intact, and so was he. He was lying there on his side, a thin fetal lump rounding out of the steel and grime. "What?" he rumbled.

I asked him the question I always seemed to be asking him: was he all right?

It took him a moment—he was working his hand free—and then he gave me the thumbs-up sign. "A-OK," he said.

The rest of the trip—through the icy Midwest, the wind-torn Rockies, and the scorching strip between Tucson and Gila Bend—was uneventful. For me, anyway. I alternately slept, ate truckstop fare designed to remove the lining of your stomach, and listened to Mink or Steve—their conversation was interchangeable—rhapsodize about Harleys, IROC Camaros, and women who went down on all fours and had "Truckers' Delite" tattooed across their buttocks. For Zoltan, it was business as usual. If he suffered from the cold, the heat, the tumbleweeds, beer cans, and fast-food containers that ricocheted off his poor lean scrag of a body day and night, he never mentioned it. True to form, he refused food and drink, though I suspected he must have had something concealed in his cape, and he never climbed down out of his cocoon, not even to move his bowels. Three days and three nights after we'd left Maine, we wheeled the big rig through the streets of Pasadena and into the parking lot outside the Rose Bowl, right on schedule.

There was a fair-sized crowd gathered, though there was no telling whether they'd come for the swap meet, the heavy-metal band we'd hired to give some punch to Zoltan's performance, or the stunt itself, but then who cared? They were there. As were the "Action News" team, the souvenir hawkers and hot-dog vendors. Grunting, his face beaded with sweat, Mink guided the truck into place alongside the twenty-five others, straining to get it as close as possible: an inch could mean the difference between life and death for Zoltan, and we all knew it.

I led a knot of cameramen to the rear of the truck so they could get some tape of Zoltan crawling out of his grapefruit bag. When they were all gathered, he stirred himself, shaking off the froth of insects and road grime, the scraps of paper and cellophane, placing first one bony foot and then the other on the pavement. His eyes were feverish behind the lenses of the goggles and when he lurched out from under the truck I had to catch his arm to prevent him from falling. "So how does it feel to conquer the roadways?" asked a microphone-jabbing reporter with moussed hair and flawless teeth. "What was the worst moment?" asked another.

Zoltan's legs were rubber. He reeked of diesel fuel, his cape was in tatters, his face smeared with sweat and grease. "Twenty-six truck," he rumbled. "The Human Fly is invincible."

And then the band started in—smokebombs, megadecibels, subhuman screeches, the works—and I led Zoltan to his dressing room. He refused a shower, but allowed the makeup girl to sponge off his face and hands. We had to cut the old outfit off him—he was too exhausted to undress himself—and then the girl helped him into the brand-new one I'd provided for the occasion. "Twenty-six truck," he kept mumbling to himself, "A-OK."

I wanted him to call it off. I did. He wasn't in his right mind, anybody could see that. And he was exhausted, beat, as starved and helpless as a refugee. He wouldn't hear of it. "Twenty-six truck," he rumbled, and when I put through a frantic last-minute call to Sol, Sol nearly swallowed the phone. "Damn straight he's going for it!" he shouted. "We got sponsors lined up here. ABC Sports wants to see the tape, for christsake." There was an outraged silence punctuated by the click of throat lozenges, and then Sol cut the connection.

Ultimately, Zoltan went for it. Mink threw open the trailer door, Zoltan fired up the motorcycle—a specially modified Harley Sportster with gas shocks and a bored engine—and one of our people signaled the band to cut it short. The effect was dynamic, the band cutting back suddenly to a punchy drum-and-bass thing and the growl of the big bike coming on in counterpoint . . . and then Zoltan sprang from the back of the trailer, his cape stiff with the breeze, goggles flashing, tires squealing. He made three circuits of the lot, coming in close on the line of trucks, dodging away from the ramp, hunched low and flapping over the handlebars. Every eye was on him. Suddenly he raised a bony fist in the air, swerved wide of the trucks in a great arcing loop that took him to the far end of the lot, and made a run for the ramp.

He was a blur, he was nothing, he was invisible, a rush of motion above the scream of the engine. I saw something—a shadow—launch itself into the thick brown air, cab after cab receding beneath it, the glint of chrome in the sun, fifteen trucks, twenty, twenty-five, and then the sight that haunts me to this day. Suddenly the shadow was gone and a blemish appeared on the broad side panel of the last truck, the one we'd taken across country, Mink's truck, and then, simultaneous with it, there was the noise. A single booming reverberation, as if the world's biggest drum had exploded, followed by the abrupt cessation of the motorcycle's roar and the sad tumbling clatter of dissociated metal.

We had medical help this time, of course, the best available: paramedics, trauma teams, ambulances. None of it did any good. When I pushed through the circle of people around him, Zoltan was lying there on the pavement like a bundle of broken twigs. The cape was twisted round his neck, and his limbs—the sorry fleshless sticks of his arms and legs—were skewed like a doll's. I bent over him as the paramedics brought up the stretcher. "Twenty-five truck next time," he whispered, "promise me." There was blood in his ears, his nostrils, his eye sockets. "Yes," I said, "yes. Twenty-five."

"No worries," he choked as they slid the stretcher under him, "the Human Fly . . . can survive . . . anything."

We buried him three days later.

It was a lonely affair, as funerals go. The uncle, a man in his seventies with the sad scrawl of time on his face, was the only mourner. The press stayed away, though the videotape of Zoltan's finale was shown repeatedly over the air and the freeze-frame photos appeared in half the newspapers in the country. I was shaken by the whole thing. Sol gave me a week off and I did some soul-searching. For a while I thought of giving up the entertainment business altogether, but I was pulled back into it despite myself. Everybody, it seemed, wanted a piece of Zoltan. And as I sat down to sort through the letters, telegrams, and urgent callback messages, the phone ringing unceasingly, the sun flooding the windows of my new well-appointed and highflown office, I began to realize that I owed it to Zoltan to pursue them. This was what he'd wanted, after all.

We settled finally on the animated series, with the usual tie-ins. I knew the producer—Sol couldn't say enough about him—and I knew he'd do quality work. Sure enough, the show premiered number one in its timeslot and it's been there ever since. Sometimes I'll get up early on a Saturday morning just to tune in, to watch the jerky figures move against a backdrop of greed and corruption, the Human Fly ascendant, incorruptible, climbing hand over hand to the top.

(1988)

ON FOR THE LONG HAUL

There was nothing wrong with his appendix—no stitch in the side, no inflammation, no pain—but Bayard was having it out. For safety's sake. He'd read an article once about an anthropologist who'd gone to Malaysia to study the social habits of the orangutan and died horribly when her appendix had burst three hundred miles from the nearest hospital; as she lay writhing in her death agony the distraught apes had hauled her halfway up a jackfruit tree, where she was found several days later by a photographer from *Life* magazine. The picture—splayed limbs, gouty face, leaves like a mouthful of teeth—was indelible with him. She'd been unprepared, that anthropologist, inattentive to the little details that can make or break you. Bayard was taking no such chances.

At their first meeting, the surgeon had been skeptical. "You're going to Montana, Mr. Wemp, not Borneo. There are hospitals there, all the modern facilities."

"It's got to go, doctor," Bayard had quietly insisted, looking up with perfect composure from the knot of his folded hands.

"Listen, Mr. Wemp. I've got to tell you that every surgical procedure, however routine, involves risk"—the doctor paused to let this sink in—"and I really feel the risks outweigh the gains in this case. All the tests are negative—we have no indication of a potential problem here."

"But doctor—" Bayard felt himself at a loss for words. How explain to this earnest, assured man with the suntanned wife, the Mercedes, and the house in Malibu that all of Los Angeles, San Francisco, New York—civilization itself—was on the brink of a catastrophe that would make the Dark Ages look like a Sunday-afternoon softball game? How intimate the horrors that lay ahead, the privation, the suffering? He remembered Aesop's fable about the ant and the grasshopper. Some would be prepared, others would not. "You just don't understand how isolated I'm going to be," he said finally.

Isolated, yes. Thirty-five acres in Bounceback, Montana, population thirty-seven. The closest town with a hospital, bank, or restaurant was Missoula, a two-and-a-half-hour drive, an hour of it on washboard dirt. Bayard would have his own well, a cleared acre for vegetable farming, and a four-room cabin with wood stove, electrical generator, and a radiation-proof cellar stocked with a five-year supply of canned and freeze-dried foodstuffs. The whole thing was the brainchild of Sam Arkson, a real-estate developer who specialized in subsistence plots, bomb shelters, and survival homes. Bayard's firm had done some PR work for one of Arkson's companies—Thrive, Inc.—and as he looked into the literature of catastrophe, Bayard had found himself growing ever more uncertain about the direction of his own life. *Remember the gas crisis?* asked one of Arkson's pamphlets. *An inconvenience, right? The have-nots stepping on the haves. But what about the food crisis around the corner? Have you thought about what you'll do when they close up the supermarkets with a sign that says "Sorry, Temporarily Out of Food"?*

Bayard would never forget the day he'd come across that pamphlet. His palms had begun to sweat as he read on, gauging the effect of nuclear war on the food and water supply, thinking of life without toilet paper, toothpaste, or condiments, summoning images of the imminent economic depression, the starving masses, the dark-skinned marauding hordes pouring across our borders from the south to take, take, take with their greedy, desperate, clutching hands. That night he'd gone home in a cold sweat, visions of apocalypse dancing in his head. Fran made him a drink, but he couldn't taste it. The girls showed him their schoolwork—the sweet, ingenuous loops of their penmanship, the pale watercolors and gold stars—and he felt the tears start up in his eyes. They were doomed, he was doomed, the world sinking like a stone. After they'd gone to bed he slipped out to the kitchen and silently pulled back the refrigerator door. Inside he found a head of deliquescing lettuce, half a gallon of milk, mayonnaise, mustard, chutney, a jar of capers so ancient it might have been unearthed in a tomb, a pint of butter-brickle ice cream, and a single Mexicali Belle TV dinner. The larder yielded two cans of pickled Chinese mushrooms, half a dozen packages of artificial rice pudding, and a lone box of Yodo Crunch cereal, three-quarters empty. He felt sick. Talk about a prolonged siege—they didn't even have breakfast.

That night his dreams had tentacles. He woke feeling strangled. The coffee was poisonous, the newspaper rife with innuendo, each story, each detail cutting into him with the sharp edge of doom. A major quake was on the way, the hills were on fire, there was murder and mayhem in Hollywood, AIDS was spreading to the heterosexual population, Kaddafi had the bomb. Outside sat the traffic. Three million cars, creeping, spitting, killing the atmosphere, inching toward gridlock. The faces of the drivers were impassive. Shift, lurch, advance, stop,

shift, lurch. Didn't they know the whole world had gone hollow, rotten like a
tooth? Didn't they know they were dead? He looked into their eyes and saw
empty sockets, looked into their faces and saw the death's head. At work it was
no better. The secretaries greeted him as if money mattered, as if there were time
to breathe, go out to Chan Dara for lunch, and get felt up in the Xerox room; his
colleagues were as bland as cue balls, nattering on about baseball, stocks, VCRs,
and food processors. He staggered down the hallway as if he'd been hit in the vitals, slamming into the sanctuary of his office like a hunted beast. And there, on
his desk, as if it were the bony pointed finger of the Grim Reaper himself, was
Arkson's pamphlet.

By two-thirty that afternoon he was perched on a chair in Sam Arkson's San
Diego office, talking hard-core survival with the impresario himself. Arkson sat
behind a desk the size of a trampoline, looking alternately youthful and fissured
with age—he could have been anywhere from thirty-five to sixty. Aggressively
tanned and conscientiously muscled, his hair cut so close to the scalp it might
have been painted on, he resembled nothing so much as a professional sweat
meister, Vic Tanny fighting the waistline bulge, Jack LaLanne with a Mohawk.
He was dressed in fatigues and wore a khaki tie. "So," he said, leaning back in
his chair and sizing up Bayard with a shrewd, unforgiving gaze, "are you on for
the long haul or do you just need a security blanket?"

Bayard was acutely conscious of his paunch, the whiteness of his skin, the
hair that trailed down his neck in soft, frivolous coils. He felt like a green recruit
under the burning gaze of the drill instructor, like an awkward dancer trying out
for the wrong role. He coughed into his fist. "The long haul."

Arkson seemed pleased. "Good," he said, a faint smile playing across his lips.
"I thought at first you might be one of these halfway types that wants a bomb
shelter under the patio or something." He gave Bayard a knowing glance. "They
might last a month or two after the blast," he said, "but what then? And what if
it's not war we're facing but worldwide economic collapse? Are they going to eat
their radiation detectors?"

This was a joke. Bayard laughed nervously. Arkson cut him off with a contemptuous snort and a wave of his hand that consigned all the timid, slipshod,
halfway Harrys of the world to an early grave. "No," he said, "I can see you're
the real thing, a one-hundred-percenter, no finger in the dike for you." He
paused. "You're a serious person, Bayard, am I right?"

Bayard nodded.

"And you've got a family you want to protect?"

Bayard nodded again.

"Okay"—Arkson was on his feet, a packet of brochures in his hand—"we're
going to want to talk hidden location, with the space, seeds, fertilizer, and tools
to grow food and the means to hunt it, and we're going to talk a five-year renew-
able stockpile of survival rations, medical supplies, and specie—and of course
weaponry."

"Weaponry?"

Arkson had looked at him as if he'd just put a bag over his head. "Tell me," he said, folding his arms so that the biceps swelled beneath his balled fists, "when the bust comes and you're sitting on the only food supply in the county, you don't really think your neighbors are going to breeze over for tea and polite chitchat, do you?"

Though Bayard had never handled a gun in his life, he knew the answer: there was a sickness on the earth and he'd have to harden himself to deal with it.

Suddenly Arkson was pointing at the ceiling, as if appealing to a higher authority to back him up. "You know what I've got up there on the roof?" he said, looming over Bayard like an inquisitor. Bayard hadn't the faintest idea.

"A Brantley B2B."

Bayard gave him a blank look.

"A chopper. Whirlybird. You know: upski-downski. And guess who flies it?" Arkson spread the brochures out on the desk in front of him, tapping a forefinger against the glossy photograph of a helicopter floating in a clear blue sky beneath the rubric ESCAPE CRAFT. "That's right, friend: me. I fly it. Leave nothing to chance, that's my motto." Bayard thumbed through the brochure, saw minijets, hovercraft, Cessnas, seaplanes and ultralights.

"I can be out of town in ten minutes. Half an hour later I'm in my compound— two hundred fenced acres, three security men, goats, cows, chickens, pigs, corn as high as your chin, wheat, barley, rye, artesian wells, underground gas and water tanks—and an arsenal that could blow away the PLO. Listen," he said, and his eyes were like a stalking cat's, "when the shit hits the fan they'll be eating each other out there."

Bayard had been impressed. He was also terrified, sick with the knowledge of his own impotence and vulnerability. The blade was poised. It could fall today, tonight, tomorrow. They had to get out. "Fran," he called as he hurried through the front door, arms laden with glossy brochures, dire broadsides, and assorted survival tomes from Arkson Publications, Ltd. "Fran!"

Fran had always been highstrung—neurotic, actually—and the sort of pure, unrefined paranoia that had suddenly infested Bayard was second nature to her. Still, she would take some persuading—he was talking about uprooting their entire life, after all—and it was up to Bayard to focus that paranoia and bring it to bear on the issue at hand. She came out of the sunroom in a tentlike swimsuit, a large, solid, plain-faced woman in her late thirties, trailing children. She gave him a questioning look while the girls, chanting "Daddy, Daddy," foamed round his legs. "We've got to talk," was all he could say.

Later, after the children had been put to bed, he began his campaign. "We're sitting on a powder keg," he said as she bent over the dishwasher, stacking plates. She looked up, blinking behind the big rectangular frames of her glasses like a frogman coming up for air. "Pardon?"

"L.A., the whole West Coast. It's the first place the Russians'll hit—if the quake doesn't drop us into the ocean first. Or the banks go under. You've read about the S&Ls, right?"

She looked alarmed. But then, she alarmed easily. Chronically overprotected as a child, cloistered in a parochial school run along the lines of a medieval nunnery, and then consigned to a Catholic girls' college that made it look liberal, she believed with all her heart in the venality of man and the perfidy and rottenness of the world. On the rare occasions when she left the house she clutched her purse like a fullback going through a gap in the line, saw all pedestrians—even white-haired grandmothers—as potential muggers, and dodged Asians, Latinos, Pakistanis, and Iranians as if they were the hordes of Genghis Khan. "What in God's name are you talking about?" she said.

"I'm talking about Montana."

"Montana?"

At this point Bayard had simply fetched his trove of doom literature and spread it across the kitchen table. "Read," he said, knowing full well the books and pamphlets could speak far more eloquently than he. In the morning he'd found her hunched over the table still, the ashtray full beside her, a copy of *Doom Newsletter* in her hand, *Panic in the Streets* and *How to Kill*, volumes I–IV, face down beside a steaming coffee mug. "But what about the girls?" she said. "What about school, ballet lessons, tennis, swimming?"

Melissa was nine, Marcia seven. The move to the hinterlands would be disruptive for them, maybe traumatic—Bayard didn't deny it—but then, so would nuclear holocaust. "Ballet lessons?" he echoed. "What good do you think ballet lessons are going to be when maniacs are breaking down the door?" And then, more gently: "Look, Fran, it's going to be hard for all of us, but I just don't see how we can stay here now that our eyes have been opened—it's like sitting on the edge of a volcano or something."

She was weakening, he could feel it. When he got home from the office she was sunk into the sofa, her eyes darting across the page before her like frightened animals. Arkson had called. Four times. "Mrs. Wemp, Fran," he'd shouted over the wire as if the barbarians were at the gate, "you've got to listen to me. I have a place for you. Nobody'll find you. You'll live forever. Sell that deathtrap and get out now before it's too late!" Toward the end of the week she went through an entire day without changing out of her nightgown. Bayard pressed his advantage. He sent the girls to the babysitter and took the day off from work to ply her with pamphlets, rhetoric and incontrovertible truths, and statistics on everything from the rising crime rate to nuclear kill ratios. As dusk fell that evening, the last choked rays of sunlight irradiating the smog till it looked like mustard gas coming in over the trenches, she capitulated. In a voice weak with terror and exhaustion, she called him into the bedroom, where she lay still as a corpse. "All right," she croaked. "Let's get out."

After Fran, the surgeon was easy. For fifteen minutes Bayard had quietly persisted while the doctor demurred. Finally, throwing his trump card, the surgeon leaned forward and said: "You're aware your insurance won't cover this, Mr. Wemp?"

Bayard had smiled. "No problem," he said. "I'll pay cash."

Two months later he and Fran sported matching abdominal scars, wore new flannel shirts and down vests, talked knowledgeably of seed sets, fertilizer, and weed killer, and resided in the distant rugged reaches of the glorious Treasure State, some four hundred miles from ground zero of the nearest likely site of atomic devastation. The cabin was a good deal smaller than what they were used to, but then, they were used to luxury condominiums, and the cabin sacrificed luxury—comfort, even—for utility. Its exterior was simulated log, designed to make the place look like a trapper's cabin to the average marauder, but the walls were reinforced with steel plates to a thickness that would withstand bazooka or antitank gun. In the basement, which featured four-foot-thick concrete walls and lead shielding, was the larder. Ranks of hermetically sealed canisters mounted the right-hand wall, each with a reassuring shelf life of ten years or more: bulk grains, wild rice, textured vegetable protein, yogurt powder, matzo meal, hardtack, lentils, bran, Metamucil. Lining the opposite wall, precisely stacked, labeled and alphabetized, were the freeze-dried entrées, from *abbacchio alla cacciatora* and *boeuf bourguignon* to shrimp Creole, turkey Tetrazzini, and *ziti alla romana*. Bayard took comfort in their very names, as a novice might take comfort in the names of the saints: Just In Case freeze-dried linguine with white clam sauce, tomato crystals from Lazarus Foods, canned truffles from Gourmets for Tomorrow, and Arkson's own Stash Brand generic foodstuffs, big plain-labeled cans that read CATSUP, SAUERKRAUT, DETERGENT, LARD. In the evenings, when the house was as quiet as the far side of the moon, Bayard would slip down into the shelter, pull the airtight door closed behind him, and spend hours contemplating the breadth, variety, and nutritional range of his cache. Sinking back in a padded armchair, his heartbeat decelerating, breathing slowed to a whisper, he would feel the calm of the womb descend on him. Then he knew the pleasures of the miser, the hoarder, the burrowing squirrel, and he felt as free from care as if he were wafting to and fro in the dark amniotic sea whence he sprang.

Of course, such contentment doesn't come cheap. The whole package—land, cabin, four-wheel-drive vehicle, arms and munitions, foodstuffs, and silver bars, DeBeers diamonds, and cowrie shells for barter—had cost nearly half a million. Arkson, whose corporate diversity put him in a league with Gulf & Western, had been able to provide everything, lock, stock, and barrel, right down to the church-key opener in the kitchen drawer and the reusable toilet paper in the bathroom. There were radiation suits, flannels, and thermal underwear from Arkson Outfitters, and weapons—including a pair of Russian-made AK-47s smuggled out of Afghanistan and an Israeli grenade launcher—from Arkson Munitions. In the driveway, from Arkson Motors, Domestic and Import, was the four-wheel-drive Norwegian-made Olfputt TC 17, which would run on anything handy, from paint thinner to rubbing alcohol, climb the north face of the Eiger in an ice storm, and pull a plow through frame-deep mud. The cabin's bookshelves were mostly given over to the how-to, survival, and self-help tomes in which Arkson Publications specialized, but there were reprints of selected classics—*Journal of the Plague Year, Hiroshima,* and *Down and Out in London and Paris*—as well. Arkson made an itemized list, tallied the whole thing up, and presented the bill to Bayard and Fran in the San Diego office.

Fran was so wrought up at this point she barely gave it a glance. She kept looking over her shoulder at the door as if in expectation of the first frenzied pillagers, and then she would glance down at the open neck of her purse and the .22-caliber Beretta Arkson had just handed her ("My gift to you, Fran," he'd said; "learn to use it"). Bayard himself was distracted. He tried to look judicious, tried to focus on the sheet of paper before him with the knowing look one puts on for garage mechanics presenting the bill for arcane mechanical procedures and labor at the rate of a hundred and twenty dollars an hour, but he couldn't. What did it matter? Until he was ensconced in his cabin he was like a crab without its shell. "Seems fair," he murmured.

Arkson had come round the desk to perch on the near edge and take his hand. "No bargain rate for survival, Bayard," he said, "no fire sales. If the price seems steep, just think of it this way: Would you put a price on your life? Or the lives of your wife and children?" He'd paused to give Bayard a saintly look, the look of the young Redeemer stepping through the doors of the temple. "Just be thankful that you two had the financial resources—and the foresight—to protect yourself."

Bayard had looked down at the big veiny tanned hand clutching his own and shaken it mechanically. He felt numb. The past few weeks had been hellish, what with packing up, supervising the movers, and making last-minute trips to the mall for things like thread, Band-Aids, and dental floss—not to mention agonizing over the sale of the house, anticipating Fran's starts and rushes of panic, and turning in his resignation at the Hooper-Munson Co., where he'd put in fourteen years and worked himself up to Senior Vice President in Charge of Reversing Negative Corporate Image. Without Arkson it would have been impossible. He'd soothed Fran, driven the children to school, called the movers, cleaners, and painters, and then gone to work on Bayard's assets with the single-mindedness of a general marshaling troops. Arkson Realty had put the condo on the market and found a buyer for the summer place in Big Bear, and Arkson, Arkson, and Arkson, Brokers, had unloaded Bayard's holdings on the stock exchange with a barely significant loss. When combined with Fran's inheritance and the money Bayard had put away for the girls' education, the amount realized would meet Thrive, Inc.'s price and then some. It was all for the best, Arkson kept telling him, all for the best. If Bayard had second thoughts about leaving his job and dropping out of society, he could put them out of his mind: society, as he'd known it, wouldn't last out the year. And as far as money was concerned, well, they'd be living cheaply from here on out.

"Fran," Arkson was saying, taking her hand now too and linking the three of them as if he were a revivalist leading them forward to the purifying water, "Bayard . . ." He paused again, overcome with emotion. "Feel lucky."

Now, two months later, Bayard could stand on the front porch of his cabin, survey the solitary expanse of his property with its budding aspen and cottonwood and glossy conifers, and take Arkson's parting benediction to heart. He did feel lucky. Oh, perhaps on reflection he could see that Arkson had shaved him on one item or another, and that the doom merchant had kindled a blaze under him and Fran that put them right in the palm of his hand, but Bayard had no regrets. He felt secure, truly secure, for the first time in his adult life, and he bent contentedly to ax or hoe, glad to have escaped the Gomorrah of the city. For her part, Fran seemed to have adjusted well too. The physical environment beyond the walls of her domain had never much interested her, and so it was principally a matter of adjusting to one set of rooms as opposed to another. Most important, though, she seemed more relaxed. In the morning, she would lead the girls through their geography or arithmetic, then read, sew, or nap in the early afternoon. Later she would walk round the yard—something she rarely did in Los Angeles—or work in the flower garden she'd planted outside the front door. At night, there was television, the signals called down to earth from the heavens by means of the satellite dish Arkson had providently included in the package.

The one problem was the girls. At first they'd been excited, the whole thing a lark, a vacation in the woods, but as the weeks wore on they became increasingly withdrawn, secretive, and, as Bayard suspected, depressed. Marcia missed Mrs. Sturdivant, her second-grade teacher; Melissa missed her best friend Nicole, Disneyland, Baskin and Robbins, and the beach, in that order. Bayard saw the pale, sad ovals of their faces framed in the gloom of the back bedroom as they hovered over twice-used coloring books, and he felt as if a stake had been driven through his heart. "Don't worry," Fran said, "give them time. They'll make the adjustment." Bayard hoped so. Because there was no way they were going back to the city.

One afternoon—it was mid-June, already hot, a light breeze discovering dust and tossing it on the hoods and windshields of the cars parked along the street— Bayard was in the lot outside Chuck's Wagon in downtown Bounceback, loading groceries into the back of the Olfputt, when he glanced up to see two men stepping out of a white Mercedes with California plates. One of them was Arkson, in his business khakis and tie. The other—tall and red-faced, skinny as a refugee in faded green jumpsuit and work boots—Bayard had never seen before. Both men stretched themselves, and then the stranger put his hands on his hips and slowly revolved a full three hundred and sixty degrees, his steady, expressionless gaze taking in the gas station, saloon, feed store, and half-deserted streets as if he'd come to seize them for nonpayment of taxes. Bayard could barely contain himself. "Sam!" he called. "Sam Arkson!" And then he was in motion, taking the lot in six animated strides, his hand outstretched in greeting.

At first Arkson didn't seem to recognize him. He'd taken the stranger's arm and was pointing toward the mountains like a tour guide when Bayard called out his name. Half turning, as if at some minor disturbance, Arkson gave him a preoccupied look, then swung back to say something under his breath to his companion. By then Bayard was on him, pumping his hand. "Good to see you, Sam."

Arkson shook numbly. "You too," he murmured, avoiding Bayard's eyes.

There was an awkward silence. Arkson looked constipated. The stranger— his face was so red he could have been apoplectic, terminally sunburned, drunk—glared at Bayard as if they'd just exchanged insults. Bayard's gaze shifted uneasily from the stranger's eyes to the soiled yellow beret that lay across his head like a cheese omelet and then back again to Arkson. "I just wanted to tell you how well we're doing, Sam," he stammered, "and . . . and to thank you—I mean it, really—for everything you've done for us."

Arkson brightened immediately. If a moment earlier he'd looked like a prisoner in the dock, hangdog and tentative, now he seemed his old self. He smiled, ducked his head, and held up his palm in humble acknowledgment. Then, running his fingers over the stubble of his crown, he stepped back a pace and introduced the ectomorphic stranger. "Rayfield Cullum," he said, "Bayard Wemp."

"Glad to meet you," Bayard said, extending his hand.

The stranger's hands never left his pockets. He stared at Bayard a moment out of his deepset yellow eyes, then turned his head to spit in the dirt. Bayard's hand dropped like a stone.

"I'd say you two have something in common," Arkson said mysteriously. And then, leaning forward and dropping his voice: "Rayfield and I are just ironing out the details on the plot next to yours. He wants in this week—tomorrow, if not sooner." Arkson laughed. The stranger's eyes lifted to engage Bayard's; his face remained expressionless.

Bayard was taken by surprise. "Plot?" he repeated.

"East and south," Arkson said, nodding. "You'll be neighbors. I've got a retired couple coming in the end of the month from Saratoga Springs—they'll be purchasing the same package as yours directly to the north of you, by that little lake."

"Package?" Bayard was incredulous. "What is this, Levittown, Montana, or something?"

"Heh-heh, very funny, Bayard." Arkson had put on his serious look, life and death, the world's a jungle, LaLanne admonishing his audience over the perils of flab. "The crunch comes, Bayard," he said, "you could support fifty people on those thirty-five acres, what with the game in those woods and the fertility of that soil. You know it as well as I do."

Now Cullum spoke for the first time, his voice a high, nagging rasp, like static. "Arkson," he said, driving nails into the first syllable, "I ain't got all day."

It was then that Melissa, giggling like a machine and with a pair of ice-cream cones thrust up like torches over her head, came tearing around the side of the building, her sister in pursuit. Marcia was not giggling. She was crying in frustration, wailing as if her heart had been torn out, and cutting the air with a stick. "Melissa!" Bayard shouted, but it was too late. Her skinny brown legs got tangled and she pitched forward into Cullum, who was just then swiveling his head round at the commotion. There was the scrape of sneakers on gravel, the glare of the sun poised motionless overhead, and then the wet, rich, fecal smear of chocolate-fudge ice cream—four scoops—on the seat of Cullum's jumpsuit. Cullum's knee buckled under the impact, and he jumped back as if he'd been struck by a snake. "Goddamnit!" he roared, and Bayard could see that his hands were shaking. "Goddamnit to hell!"

Melissa lay sprawled in the dirt. Stricken face, a thin wash of red on her scraped knee. Bayard was already bending roughly for her, angry, an apology on his lips, when Cullum took a step forward and kicked her twice in the ribs. "Little shit," he hissed, his face twisted with lunatic fury, and then Arkson had his broad arms around him, pulling him back like a handler with an attack dog.

Melissa's mouth was working in shock, the first hurt breathless shriek caught in her throat; Marcia stood white-faced behind them; Cullum was spitting out curses and dancing in Arkson's arms. Bayard might have lifted his daughter from the dirt and pressed her to him, he might have protested, threatened, waved his fist at this rabid dog with the red face, but he didn't. No. Before he could think he was on Cullum, catching him in the center of that flaming face with a fist like a knob of bone. Once, twice, zeroing in on the wicked little dog eyes and the fleshy dollop of the nose, butter, margarine, wet clay, something giving with a crack, and then a glancing blow off the side of the head. He felt Cullum's workboots flailing for his groin as he stumbled forward under his own momentum, and then Arkson was driving him up against the Mercedes and shouting something in his face. Suddenly freed, Cullum came at him, beret askew, blood bright in his nostrils, but Arkson was there, pinning Bayard to the car and shooting out an arm to catch hold of the skinny man's shirt. "Daddy!" Melissa shrieked, the syllables broken with shock and hurt.

"You son of a bitch!" Bayard shouted.

"All right now, knock it off, will you?" Arkson held them at arm's length like a pair of fighting cocks. "It's just a misunderstanding, that's all."

Bleeding, shrunk into his jumpsuit like a withered tortoise, Cullum held Bayard's gaze and dropped his voice to a hiss. "I'll kill you," he said.

Fran was aghast. "Is he dangerous?" she said, turning to peer over her spectacles at Bayard and the girls as they sat at the kitchen table. She was pouring wine vinegar from a three-gallon jug into a bowl of cucumber spears. Awkwardly. "I mean, he sounds like he escaped from a mental ward or something."

Bayard shrugged. He could still taste the tinny aftershock the incident had left in the back of his throat. A fight. He'd been involved in a fight. Though he hadn't struck anyone in anger since elementary school, hadn't even come close, he'd reacted instinctively in defense of his children. He sipped his gimlet and felt a glow of satisfaction.

"This is the man we're going to have next door to us?" Fran set the bowl on the table beside a platter of reconstituted stir-fried vegetables and defrosted tofu. The girls were subdued, staring down their straws into glasses of chocolate milk. "Well?" Fran's eyes searched him as she sat down across the table. "Do you think I can have any peace of mind with this sort of . . . of violence and lawlessness on my doorstep? Is this what we left the city for?"

Bayard speared a square of tofu and fed it into his mouth. "It's hardly on our doorstep, Fran," he said, gesturing with his fork. "Besides, I can handle him, no problem."

A week passed. Then two. Bayard saw no more of Arkson, or of Cullum, and the incident began to fade from his mind. Perhaps Cullum had soured on the deal and gone off somewhere else—or back to the hole he'd crawled out of. And what if he did move in? Arkson was right: there was so much land between them they might never lay eyes on one another, let alone compete for resources. At any rate, Bayard was too busy to worry about it. Mornings, it was second-grade geography and fourth-grade history, which meant relearning his state capitals and trying to keep his de Sotos, Coronados, and Cabeza de Vacas straight. Afternoons, he kept busy with various home-improvement projects—constructing a lopsided playhouse for the girls, fencing his vegetable garden against the mysterious agent that masticated everything he planted right down to the root, splitting and stacking wood, fumbling over the instructions for the prefab aluminum toolshed he'd mail-ordered from the Arkson Outfitters catalogue. Every third day he drove into Bounceback for groceries (he and Fran had decided to go easy on the self-subsistence business until such time as society collapsed and made it imperative) and on weekends the family would make the long trek down to Missoula for a restaurant meal and a movie. It was on one of these occasions that they bought the rabbits.

Bayard was coming out of the hardware store with a box of twopenny nails, a set of socket wrenches, and a hacksaw when he spotted Fran and the girls across the street, huddled over a man who seemed to be part of the sidewalk. The man, Bayard saw as he crossed the street to join them, was long-haired, bearded, and dirty. He had a burlap sack beside him, and the sack was moving. "Here, here," said the man, grinning up at them, and then he plunged his hand into the bag and drew out a rabbit by the ears. The animal's paws were bound with rubber bands, its fur was rat-colored. "This one here's named Duke," the man said, grinning. "He's trained."

Long-whiskered, long-eared, and long-legged, it looked more like a newborn mule than a rabbit. As the man dangled it before the girls, its paws futilely kicking and eyes big with terror, Bayard almost expected it to bray. "Good eatin', friend," the man said, giving Bayard a shrewd look.

"Daddy," Melissa gasped, "can we buy him? Can we?"

The man was down on his knees, fumbling in the sack. A moment later he extracted a second rabbit, as lanky, brown, and sickly-looking as the first. "This one's Lennie. He's trained too."

"Can we, Daddy?" Marcia chimed in, tugging at his pant leg.

Bayard looked at Fran. The girls held their breath. "Five bucks," the man said.

Down the street sat the Olfputt, gleaming like a gigantic toaster oven. Two women, a man in a cowboy hat, and a boy Melissa's age stood staring at it in awe and bewilderment. Bayard jingled the change in his pocket, hesitating. "For both," the man said.

Initially, the rabbits had seemed a good idea. Bayard was no psychologist, but he could see that these gangling flat-footed rodents, with their multiplicity of needs, with their twitching noses and grateful mouths, might help draw the girls out of themselves. He was right. From the moment they'd hustled the rabbits into the car, cut their bonds, and pressed them to their scrawny chests while Fran fretted over ticks, tularemia, and relapsing fever, the girls were absorbed with them. They fed them grass, lettuce, and the neat little pellets of rabbit food that so much resembled the neat little pellets the animals excreted. They cuddled, dressed, and brushed them. They helped Bayard construct a pair of interlocking chicken-wire cages and selected the tree from which they would hang, their thin serious faces compressed with concern over weasels, foxes, coons, coyotes. Melissa devoted less time to tormenting her sister and bemoaning the absence of her school friends; Marcia seemed less withdrawn.

For his part, Bayard too found the new pets compelling. They thumped their feet joyously when he approached their cages with lettuce or parsley, and as they nuzzled his fingers he gazed out over his cleared acre to the trees beyond and thought how this was only the beginning. He would have goats, chickens, pigs, maybe even a cow or a horse. The way he saw it, a pet today was meat on the hoof tomorrow. Hadn't they eaten horses during the First World War? Mules, oxen, dogs? Not to mention rabbits. Of course, these particular rabbits were an exception. Though in theory they were to be skinned, stewed, and eaten in time of distress, though they represented a hedge against hard times and a life-sustaining stock of protein, Bayard looked into their quiet, moist eyes and knew he would eat lentils first.

The following week Bayard took the family into Missoula for a double sci-fi/horror feature (which only helped confirm him in his conviction that the world was disintegrating) and dinner at the local Chinese restaurant. It was after dark when they got home and the Olfputt's headlights swung into the yard to illuminate two tiny figures hanging like wash from the simulated beam that ran the length of the front porch. Melissa spotted them first. "What's that?" she said.

"Where?"

"There, up on the porch."

By the time Bayard saw them it was too late. Fran had seen them too—disheveled ears and limp paws, the puny little carcasses twisting slowly round their monofilament nooses—and worse, the seven-year-old, rousing herself from sleep, had caught a nightmarish glimpse of them before he could flick off the lights. "My God," Fran whispered. They sat there a moment, the dark suffocating, no gleam of light for miles. Then Marcia began to whimper and Melissa called out his name sharply, as if in accusation, as if he alone were responsible for all the hurts and perversions of the world.

Bayard felt he was sinking. Pork fried rice and duck sauce tore at the pit of his stomach with a hellish insistence, Fran was hyperventilating, and the girls' lamentations rose in intensity from piteous bewildered bleats to the caterwauling of demons. Frightened, angry, uncomprehending, he sat there in utter blackness, his hands trembling on the wheel. When finally he turned on the parking lights and pushed open the door, Fran clutched his arm with the grip of a madwoman. "Don't go out there," she hissed.

"Don't be silly," Bayard said.

"No," she sobbed, clawing at him as if she were drowning. Her eyes raged at him in the dim light, the girls were weeping and moaning, and then she was pressing something into his hand, heavy, cold, instrument of death. "Take this."

Six or seven pickups were parked outside the T&T Cocktail Bar when Bayard rolled into downtown Bounceback. It was half past eleven, still hot, the town's solitary street light glowing like a myopic eye. As he crossed the street to the telephone outside Chuck's Wagon, Bayard could make out a number of shadowy figures in broad-brimmed hats milling around in front of the bar. There was a murmur of disembodied voices, the nagging whine of a country fiddle, stars overhead, the glow of cigarettes below. Drunks, he thought, hurrying past them. Their lives wouldn't be worth a carton of crushed eggs when the ax fell.

Bayard stalked up to the phone, tore the receiver from its cradle, and savagely dialed the number he'd scribbled across a paper napkin. He was angry, keyed up, hot with outrage. He listened to the phone ring once, twice, three times, as he cursed under his breath. This was too much. His wife was sick with fear, his children were traumatized, and all he'd worked for—security, self-sufficiency, peace of mind—was threatened. He'd had to prowl round his own home like a criminal, clutching a gun he didn't know how to use, jumping at his own shadow. Each bush was an assassin, each pocket of shadow a crouching adversary, the very trees turned against him. Finally, while Fran and the girls huddled in the locked car, he'd cut down Lennie and Duke, bundled the lifeless bodies in a towel, and hid them out back. Then Fran, her face like a sack of flour, had made him turn on all the lights till the house blazed like a stage set, insisting that he search the closets, poke the muzzle of the gun under the beds, and throw back the doors of the kitchen cabinets like an undercover cop busting drug peddlers. When he'd balked at this last precaution—the cabinets couldn't have concealed anything bigger than a basset hound—she'd reminded him of how they'd found Charlie Manson under the kitchen sink. "All right," he'd said after searching the basement, "there's nobody here. It's okay."

"It was that maniac, wasn't it?" Fran whispered, as if afraid she'd be overheard.

"Daddy," Melissa cried, "where's Lennie, and . . . and Duke?" The last word trailed off in a broken lamentation for the dead, and Bayard felt the anger like a hot nugget inside him.

"I don't know," he said, pressing Melissa to him and massaging her thin, quaking little shoulders. "I don't know." Through the doorway he could see Marcia sitting in the big armchair, sucking her thumb. Suddenly he became aware of the gun in his hand. He stared down at it for a long moment, and then, almost unconsciously, as if it were a cigarette lighter or a nail clipper, he slipped it into his pocket.

Now he stood outside Chuck's Wagon, the night breathing down his neck, the telephone receiver pressed to his ear. Four rings, five, six. Suddenly the line engaged and Arkson, his voice shrunk round a kernel of suspicion, answered with a quick tentative "Yeah?"

"Sam? It's me. Bayard."

"Who?"

"Bayard Wemp."

There was a pause. "Oh yeah," Arkson said finally, "Bayard. What can I do for you? You need anything?"

"No, I just wanted to ask you—"

"Because I know you're going to be short on hardware for harvesting, canning, and all that, and I've got a new line of meat smokers you might want to take a look at—"

"Sam!" Bayard's voice had gone shrill, and he fought to control it. "I just wanted to ask you about the guy in the beret, you know, the one you had with you up here last month—Cullum?"

There was another pause. Bayard could picture his mentor in a flame-retardant bathrobe, getting ready to turn in on a bed that converted to a life raft in the event that a second flood came over the earth while he lay sleeping. "Uh-huh. Yeah. What about him?"

"Well, did he ever buy the place? I mean, is he up here now?"

"Listen, Bayard, why not let bygones be bygones, huh? Rayfield is no different than you are—except maybe he doesn't like children, is all. He's a one-hundred-percenter, Bayard, on for the long haul like you. I'm sure he's forgot all about that little incident—and so should you."

Bayard drew a long breath. "I've got to know, Sam."

"It takes all kinds, Bayard."

"I don't need advice, Sam. Just information. Look, I can go down to the county assessor's office in the morning and get what I want."

Arkson sighed. "All right," he said finally. "Yes. He moved in yesterday."

When he turned away from the phone, Bayard felt his face go hot. Survival. It was a joke. He owned thirty-five acres of untrammeled Wild West backwoods wilderness land and his only neighbor was a psychopath who kicked children in the stomach and mutilated helpless animals. Well, he wasn't going to allow it. Society might be heading for collapse, but there were still laws on the books. He'd call the sheriff, take him to court, have him locked up.

He was halfway to his car, just drawing even with the open door of the T&T, when he became aware of a familiar sound off to his left—he turned, recognizing the distinctive high whine of an Olfputt engine. There, sitting at the curb, was an Olfputt pickup, looking like half an MX missile with a raised bed grafted to the rear end. He stopped, puzzled. This was no Ford, no Chevy, no Dodge. The Olfputt was as rare in these parts as a palanquin—he'd never seen one himself till Arkson . . . Suddenly he began to understand.

The door swung open. Cullum's face was dark—purple as a birthstain in the faint light. The engine ticked, raced, and then fell back as the car idled. The headlights seemed to clutch at the street. "Hey, hey," Cullum said. "Mr. Rocky Marciano. Mr. Streetfight."

Bayard became aware of movement in the shadows around him. The barflies, the cowboys, had gathered silently, watching him. Cullum stood twenty feet away, a rifle dangling at his side. Bayard knew that rifle, just as he'd known the Olfputt. Russian-made, he thought. AK-47. Smuggled out of Afghanistan. He felt Fran's little pistol against his thigh, weighing him down like a pocketful of change. His teeth were good, his heartbeat strong. He had a five-year supply of food in his basement and a gun in his pocket. Cullum was waiting.

Bayard took a step forward. Cullum spat in the dirt and raised the rifle. Bayard could have gone for his gun, but he didn't even know how to release the safety catch, let alone aim and fire the thing, and it came to him that even if he did know how to handle it, even if he'd fired it a thousand times at cans, bottles, rocks, and junkyard rats, he would never use it, not if all the hungry hordes of the earth were at his door.

But Cullum would. Oh yes, Cullum would. Cullum was on for the long haul.

(1983)

THE 100 FACES OF DEATH, VOLUME IV

He knew he'd really screwed up. Screwed up in a major and unforgiving way. You could see the perception solidifying in his eyes—eyes that seemed to swell out of his head like hard-cooked eggs extruded through the sockets, and the camera held steady. He was on a stage, faultlessly lit, and a banner proclaimed him RENALDO THE GREAT ESCAPE ARTIST. He was running sweat. Oozing it. His pores were huge, saturated, craters trenching his face like running sores. Suspended six feet above his head, held aloft by block and tackle, was a fused meteorite of junkyard metal the size of a truck engine, its lower surface bristling with the gleaming jagged teeth of a hundred kitchen knives annealed in the forges of Guadalajara. Renaldo's hands were cuffed to his ankles, and what looked like a tugboat anchor chain was wound round his body six or eight times and bolted to the concrete floor. His lovely assistant, a heavily made-up woman whose thighs ballooned from her lacy tutu like great coppery slabs of meat, looked as if her every tremor and waking nightmare had been distilled in the bitter secretions of that moment. This was definitely not part of the act.

"Watch this," Jamie said. "Watch this."

Janine tightened her grip on my hand. The room shrank in on us. The beer in my free hand had gone warm, and when I lifted it to my lips it tasted of yeast and aluminum. And what did I feel? I felt the way the lovely assistant looked, felt the cold charge of revulsion and exhilaration that had come over me when I'd seen my first porno movie at the age of fourteen, felt a hairy-knuckled hand slide up my throat and jerk at a little lever there.

When the video opened, over the credits, Renaldo was clenching a straw between his teeth—a straw, a single straw, yellow and stiff, the smallest part of a broom. He was leaning forward, working the straw in the tiny aperture that controlled the release mechanism of the handcuffs. But now, because he'd begun to appreciate that this wasn't his day, and that the consequences of that fact were irrevocable, his lips began to tremble and he lost his grip on the straw. The lovely assistant gave the camera a wild strained look and then made as if to dash forward and restore that essential wisp of vegetation to the artist's mouth, but it was too late. With a thick slushing sound, the sound of tires moving through wet snow, the timer released the mechanism that restrained the iron monolith, and Renaldo was no more.

Jamie said something like, "Dude really bought it," and then, "Anybody ready for a beer?"

I sat through another ninety-nine permutations of the final moment, variously lit and passionately or indifferently performed, watched the ski-masked bank robber pop his hostage's head like a grape with the aid of a .44 Magnum and then pop his own, saw the fire-eater immolate herself and the lumberjack make his final cut. Jamie, who'd seen the video half-a-dozen times, couldn't stop laughing. Janine said nothing, but her grip on my hand was unyielding. For my part, I remember going numb after the third or fourth death, but I sat there all the same, though there were ninety-six to go.

But then, who was counting?

The following weekend, my Aunt Marion died. Or "passed on," as my mother put it, a delicate euphemistic phrase that conjured up ethereal realms rather than the stark black-and-white image of damp soil and burrowing insects. My mother was in New York, I was in Los Angeles. And no, I wasn't flying in for the funeral. She cried briefly, dryly, and then hung up.

I was twenty-five at the time, a graduate of an indifferent university, a young man who went to work and made money, sought the company of young women and was perhaps too attached to the friends of his youth, Jamie in particular. I listened to the silence a moment, then phoned Janine and asked her to dinner. She was busy. What about tomorrow, then? I said. She planned to be busy then, too.

I hadn't laid eyes on my Aunt Marion in ten years. I remembered her as a sticklike woman in a wheelchair with an unsteady lip and a nose that overhung it like a cutbank, a nose that wasn't qualitatively different from my mother's and, in the fullness of generation, my own. Her death was the result of an accident— negligence, my mother insisted—and already, less than twenty-four hours after the fact, there was an attorney involved.

It seemed that Aunt Marion had been on an outing to the art museum with several other inmates of the nursing home where she'd been in residence since Nixon's presidency, and the attendant, in placing her at the head of the ramp out back of the museum dining hall, had failed to properly set the brake on the back wheels of her chair. Aunt Marion suffered from some progressive nervous disorder that had rendered her limbs useless—she was able to control her motorized chair only through the use of a joystick which she gripped between her teeth, and even then only at the best of times. Left alone at the summit of the ramp while the attendant went off to fetch another patient, Aunt Marion felt her chair begin to slip inexorably forward. The chair picked up speed, and one of the two witnesses to the accident claimed that she'd bent her face to the controls to arrest it, while the other insisted she'd done nothing at all to save herself, but had simply glided on down the ramp and into eternity with a tight little smile frozen to her face. In any case, there was blame to be assigned, very specific and undeniable blame, and a cause-and-effect reaction to explain Aunt Marion's removal from this sphere of being, and, in the end, it seemed to give my mother some measure of comfort.

Try as I might, though, I couldn't picture the face of Aunt Marion's death. My own blood was involved, my own nose. And yet it was all somehow remote, distant, and the death of Renaldo the Great stayed with me in a way Aunt Marion's could never have begun to. I don't know what I wound up doing that weekend, but in retrospect I picture the Coast Highway, an open convertible, Jamie, a series of bars with irradiated decks and patios, and women who were very much alive.

Janine passed into oblivion, as did Carmen, Eugenie and Katrinka, and Jamie went off to explore the wide bleeding world. He spent the next eight months dredging the dark corners of countries whose names changed in the interim, the sort of places where people died in the streets as regularly as flowers sprang through the soil and pigeons fouled the monuments to the generalissimo of the month. I worked. I turned over money. Somebody gave me a cat. It shat in a box under the sink and filled the house with a graveyard stink.

Jamie had been back two months before he called to invite me to a party in the vast necropolis of the San Fernando Valley. He'd found a job inculcating moral awareness in the minds of six- and seven-year-olds at the Thomas Jefferson Elementary School in Pacoima five days a week, reserving the weekends for puerile thrills. I didn't realize how much I'd missed him until I saw him standing there on the landing outside my apartment. He looked the same—rangy, bugeyed, a plucked chicken dressed in surfer's clothes—but for his nose. It was inflamed, punished, a dollop of meat grafted to his face by some crazed body snatcher. "What's with the nose?" I said, dispensing with the preliminaries.

He hesitated, working up to a slow grin under the porch light. "Got in a fight in this bar," he said. "Some dude bit it off."

They'd sewed the tip of his nose back in place—or almost in place; it would forever be canted ever so slightly to the left—but that wasn't what excited him.

He moved past me into the living room and fumbled around in his pocket for a minute, then handed me a series of snapshots, close-ups of his face shortly after the operation. I saw the starched white sheets, the nest of pillows, Jamie's triumphant leer and an odd glistening black line drawn across the bridge of his nose where the bandage should have been. The photos caught it from above, beneath, head-on and in profile. Jamie was looking over my shoulder. He didn't say a word, but his breathing was quick and shallow. "So what is it?" I said, swinging round on him. "What's the deal?"

One word, succulent as a flavored ice: "Leeches."

"Leeches?"

He held it a moment, center stage. "That's right, dude, latest thing. They use them to bring back the tiny blood vessels, capillaries and whatnot, the ones they can't tie up themselves. It's the sucking action," and he made a kissing noise. "Suck, suck, suck. I wore them around for three days, grossing the shit out of everybody in the hospital." He was looking into my eyes. Then he shrugged and turned away. "They wouldn't let me take them home, though—that was the pisser."

The party consisted of seven people—three women and four men, including us—sitting around a formal dining-room table eating carnitas and listening to inflammatory rap at a barely audible volume. The hosts were Hilary and Stefan, who had a house within hearing distance of the Ventura Freeway and taught with Jamie in Pacoima. Hilary's sister, Judy, was there, the end product of psychosomatic dieting and the tanning salon, along with her friend Marsha and a man in his forties with sprayed-up hair and a goatee whose name I never did catch. We drank Carta Blanca and shots of Cuervo Gold and ate flan for dessert. The general conversation ran to Jamie's nose, leeches, bowel movements and death. I don't know how we got into it exactly, but after dinner we gravitated toward a pair of mallowy couches the color of a Haas avocado and began our own anthology of final moments. I came back from the bathroom by way of the kitchen with a fresh beer, and Judy, sunk into her tan like something out of a sarcophagus at Karnak, was narrating the story of the two UCLA students, lovers of nature and of each other, who went kayaking off Point Dume.

It was winter, and the water was cold. There'd been a series of storms bred in the Gulf of Alaska and the hills were bleeding mud. There was frost in the Valley, and Judy's mother lost a bougainvillea she'd had for twenty years. That was the fatal ingredient, the cold. The big sharks—the great whites—generally stayed well north of the Southern California coast, up near the Bay Area, the Farallons and beyond, where the seals were. That was what they ate: seals.

In Judy's version, the couple had tied their kayaks together and they were resting, sharing a sandwich, maybe getting romantic—kissing, fondling each other through their wet suits. The shark wasn't supposed to be there. It wasn't supposed to mistake the hulls of their kayaks for the silhouettes of two fat rich hot-blooded basking seals either, but it did. The girl drowned after going faint from blood loss and the chill of the water. They never found her lover.

"Jesus," the older guy said, throwing up his hands. "It's bad enough to have to go, but to wind up as sharkshit—"

Jamie, who'd been blowing softly into the aperture of his beer bottle, looked perturbed. "But how do you know?" he demanded, settling his eyes on Judy. "I mean, were you there? Did you see it, like maybe from another boat?"

She hadn't seen it. She wasn't there. She'd read about it in the paper.

"Uh-uh," Jamie scolded, wagging his finger. "No fair. You have to have seen it, actually been there."

The older guy leaned forward, lit a cigarette and told about an accident he'd witnessed on the freeway. He was coming back from the desert on a Monday night, the end of a three-day weekend, and there was a lot of traffic, but it was moving fast. Four guys in a pickup passed him—three in the cab, the fourth outside in the bed of the truck. A motorcycle stood beside him, lashed upright in the center of the bed. They passed on the right, and they were going at a pretty good clip. Just then, feeling a little bored and left out, the guy in the back of the truck mounted the motorcycle, as a joke. He got up on the seat, leaned into the wind raking over the top of the cab and pretended he was heading into the final lap of the motocross. Unfortunately—and this was the morbid thrill of the exercise; there was always a pathetic adverb attached to the narrative, a "sadly" or "tragically" or "unfortunately" to quicken the audience's blood—unfortunately, traffic was stalled ahead, the driver hit the brakes and the erstwhile motocross champion careened into the cab and went sailing out over the side like an acrobat. And like an acrobat, miraculously, he picked himself up unhurt. The older guy paused, flicked the ash from his cigarette. But unfortunately—and there it was again—the next car hit him in the hips at sixty and flung him under the wheels of a big rig one lane over. Eight more cars hit him before the traffic stopped, and by then there wasn't much left but hair and grease.

Hilary told the story of the "Tiger Man," who stood outside the tiger exhibit at the L.A. Zoo eight hours a day, seven days a week, for an entire year, and then was discovered one morning on the limb of a eucalyptus that hung thirty feet over the open enclosure, in the instant before he lost his balance. She was working the concession stand at the time, a summer job while she was in college, and she heard the people round the tiger pit screaming and the tigers roaring and snarling and thought at first they were fighting. By the time she got there the tiger man was in two pieces and his insides were spread out on the grass like blue strings of sausage. They had to shoot one of the tigers, and that was a shame, a real shame.

Jamie was next. He started in on the story of Renaldo the Great as if it were an eyewitness account. "I was like at this circus in Guadalajara," he said, and my mind began to drift.

It was my turn next, and the only death I could relate, the only one I'd witnessed face to face and not in some voyeuristic video or the pages of *Newsweek* or *Soldier of Fortune*, a true death, the dulling of the eyes, the grip gone lax, the passing from animacy to quietus, I'd never spoken of, not to anyone. The face of it came back to me at odd moments, on waking, starting the car, sitting still in the impersonal dark of the theater before the trailers begin to roll. I didn't want to tell it. I wasn't going to. When Jamie was done, I was going to excuse myself, lock the bathroom door behind me, lean over the toilet and flush it and flush it again till they forgot all about me.

I was sixteen. I was on the swim team at school, bulking up, pushing myself till there was no breath left in my body, and I entertained visions of strutting around the community pool in the summer with a whistle round my neck. I took the Coast Guard–approved lifesaving course and passed with flying colors. It was May, an early searing day, and I wheeled my mother's tubercular Ford out along the ocean to a relatively secluded beach I knew, thinking to do some wind sprints in the sand and pit my hammered shoulders and iron legs against the elemental chop and roll of the Pacific. I never got the chance. Unfortunately. I came down off the hill from the highway and there was a Mexican kid there, nine or ten years old, frantic, in full blind headlong flight, running up the path toward me. His limbs were sticks, his eyes inflamed, and the urgency rode him like a jockey. *"Socorro!"* he cried, the syllables catching in his throat, choking him. *"Socorro!"* he repeated, springing up off his toes, and he had me by the arm in a fierce wet grip, and we were running.

The sand flared with reflected light, the surf broke away to the horizon beneath the blinding ache of the sky, I felt my legs under me, and there it was, the moment, the face of it, lying there in the wash like some elaborate offering to the gulls. A man, big-bellied and dark, his skin slick with the wet, lay facedown in the sand as if he'd been dropped from the clouds. The boy choked and pleaded, too wrought up even for tears, the story I didn't want to hear spewing out of him in a language I couldn't comprehend, and I bent to the man and turned him over.

He wasn't sleeping. No sleep ever looked like that. The eyes were rolled back in his head, white flecks of vomit clung to his lips and stained the dead drooping mustache, and his face was huge, bloated, and if it had been pumped up with gas, as if in a minute's time a week had elapsed and all the rot inside him was straining to get out. There was no one else in sight. I straddled that monstrous head, cleared the dark slab of the tongue, pressed the side of my face to the sand-studded chest. I might have heard something there, faint and deep, the whisper of the sea in a smooth scalloped shell, but I couldn't be sure.

"Mi padre," the boy cried, *"mi padre."* I was a lifesaver. I knew what to do. I knew the moment had come to pinch shut those gaping nostrils, bend my lips to the dark hole beneath the vomit-flecked mustache and breathe life into the inert form beneath me, mouth to mouth.

Mouth to mouth. I was sixteen years old. Five and a half billion of us on the planet, and here was this man, this one, this strange dark individual with the unseeing eyes and lips slick with phlegm, and I couldn't do it. I gave the boy a look, and it was just as if I'd pulled out a handgun and shot him between the eyes, and then I got to my feet in a desperate scramble—think of a kitten plucked from the sleeping nest of its siblings, all four paws lashing blindly at the air—got to my feet, and ran.

My own father died when I was an infant, killed in a plane crash, and though I studied photos of him when I was older, I always pictured him as some faceless, mangled corpse risen from the grave like the son in "The Monkey's Paw." It wasn't a healthy image, but there it was.

My mother was different. I remember her as being in constant motion, chopping things on the drainboard while the washer chugged round, taking business calls—she was an accountant—and at the same time reaching for the sponge to scrub imaginary fingerprints off the white kitchen phone, all in a simultaneous and never-ceasing whirl. She died when I was thirty-two—or "passed on," as she would have had it. I wasn't there. I don't know. But as I've heard it told, digging round the crust of politesse and euphemism like an archaeologist unearthing a bone, there was no passing to it at all, no gentle progress, no easeful journey.

She died in public, of a heart attack. An attack. A seizure. A stroke. Violent and quick, a savage rending in the chest, no passing on, no surcease, no privacy, no dignity, no hope. She was shopping. At Safeway. Five-thirty in the afternoon, the place packed to the walls, the gleaming carts, this item and that, the little choices, seventeen point five cents an ounce as opposed to twenty-two point one. She writhed on the floor. Bit her tongue in two. Died. And all those faces, every one of them alive and condemned, gazing down on her in horror, all those dinners ruined, all that time wasted at the checkout counter.

We all knew Jamie would be the first of us to go. No one doubted it, least of all Jamie himself. He courted it, flaunted it, rented his videos and tried, in his own obsessive, relentless way, to talk it to death. Every time he got in his car, even to drive to the corner for a pack of cigarettes, it was like the start of the Indianapolis 500. He picked fights, though he was thirty years old and should have known better, dove out of airplanes, wrecked a pair of hang gliders. When he took up rock climbing, he insisted on free climbs only—no gear, no ropes, no pitons, only the thin tenuous grip of fingers and toes. I hadn't seen him in two years. He'd long since left L.A., teaching, any sort of steady job, steady income, steady life. He was in Aspen, Dakar, Bangkok. Once in a while I got a dirt-smeared postcard from out of the amazing pipeline, exotic stamps, a mad trembling hasty scrawl of which the only legible term was "dude."

This was the face of Jamie's death: Studio City, a golden winter afternoon,

Jamie on a bench, waiting for the bus. It had rained the week before—the whole week—and the big twisting branches of the eucalyptus trees were sodden and heavy. They have a tendency to shear off, those branches, that's why the city keeps them trimmed back. Or used to, when there were funds for such things. A wind came up, a glorious dry-to-the-bone featherbed wind off the desert; the trees threw out their leaves and danced. And a single branch, wide around as any ordinary tree, parted company with the trunk and obliterated my friend Jamie, crushed him, made dog meat of him.

Am I too graphic? Should I soften it? Euphemize it? Pray to God in His Heaven?

When the phone rang and I heard the long-forgotten but unmistakable tones of an old high school sometime acquaintance—Victor, Victor Cashaw—I knew what he was going to say before he knew it himself. I set down the phone and gazed through the kitchen to the patio, where Linda, my wife, lay stretched out on a rattan sofa, absorbed in a magazine that revealed all the little secrets of nail acrylics and blusher and which towel to use when you wake up at his house. For all I knew, she could have been pregnant. I walked straight out the door, climbed into the car and drove down the block to Video Giant.

In a way, it was perversely gratifying to see that the *100 Faces of Death* series had grown to twenty volumes, but it was Volume IV that I wanted, only that. At home, I slipped quietly into the den—Linda was still there, still on the patio sofa, still motionless but for the beat of her eyes across the page—and inserted the cassette into the slot in the machine. It had been nine years, but I recognized Renaldo as if I'd seen him yesterday, his dilemma eternal, his sweat inexhaustible, his eyes forever glossy. I watched the lovely assistant slide toward panic, focused on the sliver of straw clenched between Renaldo's gleaming teeth. When did he realize? I wondered. Was it now? Now?

I waited till the moment came for him to drop the straw. Poor Renaldo. I froze it right there.

(1992)

LITTLE AMERICA

All he wanted was a quarter, fifty cents, a dollar maybe. The guy was a soft touch, absolutely—the softest. You could see it in the way he clutched the suitcase with his big-knuckled hairy old hands and kept blinking his eyes as if he'd just got out of bed or something. People were spilling out of the train, the usual crush—a scrawny black woman with the pale splash of a birthmark on her face and two angry-looking kids clinging to her dress, a tight little clump of pin-eared teenagers, guys with briefcases and haircuts hustling up the ramp with their chop-chop strides—and nobody had spotted the old man yet. Roger stood motionless, twenty feet from him, and waited. Out of the corner of his eye he saw Rohlich holding out his battered Orioles cap to a polyester wonder with sunglasses like a visor, and he saw the look of annoyance, the firm set of the jaw, the brush-off. Rohlich's voice came back to him like a bad radio over the squeal of the train's brakes and the scrape and clatter of shoes on the pavement and all the birdy jabber of the arriving and departing: "Hey, who bit you in the ass, man? All I wanted was a quarter—"

But the old man, the softest of touches, never moved. He stood rooted to the floor, just in front of the Baltimore sign, his watery old eyes roving over the crowd as if he was an explorer and he'd just discovered a new tribe. The man was old, Roger could see that, seventy at least, and he didn't have a clue as to where he was. Ducking his head and sidling across the floor with the crab walk he always used on touches—never come up to them directly, never freak them— Roger moved in. He was moistening his lips to make his pitch and thinking, *A buck, a buck at least,* when the old man's face suddenly lit with a smile. Roger looked over his shoulder. There was no one there. The old man was smiling at him.

"Hey," Roger crooned, ducking his head again and rolling it back up on his shoulders, "hello. I mean, how you doin'?"

He was wearing a suit, the old man, and nothing too shabby, either—probably mohair or something like that—and his hair was perfectly parted, a plumb line that showed a swath of naked pink scalp beneath. The skin was drawn tight under his cheekbones and there was something strange about his lips, but the milky eyes were focused now. On Roger. "Well, well," the old man said, and his voice was deep and hearty, with an echo to it, "good to see you again, a real pleasure." And he reached out his hand for a shake.

Roger took the hand, a dry old-man's hand, held it a moment and looked into his eyes. "Yeah, sure. Good to see you too." He'd begun to wonder if the guy was mental or whatever—he was probably looking for his nurse. Or his keeper. But that watch—that was a Movado, three hundred bucks, easy—and he had a college ring that looked like something. "Real good," Roger added, for emphasis.

"Yes," the old man said, and he smacked his lips and held the suitcase out for Roger to take. Roger could feel his heart going. This was too good to be true, a fantasy in three dimensions and Technicolor, too. He looked over his shoulder, scanned the place for cops and took the suitcase. "We'll be at the Sheraton again, then?" the old man asked.

Roger took a deep breath, his eyes uncontainable, a whole hive of bees buzzing round inside his chest—*Just get us out of here*—and said, "Yeah, the Sheraton. Of course. Just like last time, right?"

The old man tugged at his nose as if he was afraid it might drop off his face. He was studying his shoes. "Just like last time," he repeated.

One more look around, and then Roger hunched his shoulders over the suitcase and swung toward the street exit. "Follow me," he said.

The train always brought back memories—there was a rhythm to it, a discontinuous flow that seemed to peel back the layers of his mind like growth rings in a tree. One minute he was a boy hunched over the radio with his mother as his father's voice spoke to the whole U.S.A. from out of the clasp of the impermeable dark, and then he was a father himself, his step light on the cobbles of Beacon Hill, and then a grandfather, and finally an old man on a train, staring back at himself in the flicker of the window. The train did that to him. It was like a drug, a narcotic, a memory solution leaking drop by drop into his uncertain veins. And that was funny, too: he was on a train because he didn't like to fly. Richard Evelyn Byrd III, son of the greatest aviator of them all, and he didn't like to fly. Well, he was old now—he'd had enough of flying when he was a boy. A young man, really. He remembered the bright flaring skin of Antarctica, the whole ice shelf shaved close with a razor, felt the jolt of the landing and the hard sharp crack of the skis on the ice just as vividly as if they were beneath him now, saw again the light in his father's eyes and the perfect sangfroid with which he confronted all things, the best and the worst alike.

Leverett had put him on the train in Boston and his daughter-in-law was waiting for him in Washington. He repeated it to himself, aloud, as the car swayed and clicked over the rails. *Leverett. His daughter-in-law. Washington.* But no, that wasn't right. It was that pleasant young man from the Geographic Society, the one who'd been so nice about the rooms at the Sheraton, he was the one. Of course he was. A first-class reception all the way. And that was only as it should be—he, the son of the father, traveling all the way to the nation's capital for the unveiling of the new commemorative stamp honoring the man whose legend would never die, the last of the men in the old mold, the last hero. Yes. And he would talk to them about that—to Walter what's-his-name at the Geographic Society—about his father's museum. He had a reindeer-skin mukluk with him now, in his suitcase, from the 1929 expedition—just to show it to them, just as bait. There was a whole houseful of stuff back in Boston, a shrine, and it was a shame it wasn't on public display, now and permanently—and why not? For lack of a few dollars? They were financing presidents' libraries, weren't they? And paying out welfare and food stamps and whatnot? What would the Byrd Museum take? A million? Two? Well, he had his father's mukluk for them and that was worth a thousand words of pleading and haggling—ten thousand.

And then the train stopped—he felt it lurch at his insides and for an instant he thought he was up in the hard pellucid Antarctic sky all over again, and he even felt the chill of it. But the train stopped, and there was his suitcase, and he got off. Washington, D.C. The capital. He recognized the station, of course he did. But where was his daughter-in-law? Where was the car? Where was that pleasant young fellow from the Geographic Society?

The old man's voice kept nagging at him, a fruity drone that caught and swallowed itself and vomited it all back up again. Why weren't they taking the car? Were they going to walk the whole way? And his daughter-in-law, where was she? But then he'd change the subject as if he wasn't even listening to himself and the next minute he'd be rattling on about what a bracing day it was, just like high summer at the South Pole, ha ha ha, and now he was laughing or choking— it was hard to say which. Roger stayed two paces ahead of him, head down, fingers locked around the handle of the suitcase, and listened to him bluster and wheeze. "It's not much farther," he said. "You'll see your daughter-in-law, she'll be there, and everybody else, too. Here, this way," he said, and he paused to let the old man draw even with him, and then he steered him down the alley out back of the recycling center.

They were six blocks from the station now, and the throttle of Roger's heart had eased back a bit, but still, with every step he had to fight down the impulse to take the suitcase and run. That would have been the easy way. But he would have been a fool to do it and he knew the game was going to be a whole lot richer if he played it right. If he could just get the old geek into the back of the warehouse, a quiet place he knew, where the newspapers were stacked up twenty feet high, he could dig a little deeper. What else did he have besides the watch and ring? A wallet maybe? Cash? Credit cards?

At the door to the place—a big aluminum garage door that was pried up in the corner just enough to allow a no-waist man holding his breath to slip right on through—the old guy surprised him. He didn't balk at all. Just took a glance at the trash blown up against the concrete-block wall as if it was the most ordinary thing in the world, pinched in his gut and followed Roger into the dark echoing vastness of the warehouse.

And that was it: they were safe. It was over. Anything that old man had was Roger's, right on down to his undershorts, and there was nobody to say any different. Roger led him behind a column of newsprint and set the suitcase down. "Here we are," he said, turning to face the old man, "the Sheraton."

"This isn't the Sheraton," the old man said, but he didn't seem upset at all. He was grinning and his eyes were bright. "It isn't the Ritz-Carlton, either. You're pulling my leg, aren't you?"

Roger gave him back the grin. There was a long pause, during which he became aware of the distant beep-beep-beep of a forklift somewhere on the far side of the warehouse. "Yeah, sure," Roger said finally, "I was only joking, sure I was. Can't fool you, huh?" He settled himself down on a stack of newspaper and motioned for the old man to do the same. He lit a cigarette—or the stub of a cigarette he'd picked out of an ashtray at the station. He was taking his time, enjoying himself—there was no reason to rush, or to get violent, either. The old man was out there, no doubt about it.

"So what's in the suitcase?" Roger asked casually, shaking out the match and exhaling through his nostrils.

The old guy had been sitting there, as content as if he was stretched out in his easy chair back at home, smacking his lips and chuckling softly to himself, but now his face went serious. "My father's mukluk."

Roger couldn't help himself. He let out a laugh. "Your father's who?"

"Here, let me show you," the old man said, and Roger let him take the suitcase. He propped it up on his bony old knees, popped the latches and pulled back the lid to reveal a nest of garments—socks, shirts, handkerchiefs and a tweed sportcoat. Rummaging around a moment, he finally came up with what he was looking for—some kind of shoe or boot or something, made out of fur—and held it up for Roger's inspection as if it was Princess Di's tiara.

"So what did you say this was?" Roger asked, taking the thing from him and turning it over in his hand.

"My father's mukluk. For the museum."

Roger didn't know what to make of this. He pulled quietly on his cigarette a moment, then handed the thing back to him with a shrug. "Is it worth anything?"

"Ha!" the old man boomed, and Roger was afraid he was going to get to his feet and try something. "Worth anything? The very mukluk Admiral Byrd wore in Little America? The very one?" The old man drew himself up, cradling the shoe to his chest. "And I tell you something—and you can tell Walter from me," he said, lowering his voice in confidentiality. "I've got plenty more where this came from. Plenty. Notebooks, parkas, reindeer pants and finnesko boots, the sun compass itself—the very one he used to make his fix on the Pole." He rocked back on his haunches. "Yes," he murmured, and he might have been talking to himself, so oblivious was he of Roger and his surroundings, "you tell Walter. All we need is maybe a million. And that's nothing these days. Nothing."

The old man was as crazy as plant life, but that only took you so far, and though Roger had nowhere to go—hadn't had anywhere to go in maybe ten years now—he was getting impatient. "You're absolutely right," he said, cutting him off in the middle of a windy speech about his museum, and he used the phrase as an excuse to lean forward and shake the dry old hand again. But this time, unlike the first, when every eye in the station was on them, Roger expertly slipped the watch over the bony wrist and dropped it in his coat pocket, and the old man didn't know a thing about it.

Or maybe he did. His expression changed suddenly, as if he was trying to remember something. The lines stood out in his face. He looked old. Old and constipated. "I'm thirsty," he suddenly announced.

"Thirsty?" Roger roared, drunk with his own success. "Hell, so am I—what say we share a pint or two, eh? Have a party. Drink to your mukluk and your museum." He stood and patted his pockets theatrically, enjoying himself all over again—he couldn't remember the last time he'd had this much fun. "But I'm a little short. You got any cash? For a drink, I mean?"

Another facial change. The jaw clenched, the eyes caught hold of him. "You're not the young man from the Geographic Society," the old man said quietly.

"The hell I'm not," Roger protested, and he was so frisky all of a sudden he spun around twice and threw out his arms like a tap dancer rising to the finale. "Sure I am, old man, sure I am—but listen, what did you say your name was?"

"Byrd. Richard Evelyn Byrd. The third."

Oh, the solemnity of it, the dignity. He might have been announcing the King of Arabia or something. Roger laughed out loud. "Bird, huh? Tweet-tweet. Bird the Third." Then he let a hint of ugliness creep into his voice, and he stood over the old man now, no mistaking the posture: "I said, you got any cash for a drink, Bird the Third?"

The hand shook, the fingers fumbled in the jacket pocket, and there was the wallet, genuine calfskin, receptacle for the sort of notes and documents that separated people like the old man from Roger and Rohlich and all the other bleary-eyed, rotten-toothed bums and winos curled up on their sheets of cardboard across the city. In that moment, Roger almost felt sorry for the old retard—almost. But in the end, of course, he felt sorrier for himself, and in a quick swipe the wallet was his: five twenties, folded and joined with a paper clip; three ones; a return ticket, Washington to Boston. Photos: an old lady, a kid in a Little League outfit, some white-haired old duffer in a parka. And what was this, what was this? A Visa card, thin as a wafer, shiny as a pot of gold.

He was used to a cocktail before dinner—a Manhattan, generally, shaken, and with a twist instead of a cherry—and a good cabernet or pinot noir with his meal, but this was something he hadn't experienced before, this was something new. The young man passed him the bottle—*Gallo White Port,* the label read, *Alcohol 19% By Volume*—and he took a long gulping swallow that left his chin wet and his stomach burning. He was thirsty, nearly parched, and the liquid—it was cold, it was wet—went down easily, and after the first drink he didn't care what it was. When the bottle was gone, the young man produced another, and though he'd been hungry, though he hadn't eaten anything except the egg-salad sandwich and the apple his son had given him at the Boston station, the hunger faded and he felt better and better as the evening wore on. He was telling the young man about pemmican, how it was the highest-energy food man had yet to devise and how many calories you had to replace daily just to stay alive at seventy-five below, when all at once he felt as lucid as he ever had. He caught himself up so suddenly he almost choked. This wasn't the young man from the Geographic Society, not at all. There was the same fringe of patchy, youthful beard, the startled blue eyes and delicate raw skin, but the nose was all wrong and the mouth had a mean, hurtful look to it. And his clothes—they were in tatters, soaked through with the grease and leavings of the ages, reeking, an unforgivably human stink he could smell from all the way over here. "This isn't Washington," the old man said, understanding now that he'd gotten off at the wrong stop, that he was in some other city altogether, a place he didn't know, understanding that he was lost. "Is it?"

His face shining with drink, his ragged arms flailing at the air, the young man howled with manic glee, kicked at the newspapers heaped up round him and finally had to clutch his ribs tight to stop the laughter. He laughed till he began to cough, and he coughed till he brought something up and spat it on the floor. "You are out there, Bird," he said, straining at each word, and the laughter seized him again. "You are really out there."

So: he was lost. It had happened to him before, two or three times at least. A trick of the mind, that was all, one little mistake—getting off at the wrong stop, turning right instead of left—and the world became a strange and unfathomable place, terrain to explore all over again. He didn't mind. They'd come for him, Leverett and his wife, sweet girl, really, and the grandchildren, they'd find him.

But then a little wedge of concern inserted itself along the fracture line of his psyche, and it became a worry. Who was this man if he wasn't from the Geographic Society, and what did he want? And what was this place? Newspapers. Drifts of them, mountains, a whole continent, and all it was was newsprint.

He took the bottle when it came to him and he took a drink and passed it back, and there was a third member of their party now, another hand interposed between him and the young man who wasn't from the Geographic Society. Matted beard, nose like a bird of prey, eyes frozen into his head, and he didn't know him, not at all, but why did he look so familiar? He felt himself drifting. It was cold, damnably cold, for what—October, wasn't it? "Early winter this year," he murmured, but no one uttered a word in response.

The next time he noticed anything, it was the candle. He must have dozed. But there it was, the candle. A light in the wilderness. The bottle came back to him and the feeble light leapt out suddenly to illuminate the new man's face, and he knew him, knew him as well as he knew his own son and his own father. "You," he said out of the void, "I know you."

There was a low cackle, a dribble of hard-edged laughter from two ravaged throats. "Yeah, we know you, too, Bird the Third," the young man said, and his voice had changed, the tone of it, till everything he said sounded like a schoolyard taunt.

"No," the old man insisted, "not you . . . I mean"—and he looked the newcomer full in the face—"I mean you." The inspiration had flared in his brain, and he knew the man even after all these years, a great man, his father's equal almost, the only other man in the world who'd been to both poles and back again. "You're Roald Amundsen."

The laugh was ugly, almost a bark. The man showed the stubs of his teeth. He took his time, drinking, wiping his mouth with the back of his sleeve. "Shit, man, sure I am," he said, and the other one was laughing again, "and this here, your friend with the bottle, this guy's Santy Claus."

Roger was on a tear. For a full week, seven whole days and maybe more, he didn't know where he was. He hadn't had this much money, all at once, since he'd left New Jersey, when he was a kid living in that lopsided trailer with his mother and stocking the shelves at Waldbaum's. The whole thing with the old man had been unreal, the sort of score everybody dreams about but never makes, never. Oh, sure, zombies like Rohlich would tell you they were hitchhiking once and Madonna gave them a lift or some high roller in Atlantic City handed them a C-note when all they asked for was a quarter, but this was unreal, this *happened*. Those five twenties alone could have kept him flying for a month or more, but of course they'd disappeared, dropped down the hole where all of it went sooner or later—usually sooner. He didn't know where he'd been or what he'd done, but he ached all over, so it must have been good, and he needed a drink so bad he could taste it. Or couldn't taste it. Or whatever.

And shit, it was cold. Too cold for this time of year. Cold and drizzling. When he woke up an hour or so ago he'd found himself on a wet slab of cardboard out back of the fish restaurant the yuppies flocked to—Cicero's—and he didn't know how he'd got there or what he'd done the night before, and his pockets were empty. No loose change. No nothing. He'd wandered over to the mission and passed a short dog around with the black guy they called Hoops, and now he was wet through to the skin and shivering and looking for a benefactor so he could invest in the Gallo Company and warm up where it counted most. He remembered the old guy's watch then, the black Movado, and felt around in his pockets for it. It was gone. He had a further—and dimmer—recollection of pawning it and getting ten bucks for the thing and being all pissed off about it, but then he wasn't so sure—it might have been another watch and another time.

He stayed on the street for a couple hours, it got a whole lot colder, and all he came up with was ninety-two cents. By then, his thirst was driving him crazy, so he bought a can of beer and went over to the warehouse to see who was around and maybe trade up for a hit or two of wine. He saw that somebody had tried to hammer the crease out of the door and that they'd moved a whole shitload of papers out and a whole new shitload in, but other than that nothing had changed. There was nobody around, so he made himself a little igloo out of bundled newspaper, drank his beer in two swallows, and tried to stop shivering for a minute at a time.

At first he didn't hear it—or it didn't register. The place was cavernous, with a ceiling you could fly planes under and walls that went on for a block, and it was noisy, middle of the day, trucks rumbling in and out of the South Street entrance with cans and bottles, and Mr. and Mrs. Nice driving up with Sis and Bud to deliver their neat foursquare string-tied bundles of newspaper. It was noisy and he didn't hear a thing but the muted rumble of all that activity, and he wished five o'clock would come and they'd shut the place down and go home and leave him in peace, but after a while he became aware that somebody was there with him, just up the next aisle, muttering to himself in the low sweet singsong tones of the crackbrained and hopeless. Another bum. Somebody he knew maybe. A man with a short dog and maybe a bite of something scavenged from the top of the bin out back of the supermarket. He felt his spirits lift.

He pushed himself up, keeping an eye out for the watchman, and slipped up the next aisle. The papers had fallen in drifts here, sloppily stacked, and he fought his way through them in the direction of the voice, his harsh ragged breath crystallizing before him. There was a nook carved out of the wall, and he saw the back of a white head, the old withered stalk of a neck, and there he was: Bird the Third.

He was amazed. He would have thought the guy would be long gone, would have found his people, his keeper, whatever. But still, there he was, and for a moment Roger felt a surge of hope. Maybe he had something on him still, something he'd overlooked, some piece of jewelry, a pair of glasses—hell, his clothes even. But then he saw that they'd already got to him. The old retard's suit was gone, and his socks and shoes too. Somebody'd switched on him, and he was dressed in a puke-green janitor's jumpsuit and was missing a shoe—or he'd found a shoe somewhere, a torn greasy old Nike sneaker with the toes ripped out. He was pathetic. A mess. And he wasn't worth anything to anybody.

For a long while, Roger just stood there watching him. The old man was shivering, his arms wrapped around himself like coils, the bare foot discolored and bad-looking. He had that thousand-mile stare on his face, the same one you saw on some of the older guys, the Vietnam vets and whatnot. Roger's brain was working hard, and for a moment he saw himself taking the guy along to the police station and turning him in like a hero and maybe getting a reward from the guy's family or whoever. They had to be looking for him. You don't come from that world, with your haircut and your suitcase and your Movado watch, without somebody looking for you, especially if you're a little soft in the head to begin with.

It was a good idea for about eight seconds, and then it became a whole lot less good, and ten seconds further on it just plain stank. There wouldn't be any reward—maybe for Joe Average and Mr. and Mrs. Nice, maybe for them, but not for the likes of Roger. That's how things worked. There were two worlds operating here, the one where Bird the Third and all the rest of them lived, and this one, the real one, where you slept under things at ankle level and ate the crumbs they gave you. Well, fuck that. Fuck it. It was just like the credit card. He'd tried it on maybe twenty liquor stores, the ones he knew and the ones he didn't, and nobody took him for Bird the Third, no matter how much ID he showed or how hard he tried. Not the way he looked, no way. He was going to trade the thing for a bottle at this one place—*Here, you want the card, Visa Gold? Keep it*—but then the jerk behind the counter got nasty, real nasty, and confiscated the whole business, plastic, ID and all. That's how it was.

He was going to say something, goodbye or thanks for the ride or whatever, but in the end he decided against it. Somewhere, in some deep tunnel of what used to be his reality and was now somebody else's, he even felt a stab of pity and, worse, guilt. But he comforted himself with the thought that if he hadn't been there at the station, somebody else would have, and any way you looked at it Bird the Third would have wound up plucked. In the end, he just shrugged. Then he made his way off through the drifts, thinking maybe he'd just go on down to the station and check out the trains.

Oh, but it was cold. Cold to the bone. And dry. He knew the irony of it all too well—a shelf made of water, frozen and compacted over the howling eons, and not a drop to drink. It was locked in, unavailable, dry as paper. He shifted position and winced. It was his foot. He'd lost all feeling in it there for a while, but now it came back with a vengeance, a thousand hot needles radiating all the way up his leg to the thigh. That's how it was with frostbite. He'd lose his toes, he knew that, but they'd all lost toes, fingers—the great ones—even the tips of their noses. There were continents to explore, unknown corners to make known, and what was a little discomfort compared to the greatness of that?

He thought of his father in the weather shack where he'd wintered alone, the fear of that eternal blackness closing in on him like a fist, alternately freezing and asphyxiating himself on the fumes from the kerosene stove. That was greatness. That was will. That was the indomitable spirit he'd inherited. But still, it was cold, terribly, implacably, unrelentingly cold, and his foot hurt him and he felt himself drifting off to sleep. That was how it happened, that was how they died out here, numbed by the cold, seduced into sleep and forgetfulness.

He stirred, and he fought it. He beat at his thighs, hammered his hands against the meat of his arms, but he couldn't keep it up, and before long he subsided. He tried to call out, but his voice was gone, and besides, it was the coward's way—his father would never have called out. Never. No, he would have gone on into the grip of that polar night, never wavering, never halting, on and on, into the dream.

(1992)

STONES IN MY PASSWAY, HELLHOUND ON MY TRAIL

I got stones in my passway
and my road seems black as night.
I have pains in my heart,
they have taken my appetite.

—Robert Johnson (1914?–1938)

Saturday night. He's playing the House Party Club in Dallas, singing his blues, picking notes with a penknife. His voice rides up to a reedy falsetto that gets the men hooting and then down to a cavernous growl that chills the women, the hard chords driving behind it, his left foot beating like a hammer. The club's patrons—field hands and laborers—pound over the floorboards like the start of the derby, stamping along with him. Skirts fly, hats slump over eyebrows, drinks spill, ironed hair goes wiry. Overhead two dim yellow bulbs sway on their cords; the light is suffused with cigarette smoke, dingy and brown. The floor is wet with spittle and tobacco juice. From the back room, a smell of eggs frying. And beans.

Huddie Doss, the proprietor, has set up a bar in the corner: two barrels of roofing nails and a pine plank. The plank supports a cluster of gallon jugs, a bottle of Mexican rum, a pewter jigger, and three lemons. Robert sits on a stool at the far end of the room, boxed in by men in kerchiefs, women in calico. The men watch his fingers, the women look into his eyes.

It is 1938, dust bowl, New Deal. FDR is on the radio, and somebody in Robinsonville is naming a baby after Jesse Owens. Once, on the road to Natchez, Robert saw a Pierce Arrow and talked about it for a week. Another time he spent six weeks in Chicago and didn't know the World's Fair was going on. Now he plays his guitar up and down the Mississippi, and in Louisiana, Texas, and Arkansas. He's never heard of Hitler and he hasn't eaten in two days.

■ ■ ■

When he was fifteen he watched a poisoned dog tear out its entrails. It was like this:

They were out in the fields when a voice shouted, "Loup's gone mad!" and then he was running with the rest of them, down the slope and across the red dust road, past the shanties and into the gully where they dumped their trash, the dog crying high over the sun and then baying deep as craters in the moon. It was a coonhound, tawny, big-boned, the color of a lion. Robert pushed through the gathering crowd and stood watching as the animal dragged its hindquarters along the ground like a birthing bitch, the ropy testicles strung out behind. It was mewling now, the high-pitched cries sawing away at each breath, and then it was baying again, howling death until the day was filled with it, their ears and the pits of their stomachs soured with it. One of the men said in a terse, angry voice, "Go get Turkey Nason to come on down here with his gun," and a boy detached himself from the crowd and darted up the rise.

It was then that the dog fell heavily to its side, ribs heaving, and began to dig at its stomach with long racing thrusts of the rear legs. There was yellow foam on the black muzzle, blood bright in the nostrils. The dog screamed and dug, dug until the flesh was raw and its teeth could puncture the cavity to get at the gray intestine, tugging first at a bulb of it and then fastening on a lank strand like dirty wash. There was no sign of the gun. The woman beside Robert began to cry, a sound like crumpling paper. Then one of the men stepped in with a shovel in his hand. He hit the dog once across the eyes and the animal lunged for him. The shovel fell twice more and the dog stiffened, its yellow eyes gazing round the circle of men, the litter of bottles and cans and rusted machinery, its head lolling on the lean, muscular neck, poised for one terrible moment, and then it was over. Afterward Robert came close: to look at the frozen teeth, the thin, rigid limbs, the green flies on the pink organs.

Between sets Robert has been out back with a girl named Beatrice, and Ida Mae Doss, Huddie's daughter, is not happy about it. As he settles back down on the stool and reaches for his guitar, he looks up at the pine plank, the barrels, Ida Mae stationed behind the bar. She is staring at him—cold, hard, her eyes like razors. What can he do? He grins, sheepish. But then Beatrice steams in, perfumed in sweat, the blue print shift clinging like a wet sheet. She sashays through the knot of men milling around Robert and says, "Why don't you play something sweet?" Robert pumps the neck of the guitar, strikes the strings twice, and then breaks into "Phonograph Blues":

> *And we played it on the sofa and we played it 'side the wall,*
> *But, boys, my needle point got rusty and it will not play at all.*

The men nudge one another. Ida Mae looks daggers. Beatrice flounces to the center of the floor, raises her arms above her head, and begins a slow grinding shuffle to the pulse of the guitar.

No one knows how Robert got his guitar. He left Letterman's farm when he was sixteen, showed up a year and a half later with a new Harmony Sovereign. He walked into the Rooster Club in Robinsonville, Mississippi, and leaned against the wall while Walter Satter finished out his set. When Satter stepped up to the bar, Robert was at his elbow. "I heard your record," Robert said. He was short, skinny, looked closer to twelve than eighteen.

"You like it?"

"Taught me a lot."

Satter grinned.

"Mind if I sit in on the next set?"

"Sure—if you think you can go on that thing."

Robert sat in. His voice was a shower, his guitar a storm. The sweet slide leads cut the atmosphere like lightning at dusk. Satter played rhythm behind him for a while, then stepped down.

The lemons are pulp, the rum decimated, jugs lighter. Voices drift through the open door, fireflies perforate the dark rafters. It is hot as a jungle, dark as a cave. The club's patrons are quieter now—some slouched against the walls, others leaning on the bar, their fingers tapping like batons. Beatrice is an exception. She's still out in the center of the floor, head swaying to the music, heels kicking, face bright with perspiration—dancing. A glass in her hand. But suddenly she lurches to the left, her leg buckles, and she goes down. There is the shrill of breaking glass, and then silence. Robert has stopped playing. The final chord rings in the air, decapitated; a sudden unnatural silence filters through the smoke haze, descending like a judgment. Robert sets the guitar across the stool and shuffles out to where Beatrice lies on the floor. She rolls heavily to her side, laughing, muttering to herself. Robert catches her under the arms, helps her up, and guides her to a chair in the corner—and then it's over. The men start joking again, the bar gets busy, women tell stories, laugh.

Beatrice slumps in the chair, chin to chest, and begins to snore—delicate, jagged, the purr of a cat. Robert grins and pats her head—then turns to the bar. Ida Mae is there, measuring out drinks. Her eyes are moist. Robert squeezes the husk of a lemon over his glass, half fills it with rum, and presses a nickel into her palm. "What you got cooking, Ida Mae?" he says.

A thin silver chain hangs between her breasts, beneath the neckline of her cotton dress. It is ornamented with a wooden guitar pick, highly varnished, the shape of a seed.

"Got eggs," she says. "And beans."

Lubbock, Natchez, Pascagoula, Dallas, Eudora, Rosedale, Baton Rouge, Memphis, Friars Point, Vicksburg, Jonesboro, Mooringsport, Edwards, Chattanooga, Rolling Fork, Commerce, Itta Bena. Thelma, Betty Mae, Adeline, Harriet, Bernice, Ida Bell, Bertha Lee, Winifred, Maggie, Willie Mae. "Robert been driving too hard," people said. "Got to stumble."

In 1937 Franco laid siege to Madrid, the Japanese invaded Nanking, Amelia Earhart lost herself in the Pacific, and Robert made a series of recordings for Victrix Records. He was twenty-three at the time. Or twenty-two. A man from Victrix sent him train fare to New Orleans in care of the High Times Club in Biloxi. Robert slit the envelope with his penknife and ran his thumb over the green-and-silver singles while the bartender read him the letter. Robert was ecstatic. He kissed women, danced on the tables, bought a Havana cigar—but the bills whispered in his palm and he never made it to the station. A week later the man sent him a nonrefundable one-way ticket.

The man was waiting for him when the train pulled into the New Orleans station. Robert stepped off the day coach with his battered Harmony Sovereign and a cardboard valise. The stink of kerosene and coal blistered the air. Outside, automobiles stood at the curb like a dream of the twentieth century. "Walter Fagen," the man said, holding out his hand. Robert looked up at the wisps of white-blond hair, the pale irises, the red tie, and then down at a torn ticket stub on the platform. "Pleased to meet you," he mumbled. One hand was on the neck of the guitar, the other in his pocket. "Go ahead, shake," Fagen said. Robert shook.

Fagen took him to a boardinghouse, paid the big kerchief-headed woman at the door, instructed Robert to come around to the Arlington Hotel in the morning. Then he gave him a two-dollar advance. Three hours later Fagen's dinner was interrupted by a phone call from the New Orleans police: Robert was being held for disorderly conduct. Fagen hired a taxi, drove to the jailhouse, laid five silver dollars on the desk, and walked out with his recording artist. Robert's right eye was swollen closed; the guitar was gone. Robert had nothing to say. When the taxi stopped in front of the boardinghouse, Fagen gave him thirty-five cents for breakfast and told him to get a good night's sleep.

Back at the Arlington, Fagen took a seat in the dining room and reordered. He was sipping a gimlet when a boy paged him to the phone. It was Robert. "I'm lonesome," he said.

"Lonesome?"

"Yeah—there's a woman here wants forty cents and I'm a nickel short."

The voices wash around her like birds at dawn, a Greek chorus gone mad. Smoke and stale sweat, the smell of lemon. She grits her teeth. "Give me a plate of it, then, girl," he is saying. "Haven't eat in two days." Then she's in the back room, stirring beans, cracking eggs, a woman scorned. The eggs, four of them, stare up at her like eyes. Tiny embryos. On the shelf above the stove: can of pepper, saltcellar, a knife, the powder they use for rats and roaches.

Agamemnon, watch out!

Robert's dream is thick with the thighs of women, the liquid image of songs sung and songs to come, bright wire wheels and sloping fenders, swamps, trees, power lines, and the road, the road spinning out like string from a spool, like veins, blood and heart, distance without end, without horizon.

It is the last set. Things are winding down. Beatrice sags in the chair, skirt pulled up over her knees, her chest rising and falling with the soft rhythm of sleep. Beside her, a man in red suspenders presses a woman against the wall. Robert watches the woman's hands like dark animals on the man's hips. Earlier, a picker had been stabbed in the neck after a dispute over dice or women or liquor, and an old woman had fallen, drunk, and cut her head on the edge of a bench. But now things are winding down. Voices are hushed, cigarettes burn unattended, moonlight limns the windows.

Robert rests the guitar on his knee and does a song about a train station, a suitcase, and the eyes of a woman. His voice is mournful, sad as a steady rain, the guitar whining above it like a cry in the distance. "Yes!" they call out. "Robert!" Somebody whistles. Then they applaud, waves on the rocks, smoke rising as if from a rent in the earth. In response, the guitar reaches low for the opening bars of Robert's signature tune, his finale, but there is something wrong—the chords staggering like a seizure, stumbling, finally breaking off cold.

Cramps. A spasm so violent it jerks his fingers from the strings. He begins again, his voice quavering, shivered: "Got to keep moving, got to keep moving, / Hellbound on my trail." And then suddenly the voice chokes off, gags, the guitar slips to the floor with a percussive shock. His bowels are on fire. He stands, clutches his abdomen, drops to hands and knees. "Boy's had too much of that Mexican," someone says. He looks up, a sword run through him, panting, the shock waves pounding through his frame, looks up at the pine plank, the barrels, the cold, hard features of the girl with the silver necklace in her hand. Looks up, and snarls.

(1977)

THE HIT MAN

Early Years

The Hit Man's early years are complicated by the black bag that he wears over his head. Teachers correct his pronunciation, the coach criticizes his attitude, the principal dresses him down for branding preschoolers with a lit cigarette. He is a poor student. At lunch he sits alone, feeding bell peppers and salami into the dark slot of his mouth. In the hallways, wiry young athletes snatch at the black hood and slap the back of his head. When he is thirteen he is approached by the captain of the football team, who pins him down and attempts to remove the hood. The Hit Man wastes him. Five years, says the judge.

Back on the Street

The Hit Man is back on the street in two months.

First Date

The girl's name is Cynthia. The Hit Man pulls up in front of her apartment in his father's hearse. (The Hit Man's father, whom he loathes and abominates, is a mortician. At breakfast the Hit Man's father had slapped the cornflakes from his son's bowl. The son threatened to waste his father. He did not, restrained no doubt by considerations of filial loyalty and the deep-seated taboos against patricide that permeate the universal unconscious.)

Cynthia's father has silver sideburns and plays tennis. He responds to the Hit Man's knock, expresses surprise at the Hit Man's appearance. The Hit Man takes Cynthia by the elbow, presses a twenty into her father's palm, and disappears into the night.

Father's Death

At breakfast the Hit Man slaps the cornflakes from his father's bowl. Then wastes him.

Mother's Death

The Hit Man is in his early twenties. He shoots pool, lifts weights and drinks milk from the carton. His mother is in the hospital, dying of cancer or heart disease. The priest wears black. So does the Hit Man.

First Job

Porfirio Buñoz, a Cuban financier, invites the Hit Man to lunch. I hear you're looking for work, says Buñoz.

That's right, says the Hit Man.

Peas

The Hit Man does not like peas. They are too difficult to balance on the fork.

Talk Show

The Hit Man waits in the wings, the white slash of a cigarette scarring the midnight black of his head and upper torso. The makeup girl has done his mouth and eyes, brushed the nap of his hood. He has been briefed. The guest who precedes him is a pediatrician. A planetary glow washes the stage where the host and the pediatrician, separated by a potted palm, cross their legs and discuss the little disturbances of infants and toddlers.

After the station break the Hit Man finds himself squeezed into a director's chair, white lights in his eyes. The talk-show host is a baby-faced man in his early forties. He smiles like God and all His Angels. Well, he says. So you're a hit man. Tell me—I've always wanted to know—what does it feel like to hit someone?

Death of Mateo María Buñoz

The body of Mateo María Buñoz, the cousin and business associate of a prominent financier, is discovered down by the docks on a hot summer morning. Mist rises from the water like steam, there is the smell of fish. A large black bird perches on the dead man's forehead.

Marriage

Cynthia and the Hit Man stand at the altar, side by side. She is wearing a white satin gown and lace veil. The Hit Man has rented a tuxedo, extra-large, and a silk-lined black-velvet hood.

. . . Till death do you part, says the priest.

Moods

The Hit Man is moody, unpredictable. Once, in a luncheonette, the waitress brought him the meatloaf special but forgot to eliminate the peas. There was a spot of gravy on the Hit Man's hood, about where his chin should be. He looked up at the waitress, his eyes like pins behind the triangular slots, and wasted her.

Another time he went to the track with $25, came back with $1,800. He stopped at a cigar shop. As he stepped out of the shop a wino tugged at his sleeve and solicited a quarter. The Hit Man reached into his pocket, extracted the $1,800 and handed it to the wino. Then wasted him.

First Child

A boy. The Hit Man is delighted. He leans over the edge of the playpen and molds the tiny fingers around the grip of a nickel-plated derringer. The gun is loaded with blanks—the Hit Man wants the boy to get used to the noise. By the time he is four the boy has mastered the rudiments of Tae Kwon Do, can stick a knife in the wall from a distance of ten feet and shoot a moving target with either hand. The Hit Man rests his broad palm on the boy's head. You're going to make the Big Leagues, Tiger, he says.

Work

He flies to Cincinnati. To L.A. To Boston. To London. The stewardesses get to know him.

Half an Acre and a Garage

The Hit Man is raking leaves, amassing great brittle piles of them. He is wearing a black T-shirt, cut off at the shoulders, and a cotton work hood, also black. Cynthia is edging the flower bed, his son playing in the grass. The Hit Man waves to his neighbors as they drive by. The neighbors wave back.

When he has scoured the lawn to his satisfaction, the Hit Man draws the smaller leaf-hummocks together in a single mound the size of a pickup truck. Then he bends to ignite it with his lighter. Immediately, flames leap back from the leaves, cut channels through the pile, engulf it in a ball of fire. The Hit Man stands back, hands folded beneath the great meaty biceps. At his side is the three-headed dog. He bends to pat each of the heads, smoke and sparks raging against the sky.

Stalking the Streets of the City

He is stalking the streets of the city, collar up, brim down. It is late at night. He stalks past department stores, small businesses, parks, and gas stations. Past apartments, picket fences, picture windows. Dogs growl in the shadows, then slink away. He could hit any of us.

Retirement

A group of businessman-types—sixtyish, seventyish, portly, diamond rings, cigars, liver spots—throws him a party. Porfirio Buñoz, now in his eighties, makes a speech and presents the Hit Man with a gilded scythe. The Hit Man thanks him, then retires to the lake, where he can be seen in his speedboat, skating out over the blue, hood rippling in the breeze.

Death

He is stricken, shrunken, half his former self. He lies propped against the pillows at Mercy Hospital, a bank of gentians drooping round the bed. Tubes run into the hood at the nostril openings, his eyes are clouded and red, sunk deep behind the triangular slots. The priest wears black. So does the Hit Man.

On the other side of town the Hit Man's son is standing before the mirror of a shop that specializes in Hit Man attire. Trying on his first hood.

(1977)

NOT A LEG TO STAND ON

Calvin Tompkins is just lifting the soda bottle to his lips when the German-made car brakes in front of the house and the woman with the mean little eyes and the big backside climbs out in a huff. "Where'd you get that?" she demands, shoving through the hinge-sprung gate on feet so small it's astonishing they can support her. The old man doesn't know what to say. He can tell you the dimensions of the biggest hot dog ever made or Herbert Hoover's hat size, but sometimes, with the rush of things, it's all he can do to hold up his end of a conversation. Now he finds himself entirely at a loss as the big woman sways up the rotted steps to the rot-gutted porch and snatches the bottle out of his hand.

"Patio soda!" The way she says it is an indictment, her voice pinched almost to a squeal and the tiny feet stamping in outrage. "I am the only one that sells it for ten miles around here, and I want to know where you got it. Well?"

Frail as an old rooster, Calvin just gapes up at her.

She stands there a moment, her lips working in rage, the big shoulders, bosom, and belly poised over the old man in the wheelchair like an avalanche waiting to happen, then flings the bottle down in disgust. "*Mein Gott,* you people!" she says, and suddenly her eyes are wet.

It is then that Ormand, shadowed by Lee Junior, throws back the screen door with a crash and lurches out onto the porch. He's got a black bottle of German beer in his hand and he's unsteady on his feet. "What the hell's goin' on here?" he bellows, momentarily losing his footing in the heap of rags, cans, and bottles drifted up against the doorframe like detritus. Never graceful, he catches himself against the near post and sets the whole porch trembling, then takes a savage swipe at a yellow Kmart oilcan and sends it rocketing out over the railing and up against the fender of the rusted, bumper-blasted Mustang that's been sitting alongside the house as long as the old man can remember.

"You know what is going on," the woman says, holding her ground. "You know," she repeats, her accent thickening with her anger, "because you are a thief!"

Ormand is big, unshaven, dirty. At twenty-two, he already has a beer gut. "Hell I am," he says, slurring his words, and the old man realizes he's been helping himself to the pain pills again. Behind Ormand, Lee Junior bristles. He too, Calvin now sees, is clutching a black bottle.

"Thief!" the woman shouts, and then she begins to cry, her face splotched with red, the big bosom heaving. Watching her, the old man feels a spasm of alarm: why, she's nothing but a young girl. Thirty years old, if that. For a keen, sharp instant her grief cuts at him like a saw, but then he finds himself wondering how she got so fat. Was it all that blood sausage and beer she sells? All that potato salad?

Now Lee Junior steps forward. "You got no right to come around here and call us names, lady—this is private property." He is standing two feet from her and he is shouting. "Why don't you get your fat ass out of here before you get hurt, huh?"

"Yeah," Ormand spits, backing him up. "You can't come around here harassing this old man—he's a veteran, for Christ's sake. You keep it up and I'm going to have to call the police on you."

In that instant, the woman comes back to life. The lines of her face bunch in hatred, the lips draw back from her teeth, and suddenly she's screaming. *"You call the police on me!?* Don't make me laugh." Across the street a door slams. People are beginning to gather in their yards and driveways, straining to see what the commotion is about. "Pigs! Filth!" the woman shrieks, her little feet dancing in anger, and then she jerks back her head and spits down the front of Lee Junior's shirt.

The rest is confusion. There's a struggle, a stew of bodies, the sound of a blow, Lee Junior gives the woman a shove, somebody slams into Calvin's wheelchair, Ormand's voice cracks an octave, and the woman cries out in German; the next minute Calvin finds himself sprawled on the rough planks, gasping like a carp out of water, and the woman is sitting on her backside in the dirt at the foot of the stairs.

No one helps Calvin up. His arm hurts where he threw it out to break his fall, and his hip feels twisted or something. He lies very still. Below him, in the dirt, the woman just sits there mewling like a baby, her big lumpy yellow thighs exposed, her socks gray with dust, the little doll's shoes worn through the soles and scuffed like the seats on the Number 56 bus.

"Get the hell out of here!" Lee Junior roars, shaking his fist. "You . . . you fat-assed"—here he pauses for the hatred to rise up in him, his face coiled round the words—"Nazi bitch!" And then, addressing himself to Mrs. Tuxton's astonished face across the street, and to Norm Cramer, the gink in the Dodgers cap, and all the rest of them, he shouts: "And what are you lookin' at, all of you? Huh?"

Nobody says a word.

Two days later Calvin is sitting out on the porch with a brand-new white plaster cast on his right forearm, watching the sparrows in the big bearded palm across the way and rehearsing numbers by way of mental exercise—5,280 feet in a mile, eight dry quarts in a peck—when Ormand comes up round the side of the house with a satchel of tools in his hand. "Hey, Calvin, what's doin'?" he says, clapping a big moist hand on the old man's shoulder. "Feel like takin' a ride?"

Calvin glances down at his cast with its scrawl of good wishes—"Boogie Out!" Lee Junior had written—and then back at Ormand. He is thinking, suddenly and unaccountably, of the first time he laid eyes on the Orem place. Was it two years ago already? Yes, two years, come fall. He'd been living with that Mexicano family out in the Valley—rice and beans, rice and beans, till he thought he'd turn into a human burrito or blow out his insides or something—and then his daughter had found Jewel's ad in the paper and gone out and made the arrangements.

"What do you say?" Ormand is leaning over him now. "Calvin?"

"A ride?" Calvin says finally. "Where to?"

Ormand shrugs. "Oh, you know: around."

Don't expect anything fancy she'd told him, as if he had anything to say about it. But when they got there and were actually sitting in the car out front where they had a good view of the blistered paint, dead oleanders, trash-strewn yard, and reeling porch, she was the one who got cold feet. She started in on how maybe he wouldn't like these people and how maybe she ought to look a little further before they decided, but then *bang!* went the screen door and Big Lee and Ormand ambled down the steps in T-shirts and engineer boots. Big Lee folded a stick of Red Man and tucked it up alongside his teeth, Ormand was clutching a can of Safeway beer like it was grafted onto him, and both of them were grinning as if they'd just shared a dirty joke in the back of the church. And then Big Lee was reaching his callused hand in through the window to shake with Calvin. Glad to meet you, neighbor, he murmured, turning his head to spit.

Shit, Calvin had said, swiveling round to look his daughter in the eye, I like these people.

Two minutes later they're out in the street, Ormand swinging back the door of his primer-splotched pickup, the pale bulb of Mrs. Tuxton's face just visible beyond the curtains over her kitchen sink. Even with Ormand's help, the old man has trouble negotiating the eight-inch traverse from the wheelchair to the car seat, what with his bum leg and fractured forearm and the general debility that comes of living so long, but once they're under way he leans back, half closes his eyes, and gives himself up to the soothing wash of motion. Trees flit overhead, streaks of light and moving shadow, and then an open stretch and the sun, warm as a hand, on the side of his face.

Yes, he likes these people. They might have their faults—Ormand and Lee Junior are drunk three-quarters of the time (that is, whenever they're not sleeping) and they gobble up his pain pills like M&Ms—but deep down he feels more kinship with them than he does with his own daughter. At least they'll talk to him and treat him like a human being instead of something that's been dead and dug up. Hell, they even seem to like him. When they go out visiting or whatever it is they do—house to house, dusty roads, day and night—they always want to take him along. So what if he has to sit there in the car sometimes for an hour or more? At least he's out of the house.

When he looks up, they're in a strange neighborhood. Stucco houses in shades of mustard and aquamarine, shabby palms, campers and trailers and pickups parked out front. Ormand has got a fresh beer and his eyes are shrunk back in his head. He stabs at the radio buttons and a creaky fiddle comes whining through the dashboard speaker. "You been noddin' out there a bit, huh, Calvin?" he says.

The old man's teeth hurt him all of a sudden, hurt him something fierce, so that the water comes to his eyes—he wants to cry out with the pain of it, but his arm begins to throb in counterpoint and pretty soon his hip starts kicking up where he twisted it and all he can do is just clamp his jaws shut in frustration. But when the car rolls to a stop beneath a dusty old oak and Ormand slips out the door with his satchel and says, "Just hang out here for a bit, okay, Calvin? I'll be right back," the old man finds the image of the German woman rising up in his mind like a river-run log that just won't stay down, and his voice comes back to him. "Where *did* you get that soda, anyways?" he says.

"I tell you, Dad, I just don't trust these people. Now, you look what's happened to your arm, and then there's this whole business of Lee going to jail—"

Calvin is sitting glumly over a bowl of tepid corn chowder in the Country Griddle, toying with his spoon and sucking his teeth like a two-year-old. Across the bright Formica table, his daughter breaks off her monologue just long enough to take a sip of coffee and a quick ladylike nip at her tuna on rye. She's wearing an off-white dress, stockings, false eyelashes, and an expression about midway between harried and exasperated.

"He was innocent," Calvin says.

His daughter gives him an impatient look. "Innocent or not, Dad, the man is in jail—in prison—for armed robbery. And I want to know who's paying the bills and taking care of the place—I want to know who's looking after you."

"Armed robbery? The man had a screwdriver in his hand, for Christ's sake—"

"Sharpened."

"What?"

"I said it was a sharpened screwdriver."

For a moment, Calvin says nothing. He fiddles with the salt shaker and watches his daughter get the Dad-you-know-you're-not-supposed-to look on her face, and then, when he's got her off guard, he says, "Jewel."

"Jewel? Jewel what?"

"Takes care of the place. Pays the bills. Feeds me." And she does a hell of a job of it too, he's about to add, when a vast and crushing weariness suddenly descends on him. Why bother? His daughter's up here on her day off to see about his arm and snoop around till she finds something rotten. And she'll find it, all right, because she's nothing but a sack of complaints and suspicions. Her ex-husband is second only to Adolf Hitler for pure maliciousness, her youngest is going to a psychiatrist three times a week, and her oldest is flunking out of college, she's holding down two jobs to pay for the station wagon, figure-skating coaches, and orthopedic shoes, and her feet hurt. How could she even begin to understand what he feels for these people?

"Yes, and she drinks too. And that yard—it looks like something out of 'Li'l Abner.' " She's waving her sandwich now, gesturing in a way that reminds him of her mother, and it makes him angry, it makes him want to throw her across his knee and paddle her. "Dad," she's saying, "listen. I've heard of this place up near me—a woman I know whose mother is bedridden recommended it and she—"

"A nursing home."

"It's called a 'gerontological care facility' and it'll cost us seventy-five dollars more a month, but for my peace of mind—I mean, I just don't feel right about you being with these people anymore."

He bends low over his chowder, making a racket with the spoon. So what if Jewel drinks? (And she does, he won't deny it—red wine mainly, out of the gallon jug—and she's not afraid to share it, either.) Calvin drinks too. So does the president. And so does the bossy, tired-looking woman sitting across the table from him. It doesn't mean a damn thing. Even with Lee in jail, even with her two big out-of-work nephews sitting down at the table and eating like loggers or linebackers or something, Jewel manages. And with no scrimping, either. Eggs for breakfast, bologna and American cheese on white for lunch with sweet butter pickles, and meat—real meat—for supper. Damn Mexicans never gave him meat, that's for shit sure.

"Dad? Did you hear what I said? I think it's time we made a change."

"I'm going nowhere," he says, and he means it, but already the subject has lost interest for him. Thinking of Jewel has got him thinking of her ham hocks and beans, and thinking of ham hocks and beans has got him thinking of Charlottesville, Virginia, and a time before he lost his leg when he and Bobbie Bartro were drunk on a bottle of stolen bourbon and racing up the street to his mother's Sunday-afternoon sit-down dinner, where they slid into their seats and passed the mashed potatoes as if there were nothing more natural in the world. Off on the periphery of his consciousness he can hear his daughter trumpeting away, stringing together arguments, threatening and cajoling, but it makes no difference. His mind is made up.

"Dad? Are you listening?"

Suddenly the lights are blinding him, the jukebox is scalding his ears, and the weariness pressing down on him like a truckload of cement. "Take me home, Berta," he says.

He wakes to darkness, momentarily disoriented. The dreams have come at him like dark swooping birds, lifting him, taking him back, dropping him in scene after scene of disorder, threat, and sorrow. All of a sudden he's sunk into the narrow hospital bed in San Bernardino, fifty years back, his head pounding with the ache of concussion, his left leg gone at the knee. *What kind of motorcycle was it?* the doctor asks. And then he's in Bud's Grocery and General Store in Charlottesville, thirteen years old, and he's got a salami in one hand and a sixty-pound-pull hunting bow in the other and no money, and he's out the door and running before Bud can even get out from behind the counter. And then finally, in the moment of waking, there's Ruth, his wife, down on the kitchen floor in a spasm, hurt bad somewhere down in the deep of her. But wait: somehow all of a sudden she's grown fat, rearranged her features and the color of her hair— somehow she's transformed herself into the Patio-soda woman. Big, big, big. Thighs like buttermilk. *You people,* she says.

There's a persistent thumping in the floorboards, like the beat of a colossal heart, and the occasional snatch of laughter. He hears Ormand's voice, Jewel's. Then another he doesn't recognize. Ormand. Lee Junior. Laughter. Pushing himself up to a sitting position, he swings his legs around and drops heavily into the wheelchair. Then he fumbles for his glasses—1:30, reads the dimly glowing face of the clock—and knocks over the cup with his partial plate in it. He's wearing his striped pajamas. No need to bother about a bathrobe.

"Hey, Calvin—what's happening!" Ormand shouts as the old man wheels himself into the living room. Lee Junior and Jewel are sitting side by side on the couch; the Mexican kid—Calvin can never remember his name—is sprawled on the floor smoking a big yellow cigarette, and Ormand is hunched over a bottle of tequila in the easy chair. All three color TVs are on and the hi-fi is scaring up some hellacious caterwauling nonsense that sets his teeth on edge. "Come on in and join the party," Jewel says, holding up a bottle of Spañada.

For a moment he just sits there blinking at them, his eyes adjusting to the light. The numbers are in his head again—batting averages, disaster tolls, the dimensions of the Grand Coulee Dam—and he doesn't know what to say. "C'mon, Calvin," Ormand says, "loosen up."

He feels ridiculous, humbled by age. Bony as a corpse in the striped pajamas, hair fluffed out like cotton balls pasted to his head, glasses glinting in the lamplight. "Okay," he murmurs, and Jewel is up off the couch and handing him a paper cup of the sweetened red wine.

"You hear about Rod Chefalo?" the Mexican says.

"No," says Lee Junior.

"Ormand, you want to put on a movie or something I can watch?" Jewel says. One TV set, the biggest one, shows an auto race, little cars plastered with motor-oil stickers whizzing round a track as if in a children's game; the other two feature brilliantined young men with guitars.

"Drove that beat Camaro of his up a tree out in the wash."

"No shit? He wind up in the hospital or what?"

"What do you want to watch, Aunt Jewel? You just name it. I don't give a shit about any of this."

After a while, Calvin finds himself drifting. The wine smells like honeydew melons and oranges and tastes like Kool-Aid, but it gives him a nice little burn in the stomach. His daughter's crazy, he's thinking as the wine settles into him. These are good people. Nice to sit here with them in the middle of the night instead of being afraid to leave his room, like when he was with those Mexicans, or having some starched-up bitch in the nursing home dousing the lights at eight.

"You know she went to the cops?" Lee Junior's face is like something you'd catch a glimpse of behind a fence.

"The cops?" The Mexican kid darts his black eyes round the room, as if he expects the sheriff to pop up from behind the couch. "What do you mean, she went to the cops?"

"They can't do a thing," Ormand cuts in. "Not without a search warrant."

"That's right." Lee Junior reaches for his can of no-name beer, belching softly and thumping a fist against his sternum. "And to get one they need witnesses. And I tell you, any of these shitheels on this block come up against me, they're going to regret it. Don't think they don't know it either."

"That fat-assed Kraut," Ormand says, but he breaks into a grin, and then he's laughing. Lee Junior joins him and the Mexican kid makes some sort of wise-crack, but Calvin misses it. Jewel, her face noncommittal, gets up to change the channel.

"You know what I'm thinkin'?" Ormand says, grinning still. Jewel's back is turned, and Calvin can see the flicker of green and pink under her right arm as she flips through the channels on the big TV. Lee Junior leans forward and the Mexican kid waves the smoke out of his eyes and props himself up on one elbow, a cautious little smile creeping into the lower part of his face. "What?" the Mexican kid says.

Calvin isn't there, he doesn't exist, the cardboard cup is as insubstantial as an eggshell in his splotched and veiny hand as he lifts it, trembling, to his lips.

"I'm thinking maybe she could use another lesson."

■ ■ ■

In the morning, early, Calvin is awakened by the crackle and stutter of a short-wave radio. His throat is dry and his head aches, three cups of wine gone sour in his mouth and leaden on his belly. With an effort, he pushes himself up and slips on his glasses. The noise seems to be coming from outside the house—static like a storm in the desert, tinny voices all chopped and diced. He parts the curtains.

A police cruiser sits at the curb, engine running, driver's door swung open wide. Craning his neck, Calvin can get a fix on the porch and the figures of Ormand—bare chest and bare feet—and a patrolman in the uniform of the LAPD. "So what's this all about?" Ormand is saying.

The officer glances down at the toes of his boots, and then looks up and holds Ormand's gaze. "A break-in last night at the European Deli around the corner, 2751 Commerce Avenue. The proprietor"—and here he pauses to consult the metal-bound notepad in his hand—"a Mrs. Eva Henckle, thinks that you may have some information for us. . . ."

Ormand's hair is in disarray; his cheeks are dark with stubble. "No, Officer," he says, rubbing a hand over his stomach. "I'm sorry, but we didn't hear a thing. What time was that, did you say?"

The patrolman is young, no more than two or three years older than Ormand. In fact, he looks a bit like Ormand—if Ormand were to lose thirty pounds, stand up straight, get himself a shave, and cut the dark scraggly hair that trails down his back like something stripped from an animal. Ignoring the questions, the patrolman produces a stub of pencil and asks one of his own. "You live here with your aunt, is that right?"

"Uh-huh."

"And a brother, Leland Orem, Junior—is that right?"

"That's right," Ormand says. "And like I said, we were all in last night and didn't hear a thing."

"Mother deceased?"

"Yeah."

"And your father?"

"What's that got to do with the price of beans?" Ormand's expression has gone nasty suddenly, as if he's bitten into something rotten.

For a moment, the patrolman is silent, and Calvin becomes aware of the radio again: the hiss of static, and a bored, disembodied voice responding to a second voice, equally bored and disembodied. "Do you know a Jaime Luis Torres?" the patrolman asks.

Ormand hesitates, shuffling his feet on the weathered boards a minute before answering. His voice is small. "Yes," he says.

"Have you seen him recently?"

"No," Ormand lies. His voice is a whisper.

"What was that?"

"I said no."

There is another pause, the patrolman looking into Ormand's eyes, Ormand looking back. "Mrs. Henckle's place has been burglarized four times in the last three months. She thinks you and your brother might be responsible. What do you say?"

"I say she's crazy." Ormand's face is big with indignation. The officer says nothing. "She's had it in for us ever since we were in junior high and she says Lee took a bottle of beer out of the cooler—which he never did. She's just a crazy bitch and we never had nothin' to do with her."

The patrolman seems to mull over this information a moment, thoughtfully stroking the neat clipped crescent of his mustache. Then he says, "She claims she's seen you and your brother out here on the porch drinking types of German beer and soda you can't get anywhere else around here—except at her place."

"Yeah?" Ormand snarls. "And what does that prove? You want to know, I bought that stuff in downtown L.A."

"Where?"

"This place I know, I'm not sure of the street, but I could drive you right to it, no sweat. She's just crazy, is all. She don't have a leg to stand on."

"Okay, Ormand," the officer says, snapping shut his notepad. "I've got it all down here. Mind if I step inside a minute and look around?"

"You got a search warrant?"

It's a long morning. Calvin sits up in bed, trying to read an article in *The Senior Citizen* about looking and feeling younger—"Get Out and Dance!" the headline admonishes—but he has trouble concentrating. The house is preternaturally quiet. Ormand and Lee Junior, who rarely rise before noon, slammed out the door half an hour after the patrolman left, and they haven't been back since. Jewel is asleep. Calvin can hear the harsh ratcheting snores from her room up the hall.

The thing that motivates him to pull on a flannel shirt and a pair of threadbare khaki pants and lower himself into the wheelchair is hunger—or at least that's what he tells himself. Most times when Jewel overindulges her taste for red wine and sleeps through the morning, Calvin stays put until he hears her moving about in the kitchen, but today is different. It's not just that he's feeling out of sorts physically, the cheap wine having scoured his digestive tract as relentlessly as a dose of the cathartic his mother used to give him when he had worms as a boy, but he's disturbed by the events of the preceding night and early morning as well. "She could use another lesson," Ormand had said, and then, first thing in the morning, the patrolman had shown up. Down deep, deeper even than the lowest stratum of excuses and denials he can dredge up, Calvin knows it's no coincidence.

The wheels rotate under his hands as he moves out into the hallway and eases past Jewel's room. He can see her through the half-open door, still in her dress and sneakers, her head buried in a litter of bedclothes. Next door is the bathroom—he's been in there three times already—and then, on the left, the kitchen. He rolls off the carpet and onto the smooth, spattered linoleum, gliding now, pulling right to skirt an overturned bag of garbage, and wheeling up to the sink for a sip of water.

The place is a mess. Unwashed cups, glasses, plates, and silverware litter the counter, and beer bottles too—the black ones. A jar of peanut butter stands open on the kitchen table, attracting flies. There's a smear of something on the wall, the wastebasket hasn't been emptied in a week, and the room reeks of sick-sweet decay. Calvin gulps a swallow or two of water from a cup scored with black rings. Eleven A.M. and hot already. He can feel the sweat where the glasses lie flat against his temples as he glides over to the refrigerator and swings back the door.

He'd been hoping for a leftover hamburger or a hard-boiled egg, but he isn't ready for this: the thing is packed, top to bottom, with cold cuts, big blocks of cheese, bratwurst and Tiroler. *Käse,* reads the label on a wedge of white cheese, *Product of Germany. Tilsiter,* reads another. *Schmelzkäse, Mainauer, Westfälischer Schinken.* For a long moment Calvin merely sits there, the cold air in his face, the meats and blocks of cheese wrapped in white butcher's paper, stacked up taller than his head. Somehow, he doesn't feel hungry anymore. And then it hits him: something like anger, something like fear.

The refrigerator door closes behind him with an airtight hiss, flies scatter, an overturned cup on the floor spins wildly away from his right wheel, and he's back in the hallway again, but this time he's turning left into the living room. Bottles, ashtrays, crumpled newspapers, he ignores them all. On the far side of the room stands a cheap plywood door, a door he's never been through: the door to Ormand and Lee Junior's room. Sitting there evenings, watching TV, he's caught a glimpse of the cluttered gloom beyond the doorway as one or the other of the boys slams in or out, but that's about it. They've never invited him in, and he's never much cared. But now, without hesitation, he wheels himself across the room, shoves down on the door latch with the heel of his hand, and pushes his way in.

He's no fool. He knew what he would find. But still, the magnitude of it chokes up his throat and makes the blood beat in his head like a big bass drum. From one end of the room to the other, stacked up to the ceiling as if the place were a warehouse or something, are stereo sets, radios, TVs, power tools, toaster ovens, and half a dozen things Calvin doesn't even recognize except to know that they cost an arm and a leg. In one corner are cases of beer—and, yes, Patio soda—and in the other, beneath a pair of huge PA speakers, guns. Shotguns, rifles, semiautomatics, a sack full of handguns with pearly and nickel-plated grips spilled on the floor like treasure. He can't believe it. Or no, worse, he can. Shaken, he backs out of the room and pulls the door shut.

The house is silent as a tomb. But wait: is that Jewel? Calvin's underarms are soaked through, a bead of sweat drops from his nose. The house stirs itself, floorboards creak of their own accord, the refrigerator starts up with a sigh. Is that Ormand? No, there: he can hear Jewel's snores again, stutter and wheeze, faint as the hum of the flies. This is his chance: he knows what he must do.

Outside, the sun hits him like a slap in the face. Already his shoulder sockets are on fire and the cast feels like an anchor twisted round his arm. For an instant he sits there beside the door as if debating with himself, the watery old eyes scanning the street for Ormand's pickup. Then all at once he's in motion, rocking across the loose floorboards, past the mounds of debris, and down the ramp Ormand fixed up for him at the back end of the porch. Below, the ground is littered with tires and machine parts, with rags and branches and refuse, and almost immediately he finds himself hung up on something—part of an auto transmission, it looks like—but he leans over to wrestle with it, heart in his throat, fingers clawing at grease and metal, until he frees himself. Then he's out the ramshackle gate and into the street.

It's not much of a hill—a five-degree grade maybe, and fifty or sixty yards up—but to the old man it seems like Everest. So hot, his seat stuck to the chair with his own wetness, salt sweat stinging his eyes, arms pumping and elbows stabbing, on he goes. A station wagon full of kids thunders by him, and then one of those little beetle cars; up ahead, at the intersection of Tully and Commerce, he can see a man on a bicycle waiting for the light to change. Up, up, up, he chants to himself, everything clear, not a number in his head, the good and bad of his life laid out before him like an EKG chart. The next thing he knows, the hill begins to even off and he's negotiating the sidewalk and turning the corner into the merciful shade of the store fronts. It's almost a shock when he looks up and finds himself staring numbly at his gaunt, wild-haired image in the dark window of Eva's European Deli.

The door stands open. For a long moment he hesitates, watching himself in the window. His face is crazy, the glint of his glasses masking his eyes, a black spot of grease on his forehead. What am I doing? he thinks. Then he wipes his hands on his pants and swings his legs through the doorway.

At first he can see nothing: the lights are out, the interior dim. There are sounds from the rear of the shop, the scrape of objects being dragged across the floor, a thump, voices. "I got no insurance, I tell you." Plaintive, halting, the voice of the German woman. "No money. And now I owe nearly two thousand dollars for all this stock"—more heavy, percussive sounds—"all gone to waste."

Now he begins to locate himself, objects emerging from the gloom, shades drawn, a door open to the sun all the way down the corridor in back. Christ, he thinks, looking round him. The display racks are on the floor, toppled like trees, cans and boxes and plastic packages torn open and strewn from one end of the place to the other. He can make out the beer cooler against the back wall, its glass doors shattered and wrenched from the hinges. And here, directly in front of him, like something out of a newsreel about flooding along the Mississippi, a clutter of overturned tables, smashed chairs, tangled rolls of butcher's paper, the battered cash register and belly-up meat locker. But all this is nothing when compared with the swastikas. Black, bold, stark, they blot everything like some killing fungus. The ruined equipment, the walls, ceiling, floors, even the bleary reproductions of the Rhine and the big hand-lettered menu in the window: nothing has escaped the spray can.

"I am gone," the German woman says. "Finished. Four times is enough."

"Eva, Eva, Ea." The second voice is thick and doleful, a woman's voice, sympathy like going to the bathroom. "What can you do? You know how Mike and I would like to see those people in jail where they belong—"

"Animals," the German woman says.

"We know it's them—everybody on the block knows it—but we don't have the proof and the police won't do a thing. Honestly, I must watch that house ten hours a day but I've never seen a thing proof positive." At that moment, Mrs. Tuxton's head comes into view over the gutted meat locker. The hair lies flat against her temples, beauty-parlor silver. Her lips are pursed. "What we need is an eyewitness."

Now the German woman swings into view, a carton in her arms. "Yah," she says, the flesh trembling at her throat, "and you find me one in this . . . this stinking community. You're a bunch of cowards—and you'll forgive me for this, Laura—but to let criminals run scot-free on your own block, I just don't understand it. Do you know when I was a girl in Karlsruhe after the war and we found out who was the man breaking into houses on my street, what we did? Huh?"

Calvin wants to cry out for absolution: I know, I know who did it! But he doesn't. All of a sudden he's afraid. The vehemence of this woman, the utter shambles of her shop, Ormand, Lee Junior, the squawk of the police radio: his head is filling up. It is then that Mrs. Tuxton swivels round and lets out a theatrical little gasp. "My God, there's someone here!"

In the next moment they're advancing on him, the German woman in a tent-like dress, the mean little eyes sunk into her face until he can't see them, Mrs. Tuxton wringing her hands and jabbing her pointy nose at him as if it were a knife. "You!" the German woman exclaims, her fists working, the little feet in their worn shoes kneading the floor in agitation. "What are you doing here?"

Calvin doesn't know what to say, his head crowded with numbers all of a sudden. Twenty thousand leagues under the sea, a hundred and twenty pesos in a dollar, sixteen men on a dead man's chest, yo-ho-ho and one-point-oh-five quarts to a liter. "I . . . I—" he stammers.

"The nerve," Mrs. Tuxton says.

"Well?" The German woman is poised over him now, just as she was on the day she slapped the soda from his hand—he can smell her, a smell like liverwurst, and it turns his stomach. "Do you know anything about this, eh? Do you?"

He does. He knows all about it. Jewel knows, Lee Junior knows, Ormand knows. They'll go to jail, all of them. And Calvin? He's just an old man, tired, worn out, an old man in a wheelchair. He looks into the German woman's face and tries to feel pity, tries to feel brave, righteous, good. But instead he has a vision of himself farmed out to some nursing home, the women in the white caps prodding him and humiliating him, the stink of fatality on the air, the hacking and moaning in the night—

"I'm . . . I'm sorry," he says.

Her face goes numb, flesh the color of raw dough. "Sorry?" she echoes. "Sorry?"

But he's already backing out the door.

(1983)

GREEN HELL

There has been a collision (with birds, black flocks of them), an announcement from the pilot's cabin, a moment of abeyed hysteria, and then the downward rush. The plane is nosing for the ground at a forty-five-degree angle, engines wheezing, spewing smoke and feathers. Lights flash, breathing apparatus drops and dangles. Our drinks become lariats, the glasses knives. Lunch (chicken croquettes, gravy, reconstituted potatoes and imitation cranberry sauce) decorates our shirts and vests. Outside there is the shriek of the air over the wings; inside, the rock-dust rumble of grinding teeth, molar on molar. My face seems to be slipping over my head like a rubber mask. And then, horribly, the first trees become visible beyond the windows. We gasp once and then we're down, skidding through the greenery, jolted from our seats, panicked, repentant, savage. Windows strain and pop like lightbulbs. We lose our bowels. The plane grates through the trees, the shriek of branches like the keen of harpies along the fuselage, our bodies jarred, dashed and knocked like the silver balls in a pinball machine. And then suddenly it's over: we are stopped (think of a high diver meeting the board on the way down). I expect (have expected) flames.

There are no flames. There is blood. Thick clots of it, puddles, ponds, lakes. We count heads. Eight of us still have them: myself, the professor, the pilot (his arm already bound up in a sparkling white sling), the mime, Tanqueray with a twist (nothing worse than a gin drinker), the man allergic to cats (runny eyes, red nose), the cat breeder, and Andrea, the stewardess. The cats, to a one, have survived. They crouch in their cages, coated with wet kitty litter like tempura shrimp. The rugby players, all twelve of them (dark-faced, scowling sorts), are dead. Perhaps just as well.

Dazed, palms pressed to bruised organs, handkerchiefs dabbing at wounds, we hobble from the wreckage. Tanqueray is sniveling, a soft moan and gargle like rain on the roof and down the gutter. The mime makes an Emmett Kelly face. The professor limps, cradling a black briefcase with *Fiskeridirektoratets Havforskningsinstitutt* engraved in the corner. The cats, left aboard, begin to yowl. The allergic man throws back his head, sneezes.

We look around: trees that go up three hundred feet, lianas, leaves the size of shower curtains, weeds thick as a knit sweater. Step back ten feet and the plane disappears. The pilot breaks the news: we've come down in the heart of the Amazon basin, hundreds, perhaps thousands of miles from the nearest toilet.

The radio, of course, is dead.

Evening

We are back in the plane. They've sopped up the gore, switched the seats with palm fronds, buried the rugby players. Air freshener has been sprayed. The punctures (sardine tin, church key) have been plugged with life preservers, rubber life rafts. This then, will be our shelter.

Andrea, her uniform torn over the breast and slit up the leg, portions out our dinner: two of those plastic thimbles of nondairy creamer, a petrified brioche, two plastic packets of Thousand Island dressing, a cup of water and Bloody Mary mix. Apiece.

"Life has its little rewards," says Tanqueray, smacking his lips. He is a man of sagging flesh, torrid complexion, drooping into his sixth decade. There are two empty gin bottles (miniatures) on his tray.

The professor looks up at him. He pages rapidly through a Norwegian-English dictionary. "Good evening," he says. "I am well. And you?"

Tanqueray nods.

"I sink we come rain," the professor says.

The allergic man rattles a bottle of pills.

The mime makes a show of licking the plastic recesses of his Thousand Island packet.

"Foreigner, eh?" says Tanqueray.

Suddenly the pilot is on his feet. "Now listen, everybody," he booms. "I'm going to lay it on the line. No mincing words, no pussyfooting. We're in a jam. No food, no water, no medical supplies. I'm not saying we're not lucky to be alive and I'm not saying that me and the prof here ain't going to try our damnedest to get this crate in the air again . . . but I am saying we're in a jam. If we stick together, if we fight this thing—if we work like a team—we'll make it."

I watch him: the curls at his temple, sharp nose, white teeth, the set of his jaw (prognathic). I realize that we have a leader. I further realize that I detest him. I doubt that we will make it.

"A team," he repeats.

The mime makes his George-Washington-crossing-the-Delaware face.

Night

Chiggers, ticks, gnats, nits. Cicadas. Millipedes, centipedes, omnipedes, mini-pedes, pincerheads, poison toads, land leeches, skinks. Palmetto bugs. Iguanas, fer-de-lance, wolf spiders, diggers, buzzers, hissers, stinkers. Oonipids. Spitting spiders. Ants. Mites. Flits. Whips. Mosquitoes.

Morning

The gloom brightens beyond the shattered plastic windows. Things are cooing and chattering in the bushes. Weep-weep-weep. Coo-hooo, coo-hooo. I wake itching. There is a spider the size of a two-egg omelet on my chest. When I lift my hand (slowly and stealthily, like a tropism) he scrambles across my face and up over the seat.

Tanqueray (buttery-faced, pouchy slob) is snoring. I sit up. The cat man is watching me. "Good morning," he whispers. The lower half of his face, from the lips down, is the color of a plum. A birthmark. I'd taken it for a beard, but now, up close, I see the mistake.

"Sleep well?" he whispers.

I grunt, scratch.

The others are still sleeping. I can hear the professor grinding his teeth, the allergic man wheezing. Andrea and the pilot are not present. The door to the pi-lot's cabin is drawn shut. Somewhere, a cat wails.

"Hssst," says the cat man. He stands, beckons with a finger, then slips out the door. I follow.

Things hiss off in the vegetation and rattle in the trees. We slash our way to the baggage compartment, where the cat man pauses to lift the door and duck his way in. Immediately I become aware of the distinctive odor attaching to the feline body functions. I step inside.

"My beauties," says the cat man, addressing the cats. They yowl in unison and he croons to them ("little ones," "prettyfeet," "buttertails") in a primitive sort of recognition rite. I realize that the cat man is an ass.

"Let me introduce you to my wards," he says. "This"—there is a cat in his arms, its fur like cotton candy—"is Egmont. He's a Chinchilla Persian. Best of Show at Rio two weeks ago. I wouldn't take ten thousand dollars for him." He looks at me. I whistle, gauging the appropriate response. He points to the cages successively: "Joy Boy, Roos, Great Northern, Peaker, and Peaker II. Roos is an Aroostook Main Coon Cat."

"Very nice," I say, trying to picture the man as a ten-year-old hounded into a wimpy affection for cats by the tough kids, merciless on the subject of his purple face. But then suddenly my nostrils charge. He is twisting the key on a tin of herring.

"Special diet," he says. "For their coats."

Real food has not passed my lips in over twenty-four hours. At his feet, a cardboard box packed with cans: baby smoked oysters, sardines, anchovies, salmon, tuna. When he turns to feed Joy Boy I fill my pockets.

He sighs. "Gorgeous, aren't they?"

"Yes," I say. With feeling.

Afternoon

We have had a meeting. Certain propositions have been carried. Namely, that we are a society in microcosm. That tasks will be (equably) apportioned. That we will work toward a common goal. As a team.

The pilot addressed us (slingless). He spoke with the microphone at his lips, out of habit I suppose, and with his Pan Am captain's cap raked across one eyebrow. Andrea stood at his side, her fingers twined in his, her uniform like a fishnet. The rest of us occupied our seats (locked in the upright position), our seat belts fastened, not smoking. We itched, sweated, squirmed. The pilot talked of the spirit of democracy, the social contract, the state of nature, the myth of the noble savage and the mythopoeic significance of Uncle Sam. He also dwelt on the term *pilot* as image, and explored its etymology. Then, in a voice vote (yea/nay), we elected him leader.

He proceeded to assign duties. He, the pilot, would oversee food and water supplies. At the same time, he and the professor would tinker with the engine and tighten bolts. Andrea would hold their tools. The mime's job was to write our constitution. Tanqueray would see that the miniatures were emptied. (He interjected here to indicate that he would cheerfully take on the task appointed him, though it would entail tackling the inferior spirits as well as gin—taking the bad with the good, as he put it. The pilot found him out of order and made note of the comment in any case.) To the allergic man (who sagged, red and wheezing) fell the duty of keeping things tidy within the plane. The cat man and myself were designated food gatherers, with the attendant task of clearing a landing strip. Then the pilot threw the meeting open to comments from the floor.

The allergic man stood, wiping his eyes. "I insist," he said, and then fell into a coughing spasm, unable to continue until the mime delivered a number of slaps to his back with the even, flat strokes of a man beating a carpet. "I insist that the obscene, dander-spewing vermin in the baggage compartment be removed from the immediate vicinity of the aircraft." (These were the first articulate sounds he had produced. Judging from diction, cadence and the accent in which they were delivered, it began to occur to me that he must be an Englishman. My father was an Englishman. I have an unreasoning, inexorable and violent loathing for all things English.) "In fact," he continued, choking into his handkerchief, "I should like to see all the squirrelly little beggars spitted and roasted like hares, what with the state of our food supply."

The cat man's purple shaded to black. He unbuckled his seat belt, stood, stepped over to the English/allergic man, and put a fist in his eye. The pilot called the cat man out of order, and with the aid of Tanqueray and the professor, ejected him from the meeting. Oaths were exchanged. Outside, in the bush, a howler monkey imitated the shriek of a jaguar set afire.

The pilot adjourned the meeting.

Evening

It is almost pleasant: sun firing the highest leaves, flowers and vines and bearded Spanish moss like a Rousseau exhibit, the spit and crackle of the campfire, the sweet strong odor of roasting meat. Joy Boy and Peaker II are turning on spits. The cat man has been exiled, the spoils (fat pampered feline) confiscated. Much to my chagrin, he thought to make off with his cache of cat food, and had actually set loose Egmont, Peaker, Roos and Great Northern before the pilot could get to him. I told no one of the cat food. Eleven shiny tins of it lie buried not twenty feet from the nose of the plane. A reserve. A private reserve. Just in case.

There is a good deal of squabbling over the roast cat. The pilot, Andrea and the professor seem to wind up with the largest portions. Mine is among the smallest. Off in the black bank of the jungle we can hear the pariah gnashing his teeth, keening. He is taking it hard. The pilot says that he is a troublemaker anyway and that the community is better off without him. As I tear into Joy Boy's plump drumstick, I cannot help agreeing.

Night

Wispy flames tremble at the wicks of three thin birthday candles Andrea has found in the galley. Their light is sufficient for the professor. He is tinkering with the radio, and with the plane's massive battery. Suddenly the cracked speaker comes to life, sputters, coughs up a ball of static sizzling like bacon in a frying pan. The pilot is a madman. He bowls over Tanqueray, flings himself on his knees before the radio (think of altar and neophyte), snatches up the microphone and with quaking fingers switches to TRANSMIT. "Mayday, Mayday!" he shouts, "Mayday, Mayday, Mayday."

We freeze—a sound is coming back through the speaker. The professor tunes it in, the interference like a siren coming closer and then shooting off in the distance as the sound clears. It is music, a tune. Tinny mandolins, a human voice—singing. We listen, rapt, suddenly and magically in communion with the civilized world. The song ends. Then the first strains of a commercial jingle, familiar as our mothers' faces, things go better with Coke, but there's something wrong, the words in a muddle. The announcer's voice comes over—in Japanese. Radio Tokyo. Then the box goes dead. There is the smell of scorched wire, melted transistor. The pilot's jaw lists, tears start in his eyes, his knuckles whiten over the microphone. "Good morning, Mr. Yones," says the professor. "How are your wife?"

Morning

Many things to report:

1) The tools have vanished. The cat man suspected. Vengeance the motive. The pilot and the professor are off in the shadows, hunting him.

2) Tanqueray and the English/allergic man (nose clogged, eyes like open sores) have volunteered to make their way back to civilization and send succor. They are not actuated by blind heroism. The one has finished the miniatures, the other is out of epinephrine. Their chances—a drunken old man and a flabby asthmatic—are negligible. I will not miss them in any case. They are both consummate asses.

3)) The mime has begun our constitution. He sits hunched in his seat, face in pancake, looking uncannily like Bernardo O'Higgins.

4) I have made overtures to Andrea. When the pilot and the professor slipped off after the cat man, I took her aside and showed her a tin of sardines. She followed me out of the plane and through the dripping fronds and big squamate leaves. We crouched in the bush. "I had this tucked away in my suitcase," I whispered, lying. "Thought you might want to share it with me—"

She looked at me—the green of her eyes, the leafy backdrop. Her uniform had degenerated to shorts and halter, crudely knotted. Her cleavage was deep as the jungle. "Sure," she said.

"—for a consideration . . ."

"Sure."

I turned the key. The sardines were silver, the oil gold. I counted them out, half for her, half for me. We ate. She sucked her fingers, licked the corners of the tin. I watched her tongue. When she finished she looked up at me, a fat bubble of oil on her lip. "You know," she said, "you're a shit. I mean you're a real shit. Holding out, trying to bribe me. You think I'd do it with you? Listen. You nauseate me with your skinny legs and your filthy beard and your dirty little habits— I've been watching you since you got on the plane back at Rio. Think I don't know your type? Ha. You're a real shit."

What could I say? We stood. I answered her with the vilest string of expletives I could dredge up (nineteen words in all). She caught me off balance, I tumbled back into the bushes, sat studying the shift of her buttocks as she stalked off. A spider the size of a three-egg omelet darted down the neck of my shirt. I crushed him against my chest, but his bite was like an injection of fire.

Afternoon

"Been holding out on us, eh?"

"Look, I just had the one tin—you can search through my bags if you don't believe me. Go ahead."

"Damn straight I will. And I got a good mind to send you down the road with that freak-faced cat fancier too. You're sure as hell no part of this society, buddy. You never say a damn word, you don't toe your line, and now you're sequestering food. . . . You sure there's no more of it?"

"No, I swear it. I just picked up the one tin at Rio—the label caught my eye in the snack shop at the airport."

The pilot's eyes are razors, his jaw a saber. He thrusts, I parry. He paws through my things, sniffs at my sport shirts, pockets a bottle of after-shave. The big fist spasmodically clenches and slackens, bunching the collar of my shirt. The professor looks on, distant, serene. The mime is busy with his writing. Andrea stands in the background, arms crossed, a tight snake's smile on her lips.

Evening

Trees have fallen on trees here in the rain forest. *Mauritia,* orbyguia, *Euterpe,* their branches meshed with wild growths of orchids, ferns and pipers. Stands of palm. The colossal ceibas, Para nuts and sucupiras with their blue flowers high in the sun. I am feeling it, the rain forest, here in the gloom below. Sniffing it, breathing it. In the branches, tail-swinging monkeys and birds of every stripe; in the mold at my feet, two tiny armadillos, tough and black as leather. They root round my shoes, stupid piglike ratlike things. I bend toward them, a drooping statue, slow as the waning sun. My hand hangs over them. They root, oblivious. I strike.

The big one squeals (faint as a baby smothering in the night), and the smaller scuttles off, more ratlike by the second. Suddenly I am stamping, the blood pounding in my thighs, my shoes like hammers. And then I am sitting in the wet, the spiderbite swelling like a nectarine under my skin, mosquitoes black on my neck, my face, my arms, the strange crushed thing at my feet. I want to tear it, eat it raw, alone and greedy.

But I will take it back, an offering for Andrea's cold eyes and the pilot's terrible jaw. I will placate them, stay with the ship and the chance of rescue—I will shrink, and wait my chance, sly and watchful as a coiled bushmaster.

Night

I am excited, brimming with expectation—and yet stricken with fear, uncertainty, morbid presentiment. I have seen something in the bush—two eyes, a shadow, the hint of a human form. It was not the cat man, not the English/allergic man, not Tanqueray. I have said nothing to the others.

Tonight there are just three of us in the familiar dormitory: the professor, the mime, myself. A single stumpy candle gutters. The door has already closed on the pilot and Andrea. Outside, the leaves rattle with the calls of a thousand strange creatures, cooing, chattering, hissing, clucking, stirring wings, stretching toes, creeping beneath and scrabbling over: a festering backdrop for those pathogenic eyes in the bush.

Morning

Andrea, in bad humor, portions out breakfast—leg of armadillo, (charred scale, black claw), imitation roquefort dressing, a half-ration of water and sour mix. Apiece. She holds back the tail for herself. The mime, in tights and pancake, entertains us with animal impressions: walrus, swan, earthworm. Then he does a man shaving and showering in a flurry of interruptions: the phone, the doorbell, the oven timer. The professor laughs, a weird silent Scandinavian laugh. The pilot and Andrea scowl. My face is neutral.

Suddenly the pilot stands, cutting the performance short. "I've got an announcement," he says. "We might as well face it—this crate'll never fly, no matter how heroic the effort on the part of the prof and me." He hangs his head (think of Christ, nailed to the cross, neck muscles gone loose, his moment of doubt and pain)—but then suddenly he snaps to attention and glares at us, his eyes like the barrels of a shotgun. "And you want to know the reason?" (He is shouting.) "A cut-and-dried case of desertion, that's the reason. Plumface goes and disrupts the community, lets us all down—and then, as if that wasn't enough, he makes off with our tools out of sheer spite. . . . I'm not going to kid you: it looks pretty grim." (Christ again.) "Still, if we stick together—" (here he pauses, the catchword on all our lips) "—we'll lick this jungle yet.

"Now listen. Rummy and Sneezes have been gone for nearly twenty-four hours now. Anytime we could hear those choppers coming for us. So let's get out and clear 'em a landing strip, back to back, like a real community!" Andrea applauds. I seethe. The mime looks like a cross between the unknown soldier and Charles de Gaulle. The professor works his mouth, searching for a phrase.

Outside, just beyond the tail of the plane, is a patch of partially cleared ground, a consequence of the crash. In the center of this patch—undiscovered as yet by any of us—are two freshly cut stakes, set in the ground. On the tips of the stakes, like twin balls of flies or swarms of bees, poise the heads of Tanqueray and the English/allergic man, dripping.

Afternoon

A quickening series of events:
  —The Discovery. The professor faint, Andrea tough as a kibbutz woman.
  —The Discussion. The pilot, our leader, punches our shoulders in turn. Slaps our backs. He has decided to abandon the plane in the morning. We will walk back to civilization. In charade, the mime asks if we will not all be decapitated during the coming night, our blood quaffed, bones gnawed by autochthonous cannibals. The pilot steps into his cabin, returns a moment later with a pistol the size of a football. For hijackers, he explains.
  —The Preparation. We pull down the life preservers (a rain of scorpions and spiders, birds' nests, strange black hairs). They are the color of the rain slickers worn by traffic patrolmen. We will each wear one, insurance against bottomless swamps and angry copper rivers. In addition, we are each provided with a crude walking stick cum club, at one end of which we tie up our belongings, hobo fashion. The provisions are slim: we divide up nine individual packets of sugar, six of ketchup, three rippled pepper shakers. Each of us takes a plastic spoon, knife, and fork, sealed in polyethylene with a clean white napkin.
  —The Plan. We will live off the land. Eat beetle, leech, toad. We will stick together. Walk back. A team.

Evening

The mime has fallen sick. What could it be but the dreaded jungle fever? He writhes in his seat, raves (in pantomime), sweats. His makeup is a mess. The professor tends him, patting his head and crooning softly in Norwegian. Andrea and the pilot keep their distance. As do I.

We do not eat. We will need what little we have for the road. Still, around dinnertime, the pilot and Andrea mew themselves up in his cabin: they have their secrets I suppose. I have my secrets as well. As the cabin door eases shut I slip out into the penumbra of the forest floor, ferret through the stalks and creepers, dig up my hoard (the seven shiny survivors) and silently turn the key on a tin of baby smoked oysters. I pack the rest among my underwear in the tight little bundle I will carry with me in the morning.

Later, we discuss the mime's condition. He is in no shape to travel, and yet it is clear that we cannot remain where we are. In fact, all of us are in a bug-eyed rage to get away from those rotting heads and those terrible shadows and eyes,

eyes and shadows. And so, we discuss. No one mentions community, nor refers
to the group constitution. The pilot puts it to a vote: stay or leave. Mime or no
mime. He and Andrea vote to leave at dawn, regardless of the mime's condition.
If he can accompany us, fine. If not, he will have to stay behind (until we can direct a rescue party to the plane of course). I do not want to stay behind. I do not
want to carry the mime. I raise my hand. And the professor makes it unanimous,
though I doubt if he has any conception of what the vote involves. Aside, he asks
me if I can direct him to the library.

Night

Andrea and the pilot choose to sleep in the main cabin for the first time.
    We keep a bonfire burning through the darkness.
    We share sentry duty.
    The sounds of the jungle are knives punched through our chests.

Morning

I wake in a sweat. Everything still. Andrea, all leg, shoulder, navel and cleavage,
is snoring, her breath grating like bark stripped from a tree. Beside her, the pilot:
captain's cap pulled over his face, gun tucked in his belt. The professor, who had
the last watch, is curled in his chair asleep. Outside, the fire has burned to fine
white ash and a coatimundi steals across the clearing. Something is wrong—I
feel it like a bad dream that refuses to end. Then I glance over at the mime. He
looks exactly like John F. Kennedy lying in state. Dead.
    There is no time for ceremony. No time in fact for burial. The pilot, sour with
sleep, drops a blanket over the frozen white face and leads us cautiously out of
the plane, and into the bush. We shoulder our clubs, the white bundles. Our life
jackets glow in the seeping gloom. The pilot, Andrea, the professor, me. A team.
Pass the baton and run, I think, and chuckle to myself. My expectation of survival is low, but I follow anyway, and watch, and hope, and wait.
    We walk for three hours, slimed in sweat, struggling through the leaves,
creepers, tendrils, vines, shoots, stems and stalks, over the colossal rotting
trunks, into the slick algae-choked ponds. Birds and monkeys screeching in the
trees. Agoutis stumbling off at our feet. Snakes. The trails of ants. And in the festering water, a tapir, big as a pregnant horse. I develop a terrible thirst (the pilot,
of course, is custodian of our water supply). My throat is sore, lips gummed. I
think of the stories I have heard—thirst-crazed explorers plunging their heads
into those scummy pools, drinking deep of every foul and crippling disease
known to man. And I think of the six shiny tins in my pack.
    Suddenly we are stopping (halftime, I suppose). The pilot consults his com-

pass, the great jaw working. Andrea, 97 percent exposed flesh, is like a first-aid dummy. Slashes, paper cuts, welts, sweet droplets of blood, a leech or two, insects spotting her skin like a terminal case of moles. We throw ourselves down in the wet, breathing hard. Things of the forest floor instantly dart up our pantlegs, down our collars. Andrea asks the pilot if he has the vaguest fucking idea of where we're headed.

He frowns down at the compass.

She asks again.

He curses.

She holds up her middle finger.

The pilot takes a step toward her, lip curled back, when suddenly his expression goes soft. There is a look of surprise, of profound perplexity on his face, as if he'd just swallowed an ice cube. In his neck, a dart. A tiny thing, with feathers (picture a fishing lure pinned beneath his chin like a miniature bow tie). And then from the bushes, a sound like a hundred bums spitting in the gutter. Two more darts appear in the pilot's neck, a fourth and fifth in his chest. He begins to giggle as if it were a great joke, then falls to his knees, tongue caught between his teeth. We watch, horror-struck. His eyes glaze, the arms twitch at his sides, the giggles rising like a wave, cresting higher, curling, and then breaking—he drops like a piece of flotsam, face down in the mulch.

We panic. The professor screams. Andrea snatches the pilot's pistol and begins laying waste to the vegetation. I stretch out flat, secrete my head, wishing I had a blanket to pull over it. A random bullet sprays mud and leaf in my hair. The professor screams again. Andrea has shot him. In the eye. When I look up, the revolver is in her lap and she is fumbling with the magazine. There is a dart in her cheek. It is no time to lose consciousness. But I do.

Afternoon

I wake to the sound of human voices, the smell of smoke. I lie still, a wax doll, though something tears persistently at the spider-welt on my chest. My eye winks open: there is a campfire, nine or ten naked men squatting round it, eating. Gnawing at bones. Their skin is the color of stained walnut, their bodies lean as raw muscle, their lips distended with wooden disks. Each has a red band painted across his face at eye level, from the brow to the bridge of the nose, like a party mask. There is no trace of my late teammates.

I find I am suffering from anxiety, the image of the fly-blackened heads screeching through my mind like a flight of carrion birds, the quick dark voices and the sound of tooth on bone grating in my ears. I am on the verge of bolting. But at that moment I become aware of a new figure in the group—pasty white skin, red boils and blotches, a fallen, purplish mask. The cat man. Naked and flabby. His penis wrapped in bark, pubic hair plucked. I sit up. And suddenly the whole assembly is on its feet, fingers twitching at bowstrings and blowguns. The cat man motions with his hand and the weapons drop. Barefooted, he hobbles over to me, and the others turn back to their meal. "How you feeling?" he says, squatting beside me.

I crush an insect against my chest, rake my nails over the throbbing spider-welt. I opt for sincerity. "Like a piece of shit."

He looks hard at me, deciding something. A fat fluffy tabby scampers across the clearing, begins rubbing itself against his thigh. I recognize Egmont. He strokes it, working his finger under the ribbon round its neck. "Don't ask any questions," he says. And then: "Listen: I've decided to help you—you were the only one who loved my little beauties, the only one who never meant us any harm. . . ."

Evening

The last. It is nothing. I follow the brown back of my guide through the shadowy maze, always steering away from the swamps and tangles, sticking to high ground. The cat man has elected to stay behind, gone feral (once an ass, always an ass). Soured on civilization, he says, by his late experience. We have had a long talk. He whimpered and sputtered. Told me of his childhood, his morbid sensitivity—marked at birth, an outcast. He's suffered all his life, and the experi-ence with the downed plane brought it all home. The Txukahameis (that was his name for them) were different. Noble savages. They found him wandering, took him in, marveled over the beauty of his face, appointed him demichief, exacted his vengeance for him. There was a lot to like about them, he said. Home cook-ing. Sexual rites. Pet ocelots. No way he was leaving. But he wished me luck.

And so I follow the brown back. Five or six hours, and then I begin to detect it—faint and distant—the chuff and stutter of a diesel. Bulldozers, two or three of them. We draw closer, the noise swells. Step by step. I can smell the exhaust. Then my guide points in the direction of the blatting engines, parts the fronds, and vanishes.

I hurry for the building road, my blood churning, a smile cracking my lips—yes, I am thinking, the moment I step from the bush I'll be a celebrity. In a month I'll be rich. Talk shows, interviews, newspapers, magazines—a book, a film. (Birds caw, my feet rush, the bulldozers roar.) I can picture the book jacket . . . my face, jungle backdrop . . . title in red . . . *Survivor* I'll call it—or *Alive* . . . no, something with more flair, more gut appeal, something dramatic, something with suffering in it. Something like—*Green Hell.*

(1976)

ME CAGO EN LA LECHE (ROBERT JORDAN IN NICARAGUA)

"So tell me, comrade, why do you wear your hair this way?"

Robert Jordan fingered the glistening, rock-hard corona of his spiked hair (dyed mud-brown now, with khaki highlights, for the sake of camouflage) and then loosened the cap of his flask and took a long burning hit of mescal. He waited till the flame was gone from his throat and the familiar glow lit his insides so that they felt radioactive, then leaned over the campfire to address the flat-faced old man in worn fatigues. "Because I shit in the milk of my mother, that's why," he said, the mescal abrading his voice. He caressed the copper stud that lay tight against the flange of his left nostril and wiped his hands with exaggerated care on his Hussong's T-shirt. "And come to think of it," he added, "because I shit in the milk of your mother too."

The old man, flat-faced though he was, said nothing. He wasn't that old, actually—twenty-eight or -nine, Robert Jordan guessed—but poor nutrition, lack of dental care, and too much squinting into the sun gave him the look of a retired caterer in Miami Beach. The fire snapped, monkeys howled. "La reputa que lo parió," the old man said finally, turning his head to spit.

Robert Jordan didn't catch it all—he'd dropped out of college in the middle of Intermediate Spanish—but he got the gist of it all right and gave the old man the finger. "Yeah," he said, "and screw you too."

Two nights earlier the old man had come to him in the Managua bus station as he gingerly lifted his two aluminum-frame superlightweight High Sierra mountain packs down from the overhead rack and exited the bus that had brought him from Mexico City. The packs were stuffed with soiled underwear, granola bars, hair gel, and plastic explosives, and Robert Jordan was suffering from a hangover. He was also suffering from stomach cramps, diarrhea, and dehydration, not to mention the general debilitating effects of having spent two days and a night on a third-class bus with a potpourri of drunks, chicken thieves, disgruntled pigs, and several dozen puking, mewling, loose-bowled niñitos. "Over here, comrade," the old man had whispered, taking him by the arm and leading him to a bench across the square.

The old man had hovered over him as Robert Jordan threw himself down on the bench and stretched his legs. Trucks rumbled by, burros brayed, campesinos hurried about their business. "You are the gringo for this of the Cup of Soup, no?" the old man asked.

Robert Jordan regarded him steadily out of the slits of his bloodshot eyes. The old man's face was as dry and corrugated as a strip of jerky and he wore the armband of the Frente, black letters—FSLN—against a red background. Robert Jordan was thinking how good the armband would look with his Dead Kennedys tour jacket, but he'd caught the "Cup of Soup" business and nodded. That nod was all the old man needed. He broke into a grin, bent to kiss him on both cheeks, and breathed rummy fumes in his face. "I am called Bayardo," the old man said, "and I am come to take you to the border."

Robert Jordan felt bone-weary, but this was what he'd come for, so he stood and shouldered one of the packs while Bayardo took the other. In a few minutes they'd be boarding yet another bus, this one north to Jinotega and the Honduran border that lay beyond it. There Robert Jordan would rendezvous with one of the counter-counter-revolutionary bands (Contra Contra) and he would, if things went well, annihilate in a roar of flying earth clods and shattered trees a Contra airstrip and warehouse where foodstuffs—Twinkies, Lipton Cup of Soup, and Rice Krispies among them—were flown in from Texas by the CIA. Hence the codename, "Cup of Soup."

But now—now they were camped somewhere on the Nicaraguan side of the border, listening to monkeys howl and getting their asses chewed off by mosquitoes, ticks, chiggers, leeches, and everything else that crawled, swam, or flew. It began to rain. The rain, Robert Jordan understood, would be bad for his hair. He finished a granola bar, exchanged curses with the old man, and crawled into his one-man pup tent. "You take the first watch," he growled through the wall of undulating nylon in his very bad Spanish. "And the second and third too. Come to think of it, why don't you just wake me at noon."

The camp was about what you'd expect, Robert Jordan thought, setting his pack down in a clump of poisonous-looking plants. He and the old man had hiked three days through the bug factory to get here, and what was it but a few banana-leaf hovels with cigarette cartons piled outside. Robert Jordan was thinking he'd be happy to blow this dump and get back to the drugs, whores, semi-clean linen, and tequila añejo of Mexico City and points north, when a one-eyed man emerged from the near hut, his face split with a homicidal grin. His name was Ruperto, and he wore the combat boots, baggy camouflage pants, and black T-shirt that even professors in Des Moines favored these days, and he carried a Kalashnikov assault rifle in his right hand. "Qué tal, old man," he said, addressing Bayardo, and then, turning to Robert Jordan and speaking in English: "And this is the gringo with the big boom-boom. Nice hair, gringo."

Robert Jordan traded insults with him, ending with the usual malediction about shit, milk, and mothers, and then pinched his voice through his nose in the nagging whine he'd perfected when he was four. "And so where's all the blow that's supposed to be dropping from the trees out here, huh? And what about maybe a hit of rum or some tortillas or something? I mean I been tramping through this craphole for three days and no sooner do I throw my pack down than I get some wiseass comment about my hair I could've stayed in Montana and got from some redneck cowboy. Hey," he shouted, leaning into Ruperto's face and twisting his voice till it broke in a snarl, "screw you too, Jack."

Ruperto said nothing. Just smiled his homicidal smile, one eye gleaming, the other dead in a crater of pale, scarred flesh. By now the others had begun to gather—Robert Jordan counted six of them, flat-faced Indians all—and a light rain was sizzling through the trees. "You want hospitality," Ruperto said finally, "go to Howard Johnson's." He spat at his feet. "Your mother," he said, and then turned to shout over his shoulder. "Muchacha!"

Everyone stopped dead to watch as the girl in skintight fatigues stepped out of the hut, shadowed by an older woman with the build of a linebacker. "Sí?" the girl said in a voice that inflamed Robert Jordan's groin.

Ruperto spat again. "Bring the gringo some chow."

"The Cup of Soup?" the girl asked.

Ruperto winked his mad wet eye at Robert Jordan. "Sí," he grunted, "the Cup of Soup."

As he lay in his pup tent that night, his limbs entwined in the girl's—her name was either Vidaluz or Concepción, he couldn't remember which—Robert Jordan thought of his grandmother. She was probably the only person in the world he didn't hate. His mother was a real zero, white wine and pasta salad all the way, and his friends back in Missoula were a bunch of dinks who thought Bryan Adams was god. His father was dead. When the old man had sucked on the barrel of his 30.06 Winchester, Robert was fourteen and angry. His role model was Sid Vicious and he was into glue and Bali Hai. It was his grandmother—she was Andalusian, really cool, a guerrilla who'd bailed out of Spain in the '30s, pregnant with Robert Jordan II—who listened patiently to his gripes about the school jocks and his wimpy teachers and bought him tire chains to wrap around his boots. They sat for hours together listening to the Clash's *Sandinista* album, and when he blew off the tips of his pinky and ring fingers with a homemade bomb, it was she who gave him his first pair of studded black leather gloves. And what was best about her—what he liked more than anything else—was that she didn't take any shit from anybody. Once, when her third husband, Joe Thunderbucket, called her "Little Rabbit," she broke his arm in three places. It was she more than anyone who'd got him into all this revolution business—she and the Clash, anyway. And of course, he'd always loved dynamite.

He lay there, slapping mosquitoes, his flesh sticky against the girl's, wondering what his grandmother was doing now, in the dark of this night before his first offensive. It was a Tuesday, wasn't it? That was bingo night on the reservation, and she usually went with Joe's sister Leona to punch numbers and drink boilermakers at the bingo hall. He pictured her in her black mantilla, her eyes cold and hard and lit maybe a little with the bourbon and Coors, and then he woke up Concepción or Vidaluz and gave it to her again, all his anger focused in the sharp tingling stab and rhythm of it.

It was still dark when the old man woke him. "Son of a bitch," Robert Jordan muttered. His hair was crushed like a Christmas-tree ornament and there was a sour metallic taste in his mouth. He didn't mind fighting for the revolution, but this was ridiculous—it wasn't even light yet. "Ándale," the old man said, "the Cup of Soup awaits."

Are you out of your gourd, or what?" Robert Jordan twisted free of the girl and checked his watch. "It's four-fifteen, for christ's sake."

The old man shrugged. "Qué puta es la guerra," he said. "War's a bitch."

And then the smell of woodsmoke and frijoles came to him over Ruperto's high crazed whinny of a laugh, the girl was up and out of his sleeping bag, strolling heavy-haunched and naked across the clearing, and Robert Jordan was reaching for his hair gel.

After breakfast—two granola bars and a tin plate of frijoles that looked and tasted like humus—Robert Jordan vomited in the weeds. He was going into battle for the first time and he didn't have the stomach for it. This wasn't like blowing the neighbors' garbage cans at 2:00 A.M. or ganging up on some jerk in a frat jacket, this was the real thing. And what made it worse was that they couldn't just slip up in the dark, attach the plastique with a timer, and let it rip when they were miles away—oh, no, that would be too simple. His instructions, carried by the old man from none other than Ruy Ruiz, the twenty-three-year-old Sandinista poet in charge of counter-counter-revolutionary activities and occasional sestinas, were to blow it by hand the moment the cargo plane landed. Over breakfast, Robert Jordan, angry though he was, had begun to understand that there was more at risk here than his coiffure. There could be shooting. Rocket fire. Grenades. A parade of images from all the schlock horror films he'd ever seen—exploding guts, melting faces, ragged ghouls risen from the grave—marched witheringly through his head and he vomited.

"Hey, gringo," Ruperto called in English, "suck up your cojones and let's hit it."

Robert Jordan cursed him weakly with a barrage of shits and milks, but when he turned round to wipe the drool from his face he saw that Ruperto and his big woman had led a cluster of horses from the jungle. The big woman, her bare arms muscled like a weightlifter's, approached him leading a gelding the size of a buffalo. "Here, gringo," she breathed in her incongruously feminine voice, "mount up."

"Mount?" Robert Jordan squeaked in growing panic. "I thought we were walking."

The truth was, Robert Jordan had always hated horses. Growing up in Montana it was nothing but horses, horses, horses, morning, noon, and night. Robert Jordan was a rebel, a punk, a free spirit—he was no cowboy dildo—and for him it was dirt bikes and dune buggies. He'd been on horseback exactly twice in his life and both times he'd been thrown. Horses: they scared him. Anything with an eye that big—

"Vámonos," Ruperto snapped. "Or are you as gutless as the rest of the gringo wimps they send us?"

"Leche," Robert Jordan whinnied, too shaken even to curse properly. And then he was in the saddle, the big, broad-beamed monster of a horse peering back at him out of the flat wicked discs of its eyes, and they were off.

Hunkered down in the bug factory, weeds in his face, his coccyx on fire, and every muscle, ligament, and tendon in his legs and ass beaten to pulp by the hammer of the horse's backbone, Robert Jordan waited for the cargo plane. He was cursing his grandmother, the Sandinistas, the Clash, and even Sid Vicious. This was, without doubt, the stupidest thing he'd ever done. Still, as he crouched there with the hard black plastic box of the detonator in his hand, watching the potbellied crewcut rednecks and their runty flat-faced Indian allies out on the landing strip, he felt a surge of savage joy: he was going to blow the motherfuckers to Mars and back.

Ruperto was somewhere to his left, dug in with the big woman and their Kalashnikovs. Their own flat-faced Indians, led by the flat-faced old man, were down to the right somewhere, bristling with rifles. The charges were in place—three in the high grass along the runway median and half a dozen under the prefab aluminum warehouse itself. The charges had been set by a scampering Ruperto just before dawn while the lone sentry dreamed of cold cerveza and a plate of fried dorado and banana chips. Ruperto had set them because when the time came Robert Jordan's legs hadn't worked and that was bad. Ruperto had called him a cheesebag, a faggot, and worse, and he'd lost face with the flat-faced Indians and the old man. But that was then, this was now.

Suddenly he heard it, the distant drone of propellers like the hum of a giant insect. He caressed the black plastic box, murmuring "Come on, baby, come on," all the slights and sneers he'd ever suffered, all the head slaps and gibes about his hair, his gloves, and his boots, all the crap he'd taken from his yuppie bitch of a mother and those dickheads at school—all of it had come down to this. If the guys could only see him now, if they could only see the all-out, hellbent, super-destructive, radical mess he was about to make . . . Yes! And there it was, just over the treetops. Coming in low like a pregnant goose, stuffed full of Twinkies. He began counting down: ten, nine, eight . . .

The blast was the most beautiful thing he'd ever witnessed. One minute he was watching the plane touch down, its wings and fuselage unmarked but for the painted-over insignia of the Flying Tigers, the world still and serene, the sack-bellies standing back expectantly, already tasting that first long cool Bud, and then suddenly, as if he'd clapped another slide in the projector, everything disappeared in a glorious killing thunderclap of fire and smoke. Hot metal, bits of molten glass and god knew how many Twinkies, Buds, and Cups of Soup went rocketing into the air, scorching the trees, and streaming down around Robert Jordan like a furious hissing rain. When the smoke cleared there was nothing left but twisted aluminum, the burned-out hulk of the plane, and a crater the size of Rockefeller Center. From the corner of his eye Robert Jordan could see Ruperto and the big woman emerge cautiously from the bushes, weapons lowered. In a quick low crouch they scurried across the open ground and stood for a moment peering into the smoking crater, then Ruperto let out a single shout of triumph— "Yee-haw!"—and fired off a round in the air.

It was then that things got hairy. Someone opened up on them from the far side of the field—Contra Contra Contra, no doubt—and Ruperto went down. The flat-faced Indians let loose with all they had and for a minute the air screamed like a thousand babies torn open. The big woman threw Ruperto over her shoulder and flew for the jungle like a wounded crab. "Ándale!" she shouted and then the firing stopped abruptly as everyone, Robert Jordan included, bolted for the horses.

When he saw the fist-sized chunk torn out of Ruperto's calf, Robert Jordan wanted to vomit. So he did. The horses were half crazy from the blast and the rat-tat-tat of the Kalashnikovs and they stamped and snorted like fiends from hell. God, he hated horses. But he was puking, Ruperto's wound like raw meat flecked with dirt and bone, and the others were leaping atop their mounts, faces pulled tight with panic. Now there was firing behind them again and he straight-ened up and looked for his horse. There he was, Diablo, jerking wildly at his tether and kicking out his hoofs like a doped-up bronc at the rodeo. Shit. Robert Jordan wiped his lips and made a grab for the reins. It was a mistake. He might just as well have stabbed the horse with a hot poker—in that instant Diablo reared, snapped his tether, and brought all of his wet steaming nine hundred and fifty-eight pounds squarely down on Robert Jordan's left foot.

The sound of his toes snapping was unmusical and harsh and the pain that accompanied it so completely demanding of his attention that he barely noticed the retreating flanks of Diablo as he lashed off through the undergrowth. Robert Jordan let out a howl and broke into a string of inspired curses in two languages and then sat heavily, cradling his foot. The time he'd passed out having his nose pierced flashed through his mind and then the tears started up in his eyes. Stupid, stupid, stupid, he thought. And then he remembered where he was and who was shooting at him from across the field and he looked up to see his comrades already mounted—Ruperto included—and giving him a quick sad look. "Too bad, gringo," Ruperto said, grinning crazily despite the wound, "but it looks like we're short a horse."

"My toes, my toes!" Robert Jordan cried, trying to stand and falling back again.

Rat-tat. Rat-tat-tat, sang the rifles behind them.

Ruperto and his big woman spoke to their horses and they were gone. So too the flat-faced Indians. Only the old man lingered a moment. Just before he lashed his horse and disappeared, he leaned down in the saddle and gave Robert Jordan a wistful look. "Leche," he said, abbreviating the curse, "but isn't war a bitch."

(1987)

THE APE LADY IN RETIREMENT

Somehow, she found herself backed up against the artichoke display in the fruit-and-vegetable department at Waldbaum's, feeling as lost and hopeless as an orphan. She was wearing her dun safari shorts and matching workshirt; the rhino-hide sandals she'd worn at the Makoua Reserve clung to the soles of her pale splayed tired old feet. Outside the big plate-glass windows, a sullen, grainy snow had begun to fall.

Maybe that was it, the snow. She was fretting over the vegetables, fumbling with her purse, the grocery list, the keys to the rheumatic Lincoln her sister had left her, when she glanced up and saw it, this wonder, this phenomenon, this dishwater turned to stone, and for the life of her she didn't know what it was. And then it came to her, the word chipped from the recesses of her memory like an old bone dug from the sediment: *snow*. Snow. What had it been—forty years?

She gazed out past the racks of diet cola and facial cream, past the soap-powder display and the thousand garish colors of the products she couldn't use and didn't want, and she was lost in a reminiscence so sharp and sudden it was like a blow. She saw her sister's eyes peering out from beneath the hood of her snowsuit, the drifts piled high over their heads, hot chocolate in a decorated mug, her father cursing as he bent to wrap the chains round the rear wheels of the car . . . and then the murmur of the market brought her back, the muted din concentrated now in a single voice, and she was aware that someone was addressing her. "Excuse me," the voice was saying, "excuse me."

She turned, and the voice took on form. A young man—a boy, really—short, massive across the shoulders, his dead-black hair cut close in a flattop, was standing before her. And what was that in his hand? A sausage of some sort, pepperoni, yes, and another word came back to her. "Excuse me," he repeated, "but aren't you Beatrice Umbo?"

She was. Oh, yes, she was—Beatrice Umbo, the celebrated ape lady, the world's foremost authority on the behavior of chimpanzees in the wild, Beatrice Umbo, come home to Connecticut to retire. She gave him a faint, distant smile of recognition. "Yes," she said softly, with a trace of the lisp that had clung to her since childhood, "and it's just terrible."

"Terrible?" he echoed, and she could see the hesitation in his eyes. "I'm sorry," he said, grinning unsteadily and thumping the pepperoni against his thigh, "but we read about you in school, in college, I mean. I even read your books, the first one, anyway—*Jungle Dawn*?"

She couldn't respond. It was his grin, the way his upper lip pulled back from his teeth and folded over his incisors. He was Agassiz, the very picture of Agassiz, and all of a sudden she was back in the world of leaves, back in the Makoua Reserve, crouched in a huddle of chimps. "Are you all right?" he asked.

"Of course I'm all right," she snapped, and at that moment she caught a glimpse of herself in the mirror behind the halved cantaloupes. The whites of her eyes were stippled with yellow, her hair was like a fright wig, her face as rutted and seamed as an old saddlebag. Even worse, her skin had the oddest citrus cast to it, a color about midway between the hue of a grapefruit and an orange. She didn't look well, she knew it. But then what could they expect of a woman who'd devoted her life to science and survived dysentery, malaria, schistosomiasis, hepatitis and sleeping sickness in the process, not to mention the little things like the chiggers that burrow beneath your toenails to lay their eggs. "I mean the fruit," she said, trying to bite back the lisp. "The fruit is terrible. No yim-yim," she sighed, gesturing toward the bins of tangerines, kumquats, and pale seedless grapes. "No wild custard apple or tiger peach. They haven't even got passionfruit."

The boy glanced down at her cart. There were fifty yams—she'd counted them out herself—six gallons of full-fat milk, and a five-pound block of cheese buried in its depths. All the bananas she could find, ranging in color from burnished green to putrescent black, were piled on top in a great towering pyramid that threatened to drop the bottom out of the thing. "They've got Italian chestnuts," he offered, looking up again and showing off his teeth in that big tentative grin. "And in a month or so they'll get those little torpedo-shaped things that come off the cactuses out west—prickly pear, that's what they call them."

She cocked her head to give him an appreciative look. "You're very sweet," she said, the lisp creeping back into her voice. "But you don't understand—I've got a visitor coming. A permanent visitor. And he's very particular about what he eats."

"I'm Howie Kantner," he said suddenly. "My father and me run Kantner Construction?"

She'd been in town less than a week, haunting the chilly cavernous house her mother had left her sister and her sister had left her. She'd never heard of Kantner Construction.

The boy ducked his head as if he were genuflecting, told her how thrilled he was to meet her, and turned to go—but then he swung back round impulsively. "Couldn't you . . . I mean, do you think you'll need some help with all those bananas?"

She pursed her lips.

"I just thought . . . the boxboys are the pits here and you're so . . . casually dressed for the weather and all . . ."

"Yes," she said slowly, "yes, that would be very nice," and she smiled. She was pleased, terribly pleased. A moment earlier she'd felt depressed, out of place, an alien in her own hometown, and now she'd made a friend. He waited for her behind the checkout counter, this hulking, earnest college boy, this big post-adolescent male with the clipped brow and squared shoulders, and she beamed at him till her gums ached, wondering what he'd think if she told him he reminded her of a chimp.

Konrad was late. They'd told her three, but it was past five already and there was no sign of him. She huddled by the fire, draped in an afghan she'd found in a trunk in the basement, and listened to the clank and wheeze of the decrepit old oil burner as it switched itself fitfully on and off. It was still snowing, snow like a curse, and she wished she were back in her hut at Makoua with the monsoon hammering at the roof. She looked out the window and thought she was on the moon.

It was close to seven when the knock at the door finally came. She'd been dozing, the notes for her lecture series scattered like refuse at her feet, the afghan drawn up tight around her throat. Clutching the title page as if it were a lifejacket tossed her on a stormy sea, she rose from the chair with a click of her arthritic knees and crossed the room to the door.

Though she'd swept the porch three times, the wind kept defeating her efforts, and when she'd pulled back the door she found Konrad standing in a drift up to his knees. He was huge—far bigger than she'd expected—and the heavy jacket, scarf, and gloves exaggerated the effect. His trainer or keeper or whatever she was stood behind him, grinning weirdly, her arms laden with groceries. Konrad was grinning too, giving her the low closed grin she'd been the first to describe in the wild: it meant he was agitated but not yet stoked to the point of violence. His high-pitched squeals—*eeeee! eeeee! eeeee!*—filled the hallway.

"Miss Umbo?" the girl said, as Konrad, disdaining introductions, flung his knuckles down on the hardwood floor and scampered for the fire. "I'm Jill," the girl said, trying simultaneously to shake hands, pass through the doorframe, and juggle the bags of groceries.

Beatrice was still trying to get over the shock of seeing a chimpanzee in human dress—and one so huge: he must have stood better than four and a half feet
and weighed close to 180—and it was a moment before she could murmur a
greeting and offer to take one of the bags of groceries. The door slammed shut
and the girl followed her into the kitchen while Konrad slapped his shoulders
and stamped round the fireplace.

"He's so . . . so big," Beatrice said, depositing the bag on the oak table in the
kitchen.

"I guess," the girl said, setting her bags down with a shrug.

"And what is all this?" Beatrice gestured at the groceries. She caught a glance
of Konrad through the archway that led into the living room: he'd settled into
her armchair and was studiously bent over her notes, tearing the pages into thin
white strips with the delicate tips of his black leather fingers.

"Oh, this," the girl said, brightening. "This is the stuff he likes to eat," dipping into the near bag and extracting one box after another as if they were exhibits at a trial, "Carnation Instant Breakfast, cheese nachos, Fruit Roll-Ups,
Sugar Daffies . . ."

"Are you—?" Beatrice hesitated, wondering how to phrase the question.
"What I mean is, you're his trainer, I take it?"

The girl must have been in her mid-twenties, though she looked fourteen.
Her hair was limp and blond, her eyes too big for her face. She was wearing
faded jeans, a puffy down vest over a flannel shirt, and a pair of two-hundred-
dollar hiking boots. "Me?" she squealed, and then she blushed. Her voice
dropped till it was nearly inaudible: "I'm just the person that cleans up his cage
and all and I've always had this like way with animals. . . ."

Beatrice was shocked. Shocked and disgusted. It was worse than she'd suspected. When she agreed to take Konrad, she knew she'd be saving him from the
sterility of a cage, from the anomie and humiliation of the zoo. And those were
the very terms—*anomie* and *humiliation*—she'd used on the phone with his former trainer, with the zookeeper himself. For Konrad was no run-of-the-mill
chimp snatched from the jungle and caged for the pleasure of the big bland
white apes who lined up to gawk at him and make their little jokes at the expense of his dignity—though that would have been crime enough—no, he was
special, extraordinary, a chimp made after the image of man.

Raised as a human, in one of those late-sixties experiments Beatrice deplored, he'd been bathed, dressed, and pampered, taught to use cutlery and sit at
a table, and he'd mastered 350 of the hand signals that constituted American
Sign Language. (This last especially appalled her—at one time he could actually
converse, or so they said.) But when he grew into puberty at the age of seven,
when he developed the iron musculature and crackling sinews of the adolescent
male who could reduce a room of furniture to detritus in minutes or snap the fe-
mur of a linebacker as if it were tinder, it was abruptly decided that he could be
human no more. They took away his trousers and shoes, his stuffed toys and his

color TV, and the overseers of the experiment made a quiet move to shift him to the medical laboratories for another, more sinister, sort of research. But he was famous by then and the public outcry landed him in the zoo instead, where they made a sort of clown of him, isolating him from the other chimps and dressing him up like something in a toy-store window. There he'd languished for twenty-five years, neither chimp nor man.

Twenty-five years. And with people like this moon-eyed incompetent to look after him. It *was* a shock. "You mean to tell me you've had no training?" Beatrice demanded, the outrage constricting her throat till she could barely choke out the words. "None at all?"

The girl gave her a meek smile and a shrug of the shoulders.

"You've had nutritional training, certainly—you must have studied the dietary needs of the wild chimpanzee, at the very least . . ." and she gestured disdainfully at the bags of junk food, of salt and fat and empty calories.

The girl murmured something, some sort of excuse or melioration, but Beatrice never heard it. A sudden movement from the front room caught her eye, and all at once she remembered Konrad. She turned away from the girl as if she didn't exist and focused her bright narrow eyes on him, the eyes that had captured every least secret of his wild cousins, the rapt unblinking eyes of the professional voyeur.

The first thing she noticed was that he'd finished with her notes, the remnants of which lay strewn about the room like confetti. She saw too that he was calm now, at home already, sniffing at the afghan as if he'd known it all his life. Oblivious to her, he settled into the armchair, draped the afghan over his knees, and began fumbling through the pockets of his overcoat like an absent-minded commuter. And then, while her mouth fell open and her eyes narrowed to pinpricks, he produced a cigar—a fine, green, tightly rolled panatela—struck a match to light it, and lounged back in an aureole of smoke, his feet, bereft now of the plastic galoshes, propped up luxuriously on the coffee table.

It was a night of stinging cold and subarctic wind, but though the panes rattled in their frames, the old house retained its heat. Beatrice had set the thermostat in the high eighties and she'd built the fire up beneath a cauldron of water that steamed the walls and windows till they dripped like the myriad leaves of the rain forest. Konrad was naked, as nature and evolution had meant him to be, and Beatrice was in the clean, starched khakis she'd worn in the bush for the past forty years. Potted plants—cane, ficus, and dieffenbachia—crowded the hallway, spilled from the windowsills, and softened the corners of each of the downstairs rooms. In the living room, the TV roared at full volume, and Konrad stood before it, excited, signing at the screen and emitting a rising series of pant hoots: *"Hoo-hoo, hoo-ah-hoo-ah-hoo!"*

Watching from the kitchen, Beatrice felt her face pucker with disapproval.

This TV business was no good, she thought, languidly stirring vegetables into a pot of chicken broth. Chimps had an innate dignity, an eloquence that had nothing to do with sign language, gabardine, color TV, or nacho chips, and she was determined to restore it to him. The junk food was in the trash, where it belonged, along with the obscene little suits of clothes the girl had foisted on him, and she'd tried unplugging the TV set, but Konrad was too smart for her. Within thirty seconds he'd got it squawking again.

"*Eee-eee!*" he shouted now, slapping his palms rhythmically on the hardwood floor.

"Awright," the TV said in its stentorian voice, "take the dirty little stool pigeon out back and extoiminate him."

It was an unfortunate thing for the TV to say, because it provoked in Konrad a reaction that could only be described as a frenzy. Whereas before he'd been excited, now he was enraged. "*Wraaaaa!*" he screamed in a pitch no mere human could duplicate, and he charged the screen with a stick of firewood, every hair on his body sprung instantly erect. Good, she thought, stirring her soup as he flailed at the oak-veneer cabinet and choked the voice out of it, good, good, good, as he backed away and bounced round the room like a huge India-rubber ball, the stick slapping behind him, his face contorted in a full open grin of incendiary excitement. Twice over the sofa, once up the banister, and then he charged again, the stick beating jerkily at the floor. The crash of the screen came almost as a relief to her—at least there'd be no more of that. What puzzled her, though, what arrested her hand in mid-stir, was Konrad's reaction. He stood stock-still a moment, then backed off, pouting and tugging at his lower lip, the screams tapering to a series of squeaks and whimpers of regret.

The moment the noise died, Beatrice became aware of another sound, low-pitched and regular, a signal it took her a moment to identify: someone was knocking at the door. Konrad must have heard it too. He looked up from the shattered cabinet and grunted softly, "*Urk,*" he said, "*urk, urk,*" and lifted his eyes to Beatrice's as she backed away from the stove and wiped her hands on her apron.

Who could it be, she wondered, and what must they have thought of all that racket? She hung her apron on a hook, smoothed back her hair, and passed into the living room, neatly sidestepping the wreckage of the TV. Konrad's eyes followed her as she stepped into the foyer, flicked on the porch light, and swung back the door.

"Hello? Miss Umbo?"

Two figures stood bathed in yellow light before her, hominids certainly, and wrapped in barbaric bundles of down, fur, and machine-stitched nylon. "Yes?"

"I hope you don't . . . I mean, you probably don't remember me," said the squatter of the two figures, removing his knit cap to reveal the stiff black brush cut beneath, "but we met a couple weeks ago at Waldbaum's? I'm Howie, Howie Kantner?"

Agassiz, she thought, and she saw his unsteady grin replicated on the face of the figure behind him.

"I hope it isn't an imposition, but this is my father, Howard," and the second figure, taller, less bulky in the shoulders, stepped forward with a slouch and an uneasy shift of his eyes that told her he was no longer the dominant male. "Pleased to meet you," he said in a voice ruined by tobacco.

She was aware of Konrad behind her—he'd pulled himself into the precarious nest he'd made in the coat tree of mattress stuffing and strips of carpeting from the downstairs hallway—and her social graces failed her. She didn't think to ask them in out of the cold till Howie spoke again. "I—I was wondering," he stammered, "my father's a big fan of yours, if you would sign a book for him?"

Smile, she told herself, and the command influenced her facial muscles. Ask them to come in. "Come in," she said, "please," and then she made a banal comment about the weather.

In they came, stamping and shaking and picking at their clothing, massive but obsequious, a barrage of apologies—"so late"; "we're not intruding?"; "did she mind?"—exploding around them. They exchanged a glance and wrinkled up their noses at the potent aroma and high visibility of Konrad. Howard Sr. clutched his book, a dog-eared paper edition of *The Wellsprings of Man*. From his coat tree, which Beatrice had secured to the high ceilings with a network of nylon tow rope, Konrad grunted softly. "No, not at all," she heard herself saying, and then she asked them if they'd like a cup of hot chocolate or tea.

Seated in the living room and divested of their impressive coats and ponderous boots, scarves, gloves, and hats, father and son seemed subdued. They tried not to look at the ruined TV or at the coat tree or the ragged section of bare plaster where Konrad had stripped the flowered wallpaper to get at the stale but piquant paste beneath. Howie was having the hot chocolate; Howard Sr., the tea. "So how do you like our little town?" Howard Sr. asked as she settled into the armchair opposite him.

She hadn't uttered a word to a human being since Konrad's companion had left, and she was having difficulty with the amenities expected of her. Set her down amidst a convocation of chimps or even a troop of baboons and she'd never commit a faux pas or gaucherie, but here she felt herself on uncertain ground. "Hate it," she said.

Howard Sr. seemed to mull this over, while unbeknownst to him, Konrad was slipping down from the coat tree and creeping up at his back. "Is it that bad," he said finally, "or is it the difference between Connecticut and the, the—" He was interrupted by the imposition of a long, sinuous, fur-cloaked arm which snaked under his own to deftly snatch a pack of cigarettes from his shirt pocket. Before he could react, the arm was gone. *"Eeeee!"* screamed Konrad, *"eeee-eeee!,"* and he retreated to the coat tree with his booty.

Beatrice rose immediately to her feet, ignoring the sharp pain that ground at her kneecaps, and marched across the room. She wouldn't have it, one of *her* chimps indulging a filthy human habit. Give it here, she wanted to say, but then she wouldn't have one of her chimps responding to human language either, as if he were some fawning lapdog or neutered cat. *"Whoo-oo-oogh,"* she coughed at him.

"Wraaaaa!" he screamed back, bouncing down from his perch and careening round the room in a threat display, the cigarettes clutched tightly to his chest. She circled him warily, aware that Howie and his father loomed behind her now, their limbs loose, faces set hard. "Miss Umbo," Howie's voice spoke at her back, "do you need any help there?"

It was then that Konrad tore round the room again—up over the couch, the banister, up the ropes and down—and Howard Sr. made a calculated grab for him. "No!" Beatrice cried, but the warning was superfluous: Konrad effortlessly eluded the old man's clumsy swipe, bounced twice, and was back up in the coat tree before he could blink his eyes.

"Heh, heh," Howard Sr. laughed from the top of his throat, "frisky little fella, isn't he?"

Beatrice stood before him, trying to catch her breath. "You don't," she began, wondering how to put it, "you don't want to, uh, obstruct him when he displays."

Howie, the son, looked bemused.

"You don't, I think, appreciate the strength of this creature. A chimpanzee— a full-grown male, as Konrad is—is at least three times as strong as his human counterpart. Now certainly, I'm sure he wouldn't deliberately hurt anyone—"

"Hurt us?" Howie exclaimed, involuntarily flexing his shoulders. "I mean, he barely comes up to my chest."

A contented grunt escaped Konrad at that moment. He lay sprawled in his nest, the rubbery soles of his prehensile feet blackly dangling. He'd wadded up the entire pack of cigarettes and tucked it beneath his lower lip. Now he extracted the wad of tobacco and paper, sniffed it with an appreciative roll of his eyes, and replaced it between cheek and gum. Beatrice sighed. She looked at Howie, but didn't have the strength to respond.

Later, while Konrad snored blissfully from his perch and the boy and his father had accepted first one bowl of chicken soup and then another, and the conversation drew away from the prosaic details of Beatrice's life in Connecticut— and did she know Tiddy Brohmer and Harriet Dillers?—and veered instead toward Makoua and the Umbo Primate Center, Howard Sr. brought up the subject of airplanes. He flew, and so did his son. He'd heard about the bush pilots in Africa and wondered about her experience of them.

Beatrice was so surprised she had to set down her tea for fear of spilling it. "You fly?" she repeated.

Howard Sr. nodded and leveled his keen glistening gaze on her. "Twenty-two

hundred and some-odd hours' worth," he said. "And Howie. He's a regular fanatic. Got his license when he was sixteen, and since we bought the Cessna
there's hardly a minute when he's on the ground."

"I love it," Howie asserted, crouched over his massive thighs on the very edge
of the chair. "I mean, it's my whole life. When I get out of school I want to restore classic aircraft. I know a guy who's got a Stearman."

Beatrice warmed up her smile. All at once she was back in Africa, 2,500 feet
up, the land spread out like a mosaic at her feet. Champ, her late husband, had
taken to planes like a chimp to trees, and though she'd never learned to fly herself, she'd spent whole days at a time in the air with him, spying out chimp habitat in the rich green forests of Cameroon, the Congo, and Zaire or coasting
above the golden veldt to some distant, magical village in the hills. She closed
her eyes a moment, overcome with the intensity of the recollection. Champ,
Makoua, the storms and sunsets and the close, savage, unimpeachable society of
the apes—it was all lost to her, lost forever.

"Miss Umbo?" Howie was peering into her eyes with an expression of concern, the same expression he'd worn that afternoon in Waldbaum's when he'd
asked if she needed help with the bananas.

"Miss Umbo," he repeated, "anytime you want to see Connecticut from the
air, just you let me know."

"That's very kind of you," she said.

"Really," and he grinned Agassiz's grin, "it'd be a pleasure."

Things were sprouting from the dead dun earth—crocuses, daffodils, nameless
buds and strange pale fingertips of vegetation—by the time the first of her scheduled lectures came round. It was an evening lecture, open to the public, and held
in the Buffon Memorial Auditorium of the State University. Her topic was "Tool
Modification in the Chimps of the Makoua Reserve," and she'd chosen fifty color
slides for illustration. For a while she'd debated wearing one of the crepe-de-
chine dresses her sister had left hanging forlornly in the closet, but in the end she
decided to stick with the safari shorts.

As the auditorium began to fill, she stood rigid behind the curtain, deaf to the
chatter of the young professor who was to introduce her. She watched the crowd
gather—blank-faced housewives and their paunchy husbands, bearded professors, breast-thumping students, the stringy, fur-swathed women of the Anthro-
pology Club—watched them command their space, choose their seats, pick at
themselves, and wriggle in their clothing. "I'll keep it short," the young professor
was saying, "some remarks about your career in general and the impact of your
first two books, then maybe two minutes on Makoua and the Umbo Primate
Center, is that all right?" Beatrice didn't respond. She was absorbed in the dy-
namics of the crowd, listening to their chatter, observing their neck-craning and
leg-crossing, watching the furtive plumbing of nostrils and sniffing of armpits,

the obsessive fussing with hair and jewelry. Howie and his father were in the second row. By the time she began, it was standing room only.

It went quite well at first—she had that impression, anyway. She was talking of what she knew better than anyone else alive, and she spoke with a fluency and grace she couldn't seem to summon at Waldbaum's or the local Exxon station. She watched them—fidgeting, certainly, but patient and intelligent, all their primal needs—their sexual urges, the necessity of relieving themselves and eating to exhaustion—sublimated beneath the spell of her words. Agassiz, she told them about Agassiz, the first of the wild apes to let her groom him, dead twenty years now. She told them of Spenser and Leakey and Darwin, of Lula, Pout, and Chrysalis. She described how Agassiz had fished for termites with the stem of a plant he'd stripped of leaves, how Lula had used a stick to force open the concrete bunkers in which the bananas were stored, and how Clint, the dominant male, had used a wad of leaves as a spoon to dip the brains from the shattered skull of a baby baboon.

The problem arose when she began the slide show. For some reason, perhaps because the medium so magnified the size of the chimps and he felt himself wanting in comparison, Konrad threw a fit. (She hadn't wanted to bring him, but the last time she'd left him alone he'd switched on all the burners of the stove, overturned and gutted the refrigerator, and torn the back door from its hinges—all this prior to committing a rash of crimes, ranging from terrorizing Mrs. Binchy's Doberman to crushing and partially eating a still-unidentified angora kitten.) He'd been sitting just behind the podium, slouched in a folding chair around which Doris Beatts, the young professor, had arranged an array of fruit, including a basket of yim-yim flown in for the occasion. "Having him onstage is a terrific idea," she'd gushed, pumping Beatrice's hand and flashing a zealot's smile that showed off her pink and exuberant gums. "What could be better? It'll give the audience a real frisson, having a live chimp sitting there."

Yes, it gave them a frisson, all right.

Konrad had been grunting softly to himself and working his way happily through the yim-yim, but no sooner had the lights been dimmed and the first slide appeared than he was up off the chair with a shriek of outrage. Puffed to twice his size, he swayed toward the screen on his hind legs, displaying at the gigantic chimp that had suddenly materialized out of the darkness. *"Wraaaaa!"* he screamed, dashing the chair to pieces and snatching up one of its jagged legs to whirl over his head like a club. There was movement in the front row. A murmur of concern—concern, not yet fear—washed through the crowd. *"Woo-oo-oogh,"* Beatrice crooned, trying to calm him. "It's all right," she heard herself saying through the speakers that boomed her voice out over the auditorium. But it wasn't all right. She snapped to the next slide, a close-up of Clint sucking termites from a bit of straw, and Konrad lost control, throwing himself at the screen with a screech that brought the audience to its feet.

Up went the lights. To an individual, the audience was standing. Beatrice didn't have time to catalogue their facial expressions, but they ran the gamut from amusement to shock, terror, and beyond. One woman—heavyset, with arms like Christmas turkeys and black little deepset eyes—actually cried out as if King Kong himself had broken loose. And Konrad? He stood bewildered amidst the white tatters of the screen, his fur gone limp again, his knuckles on the floor. For a moment, Beatrice actually thought he looked embarrassed.

Later, at the reception, people crowded round him and he took advantage of the attention to shamelessly cadge cigarettes, plunder the canapé trays, and guzzle Coca-Cola as if it were spring water. Beatrice wanted to put a stop to it— he was demeaning himself, the clown in the funny suit with his upturned palm thrust through the bars of his cage—but the press around her was terrific. Students and scholars, a man from the local paper, Doris Beatts and her neurasthenic husband, the Kantners, father and son, all bombarding her with questions: Would she go back? Was it for health reasons she'd retired? Did she believe in UFOs? Reincarnation? The New York Yankees? How did it feel having a full-grown chimp in the house? Did she know Vlastos Reizek's monograph on the seed content of baboon feces in the Kalahari? It was almost ten o'clock before Konrad turned away to vomit noisily in the corner and Howie Kantner, beaming sunnily and balancing half a plastic cup of warm white wine on the palm of one hand, asked her when they were going to go flying.

"Soon," she said, watching the crowd part as Konrad, a perplexed look on his face, bent to lap up the sour overflow of his digestive tract.

"How about tomorrow?" Howie said.

"Tomorrow," Beatrice repeated, struck suddenly with the scent of the rain forest, her ears ringing with the call of shrike and locust and tree toad. "Yes," she lisped, "that would be nice."

Konrad was subdued the next day. He spent the early morning halfheartedly tearing up the carpet in the guest room, then brooded over his nuts and bananas, all the while pinning Beatrice with an accusatory look, a look that had nacho chips and Fruit Roll-Ups written all over it. Around noon, he dragged himself across the floor like a hundred-year-old man and climbed wearily into his nest. Beatrice felt bad, but she wasn't about to give in. They'd made him schizophrenic—neither chimp nor man—and if there was pain involved in reacquainting him with his roots, with his true identity, there was nothing she could do about it. Besides, she was feeling schizophrenic herself. Konrad was a big help— the smell of him, the silken texture of his fur as she groomed him, the way he scratched around in the basement when he did his business—but still she felt out of place, still she missed Makoua with an ache that wouldn't go away, and as the days accumulated like withered leaves at her feet, she found herself wishing she'd stayed on there to die.

Howie appeared at ten of three, his rust-eaten Datsun rumbling at the curb, the omnipresent grin on his lips. It was unseasonably warm for mid-April and he wore a red T-shirt that showed off the extraordinary development of his pectorals, deltoids, and biceps; a blue windbreaker was flung casually over one shoulder. "Miss Umbo," he boomed as she answered the door, "it's one perfect day for flying. Visibility's got to be twenty-five miles or more. You ready?"

She was. She'd been looking forward to it, in fact. "I hope you don't mind if I bring Konrad along," she said.

Howie's smile faded for just an instant. Konrad stood at her side, his lower lip unfurled in a pout. *"Hoo-hoo,"* he murmured, eyes meek and round. Howie regarded him dubiously a moment, and then the grin came back. "Sure," he said, shrugging. "I don't see why not."

It was a twenty-minute ride to the airport. Beatrice stared out the window at shopping centers, car lots, Burger King and Stereo City, at cemeteries that stretched as far as she could see. Konrad sat in back, absorbed in plucking cigarette butts from the rear ashtray and making a neat little pile of them on the seat beside him. Howie was oblivious. He kept up a steady stream of chatter the whole way, talking about airplanes mostly, but shading into his coursework at school and how flipped out his anthro prof would be when she heard he was taking Beatrice flying. For her part, Beatrice was content to let the countryside flash by, murmuring an occasional "Yes" or "Uh-huh" when Howie paused for breath.

The airport was tiny, two macadam strips in a grassy field, thirty or forty airplanes lined up in ragged rows, a cement-block building the size of her basement. A sign over the door welcomed them to Arkbelt Airport. Howie pushed the plane out onto the runway himself and helped Beatrice negotiate the high step up into the cockpit. Konrad clambered into the back and allowed Beatrice to fasten his seatbelt. For a long while they sat on the ground, as Howie, grinning mechanically, revved the engine and checked this gauge or that.

The plane was a Cessna 182, painted a generic orange and white and equipped with dual controls, autopilot, a storm scope, and four cramped vinyl seats. It was about what she'd expected—a little shinier and less battered than Champ's Piper, but no less noisy or bone-rattling. Howie gunned the engine and the plane jolted down the runway with an apocalyptic roar, Beatrice clinging to the plastic handgrip till she could taste her breakfast in the back of her throat. But then they lifted off like gods, liberated from the grip of the earth, and Connecticut swelled beneath them, revealing the drift and flow of its topology and the hidden patterns of its dismemberment.

"Beautiful," she screamed over the whine of the engine.

Howie worked the flaps and drew the yoke toward him. They banked right and rose steadily. "See that out there?" he shouted, pointing out her window to where the ocean threw the sky back at them. "Long Island Sound."

From just behind her, Konrad said: *"Wow-wow, er-er-er-er!"* The smell of him, in so small a confine, was staggering.

"You want to sightsee here," Howie shouted, "maybe go over town and look for your house and the university and all, or do you want to go out over the Island a ways and then circle back?"

She was dazzled, high in the empyrean, blue above, blue below. "The Island," she shouted, exhilarated, really exhilarated, for the first time since she'd left Africa.

Howie leveled off the plane and the tan lump of Long Island loomed ahead of them. "Great, huh?" he shouted, gesturing toward the day like an impresario, like the man who'd made it. Beatrice beamed at him, "Woooo!" Howie said, pinching his nostrils and making an antic face. "He's ripe today, Konrad, isn't he?"

"Forty years," Beatrice laughed, proud of Konrad, proud of the stink, proud of every chimp she'd ever known, and proud of this boy Howie too—why, he was nothing but a big chimp himself. It was then—while she was laughing, while Howie mugged for her and she began to feel almost whole for the first time since she'd left Makoua—that the trouble began. Like most trouble, it arose out of a misunderstanding. Apparently, Konrad had saved one of the butts from Howie's car, and when he reached out nimbly to depress the cigarette lighter, Howie, poor Howie, thought he was going for the controls and grabbed his wrist.

A mistake.

"No!" Beatrice cried, and immediately the tug of war spilled over into her lap. "Let go of him!"

"Eeeee! Eeeee!" Konrad shrieked, his face distended in the full open grin of high excitement, already stoked to violence. She felt the plane dip out from under her as Howie, his own face gone red with the rush of blood, struggled to keep it on course with one hand while fighting back Konrad with the other. It was no contest. Konrad slipped Howie's grasp and then grabbed *his* wrist, as if to say, "How do you like it?"

"Get off me, goddamnit!" Howie bellowed, but Konrad didn't respond. Instead, he jerked Howie's arm back so swiftly and suddenly it might have been the lever of a slot machine; even above the noise of the engine, Beatrice could hear the shoulder give, and then Howie's bright high yelp of pain filled the compartment. In the next instant Konrad was in front, in the cockpit, dancing from Beatrice's lap to Howie's and back again, jerking at the controls, gibbering and hooting and loosing his bowels in a frenzy like nothing she'd ever seen.

"Son of a bitch!" Howie was working up a frenzy of his own, the plane leaping and bucking as he punched in the autopilot and hammered at the chimp with his left hand, the right dangling uselessly, his eyes peeled back in terror. *"Hoo-ah-hoo-ah-hoo!"* Konrad hooted, spewing excrement and springing into Beatrice's lap. For an instant he paused to shoot Howie a mocking glance and then he snatched the yoke to his chest and the plane shot up with a clattering howl while Howie flailed at him with the heavy meat of his fist.

Konrad took the first two blows as if he didn't notice them, then abruptly dropped the yoke, the autopilot kicking in to level them off. Howie hit him again and Beatrice knew she was going to die. *"Er-er,"* Konrad croaked experimentally, and Howie, panic in his face, hit him again. And then, as casually as he might have reached out for a yam or banana, Konrad returned the blow and the plane jerked with the force of it. *"Wraaaaa!"* Konrad screamed, but Howie didn't hear him. Howie was unconscious. Unconscious, and smeared with shit. And now, delivering the coup de grâce, Konrad sprang to his chest, snatched up his left hand—the hand that had pummeled him—and bit off the thumb. A snap of the jaws and it was gone. Howie's heart pumped blood to the wound.

In that moment—the moment of Howie's disfigurement—Beatrice's own heart turned over in her chest. She looked at Konrad, perched atop poor Howie, and at Howie, who even in repose managed to favor Agassiz. They were beyond Long Island now, headed out to sea, high over the Atlantic. Champ had tried to teach her to fly, but she'd had no interest in it. She looked at the instrument panel and saw nothing. For a moment the idea of switching on the radio came into her head, but then she glanced at Konrad and thought better of it.

Konrad was looking into her eyes. The engine hummed, Howie's head fell against the door, the smell of Konrad—his body, his shit—filled her nostrils. They had five hours' flying time, give or take a few minutes, that much she knew. She looked out over the nose of the plane to where the sea swallowed up the rim of the world. Africa was out there, distant and serene, somewhere beyond the night that fell like an ax across the horizon. She could almost taste it.

"Urk," Konrad said, and he was still looking at her. His eyes were soft now, his breathing regular. He sat atop Howie in a forlorn slouch, the cigarette forgotten, the controls irrelevant, nothing at all. *"Urk,"* he repeated, and she knew what he wanted, knew in a rush of comprehension that took her all the way back to Makoua and that first, long-ago touch of Agassiz's strange spidery fingers.

She held his eyes. The engine droned. The sea beneath them seemed so still you could walk on it, so soft you could wrap yourself up in it. She reached out and touched his hand. *"Urk,"* she said.

(1988)

DE RERUM NATURA

The inventor is in his laboratory, white smock, surgical mask, running afoul of the laws of nature. Schlaver and Una Moss are with him, bent over the Petri dishes and dissecting pans like conspirators. Overhead, the hum of the fluorescent lights.

He snaps his hands into the rubber gloves, flashes the scalpel. His touch is quick, sure, steady as a laser. The blade eases through the shaved skin of the abdomen, his fingers flutter, vessels are clamped, ligatures tied. Una is there, assisting with sponges and retractors. The Inventor's eyes burn over the mask like the eyes of an Arab terrorist. A single sweatpearl stands on his forehead. Strapped to the table before him, teats sleepy with milk, irises sinking, the sedated sow gargles through her crusted nostrils, stirs a bristling hock. Una pats the pink hoof.

Then he is speaking, the tones measured, smooth, the phrases clipped. Schlaver moves in, draws off the amniotic fluid. Una takes the forceps, offers the scalpel. The Inventor slits the sack, reaches in, pulls his prize from the steaming organs. He slaps the wet nates: the wrinkled little creature shrieks, and then again, its electric wail poking into mason jars, behind filing cabinets, rattling the loose screws in the overhead lights. Una and Schlaver tear off their masks and cheer. The Inventor hefts his latest coup, a nine-pound-three-ounce boy, red as a ham and perfect in every detail: his firstborn son and heir. The black eyes grin above the mask.

From *The Life:*

To say merely that he was a prodigy would mock the insufficiency of language. At five he was teaching in the temple. By age seven he had built his first neutron smasher, developed a gnat-sized bugging device that could pick up a whispered conversation at two miles and simultaneously translate it into any one of thirteen languages, and devised a sap-charging system which fomented rapid growth in deciduous trees of the temperate zone.* At nine he was admitted to MIT, where he completed advanced degrees in physics and mathematics prior to his thirteenth year. During the course of the next eleven months he studied surgical medicine at Johns Hopkins.

At fifteen he stunned the world with his first great advance, the stoolless cat, which brought him the financial independence to sustain his subtler and more meaningful future work. Through an accelerated but painstaking process of selective breeding he had overseen the evolution of a strain of common housecat—the usual attributes intact—which never in the course of its normal lifespan was actuated by the physiological demands of micturition or defecation. Within six months after its introduction the major producers of cat litter had thrown in the towel and pet shops were opening next to every liquor store in the country. His photograph (contemplative, the horn-rims) appeared on the covers of *Newsweek* and *Time* during the same week. He was hailed. "An Edison for the Seventies," "The Pragmatist's Einstein," they said. Housewives clamored. The Russians awarded him the Star of Novgorod. Encouraged, he went on to develop the limbless, headless, tailless strain that has since become an international institution. A tribute to his disinterestedness: "Under no circumstance, no matter how attractive the inducement," he said, "will I be persuaded to breed out the very minimal essence of the feline—I refer to its purr."†

He is in his study, musing over the morning's mail. The mail, corners, edges, inks and stamps like the tails of tropical birds, lies across his desk in a welter. In his hand, the paper knife. He selects an envelope printed in a blue and yellow daisy pattern.

It is a threat.

Next he picks up a business envelope, imprinted with the name and logo (an ascending rocket) of his son's school: WERNHER VON BRAUN ELEMENTARY SCHOOL. It is a letter from his son's teacher. She is alarmed at what appears to be a worsening deformity of the boy's feet (so misshapen as almost to resemble hoofs, she says) and hopes that his father will have the matter looked into. She is also

---

*The oaks and willows shadowing the home of Helmut Holtz, his first tutor, have attained heights in excess of three hundred feet, and continue to grow at an annual rate of nine feet, three and three quarters inches.

†In Finland, for example, a 10.3 annual per capita consumption of the Furballs (pat. trade name) is indicated. At Reykjavik they are sold on the street corner. An American Porno Queen posed nude in a sea of Furballs for a still-controversial spread in a men's publication. And the Soviet Premier has forgone bedclothes for them. His explanation: "Can you make to purr the electric blanket?"

concerned with his behavior. The boy has, it seems, been making disruptive noises in the classroom. A sort of whinnying or chuffing. The Inventor carefully folds the letter, tucks it into the pocket of his shirt. At that moment the double doors yawn and Una Moss, in deshabille, ambles in behind the tea cart. Her pet python, weaving a turgid *S* in the rug behind her, stops at the door.

She pours the Inventor's tea (two lumps) while he frowns at the mail. As she turns to leave, he speaks. "Una?" She looks, puckers a moue. "What is this business with the boy? It seems he's been emitting those noises in the schoolroom." Una's expression irons to the serious. "We can't have that," he says. "Will you speak with him?"

"Of course, pumpkin."

He looks down again. The door closes behind Una, a gentle click, and he turns back to the mail. A brown-paper parcel catches his eyes. The paper knife makes a neat incision and he extracts the contents: a hardcover book. No letter, no inscription. *The Island of Dr. Moreau* by H. G. Wells. He folds back the page, begins to read.

From *The Life:*

His second major breakthrough was also a humanitarian effort. A committee from the Gandhi Foundation had come to him asking for a solution to the problem of world hunger. He told them he would consider their petition, though engaged in other projects at the time. That afternoon, while he was rooting through a local wrecking yard in search of a tailpipe replacement for his automobile, the solution rushed on him like a firestorm. "Of course," he was heard to mutter. He retraced his steps to the proprietor's blistered shed. There he borrowed a #2 faucet wrench, ball peen hammer and screwdriver. He then removed the tailpipe from a sandwiched auto of identical make and model to his own. This involved twelve minutes, thirty-seven seconds, as near as investigators have been able to determine. In the short space of this time he had worked out the complicated structural formulae which resulted in one of mankind's biggest boons—that is to say, he discovered the method by which a given tonnage of spotted chrome and rusted steel could be converted to an equivalent weight of porterhouse steak.

He is at Horn & Hardart, surrounded by strangers. The boy sits across from him, head down, heels swinging, fingers fluffed with the meringue from his third slice of pie. Una's handbag perches like a sentinel at the edge of the table. Suddenly the boy begins to grunt: hurp-hurp-hurp. The Inventor looks uncomfortable. He raises a finger to his lips—but the grunting cracks an octave and the boy pins the plate to the table, begins licking. The Inventor remonstrates. The plate rattles on the Formica. Heads turn. The Inventor stands, looking for Una. Then strides to the bank of tiny windows and stainless steel doors, fishing in his pocket for coins. Behind him the grunting increases in volume. He peers into each window until he finds a slice of lemon meringue pie, yellow sliver, brown peaks. He puts the coins in the slot, tugs at the door. It does not open. He tugs harder, taps at the glass, tries another coin. There is the slap of the boy's plate on the tiles, and then his angry wail. A middle-aged woman, a stranger, is trying to comfort him. The Inventor's armpits are moist. He jerks at the door, tries to spring it with his penknife. The howls at his back, the ripe flush of the woman's face. And then, from the Ladies' Room, Una. Like a savior. Green eyeshade, black caftan, copper anklets.

From *The Life:*

The Inventor's marriage with Roxanne Needelman was never consummated. She was twenty-nine, a laboratory assistant, twice married and widowed. He was eighteen, raw, ingenuous, in the first flush of his monumental success with the stoolless cat. After a disastrous honeymoon at Olduvai Gorge the two set up separate households. Three years later the marriage was terminated. The Inventor, immersed in his work, retired to his estate in northern Westchester.

During the course of the next five years he lived and worked alone, perfecting the Autochef and laying the theoretical groundwork for expanding the minute. On the eve of his twenty-sixth birthday he began his association with Yehudi Schlaver, the German-born physicist who would be with him to the end. Two years later, on a rainy April evening, the front buzzer sounded through the umbrageous corridors of the Westchester mansion. At the door, Una Moss. She was wearing a backpack. Two tote bags lay at her feet. She had followed the Great Man's career, saved the clippings from over fifty periodicals, and now she had come to live with him. The Inventor stood in the doorway, his brow square as the spine of a book. He pushed open the door.

Una, Schlaver, the Inventor, his son. They stand at the rail of the Dayliner, in identical London Fog overcoats. On their way to Bear Mountain, for an outing. The air like bad breath, sky black, the water thick and dun-colored. An amateur photographer, passing in a small craft, recognizes the celebrated faces and takes a snapshot: Una, eyes shaded in purple, the rock python wrapped under her chin like primordial jewelry and disappearing in the folds of her overcoat, its head visible beneath the sleeve; Schlaver, small, gray, nondescript; the Great Man, his blocklike brow, the creases like chains running deep into the hairline, the black eyes pinched behind the horn-rims, the point of the beard, lank arms, stooped back; and the boy, feet concealed in custom-built boots, ears already growing to the point and peeping like tongues from beneath the bristling hair. Waves lap, the deck rises, dips. Una, Schlaver and the boy wave. The Inventor hangs his head and disgorges the contents of his stomach.

At the dock, the boy darts ahead, repeatedly stumbling in his boots. Schlaver and Una follow, the one taking charge of the Inventor's compass, calculator and notebooks, the other dragging a picnic basket. The Inventor, sulking, brings up the rear. It begins to drizzle.

A picnic table, prettily reflecting inverted treetops in a sheen of rainwater. The three, collars up, noses dripping, chewing stolidly. In silence. The boy, boots in hand, merrily roots among the wildflowers, nudging at the wet red earth with the bridge of his nose. "Screee-honk-honk," he says, at intervals. The Inventor looks unutterably depressed. He stands, buckles the belt round his raincoat. "Una. I will take a short walk. I wish to be alone, and to be among the trees and mosses." He strides off, into the black bank of pine and beech. Continues on, deep in thought. The trees look alike. He loses his way. When night falls, Una and Schlaver become alarmed. They step into the shadows of the first trees and halloo. There is no answer.

In the morning, search parties are organized. Bloodhounds, state police, Boy Scout troops, helicopters, flares. The Governor mobilizes the National Guard. The Vice President flies in. The voice of the Inventor's mother (a wizened old woman in a babushka) is boomed through enormous loudspeakers. Woodsmen begin felling trees, burning off ground cover. The Inventor has vanished.

Forty days later, Una, who alone has refused to give up the search, is struggling down a slick and rock-strewn slope. Again, rain falls. Again, she wears the overcoat. Again, she accommodates the reptile (the head a comfort in her hand). At the base of the hill, a swamp. Her boots slosh through the clots of algae, heels tug against the suck of the mud. She looks up to flail at a spider web and there he is, squatting naked in a ring of skunk cabbage, his back dancing with mosquito and fly. The glasses are gone, the black eyes crazed and bloodshot. "Here," she says, and holds out her hand. He looks up at her, confused, then slowly lifts his hand to hers, loses his fingers in the triangular black mouth of the snake.

From *The Life:*

The now infamous "Bear Mountain Sojourn" marked the decline of the Inventor's practical humanitarian phase. He called a press conference, announced his intention of permanently retiring to his home in suburban Westchester for the purpose of undertaking his great work, a work which would "spiritually edify the race of men as [his] previous work had materially edified them." For seven years nothing was heard of him. Of course there were the usual garbage sifters and mail steamers, the reports from the Inventor's few privileged friends, the speculations of the press. And from time to time paparazzi came up with photographs of the Great Man: brooding on the bedroom fire escape, rooting in the turf with his son, sending up frozen slashes of foam (his slick arm poised) while swimming laps in the pool. Still, he was all but lost to the public eye.

It was during the Seven Years of Silence that a nefarious innovation with enormous market potential appeared briefly in this country and in two Western European nations: a colorless, tasteless liquid, which, when combined with food or drink, reduced the ingestor to a heap of desiccated flakes. When the flakes were moistened, the desiccatee would regain his/her normal structure, totally free of side effects. Abuses of the product were legion.* And though the FDA banned its sale minutes after it was first made available commercially, it was readily obtainable on the black market and even today continues suspect in any number of unsolved kidnappings and missing-persons cases. Rumor attributed its invention to the Great Man. Schlaver read a statement denying his associate's participation in the development of the chemical and asserting how deeply the Inventor deplored the discovery of a product so potentially pernicious. But rumor is not easily squelched, and the whole affair left a bad taste.

He is dozing in an armchair, three Furballs purring in his lap. In the hall, the sound of his son's hoofs like a drumbeat on the linoleum. His eyes flutter open, caught in the rift between consciousness and the deeps. He stands. Gropes for his glasses. Una lies asleep on the davenport, the snake coiled round her like a meandering stream. He finds the tail. It stiffens under his fingers, then goes limp. He heaves, fireman and firehose: the coils spin to the carpet. "What's up?" Una murmurs. He is unbuttoning her smock. The python lies on the floor, dead weight, quietly digesting its bimonthly rabbit. The Inventor climbs atop her, arching over her stiff as a mounted butterfly. "I had a dream," he says.

From *The Life:*

It is now known that Una Moss was not the mother of the Inventor's peculiarly deformed son. In fact, as Sissler and Teebe have shown in *The Brewing Storm*, their perceptive study of his last years, the Inventor and Miss Moss were never sexually intimate. The reason is simple: the Great Man was impotent.

The son remains a problem.

The Inventor stands in the rain, surrounded by marble monuments: angels, christs, bleeding hearts. Una and the boy at his side. Their overcoats. Bowed heads. The smell of mold, the open hole. The man in black reading from a book.

---

*A Cincinnati man, J. Leonard Whist, was prosecuted for possession of a controlled substance, intent to do great bodily harm, and bigamy, when police found that he had married four times, desiccated each of his wives, and reconstituted them as the whim took him.

It is Schlaver's funeral. Cardiac arrest. The Inventor lingers after the others have gone, the rain slanting down, and watches the attendants as they slap the muddy earth on the coffin, scrape it into the corners, tamp the reddish mound that rises above the grass like bread in a pan. He stands there for a long while, the eyes black, elbow tucked, fist under chin. Suddenly he turns and hurries back to the limousine. Una and the boy are there, the windows fogged. He snaps open his notebook and begins scrawling equations across the page.

Three days later Schlaver is leaning back in an armchair at the Westchester house, surrounded by reporters, lights, TV cameras. He is in his bathrobe, looking much as he did before death. The medical world is astounded. The press calls it a hoax. The Inventor stands in the shadows, grinning.

From *The Life:*

There were threatening phone calls. Windows were broken. The house egged. The boy came home from school, blood on the seat of his pants. His tail had been clipped. In the shower room. It had been a pink tail, almost translucent, curled in three tight coils like an angleworm, or the breath of a serpent.

The interviewer clears his throat, blows his nose in a checked handkerchief, fiddles with the controls of the portable tape recorder. Una sits cross-legged on the carpet, barefoot, a ring on each toe. She is lining up dominoes on the coffee table, standing them on end in a winding file. The Inventor is in his armchair; he is wearing a flannel shirt, sipping sherry. "And which of your myriad inventions," says the interviewer, "gives you the greatest personal satisfaction?" The Inventor looks down at the carpet, his fingers massaging the Furball in his lap. The wheels of the recorder whir, faint as the whine of a mosquito. "Those to come," he says. "Those that exist *ab ovo,* that represent possibility, moments of chemical reaction, epiphanies great and small. You must see of course that invention makes metaphor a reality, fixes—" but then he is interrupted by the clack of tumbling dominoes, regular as a second hand, beating like a train rushing over a bad spot in the rail. Una looks up, smiling, serene, her lips fat as things stung. The final domino totters. "Yes," says the Inventor. "Where were we?"

A Jewish star has been burned on his lawn. The Inventor is puzzled. He is not Jewish.

From *The LIfe:*

The great work which had brooded so long on the Great Man's horizon came like Apocalypse. The world's ears stung. The work was met with cries of outrage, despair, resentment. Never, said his critics, have the hopes, the illusions, the dignity of mankind been so deflated in a single callous swipe.

Fact, brutal undeniable naked fact, ate like a canker at all our hearts, they said. Who will reclothe our illusions? they asked. His friends hung their heads and feebly praised his candor. Others persisted in calling it a canard. It was no canard. How he had done it no one could begin to imagine. But there were the formulas for the experts to wonder at, and there, for all the world to see, were the slides. The color slides of God dead.

1) God, his great white beard, gauzy dressing gown, one arm frozen at half-mast. Supine. His mouth agape. Nebular backdrop.

2) A top view. God stretching below the lens like a colossus, purple mountains' majesty, from sea to shining sea. Cloud foaming over his brow, hissing up from beneath his arms, legs, crotch.

3) The closeup. Eye sockets black, nostrils collapsed, the stained hairs of the beard, lips gone, naked hideous teeth.

Night. Insects scraping their hind legs together, things stirring in the grass. Then the first cries, the flare of the torches. The earthquaking roar of the crowd. His neighbors are in the street, garden rakes and edgers poking over their massed heads, Yorkies and Schnauzers yanking them forward at the ends of leashes. Linked arm in arm, chanting "The Battle Hymn of the Republic," they come on, wrenching the great iron gates from their hinges, crushing through the beds of peonies, the banks of shrubbery, their faces savage and misaligned in the glare of the torches. Then the crash of the windows like a fever, the jeers of the women and children, husky brays of the men. And then the flames licking at the redwood planking, fluttering through the windows to chew at the drapes and carpets. The flash of Molotovs, the thunder of the little red cans of gasoline from a hundred lawn mowers. "Yaaaar!" howls the canaille at the first concussion. "Yaaaar!"

He is there. In the upper window. Una, Schlaver and the boy struggling to reach him from the fire escape. The flames, licking up twenty, thirty feet, framing the window like jagged teeth. The granite forehead, wisp of a beard, black eyes swimming behind the bottle lenses. Suddenly a cloud of smoke, dark as burning rubber, swells up and obscures the window. The crowd roars. When the smoke passes, the window is empty. Una's scream. Then the groan of the beams, the house collapsing in on itself with a rush of air, the neon cinders shooting high against the black and the stars, like the tails of a thousand Chinese rockets.

(1976)

THE EXTINCTION TALES

I will show you fear in a handful of dust.

—T. S. Eliot, *The Waste Land*

He was in his early fifties, between jobs, his wife dead ten years. When he saw the position advertised in the Wellington paper it struck him as highly romantic, and he was immediately attracted to it.

LIGHTHOUSEKEEPER. Stephen Island. References. Inquire T. H. Penn, Maritime Authority.

He took it. Sold his furniture, paid the last of the rent, filled two duffel bags with socks and sweaters and his bird-watcher's guide, and hired a cart. Just as he was leaving, a neighbor approached him with something in her arms: pointed ears, yellow eyes. Take it, she said. For company. He slipped the kitten into the breast of his pea coat, waved, and started off down the road.

Stephen Island is an eruption of sparsely wooden rock seventeen miles northwest of Wellington. It is uninhabited. At night the constellations wheel over its quarter-mile radius like mythical beasts.

The man was to be relieved for two weeks every six months. He planted a garden, read, fished, smoked by the sea. The cat grew to adolescence. One afternoon it came to him with a peculiar bird clenched in its teeth. The man took the bird away, puzzled over it, and finally sent it to the national museum at Wellington for identification. Three weeks later a reply came. He had discovered a new species: the Stephen Island wren. In the interim the cat had brought him fourteen more specimens of the odd little buff and white bird. The man never saw one of the birds alive. After a while the cat stopped bringing them.

In 1945, when the Russians liberated Auschwitz, they found 129 ovens in the crematorium. The ovens were six feet long, two feet high, one and a half feet wide.

The Union Pacific Railroad had connected New York, Chicago and San Francisco, Ulysses S. Grant was stamping about the White House in hightop boots, Jay Gould was buying up gold and Jared Pink was opening a butcher shop in downtown Chicago.

PINK'S POULTRY, BEEF AND GAME

The town was booming. Barouches and cabriolets at every corner, men in beavers and frock coats lining the steps of the private clubs, women in bustles, bonnets and flounces giving teas and taking boxes at the theater. Thirty-room mansions, friezes, spires, gargoyles, the opera house, the exchange, shops, saloons, tenements. In the hardpan streets men and boys trailed back from the factories, stockyards, docks, their faces mapped in sweat and soot and the blood of animals.

All of them ate meat. Pink provided it. Longhorns from Texas, buffalo from the plains, deer, turkey, pheasant and pigeon from Michigan and Illinois. They stormed his shop, the bell over the door rushing and trilling as they bought up everything he could offer them, right down to the scraps in the brine barrels. Each day he sold out his stock and in the morning found himself at the mercy of his suppliers. A pre-dawn trip to the slaughterhouse for great swinging sides of beef, livers and tripe, blood for pudding, intestine for sausage. And then twice a week to meet the Michigan Line and long low boxcars strung with dressed deer and piled deep with pigeons stinking of death and excrement. Unplucked, their feathers a nightmare, they filled the cars four feet deep and he would bring a boy along to shovel them into his wagon. They sold like a dream.

When his supplier tripled the price per bird Pink sent his brother Seth up to the nesting grounds near Petoskey, Michigan. As Seth's train approached Petoskey the sky began to darken. He checked his pocket watch: it was three in the afternoon. He leaned over the man beside him to look out the window. The sky was choked with birds, their mass blotting the sun, the drone of their wings and dry rattling feathers audible over the chuff of the engine. Seth whistled. Are those—? he said. Yep, said the man. Passenger pigeons.

Seth wired his brother from the Petoskey station. Two days later he and Jared were stalking the nesting ground with a pair of Smith & Wesson shotguns and a burlap sack. They were not alone. The grove was thronged with hunters, hundreds of them, drinking, shooting, springing traps and tossing nets. Retrievers barked, shotguns boomed. At the far edge of the field women sat beneath parasols with picnic lunches.

Jared stopped to watch an old man assail the crown of a big-boled chestnut with repeated blasts from a brace of shotguns. A grim old woman stood at the man's elbow, reloading, while two teenagers scrambled over the lower branches of the tree, dropping nestlings to the ground. Another man, surrounded by dirt-faced children, ignited a stick of dynamite and pitched it into a tree thick with roosting birds. A breeze ruffled the leaves as the spitting cylinder twisted through them, pigeons cooing and clucking in the shadows—then there was a flash, and a concussion that thundered over the popping of shotguns from various corners of the field. Heads turned. The smoke blew off in a clot. Feathers, twigs, bits of leaf and a fine red mist began to settle. The children were already beneath the tree, on their hands and knees, snatching up the pigeons and squab as they fell to earth like ripe fruit.

Overhead the sky was stormy with displaced birds. Jared fired one barrel, then the other. Five birds slapped down, two of them stunned and hopping. He rushed them, flailing with the stock of his gun until they lay still. He heard Seth fire behind him. The flock was the sky, shrieking and reeling, panicked, the chalky white excrement like a snowstorm. Jared's hair and shoulders were thick with it, white spots flecked his face. He was reloading. There's got to be a better way, he said.

Three weeks later he and his brother returned to Petoskey. They rode out to the nesting grounds in a horse-drawn wagon, towing an old Civil War cannon behind them. In the bed of the wagon lay a weighted hemp net, one hundred feet square, and a pair of cudgels. Strips of cotton broadcloth had been sewed into the center of the net to catch the wind and insure an even descent, but the net fouled on its maiden flight and Seth had to climb a silver maple alive with crepitating pigeons to retrieve it. They refolded the net, stuffed it into the mouth of the cannon, and tried again. This time they were successful: Seth flushed the birds from the tree with a shotgun blast, the cannon roared, and Jared's net caught them as they rose. Nearly two thousand pigeons lay tangled in the mesh, their distress calls echoing through the trees, metallic and forlorn. The two brothers stalked over the grounded net with their cudgels, crushing the heads of the survivors. When the net had ceased to move and the blood had begun to settle into abstract patterns in the broadcloth, they dropped their cudgels and embraced, hooting and laughing like prospectors on a strike. We'll be rich! Seth shouted.

He was right. Within six months PINK'S POULTRY, BEEF AND GAME was turning over as many as seventeen thousand pigeons a day, and Jared opened a second and then a third shop before the year was out. Seth oversaw the Petoskey operation and managed one of the new shops. Two years later Jared opened a restaurant and a clothing store and began investing in a small Ohio-based petroleum company called Standard Oil. By 1885 he was worth half a million dollars and living in an eighteen-room mansion in Highland Park, just down the street from his brother Seth.

On a September afternoon in 1914, when Jared Pink was seventy-two, a group of ornithologists was gathered around a cage at the Cincinnati zoo. Inside the cage was a passenger pigeon named Martha, and she was dying of old age. The bird gripped the wire mesh with her beak and stiffened. She was the last of her kind on earth.

The variola virus, which causes smallpox, cannot exist outside the human body. It is now, as the result of pandemic immunization, on the verge of extinction.

Numerous other lifeforms have disappeared in this century, among them the crested shelduck, Carolina parakeet, Kittlitz's thrust, Molokai oo, huia, Toolach wallaby, freckled marsupial mouse, Syrian wild ass, Schomburgk's deer, rufous gazelle, bubal hartebeest and Caucasian wisent.

George Robertson was infused with the spirit of Christianity. When he arrived in Tasmania in 1835, the island's autochthonous population had been reduced from seven thousand to less than two hundred in the course of the thirty-two years that the British colony at Risdon had been in existence. The original settlers, a group of convicts under the supervision of Lieutenant John Bowen, had hunted the native Tasmanians as they would have hunted wolves or rats or any other creatures that competed for space and food. George Robertson had come to save them.

Picture him: thirty, eyes like rinse water, hair bleached white in the sun, the tender glossy skin showing through the molt of nose and cheekbone. A gangling tall man who walked with a limp and carried an umbrella everywhere he went. He was an Anglican clergyman. His superiors had sent him to the island on a mission of mercy: to save the aboriginal Tasmanians from extinction and perdition both. Robertson had leaped at the opportunity. He would be a paraclete, a leader, an arm of God. But when he stepped ashore at Risdon, he found that no one had seen a native Tasmanian—alive or dead—in nearly five years. Like the thylacines and wombats, they had withdrawn to the desolate slopes of the interior.

The one exception was a native woman called Trucanini who had been captured five years earlier and integrated into colonial life as a servant to the governor. When John Bowen had organized a line of beaters to sweep the bush and exterminate the remaining "black crows," the drive had turned up only two Tasmanians—Trucanini and her mother, who were discovered sleeping beneath a log. The others had vanished. Trucanini's mother was an old woman, blind and naked, her skin ropy and cracked. Bowen left her to die.

The day he landed, Robertson limped up to the back door of the governor's manor house, umbrella tucked under his arm, stepped into the kitchen and led Trucanini out into the courtyard. She was in her early forties, toothless, her nose splayed, cheeks and forehead whorled with tattoos. Robertson embraced her, forced her to her knees in the sand and taught her to pray. A week later the two of them struck off into the bush, unarmed, in search of the remnants of her tribe.

It took him four years. The governor had declared him legally dead, his mother back in Melbourne had been notified, a marker had been placed in the cemetery. Then one afternoon, in the teeth of a slashing monsoon, Robertson strode up the governor's teakwood steps followed by one hundred eighty-seven hungry aboriginal Christians. Wooden crosses dangled from their necks, their heads were bowed, palms laid together in prayer. The rains washed over them like a succession of waterfalls. Robertson asked for safe conduct to Flinders Island; the governor granted it.

The Tasmanians were a Stone Age society. They wore no clothes, lived in the open, foraged for food. Robertson clothed them, built huts and lean-tos, taught them to use flint, cultivate gardens, bury their excrement. He taught them to pray, and he taught them to abandon polygamy for the sacrament of marriage. They were shy, tractable people, awed and bewildered by their white redeemer, and they did their best to please him. There was one problem, however. They died like mayflies. By 1847 there were less than forty of them left. Twelve years later there were two: Trucanini, now long past menopause, and her fifth husband, William Lanne.

Robertson stuck it out, though he and Trucanini moved back into Risdon when William Lanne went off on a six-month whaling voyage. There they waited for Lanne's return, and Robertson prayed for the impossible—that Trucanini would bear a child. But then he realized that she would have to bear at least one other and then that the children would have to live in incest if the race were to survive. He no longer knew what to pray for.

When Lanne's ship dropped anchor, Robertson was waiting. He took the wizened little tattooed man by the elbow and walked him to Trucanini's hut, then waited at a discreet distance. After an hour he went home to bed. In the morning Lanne was found outside the supply store, a casket of rum and a tin cup between his legs. His head was cocked back, and his mouth, which hung open, was a cauldron of flies.

Seven years later Trucanini died in bed. And George Robertson gave up the cloth.

Concerning the higher primates: there are now on earth circa 25,000 chimpanzees, 5,000 gorillas, 3,000 orangutans, and 4,000,000,000 men.

Didus ineptus, the dodo. A flightless pigeon the size of a turkey, extinct 1648. All that remains of it today is a foot in the British museum, a head in Copenhagen, and a quantity of dust.

Suns fade, and planets wither. Solar systems collapse. When the sun reaches its red-giant stage in five billion years it will flare up to sear the earth, ignite it like a torch held to a scrap of newsprint, the seas evaporated, the forests turned to ash, the ragged Himalayan peaks fused and then converted to dust, cosmic dust. What's a species here, a species there? This is where extinction becomes sublime.

Listen: when my father died I did not attend the funeral. Three years later I flew in to visit with my mother. We drank vodka gimlets, and I was suddenly seized with a desire to visit my father's grave. It was 10 P.M., December, snow fast to the frozen earth. I asked her which cemetery. She thought I was joking.

I drove as far as the heavy-link chain across the main gate, then stepped out of the car into a fine granular snow. My fingers slipped the switch of the flashlight through woolen gloves and I started for section 220F. The ground stretched off, leprous white, broken by the black scars of the monuments. It took nearly an hour to find, the granite markers alike as pebbles on a beach, names and dates, names and dates. I trailed down 220F, the light playing off stone and statue. Then I found it. My father's name in a spot of light. I regarded the name: a three-part name, identical to my own. The light held, snowflakes creeping through the beam like motes of dust. I extinguished the light.

(1977)

THE FOG MAN

He came twice a week, rattling through the development in an army-surplus jeep, laying down a roiling smoke screen that melted the trees into oblivion, flattened hills and swallowed up houses, erased Fords, Chevies and Studebakers as if they were as insubstantial as the air itself, and otherwise transformed the world to our satisfaction. Shrubs became dinosaurs, lampposts giraffes, the blacktop of the streets seethed like the surface of the swamp primeval. Our fathers stood there on their emerald lawns, hoses dripping, and they waved languidly or turned their backs to shoot a sparkling burst at the flower beds or forsythias. We took to our bikes, supercharged with the excitement of it, and we ran just behind him, the fog man, wheeling in and out of the tight billowing clouds like fighter pilots slashing across the sky or Grand Prix racers nosing in for the lead on that final excruciating lap. He gave us nothing except those moments of transfiguration, but we chased him as single-mindedly as we chased the ice-cream man in his tinkling white truck full of Drumsticks and Eskimo Pies, chased him till he'd completed his tour of the six connecting streets of the development—up one side and down the other—and lurched across the highway, trailing smoke, for the next.

And then the smoke settled, clinging to the dewy wet grass, the odor of smoldering briquettes fought over the top of the sweet narcotic smell of it, and we were gone, disseminated, slammed behind identical screen doors, in our identical houses, for the comfort and magic of the TV. My father was there, always there, propped up in his recliner, one hand over his eyes to mask an imaginary glare, the other clutched round his sweating drink. My mother was there too, legs tucked under her on the couch, the newspaper spread in her lap, her drink on the cluttered table beside her.

"The fog man was just here," I would announce. I didn't expect a response, really—it was just something to say. The show on TV was about a smiling family. All the shows were about smiling families. My mother would nod.

One night I appended a question. "He's spraying for bugs, right?" This much I knew, this much had been explained to me, but I wanted confirmation, affirmation, I wanted reason and meaning to illuminate my life.

My father said nothing. My mother looked up. "Mosquitoes."

"Yeah, that's what I thought—but how come there's so many of them then? They bit right through my shirt on the front porch."

My mother tapped at her cigarette, took a sip of her drink. "You can't get them all," she said.

It was at about this time that the local power company opened the world's first atomic power plant at Indian Point. Ten years earlier nuclear fission had been an instrument of war and destruction; now it was safe, manageable; now it would warm our houses and light our lights and power our hi-fis and toasters and dishwashers. The electric company took pains to ensure that the community saw it that way. It was called public relations.

I didn't know the term then. I was eleven years old, in my first week of my last year of elementary school, and on my way to the power plant in a school bus crammed to the yawning windows with my excitable classmates. This was known as a field trip. The previous year we'd been to a farm in Brewster and the Museum of Natural History in New York. We were starting early this year, but it was all due to the fact of this astonishing new technological force set down amongst us, this revolution in the production of electricity and the streamlining of our lives. We didn't know what to expect.

The bus rumbled and belched fumes. I sat on the hard cracked leatherette seat beside Casper Mendelson and watched the great gray concrete dome rise up out of the clutch of the trees, dominating the point and the placid broad fish-stinking river beyond it. It was impressive, this huge structure inside of which the titanic forces of the universe were pared down to size. Casper said that it could blow up, like the bomb they'd dropped on the Japanese, and that it would take all of Peterskill and Westchester with it. The river would turn to steam and there'd be nothing left but a crater the size of the Grand Canyon and we'd all be melted in our beds. I gaped out the window at the thing, awestruck, the big dome keeping a lid on all that seething complexity, and I was impressed, but I couldn't help thinking of the point's previous incarnation as an amusement park, a place of strung lights, cotton candy and carousels. Now there was this gray dome.

They led us into a little brightly lit building full of colorful exhibits, where we handled things that were meant to be handled, scuffed the gleaming linoleum floors and watched an animated short in which Johnny Atom splits himself in two and saves the world by creating electricity. The whole thing was pretty dull, aside from the dome itself and what Casper had said about it, and within the hour my classmates were filling the place with the roar of a stampede, breaking the handles off things, sobbing, skipping, playing tag and wondering seriously about lunch—which, as it turned out, we were to have back at school, in the cafeteria, after which we were expected to return to our classrooms and discuss what we'd learned on our field trip.

I remember the day for the impression that imposing gray dome made on me, but also because it was the first chance I got to have a look at Maki Duryea, the new girl who'd been assigned to the other sixth-grade section. Maki was black— or not simply black, but black and Oriental both. Her father had been stationed in Osaka during the occupation; her mother was Japanese. I watched her surreptitiously that morning as I sat in the rear of the bus with Casper. She was somewhere in the middle, sitting beside Donna Siprelle, a girl I'd known all my life. All I could make out was the back of her head, but that was enough, that alone was a revelation. Her hair was an absolute, unalloyed, interstellar black, and it disappeared behind the jutting high ridge of the seat back as if it might go on forever. It had hung iron straight when we first climbed aboard the bus that morning, but on the way back it was transformed, a leaping electric snarl that engulfed the seat and eclipsed the neat little ball of yellow curls that clung to the back of Donna Siprelle's head. "Maki Duryea, Maki Duryea," Casper began to chant, though no one could hear him but me in the pandemonium of that preprandial school bus. Annoyed, I poked him with a savage elbow but he kept it up, louder now, to spite me.

There were no blacks in our school, there were no Asians or Hispanics. Italians, Poles, Jews, Irish, the descendants of the valley's Dutch and English settlers, these we had, these we were, but Maki Duryea was the first black—and the first Asian. Casper's father was Jewish, his mother a Polish Catholic. Casper had the soaring IQ of a genius, but he was odd, skewed in some deep essential way that set him apart from the rest of us. He was the first to masturbate, the first to drink and smoke, though he cared for neither. He caused a panic throughout the school when he turned up missing one day after lunch and was found, after a room-by-room, locker-by-locker search, calmly reading on the fire escape; he burst from his chair at the back of the classroom once and did fifty frantic squat-thrusts in front of the hapless teacher and then blew on his thumb till he passed out. He was my best friend.

He turned to me then, on the bus, and broke off his chant. His eyes were the color of the big concrete dome, his head was shaved to a transparent stubble. "She stinks," he said, grinning wildly, his eyes leaping at my own. "Maki Duryea, Maki Duryea, Maki Duryea"—he took up the chant again before subsiding into giggles. "They don't smell like we do."

■ ■ ■

My family was Irish. Irish, that's all I knew. A shirt was cotton or it was wool. We were Irish. No one talked about it, there was no exotic language spoken in the house, no ethnic dress or cuisine, we didn't go to church. There was only my grandfather.

He came that year for Thanksgiving, a short big-bellied man with close-cropped white hair and glancing white eyebrows and a trace of something in his speech I hadn't heard before—or if I had it was in some old out-of-focus movie dredged up for the TV screen, nothing I would have remembered. My grandmother came too. She was spindly, emaciated, her skin blistered with shingles, a diabetic who couldn't have weighed more than ninety pounds, but there was joy in her and it was infectious. My father, her son, woke up. A festive air took hold of the house.

My grandfather, who years later dressed in a suit for my father's funeral and was mistaken for a banker, had had a heart attack and he wasn't drinking. Or rather, he was strictly enjoined from drinking, and my parents, who drank themselves, drank a lot, drank too much, took pains to secrete the liquor supply. Every bottle was removed from the cabinet, even the odd things that hadn't been touched in years—except by me, when I furtively unscrewed the cap of this or that and took a sniff or touched my tongue tentatively to the cold hard glass aperture—and the beer disappeared from the refrigerator. I didn't know what the big deal was. Liquor was there, a fact of life, it was unpleasant and adults indulged in it as they indulged in any number of bizarre and unsatisfactory practices. I kicked a football around the rock-hard frozen lawn.

And then one afternoon—it was a day or two before Thanksgiving and my grandparents had been with us a week—I came in off the front lawn, my fingers numb and nose running, and the house was in an uproar. A chair was overturned in the corner, the coffee table was slowly listing over a crippled leg and my grandmother was on the floor, frail, bunched, a bundle of sticks dropped there in a windstorm. My grandfather stood over her, red-faced and raging, while my mother snatched at his elbow like a woman tumbling over the edge of a cliff. My father wasn't home from work yet. I stood there in the doorway, numb from the embrace of the wind, and heard the inarticulate cries of those two women against the oddly inflected roars of that man, and I backed out the door and pulled it closed behind me.

The next day my grandfather, sixty-eight years old and stiff in the knees, walked two miles in twenty-degree weather to Peterskill, to the nearest liquor store. It was dark, suppertime, and we didn't know where he was. "He just went out for a walk," my mother said. Then the phone rang. It was the neighbor two doors down. There was a man passed out in her front yard—somebody said we knew him. Did we?

I spent the next two days—Thanksgiving and the day after—camping in the sorry patch of woods at the end of the development. I wasn't running away, nothing as decisive or extreme as that—I was just camping, that was all. I gnawed cold turkey up there in the woods, lifted congealed stuffing to my mouth with deadened fingers. In the night I lay shivering in my blankets, never colder before or since.

We were Irish. I was Irish.

That winter, like all winters in those days, was interminable, locked up in the grip of frozen slush and exhaust-blackened snow. The dead dark hours of school were penance for some crime we hadn't yet committed. The TV went on at three-thirty when we got home from school, and it was still on when we went to bed at nine. I played basketball that winter in a league organized by some of the fathers in the development, and three times a week I walked home from the fungus-infested gym with a crust of frozen sweat in my hair. I grew an inch and a half, I let my crewcut grow out and I began to turn up the collar of my ski jacket. I spent most of my time with Casper, but in spite of him, as the pale abbreviated days wore on, I found myself growing more and more at ease with the idea of Maki Duryea.

She was still foreign, still exotic, still the new kid and worse, much worse, the whole business complicated by the matter of her skin color and her hair and the black unblinking depths of her eyes, but she was there just like the rest of us and after a while it seemed as if she'd always been there. She was in the other section, but I saw her on the playground, in the hallway, saw her waiting on line in the cafeteria with a tray in her hands or struggling up the steps of the school bus in a knit hat and mittens no different from what the other girls wore. I didn't have much to say to any of the girls really, but I suppose I must have said things to her in passing, and once, coming off the playground late, I found myself wedged up against her on the crowded school bus. And then there was the time the dancing teacher, with a casual flick of her wrist, paired me off with her.

Everything about dancing was excruciating. It was not kickball, it was not basketball or bombardment. The potential for embarrassment was incalculable. We were restless and bored, the gymnasium was overheated against the sleet that rattled at the windows, and the girls, entranced, wore peculiar little smiles as Mrs. Feldman demonstrated the steps. The boys slouched against one adamantine wall, poking one another, shuffling their feet and playing out an elaborate ritual to demonstrate that none of this held the slightest interest for them, for us, though it did, and we were nervous about it despite ourselves. Alone, of all the two classes combined, Casper refused to participate. Mrs. Feldman sent him to the principal's office without so much as a second glance, chose partners arbitrarily for the remainder of the class and started up the ancient phonograph and the arcane scratchy records of songs no one knew and rhythms no one could follow, and before I was fully cognizant of what was happening I found myself clutching Maki Duryea's damp palm in my own while my arm lay like a dead thing across the small of her back. She was wearing a sweater thick enough for Arctic exploration and she was sweating in the choking humid jungle atmosphere of the gymnasium. I could smell her, but despite what Casper had said the heat of her body gave off a luxurious yeasty soporific odor that held me spellbound and upright through the droning eternity of the record.

The dance, the big dance that all this terpsichorean instruction was leading up to, was held on February 29, and Mrs. Feldman, in an evil twist of fate, decided to honor custom and have the girls invite the boys as their partners. We did perspective drawing in art class—great lopsided vistas of buildings and avenues dwindling in the distance—while the girls made up the invitations with strips of ribbon, construction paper and paste. My mind was on basketball, ice fishing, the distant trembling vision of spring and summer and liberation from Mrs. Feldman, the gym and the cafeteria and all the rest, and I was surprised, though I shouldn't have been, when Maki's invitation arrived. I didn't want to go. My mother insisted. My father said nothing.

And then the telephone began to ring. My mother answered each call with quiet determination, immovable, unshakable, whispering into the phone, doodling on a pad, lifting the drink or a cigarette to her lips. I don't know what she said exactly, but she was talking to the other mothers, the mothers of sons who hadn't been invited to the dance by Maki Duryea, and she was explaining to them precisely how and why she could and would allow her son to go to the dance with a Negro. In later years, as the civil-rights movement arose and Malcolm X and Martin Luther King fell and the ghettoes burned, she never had much to say about it, but I could feel her passion then, on the telephone, in the cool insistent rasp of her voice.

I went to the dance with Maki Duryea. She wore a stiff organdy dress with short sleeves that left her looking awkward and underdressed and I wore a tie and sportcoat and arranged my hair for the occasion. I held her and I danced with her, though I didn't want to, though I snapped at her when she asked if I wanted a brownie and a cup of punch, though I looked with envy and longing to the streamer-draped corner where Casper alternately leered at me and punched Billy Bartro in the shoulder; I danced with her, but that was it, that was as far as I could go, and I didn't care if the snow was black and the dome blew off the reactor and Johnny Atom came and melted us all in our sleep.

It was a late spring and we tried to force it by inaugurating baseball season while the snow still lingered atop the dead yellow grass and the frozen dirt beneath it. We dug out balls and mitts and stood in the street in T-shirts, gooseflesh on our arms, shoulders quaking, a nimbus of crystallized breath suspended over our heads. Casper didn't play ball—foot, hand, base or basket—and he stood hunched in his jacket, palming a cigarette and watching us out of his mocking gray eyes. I caught cold and then flu and stayed in bed a week. On the first of

April I went trout fishing, a ritual of spring, but the day was gloomy and lowering, with a stiff wind and temperatures in the twenties. I cast a baited hook till my arm lost all sensation. The trout might as well have been extinct.

Since the time of the dance I'd had nothing to do with Maki Duryea. I wouldn't even look at her. If she'd suddenly exploded in flames on the playground or swelled up to the size of a dirigible I wouldn't have known. I'd taken a steady stream of abuse over the dance episode, and I was angry and embarrassed. For a full month afterward I was the object of an accelerated program of ear snapping and head knuckling, the target of spitballs and wads of lined notebook paper with crude hearts scrawled across their rumpled interiors, but we were innocent then, and no one used the epithets we would later learn, the language of hate and exclusion. They turned on me because I had taken Maki Duryea to the dance—or rather, because I had allowed her to take me—and because she was different and their parents disapproved in a way they couldn't yet define. I resented her for it, and I resented my mother too.

And so, when the rumors first began to surface, I took a kind of guilty satisfaction in them. There had been trouble at Maki's house. Vandals—and the very term gave me a perverse thrill—vandals had spray-painted racial slurs on the glistening black surface of their macadam driveway. My mother was incensed. She took her drink and her cigarettes and huddled over the phone. She even formed a committee of two with Casper's mother (who was one of the few who hadn't phoned over the dance invitation), and they met a time or two in Casper's living room to drink a clear liquid in high-stemmed glasses, tap their cigarettes over ashtrays and lament the sad state of the community, the development, the town, the country, the world itself.

While our mothers were wringing their hands and buzzing at one another in their rasping secretive voices, Casper took me aside and showed me a copy of the local newspaper, flung on the lawn not five minutes earlier by Morty Solomon as he weaved up the street on his bicycle. I didn't read newspapers. I didn't read books. I didn't read anything. Casper forced it into my hands and there it was, the rumor made concrete: VANDALS STRIKE AGAIN. This time, a cross had been burned on the Duryea lawn. I looked up at Casper in amazement. I wanted to ask him what that meant, a cross—a cross was religious, wasn't it, and this didn't have anything to do with religion, did it?—but I felt insecure in my confusion and I held back.

"You know what we ought to do?" he said, watching me closely.

I was thinking of Maki Duryea, of her hair and her placid eyes, thinking of the leaping flames and the spray paint in the driveway. "What?"

"We ought to egg them."

"But—" I was going to ask how we could egg them if we didn't know who did it, but then I caught the startling perverse drift of what he was suggesting and in my astonishment I blurted, "But why?"

He shrugged, ducked his head, scuffed a foot on the carpet. We were in the

hallway, by the telephone stand. I heard my mother's voice from the room beyond, though the door was closed and she was talking in a whisper. The voice of
Casper's mother came right back at her in raspy collusion. Casper just stared at
the closed door as if to say, *There, there's your answer.*

After a moment he said, "What's the matter—you afraid?"

I was twelve now, twelve and a half. How could anyone at that age admit to
fear? "No," I said. "I'm not afraid."

The Duryea house lay outside the confines of the development. It was a rental
house, two stories over a double garage in need of paint and shingles, and it sat
on a steep rutted dirt road half a mile away. There were no streetlights along that
unfinished road and the trees overhung it so that the deepest shadows grew
deeper still beneath them. It was a warm, slick, humid night at the end of May,
the sort of night that surprises you with its richness and intensity, smells height-
ened, sounds muffled, lights blurred to indistinction. When we left Casper's it
was drizzling.

Casper bought the eggs, two dozen, at the corner store out on the highway.
His parents were rich—rich compared to mine, at any rate—and he always
seemed to have money. The storekeeper was a tragic-looking man with purple
rings of puffed flesh beneath his eyes and a spill of gut that was like an avalanche
under the smeared white front of his apron. Casper slipped two cigars into his
pocket while I distracted the man with a question about the chocolate milk—did
it come in a smaller size?

As we started up the dirt road, eggs in hand, Casper was strangely silent.
When a dog barked from the driveway of a darkened house he clutched my arm,
and a moment later, when a car turned into the street, he pulled me into the
bushes and crouched there, breathing hard, till the headlights faded away. "Maki
Duryea," he whispered, chanting it as he'd chanted it a hundred times before,
"Maki Duryea, Maki Duryea." My heart was hammering. I didn't want to do this.
I didn't know why I was doing it, didn't yet realize that the whole purpose of the
exercise was to invert our parents' values, trash them, grind them into the dirt,
and that all ethical considerations were null in the face of that ancient imperative. I was a freedom fighter. The eggs were hand grenades. I clutched them to
my chest.

We hid ourselves in the wild tangle of shrubs gone to seed outside the house
and watched the steady pale lighted windows for movement. My hair hung limp
with the drizzle. Casper squatted over his ankles and fingered his box of eggs.
I could barely make him out. At one point a figure passed in front of the
window—I saw the hair, the mat of it, the sheen—and it might have been
Maki, but I wasn't sure. It could have been her mother. Or her sister or aunt or
grandmother—it could have been anybody. Finally, when I was as tired of
crouching there in the bushes as I've ever been tired of being anywhere, even the

dentist's, the lights flicked off. Or no, they didn't just flick off—they exploded in darkness and the black torrent of the night rushed in to engulf the house.

Casper rose to his feet. I heard him fumbling with his cardboard carton of eggs. We didn't speak—speech would have been superfluous. I rose too. My eggs, palpable, smooth, fit the palm of my hand as if they'd been designed for it. I raised my arm—baseball, football, basketball—and Casper stirred beside me. The familiar motion, the rush of air: I will never forget the sound of that first egg loosing itself against the front of the house, a wetness there, a softness, the birth of something. No weapon, but a weapon all the same.

The summer sustained me. Hot, unfettered, endless. On the first day of vacation I perched in an apple tree at the end of the cul-de-sac that bordered the development and contemplated the expanse of time and pleasure before me, and then it was fall and I was in junior high. Maki Duryea had moved. I'd heard as much from Casper, and one afternoon, at the end of summer, I hiked up that long rutted dirt road to investigate. The house stood empty. I climbed the ridge behind it to peer in through the naked windows and make sure. Bare floors stretched to bare walls.

And then, in the confusion of the big parking lot at the junior high where fifty buses deposited the graduates of a dozen elementary schools, where I felt lost and out of place and shackled in a plaid long-sleeved shirt new that morning from the plastic wrapping, I saw her. She sprang down from another bus in a cascade of churning legs and arms and anxious faces, a bookbag slung over one shoulder, hair ironed to her waist. I couldn't move. She looked up then and saw me and she smiled. Then she was gone.

That night, as I slapped a hard black ball against the side of the house, thinking nothing, I caught a faint electrifying whiff of a forgotten scent on the air, and there he was, the fog man, rattling by the house in his open jeep. My bike lay waiting at the curb and my first impulse was to leap for it, but I held off. There was something different here, something I couldn't quite place at first. And then I saw what it was: the fog man was wearing a mask, a gas mask, the sort of thing you saw in war movies. He'd collected the usual escort of knee-pumping neighborhood kids by the time he'd made his second pass down the street in front of our house, and I'd moved to the curb now to study this phenomenon, this subtle alteration in the texture of things. He looked different in the mask, sinister somehow, and his eyes seemed to glitter.

The fog obliterated the houses across from me, the wheeling children vanished, the low black roiling clouds melted toward me across the perfect sweep of the lawn. And then, before I knew what I was doing, I was on my bike with the rest of them, chasing the fog man through the mist, chasing him as if my life depended on it.

(1989)

DROWNING

In this story, someone will drown. Yet there will be no apparent reason for this drowning—it will not for example be attributable to suicide, murder, divine retribution—nor even such arcana as current and undertow. It will instead be like so many events of the future: inexplicable, incomprehensible. Nonetheless, it will occur.

There is a girl alone on the beach, a mere inkspot in the white: nothing really, when compared with the massive dunes that loom behind her and the sea, dark and implacable, which stretches before her to Europe and Africa. She is lying there on her back, eyes closed, her body loose, toes pointing straight out to the water. Her skin glistens with oil, tanned deep as a ripe pear. And she wears a white bikini: two strips of cloth as dazzlingly white in this sun as the sand itself. She is after an effect, a contrast.

Now she sits up, the taut line of her abdomen bunching in soft creases, and glances slyly around. No one in sight up and down the beach, for miles perhaps—the only sign of life the gull beating overhead, muttering in its prehistoric voice. Her hands reach behind for the strings to the bikini halter—the elbows strain out in sharp triangles and her back arches, throwing her chest forward. She feels a quick pulse of excitement as her breasts fall free and the sea breeze tickles against them. She's brown here too—a shade lighter than her shoulders and abdomen, but still tanned deeply.

She falls back on her elbows, face to the sun, the hair soft down her back and into the sand. The gull is gone now, and the only sounds are the hiss of the foam and the plangent thunder of the breakers smoothing rock a hundred yards out.

She steals another look round—a good long one, over her shoulders and up to the peaks of the dunes. No one. "Why not?" she thinks. "Why not?" And her thumbs ease into the elastic band that girds her hips, working it down, kicking her legs free of it, stretching and spreading herself to the sun. But here she is white, ridiculously white, white as the bikini, white as the breakers.

Then she lets her head fall back again, closes her eyes, points her toes. But she can't hold it for long—she feels something, a racing inside that makes her breath quick—and she raises her head to look long down her body: the breasts high on her chest, the sharp declivity of the rib cage, the smooth abdomen, the tightly wound hairs. The sun on her body is languid, warm: a massage. At her side: the tanning oil, cooking in the sun. She uncaps the plastic bottle, squeezes, feels the hot spurt of it across her chest. Then her palms are smoothing over the skin in a slow circular motion and she remembers how they'd all studied her with their hot faces while she sat above them, a Greek statue, staring out the window. From their expressions she could tell it wasn't like sketching a professional model—they'd seen her around campus so many times and so many times had looked up her skirt and down her blouse, undressing her with their eyes. And then suddenly, a shock: there she was. She thinks of those faces, those nervous hands, hairy wrists. And laughs, laughs while her fingers move in the ripening sun—smoothly, thrillingly—over her body.

Five hundred yards down the beach, the man ends his hike and approaches the water's edge. He kicks about in the sand while the soft foaming fringe shoots over his toes, up to his ankles and on past to retrace a broad ellipse in the sand behind him. He seems satisfied with the spot. Everything pleasantly symmetrical: the dark line of the high tide, the rounded peaks of the dunes, the fanned circular waves riding it on an infinity of waves, each identical to the first. Yes, he is satisfied, and like any other bather he wades in, the water rising gradually up his thin pale legs. But he is an anomaly here—his skin shows no trace of a tan—not the smallest freckle. Is this then his first day on the beach? He looks unhealthy and thin, too white in this flashing sun.

He wades deeper and the water washes level with his groin, the roll of the waves gently floating his genitals. The sensation, after the first shock, is cool and smooth, like the breath of an air conditioner. Is he aware, as he turns his head to look down the beach, that the girl, drowsing now despite herself, is naked and alone—defenseless even? I think not. There is certainly something down there in the distance, obscured by the glare and heat haze. Something dark, a stain in the whiteness. But really, it's none of his concern. The waves lap at his underarms, splash up into his beard—and then he dives smooth into the next tall one, spearing through like a dolphin. He kicks powerfully and speeds through the incoming peaks until he is a considerable distance from shore. From his performance in the water, it is apparent that this is his element, that the paleness he displayed on the beach has no bearing here. Far from shore, his head is a buoy, tentatively riding up on the distant blinding whitecaps.

She strolled into the classroom in a short white smock. The hem of the smock defined a sharp line across the rise of her buttocks. It lifted and fell with each deliberate step. The art students, the ones who'd absently sketched a dozen models before her, now practically leaped from their chairs. She recognized nearly all of them from around campus, had ignored their slick hungry looks on countless occasions. She knew the girls too—they colored a bit when she entered, shifted in their seats from buttock to buttock. A few glared. But she just strolled, calmly, confidently, her chest thrust forward, just strolled right to the center of the room, yawned a brief yawn and then unbuttoned the smock, and let it fall to the floor.

In the broad expanse of the dunes a pair of wide feet wanders, kicking channels in the hot sand, becoming buried and unburied alternately as they are lifted from one spot to the next. Bobbing along, just ahead of the shuffling feet, is a circular shadow. Its unwitting creator is an obese young man, dressed in T-shirt and bathing trunks—the baggy boxer type with a broad red stripe on each side. Clenched in his left hand is a towel. Every few moments the towel rises to his face and flaps about in an effort to mop up the perspiration. Brackish creeks and streams and rivulets wash over the globe of his torso and down his legs to dot the sand. He apparently has come a good distance, but why through the harsh dunes? If, as I suspect, he is looking for a secluded stretch of sea for bathing, why doesn't he walk along the beach, where temperatures are cooler and footing easier?

He approaches the crest of the final dune blocking his way to the beach, the sea breeze stiff in his nostrils and cool against his face. Feet splayed, his legs attack the slope—the band of ocean visible over the lip of the dune grows wider, opening like an eye, with each plodding step upward. Finally, with a great wet heave of breath, he reaches the summit. Ah! The wind in his hair, the sea, the lone gull coasting overhead, solitude! But no, there below him is . . . a female! Nude and asleep! He starts back, vanishes. And then, on his belly in the sand, takes a lingering look. Her breasts, flattened with gravity, nipples pointing heavenward, her black-haired pubes! Beneath him, another part of the body, just a small appendage, adds itself to the general tumescence.

One hour. They had one hour to leer to their hearts' content—she wasn't even watching—her gaze was fixed on the bell tower out the window and across the campus. They were crowding in, faces blank, scholars. Scholars operating under the premise that she was just a specimen, headless and mindless, a physique, a painted beetle fixed beneath a microscope.

She knew better.

Tomorrow they wouldn't dare approach her, yet they'd stare even harder, straining to see up her skirt and down her blouse, grinning like jackals. They'd leer and joke as if she were some kind of freak. And she would be distant, haughty. They'd had their hour, and that was that. The closest any of them would ever come to her. In bed in the dark they would fitfully strain to summon her image, but like all mental pictures it would come in flashes, a film out of frame. She knew all this, and as she posed that day the faintest trace of a smile rounded her lips: inscrutably.

All his life he'd been forced to contend with sniggers, grinning faces, pointed fingers. People looked on him as a bad joke—a caricature of themselves, some sort of cosmic admonition to keep their noses clean. They laughed to cover their horror, laughed, imagining their own eyes pinched behind those sagging cheeks and chins. And often as not they resorted to violent pranks. He had for instance been obliged to discontinue regular attendance at the high school when he found he couldn't walk the halls without having his head slapped from behind by some invisible hand or having the books pushed from his arms to spray beneath hundreds of trampling feet. On one occasion eight or nine lean toughs had lined the wall outside his chemistry class, and when he emerged had enthusiastically decorated his physiognomy with lemon chiffon, coconut custard and Boston cream. After that, his parents decided that perhaps home tutoring would be more viable.

Since the time of these experiences he had very rarely entertained the company of others, had very rarely in fact left his parents' home. In the winter it was the apartment, in the summer the beach house. His social phobia was so overwhelming that he refused to show himself in public under any circumstance, not even in so trivial a role as picking up half a pound of pastrami at the delicatessen around the corner or taking the wash to the laundromat. He was a hermit, a monk, a solipsist. In the summer he would walk for miles through the dunes so he could swim alone without fear of exposing himself to ridicule, the preponderance of his flesh displayed in a swimsuit.

The upshot of all this is that he had, at the time of this story, reached the age of twenty-one years without ever having been laid. He had never been on a date, had never brushed a cheek against his own, had never squeezed a sweating palm or tit.

He stands, decides to have a closer look. But what if she should wake? The thought attenuates his resolve and he freezes there at the dune's crest, staring, obsessed. Just like in the nudist magazines. Masturbatory fantasies recur, charge through his head like rams—this is just the situation he had always pictured alone in his room, pulling furiously at his pud.

Soon he becomes increasingly conscious of the heat and removes his T-shirt, dropping it carelessly beside him, his attention fixed on the browned peaks below. He starts stealthily down the slope: a sly beast stalking its prey. But in a moment he's sliding down out of control, a truckload of sand following him. The seat of his trunks fills with it. At the base of the dune he recovers himself, jumps up, afraid to breathe, his rear abraded and an uncomfortable projection straining against the zipper of his trunks. The trunks begin to annoy him: he removes them.

A course of action is not entirely clear to him, but he moves closer anyhow, now as naked as she. The breasts swell gently with her sleep, the legs stir, the tongue peeps out to moisten her lips. And then suddenly the feathery warmth of the sun becomes a hot oppressive burden and she wakes to a huge childish face in her own and an insistent poking between her thighs. She shrieks, pushes wildly at that fat face. But she's pinned beneath a truck, she's been involved in an accident, that's it, a mountain has fallen and she's trapped beneath it. (Sure he's embarrassed but how can he stop now, the blood swelling up in him as it is?)

Cheeks clawed and gashed, eardrums aching, sweating like a frosted goblet, he drives relentlessly on. He inserts a massive fist in her mouth to quiet the wailing, and inadvertently, as he stiffens toward his moment of truth, he shoves increasingly harder, her head smoothing a depression in the sand—a basin for the blood that seeps from her mashed lips, loosened teeth. She gasps, croaks for air. Below, the white triangle is smothered beneath a sea of convulsively heaving flesh, and furtively, deep within, it too begins to bleed.

"Hey!" yell the fishermen. (They'd been poking around up the shore, drinking beer from a cooler, hunting in a half-assed way for stripers or porgies or blues.) "Hey!" And then they begin running toward what looks like a giant sea turtle digging frantically to bury its eggs.

His head rears up in surprise. With a grunt he disengages himself from her body and his fist from her mouth. An enamel cap, embedded between the second and third knuckles of his left hand, comes with it. He stands there for a blind moment, naked, dripping blood, caught in the act of committing an atrocity. He feels shame, mortification, guilt, remorse, self-denigration—and a rabid animal impulse to escape at any cost. He lumbers in a panic toward the sea, his only possible refuge. The fishermen reach the girl just as he is parting the waves, a colossal preterrestrial creature more at home in the sea than on land. "Hey!" the fishermen shout. But he is gone, paddling furiously, smashing the waves like an icebreaker. Deeper and deeper, farther and farther from his pursuers and his own fat life.

The fishermen are standing in the surf, their shoes and pants wet. They bellow a few drunken imprecations but he is already too distant to care. He drifts off on the waves, a great lump of sperm seeking to impregnate the sea. The fishermen turn back to the whimpering girl. One gently cups his hand under her chin while the other removes his trousers and sets to her.

Far out to sea, far beyond the churning fat boy and the rapacious fishermen, that strange pale creature floats, peacefully drowsing. His beard and long hair fan out in the water, become masses of seaweed. A chance wave, peaking higher than the others, rolls over him and he swallows a quantity of water. The next buries him. He has had no warning, no chance to cry for help, no hope that help would be available. Quite simply then, he drowns. A random event, one that I imagine, considering the world as a whole, is quite common.

The fat boy creeps home naked through the dark dunes, miles from where he had first encountered the girl. His feet and lower legs are lacerated from the stiff dune grass which bites into each blind step. In all, he feels a vague sense of shame, but also a certain exhilaration. After all, he's finally made the first palpable step in overcoming his social inadequacy.

The fishermen are at home, watching color TV. They feel a deep and abiding sense of accomplishment, of fulfillment—though they returned home this afternoon with an empty porgy basket.

The girl sleeps a heavy drugged sleep, enfolded in the astringently white hospital sheets. Her tan contrasts nicely with them. The breath passes gently through her parted lips, lips battered and brown with dried blood. A gray-haired man (her father?) sits beside her, patting her sleeping hand.

The thin man, the pale one, is jerked spasmodically by the underwater currents, tangled in a bed of weed. The crabs have long since discovered him and are rattling their ancient horny shells about his flesh, delighted with the unexpected treat. The tide is washing in, and the drowned man with it. Eventually, I suspect, what is left of him will come to rest on the beach, a few yards away from a curious red-brown stain in the bleached sand. The half-cleaned skeletons and carapaces of other strange creatures lie there too, waiting for the morning's gulls.

(1971)

RARA AVIS

It looked like a woman or a girl perched there on the roof of the furniture store, wings folded like a shawl, long legs naked and exposed beneath a skirt of jagged feathers the color of sepia. The sun was pale, poised at equinox. There was the slightest breeze. We stood there, thirty or forty of us, gaping up at the big motionless bird as if we expected it to talk, as if it weren't a bird at all but a plastic replica with a speaker concealed in its mouth. Sidor's Furniture, it would squawk, loveseats and three-piece sectionals.

I was twelve. I'd been banging a handball against the side of the store when a man in a Studebaker suddenly swerved into the parking lot, slammed on his brakes, and slid out of the driver's seat as if mesmerized. His head was tilted back, and he was shading his eyes, squinting to focus on something at the level of the roof. This was odd. Sidor's roof—a flat glaring expanse of crushed stone and tar relieved only by the neon characters that irradiated the proprietor's name—was no architectural wonder. What could be so captivating? I pocketed the handball and ambled round to the front of the store. Then I looked up.

There it was: stark and anomalous, a relic of a time before shopping centers, tract houses, gas stations and landfills, a thing of swamps and tidal flats, of ooze, fetid water, and rich black festering muck. In the context of the minutely ordered universe of suburbia, it was startling, as unexpected as a downed meteor or the carcass of a woolly mammoth. I shouted out, whooped with surprise and sudden joy.

Already people were gathering. Mrs. Novak, all three hundred pounds of her, was lumbering across the lot from her house on the corner, a look of bewilderment creasing her heavy jowls. Robbie Matechik wheeled up on his bike, a pair of girls emerged from the rear of the store with jump ropes, an old man in baggy trousers struggled with a bag of groceries. Two more cars pulled in, and a third stopped out on the highway. Hopper, Moe, Jennings, Davidson, Sebesta: the news echoed through the neighborhood as if relayed by tribal drums, and people dropped rakes, edgers, pruning shears, and came running. Michael Donadio, sixteen years old and a heartthrob at the local high school, was pumping gas at the station up the block. He left the nozzle in the customer's tank, jumped the fence, and started across the blacktop, weaving under his pompadour. The customer followed him.

At its height, there must have been fifty people gathered there in front of Sidor's, shading their eyes and gazing up expectantly, as if the bird were the opening act of a musical comedy or an ingenious new type of vending machine. The mood was jocular, festive even. Sidor appeared at the door of his shop with two stockboys, gazed up at the bird for a minute, and then clapped his hands twice, as if he were shooing pigeons. The bird remained motionless, cast in wax. Sidor, a fleshless old man with a monk's tonsure and liver-spotted hands, shrugged his shoulders and mugged for the crowd. We all laughed. Then he ducked into the store and emerged with an end table, a lamp, a footstool, motioned to the stockboys, and had them haul out a sofa and an armchair. Finally he scrawled BIRD WATCHER'S SPECIAL on a strip of cardboard and taped it to the window. People laughed and shook their heads. "Hey, Sidor," Albert Moe's father shouted, "where'd you get that thing—the Bronx Zoo?"

I couldn't keep still. I danced round the fringe of the crowd, tugging at sleeves and skirts, shouting out that I'd seen the bird first—which wasn't strictly true, but I felt proprietary about this strange and wonderful creature, the cynosure of an otherwise pedestrian Saturday afternoon. Had I seen it in the air? people asked. Had it moved? I was tempted to lie, to tell them I'd spotted it over the school, the firehouse, the used-car lot, a hovering shadow, wings spread wider than the hood of a Cadillac, but I couldn't. "No," I said, quiet suddenly. I glanced up and saw my father in the back of the crowd, standing close to Mrs. Schlecta and whispering something in her ear. Her lips were wet. I didn't know where my mother was. At the far end of the lot a girl in a college sweater was leaning against the fender of a convertible while her boyfriend pressed himself against her as if he wanted to dance.

Six weeks earlier, at night, the community had come together as it came together now, but there had been no sense of magic or festivity about the occasion. The Novaks, Donadios, Schlectas, and the rest—they gathered to watch an abandoned house go up in flames. I didn't dance round the crowd that night. I stood beside my father, leaned against him, the acrid, unforgiving stink of the smoke almost drowned in the elemental odor of his sweat, the odor of armpit and crotch and secret hair, the sematic animal scent of him that had always repelled me—until that moment. Janine McCarty's mother was shrieking. Ragged and torn, her voice clawed at the starless night, the leaping flames. On the front lawn, just as they backed the ambulance in and the crowd parted, I caught a glimpse of Janine, lying there in the grass. Every face was shouting. The glare of the fire tore disordered lines across people's eyes and dug furrows in their cheeks.

There was a noise to that fire, a killing noise, steady and implacable. The flames were like the waves at Coney Island—ghost waves, insubstantial, yellow and red rather than green, but waves all the same. They rolled across the foundation, spat from the windows, beat at the roof. Wayne Sanders was white-faced. He was a tough guy, two years older than I but held back in school because of mental sloth and recalcitrance. Police and firemen and wild-eyed neighborhood men nosed round him, excited, like hounds. Even then, in the grip of confusion and clashing voices, safe at my father's side, I knew what they wanted to know. It was the same thing my father demanded of me whenever he caught me—in fact or by report—emerging from the deserted, vandalized, and crumbling house: What were you doing in there?

He couldn't know.

Spires, parapets, derelict staircases, closets that opened on closets, the place was magnetic, vestige of an age before the neat rows of ranches and Cape Cods that lined both sides of the block. Plaster pulled back from the ceilings to reveal slats like ribs, glass pebbled the floors, the walls were paisleyed with aerosol obscenities. There were bats in the basement, rats and mice in the hallways. The house breathed death and freedom. I went there whenever I could. I heaved my interdicted knife end-over-end at the lintels and peeling cupboards, I lit cigarettes and hung them from my lower lip, I studied scraps of pornographic magazines with a fever beating through my body. Two days before the fire I was there with Wayne Sanders and Janine. They were holding hands. He had a switchblade, stiff and cold as an icicle. He gave me Ex-Lax and told me it was chocolate. Janine giggled. He shuffled a deck of battered playing cards and showed me one at a time the murky photos imprinted on them. My throat went dry with guilt.

After the fire I went to church. In the confessional the priest asked me if I practiced self-pollution. The words were formal, unfamiliar, but I knew what he meant. So, I thought, kneeling there in the dark, crushed with shame, there's a name for it. I looked at the shadowy grille, looked toward the source of the soothing voice of absolution, the voice of forgiveness and hope, and I lied. "No," I whispered.

And then there was the bird.

It never moved, not once, through all the commotion at its feet, through all the noise and confusion, all the speculation regarding its needs, condition, origin, species: it never moved. It was a statue, eyes unblinking, only the wind-rustled feathers giving it away for flesh and blood, for living bird. "It's a crane," somebody said. "No, no, it's a herring—a blue herring." Someone else thought it was an eagle. My father later confided that he believed it was a stork.

"Is it sick, do you think?" Mrs. Novak said.

"Maybe it's broke its wing."

"It's a female," someone insisted. "She's getting ready to lay her eggs."

I looked around and was surprised to see that the crowd had thinned considerably. The girl in the college sweater was gone, Michael Donadio was back across the street pumping gas, the man in the Studebaker had driven off. I scanned the crowd for my father: he'd gone home, I guessed. Mrs. Schlecta had disappeared too, and I could see the great bulk of Mrs. Novak receding into her house on the corner like a sea lion vanishing into a swell. After a while Sidor took his lamp and end table back into the store.

One of the older guys had a rake. He heaved it straight up like a javelin, as high as the roof of the store, and then watched it slam down on the pavement. The bird never flinched. People lit cigarettes, shuffled their feet. They began to drift off, one by one. When I looked around again there were only eight of us left, six kids and two men I didn't recognize. The women and girls, more easily bored or perhaps less interested to begin with, had gone home to gas ranges and hopscotch squares: I could see a few of the girls in the distance, on the swings in front of the school, tiny, their skirts rippling like flags.

I waited. I wanted the bird to flap its wings, blink an eye, shift a foot; I wanted it desperately, wanted it more than anything I had ever wanted. Perched there at the lip of the roof, its feet clutching the drainpipe as if welded to it, the bird was a coil of possibility, a muscle relaxed against the moment of tension. Yes, it was magnificent, even in repose. And, yes, I could stare at it, examine its every line, from its knobbed knees to the cropped feathers at the back of its head, I could absorb it, become it, look out from its unblinking yellow eyes on the street grown quiet and the sun sinking behind the gas station. Yes, but that wasn't enough. I had to see it in flight, had to see the great impossible wings beating in the air, had to see it transposed into its native element.

Suddenly the wind came up—a gust that raked at our hair and scattered refuse across the parking lot—and the bird's feathers lifted like a petticoat. It was then that I understood. Secret, raw, red and wet, the wound flashed just above the juncture of the legs before the wind died and the feathers fell back in place.

I turned and looked past the neighborhood kids—my playmates—at the two men, the strangers. They were lean and seedy, unshaven, slouching behind the brims of their hats. One of them was chewing a toothpick. I caught their eyes: they'd seen it too.

I threw the first stone.

(1981)

THE OVERCOAT II

There was a commotion near the head of the queue, people shouting, elbowing one another, wedging themselves in, and bracing for the inevitable shock wave that would pulse through the line, tumbling children, pregnant women, and unsuspecting old pensioners like dominoes. Akaky craned his neck to see what was happening, but he already knew: they were running out of meat. Two and a half hours on line for a lump of gristly beef to flavor his kasha and cabbage, nearly a hundred people ahead of him and Lenin knows how many behind, and they had to go and run out.

It was no surprise. The same thing had happened three days ago, last week, last month, last year. A cynic might have been led to grumble, to disparage the farmers, the truckers, the butchers and butchers' assistants, to question their mental capacity and cast aspersions on their ancestry. But not Akaky. No, he was as patient and enduring as the limes along the Boulevard Ring, and he knew how vital personal sacrifice was to the Soviet socialist workers' struggle against the forces of Imperialism and Capitalist Exploitation. He knew, because he'd been told. Every day. As a boy in school, as an adolescent in the Young Pioneers, as an adult in on-the-job political-orientation sessions. He read it in *Pravda* and *Izvestia*, heard it on the radio, watched it on TV. Whizz, whir, clack-clack-clack: the voice of Lenin was playing like a tape recording inside his head. "Working People of the Soviet Union! Struggle for a communist attitude toward labor. Hold public property sacred and multiply it!"

"Meat," cried a voice behind him. He squirmed round in disbelief—how could anyone be so insensitive as to voice a complaint in public?—and found himself staring down at the shriveled husk of an old woman, less than five feet tall, her babushkaed head mummy-wrapped against the cold. She was ancient,

older than the Revolution, a living artifact escaped from the Museum of Serf Art.
Akaky's mouth had dropped open, the word "Comrade" flying to his lips in gentle remonstrance, when the man in front of him, impelled by the estuarine wash
of the crowd, drove him up against the old woman with all the force of a runaway tram. Akaky clutched at her shoulders for balance, but she was ready for
him, lowering her head and catching him neatly in the breastbone with the rock-
hard knot in the crown of her kerchief. It was as if he'd been shot. He couldn't
breathe, tried to choke out an apology, found himself on the pavement beneath a
flurry of unsteady feet. The old woman towered over him, her face as stolid and
impassive as the monumental bust of Lenin at the Party Congress. "Meat," she
cried, "meat!"

Akaky stayed on another quarter of an hour, until a cordon of policemen
marched up the street and superintended the closing of the store. It was 9:00
P.M. Akaky was beat. He'd been standing in one line or another since 5:30, when
he left the ministry where he worked as file clerk, and all he had to show for it
was eight russet potatoes, half a dozen onions, and twenty-six tubes of Czecho-
slovakian toothpaste he'd been lucky enough to blunder across while looking for
a bottle of rubbing alcohol. Resigned, he started across the vacant immensity of
Red Square on his way to Herzen Street and the Krasnaya Presnya district where
he shared a communal apartment with two families and another bachelor. Normally he lingered a bit when crossing the great square, reveling in the majesty of
it all—from the massive blank face of the Kremlin wall to the Oriental spires of
Pokrovsky Cathedral—but now he hurried, uncommonly stung by the cold.

One foot after the next, a sharp echo in the chill immensity, ice in his nostrils,
his shoulders rattling with the cold that clutched at him like a hand. What was it:
twenty, twenty-five below? Why did it seem so much colder tonight? Was he
coming down with something? One foot after the next, rap-rap-rap, and then he
realized what it was: the overcoat. Of course. The lining had begun to come
loose, peeling back in clumps as if it were an animal with the mange—he'd noticed it that morning, in the anteroom at the office—balls of felt dusting his
shoes and trouser cuffs like snow. The coat was worthless, and he'd been a fool
to buy it in the first place. But what else was there? He'd gone to the Central Department Store in response to a notice in the window—"Good Quality Soviet
Made Winter Coats"—at a price he could afford. He remembered being surprised over the shortness and sparseness of the line, and over the clerk's bemused expression as he handed him the cloth coat. "You don't want this," the
clerk had said. The man was Akaky's age, mustachioed. He was grinning.

Akaky had been puzzled. "I don't?"

"Soviet means shoddy," the man said, cocky as one of the American delin-
quents Akaky saw rioting on the televised news each night.

Akaky's face went red. He didn't like the type of person who made light of
official slogans—in this case, "Soviet Means Superior"—and he was always
shocked and embarrassed when he ran across one of these smug apostates.

The man rubbed his thumb and forefingers together. "I'll have something really nice here, well-made, stylish, a coat that will hold up for years after this *shtampny* is in the rubbish heap. If you want to meet me out back, I think I can, ah, arrange something for you—if you see what I mean?"

The shock and outrage that had seized Akaky at that moment were like an electric jolt, like the automatic response governed by electrodes implanted in the brains of dogs and monkeys at the State Lab. He flushed to the apex of his bald spot. "How dare you insinuate—" he sputtered, and then choked off, too wrought up to continue. Turning away from the clerk in disgust, he snatched up the first overcoat at random and strode briskly away to join the swollen queue on the payment line.

And so he was the owner of a shabby, worthless garment that fit him about as snugly as a circus tent. The lining was in tatters and the seam under the right arm gaped like an open wound. He should have been more cautious, he should have controlled his emotions and come back another day. Now, as he hurried up Herzen Street, reflexively clutching his shoulders, he told himself that he'd go to see Petrovich the tailor in the morning. A stitch here, a stitch there, maybe a reinforced lining, and the thing would be good as new. Who cared if it was ill-fitting and outdated? He was no fashion plate.

Yes, he thought, Petrovich. Petrovich in the morning.

Akaky was up at 7:00 the next morning, the faintly sour odor of a meatless potato-onion soup lingering in unexpected places, the room numb with cold. It was dark, of course, dark till 9:00 A.M. this time of year, and then dark again at 2:30 in the afternoon. He dressed by candlelight, folded up the bed, and heated some kasha and spoiled milk for breakfast. Normally he had breakfast in his corner of the kitchen, but this morning he used the tiny camp stove in his room, reluctant to march down the hallway and disturb the Romanovs, the Yeroshkins or old Studniuk. As he slipped out the door ten minutes later, he could hear Irina Yeroshkina berating her husband in her pennywhistle voice: "Up, Sergei, you drunken lout. Get up. The factory, Sergei. Remember, Sergei? Work? You remember what that is?"

It was somewhere around thirty below, give or take a degree. Akaky was wearing two sweaters over his standard-brown serge suit (the office wags called it "turd brown"), and still the cold made him dance. If it was any consolation, the streets were alive with other dancers, shudderers, sprinters, and vaulters, all in a delirious headlong rush to get back inside before they shattered like cheap glass. Akaky was not consoled. His throat was raw and his eyelids crusted over by the time he flung himself into Petrovich's shop like Zhivago escaped from the red partisans.

Petrovich was sitting beneath a single brown lightbulb in a heap of rags and scraps of cloth, the antique pedal sewing machine rising up out of the gloom beside him like an iron monster. He was drunk. Eight o'clock in the morning, and he was drunk. "Well, well, well," he boomed, "an early customer, eh? What's it this time, Akaky Akakievich, your cuffs unraveling again?" And then he was laughing, choking away like a tubercular horse.

Akaky didn't approve of drinking. He lived a quiet, solitary existence (as solitary as the six Yeroshkin brats would allow), very rarely had occasion to do any social drinking, and saw no reason to drink alone. Sure, he had a shot of vodka now and again to ward off the cold, and he'd tasted champagne once when his sister had got married, but in general he found drinking repugnant and always got a bit tongue-tied and embarrassed in the presence of someone under the influence. "I . . . I . . . I was, uh, wondering if—"

"Spit it out," Petrovich roared. The tailor had lost an eye when he was eighteen, in the Hungarian police action—he'd poked his head up through the top hatch of his tank and a Magyar patriot had nailed him with a dexterously flung stone—and his good eye, as if in compensation, seemed to have grown to inhuman proportions. He fixed Akaky with his bulging protoplasmic mass and cleared his throat.

"—wondering if you could, ah, patch up the lining of my, ah, overcoat."

"Trash," Petrovich said.

Akaky held the coat open like an exhibitionist. "Look: it's not really that bad, just peeling back a little. Maybe you could, ah, reinforce the lining and—"

"Trash, *shtampny, brak.* You're wearing a piece of Soviet-bungled garbage, a fishnet, rotten through to the very thread of the seams. I can't fix it."

"But—"

"I won't. It wouldn't last you the winter. Nope. The only thing to do is go out and get yourself something decent."

"Petrovich." Akaky was pleading. "I can't afford a new coat. This one cost me over a month's salary as it is."

The tailor had produced a bottle of vodka. He winked his eye closed in ecstasy as he took a long pull at the neck of it. When he righted his head he seemed to have trouble focusing on Akaky, addressing himself to a point in space six feet to the left of him.

"I'll make you one," he said, pounding at his rib cage and belching softly. "Down-lined, fur collar. Like they wear in Paris."

"But, but . . . I can't afford a coat like that—"

"What are you going to do, freeze? Listen, Akaky Akakievich, you couldn't get a coat like this for five hundred rubles on the black market."

Black market. The words made Akaky cringe, as if the tailor had spouted some vile epithet: *faggot, pederast,* or *CIA.* The black market was flourishing, oh yes, he knew all about it, all about the self-centered capitalist revisionists who sold out the motherland for a radio or a pair of blue jeans or—or an overcoat. "Never," he said. "I'd rather wear rags."

"Hey, hey: calm down, Akaky, calm down. I said I *could* get you one, not that I would. No, for five-fifty I'll make you one."

Five hundred and fifty rubles. Nearly three months' salary. It was steep, it was outrageous. But what else could he do? Go back to the department store for another piece of junk that would fall apart in a year? He stepped back into the tailor's line of vision.

"Are you absolutely sure you can't fix this one?"

Petrovich shook his massive head. "No way."

"All right," Akaky said, his voice a whisper. "When could you have it done?"

"One week from today."

"One week? Isn't that awfully fast work?"

The tailor grinned at him, and winked his bloated eye. "I have my methods," he said. "Rely on me."

At the office that morning, while he crouched shuddering over the radiator in his worn overcoat, ragged sweaters, and standard-brown serge suit, Akaky became aware of a disturbance at his back: strident whispers, giggling, derisive laughter. He turned to look up into the grinning, wet-lipped faces of two of the younger clerks. They were wearing leather flight jackets with fur collars and blue jeans stamped prominently with the name of an American Jewish manufacturer, and they were staring at him. The shorter one, the blond, tossed his head arrogantly and made an obscene comment, something to do with mothers, sexual intercourse, and Akaky's Soviet-made overcoat. Then he put a finger to his head in a mock salute and sauntered through the main door, closely tailed by his tall cohort. Akaky was puzzled at first, then outraged. Finally, he felt ashamed. Was he really such a sight? Shoulders hunched, he ducked down the hallway to the lavatory and removed overcoat and sweaters in the privacy of one of the stalls.

Akaky took his afternoon break in the window of a gloomy downstairs hallway rather than endure the noisy, overcrowded workers' cafeteria. He munched a dry onion sandwich (he hadn't seen butter in weeks), drank weak tea from a thermos, and absently scanned the *Izvestia* headlines. RECORD GRAIN HARVEST; KAMA RIVER TRUCK PLANT TRIPLES OUTPUT; AMERICAN NEGROES RIOT. When he got back to his desk he knew immediately that something was wrong—he sensed it, and yet he couldn't quite put a finger on it. The others were watching him: he looked up, they looked down. What was it? Everything was in place on his desk—the calendar, the miniature of Misha the Olympic bear, his citation from the Revolutionary Order of United Soviet File Clerks for his twenty-five years of continuous service . . . and then it occurred to him: he was late. He'd dozed over lunch, and now he was late getting back to his desk.

Frantic, he jerked round to look at the clock, and saw in that instant both that he was as punctual as ever and that a terrible, shaming transformation had come over the life-size statue of Lenin that presided over the room like a guardian angel. Someone, some jokester, some flunky, had appropriated Akaky's overcoat and draped it over the statue's shoulders. This was too much. The bastards, the thoughtless, insensitive bastards. Akaky was on his feet, his face splotched with humiliation and anger. "How could you?" he shouted. A hundred heads looked up. "Comrades: how could you do this to me?"

They were laughing. All of them. Even Turpentov and Moronov, so drunk they could barely lift their heads, even Rodion Mishkin, who sometimes played a game of chess with him over lunch. What was wrong with them? Was poverty a laughing matter? The overcoat clung to Lenin's shoulders like a growth, the underarm torn away, a long tangled string of felt depending from the skirts like a tail. Akaky strode across the room, mounted the pedestal and retrieved his coat. "What is it with you?" he sputtered. "We're all proletarians, aren't we?" For some reason, this fired up the laughter again, a wave of it washing over the room like surf. The blond tough, the punk, was smirking at him from the safety of his desk across the room; Moronov was jeering from beneath his red, vodka-swollen nose. "Citizens!" Akaky cried. "Comrades!" No effect. And then, shot through with rage and shame and bewilderment, he shouted as he had never shouted in his life, roared like an animal in a cage: "Brothers!" he bellowed.

The room fell silent. They seemed stunned at his loss of control, amazed to see that this little man who for twenty-five years had been immovable, staid as a statue, was made of flesh and blood after all. Akaky didn't know what he was doing. He stood there, the coat in one hand, the other clutching Lenin's shoulder for support. All at once something came over him—he suddenly felt heroic, an orator, felt he could redeem himself with words, shame them with a spontaneous speech, take to the pulpit like one of the revolutionary sailors of the *Potemkin*. "Brothers," he said, more softly, "don't you realize—"

There was a rude noise from the far side of the room. It was the blond tough, razzing him. The tall one took it up—his accomplice—and then Turpentov, and in an instant they were all laughing and jeering again. Akaky stepped down from the pedestal and walked out the door.

As rooms go—even in apartment-starved Moscow—Akaky's was pretty small, perhaps half a size larger than the one that drove Raskolnikov to murder. Actually, it was the foyer of the gloomy four-room apartment he shared with the eight Yeroshkins, five Romanovs, and old Studniuk. The room's main drawback, of course, was that anyone entering or leaving the apartment had to troop through it: Sergei Yeroshkin, on the tail end of a three-day drunk; Olga Romanov, necking with her boyfriend at the door while a whistling draft howled through the room and Akaky tried fitfully to sleep; old Studniuk's ancient, unsteady cronies lurching through the door like elephants on their way to the burial ground. It was intolerable. Or at least it would have been, had Akaky given it any thought.

But it never occurred to him to question his lot in life or to demand that he and Studniuk switch rooms on a rotating basis or to go out and look for more amenable living quarters. He was no whining, soft-in-the-middle bourgeois, he was a hard-nosed revolutionary communist worker and an exemplary citizen of the Union of Soviet Socialist Republics. When industrial production goals were met, the party leaders would turn their attention to housing. Until then, there was no sense in complaining. Besides, if he really wanted privacy, he could duck into the coat closet.

Now, coming up the steps and into the still, darkened apartment, Akaky felt like an intruder in his own home. It was two-fifteen in the afternoon. He hadn't been home at this hour in thirteen years, not since the time he'd come down with a double attack of influenza and bronchitis, and Mother Gorbanyevskaya (she'd had Studniuk's room then) had nursed him with lentil soup and herb tea. He closed the door on silence: the place was deserted, the dying rays of the sun suffusing the walls with a soft eerie light, the samovar a lurking presence, shadows in the corners like spies and traducers. Without a pause, Akaky unfolded his bed, undressed, and pulled the covers up over his head. He had never felt more depressed and uncertain in his life: the injustice of it, the pettiness. He was a good man, true to the ideals of the Revolution, a generous man, inoffensive, meek: why did they have to make him their whipping boy? What had he done?

His thoughts were interrupted by the sound of a key turning in the lock. What now? he thought, stealing a glance at the door. The lock rattled, the bolt slid back, and old Studniuk was standing there in the doorway, blinking in bewilderment, a swollen string bag over his shoulder. "Akaky Akakievich?" he said. "Is that you?"

From beneath the blankets, Akaky grunted in assent.

"Blessed Jesus," the old man shouted, "what is it: have you gone rotten in the stomach, is that it? Have you had an accident?" Studniuk had shut the door and was standing over the bed now: Akaky could feel the old man's trembling fingertips on the bedspread. "Talk to me, Akaky Akakievich—are you all right? Should I call a doctor?"

Akaky sat up. "No, no, Trifily Vladimirovich, no need. I'm ill, that's all. It'll pass."

With a crack of his ancient knees, old Studniuk lowered himself to the corner of the bed and peered anxiously into Akaky's face. The string bag lay at his feet, bulging with cabbages, carrots, cheese, butter, bread, bottles of milk, and squarish packages wrapped in butcher's paper. After a long moment, the old man pulled a pouch of tobacco from his shirt pocket and began to roll a cigarette. "You don't look sick," he said.

All his life, Akaky had put a premium on truthfulness. When he was fifteen and assistant treasurer of the Young Pioneers, two of his co-workers had misappropriated the funds from a collection drive and no one in the group would expose them until Akaky came forward. The group leader had given him a citation for revolutionary rectitude which he still kept in a box with his school diploma and a photograph of his mother at the Tolstoi Museum. He looked Studniuk in the eye. "No," he said. "I'm not sick. Not physically anyway."

The old man rolled another cigarette with his clonic fingers, tucked the finished product behind his ear along with the first, and produced a handkerchief the size of a dish towel. He thoughtfully plumbed his nostrils while Akaky, in a broken voice, narrated the sad tale of his humiliation at the office. When Akaky was finished, the old man carefully folded up the handkerchief, tucked it in his shirt pocket, and extracted a paring knife from his sleeve. He cut the rind from a round of cheese and began sucking at bits of it while slowly shaking his head back and forth. After a while he said, "I've got some advice for you."

Studniuk was the patriarch of the apartment complex, ageless, a man who didn't have to look at newsreels to see history: it played in his head. He'd been there. For fifty-two years he'd worked in the First State Bearing Plant, present at its opening, a face in the crowd while successive generations of leaders came and went—Kerensky, Lenin, Trotsky, Stalin, Khrushchev. No one knew how old he was, or how he managed to live so well. He was jaunty, big-shouldered, bald as a fire hydrant; his nose had been broken so many times it looked like a question mark. Suddenly he was laughing, a sound like wind in the grass.

"You know," the old man said, fighting for control, "you're a good man, Akaky Akakievich, but you're an ass." Studniuk looked him full in the face, as hard and squint-eyed as a snapping turtle. "An ass," he repeated. "Don't you know that nobody gives half a shit about all this party business any more? Huh? Are you blind, son, or what? Where do you think I got all this?" he said, nodding at the sack of food with a belligerent jerk of his neck.

Akaky felt as if he'd been slapped in the face. The words were on his lips—"Betrayer, backslider"—but the old man cut him off. "Yes, that's right: wheeling and dealing on the black market. And you're a damn fool and an ass if you don't go out there and get everything you can, because it's for shit sure there ain't no comrade commissioner going to come round and give it to you."

"Get out of my room, Studniuk," Akaky said, his heart pounding wildly at his rib cage. "I'm sorry. But, please get out."

Wearily, the old man got to his feet and gathered up his things. He hesitated in the hallway, the ravaged nose glowing in the shadows like something made of luminescent wax. "I'll tell you why they hate you, Akaky Akakievich, you want to know why? Because you're a stick in the mud, because you're a holier-than-thou, because you're a party tool, that's why. Because you go around in that goddamned flapping overcoat like a saint or something, that's why." The old man shook his head, then turned and receded into the gloom of the hallway.

Akaky didn't hear him leave. He was biting his lip and pressing his hands to his ears with a fierce, unrelenting pressure, with the strict stoic rectitude of saints and martyrs and revolutionary heroes.

■ ■ ■

Petrovich was true to his word: the overcoat was ready in a week. It was a week to the day, in fact, that Akaky appeared at the tailor's shop, full of misgivings and clutching a wad of ruble notes as if he expected them to wriggle through his fingers like worms or sprout wings and flutter up in his face. He'd exhausted his savings and sold his antique Tovstonogov Star TV set to come up with the money, a real hardship considering how inflexible his budget was. (For the past twenty-two years he'd been sending half of each paycheck to his invalid mother in the Urals. It seemed there'd been some sort of mysterious calamity in the area and the authorities had had to relocate her entire village. Ever since, she'd been pale and listless, her hair had fallen out, and she complained that her bones felt as if they'd gone hollow, like a bird's.) The tailor was expecting him. "Akaky Akakievich," he shouted, rubbing his hands together and ushering him into the shop, "come in, come in."

Akaky shook Petrovich's hand and then stood uneasily in the center of the shop while the tailor ducked into the back room to fetch the coat. Left alone, Akaky found himself surveying the place with a discerning eye, as if it were the shop he was buying and not merely an overcoat. The place was shabby, no question about it. Cracks rent the plaster like fault lines, soiled rags and odd scraps of cloth puddled up round his ankles like the aftermath of an explosion in a textile plant, a dish of roach poison glistened in the corner, pincushioned with the yellow husks of dead and dying insects. Could a man who worked in such squalor produce anything worthwhile—anything worth five hundred and fifty rubles?

There was a rustle of wrapping paper and Petrovich was at his side, holding out a loosely wrapped package in both arms, as if it were an offering. Akaky felt his stomach sink. The tailor swept an armful of half-finished garments to the floor and laid the package on the table. It was wrapped in soft white tissue paper, the sort of paper you see at Christmas, but then only in the store windows. Akaky reached out to touch it, and the tailor swept back the paper with a flourish.

Akaky was stunned. He was staring down at the overcoat of a prince, as fine as the one the Secretary himself wore, so handsome it was almost indecent. "You can't—" he began, but he couldn't find the words.

"Camel's hair," Petrovich said, winking his enormous eye. "That's genuine fox, that collar. And look at the lining."

Akaky looked. The lining was quilted with down.

"You don't think you'll be warm in that?" Petrovich said, breathing vodka fumes in his face and nudging him, "eh, Akaky Akakievich, eh?"

It's such a small thing, an overcoat, a necessity of life—what's to be so excited about? Akaky told himself as he slid into the coat and followed Petrovich

into the back room to stand before the speckled mirror. What he saw reflected
there drove the last vestige of composure from his body. . . . He looked . . . magnificent, dignified, like a member of the Politburo or the manager of the National
Hotel, like one of the bigwigs themselves. He couldn't help himself, he was grinning, he was beaming.

Akaky was late to work that morning for the first time in anyone's memory. He
strolled in at quarter past the hour, as though oblivious of the time, nodding be-
nignly at this clerk or that. What was even more remarkable, from his fellow
clerks' point of view, was the way he was dressed—they recognized the cracked
imitation vinyl gloves, the standard-brown serge trousers, and the great woolly
black hat that clung to his head like an inflated rodent—but the overcoat, the
fox-trimmed camel's-hair overcoat, really threw them. Was this Akaky A. Bashmachkin, party tool and office drudge, strutting through the corridors like a
coryphée with the Bolshoi, like an Olympic shot putter, like one of the *appa-
ratchiki?* Had he been elevated to a supervisory position, was that it? Had he
come into a fortune, held up a bank? A few heads turned toward the door, half
expecting a cordon of KGB men to burst in and lead him away in disgrace.

No one had said a word to Akaky since the incident of a week before, but
now, with furtive glances over their shoulders for the supervisor, Turpentov, Moronov, and Volodya Smelyakov—the elder statesman of the office, hoary-headed,
toothless, and two months from retirement—gathered round Akaky's desk.
"Good morning, Akaky Akakievich," Moronov slurred, his tongue already thickening from his morning pick-me-up, "nice day, isn't it?" Moronov's eyes were red
as a pearl diver's. Beyond the windows the sky was like steel wool, the wind was
raging, and the temperature rapidly plunging from a high of minus twenty-eight
degrees.

Akaky had no reason to be cordial to Moronov, nor did he approve of
his drinking, but instead of fixing him with his usual bland and vaguely disap-
proving stare, he smiled, the upper lip drawing back from his teeth as if by the
operation of some hidden, uncontrollable force. He couldn't help it. He felt marvelous, felt like a new man, and not even Moronov, nor even the jeering blond
tough, could sour his mood. The fact was, he was late because he'd lingered on
the streets, despite the cold, to examine his reflection in shop windows and try
out his new, magnanimous big-shot's grin on strangers in Red Square. On a
whim, he'd stopped in at a tourist shop for an outrageously overpriced cup of
coffee and sweet bun. So what if he was late one morning out of five thousand?
Would the world collapse round him?

Old man Smelyakov cleared his throat and smacked his gums amicably.
"Well, well, well," he said in the voice of a throttled bird, "what a lovely, lovely,
ah"—the word seemed to stick in his throat—"overcoat you have there, Akaky
Akakievich."

"Yes," Akaky said, slipping out of the coat and hanging it reverently on the hook beside the desk, "yes it is." Then he sat down and began shuffling through a sheaf of papers.

Turpentov tugged at his knuckles. His voice was harsh, like a great whirring mill saw bogged down in a knotty log. "You wouldn't want to trust that to the workers' cloakroom, now would you," he said, making a stab at jocularity. "I mean, it's so ritzy and all, so expensive-looking."

Akaky never even glanced up. He was already cranking the first report into his antiquated Rostov Bear typewriter. "No," he said, "no, I wouldn't."

During the afternoon break, Akaky took his lunch amid the turmoil of the workers' cafeteria, rather than in the solitary confines of the lower hallway. On the way in the door, he'd nearly run head-on into the surly blond youth and had stiffened, expecting some sort of verbal abuse, but the blond merely looked away and went about his business. Akaky found a spot at one of the long imitation Formica tables and was almost immediately joined by Rodion Mishkin, his some-time chess partner, who squeezed in beside him with a lunchbox in one hand and a copy of *Novy Mir* in the other. Mishkin was a thin, nervous man in wire-rimmed spectacles, who carried a circular yellow patch of hardened skin on his cheek like a badge and looked as if he should be lecturing on molecular biology at the Academy of Sciences. He had a habit of blowing on his fingertips as he spoke, as if he'd just burned them or applied fresh nail polish. "Well," he said with a sigh as he eased down on the bench and removed a thickly buttered sausage sandwich from his lunchbox, "so you've finally come around, Akaky Akakievich."

"What do you mean?" Akaky said.

"Oh come on, Akaky, don't be coy."

"Really, Rodion Ivanovich, I have no idea what you're talking about."

Mishkin was grinning broadly, his gold fillings glistening in the light, grinning as if he and Akaky had just signed some nefarious pact together. "The overcoat, Akaky, the overcoat."

"Do you like it?"

Mishkin blew on his fingers. "It's first-rate."

Akaky was grinning now too. "You wouldn't believe it—I had it custom-made, but I suppose you can see that in the lines and the distinction of it. A tailor I know, lives in squalor, but he put it together for me in less than a week."

It was as if Mishkin's fingertips had suddenly exploded in flame: he was puffing vigorously at them and waving his hands from the wrist. "Oh come off it, Akaky—you don't have to put on a show for me," he said, simultaneously flailing his fingers and nudging Akaky with a complicitous elbow.

"It's the truth," Akaky said. And then: "Well, I guess it wouldn't be fair to say *less* than a week—it took him a full seven days, actually."

"All right, all right," Mishkin snapped, bending to his sandwich, "have it any way you want. I don't mean to pry."

Puzzled at his friend's behavior, Akaky looked up to see that a number of heads were turned toward them. He concentrated on his sandwich: raw turnip and black bread, dry.

"Listen," Mishkin said after a while, "Masha and I are having a few people from the office over tonight—for some dinner and talk, maybe a hand or two at cards. Want to join us?"

Akaky never went out at night. Tickets to sporting events, films, concerts, and the ballet were not only beyond his means but so scarce that only the *appa-ratchiki* could get them in any case, and since he had no friends to speak of, he was never invited for dinner or cards. In all the years he'd known Rodion Ivanovich the closest they'd come to intimacy was an occasional exchange on sports or office politics over a lunchtime game of chess. Now Rodion was inviting him to his house. It was novel, comradely. The idea of it—of dinner out, conversation, the company of women other than the dreary Romanov wife and daughter or the vituperative Mrs. Yeroshkina—suddenly burst into flower in his head and flooded his body with warmth and anticipation. "Yes," he said finally, "yes, I'd like that very much."

After work, Akaky spent two hours in line at the grocery, waiting to buy a small box of chocolates for his hostess. He had only a few rubles left till payday, but remembered reading somewhere that the thoughtful dinner guest always brought a little gift for the hostess—chocolates, flowers, a bottle of wine. Since he wasn't a drinker, he decided against the wine, and since flowers were virtually impossible to obtain in Moscow at this time of year, he settled on candy—a nice little box of chocolates with creme centers would be just the thing. Unfortunately, by the time he got to the head of the line, every last chocolate in the store had been bought up, and he was left with a choice between penny bubble gum and a rock-hard concoction of peppermint and butterscotch coated in a vaguely sweet soya substance that sold for two to the kopeck. He took ten of each.

As he hurried up Chernyshevsky Street, clutching the scrap of paper on which Mishkin had scrawled his address, Akaky was surprised by a sudden snow squall. He'd thought it was too cold for snow, but there it was, driving at him like a fusillade of frozen needles. Cocking the hat down over his brow and thrusting his hands deep in his pockets, he couldn't help smiling—the overcoat was marvelous, repelling the white crystals like a shield, and he was as warm as if he were home in bed. He was thinking of how miserable he'd have been in the old overcoat, shivering and stamping, dashing in and out of doorways like a madman, his bones rattling and nose running—when suddenly he felt an arm slip through his. Instinctively, he jerked back and found himself staring into the perfect oval of a young woman's face; she had hold of his arm and was matching him stride for stride as if they were old acquaintances out for an evening stroll. "Cold night," she breathed, looking up into his eyes.

Akaky didn't know what to do. He stared into her face with fascination and horror—what was happening to him?—captivated by her candid eyes and mascaraed lashes, the blond curls fringing her fur cap, the soft wet invitation of her Western lipstick. "I—I beg your pardon?" he said, trying to draw his hand from his pocket.

She had a firm grip on him. "You're so handsome," she said. "Do you work at the ministry? I love your coat. It's so, so elegant."

"I'm sorry," he said, "I've—"

"Would you like to take me out?" she said. "I'm available tonight. We could have a drink and then later—" She narrowed her eyes and squeezed his hand, still buried in the overcoat pocket.

"No, no," he said, his voice strained and unfamiliar in his ears, as if he'd suddenly been thrust into a stranger's body, "no, you see I can't really, I—I'm on my way to a dinner engagement."

They were stopped now, standing as close as lovers. She looked up at him imploringly, then said something about money. The snow blew in their faces, their breath mingled in clouds. Suddenly Akaky was running, hurtling headlong up the street as if a legion of gypsy violinists and greedy yankee moneylenders were nipping at his heels, his heart drumming beneath the standard-brown serge suit, the layers of down, and the soft, impenetrable elegance of his camel's-hair overcoat.

"Akaky Akakievich, how good to see you." Rodion stood at the door, blowing on his fingertips. Beside him, a short, broad-faced woman in an embroidered dressing gown, whom Akaky took to be his wife. "Masha," Rodion said by way of confirmation, and Akaky made a quick little bow and produced the bag of sweets. To his consternation, he saw that in the confusion on the street it had gotten a bit crushed, and that some of the soya substance had begun to stain the bottom of the white confectioner's bag. Masha's smile bloomed and faded as quickly as an accelerated film clip of horticultural miracles. "You shouldn't have," she said.

The apartment was magnificent, stunning, like nothing Akaky could have imagined. Three and a half rooms, abundantly furnished, with oil paintings on the walls—and they had it all to themselves. Rodion showed him around the place. There was a new stove and refrigerator, a loveseat in the front room. Little Ludmila lay sleeping on a cot in the bedroom. "Really, Rodion Ivanovich, I'm impressed," Akaky said, wondering how his friend managed to live so well. It was true that Rodion, as Deputy Assistant to the Chief File Clerk of the Thirty-second Bureau, made somewhat more than he did, and true too that Akaky was effectively operating on half pay because of his mother, but still, this was real opulence as far as he was concerned. Rodion was showing him the Swiss cuckoo clock. "It's very kind of you to say that, Akaky. Yes"—puffing at his fingers—"we find it comfortable."

There were a number of courses at dinner: a clear broth; fish in cream sauce; pickled sausages, white bread, and cheese; chicken, *galushki,* and Brussels sprouts. Rodion poured vodka and French wine throughout the meal, and afterward served a cherry cake and coffee. Akaky recognized some of the other guests from the office—faces but not names—and found himself engaged in a conversation with a man beside him over the melodic virtues of Dixieland jazz as opposed to the dissonance of free jazz. Akaky had never heard of either variety of jazz—in fact, he only vaguely knew what jazz was, a degenerate Negro sort of thing from America, with blaring horns and saxophones—but he smiled agreeably and asked an occasional question, while the man expatiated on one school of musical thought or another. Timidly, Akaky began to sip at the glass of wine before him; each time he turned around the glass was full again, and Rodion was beaming at him from the head of the table. He began to feel a depth of warmth and gratitude toward these people gathered around him, his comrades, men and women whose interests and knowledge ranged so far, whose wit flowed so easily: at one point he realized how much he'd been missing, felt that until now life had been passing him by. When Rodion proposed a toast to Masha—it was her birthday—Akaky was the first to raise his glass.

After the coffee, there was more vodka, a few hands of cards, and a good uproarious sing-along, all the old tunes Akaky had sung as a boy rising up from some deep hollow in him to burst forth as if he rehearsed them every day. He never missed a beat. When, finally, he thought to look at his watch, he was shocked to see that it was past one in the morning. Rodion's eyes were bloodshot, and the patch of skin on his cheek seemed to have concentrated all the color in his face; Masha was nowhere to be seen, and only one other guest remained—the jazz man—snoring peaceably in the corner. Akaky leaped to his feet, thanked Rodion profusely—"Best time I've had in years, in *years,* Rodion Ivanovich"—and hurried out into the desolate streets.

It was still snowing. Silently, stealthily, while Akaky had been pulling strips of chicken from the bone, raising his glass and singing "How high the shrubless crags!" the snow had been steadily accumulating, until now it spread a flat, even finish over streets, stairways, and rooftops and clung like dander to the hoods of automobiles and the skeletons of neglected bicycles. Whistling, Akaky kicked through the ankle-deep powder, for once unmindful of his cracked imitation plastic galoshes and disintegrating gloves, the fox collar as warm as a hand against the back of his neck. As he turned into Red Square, he was thinking how lucky he was.

It was ghostly, the square, as barren as the surface of the moon, trackless and white. Behind him, Pokrovsky Cathedral, like some shrouded Turkish dream; ahead the dark bank of the Lenin Mausoleum and the soft, snow-blurred lights of the city. He was just passing the mausoleum when two men materialized before him. The one was tall, cheekbones like slashes, with a fierce Oriental mustache that disappeared in the folds of his muffler; the other was hooded and slight. "Comrade," snarled the taller man, rushing at him out of the gloom, "that's my coat you've got there."

"No," Akaky said, "no, you must be mistaken," but the man had already taken hold of his collar and presented him with a bare fist the size of a football. The fist wavered under Akaky's nose for an instant, then dropped into the darkness and hammered him three or four times in the midsection. Suddenly Akaky was on the ground, crying out like an abandoned infant, while the big man rolled him over and his accomplice tugged at the sleeve of the overcoat. Ten seconds later it was over. Akaky lay on the ground in his standard-brown serge suit and imitation plastic galoshes, doubled up in the fetal position, gasping for breath. The thugs were gone. In the near distance, the Kremlin wall drew a white line across the night. The snow sifted down with a hiss.

How he made it home that night, Akaky would never know. For a long while he merely lay there in the snow, stunned by the enormity of the crime against him, some last fiber of his faith and conviction frayed to the breaking point. He remembered the feel of the snowflakes brushing his lips and melting against his eyelids, remembered feeling warm and cozy despite it, remembered the overwhelming, seductive craving for oblivion, for sleep and surcease. As he lay there, drifting between consciousness and absence, the words of the First Secretary began to echo in his ears, over and over, a record stuck in the groove: "Our goal is to make the life of the Soviet people still better, still more beautiful, and still more happy." Oh yes, oh yes, he thought, lying there on the ground. And then the man and woman had come along—or was it two men and a woman?—practically tripping over him in the dark. "My God," the woman had gasped, "it's a poor murdered man!"

They helped him to his feet, brushed the snow from his clothes. He was mad with the cold, with the hunger for justice—who said the world was fair or that everyone played by the same rules?—delirious with the fever of purpose. "The police!" he sputtered as a gloved hand held a flask of vodka to his lips. "I've been robbed." They were solicitous, these people, faces and voices emerging dreamlike from the banks of swirling snow, but they were cautious too—distant even. (It was as though they weren't quite sure what to make of his story—was he the victimized citizen he claimed to be, or merely a gibbering kopeck wheedler on the tail end of a drinking spree?) They guided him to the nearest precinct station and left him on the steps.

Pockets and cuffs heavy with snow, his eyebrows frosted over and lower lip quivering with indignation, Akaky burst through the massive double doors and into the cavernous anteroom of the Bolshaya Ordynka police station. It was about 3:00 A.M. Four patrolmen stood in the corner beneath the Soviet flag, drinking tea and joking in low tones; another pair sat together in the front row of an interminable file of benches, playing backgammon. At the far end of the chamber, on a dais, a jowly officer with thickly lidded eyes sat behind a desk the size of a pickup truck.

Akaky trotted the length of the room, a self-generated wind flapping round him, bits of compacted snow flying from his suit. "I've been beaten and robbed!" he cried, his voice strangely constricted, as if someone had hold of his windpipe. "In a public place. In Red Square. They took, they took"—here he felt himself racked by deep quaking bursts of sorrow so that he had to fight back the tears— "they took my overcoat!"

The desk sergeant looked down at him, immense, inscrutable, his head as heavy and shaggy as a circus bear's. Behind him, a great faded mural depicted Lenin at the helm of the ship of state. After a long moment of absolute, drenching silence, the sergeant pressed a chubby hand to his eyes, then rattled some papers and waited for the clerk to appear at his side. The clerk, also in uniform, looked to be about eighteen or nineteen, his face cratered with acne. "You will fill out this form, comrade, delineating the salient details," the clerk said, handing Akaky eight or ten pages of printed matter and an imitation ballpoint pen, "and then you will return at ten o'clock sharp tomorrow morning."

Akaky sat over the form—Place of Employment, Birthdate, Mother's Name and Shoe Size, Residence Permit Number, Previous Arrest Record—until past four in the morning. Then he handed it to the clerk, absently gathered up his hat and gloves, and wandered out into the teeth of the storm, as dazed and unsteady as the sole survivor of a shipwreck.

Akaky woke with a start at quarter past nine the following morning, the Ukrainian-made alarm clock having failed to go off on schedule. He was late for work, late for his appointment at the police station; his throat ached, a phlegmy cough clenched at his chest, and, worst of all, his overcoat was gone—gone, vanished, pilfered, three months' salary down the drain. It hit him all at once, in the instant of waking, and he fell back against the pillow, paralyzed, crushed under the weight of catastrophe and loss of faith. "Vladimir Ilyich Lenin!" he cried, taking the great man's name in vain as the six smirking Yeroshkin brats trundled by his bed on their way to school, "what am I going to do now?"

If he could have buried himself then and there, piled the dirt eight feet high atop his bed, he would have done it. What was the sense in going on? But then he thought of the police—perhaps they'd apprehended the thieves, put them behind bars where they belonged; perhaps they'd recovered his overcoat. He pictured the bearlike sergeant handing it to him with his apologies, and then commending him for his alert description of the crime's perpetrators and the swift and unhesitating way in which he'd filled out the crime report. As he pulled on the standard-brown serge trousers and imitation plastic boots, the image of the coat filled his consciousness and for a minute he was lost in reverie, remembering its softness, its lines, its snug and simple elegance. How long had he owned it—less than twenty-four hours? He wanted to cry.

His hand trembled as he knotted the olive-drab tie, finger-combed his hair, and tried to reach the office on Irina Yeroshkina's telephone. "Hello? Kropotkin's Laundry. May I be of assistance?" He hung up, dialed again. A voice immediately came over the wire, no salutation or identification, reading a list of numbers in a harsh, consonant-thick accent: "*dva-dyevy-at-odin-chyetirye-dva-dva—*" Akaky's stomach was on fire, his head pumped full of helium. He slammed down the receiver, snatched up the sad, ragged tatters of his Soviet-made overcoat, and hurried out the door.

It was three minutes past ten when he hurtled through the doors of the police station like a madman, out of breath, racked with shivers and trailing a dirty fringe of knotted felt lining. He ran headlong into a hunched old grandmother in a babushka—what was it about her that looked so familiar?—and realized with a start that the room that had been so empty just six hours ago was now thronged with people. The old woman, who called him a rude name and set down a bag of beets to give him a clean two-armed shove, was standing in an endless, snaking line that cut back on itself and circled the room twice. Akaky followed the line to the end and asked a man in knee boots and Tatar hat what was going on. The man looked up from the chess puzzle he'd been studying and fixed Akaky with a cold eye. "I assume you have a crime to report, comrade?"

Akaky bit his lower lip. "They took my overcoat."

The man held up a closely inscribed form. "Have you picked up your report yet?"

"Well, no, I—"

"First door to your left," the man said, turning back to his puzzle. Akaky looked in the direction the man had indicated and saw that a line nearly as long as the first was backed up outside the door. His stomach turned over like an egg in a skillet. This was going to be a wait.

At four-thirty, just when Akaky had begun to despair of gaining admission to the inner sanctum of the police headquarters or of ever seeing his overcoat again, a man in the uniform of the OBKhSS marched down the line to where Akaky was standing, snapped his heels together, and said: "Akaky A. Bashmachkin?" The OBKhSS was a branch of the Ministry of Internal Security, officially designated "The Department for the Struggle Against the Plundering of Socialist Property." Its job, as Akaky was reminded each day in the newspapers and on TV, was to curtail black-market activities by cracking down on the pirating of the people's goods to pay for foreign luxury items smuggled into the country. "Yes." Akaky blinked. "I—I've lost an overcoat."

"Come with me, please." The man spun on one heel and stamped off in the direction from which he'd come, Akaky hurrying to keep up. They breezed by the sixty or so scowling citizens who made up the forward section of the line, passed through the heavy wooden door into a room swarming with victims, suspects, police officers, and clerks, and then through a second door, down a hallway, and finally into a long, low-ceilinged room dominated by a glossy conference table. A single man sat at the head of the table. He was bald-headed, clean-shaven, dressed in slippers, slacks, and sports shirt. "Have a seat," he said, indicating a chair at the near end of the table. And then, to the OBKhSS man: "Watch the door, will you, Zamyotov?"

"Now," he said, clearing his throat, and consulting the form on the table before him, "you're Akaky A. Bashmachkin, is that right?" His voice was warm, fraternal, spilling over the room like sugared tea. He could have been a country physician, a writer of children's books, the genial veterinarian who'd tended the old cow Akaky's grandmother had kept tethered outside the door when he was a boy in the Urals. "I'm Inspector Zharyenoye, Security Police," he said.

Akaky nodded impatiently. "They've taken my overcoat, sir."

"Yes," said Zharyenoye, leaning forward, "why don't you tell me about it."

Akaky told him. In detail. Told him of the mockery he'd been exposed to at the office, of Petrovich's promise, of the overcoat itself, and of the brutal, uncommunist spirit of the men who'd taken it from him. His eyes were wet when he was finished.

Zharyenoye had listened patiently throughout Akaky's recitation, interrupting him only twice—to ask Petrovich's address and to question what Akaky was doing in Red Square at one-thirty in the morning. When Akaky was finished, Zharyenoye snapped his fingers and the antiplunderer from the OBKhSS stepped into the room and laid a package on the table. The inspector waved his hand, and the man tore back the wrapping paper.

Akaky nearly leaped out of his chair: there, stretched out on the table before him, as pristine and luxurious as when he'd first laid eyes on it, was his overcoat. He was overjoyed, jubilant, he was delirious with gratitude and relief. Suddenly he was on his feet, pumping the OBKhSS man's hand. "I can hardly believe it," he exclaimed. "You've found it, you've found my overcoat!"

"One moment, Comrade Bashmachkin," the inspector said. "I wonder if you might positively identify the coat as the one you were deprived of early this morning. Has your name been sewed into the lining perhaps? Can you tell me what the pockets contain?"

Akaky wanted to kiss the inspector's bald pate, dance him round the room: how good the policemen were, how efficient and dedicated and clever. "Yes, yes, of course. Um, in the right front pocket there's an article clipped from the paper on cheese production in Chelyabinsk—my grandmother used to make her own."

Zharyenoye went through the pockets, extracting seven kopecks, a pocket comb, and a neatly folded page of newsprint. He read the headline: " 'Cheese

Production Up.' Well, I guess that proves ownership incontrovertibly, wouldn't you say, Mr. Zamyotov?—unless Comrade Bashmachkin is a clairvoyant." The inspector gave a little laugh; Zamyotov, humorless as a watchdog, grunted his concurrence.

Akaky was grinning. Grinning like a cosmonaut on parade, like a schoolboy accepting the Karl Marx solidarity prize before the assembled faculty and student body. He stepped forward to thank the inspector and collect his overcoat, but Zharyenoye, suddenly stern-faced, waved him off. He had a penknife in his hand, and he was bending over the coat. Akaky looked on, bewildered, as the inspector carefully severed a number of stitches fastening the lining to the inner collar of the coat. With an impeccably manicured thumbnail, Zharyenoye prized a label from beneath the lining. Akaky stared down at it. Black thread, white acetate; MADE IN HONG KONG.

The animation had gone out of the inspector's voice. "Perhaps you'd better sit down, comrade," he said.

From that moment on, Akaky's life shifted gears, lurching into a rapid and inexorable downward spiral. The inspector had finally let him go—but only after a three-hour grilling, a lecture on civic duty, and the imposition of a one-hundred-ruble fine for receiving smuggled goods. The overcoat, of course, became the property of the Soviet government. Akaky left the conference room in a daze—he felt as if he'd been squeezed like a blister, flattened like a fly. His coat was gone, yes—that was bad enough. But everything he believed in, everything he'd worked for, everything he'd been taught from the day he took his first faltering steps and gurgled over a communal rattle—that was gone too. He wandered the streets for hours, in despair, a stiff, relentless wind poking fingers of ice through the rotten fabric of his Soviet-made overcoat.

The cold he'd picked up in Red Square worsened. Virulent, opportunistic, the microbes began to work in concert, and the cold became flu, bronchitis, pneumonia. Akaky lay in his bed, ravaged with fever, unable to breathe—he felt as if someone had stuffed a sock down his throat and stretched him out on the stove to simmer. Mrs. Romanova tried to feed him some borscht; Irina Yeroshkina berated him for letting himself go. Her husband called a doctor, a young woman who'd been trained in Yakutsk and seemed to have a great deal of trouble inserting the thermometer and getting a temperature reading. She prescribed rest and a strong emetic.

At one point in his delirium Akaky imagined that three or four of the Yeroshkin children were having a game of darts over his bed; another time he was certain that the blond tough from the office was laughing at him, urging him to pull on his cracked imitation plastic galoshes and come back to work like a man. Old Studniuk was with him when the end came. The patriarch was leaning

over him, his head blazing like the summer sun, his voice tense and querulous—
he was lecturing: "Oh, you ass, you young ass—didn't I tell you so? The blindness, the blindness." The old gums smacked like thunder; the whole world
shrieked in Akaky's ears. "I suppose you think they built that wall in Berlin to
keep people out, eh? Eh?" Studniuk demanded, and suddenly Akaky was crying
out, his voice choked with terror and disbelief—he must have been reliving the
scene in Red Square, his feet pounding the pavement, fingers clutching at the
Kremlin wall, the thieves at his heels—"Faster!" he shouted, "faster! Someone
get me a ladder!" And then he was quiet.

There were no ghosts haunting Moscow that winter, no vengeful, overcoat-
snatching wraiths driven from uneasy graves to settle the score among the living.
Nor was there any slowdown in the influx of foreign-made overcoats pouring
across the Finnish border, channeled through the maze of docks at Odessa,
packed like herring in the trunks of diplomats' wives and the baggage of party
officials returning from abroad. No, life went on as usual. Zhigulis hummed
along the streets, clerks clerked and writers wrote, old Studniuk unearthed an
antediluvian crony to take over Akaky's room and Irina Yeroshkin found herself
pregnant again. Rodion Mishkin thought of Akaky from time to time, shaking
his head over a tongue sandwich or pausing for a moment over his lunchtime
chess match with Grigory Stravrogin, the spunky blond lad they'd moved up to
Akaky's desk, and Inspector Zharyenoye had a single nightmare in which he
imagined the little clerk storming naked into the room and repossessing his overcoat. But that was about it. Rodion soon forgot his former colleague—Grigory's
gambits were so much more challenging—and Zharyenoye opened his closet
the morning after his odd little dream to find the overcoat where he'd left it—
hanging undisturbed between a pair of sports shirts and his dress uniform. The
inspector never had another thought of Akaky Akakievich as long as he lived,
and when he wore the overcoat in the street, proud and triumphant, people invariably mistook him for the First Secretary himself.

                                                                    (1981)

MEXICO

He didn't know much about Mexico, not really, if you discount the odd margarita and a determined crawl through the pages of *Under the Volcano* in an alcoholic haze twenty years ago, but here he was, emerging pale and heavy from the sleek envelope of the airliner and into the fecund embrace of Puerto Escondido. All this—the scorching blacktop, the distant arc of the beach, the heat, the scent of the flowers and jet fuel, and the faint lingering memory of yesterday's fish—was an accident. A happy accident. A charity thing at work—give five bucks to benefit the Battered Women's Shelter and win a free trip for two to the jewel of Oaxaca. Well, he'd won. And to save face and forestall questions he told everybody he was bringing his girlfriend along, for two weeks of R&R—Romance and Relaxation. He even invented a name for her—Yolanda—and yes, she was Mexican on her mother's side, gray eyes from her father, skin like burnished copper, and was she ever something in bed . . .

There were no formalities at the airport—they'd taken care of all that in Mexico City with a series of impatient gestures and incomprehensible commands— and he went through the heavy glass doors with his carry-on bag and ducked into the first cab he saw. The driver greeted him in English, swiveling around to wipe an imaginary speck of dust from the seat with a faded pink handkerchief. He gave a little speech Lester couldn't follow, tossing each word up in the air as if it were a tight-stitched ball that had to be driven high over the fence, then shrank back into himself and said "Where to?" in a diminished voice. Lester gave the name of his hotel—the best one in town—and sat back to let the ripe breeze wash over his face.

He was sweating. Sweating because he was in some steaming thick tropical place and because he was overweight, grossly overweight, carrying fifty pounds too many and all of it concentrated in his gut. He was going to do something about that when he got back to San Francisco—join a club, start jogging, whatever—but right now he was just a big sweating overweight man with big bare pale legs set like stanchions in the floor of the cab and a belly that soaked right through the front of his cotton-rayon open-necked shirt with the blue and yellow parrots cavorting all over it. But there was the beach, scalloped and white and chasing along beside the car, palm trees and a hint of maritime cool, and before ten minutes had ticked off his watch he was at the hotel, paying the driver from a wad of worn velvety bills that didn't seem quite real. The driver had no problem with them—the bills, that is—and he accepted a fat velvety tip too, and seven and a half minutes after that Lester was sitting in the middle of a shady tiled dining room open to the sea on one side and the pool on the other, a room key in his pocket and his first Mexican cocktail clenched in his sweating fist.

He'd negotiated the cocktail with the faintest glimmer of half-remembered high-school Spanish—jooze *naranja,* soda cloob and vodka, tall, with ice, *hielo,* yes, *hielo*—and a whole repertoire of mimicry he didn't know he possessed. What he'd really wanted was a greyhound, but he didn't know the Spanish word for grapefruit, so he'd fallen back on the orange juice and vodka, though there'd been some confusion over the meaning of the venerable Russian term for clear distilled spirits until he hit on the inspiration of naming the brand, Smirnoff. The waitress, grinning and nodding while holding herself perfectly erect in her starched white peasant dress, repeated the brand name in a creaking singsong voice and went off to fetch his drink. Of course, by the time she set it down in front of him it was already half-gone and he immediately ordered another and then another, until for the first twenty minutes or so he had the waitress and bartender working in perfect synchronization to combat his thirst and any real or imagined pangs he might have suffered on the long trip down.

After the fifth drink he began to feel settled, any anxiety over traveling dissolved in the sweet flow of alcohol and juice. He was pleased with himself. Here he was, in a foreign country, ordering cocktails like a native and contemplating a bite to eat—guacamole and nachos, maybe—and then a stroll on the beach and a nap before cocktails and dinner. He wasn't sweating anymore. The waitress was his favorite person in the world, and the bartender came next.

He'd just drained his glass and turned to flag down the waitress—one more, he was thinking, and then maybe the nachos or a shrimp cocktail—when he noticed that the table at the far end of the veranda was occupied. A woman had slipped in while he was gazing out to sea, and she was seated facing him, bare-legged, in a rust-colored bikini and a loose black robe. She looked to be about thirty, slim, muscular, with a high tight chest and feathered hair that showed off her bleeding eyes and the puffed bow of her mouth. There was a plate of something steaming at her elbow—fish, it looked like, the specialty of the house, breaded, grilled, stuffed, baked, fried, or sautéed with peppers, onions, and cilantro—and she was drinking a margarita rocks. He watched in fascination for a minute—semidrunken fascination—until she looked up, chewing, and he turned away to stare out over the water as if he were just taking in the sights like any other calm and dignified tourist.

He was momentarily flustered when the waitress appeared on his left to ask if he wanted another drink, but he let the alcohol sing in his veins and said, "Why not?—*¿Porqué no?*"—and the waitress giggled and went off with her increasingly admirable rump moving at the center of that long white gown. When he stole another glance at the woman in the corner, she was still looking his way. He smiled. She smiled back. He turned away again and bided his time, but when his drink came he tossed some money on the table, rose massively from the chair and tottered across the room.

"Hi," he said, looming over the chewing woman, the drink rigid in his hand, his teeth clenched around a defrosted smile. "I mean, *Buenos tardes.* Or *noches.*"

He watched her face for a reaction, but she just stared at him.

"Uh, *¿Cómo está Usted?* Or *tú. ¿Cómo estás tú?*"

"Sit down, why don't you," she said in a voice that was as American as Hillary Clinton's. "Take a load off."

Suddenly he felt dizzy. His drink had somehow concentrated itself till it was as dense as a meteorite. He pulled out a chair and sat heavily. "I thought . . . I thought you were—?"

"I'm Italian," she said. "From Buffalo originally. All four of my grandparents came from Tuscany. That's where I get my exotic Latin looks." She let out a short bark of a laugh, forked up a slab of fish and began chewing vigorously, all the while studying him out of eyes that were like two scalpels.

He finished his drink in a gulp and looked over his shoulder for the waitress. "You want another one?" he asked, though he saw she hadn't half-finished her first.

Still chewing, she smiled up at him. "Sure."

When the transaction was complete and the waitress had presented them with two fresh drinks, he thought to ask her name, but the silence had gone on too long and when they both began to speak at the same time, he deferred to her. "So what do you do for a living?" she asked.

"Biotech. I work for a company in the East Bay—Oakland, that is."

Her eyebrows lifted. "Really? Is that like making potatoes that walk around the kitchen and peel themselves, that sort of thing? Cloning sheep? Two-headed dogs?"

Lester laughed. He was feeling good. Better than good. "Not exactly."

"My name's Gina," she said, reaching out her hand, "but you might know me as 'The Cheetah.' Gina 'The Cheetah' Caramella?"

He took her hand, which was dry and small and nearly lost in his own. He was drunk, gloriously drunk, and so far he hadn't been ripped off by the Federales or assailed by the screaming shits or leached dry by malarial mosquitoes and vampire bats or any of the other myriad horrors he'd been warned against, and that made him feel pretty near invulnerable. "What do you mean—you're an actress?"

She gave a little laugh. "I wish." Ducking her head, she chased the remnants of the fish round the plate with her fork and the plane of her left index finger. "No," she said, "I'm a boxer."

The alcohol percolated through him. He wanted to laugh, but he fought down the urge. "A boxer? You don't mean like *boxing*, do you? Fisticuffs? Pugilism?"

"Twenty-three, two, and one," she said. She took a sip of her drink. Her eyes were bright. "What I'm doing right now is agonizing over my defeat two weeks ago at the Shrine by one of the queen bitches in the game, DeeDee DeCarlo, and my manager thought it would be nice for me to just get away for a bit, you know what I mean?"

He was electrified. He'd never met a female boxer before—hadn't even known there was such a thing. Mud-wrestling he could see—in fact, since his wife died he'd become a big fan, Tuesday nights and sometimes on Fridays—but boxing? That wasn't a woman's sport. It was crazy. Drunkenly, he scrutinized her face, and it was a good face, a pretty face, but for the bridge of her nose, a tell-tale depression there, just the faintest misalignment—and sure, sure, how had he missed it? "But doesn't it hurt? . . . I mean, when you get punched in the . . . body punches, I mean?"

"In the tit?"

He just nodded.

"Sure it hurts, what do you think? But I wear a padded bra, wrap 'em up, pull 'em flat across the rib cage so my opponent won't have a clear target, but really, it's the abdominal blows that take it out of you," and she was demonstrating with her hands now, the naked slope of her belly and the slit of her navel, abs of steel, but nothing like those freakish female bodybuilders they threw at you on ESPN, nice abs, nice navel, nice, nice, nice.

"You doing anything for dinner tonight?" he heard himself say.

She looked down at the denuded plate before her, nothing left but lettuce, don't eat the lettuce, never eat the lettuce, not in Mexico. She shrugged. "I guess I could . . . I guess in a couple hours."

He lifted the slab of his arm and consulted his watch with a frown of concentration. "Nine o'clock?"

She shrugged again. "Sure."

"By the way," he said. "I'm Lester."

April had been dead two years now. She'd been struck and killed by a car a block from their apartment, and though the driver was a teenage kid frozen behind the wheel of his father's Suburban, it wasn't entirely his fault. For one thing, April had stepped out in front of him, twenty feet from the crosswalk, and as if that wasn't bad enough, she was blindfolded at the time. Blindfolded and feeling her way with one of those flexible fiberglass sticks the blind use to register the world at their feet. It was for a psychology course she was taking at San Francisco State—"Strategies of the Physically Challenged." The professor had asked for two volunteers to remain blindfolded for an entire week, even at night, even in bed, no cheating, and April had been the first to raise her hand. She and Lester had been married for two years at the time—his first, her second—and now she was two years dead.

Lester had always been a drinker—and, for that matter, an abuser of recreational drugs—but after April's death he seemed to enjoy drinking less and need it more, as if he were lowering himself hand over hand down a long tapering rope that led to some dark place reeking of vomit and vodka fumes. He knew it, and he fought it. Still, when he got back to his room, sailing on the high of his chance meeting with Gina—Gina the Cheetah—he couldn't help digging out the bottle of Herradura he'd bought in the duty-free and taking a good long cleansing hit.

There was no TV in the room, but the air conditioner worked just fine and he stood in front of it awhile before he stripped off his sodden shirt, applied a fresh towel to his face and the swell of his gut and stepped into the shower. The water was tepid, but it did him good. He shaved, brushed his teeth, and repositioned himself in front of the air conditioner. When he saw the bottle standing there on the night table, he thought he'd have just one more hit—just one—because he didn't want to be utterly wasted when he took Gina the Cheetah out for dinner. But then he looked at his watch and saw that it was only seven-twenty, and figured what the hell, two drinks, three, he just wanted to have a good time. Too wired to sleep, he flung himself down on the bed like a big wet dripping fish and began poking through the yellowed paperback copy of *Under the Volcanco* he'd brought along because he couldn't resist the symmetry of it. What else was he going to read in Mexico—Proust?

" '*No se puede vivir sin amor,*' " he read, 'You can't live without love,' and he saw April stepping out into the street with her puny fiberglass stick and the black velvet sleep mask pulled tight over her eyes. But he didn't like that picture, not at all, so he took another drink and thought of Gina. He hadn't had a date in six months and he was ready. And who knew?—anything could happen. Especially on vacation. Especially down here. He tipped back the bottle, and then he flipped to the end of the book, where the Consul, cored and gutted and beyond all hope, tumbles dead down the ravine and they throw the bloated corpse of a dog down after him.

The first time Lester had read it, he thought it was kind of funny, in a grim sort of way. But now he wasn't so sure.

■ ■ ■

Gina was waiting for him at the bar when he came down at quarter to nine. The place was lit with paper lanterns strung from the thatched ceiling, there was the hint of a breeze off the ocean, the sound of the surf, a smell of citrus and jasmine. All the tables were full, people leaning into the candlelight over their fish and margaritas and murmuring to each other in Spanish, French, German. It was good. It was perfect. But as Lester ascended the ten steps from the patio and crossed the room to the bar, his legs felt dead, as if they'd been shot out from under him and then magically reattached, all in the space of an instant. Food. He needed food. Just a bite, that was all. For equilibrium.

"Hey," he said, nudging Gina with his shoulder.

"Hey," she said, flashing a smile. She was wearing shorts and heels and a blue halter top glistening with tiny blue beads. He was amazed at how small she was—she couldn't have weighed more than a hundred pounds. April's size. April's size exactly.

He ordered an Herradura and tonic, his forearms laid out like bricks on the bar. "You weren't kidding before," he said, turning to her, "—about boxing, I mean? Don't take offense, but you're so—well, small. I was just wondering, you know—?"

She looked at him a long moment, as if debating with herself. "I'm a flyweight, Les," she said finally. "I fight other flyweights, just like in the men's division, you know? This is how big God made me, but you come watch me some night and you'll see it's plenty big enough."

She wasn't smiling, and somewhere on the free-floating periphery of his mind he realized he'd made a blunder. "Yeah," he said, "of course. Of course you are. Listen, I didn't mean to—but why boxing? Of all the things a woman could do . . ."

"What? You think men have a patent on aggression? Or excellence?" She let her eyes sail out over the room, hard eyes, angry eyes, and then she came back to him. "Look, you hungry or what?"

Lester swirled the ice in his drink. It was time to defuse the situation, but quick. "Hey," he said, smiling for all he was worth, "I'd like to tell you I'm on a diet, but I like eating too much for that—and plus, I haven't had a thing since that crap they gave us on the plane, dehydrated chicken and rice that tasted like some sort of by-product of the vulcanizing process. So yeah, let's go for it."

"There's a place up the beach," she said, "in town. I hear it's pretty good—Los Crotos? Want to try it?"

"Sure," he said, but the deadness crept back into his legs. Up the beach? In town? It was dark out there and he didn't speak the language.

She was watching him. "If you don't want to, it's no big deal," she said, finishing off her drink and setting the glass down with a rattle of ice that sounded like nothing so much as loose teeth spat into a cup. "We can just eat here. The thing is, I've been here two days now and I'm a little bored with the menu—you know, fish, fish, and more fish. I was thinking maybe a steak would sound nice."

"Sure," he said. "Sure, no problem."

And then they were out on the beach, Gina barefoot at his side, her heels swinging from one hand, purse from the other. The night was dense and sustaining, the lights muted, palms working slowly in the breeze, empty *palapas* lined up along the high-water mark like the abandoned cities of a forgotten race. Lester shuffled through the deep sand, his outsized feet as awkward as snowshoes, while children and dogs chased each other up and down the beach in a blur of shadow against the white frill of the surf and knots of people stood in the deeper shadows of the palms, laughing and talking till the murmur of conversation was lost in the next sequence of breakers pounding the shore. He wanted to say something, anything, but his brain was impacted and he couldn't seem to think, so they walked in silence, taking it all in.

When they got to the restaurant—an open-air place set just off a shallow lagoon that smelled powerfully of seawrack and decay—he began to loosen up. There were tables draped in white cloth, the waiter was solicitous and grave and he accepted Lester's mangled Spanish with equanimity. Drinks appeared. Lester was in his element again. "So," he said, leaning into the table and trying to sound as casual as he could while Gina squeezed a wedge of lime into her drink and let her shoe dangle from one smooth slim foot, "you're not married, are you? I mean, I don't see a ring or anything—"

Gina hunched her shoulders, took a sip of her drink—they were both having top-shelf margaritas, blended—and gazed out on the dark beach. "I used to be married to a total idiot," she said, "but that was a long time ago. My manager, Jerry O'Connell—he's Irish, you know? From Cork City? In Ireland?—him and me had a thing for a while, but I don't know anymore. I really don't." She focused on him. "What about you?"

He told her he was a widower and watched her eyes snap to attention. Women loved to hear that—it got all their little wheels and ratchets turning—because it meant he wasn't damaged goods like all the other hairy-chested cretins out there, but tragic, just tragic. And needy. She asked how it had happened, a sink of sympathy and morbid female curiosity, and he told her the story of the kid in the Suburban and the wet pavement and how the student volunteers were supposed to have a monitor with them at all times, but not April, because she just shrugged it off—she wanted an authentic experience, and that was what she got all right. His throat seemed to thicken when he got to that part, the irony of it, and what with the cumulative weight of the cocktails, the reek of the lagoon, and the strangeness of the place—Mexico, his first day in Mexico—he nearly broke down. "I wasn't there for her," he said. "That's the bottom line—I wasn't there."

Gina was squeezing his hand. "You must have really loved her."

"Yeah," he said, "I did." And he had loved her, he was sure of it, though he had trouble picturing her anymore, her image drifting through his consciousness like something blown by a steady wind.

Another drink came. They ordered dinner, a respite from the intensity of what he was trying to convey, and then Gina told him her own tale of woe, the alcoholic mother, the brother shot in the face when he was mistaken for a gang member, the way she'd excelled in high school sports and nowhere to go with it, two years at the community college and a succession of mind-numbing jobs till Jerry O'Connell plucked her from anonymity and made her into a fighter. "I want to be the best," she said, "number one—and I won't settle for anything less."

"You're beautiful," he said.

She looked at him. Her drink was half gone. "I know," she said.

By the time they were finished with dinner and they'd had a couple of after-dinner drinks, he was feeling unbeatable again. It was quarter past eleven and the solicitous waiter wanted to go home. Lester wanted to go home too—he wanted to take Gina up to his room and discover everything there was to know about her. He lurched suddenly to his feet and threw a fistful of money at the table. "Want to go?" he said, the words sticking to the roof of his mouth.

She rose unsteadily from her seat and leaned into him while she adjusted the strap of her right heel. "Think we should take a cab?" she said.

"A cab? We're just up the other end of the beach—"

She was staring up at him, small as a child, her head thrown back to take in the spread and bulk of him. "Didn't you see that notice in your room—on the bathroom door? I mean, it sounds almost funny, the way they worded it, but still, I wonder."

"Notice? What notice?" He found he was sweating again. He just looked at her.

She fished around in her purse until she came up with a folded slip of paper. "Here," she said, "I wrote it down because it was so bizarre: 'The management regrets to inform you that the beach area is unsafe after dark because of certain criminal elements the local authorities are sadly unable to suppress and advises that all guests should take a taxi when returning from town.' "

"Are you kidding? Criminal elements? This place is a sleepy little village in the middle of nowhere—they ought to try the Tenderloin if they want to see criminal elements. And besides, besides"—he was losing his train of thought— "besides . . ."

"Yes?"

"There's nobody in the whole country taller than five-four, as far as I can see." He laughed. He couldn't help himself. *Criminal elements!* And he was still shaking his head as they stepped out into the night.

Call it hubris.

They hadn't gone two hundred yards, the night deepening, dogs howling in the hills, a potent fecal stench rising from the lagoon, and every star set firmly in its track, when they were jumped. It was nothing like the way Lester had visualized it while stalking home after the bars closed on 24th Street, half-hoping some sorry shithead would come up on him so he could break him in two—no words, no warning, no *Give me your wallet* or *I've got a gun* or *This is a stickup.* One minute he was trudging through the sand, a drunken arm draped hopefully over Gina's shoulder, and the next he was on the ground, two pairs of booted feet lashing diligently at his face and ribs while a whole fluttering rush of activity washed around him, as if a flock of birds had burst up off the ground in a panic. He heard a grunt, a curse, the unmistakable crack of bone and cartilage rearranging itself, and it was Gina, Gina the Cheetah, whaling away at the shadows with both fists as he shoved himself up out of the sand and the boots suddenly stopped kicking and fled.

"You all right?" she said, and he could hear her hard steady breathing over the hammering of the waves.

He was cursing into the night—"Sons of bitches! Motherfuckers! I'll kill you!"—but it was all bluster, and he knew it. Worse, so did she.

"Yeah," he said finally, his chest heaving, the booze and adrenaline pulsing in his temples till the blood vessels there felt like big green garden hoses crawling up both sides of his head. "Yeah, I'm okay . . . I took a few kicks in the face maybe . . . and I think—I think they got my wallet . . ."

"Here," she said, her voice oddly calm, "are you sure?" And then she was crouching, feeling around in the sand with spread fingers.

He joined her, glad to be down on his hands and knees and relieved of the effort of holding himself up, which suddenly seemed like such an unnecessary burden, and too much, way too much, to ask of his moribund legs. His wallet? He didn't give a shit about any wallet. The sand was cool and the regular thump of the waves conveyed itself to him in the most immediate and prescient way.

"Les?" She was standing now, obscuring the stars. He couldn't make out her face. "You sure you're all right?"

From a great reeling distance he heard himself say, "Yeah, I'm fine."

Her voice was insistent, the voice of an intimate, a wife, a lover. "Come on, Les, get up. You can't stay here. It's not safe."

"Okay," he said. "Sure. Just give me a minute."

Then there was a brightness, a burning hot soldered light fused to the cracks of the blinds, and he woke to find himself in his bed—his Mexican bed, in his Mexican hotel, in Mexico. Alone. Without Gina, that is. The first thing he did was check his watch. There it was, clinging like a manacle to his wrist, dividing his naked forearm from his meaty pale hand and indifferently announcing the time: two-thirty-two. All right. He heaved himself up to a sitting position, drained the

plastic water bottle he discovered behind the tequila on the night table, and took
a minute to assess the situation.

There was a rumor of pain between his ribs, where, he began to recall, two
pairs of sharp-toed boots had repeatedly inserted themselves in the waning hours
of the previous night, but that was nothing compared to his face. It seemed to
ache all over, from his hairline to his jaw. He reached a hand to his cheek and felt
a tenderness there, and then he worked his jaw till the pain became too much for
him. His right eye was swollen closed, there was a drumming in his head and a
vague nauseous feeling creeping up the back of his throat. To top it off, his wallet was missing.

Now he'd have to call up and cancel his credit cards, a real hassle, and he
was a fool and an idiot and he cursed himself twice over, but it wasn't the end of
the world—he had ten thin crisp hundreds hidden away in his carry-on bag, or
his shaving kit, actually, where no one would think to look for them. It could
have been worse, he was thinking, but he couldn't get much beyond that. How
had he managed to get himself back last night? Or had Gina managed it? The
thought made him burn with shame.

He took a tepid shower, clapped on a pair of coruscating silver-lensed sunglasses to mask the desecration of his eye, and limped down to the restaurant.
She wasn't there, and that was all right for the moment—he needed time to pull
himself together before he could face her. The waitress was there, though, eternally responsive to his needs, wearing another down-to-the-toes peasant dress,
this time in a shade of blue so pale it barely registered. She smiled and chirped at
him and he ordered two tall Smirnoff and *naranja* with soda cloob and three
fried eggs with tortillas and a fiery serrano salsa that cleared his airways and no
doubt about it. He ate and drank steadily, hoping to dull the throbbing in his
head, and when he looked up idly at the sea stretching beyond the veranda, he
saw nothing but a desert of water. He had a third cocktail for equilibrium, then
went down to the front desk and asked the attendant there if she knew which
room Gina was staying in.

"Gina?" the woman echoed, giving him a blank look. "What family name,
please?"

He had no idea. She'd told him, but it was gone now, obliterated by vodka,
tequila, and half a dozen kicks to the head. All he could think of was her professional name. " 'The Cheetah'?" he tried. " 'Gina the Cheetah'?"

The woman's hair was pulled back in a bun, her blouse buttoned up to her
throat. She studied him a long moment. "I'm sorry," she said. "I can't help you."

"Gina," he repeated, and his voice got away from him a bit. "How many
Ginas could there be in this place, for Christ's sake?"

When she answered this time, she spoke in Spanish, and then she turned
away.

He began a methodical search of the place, from pool to bar and back again, suddenly desperate—he had to explain to Gina about last night, joke it away, rationalize, apologize, spin shit into gold; she had to understand that he was down before he knew what hit him, that he was drunk and his judgment was impaired and if the circumstances were different he would have wiped the beach with those scumbags, he would have. Startled faces gaped up at him from the recliners around the pool, maids in pale green uniforms flattened themselves to the walls, he was sweating, he was huge, and where was she? And then he was out in the blast of the midday sun, searching through the *palapas* on the beach, hundreds of *palapas,* and practically every one with a sunburned tourist lounging beneath it. Soon he was sunburned himself, sweating rivulets and breathing hard, so he stripped off his shirt, threw himself into the waves and came up dripping to the nearest unoccupied *palapa* and sent a skinny little girl scurrying away to provide him with a piss-warm beer.

Several piss-warm beers later, he began to feel like himself again—and so what if he'd lost his shirt somewhere in the surf and the slope of his gut was as orange as a kumquat? He was in Mexico and he was drunk and he was going to go back to the hotel and find Gina and make it up to her, ask her to dinner, take a cab—a whole fleet of cabs—and buy her all the steak and lobster she could hold. It was past six by the time he got back to the hotel, and he went directly to the bar. She wasn't there, so he figured he'd just station himself at a table that commanded a view of the walkway to the rooms, and wait till she came back from wherever she was.

They served him even though he wasn't wearing a shirt—nobody in Mexico cared whether you had a shirt or not; you didn't need shoes either, just feet and flesh and money. He drank tequila with wedges of lime and some true cold beers, and when the shadows began to lengthen he made the mistake of removing his sunglasses and frightening the waitress with his eye. By now, the place had begun to fill up, burned noses and seared shoulders, women in various states of deshabille, but still no Gina. He decided to make another foray up the beach to see if she'd maybe taken one of the water taxis over to Puerto Angel or Carizalillo and was only now coming back.

The sun was hanging on a string just over the horizon, pink and lurid, and the tourists were busy packing up their sunblock and towels and paperback novels while the dark people, the ones who lived here year-round and didn't know what a vacation was, began to drift out of the trees with their children and their dogs to reclaim their turf. He smelled crushed flowers, the immitigable salt of the sea, fish fried in oil, shit. He kept walking, intent on the way his toes grabbed and released the sand, and he'd got halfway to the boats before he realized he'd left his sunglasses back on the table at the bar. No matter. He never even broke stride. They were nothing to him, one more possession, one more thing he could slough off like so much dead skin, like April's desk and her clothes and the straw baskets and pottery she'd decorated the apartment with. Besides, there was hardly any glare off the water now and these people, these coppery dark little grimacing Indians who seemed to sprout up all over the beach once the sun began to close down, they needed to see him, with his flaming belly and his crusted cheekbone and savage eye, because this was what their criminal elements had done to him and he was wearing the evidence of it like a badge. *Fuck you*, he was muttering under his breath, *fuck you all.*

At some point, Lester looked up to orient himself and saw that he was just opposite the restaurant from last night. There it sat, squat amid the trees, its lights reflected on the surface of the lagoon. A soft glow lit the bar, which he could just make out, figures there, movement, cocktail hour. He had a sudden intimation that Gina was in there, her dark head bent over a table in back, a drunken intimation that counted absolutely for nothing, but he acted on it, slashing through the fetid lagoon in his sandals and shorts, mounting the three steps from the beach and drifting across the creaking floorboards to the bar.

It wasn't Gina seated at the table but a local woman, the proprietress no doubt, totting up figures in a ledger; she raised her head when he walked in, but looked right through him. There were three men at the bar, some sort of police, in black shirts and trousers, one of them wearing dark glasses though there was no practical reason for them at this hour. They were smoking and talking quietly, in soft rasping voices. A plastic half-gallon jug of tequila stood before them on the bar, amid a litter of plates and three water glasses half-full of silvery liquid. They ignored Lester. He didn't exist, despite the evidence of his bulging eye and cracked face, the swell of his sunburned belly and the salt-encrusted hair that stood straight out from his head like a fright wig. Lester addressed the bartender. "Margarita rocks," he said. "With *hielo.*"

He sipped his drink, profoundly drunk now, but drunk for a reason—two reasons. Or three. For one thing, he had pain to kill, physical pain, and for another he was on vacation, and if you can't be legitimately wasted on your vacation, then when can you be? The third reason was Gina. He'd come so close, and then he'd blown it. *Criminal elements.* He glanced up at the cops with an idle curiosity that turned sour almost immediately: where had they been when he needed them? Why weren't they out on the beach at night, making the town safe for overweight gringos and their quick-fisted little gringa companions?

And then he noticed something that made his heart skip a beat: the boots. These guys were wearing boots, sharp-toed boots with silver toe-caps, the only boots in town. Nobody in Puerto Escondido wore boots. They could barely afford sandals, fishermen who earned their living with a hook and thirty feet of line wrapped around an empty two-liter Pepsi bottle, maids and itinerant merchants, dirt farmers from the hills. Boots? They were as likely to have Armani blazers, silk shirts, and monogrammed boxer shorts. Understanding came down like a hammer. He had to find Gina, had to tell her.

Dusk now, children everywhere, dogs, fishermen up to their chests in the rolling water, bats swooping, sand fleas leaping away from the blind advance of his feet. The steady flow of alcohol had invigorated him—he was feeling no pain, none at all—though he realized he'd have to eat something soon, and clean himself up, especially if he was going to see Gina, because his whole body was seething and rushing, and everything, from the palms to the *palapas* to the rocks scattered along the shore, seemed to have grown fur. Or fuzz. Peach fuzz. Peach fuzz on everything.

That really got to him, the peach fuzz—the conceit of it—and though he was angry and upset and had a big revelation to lay on Gina, he couldn't help chuckling to himself and shaking his head in a wide rueful arc. That was when he stepped in the hole and went down awkwardly on his right side, his face plowing a furrow in the loose sand, and the bad eye, wet with fluid, picking up a fine coating of sharp white granules. But it was no problem, no problem at all. He rolled over and lay on his back awhile, laughing softly to himself. *Criminal elements,* he thought, and he was speaking the thought aloud as people stepped around him in the sand, *sure, sure. And I'm the Pope in Rome.*

When he finally got back to the hotel, to the palm-fringed courtyard with the reception desk and the bar/restaurant off to his right and the pool and guest rooms to his left, he hesitated. Just stood there glistening in the muted light like a statue erected in honor of the befuddled tourist. On the one hand, he was struck by the impulse to go back to his room, wash the grit from his body, do something with his hair and fish another shirt out of his bag; on the other, he felt an equally strong urge to poke his head in the bar for a minute—just a minute—to see if Gina was there. Ultimately, it was no contest. Up the stairs he went, feet thundering on the planks, the sand sparkling all over him as if he'd been dipped in sugar.

There. There was the waitress, giving him an odd look—a blend of hopefulness and horror—and the thicket of heads bent over plates and glasses, the air heavy as water, the bartender looking up sharply. Ever hopeful, Lester lurched out onto the floor.

This time he got lucky: Gina was sitting at a table just around the corner of the bar, the farthest table out on the veranda, her legs crossed at the knee, one shoe dangling from her toes. There was music playing somewhere, a faint hum of it leaking in out of the night, Mexican music, shot full of saccharine trumpets and weeping violins. It was a romantic moment, or it could have been. But Gina didn't see him coming—she was turned the other way, in profile, the sea crashing behind her, her hair hanging limp to her shoulders—and it wasn't till he'd rounded the end of the bar that he saw she wasn't alone. There was a man sitting across from her, a drink in one hand, cigarette in the other. Lester saw a dangle of red hair, muscles under a Lollapalooza T-shirt, the narrow face of an insect.

In the next instant he loomed up on the table, pulled out a chair and dropped into it with a thump that reverberated the length of the dining room. "Gina, listen," he said, as if they were right in the middle of a conversation and the man with the insect face didn't exist, "about last night, and you're not going to believe this, but it was—"

And then he faltered. Gina's mouth was hanging open—and this was a mouth that could cushion any blow, a mouth that knew the taste of leather and the shock of the punch that came out of nowhere. "Christ, Les," she said, "what happened to you—you're a mess. Have you looked in the mirror?"

He watched her exchange a glance with the man across the table, and then he was talking again, trying to get it out, the night, the way they'd come at him, and they weren't just your average muggers, they were the law for christ's sake and how could anybody expect him to defend her from that?

"Les," she was saying, "Les, I think you've had too much to drink—"

"I'm trying to tell you something," he said, and his own voice sounded strange to him, distant and whining, the voice of a loser, a fat man, the maker of bad guesses and worse decisions.

That was when the red-haired man spoke up, his eyes twitching in his head. "Who is this jerk, anyway?"

Gina—Gina the Cheetah—gave him a look that was like a left jab. "Shut up, Jerry," she said. And then, turning back to Lester, "Les, this is Jerry—my manager?" She tried to inject a little air into her voice, though he could see she wasn't up to it: "Seems like he can't live without his meal ticket, even for three days."

Jerry slouched in his chair. He had nothing to say.

Lester looked from Gina to Jerry and back again. He was very far gone, he knew that, but still, even through his haze, he was beginning to see something in those two faces that shut him out, that slammed the door with a bang and turned the key in the lock. He had no right to Gina or this table or this hotel either. He was nothing. He couldn't even make it through the first round.

Gina's voice came to him as if from a great distance—"Les, really, maybe you ought to go and lay down for a while"—and then he was on his feet. He didn't say Yes or No or even See you later—he just turned away from the table, wove his way through the restaurant, down the stairs, and back out into the night.

It was fully dark now, black dark, and the shadows had settled under the skeletons of the trees. He wasn't thinking about Gina or Jerry or the empty apartment on 24th Street or even April and the kid in the Suburban. There was no justice, no revenge, no reason—there was just this, just the beach and the night and the criminal elements. And when he got to the place by the lagoon and the stink of decay rose to his nostrils, he went straight for the blackest clot of shadow and the rasping murmur at the center of it. "You!" he shouted, all the air raging in his lungs. "Hey, you!"

(1997)

· III ·

And Everything in Between

BEAT

Yeah, I was Beat. We were all Beat. Hell, I'm Beat now—is, was, and always will be. I mean, how do you stop? But this isn't about me—I'm nobody, really, just window-dressing on the whole mother of Bop freight-train-hopping holy higher than Tokay Beat trip into the heart of the American night. No, what I wanted to tell you about is Jack. And Neal and Allen and Bill and all the rest, too, and how it all went down, because I was there, I was on the scene, and there was nobody Beater than me.

Picture this: seventeen years old, hair an unholy mess and a little loden-green beret perched up on top to keep it in place, eighty-three cents in my pocket and a finger-greased copy of *The Subterraneans* in my rucksack along with a Charlie Parker disc with enough pops, scratches and white noise worked into the grooves to fill out the soundtrack of a sci-fi flick, hitched all the way from Oxnard, California, and there I am on Jack's front porch in Northport, Long Island, December twenty-three, nineteen fifty-eight. It's cold. Bleak. The town full of paint-peeling old monster houses, gray and worn and just plain old, like the whole horse-blindered tired-out East Coast locked in its gloom from October to April with no time off for good behavior. I'm wearing three sweaters under my Levi's jacket and still I'm holding on to my ribs and I can feel the snot crusting round my nostrils and these mittens I bummed from an old lady at the Omaha bus station are stiff with it, and I knock, wondering if there's an officially cool way to knock, a hipster's way, a kind of secret Dharma Bums code-knock I don't know about.

Knock-knock. Knockata-knockata, knock-knock-knock.

My first surprise was in store: it wasn't Jack, the gone hep satori-seeking poet god of the rails and two-lane blacktop, who answered the door, but a big blocky old lady with a face like the bottom of a hiking boot. She was wearing a dress the size of something you'd drape over a car to keep the dust off it, and it was composed of a thousand little red and green triangles with gold trumpets and silver angels squeezed inside of them. She gave me the kind of look that could peel the tread off a recapped tire, the door held just ajar. I shuddered: she looked like somebody's mother.

My own mother was three thousand miles away and so square she was cubed; my dog, the one I'd had since childhood, was dead, flattened out by a big rig the week earlier; and I'd flunked English, History, Calculus, Art, Phys. Ed., Music and Lunch. I wanted adventure, the life of the road, freewheeling chicks in berets and tea and bongos and long Benzedrine-inflected bullshit sessions that ran on into morning, I wanted Jack and everything he stood for, and here was this old lady. "Uh," I stammered, fighting to control my voice, which was just then deepening from the adolescent squeak I'd had to live with since consciousness had hit, "does, uh, Jack Kerouac live here, I mean, by any chance?"

"Go back where you came from," the old lady said. "My Jacky don't have time for no more of this nonsense." And that was it: she shut the door in my face.

My Jacky!

It came to me then: this was none other than Jack's mother, the Bop-nurturing freewheeling wild Madonna herself, the woman who'd raised up the guru and given him form, mother of us all. And she'd locked me out. I'd come three thousand miles, her Jacky was my Jack, and I was cold through to the bone, stone broke, scared, heartsick and just about a lungful of O_2 away from throwing myself down in the slush and sobbing till somebody came out and shot me. I knocked again.

"Hey, Ma," I heard from somewhere deep inside the house, and it was like the rutting call of some dangerous beast, a muted angry threatening Bop-benny-and-jug-wine roar, the voice of the man himself, "what the hell is this, I'm trying to concentrate in here."

And then the old lady: "It ain't nothing, Jacky."

Knock-knock. Knockata-knockata, knock-knock-knock. I paradiddled that door, knocked it and socked it, beat on it like it was the bald flat-topped dome of my uptight pencil-pushing drudge of a bourgeois father himself, or maybe Mr. Detwinder, the principal at Oxnard High. I knocked till my knuckles bled, a virtuoso of knocking, so caught up in the rhythm and energy of it that it took me a minute to realize the door was open and Jack himself standing there in the doorway. He looked the way Belmondo tried to look in *Breathless*, loose and cool in a rumpled T-shirt and jeans, with a smoke in one hand, a bottle of muscatel in the other.

I stopped knocking. My mouth fell open and the snot froze in my nostrils. "Jack Kerouac," I said.

He let a grin slide down one side of his mouth and back up the other. "Nobody else," he said.

The wind shot down my collar, I caught a glimpse of colored lights blinking on and off in the room behind him, and suddenly it was all gushing out of me like something I'd been chewing over and digesting all my life: "I hitched all the way from Oxnard and my name's Wallace Pinto but you can call me Buzz and I just wanted to say, I just wanted to tell you—"

"Yeah, yeah, I know," he said, waving a hand in dismissal, and he seemed unsteady on his muscatel-impaired feet, the smoke curling up to snatch at his cracked blue squinting eyes, the words slow on his lips, heavy, weighted and freighted with the deep everlasting bardic wisdom of the road, the cathouse and the seaman's bar, "but I tell you, kid, you keep drumming on the door like that you're going to end up in the hospital"—a pause—"or maybe a jazz combo." I just stood there in a kind of trance until I felt his hand—his Dharma Bum Subterranean On the Road Bop-master's gone Mexican-chick-digging hand—take hold of my shoulder and tug me forward, over the threshold and into the house. "You ever been introduced to a true and veritable set of tight-skinned bongos?" he asked, throwing an arm over my shoulder as the door slammed behind us.

Two hours later we were sitting there in the front room by this totally gone Christmas tree bedecked with cherubim and little Christs and the like, indulging in a poor boy and a joint or two of Miss Green, my Charlie Parker record whizzing and popping on the record player and a whole big pile of red and green construction-paper strips growing at our feet. We were making a chain to drape over the Beatest tree you ever saw and the music was a cool breeze fluttering full of Yardbird breath and the smell of ambrosia and manna crept in from the kitchen where Mémère, the Beat Madonna herself, was cooking up some first-rate mouthwatering Canuck-style two-days-before-Christmas chow. I hadn't eaten since New Jersey, the morning before, and that was only some pretty piss-poor diner hash fries and a runny solitary egg, and I was cutting up little strips of colored paper and pasting them in little circles as Jack's chain grew and my head spun from the wine and the weed.

That big old lady in the Christmas dress just kind of vanished and the food appeared, and we ate, Jack and I, side by side, left our Beat plates on the sofa, threw our chain on the tree and were just pawing through the coats in the front hallway for another poor boy of sweet Tokay wine when there was a knock at the door. This knock wasn't like my knock. Not at all. This was a delicate knock, understated and minimalistic, but with a whole deep continent of passion and expectation implicit in it—in short, a feminine knock. "Well," Jack said, his face lit with the Beatest joy at discovering the slim vessel of a pint bottle in the inside pocket of his seaman's pea coat, "aren't you going to answer it?"

"Me?" I said, grinning my Beatest grin. I was in, I was part of it all, I was Jack's confidant and compatriot, and we were in the front hallway of his pad in Northport, Long Island, a fine hot steaming mother-of-Jack-prepared meal in our gone Beat guts, and he was asking me to answer the door, me, seventeen years old and nobody. "You mean it?" and my grin widened till I could feel the creeping seeping East Coast chill all the way back to my suburban-dentist-filled molars.

Jack, uncapping, tipping back, passing the bottle: "That's a chick knock, Buzz."

Me: "I love chicks."

Jack: "A gone lovely spring flower of a beret-wearing flipped long-legged coltish retroussé-nosed and run-away-from-home-to-big-Jack-Kerouac chick knock."

Me: "I am crazy for gone lovely spring flower beret-wearing flipped long-legged coltish retroussé-nosed run-away-from-home-to-big-Jack-Kerouac chicks."

Jack: "Then answer it."

I pulled open the door and there she was, all the above and more, sixteen years old with big ungulate eyes and Mary Travers hair. She gave me a gaping openmouthed look, taking in my loden-green beret, the frizzed wildness of my hair sticking out from under it, my Beat Levi's jacket and jeans and my tea-reddened joyous hitching-all-the-way-from-Oxnard eyes. "I was looking for Jack," she said, and her voice was cracked and scratchy and low. She dropped her gaze.

I looked to Jack, who stood behind me, out of her line of vision, and asked a question with my eyebrows. Jack gave me his hooded smoldering dust-jacket-from-hell look, then stepped forward, took the poor boy from me and loomed over the now-eye-lifting chick and chucked her chin with a gone Beat curling in-dex finger. "Coochie-coochie-coo," he said.

Her name was Ricky Keen (Richarda Kinkowski, actually, but that's how she in-troduced herself), she'd hitchhiked all the way down from Plattsburgh and she was as full of hero-worship and inarticulate praise as I was. "Dean Moriarty," she said at the end of a long rambling speech that alluded to nearly every line Jack had written and half the Zoot Sims catalogue, "he's the coolest. I mean, that's who I want to make babies with, absolutely."

There we were, standing in the front hallway listening to this crack-voiced ungulate-eyed long gone Beat-haired sixteen-year-old chick talk about mak-ing babies with Charlie Parker riffing in the background and the Christmas lights winking on and off and it was strange and poignant. All I could say was "Wow," over and over, but Jack knew just what to do. He threw one arm over my shoulder and the other over the chick's and he thrust his already-bloating and booze-inflamed but quintessentially Beat face into ours and said, low and rumbly, "What we need, the three of us hepsters, cats and chicks alike, is a consciousness-raising all-night bull session at the indubitable pinnacle of all neighborhood Bodhisattva centers and bar and grills, the Peroration Pub, or, as the fellaheen know it, Ziggy's Clam House. What do you say?"

What did we say? We were speechless—stunned, amazed, moved almost to tears. The man himself, he who had practically invented the mug, the jug and the highball and lifted the art of getting sloshed to its Beat apotheosis, was asking us, the skinny underage bedraggled runaways, to go out on the town for a night of wild and prodigious Kerouackian drinking. All I could manage was a nod of assent, Ricky Keen said, "Yeah, sure, like wow," and then we were out in the frozen rain, the three of us, the streets all crusted with ugly East Coast ice, Ricky on one side of Jack, me on the other, Jack's arms uniting us. We tasted freedom on those frozen streets, passing the bottle, our minds elevated and feverish with the fat spike of Mary Jane that appeared magically between Jack's thumb and forefinger and the little strips of Benzedrine-soaked felt he made us swallow like a sacrament. The wind sang a dirge. Ice clattered down out of the sky. We didn't care. We walked eight blocks, our Beat jackets open to the elements, and we didn't feel a thing.

Ziggy's Clam House loomed up out of the frozen black wastes of the Long Island night like a ziggurat, a holy temple of Beat enlightenment and deep soul truths, lit only by the thin neon braids of the beer signs in the windows. Ricky Keen giggled. My heart was pounding against my ribs. I'd never been in a bar before and I was afraid I'd make an ass of myself. But not to worry: we were with Jack, and Jack never hesitated. He hit the door of Ziggy's Clam House like a fullback bursting through the line, the door lurched back on its hinges and embedded itself in the wall, and even as I clutched reflexively at the eighty-three cents in my pocket Jack stormed the bar with a roar: "Set up the house, barkeep, and all you sleepy fellaheen, the Beat Generation has arrived!"

I exchanged a glance with Ricky Keen. The place was as quiet as a mortuary, some kind of tacky Hawaiian design painted on the walls, a couple of plastic palms so deep in dust they might have been snowed on, and it was nearly as dark inside as out. The bartender, startled by Jack's joyous full-throated proclamation of Beat uplift and infectious Dionysian spirit, glanced up from the flickering blue trance of the TV like a man whose last stay of execution has just been denied. He was heavy in the jowls, favoring a dirty white dress shirt and a little bow tie pinned like a dead insect to his collar. He winced when Jack brought his Beat fist down on the countertop and boomed, "Some of everything for everybody!"

Ricky Keen and I followed in Jack's wake, lit by our proximity to the centrifuge of Beatdom and the wine, marijuana and speed coursing through our gone adolescent veins. We blinked in the dim light and saw that the everybody Jack was referring to comprised a group of three: a sad mystical powerfully made-up cocktail waitress in a black tutu and fishnet stockings and a pair of crewcut Teamster types in blue workshirts and chinos. The larger of the two, a man with a face like a side of beef, squinted up briefly from his cigarette and growled. "Pipe down, asshole—can't you see we're trying to concentrate here?" Then the big rippled neck rotated and the head swung back round to refixate on the tube.

Up on the screen, which was perched between gallon jars of pickled eggs and Polish sausage, Red Skeleton was mugging in a Santa Claus hat for all the dead vacant mindless living rooms of America, and I knew, with a deep sinking gulf of overwhelming un-Beat sadness, that my own triple-square parents, all the way out in Oxnard, were huddled round the console watching this same rubbery face go through its contortions and wondering where their pride and joy had got himself to. Ricky Keen might have been thinking along similar lines, so sad and stricken did she look at that moment, and I wanted to put my arms around her and stroke her hair and feel the heat of her Beat little lost body against my own. Only Jack seemed unaffected. "Beers all around," he insisted, tattooing the bar with his fist, and even before the bartender could heave himself up off his stool to comply Jack was waking up Benny Goodman on the jukebox and we were pooling our change as the Teamsters sat stoically beside their fresh Jack-bought beers and the cocktail waitress regarded us out of a pair of black staved-in eyes. Of course, Jack was broke and my eighty-three cents didn't take us far, but fortunately Ricky Keen produced a wad of crumpled dollar bills from a little purse tucked away in her boot and the beer flowed like bitter honey.

It was sometime during our third or fourth round that the burlier of the two Teamster types erupted from his barstool with the words *Communist* and *faggot* on his lips and flattened Jack, Ricky and me beneath a windmill of punches, kicks and elbow chops. We went down in a marijuana-weakened puddle, laughing like madmen, not even attempting to resist as the other Teamster, the bartender and even the waitress joined in. Half a purple-bruised minute later the three of us were out on the icy street in a jumble of limbs and my hand accidentally wandered to Ricky Keen's hard little half-formed breast and for the first time I wondered what was going to become of me, and, more immediately, where I was going to spend the night.

But Jack, heroically Beat and muttering under his breath about squares and philistines, anticipated me. Staggering to his feet and reaching down a Tokay-cradling spontaneous-prose-generating railroad-callused hand first to Ricky and then to me, he said, "Fellow seekers and punching bags, the road to Enlightenment is a rocky one, but tonight, tonight you sleep with big Jack Kerouac."

I woke the next afternoon on the sofa in the living room of the pad Jack shared with his Mémère. The sofa was grueling terrain, pocked and scoured by random dips and high hard draft-buffeted plateaus, but my stringy impervious seventeen-year-old form had become one with it in a way that approached bliss. It was, after all, a sofa, and not the cramped front seat of an A & P produce truck or road-hopping Dodge, and it had the rugged book-thumbing late-night-crashing bongo-thumping joint-rolling aura of Jack to recommend and sanctify it. So what if my head was big as a weather balloon and the rest of me felt like so many pounds and ounces of beef jerky? So what if I was nauseated from cheap wine and tea and Benzedrine and my tongue was stuck like Velcro to the roof of my mouth and Ricky Keen was snoring on the floor instead of sharing the sofa with me? So what if Bing Crosby and Mario Lanza were blaring square Christmas carols from the radio in the kitchen and Jack's big hunkering soul of a mother maneuvered her shouldery bulk into the room every five seconds to give me a look of radiant hatred and motherly impatience? So what? I was at Jack's. Nirvana attained.

When finally I threw back the odd fuzzy Canuck-knitted detergent-smelling fully Beat afghan some kind soul—Jack?—had draped over me in the dim hours of the early morning, I became aware that Ricky and I were not alone in the room. A stranger was fixed like a totem pole in the armchair across from me, a skinny rangy long-nosed Brahmin-looking character with a hundred-mile stare and a dull brown Beat suit that might have come off the back of an insurance salesman from Hartford, Connecticut. He barely breathed, squinting glassy-eyed into some dark unfathomable vision like a man trying to see his way to the end of a tunnel, as lizardlike a human as I'd ever seen. And who could this be, I wondered, perched here rigid-backed in Jack's gone Beat pad on the day before Christmas and communing with a whole other reality? Ricky Keen snored lightly from her nest on the floor. I studied the man in the chair like he was a science project or something, until all at once it hit me: this was none other than Bill himself, the marksman, freighted all the way across the Beat heaving blue-cold Atlantic from Tangier to wish Jack and his Beat Madonna a Merry Christmas and a Happy New Year!

"Bill!" I cried, leaping up from the sofa to pump his dead wooden hand, "this is . . . I mean, I can't tell you what an honor," and I went on in that gone worshipful vein for what must have been ten minutes, some vestige of the Benzedrine come up on me suddenly, and Ricky Keen snapped open her pure golden eyes like two pats of butter melting into a pile of pancakes and I knew I was hungry and transported and headachy and Bill never blinked an eye or uttered a word.

"Who's that?" Ricky Keen breathed in her scratchy cracked throat-cancery rasp that I'd begun to find incredibly sexy.

" 'Who's that?' " I echoed in disbelief. "Why, it's Bill."

Ricky Keen stretched, yawned, readjusted her beret. "Who's Bill?"

"You mean you don't know who Bill is?" I yelped, and all the while Bill sat there like a corpse, his irises drying out and his lips clamped tight round the little nugget of his mouth.

Ricky Keen ignored the question. "Did we eat anything last night?" she rasped. "I'm so hungry I could puke."

At that moment I became aware of a sharp gland-stimulating gone wild smell wafting in from the kitchen on the very same Beat airwaves that carried the corny vocalizations of Bing and Mario: somebody was making flapjacks!

Despite our deep soul brother- and sisterhood with Jack and his Mémère, Ricky and I were nonetheless a little sketchy about just bursting into the kitchen and ingratiating our way into a plate of those flapjacks, so we paused to knock on the hinge-swinging slab of the kitchen door. There was no response. We heard Mario Lanza, the sizzle of grease in the pan and voices, talking or chanting. One of them seemed to be Jack's, so we knocked again and boldly pushed open the door.

If there was a climax to all that had come before, a Beat epiphany and holy epitomized moment, this was it: Jack was there at the kitchen table and his mother at the stove, yes, but there was a third person present, arrived among us like one of the bearded mystics out of the East. And who could it be with that mad calculating bug-eyed big-lipped look of Zen wisdom and froglike beauty? I knew in an instant: it was Allen. Allen himself, the poet laureate of Beatdom, come all the way from Paris for this far-out moment with Jack and his mother in their humble little Beat kitchen on the cold North Shore of Long Island. He was sitting at the table with Jack, spinning a dreidel and singing in a muddy moist sweet-wine-lubricated voice:

> Dreidel, dreidel, dreidel,
> I made it out of clay,
> And when it's dry and ready,
> Then Dreidel I will play.

Jack waved Ricky and me into the room and pushed us down into two empty chairs at the kitchen table. "Flipped," he murmured as the dreidel spun across the tabletop, and he poured us each a water glass of sticky Mogen David blackberry wine and my throat seized at the taste of it. "Drink up, man, it's Christmas!" Jack shouted, thumping my back to jolt open the tubes.

That was when Mémère came into the picture. She was steaming about something, really livid, her shoulders all hunched up and her face stamped with red-hot broiling uncontainable rage, but she served the flapjacks and we ate in Beat communion, fork-grabbing, syrup-pouring and butter-smearing while Allen rhapsodized about the inner path and Jack poured wine. In retrospect, I should have been maybe a hair more attuned to Jack's mother and her moods, but I shoved flapjacks into my face, reveled in Beatdom and ignored the piercing glances and rattling pans. Afterward we left our Beat plates where we dropped them and rushed into the living room to spin some sides and pound on the bongos while Allen danced a disheveled dance and blew into the wooden flute and Bill looked down the long tunnel of himself.

What can I say? The legends were gathered, we cut up the Benzedrine inhalers and swallowed the little supercharged strips of felt inside, feasted on Miss Green and took a gone Beat hike to the liquor store for more wine and still more. By dark I was able to feel the wings of consciousness lift off my back and my memory of what came next is glorious but hazy. At some point—eight? nine?—I was aroused from my seventeen-year-old apprentice-Beat stupor by the sound of sniffling and choked-back sobs, and found myself looking up at the naked-but-for-a-seaman's-peacoat form of Ricky Keen. I seemed to be on the floor behind the couch, buried in a litter of doilies, antimacassars and sheets of crumpled newspaper, the lights from the Christmas tree riding up the walls and Ricky Keen standing over me with her bare legs, heaving out chesty sobs and using the ends of her long gone hair to dab at the puddles of her eyes. "What?" I said. "What is it?" She swayed back and forth, rocking on her naked feet, and I couldn't help admiring her knees and the way her bare young hitchhiking thighs sprouted upward from them to disappear in the folds of the coat.

"It's Jack," she sobbed, the sweet rasp of her voice catching in her throat, and then she was behind the couch and kneeling like a supplicant over the jean-clad poles of my outstretched legs.

"Jack?" I repeated stupidly.

A moment of silence, deep and committed. There were no corny carols seeping from the radio in the kitchen, no wild tooth-baring jazz or Indian sutras roaring from the record player, there was no Allen, no Jack, no Mémère. If I'd been capable of sitting up and thrusting my head over the back of the sofa I would have seen that the room was deserted but for Bill, still locked in his comatose reverie. Ricky Keen sat on my knees. "Jack won't have me," she said in a voice so tiny I was hardly aware she was speaking at all. And then, with a pout: "He's drunk."

Jack wouldn't have her. I mulled fuzzily over this information, making slow drawn-out turtlelike connections while Ricky Keen sat on my knees with her golden eyes and Mary Travers hair, and finally I said to myself, If Jack won't have her, then who will? I didn't have a whole lot of experience along these lines—my adventures with the opposite sex had been limited to lingering dumbstruck classroom gazes and the odd double-feature grope—but I was willing to learn. And eager, oh yes.

"It's such a drag being a virgin," she breathed, unbuttoning the coat, and I sat up and took hold of her—clamped my panting perspiring sex-crazed adolescent self to her, actually—and we kissed and throbbed and explored each other's anatomies in a drifting cloud of Beat bliss and gone holy rapture. I was lying there, much later, tingling with the quiet rush and thrill of it, Ricky breathing softly into the cradle of my right arm, when suddenly the front door flew back and the world's wildest heppest benny-crazed coast-to-coasting voice lit the room like a brushfire. I sat up. Groped for my pants. Cradled a startled Ricky head.

"Ho, ho, ho!" the voice boomed, "All you little boysies and girlsies been good? I been checkin' my list!"

I popped my head over the couch and there he was, cool and inexplicable. I couldn't believe my eyes: it was Neal. Neal escaped from San Quentin and dressed in a street-corner-Santa outfit, a bag full of booze, drugs, cigarettes and canned hams slung over his back, his palms hammering invisible bongos in the air. "Come out, come out, wherever you are!" he cried, and broke down in a sea of giggles. "Gonna find out who's naughty and nice, yes indeed!"

At that moment Jack burst in from the kitchen, where he and Allen had been taking a little catnap over a jug of wine, and that was when the really wild times began, the back-thumping high-fiving jumping jiving tea-smoking scat-singing Beat revel of the ages. Ricky Keen came to life with a snort, wrapped the jacket round her and stepped out from behind the couch like a Beat princess, I reached for the wine, Jack howled like a dog and even Bill shifted his eyes round his head in a simulacrum of animacy. Neal couldn't stop talking and drinking and smoking, spinning round the room like a dervish, Allen shouted "Miles Davis!" and the record player came to life, and we were all dancing, even Bill, though he never left his chair.

That was the crowning moment of my life—I was Beat, finally and absolutely—and I wanted it to go on forever. And it could have, if it wasn't for Jack's mother, that square-shouldered fuming old woman in the Christmas dress. She was nowhere to be seen through all of this, and I'd forgotten about her in the crazed explosion of the moment—it wasn't till Jack began to break down that she materialized again.

It was around twelve or so. Jack got a little weepy, sang an a capella version of "Hark the Herald Angels Sing" and tried to talk us all into going to the midnight mass at St. Columbanus' church. Allen said he had no objection, except that he was Jewish, Neal derided the whole thing as the height of corny bourgeois sentimentality, Bill was having trouble moving his lips and Ricky Keen said that she was Unitarian and didn't know if she could handle it. Jack, tears streaming down his face, turned to me. "Buzz," he said, and he had this wheedling crazed biggest-thing-in-the-world sort of edge to his voice, "Buzz, you're a good Catholic, I know you are—what do you say?"

All eyes focused on me. Silence rang suddenly through the house. I was three sheets to the wind, sloppy drunk, seventeen years old. Jack wanted to go to midnight mass, and it was up to me to say yea or nay. I just stood there, wondering how I was going to break the news to Jack that I was an atheist and that I hated God, Jesus, and my mother, who'd made me go to parochial school five days a week since I'd learned to walk and religious instruction on Sundays to boot. My mouth moved, but nothing came out.

Jack was trembling. A tic started in over his right eye. He clenched his fists. "Don't let me down, Buzz!" he roared, and when he started toward me Neal tried to stop him, but Jack flung him away as if he was nothing. "Midnight mass, Buzz, midnight!" he boomed, and he was standing right there in front of me, gone Beat crazy, and I could smell the booze on his stinking Beat breath. He dropped his voice then. "You'll rot in hell, Buzz," he hissed, "you'll rot." Allen reached for his arm, but Jack shook him off. I took a step back.

That was when Mémère appeared.

She swept into the room like something out of a Japanese monster flick, huge in her nightdress, big old Jack-mothery toes sticking out beneath it like sausages, and she went straight to the fireplace and snatched up the poker. "Out!" she screamed, the eyes sunk back in her head, "get out of my house, you queers and convicts and drug addicts, and you"—she turned on me and Ricky—"you so-called fans and adulators, you're even worse. Go back where you came from and leave my Jacky in peace." She made as if to swing the poker at me and I reflexively ducked out of the way, but she brought it down across the lamp on the table instead. There was a flash, the lamp exploded, and she drew back and whipped the poker like a lariat over her head. "Out!" she shrieked, and the whole group, even Bill, edged toward the door.

Jack did nothing to stop her. He gave us his brooding lumberjack Beat posing-on-the-fire-escape look, but there was something else to it, something new, and as I backpedaled out the door and into the grimy raw East Coast night, I saw what it was—the look of a mama's boy, pouty and spoiled. "Go home to your mothers, all of you," Mémère yelled, shaking the poker at us as we stood there drop-jawed on the dead brown ice-covered pelt of the lawn. "For god's sake," she sobbed, "it's Christmas!" And then the door slammed shut.

I was in shock. I looked at Bill, Allen, Neal, and they were as stunned as I was. And poor Ricky—all she had on was Jack's pea coat and I could see her tiny bare perfect-toed Beat chick feet freezing to the ground like twin ice sculptures. I reached up to adjust my beret and realized it wasn't there, and it was like I'd had the wind knocked out of me. "Jack!" I cried out suddenly, and my creaking adolescent voice turned it into a forlorn bleat. "Jack!" I cried, "Jack!" but the night closed round us and there was no answer.

What happened from there is a long story. But to make it short, I took Mémère's advice and went home to my mother, and by the time I got there Ricky had already missed her period. My mother didn't like it but the two of us moved into my boyhood room with the lame college pennants and dinosaur posters and whatnot on the walls for about a month, which is all we could stand, and then Ricky took her gone gorgeous Beat Madonna-of-the-streets little body off to an ultra-Beat one-room pad on the other end of town and I got a job as a brakeman on the Southern Pacific and she let me crash with her and that was that. We smoked tea and burned candles and incense and drank jug wine and made it till we damn near rubbed the skin off each other. The first four boys we named Jack, Neal, Allen and Bill, though we never saw any of their namesakes again except Allen, at one of his poetry readings, but he made like he didn't know us. The first of the girls we named Gabrielle, for Jack's mother, and after that we seemed to kind of just lose track and name them for the month they were born, regardless of sex, and we wound up with two Junes—June the Male and June the Female— but it was no big thing.

Yeah, I was Beat, Beater than any of them—or just as Beat, anyway. Looking back on it now, though, I mean after all these years and what with the mortgage payments and Ricky's detox and the kids with their college tuition and the way the woodworking shop over the garage burned down and how stinking close-fisted petit-bourgeois before-the-revolution pig-headed cheap the railroad disability is, I wonder now if I'm not so much Beat anymore as just plain beat. But then, I couldn't even begin to find the words to describe it to you.

(1993)

HARD SELL

So maybe I come on a little strong.

"Hey, babes," I say to him (through his interpreter, of course, this guy with a face like a thousand fists), "the beard's got to go. And that thing on your head too—I mean I can dig it and all; it's kinda wild, actually—but if you want to play with the big boys, we'll get you a toup." I wait right here a minute to let the interpreter finish his jabbering, but there's no change in the old bird's face—I might just as well have been talking to my shoes. But what the hey, I figure, he's paying me a hundred big ones up front, the least I can do is give it a try. "And this *jihad* shit, can it, will you? I mean that kinda thing might go down over here but on Santa Monica Boulevard, believe me, it's strictly from hunger."

Then the Ayatollah looks at me, one blink of these lizard eyes he's got, and he says something in his throat-cancer rasp—he's tired or he needs an enema or something—and the interpreter stands, the fourteen guys against the wall with the Uzis stand, some character out the window starts yodeling the midday prayers, and I stand too. I can feel it, instinctively—I mean, I'm perceptive, you know that, Bob—that's it for the day. I mean, nothing. Zero. Zilch. And I go out of there shaking my head, all these clowns with the Uzis closing in on me like piranha, and I'm thinking how in christ does this guy expect to upgrade his image when half the country's in their bathrobe morning, noon, and night?

Okay. So I'm burned from jet lag anyway, and I figure I'll write the day off, go back to the hotel, have a couple Tanqueray rocks, and catch some z's. What a joke, huh? They don't have Tanqueray, Bob. Or rocks either. They don't have Beefeater's or Gordon's—they don't have a bar, for christsake. Can you believe it—the whole damn country, the cradle of civilization, and it's dry. All of a sudden I'm beginning to see the light—this guy really *is* a fanatic. So anyway I'm sitting at this table in the lobby drinking grape soda—yeah, grape soda, out of the can—and thinking I better get on the horn with Chuck back in Century City, I mean like I been here what—three hours?—and already the situation is going down the tubes, when I feel this like pressure on my shoulder.

I turn around and who is it but the interpreter, you know, the guy with the face. He's leaning on me with his elbow. Like I'm a lamppost or something, and he's wearing this big shit-eating grin. He's like a little Ayatollah, this guy—beard, bathrobe, slippers, hat, the works—and he's so close I can smell the roots of his hair.

"I don't like the tone you took with the Imam," he says in this accent right out of a Pepperidge Farm commercial, I mean like Martha's Vineyard all the way, and then he slides into the chair across from me. "This is not John Travolta you're addressing, my very sorry friend. This is the earthly representative of the Qā'im, who will one day come to us to reveal the secrets of the divinity, Allah be praised." Then he lowers his voice, drops the smile, and gives me this killer look. "Show a little respect," he says.

You know me, Bob—I don't take shit from anybody, I don't care who it is, Lee Iacocca, Steve Garvey, Joan Rivers (all clients of ours, by the way), and especially not from some nimrod that looks like he just walked off the set of *Lawrence of Arabia*, right? So I take a long swallow of grape soda, Mr. Cool all the way, and then set the can down like it's a loaded .44. "Don't tell me," I go, "—Harvard, right?"

And the jerk actually smiles, "Class of '68."

"Listen, pal," I start to say, but he interrupts me.

"The name is Hojatolislam."

Hey, you know me, I'm good with names—have to be in this business. But Hojatolislam? You got to be kidding. I mean I don't even attempt it. "Okay," I say, "I can appreciate where you're coming from, the guy's a big deal over here, yeah, all right . . . but believe me, you take it anyplace else and your Ayatollah's got about as positive a public image as the Son of Sam. That's what you hired us for, right? Hey, I don't care what people think of the man, to me, I'm an agnostic personally, and this is just another guy with a negative public perception that wants to go upscale. And I'm going to talk to him. Straight up. All the cards on the table."

And then you know what he does, the chump? He says I'm crass. (Crass—and I'm wearing an Italian silk suit that's worth more than this joker'll make in six lifetimes and a pair of hand-stitched loafers that cost me . . . but I don't even want to get into it.) Anyway, I'm crass. I'm going to undermine the old fart's credibility, as if he's got any. It was so-and-so's party that wanted me in—to make the Ayatollah look foolish—and he, Hojatolislam, is going to do everything in his power to see that it doesn't happen.

"Whoa," I go, "don't let's mix politics up in this. I was hired to do a job here and I'm going to do it, whether you and the rest of the little ayatollahs like it or not."

Hoji kinda draws himself up and gives me this tight little kiss-my-ass smile. "Fine," he says, "you can do what you want, but you know how much of what you said this morning came across? In *my* translation, that is?"

Then it dawns on me: no wonder the Ayatollah looks like he's in la-la land the whole time I'm talking to him—nothing's getting through. "Let me guess," I say.

But he beats me to it, the son of a bitch. He leans forward on his elbows and makes this little circle with his thumb and index finger and then holds it up to his eye and peeks through it—real cute, huh?

I don't say a word. But I'm thinking, Okay, pal, you want to play hardball, we'll play hardball.

So it sounds like I'm in pretty deep, right? You're probably thinking it's tough enough to market this turkey to begin with, let alone having to deal with all these little ayatollahs and their pet gripes. But the way I see it, it's no big problem. You got to ask yourself, What's this guy got going for him? All right, he's a fanatic. We admit it. Up front. But hell, you can capitalize on anything. Now the big thing about a fanatic is he's sexy—look at Hitler, Stalin, with that head of hair of his, look at Fidel—and let's face it, he's got these kids, these so-called martyrs of the revolution, dying for him by the thousands. The guy's got charisma to burn, no doubt about it. Clean him up and put him in front of the TV cameras, that's the way I see it—and no, I'm not talking Merv Griffin and that sort of thing; I mean I can't feature him up there in a luau shirt with a couple of gold chains or anything like that—but he could show some chest hair, for christsake. I mean he's old, but hell, he's a pretty sexy guy in his way. A power trip like that, all those kids dying in the swamps, giving the Iraqis hell, that's a very sexy thing. In a weird way, I mean. Like it's a real turn-on. Classic. But my idea is maybe get him a gig with GTE or somebody. You know, coach up his English like with that French guy they had on selling perfume a couple years back, real charming, sweet-guy kinda thing, right? No, selling the man is the least of my worries. But if I can't talk to him, I'm cooked.

So I go straight to my room and get Chuck on the horn. "Chuck," I tell him, "they're killing me over here. Send me an interpreter on the next plane, will you? Somebody that's on our side."

Next morning, there's a knock on my door. It's this guy about five feet tall and five feet wide, with this little goatee and kinky hair all plastered down on his head. His name's Parviz. Yesterday he's selling rugs on La Brea, today he's in Tehran. Fine. No problem. Only thing is he's got this accent like Akim Tamiroff, I mean I can barely understand him myself, he's nodding off to sleep on me, and

I've got an appointment with the big guy at one. There's no time for formalities, and plus the guy doesn't know from shit about PR anyway, so I sit him down and wire him up with about sixty cups of crank and then we're out the door.

"Okay, Parviz," I say, "let's run with it."

Of course, we don't even get in the door at the Ayatollah's place and these creeps with the Uzis have Parviz up against the wall, feeling him up and jabbering away at him in this totally weird language of theirs—sounds like a tape loop of somebody clearing their throat. I mean, they feel me up too, but poor Parviz, they strip him down to his underwear—this skinny-strap T-shirt with his big pregnant gut hanging out and these boxer shorts with little blue parrots on them—and the guy's awake now, believe me. Awake, and sweating like a pig. So anyway, they usher us into this room—different room, different house than yesterday, by the way—and there he is, the Ayatollah, propped up on about a hundred pillows and giving us his lizard-on-a-rock look. Hoji's there too, of course, along with all the other Ayatollah clones with their raggedy beards and pillbox hats.

Soon as Hoji gets a load of Parviz though, he can see what's coming and he throws some kind of fit, teeth flashing in his beard, his face bruised up like a bag of bad plums, pissing and moaning and pointing at me and Parviz like we just got done raping his mother or something. But hey, I've taken some meetings in my time and if I can't handle it, Bob, I mean who can? So I just kinda brush right by Hoji, a big closer's smile on my face, and shake the old bird's hand, and I mean nobody shakes his hand—nobody's laid skin on him in maybe ten years, at least since the revolution, anyway. But I figure the guy used to live in Paris, right? He's gotta have a nose for a good bottle of wine, a plate of crayfish, Havana cigars, the track, he's probably dying for somebody to press some skin and shoot the bull about life in the civilized world. So I shake his hand and the room tenses up, but at least it shuts up Hoji for a minute and I see my opening. "Parviz," I yell over my shoulder, "tell him that I said we both got the same goal, which is positive name/face recognition worldwide. I mean billboards on Sunset, the works, and if he listens to me and cleans up his act a little, I'm ninety-nine percent sure we're going home."

Well, Parviz starts in and right away Hoji cuts him off with this high-octane rap, but the Ayatollah flicks his eyes and it's like the guy just had the tongue ripped out of his head, I mean incredible, bang, that's it. Hoji ducks his head and he's gone. And me, I'm smiling like Mr. Cool. Parviz goes ahead and finishes and the old bird clears his throat and croaks something back.

I'm not even looking at Parviz, just holding the Ayatollah's eyes—by the way, I swear he dyes his eyebrows—and I go, "What'd he say?"

And Parviz tells me. Twice. Thing is, I can't understand a word he says, but the hell with it, I figure, be positive, right? "Okay," I say, seeing as how we're finally getting down to brass tacks, "about the beard. Tell him beards went out with Jim Morrison—and the bathrobe business is kinda kinky, and we can play to that if he wants, but wouldn't he feel more comfortable in a nice Italian knit?"

The big guy says nothing, but I can see this kinda glimmer in his eyes and I know he's digging it, I mean I can feel it, and I figure we'll worry about the grooming later and I cut right to the heart of it and lay my big idea on him, the idea that's going to launch the whole campaign.

This is genius, Bob, you're going to love it.

I ask myself, How do we soften this guy a little, you know, break down the barriers between him and the public, turn all that negative shit around? And what audience are we targeting here? Think about it. He can have all the camel drivers and Kalashnikov toters in the world, but let's face it, the bottom line is how does he go down over here and that's like nowheresville. So my idea is this: baseball. Yeah, baseball. Where would Castro be without it? What can the American public relate to—and I'm talking the widest sector now, from the guys in the boardroom to the shlump with the jackhammer out the window there—better than baseball? Can you dig it: the Ayatollah's a closet baseball fan, but his people need him so much—love him, a country embattled, he's like a Winston Churchill to them—they won't let him come to New York for a Yankee game. Can you picture it?

No? Well, dig the photo. Yeah. From yesterday's *New York Times.* See the button here, on his bathrobe? Well, maybe it is a little fuzzy, AP is the pits, but that's a "Go Yankees!" button I gave him myself.

No, listen, he liked it, Bob, he liked it. I could tell. I mean I lay the concept on him and he goes off into this fucking soliloquy, croaking up a storm, and then Parviz tells me it's okay but it's all over for today, he's gotta have his hat surgically removed or something, and the guys with the Uzis are closing in again . . . but I'm seeing green, Bob, I'm seeing him maybe throwing out the first ball this spring, Yankees versus the Reds or Pirates—okay, okay, wrong league—the Birds, then—I'm telling you, the sun on his face, Brooks Brothers draping his shoulders, the cameras whirring, and the arc of that ball just going on and on, out over the grass, across the airwaves and into the lap of every regular Joe in America.

Believe me, Bob, it's in the bag.

(1987)

THE MIRACLE AT BALLINSPITTLE

There they are, the holybugs, widows in their weeds and fat-ankled mothers with palsied children, all lined up before the snotgreen likeness of the Virgin, and McGahee and McCarey among them. This statue, alone among all the myriad three-foot-high snotgreen likenesses of the Virgin cast in plaster by Finnbar Finnegan & Sons, Cork City, was seen one grim March afternoon some years back to move its limbs ever so slightly, as if seized suddenly by the need of a good sinew-cracking stretch. Nuala Nolan, a young girl in the throes of Lenten abnegation, was the only one to witness the movement—a gentle beckoning of the statue's outthrust hand—after a fifteen-day vigil during which she took nothing into her body but Marmite and soda water. Ever since, the place has been packed with tourists.

Even now, in the crowd of humble countrymen in shit-smeared boots and knit skullcaps, McGahee can detect a certain number of Teutonic or Manhattanite faces above cableknit sweaters and pendant cameras. Drunk and in debt, on the run from a bad marriage, two DWI convictions, and the wheezy expiring gasps of his moribund mother, McGahee pays them no heed. His powers of concentration run deep. He is forty years old, as lithe as a boxer though he's done no hard physical labor since he took a construction job between semesters at college twenty years back, and he has the watery eyes and doleful, doglike expression of the saint. Twelve hours ago he was in New York, at Paddy Flynn's, pouring out his heart and enumerating his woes for McCarey, when McCarey said, "Fuck it, let's go to Ireland." And now here he is at Ballinspittle, wearing the rumpled Levi's and Taiwanese sportcoat he'd pulled on in his apartment yesterday morning, three hours off the plane from Kennedy and flush with warmth from the venerable Irish distillates washing through his veins.

McCarey—plump, stately McCarey—stands beside him, bleary-eyed and impatient, disdainfully scanning the crowd. Heads are bowed. Infants snuffle. From somewhere in the distance come the bleat of a lamb and the mechanical call of the cuckoo. McGahee checks his watch: they've been here seven minutes already and nothing's happened. His mind begins to wander. He's thinking about orthodontia—thinking an orthodontist could make a fortune in this country—when he looks up and spots her, Nuala Nolan, a scarecrow of a girl, an anorectic, bones-in-a-sack sort of girl, kneeling in front of the queue and reciting the Mysteries in a voice parched for food and drink. Since the statue moved she has stuck to her diet of Marmite and soda water until the very synapses of her brain have become encrusted with salt and she raves like a mariner lost at sea. McGahee regards her with awe. A light rain has begun to fall.

And then suddenly, before he knows what's come over him, McGahee goes limp. He feels lightheaded, transported, feels himself sinking into another realm, as helpless and cut adrift as when Dr. Beibelman put him under for his gallbladder operation. He breaks out in a sweat. His vision goes dim. The murmur of the crowd, the call of the cuckoo, and the bleat of the lamb all meld into a single sound—a voice—and that voice, ubiquitous, timeless, all-embracing, permeates his every cell and fiber. It seems to speak through him, through the broad-beamed old hag beside him, through McCarey, Nuala Nolan, the stones and birds and fishes of the sea. "Davey," the voice calls in the sweetest tones he has ever heard. "Davey McGahee, come to me, come to my embrace."

As one, the crowd parts, a hundred stupefied faces turned toward him, and there she is, the Virgin, snotgreen no longer but radiant with the aquamarine of actuality, her eyes glowing, arms beckoning. McGahee casts a quick glance around him. McCarey looks as if he's been punched in the gut, Nuala Nolan's skeletal face is clenched with hate and jealousy, the humble countrymen and farmwives stare numbly from him to the statue and back again . . . and then, as if in response to a subconscious signal, they drop to their knees in a human wave so that only he, Davey McGahee, remains standing. "Come to me," the figure implores, and slowly, as if his feet were encased in cement, his head reeling and his stomach sour, he begins to move forward, his own arms outstretched in ecstasy.

The words of his catechism, forgotten these thirty years, echo in his head: "Mother Mary, Mother of God, pray for us sinners now and at the hour of our—"

"Yesssss!" the statue suddenly shrieks, the upturned palm curled into a fist, a fist like a weapon. "And you think it's as easy as that, do you?"

McGahee stops cold, hovering over the tiny effigy like a giant, a troglodyte, a naked barbarian. Three feet high, grotesque, shaking its fists up at him, the thing changes before his eyes. Gone is the beatific smile, gone the grace of the eyes and the faintly mad and indulgent look of the transported saint. The face is a gargoyle's, a shrew's, and the voice, sharpening, probing like a dental tool, suddenly bears an uncanny resemblance to his ex-wife's. "Sinner!" the gargoyle hisses. "Fall on your knees!"

The crowd gasps. McGahee, his bowels turned to ice, pitches forward into the turf. "No, no, no!" he cries, clutching at the grass and squeezing his eyes shut. "Hush," a new voice whispers in his ear, "look. You must look." There's a hand on his neck, bony and cold. He winks open an eye. The statue is gone and Nuala Nolan leans over him, her hair gone in patches, the death's-head of her face and suffering eyes, her breath like the loam of the grave. "Look, up there," she whispers.

High above them, receding into the heavens like a kite loosed from a string, is the statue. Its voice comes to him faint and distant—"Behold . . . now . . . your sins . . . and excesses . . ."—and then it dwindles away like a fading echo.

Suddenly, behind the naked pedestal, a bright sunlit vista appears, grapevines marshaled in rows, fields of barley, corn, and hops, and then, falling from the sky with thunderous crashes, a succession of vats, kegs, hogsheads, and buckets mounting up in the foreground as if on some phantom pier piled high with freight. *Boom, boom, ka-boom, boom,* down they come till the vista is obscured and the kegs mount to the tops of the trees. McGahee pushes himself up to his knees and looks around him. The crowd is regarding him steadily, jaws set, the inclemency of the hanging judge sunk into their eyes. McCarey, kneeling too now and looking as if he's just lurched up out of a drunken snooze to find himself on a subway car on another planet, has gone steely-eyed with the rest of them. And Nuala Nolan, poised over him, grins till the long naked roots of her teeth gleam beneath the skirts of her rotten gums.

"Your drinking!" shrieks a voice from the back of the throng, his wife's voice, and there she is, Fredda, barefoot and in a snotgreen robe and hood, wafting her way through the crowd and pointing her long accusatory finger at his poor miserable shrinking self. "Every drop," she booms, and the vast array of vats and kegs and tumblers swivels to reveal the signs hung from their sweating slats— GIN, BOURBON, BEER, WHISKEY, SCHNAPPS, PERNOD—and the crowd lets out a long exhalation of shock and lament.

The keg of gin. Tall it is and huge, its contents vaguely sloshing. You could throw cars into it, buses, tractor trailers. But no, never, he couldn't have drunk that much gin, no man could. And beside it the beer, frothy and bubbling, a cauldron the size of a rest home. "No!" he cries in protest. "I don't even like the taste of the stuff."

"Yes, yes, yes," chants a voice beside him. The statue is back, Fredda gone. It speaks in a voice he recognizes, though the wheezy, rheumy deathbed rasp of it has been wiped clean. "Ma?" he says, turning to the thing.

Three feet tall, slick as a seal, the robes flowing like the sea, the effigy looks up at him out of his mother's face in miniature. "I warned you," the voice leaps out at him, high and querulous, "out behind the 7-Eleven with Ricky Reitbauer and that criminal Tommy Capistrano, cheap wine and all the rest."

"But Mom, *Pernod?*" He peers into the little pot of it, a pot so small you couldn't boil a good Safeway chicken in it. There it is. Pernod. Milky and unclean. It turns his stomach even to look at it.

"Your liver, son," the statue murmurs with a resignation that brings tears to his eyes, "just look at it."

He feels a prick in his side and there it is, his liver—a poor piece of cheesy meat, stippled and striped and purple—dangling from the plaster fingers. "God," he moans. "God Almighty."

"Rotten as your soul," the statue says.

McGahee, still on his knees, begins to blubber. Meaningless slips of apology issue from his lips—"I didn't mean . . . it wasn't . . . how could I know?"—when all of a sudden the statue shouts "Drugs!" with a voice of iron.

Immediately the scene changes. The vats are gone, replaced with bales of marijuana, jars of pills in every color imaginable, big, overbrimming tureens of white powder, a drugstore display of airplane glue. In the background, grinning Laotians, Peruvian peasants with hundreds of scrawny children propped like puppets on their shoulders.

"But, but—" McGahee stutters, rising to his feet to protest, but the statue doesn't give him a chance, won't, can't, and the stentorian voice—his wife's, his mother's, no one's and everyone's, he even detects a trace of his high-school principal's in there—the stentorian voice booms: "Sins of the Flesh!"

He blinks his eyes and the Turks and their bales are gone. The backdrop now is foggy and obscure, dim as the mists of memory. The statue is silent. Gradually the poor sinner becomes aware of a salacious murmur, an undercurrent of moaning and panting, and the lubricious thwack and whap of the act itself. "Davey," a girl's voice calls, tender, pubescent, "I'm scared." And then his own voice, bland and reassuring: "I won't stick it in, Cindy, I won't, I swear . . . or maybe, maybe just . . . just an inch . . ."

The mist lifts and there they are, in teddies and negligees, in garter belts and sweat socks, naked and wet and kneading their breasts like dough. "Davey," they moan, "oh, Davey, fuck me, fuck me, fuck me," and he knows them all, from Cindy Lou Harris and Betsy Butler in the twelfth grade to Fredda in her youth and the sad and ugly faces of his one-night stands and chance encounters, right on up to the bug-eyed woman with the doleful breasts he'd diddled in the rest room on the way out from Kennedy. And worse. Behind them, milling around in a mob that stretches to the horizon, are all the women and girls he'd ever lusted after, even for a second, the twitching behinds and airy bosoms he'd stopped to admire on the street, the legs he'd wanted to stroke and lips to press to his own. McCarey's wife, Beatrice, is there and Fred Dolby's thirteen-year-old daughter, the woman with the freckled bosom who used to sunbathe in the tiger-skin bikini next door when they lived in Irvington, the girl from the typing pool, and the outrageous little shaven-headed vixen from Domino's Pizza. And as if that weren't enough, there's the crowd from books and films too. Linda Lovelace,

Sophia Loren, Emma Bovary, the Sabine women and Lot's wife, even Virginia Woolf with her puckered foxy face and the eyes that seem to beg for a good slap on the bottom. It's too much—all of them murmuring his name like a crazed chorus of Molly Blooms, and yes, she's there too—and the mob behind him hissing, hissing.

He glances at the statue. The plaster lip curls in disgust, the adamantine hand rises and falls, and the women vanish. "Gluttony!" howls the Virgin and all at once he's surrounded by forlornly mooing herds of cattle, sad-eyed pigs and sheep, funereal geese and clucking ducks, a spill of scuttling crabs and claw-waving lobsters, even the odd dog or two he'd inadvertently wolfed down in Tijuana burritos and Cantonese stir-fry. And the scales—scales the size of the Washington Monument—sunk under pyramids of ketchup, peanut butter, tortilla chips, truckloads of potatoes, onions, avocados, peppermint candies and after-dinner mints, half-eaten burgers and fork-scattered peas, the whole slithering wasteful cornucopia of his secret and public devouring. "Moooooo," accuse the cows. "Stinker!" "Pig!" "Glutton!" cry voices from the crowd.

Prostrate now, the cattle hanging over him, letting loose with their streams of urine and clots of dung, McGahee shoves his fists into his eyes and cries out for mercy. But there is no mercy. The statue, wicked and glittering, its tiny twisted features clenching and unclenching like the balls of its fists, announces one after another the unremitting parade of his sins: "Insults to Humanity, False Idols, Sloth, Unclean Thoughts, The Kicking of Dogs and Cheating at Cards!"

His head reels. He won't look. The voices cry out in hurt and laceration and he feels the very ground give way beneath him. The rest, mercifully, is a blank.

When he comes to, muttering in protest—"False idols, I mean like an autographed picture of Mickey Mantle, for christsake?"—he finds himself in a cramped mud-and-wattle hut that reeks of goat dung and incense. By the flickering glow of a bank of votary candles, he can make out the bowed and patchy head of Nuala Nolan. Outside it is dark and the rain drives down with a hiss. For a long moment, McGahee lies there, studying the fleshless form of the girl, her bones sharp and sepulchral in the quavering light. He feels used up, burned out, feels as if he's been cored like an apple. His head screams. His throat is dry. His bladder is bursting.

He pushes himself up and the bony demi-saint levels her tranced gaze on him, "Hush," she says, and the memory of all that's happened washes over him like a typhoon.

"How long have I—?"

"Two days." Her voice is a reverent whisper, the murmur of the acolyte, the apostle. "They say the Pope himself is on the way."

"The Pope?" McGahee feels a long shiver run through him.

Nods the balding death's-head. The voice is dry as husks, wheezy, but a girl's voice all the same, and an enthusiast's. "They say it's the greatest vision vouch-safed to man since the time of Christ. Two hundred and fifteen people witnessed it, every glorious moment, from the cask of gin to the furtive masturbation to the ace up the sleeve." She's leaning over him now, inching forward on all fours, her breath like chopped meat gone bad in the refrigerator; he can see, through the tattered shirt, where her breasts used to be. "Look," she whispers, gesturing toward the hunched low entranceway.

He looks and the sudden light dazzles him. Blinking in wonder, he creeps to the crude doorway and peers out. Immediately a murmur goes up from the crowd—hundreds upon hundreds of them gathered in the rain on their knees—and an explosion of flash cameras blinds him. Beyond the crowd he can make out a police cordon, vans and video cameras, CBS, BBC, KDOG, and NPR, a face above a trenchcoat that could once belong to Dan Rather himself. "Holy of holies!" cries a voice from the front of the mob—he knows that voice—and the crowd takes it up in a chant that breaks off into the Lord's Prayer. Stupefied, he wriggles out of the hut and stands, bathed in light. It's McCarey there before him, reaching out with a hundred others to embrace his ankles, kiss his feet, tear with trembling devoted fingers at his Levi's and Taiwanese tweed—Michael McCarey, adulterer, gambler, drunk and atheist, cheater of the IRS and bane of the Major Deegan—hunkered down in the rain like a holy supplicant. And there, not thirty feet away, is the statue, lit like Betelgeuse and as inanimate and snot-green as a stone of the sea.

Rain pelts McGahee's bare head and the chill seizes him like a claw jerking hard and sudden at the ruined ancient priest-ridden superstitious root of him. The flashbulbs pop in his face, a murmur of Latin assaults his ears, Sister Mary Magdalen's unyielding face rises before him out of the dim mists of eighth-grade math . . . and then the sudden imperious call of nature blinds him to all wonder and he's staggering round back of the hut to relieve himself of his two days' accumulation of salts and uric acid and dregs of whiskey. Stumbling, fumbling for his zipper, the twin pains in his groin like arrows driven through him, he jerks out his poor pud and lets fly.

"Piss!" roars a voice behind him, and he swivels his head in fright, helpless before the stream that issues from him like a torrent. The crowd falls prostrate in the mud, cameras whir, voices cry out. It is the statue, of course, livid, jerking its limbs and racking its body like the image of the Führer in his maddest denunciation. "Piss on sacred ground, will you," rage the plaster lips in the voice of his own father, that mild and pacifistic man, "you unholy insect, you whited sepulcher, you speck of dust in the eye of your Lord and maker!"

What can he do? He clutches himself, flooding the ground, dissolving the hut, befouling the bony scrag of the anchorite herself.

"Unregenerate!" shrieks the Virgin. "Unrepentant! Sinner to the core!"

And then it comes.

The skies part, the rain turns to popcorn, marshmallows, English muffins, the light of seven suns scorches down on that humble crowd gathered on the sward, and all the visions of that first terrible day crash over them in hellish simulcast. The great vats of beer and gin and whiskey fall to pieces and the sea of booze floats them, the cattle bellowing and kicking, sheep bleating and dogs barking, despoiled girls and hardened women clutching for the shoulders of the panicked communicants as for sticks of wood awash in the sea, Sophia Loren herself and Virginia Woolf, Fredda, Cindy Lou Harris and McCarey's wife swept by in a blur, the TV vans overturned, the trenchcoat torn from Dan Rather's back, and the gardai sent sprawling—"Thank God he didn't eat rattlesnake," someone cries—and then it's over. Night returns. Rain falls. The booze sinks softly into the earth, food lies rotting in clumps. A drumbeat of hoofs thunders off into the dark while fish wriggle and escargots creep, and Fredda, McCarey, the shaven-headed pizza vixen, and all the gap-toothed countrymen and farm wives and palsied children pick themselves up from the ground amid the curses of the men cheated at cards, the lament of the fallen women, and the mad frenzied chorus of prayer that speaks over it all in the tongue of terror and astonishment.

But oh, sad wonder, McGahee is gone.

Today the site remains as it was that night, fenced off from the merely curious, combed over inch by inch by priests and parapsychologists, blessed by the Pope, a shrine as reverenced as Lourdes and the Holy See itself. The cattle were sold off at auction after intensive study proved them ordinary enough, though brands were traced to Montana, Texas, and the Swiss Alps, and the food—burgers and snowcones, rib roasts, Fig Newtons, extra dill pickles, and all the rest—was left where it fell, to feed the birds and fertilize the soil. The odd rib or T-bone, picked clean and bleached by the elements, still lies there on the ground in mute testimony to those three days of tumult. Fredda McGahee Meyerowitz, Herb Bucknell and others cheated at cards, the girl from the pizza parlor and the rest were sent home via Aer Lingus, compliments of the Irish government. What became of Virginia Woolf, dead forty years prior to these events, is not known, nor the fate of Emma Bovary either, though one need only refer to Flaubert for the best clue to this mystery. And of course, there are the tourism figures—up a whopping 672 percent since the miracle.

McCarey has joined an order of Franciscan monks, and Nuala Nolan, piqued no doubt by her supporting role in the unfolding of the miracle, has taken a job in a pastry shop, where she eats by day and prays for forgiveness by night. As for Davey McGahee himself, the prime mover and motivator of all these enduring mysteries, here the lenses of history and of myth and miracology grow obscure. Some say he descended into a black hole of the earth, others that he evaporated, while still others insist that he ascended to heaven in a blaze of light, Saint of the Common Sinner.

For who hasn't lusted after woman or man or drunk his booze and laid to rest whole herds to feed his greedy gullet? Who hasn't watched them starve by the roadside in the hollows and waste places of the world and who among us hasn't scoffed at the credulous and ignored the miracle we see outside the window every day of our lives? Ask not for whom the bell tolls—unless perhaps you take the flight to Cork City, and the bus or rented Nissan out to Ballinspittle by the Sea, and gaze on the halfsize snotgreen statue of the Virgin, mute and unmoving all these many years.

(1987)

TOP OF THE FOOD CHAIN

The thing was, we had a little problem with the insect vector there, and believe me, your tamer stuff, your Malathion and pyrethrum and the rest of the so-called environmentally safe products didn't begin to make a dent in it, not a dent, I mean it was utterly useless—we might as well have been spraying with Chanel No. 5 for all the good it did. And you've got to realize these people were literally covered with insects day and night—and the fact that they hardly wore any clothes just compounded the problem. Picture if you can, gentlemen, a naked little two-year-old boy so black with flies and mosquitoes it looks like he's wearing long johns, or the young mother so racked with the malarial shakes she can't even lift a diet Coke to her lips—it was pathetic, just pathetic, like something out of the Dark Ages. . . . Well, anyway, the decision was made to go with DDT. In the short term. Just to get the situation under control, you understand.

Yes, that's right, Senator, *DDT:* Dichlorodiphenyltrichloroethane.

Yes, I'm well aware of that fact, sir. But just because *we* banned it domestically, under pressure from the birdwatching contingent and the hopheads down at the EPA, it doesn't necessarily follow that the rest of the world—especially the developing world—is about to jump on the bandwagon. And that's the key word here, Senator: *developing.* You've got to realize this is Borneo we're talking about here, not Port Townsend or Enumclaw. These people don't know from square one about sanitation, disease control, pest eradication—or even personal hygiene, if you want to come right down to it. It rains a hundred and twenty inches a year, minimum. They dig up roots in the jungle. They've still got headhunters along the Rajang River, for god's sake.

And please don't forget they *asked* us to come in there, practically begged us—and not only the World Health Organization, but the Sultan of Brunei and the government in Sarawak too. We did what we could to accommodate them and reach our objective in the shortest period of time and by the most direct and effective means. We went to the air. Obviously. And no one could have foreseen the consequences, no one, not even if we'd gone out and generated a hundred environmental-impact statements—it was just one of those things, a freak occurrence, and there's no defense against that. No that I know of, anyway. . . .

Caterpillars? Yes, Senator, that's correct. That was the first sign: caterpillars.

But let me backtrack a minute here. You see, out in the bush they have these roofs made of thatched palm leaves—you'll see them in the towns too, even in Bintulu or Brunei—and they're really pretty effective, you'd be surprised. A hundred and twenty inches of rain, they've got to figure a way to keep it out of the hut, and for centuries, this was it. Palm leaves. Well, it was about a month after we sprayed for the final time and I'm sitting at my desk in the trailer thinking about the drainage project at Kuching, enjoying the fact that for the first time in maybe a year I'm not smearing mosquitoes all over the back of my neck, when there's a knock at the door. It's this elderly gentleman, tattooed from head to toe, dressed only in a pair of running shorts—they love those shorts, by the way, the shiny material and the tight machine-stitching, the whole country, men and women and children, they can't get enough of them. . . . Anyway, he's the headman of the local village and he's very excited, something about the roofs—*atap,* they call them. That's all he can say, *atap, atap,* over and over again.

It's raining, of course. It's always raining. So I shrug into my rain slicker, start up the 4×4 and go have a look. Sure enough, all the *atap* roofs are collapsing, not only in his village, but throughout the target area. The people are all huddled there in their running shorts, looking pretty miserable, and one after another the roofs keep falling in, it's bewildering, and gradually I realize the headman's diatribe has begun to feature a new term I was unfamiliar with at the time—the word for caterpillar, as it turns out, in the Iban dialect. But who was to make the connection between three passes with the crop duster and all these staved-in roofs?

Our people finally sorted it out a couple weeks later. The chemical, which, by the way, cut down the number of mosquitoes exponentially, had the unfortunate side effect of killing off this little wasp—I've got the scientific name for it somewhere in my report here, if you're interested—that preyed on a type of caterpillar that in turn ate palm leaves. Well, with the wasps gone, the caterpillars hatched out with nothing to keep them in check and chewed the roofs to pieces, and that was unfortunate, we admit it, and we had a real cost overrun on replacing those roofs with tin . . . but the people were happier, I think, in the long run, because let's face it, no matter how tightly you weave those palm leaves, they're just not going to keep the water out like tin. Of course, nothing's perfect, and we had a lot of complaints about the rain drumming on the panels, people unable to sleep and what-have-you. . . .

Yes, sir, that's correct—the flies were next.

Well, you've got to understand the magnitude of the fly problem in Borneo, there's nothing like it here to compare it with, except maybe a garbage strike in New York. Every minute of every day you've got flies everywhere, up your nose, in your mouth, your ears, your eyes, flies in your rice, your Coke, your Singapore sling and your gin rickey. It's enough to drive you to distraction, not to mention the diseases these things carry, from dysentery to typhoid to cholera and back round the loop again. And once the mosquito population was down, the flies seemed to breed up to fill in the gap—Borneo wouldn't be Borneo without some damned insect blackening the air.

Of course, this was before our people had tracked down the problem with the caterpillars and the wasps and all of that, and so we figured we'd had a big success with the mosquitoes, why not a series of ground sweeps, mount a fogger in the back of a Suzuki Brat and sanitize the huts, not to mention the open sewers, which as you know are nothing but a breeding ground for flies, chiggers and biting insects of every sort. At least it was an error of commission rather than omission. At least we were trying.

I watched the flies go down myself. One day they were so thick in the trailer I couldn't even *find* my paperwork, let alone attempt to get through it, and the next they were collecting on the windows, bumbling around like they were drunk. A day later they were gone. Just like that. From a million flies in the trailer to none. . . .

Well, no one could have foreseen that, Senator.

The geckos ate the flies, yes. You're all familiar with geckos, I assume, gentlemen? These are the lizards you've seen during your trips to Hawaii, very colorful, patrolling the houses for roaches and flies, almost like pets, but of course they're wild animals, never lose sight of that, and just about as unsanitary as anything I can think of, except maybe flies.

Yes, well don't forget, sir, we're viewing this with twenty-twenty hindsight, but at the time no one gave a thought to geckos or what they ate—they were just another fact of life in the tropics. Mosquitoes, lizards, scorpions, leeches—you name it, they've got it. When the flies began piling up on the windowsills like drift, naturally the geckos feasted on them, stuffing themselves till they looked like sausages crawling up the walls. Where before they moved so fast you could never be sure you'd seen them, now they waddled across the floor, laid around in the corners, clung to the air vents like magnets—and even then no one paid much attention to them till they started turning belly-up in the streets. Believe me, we confirmed a lot of things there about the buildup of these products as you move up the food chain and the efficacy—or lack thereof—of certain methods, no doubt about that. . . .

The cats? That's where it got sticky, really sticky. You see, nobody really lost any sleep over a pile of dead lizards—though we did the tests routinely and the tests confirmed what we'd expected, that is, the product had been concentrated in the geckos because of the sheer number of contaminated flies they'd consumed. But lizards are one thing and cats are another. These people really have an affection for their cats—no house, no hut, no matter how primitive, is without at least a couple of them. Mangy-looking things, long-legged and scrawny, maybe, not at all the sort of animal you'd see here, but there it was: they loved their cats. Because the cats were functional, you understand—without them, the place would have been swimming in rodents inside of a week.

You're right there, Senator, yes—that's exactly what happened.

You see, the cats had a field day with these feeble geckos—you can imagine, if any of you have ever owned a cat, the kind of joy these animals must have experienced to see their nemesis, this ultra-quick lizard, and it's just barely creeping across the floor like a bug. Well, to make a long story short, the cats ate up every dead and dying gecko in the country, from snout to tail, and then the cats began to die . . . which to my mind would have been no great loss if it wasn't for the rats. Suddenly there were rats everywhere—you couldn't drive down the street without running over half-a-dozen of them at a time. They fouled the grain supplies, fell in the wells and died, bit infants as they slept in their cradles. But that wasn't the worst, not by a long shot. No, things really went down the tube after that. Within the month we were getting scattered reports of bubonic plague, and of course we tracked them all down and made sure the people got a round of treatment with antibiotics, but still we lost a few and the rats kept coming. . . .

It was my plan, yes. I was brainstorming one night, rats scuttling all over the trailer like something out of a cheap horror film, the villagers in a panic over the threat of the plague and the stream of nonstop hysterical reports from the interior—people were turning black, swelling up and bursting, that sort of thing—well, as I say, I came up with a plan, a stopgap, not perfect, not cheap; but at this juncture, I'm sure you'll agree, something had to be implemented.

We wound up going as far as Australia for some of the cats, cleaning out the SPCA facilities and what-have-you, though we rounded most of them up in Indonesia and Singapore—approximately fourteen thousand in all. And yes, it cost us—cost us upfront purchase money and aircraft fuel and pilots' overtime and all the rest of it—but we really felt there was no alternative. It was like all nature had turned against us.

And yet still, all things considered, we made a lot of friends for the U.S.A. the day we dropped those cats, and you should have seen them, gentlemen, the little parachutes and harnesses we'd tricked up, fourteen thousand of them, cats in every color of the rainbow, cats with one ear, no ears, half a tail, three-legged cats, cats that could have taken pride of show in Springfield, Massachusetts, and all of them twirling down out of the sky like great big oversized snowflakes. . . .

It was something. It was really something.

Of course, you've all seen the reports. There were other factors we hadn't counted on, adverse conditions in the paddies and manioc fields—we don't to this day know what predatory species were inadvertently killed off by the initial sprayings, it's just a mystery—but the weevils and whatnot took a pretty heavy toll on the crops that year, and by the time we dropped the cats, well, the people were pretty hungry, and I suppose it was inevitable that we lost a good proportion of them right then and there. But we've got a CARE program going there now, and something hit the rat population—we still don't know what, a virus, we think—and the geckos, they tell me, are making a comeback.

So what I'm saying is, it could be worse, and to every cloud a silver lining, wouldn't you agree, gentlemen?

(1992)

THE HECTOR QUESADILLA STORY

He was no Joltin' Joe, no Sultan of Swat, no Iron Man. For one thing, his feet hurt. And God knows no legendary immortal ever suffered so prosaic a complaint. He had shin splints too, and corns and ingrown toenails and hemorrhoids. Demons drove burning spikes into his tailbone each time he bent to loosen his shoelaces, his limbs were skewed so awkwardly that his elbows and knees might have been transposed and the once-proud knot of his *frijole*-fed belly had fallen like an avalanche. Worse: he was old. Old, old, old, the graybeard hobbling down the rough-hewn steps of the senate building. The Ancient Mariner chewing on his whiskers and stumbling in his socks. Though they listed his birthdate as 1942 in the program, there were those who knew better: it was way back in '54, during his rookie year for San Buitre, that he had taken Asunción to the altar, and even in those distant days, even in Mexico, twelve-year-olds didn't marry.

When he was younger—really young, nineteen, twenty, tearing up the Mexican League like a saint of the stick—his ears were so sensitive he could hear the soft rasping friction of the pitcher's fingers as he massaged the ball and dug in for a slider, fastball, or change-up. Now he could barely hear the umpire bawling the count in his ear. And his legs. How they ached, how they groaned and creaked and chattered, how they'd gone to fat! He ate too much, that was the problem. Ate prodigiously, ate mightily, ate as if there were a hidden thing inside him, a creature all of jaws with an infinite trailing ribbon of gut. *Huevos con chorizo* with beans, *tortillas, camarones* in red sauce, and a twelve-ounce steak for breakfast, the chicken in *mole* to steady him before afternoon games, a sea of beer to wash away the tension of the game and prepare his digestive machinery for the flaming *machaca*-and-pepper salad Asunción prepared for him in the blessed evenings of the home stand.

Five foot seven, one hundred eighty-nine and three-quarters pounds. Hector Hernán Jesús y María Quesadilla. Little Cheese, they called him. Cheese, Cheese, Cheesus, went up the cry as he stepped in to pinch-hit in some late-inning crisis, Cheese, Cheese, Cheesus, building to a roar until Chavez Ravine resounded as if with the holy name of the Savior Himself when he stroked one of the clean line-drive singles that were his signature or laid down a bunt that stuck like a finger in jelly. When he fanned, when the bat went loose in the fat brown hands and he went down on one knee for support, they hissed and called him *Viejo*.

One more season, he tells himself, though he hasn't played regularly for nearly ten years and can barely trot to first after drawing a walk. One more. He tells Asunción too—*One more, one more*—as they sit in the gleaming kitchen of their house in Boyle Heights, he with his Carta Blanca, she with her mortar and pestle for grinding the golden, petrified kernels of maize into flour for the tortillas he eats like peanuts. *Una más*, she mocks. What do you want, the Hall of Fame? Hang up your spikes, Hector.

He stares off into space, his mother's Indian features flattening his own as if the legend were true, as if she really had taken a spatula to him in the cradle, and then, dropping his thick lids as he takes a long slow swallow from the neck of the bottle, he says: Just the other day, driving home from the park, I saw a car on the freeway, a Mercedes with only two seats, a girl in it, her hair out back like a cloud, and you know what the license plate said? His eyes are open now, black as pitted olives. Do you? She doesn't. Cheese, he says. It said Cheese.

Then she reminds him that Hector Jr. will be twenty-nine next month and that Reina has four children of her own and another on the way. You're a grandfather, Hector—almost a great-grandfather, if your son ever settled down. A moment slides by, filled with the light of the sad, waning sun and the harsh Yucatecan dialect of the radio announcer. *Hombres* on first and third, one down. *Abuelo*, she hisses, grinding stone against stone until it makes his teeth ache. Hang up your spikes, *abuelo*.

But he doesn't. He can't. He won't. He's no grandpa with hair the color of cigarette stains and a blanket over his knees, he's no toothless old gasser sunning himself in the park—he's a big-leaguer, proud wearer of the Dodger blue, wielder of stick and glove. How can he get old? The grass is always green, the lights always shining, no clocks or periods or halves or quarters, no punch-in and punch-out: this is the game that never ends. When the heavy hitters have fanned and the pitcher's arms gone sore, when there's no joy in Mudville, taxes are killing everybody, and the Russians are raising hell in Guatemala, when the manager paces the dugout like an attack dog, mind racing, searching high and low for the canny veteran to go in and do single combat, there he'll be—always,

always, eternal as a monument—Hector Quesadilla, utility infielder, with the .296 lifetime batting average and service with the Reds, Phils, Cubs, Royals, and L.A. Dodgers.

So he waits. Hangs on. Trots his aching legs round the outfield grass before the game, touches his toes ten agonizing times each morning, takes extra batting practice with the rookies and slumping millionaires. Sits. Watches. Massages his feet. Waits through the scourging road trips in the Midwest and along the East Coast, down to muggy Atlanta, across to stormy Wrigley, and up to frigid Candlestick, his gut clenched round an indigestible cud of meatloaf and instant potatoes and wax beans, through the terrible night games with the alien lights in his eyes, waits at the end of the bench for a word from the manager, for a pat on the ass, a roar, a hiss, a chorus of cheers and catcalls, the marimba pulse of bat striking ball, and the sweet looping arc of the clean base hit.

And then comes a day, late in the season, the homeboys battling for the pennant with the big-stick Braves and the sneaking Jints, when he wakes from honeyed dreams in his own bed that's like an old friend with the sheets that smell of starch and soap and flowers, and feels the pain stripped from his body as if at the touch of a healer's fingertips. Usually he dreams nothing, the night a blank, an erasure, and opens his eyes on the agonies of the martyr strapped to a bed of nails. Then he limps to the toilet, makes a poor discolored water, rinses the dead taste from his mouth, and staggers to the kitchen table, where food, only food, can revive in him the interest in drawing another breath. He butters tortillas and folds them into his mouth, spoons up egg and melted jack cheese and *frijoles refritos* with the green *salsa*, lashes into his steak as if it were cut from the thigh of Kerensky, the Atlanta relief ace who'd twice that season caught him looking at a full-count fastball with men in scoring position. But not today. Today is different, a sainted day, a day on which sunshine sits in the windows like a gift of the Magi and the chatter of the starlings in the crapped-over palms across the street is a thing that approaches the divine music of the spheres. What can it be?

In the kitchen it hits him: *pozole* in a pot on the stove, *carnitas* in the saucepan, the table spread with sweetcakes, *buñuelos,* and the little marzipan *dulces* he could kill for. *Feliz cumpleaños,* Asunción pipes as he steps through the doorway. Her face is lit with the smile of her mother, her mother's mother, the line of gift givers descendant to the happy conquistadors and joyous Aztecs. A kiss, a *dulce,* and then a knock at the door and Reina, fat with life, throwing her arms around him while her children gobble up the table, the room, their grandfather, with eyes that swallow their faces. Happy birthday, Daddy, Reina says, and Franklin, her youngest, is handing him the gift.

And Hector Jr.?

But he doesn't have to fret about Hector Jr., his firstborn, the boy with these same great sad eyes who'd sat in the dugout in his Reds uniform when they lived in Cincy and worshiped the pudgy icon of his father until the parish priest had to straighten him out on his hagiography; Hector Jr., who studies English at

USC and day and night writes his thesis on a poet his father has never heard of, because here he is, walking in the front door with his mother's smile and a store-wrapped gift—a book, of course. Then Reina's children line up to kiss the *abuelo*—they'll be sitting in the box seats this afternoon—and suddenly he knows so much: he will play today, he will hit, oh yes, can there be a doubt? He sees it already. Kerensky, the son of a whore. Extra innings. Koerner or Manfredonia or Brooksie on third. The ball like an orange, a mango, a muskmelon, the clean swipe of the bat, the delirium of the crowd, and the gimpy *abuelo,* a bigleaguer still, doffing his cap and taking a tour of the bases in a stately trot, Sultan for a day.

Could things ever be so simple?

In the bottom of the ninth, with the score tied at five and Reina's kids full of Coke, hot dogs, peanuts, and ice cream and getting restless, with Asunción clutching her rosary as if she were drowning and Hector Jr.'s nose stuck in some book, Dupuy taps him to hit for the pitcher with two down and Fast Freddie Phelan on second. The eighth man in the lineup, Spider Martinez from Muchas Vacas, D.R., has just whiffed on three straight pitches, and Corcoran, the Braves' left-handed relief man, is all of a sudden pouring it on. Throughout the stadium a hush has fallen over the crowd, the torpor of suppertime, the game poised at apogee. Shadows are lengthening in the outfield, swallows flitting across the face of the scoreboard, here a fan drops into his beer, there a big mama gathers up her purse, her knitting, her shopping bags and parasol, and thinks of dinner. Hector sees it all. This is the moment of catharsis, the moment to take it out.

As Martinez slumps toward the dugout, Dupuy, a laconic, embittered man who keeps his suffering inside and drinks Gelusil like water, takes hold of Hector's arm. His eyes are red-rimmed and paunchy, doleful as a basset hound's. Bring the runner in, champ, he rasps. First pitch fake a bunt, then hit away. Watch Booger at third. Uh-huh, Hector mumbles, snapping his gum. Then he slides his bat from the rack—white ash, tape-wrapped grip, personally blessed by the archbishop of Guadalajara and his twenty-seven acolytes—and starts for the dugout steps, knowing the course of the next three minutes as surely as his blood knows the course of his veins. The familiar cry will go up—Cheese, Cheese, Cheesus—and he'll amble up to the batter's box, knocking imaginary dirt from his spikes, adjusting the straps of his golf gloves, tugging at his underwear, and fiddling with his battling helmet. His face will be impenetrable. Corcoran will work the ball in his glove, maybe tip back his cap for a little hair grease, and then give him a look of psychopathic hatred. Hector has seen it before. Me against you. My record, my career, my house, my family, my life, my mutual funds and beer distributorship against yours. He's been hit in the elbow, the knee, the groin, the head. Nothing fazes him. Nothing. Murmuring a prayer to Santa Griselda, patroness of the sun-blasted Sonoran village where he was born like a heat blister on his mother's womb, Hector Hernán Jesús y María Quesadilla will step into the batter's box, ready for anything.

But it's a game of infinite surprises.

Before Hector can set foot on the playing field, Corcoran suddenly doubles up in pain, Phelan goes slack at second, and the catcher and shortstop are hustling out to the mound, tailed an instant later by trainer and pitching coach. First thing Hector thinks is groin pull, then appendicitis, and finally, as Corcoran goes down on one knee, poison. He'd once seen a man shot in the gut at Obregón City, but the report had been loud as a thunderclap, and he hears nothing now but the enveloping hum of the crowd. Corcoran is rising shakily, the trainer and pitching coach supporting him while the catcher kicks meditatively in the dirt, and now Mueller, the Atlanta *cabeza,* is striding big-bellied out of the dugout, head down as if to be sure his feet are following orders. Halfway to the mound, Mueller flicks his right hand across his ear quick as a horse flicking its tail, and it's all she wrote for Corcoran.

Poised on the dugout steps like a bird dog, Hector waits, his eyes riveted on the bullpen. Please, he whispers, praying for the intercession of the Niño and pledging a hundred votary candles—at least, at least. Can it be?—yes, milk of my mother, yes—Kerensky himself strutting out onto the field like a fighting cock. Kerensky!

Come to the birthday boy, Kerensky, he murmurs, so certain he's going to put it in the stands he could point like the immeasurable Bambino. His tired old legs shuffle with impatience as Kerensky stalks across the field, and then he's turning to pick Asunción out of the crowd. She's on her feet now, Reina too, the kids come alive beside her. And Hector Jr., the book forgotten, his face transfigured with the look of rapture he used to get when he was a boy sitting on the steps of the dugout. Hector can't help himself: he grins and gives them the thumbs-up sign.

Then, as Kerensky fires his warm-up smoke, the loudspeaker crackles and Hector emerges from the shadow of the dugout into the tapering golden shafts of the late-afternoon sun. That pitch, I want that one, he mutters, carrying his bat like a javelin and shooting a glare at Kerensky, but something's wrong here, the announcer's got it screwed up: BATTING FOR RARITAN, NUMBER 39, DAVE TOOL. What the—? And now somebody's tugging at his sleeve and he's turning to gape with incomprehension at the freckle-faced batboy, Dave Tool striding out of the dugout with his big forty-two-ounce stick, Dupuy's face locked up like a vault, and the crowd, on its feet, chanting Tool, Tool, Tool! For a moment he just stands there, frozen with disbelief. Then Tool is brushing by him and the idiot of a batboy is leading him toward the dugout as if he were an old blind fisherman poised on the edge of the dock.

He feels as if his legs have been cut out from under him. Tool! Dupuy is yanking him for Tool? For what? So he can play the lefty-righty percentages like some chess head or something? Tool, of all people, Tool, with his thirty-five

home runs a season and lifetime B.A. of .234; Tool, who's worn so many uniforms they had to expand the league to make room for him—what's he going to
do? Raging, Hector flings down his bat and comes at Dupuy like a cat tossed in a
bag. You crazy, you jerk, he sputters. I woulda hit him. I woulda won the game. I
dreamed it. And then, his voice breaking: It's my birthday, for Christ's sake!

But Dupuy can't answer him, because on the first pitch Tool slams a real
worm burner to short and the game is going into extra innings.

By seven o'clock, half the fans have given up and gone home. In the top of
the fourteenth, when the visitors came up with a pair of runs on a two-out pinch-
hit home run, there was a real exodus, but then the Dodgers struck back for two
to knot it up again. Then it was three up and three down, regular as clockwork.
Now, at the end of the nineteenth, with the score deadlocked at seven all and the
players dragging themselves around the field like gut-shot horses, Hector is beginning to think he may get a second chance after all. Especially the way Depuy's
been using up players like some crazy general on the Western Front, yanking
pitchers, juggling his defense, throwing in pinch runners and pinch hitters until
he's just about gone through the entire roster. Asunción is still there among the
faithful, the foolish, and the self-deluded, fumbling with her rosary and
mouthing prayers for Jesus Christ Our Lord, the Madonna, Hector, the home
team, and her departed mother, in that order. Reina too, looking like the survivor
of some disaster, Franklin and Alfredo asleep in their seats, the *niñitas* gone off
somewhere—for Coke and dogs, maybe. And Hector Jr. looks like he's going to
stick it out too, though he should be back in his closet writing about the mystical
so-and-so and the way he illustrates his poems with gods and men and serpents.
Watching him, Hector can feel his heart turn over.

In the bottom of the twentieth, with one down and Gilley on first—he's a
starting pitcher but Dupuy sent him in to run for Manfredonia after Manfredonia
jammed his ankle like a turkey and had to be helped off the field—Hector pushes
himself up from the bench and ambles down to where Dupuy sits in the corner,
contemplatively spitting a gout of tobacco juice and saliva into the drain at his
feet. Let me hit, Bernard, come on, Hector says, easing down beside him.

Can't, comes the reply, and Dupuy never even raises his head. Can't risk it,
champ. Look around you—and here the manager's voice quavers with uncertainty, with fear and despair and the dull edge of hopelessness—I got nobody
left. I hit you, I got to play you.

No, no, you don't understand—I'm going to win it. I swear.

And then the two of them, like old bankrupts on a bench in Miami Beach,
look up to watch Phelan hit into a double play.

A buzz runs through the crowd when the Dodgers take the field for the top
of the twenty-second. Though Phelan is limping, Thorkelsson's asleep on his
feet, and Dorfman, fresh on the mound, is the only pitcher left on the roster, the
moment is electric. One more inning and they tie the record set by the Mets and

Giants back in '64, and then they're making history. Drunk, sober, and then drunk again, saturated with fats and nitrates and sugar, the crowd begins to come to life. Go, Dodgers! Eat shit! Yo Mama! Phelan's a bum!

Hector can feel it too. The rage and frustration that had consumed him back in the ninth are gone, replaced by a dawning sense of wonder—he could have won it then, yes, and against his nemesis Kerensky too—but the Niño and Santa Griselda have been saving him for something greater. He sees it now, knows it in his bones: he's going to be the hero of the longest game in history.

As if to bear him out, Dorfman, the kid from Albuquerque, puts in a good inning, cutting the bushed Braves down in order. In the dugout, Doc Pusser, the team physician, is handing out the little green pills that keep your eyes open and Dupuy is blowing into a cup of coffee and staring morosely out at the playing field. Hector watches as Tool, who'd stayed in the game at first base, fans on three pitches, then he shoves in beside Dorfman and tells the kid he's looking good out there. With his big cornhusker's ears and nose like a tweezer, Dorfman could be a caricature of the green rookie. He says nothing. Hey, don't let it get to you, kid—I'm going to win this one for you. Next inning or maybe the inning after. Then he tells him how he saw it in a vision and how it's his birthday and the kid's going to get the victory, one of the biggest of all time. Twenty-four, twenty-five innings maybe.

Hector had heard of a game once in the Mexican League that took three days to play and went seventy-three innings, did Dorfman know that? It was down in Culiacán. Chito Martí, the converted bullfighter, had finally ended it by dropping down dead of exhaustion in center field, allowing Sexto Silvestro, who'd broken his leg rounding third, to crawl home with the winning run. But Hector doesn't think this game will go that long. Dorfman sighs and extracts a bit of wax from his ear as Pantaleo, the third-string catcher, hits back to the pitcher to end the inning. I hope not, he says, uncoiling himself from the bench; my arm'd fall off.

Ten o'clock comes and goes. Dorfman's still in there, throwing breaking stuff and a little smoke at the Braves, who look as if they just stepped out of *The Night of the Living Dead.* The home team isn't doing much better. Dupuy's run through the whole team but for Hector, and three or four of the guys have been in there since two in the afternoon; the rest are a bunch of ginks and gimps who can barely stand up. Out in the stands, the fans look grim. The vendors ran out of beer an hour back, and they haven't had dogs or kraut or Coke or anything since eight-thirty.

In the bottom of the twenty-seventh Phelan goes berserk in the dugout and Dupuy has to pin him to the floor while Doc Pusser shoves something up his nose to calm him. Next inning the balls-and-strikes ump passes out cold, and Dorfman, who's beginning to look a little fagged, walks the first two batters but manages to weasel his way out of the inning without giving up the go-ahead run. Meanwhile, Thorkelsson has been dropping ice cubes down his trousers to keep awake, Martinez is smoking something suspicious in the can, and Ferenc Fortnoi, the third baseman, has begun talking to himself in a tortured Slovene dialect. For his part, Hector feels stronger and more alert as the game goes on. Though he hasn't had a bite since breakfast he feels impervious to the pangs of hunger, as if he were preparing himself, mortifying his flesh like a saint in the desert.

And then, in the top of the thirty-first, with half the fans asleep and the other half staring into nothingness like the inmates of the asylum of Our Lady of Guadalupe, where Hector had once visited his halfwit uncle when he was a boy, Pluto Morales cracks one down the first-base line and Tool flubs it. Right away it looks like trouble, because Chester Bubo is running around right field looking up at the sky like a birdwatcher while the balls snakes through the grass, caroms off his left foot, and coasts like silk to the edge of the warning track. Morales meanwhile is rounding second and coming on for third, running in slow motion, flat-footed and hump-backed, his face drained of color, arms flapping like the undersize wings of some big flightless bird. It's not even close. By the time Bubo can locate the ball, Morales is ten feet from the plate, pitching into a face-first slide that's at least three parts collapse, and that's it, the Braves are up by one. It looks black for the hometeam. But Dorfman, though his arm has begun to swell like a sausage, shows some grit, bears down, and retires the side to end the historic top of the unprecedented thirty-first inning.

Now, at long last, the hour has come. It'll be Bubo, Dorfman, and Tool for the Dodgers in their half of the inning, which means that Hector will hit for Dorfman. I been saving you, champ, Dupuy rasps, the empty Gelusil bottle clenched in his fist like a hand grenade. Go on in there, he murmurs, and his voice fades away to nothing as Bubo pops the first pitch up in back of the plate. Go on in there and do your stuff.

Sucking in his gut, Hector strides out onto the brightly lit field like a nineteen-year-old, the familiar cry in his ears, the haggard fans on their feet, a sickle moon sketched in overhead as if in some cartoon strip featuring drunken husbands and the milkman. Asunción looks as if she's been nailed to the cross, Reina wakes with a start and shakes the little ones into consciousness, and Hector Jr. staggers to his feet like a battered middleweight coming out for the fifteenth round. They're all watching him. The fans whose lives are like empty sacks, the wife who wants him home in front of the TV, his divorced daughter with the four kids and another on the way, his son, pride of his life, who reads for the doctor of philosophy while his crazy *padrecito* puts on a pair of long stockings and chases around after a little white ball like a case of arrested development. He'll show them. He'll show them some *cojones*, some true grit and desire: the game's not over yet.

On the mound for the Braves is Bo Brannerman, a big mustachioed machine of a man, normally a starter but pressed into desperate relief service tonight. A fine pitcher—Hector would be the first to admit it—but he just pitched two nights ago and he's worn thin as wire. Hector steps up to the plate, feeling legendary. He glances over at Tool in the on-deck circle, and then down at Booger, the third-base coach. All systems go. He cuts at the air twice and then watches Brannerman rear back and release the ball: strike one. Hector smiles. Why rush things? Give them a thrill. He watches a low outside slider that just about bounces to even the count, and then stands like a statue as Brannerman slices the corner of the plate for strike two. From the stands, a chant of *Viejo, Viejo,* and Asunción's piercing soprano, Hit him, Hector!

Hector has no worries, the moment eternal, replayed through games uncountable, with pitchers who were over the hill when he was a rookie with San Buitre, with pups like Brannerman, with big-leaguers and Hall of Famers. Here it comes, Hector, 92 MPH, the big *gringo* trying to throw it by you, the matchless wrists, the flawless swing, one terrific moment of suspended animation—and all of a sudden you're starring in your own movie.

How does it go? The ball cutting through the night sky like a comet, arching high over the center fielder's hapless scrambling form to slam off the wall while your legs churn up the basepaths, you round first in a gallop, taking second, and heading for third . . . but wait, you spill hot coffee on your hand and you can't feel it, the demons apply the live wire to your tailbone, your legs give out and they cut you down at third while the stadium erupts in howls of execration and abuse and the *niñitos* break down, faces flooded with tears of humiliation, Hector Jr. turning his back in disgust and Asunción raging like a harpy, *Abuelo! Abuelo! Abuelo!*

Stunned, shrunken, humiliated, you stagger back to the dugout in a maelstrom of abuse, paper cups, flying spittle, your life a waste, the game a cheat, and then, crowning irony, that bum Tool, worthless all the way back to his washerwoman grandmother and the drunken muttering whey-faced tribe that gave him suck, stands tall like a giant and sends the first pitch out of the park to tie it. Oh, the pain. Flat feet, fire in your legs, your poor tired old heart skipping a beat in mortification. And now Dupuy, red in the face, shouting: The game could be over but for you, you crazy gimpy old beaner washout! You want to hide in your locker, bury yourself under the shower-room floor, but you have to watch as the next two men reach base and you pray with fervor that they'll score and put an end to your debasement. But no, Thorkelsson whiffs and the new inning dawns as inevitably as the new minute, the new hour, the new day, endless, implacable, world without end.

But wait, wait: who's going to pitch? Dorfman's out, there's nobody left, the astonishing thirty-second inning is marching across the scoreboard like an invading army, and suddenly Dupuy is standing over you—no, no, he's down on one knee, begging. Hector, he's saying, didn't you use to pitch down in Mexico when you were a kid, didn't I hear that someplace? Yes, you're saying, yes, but that was—

And then you're out on the mound, in command once again, elevated like

some half-mad old king in a play, and throwing smoke. The first two batters go
down on strikes and the fans are rabid with excitement. Asunción will raise a
shrine, Hector Jr. worships you more than all the poets that ever lived, but can
it be? You walk the next three and then give up the grand slam to little Tommy
Oshimisi! Mother of God, will it never cease? But wait, wait, wait: here comes
the bottom of the thirty-second and Brannerman's wild. He walks a couple, gets
a couple out, somebody reaches on an infield single and the bases are loaded for
you, Hector Quesadilla, stepping up to the plate now like the Iron Man himself.
The wind-up, the delivery, the ball hanging there like a *piñata*, like a birthday
gift, and then the stick flashes in your hands like an archangel's sword, and the
game goes on forever.

(1983)

WE ARE NORSEMEN

We are Norsemen, hardy and bold. We mount the black waves in our doughty sleek ships and go a-raiding. We are Norsemen, tough as stone. At least some of us are. Myself, I'm a skald—a poet, that is. I go along with Thorkell Son of Thorkell the Misaligned and Kolbein Snub when they sack the Irish coast and violate the Irish children, women, dogs and cattle and burn the Irish houses and pitch the ancient priceless Irish manuscripts into the sea. Then I sing about it. Doggerel like this:

> *Fell I not nor failed at*
> *Fierce words, but my piercing*
> *Blade mouth gave forth bloody*
> *Bane speech, its harsh teaching.*

Catch the kennings? That's the secret of this skaldic verse—make it esoteric and shoot it full of kennings. Anyway, it's a living.

But I'm not here to carp about a skald's life, I'm here to make art. Spin a tale for posterity. Weave a web of mystery.

That year the winter ran at us like a sword, October to May. You know the sort of thing: permafrosting winds, record cold. The hot springs crusted over, birds stiffened on the wing and dropped to the earth like stones, Thorkell the Old froze to the crossbar in the privy. Even worse: thin-ribbed wolves yabbered on our doorstep, chewed up our coats and boots, and then—one snowy night—made off with Thorkell the Young. It was impossible. We crouched round the fire, thatch leaking and froze our norns off. The days were short, the mead barrel deep. We drank, shivered, roasted a joint, told tales. The fire played off our faces, red-gold and amber, and we fastened on the narrator's voice like a log on a dark sea, entranced, falling in on ourselves, the soft cadences pulling us through the waves, illuminating shorelines, battlefields, mountains of plunder. Unfortunately, the voice was most often mine. Believe me, a winter like that a skald really earns his keep—six months, seven days a week, and an audience of hardbitten critics with frost in their beards. The nights dragged on.

One bleak morning we saw that yellow shoots had begun to stab through the cattle droppings in the yard—we stretched, yawned, and began to fill our boats with harrying matériel. We took our battle axes, our throwing axes, our hewing axes, our massive stroke-dealing swords, our disemboweling spears, a couple of strips of jerky and a jug of water. As I said, we were tough. Some of us wore our twin-horned battle helmets, the sight of which interrupts the vital functions of our victims and enemies and inspires high-keyed vibrato. Others of us, in view of fifteen-degree temperatures and a stiff breeze whitening the peaks of the waves, felt that the virtue of toughness had its limits. I decided on a lynx hat that gave elaborate consideration to the ears.

We fought over the gravel brake to launch our terrible swift ship. The wind shrieked of graves robbed, the sky was a hearth gone cold. An icy froth soaked us to the waist. Then we were off, manning the oars in smooth Nordic synch, the ship lurching through rocky breakers, heaving up, slapping down. The spray shot needles in our eyes, the oars lifted and dipped. An hour later the mainland winked into oblivion behind the dark lids of sea and sky.

There were thirteen of us: Thorkell Son of Thorkell the Misaligned, Thorkell the Short, Thorkell Thorkellsson, Thorkell Cat, Thorkell Flat-Nose, Thorkell-neb, Thorkell Ale-Lover, Thorkell the Old, Thorkell the Deep-minded, Ofeig, Skeggi, Grim, and me. We were tough. We were hardy. We were bold.

Nonetheless the voyage was a disaster. A northeaster roared down on us like a herd of drunken whales and swept us far off course. We missed our landfall— Ireland—by at least two hundred miles and carried past into the open Atlantic. Eight weeks we sailed, looking for land. Thorkell the Old was bailing one gray afternoon and found three menhaden in his bucket. We ate them raw. I speared an albatross and hung it round my neck. It was no picnic.

Then one night we heard the cries of gulls like souls stricken in the dark. Thorkell Ale-Lover, keen of smell, snuffed the breeze. "Landfall near," he said. In the morning the sun threw our shadows on a new land—buff and green, slabs of gray, it swallowed the horizon.

"Balder be praised!" said Thorkell the Old.

"Thank Frigg," I said.

We skirted the coast, looking for habitations to sack. There were none. We'd discovered a wasteland. The Thorkells were for putting ashore to replenish our provisions and make sacrifice to the gods (in those days we hadn't yet learned to swallow unleavened bread and dab our foreheads with ashes. We were real primitives). We ran our doughty sleek warship up a sandy spit and leapt ashore, fierce as flayed demons. It was an unnecessary show of force, as the countryside was desolate, but it did our hearts good.

The instant my feet touched earth the poetic fit came on me and I composed this verse:

> New land, new-found beyond
> The mickle waves by fell
> Men-fish, their stark battle
> Valor failèd them not.

No *Edda,* I grant you—but what can you expect after six weeks of bailing? I turned to Thorkell Son of Thorkell the Misaligned, my brain charged with creative fever. "Hey!" I shouted, "let's name this new-found land!" The others crowded round. Thorkell son of Thorkell the Misaligned looked down at me (he was six four, his red beard hung to his waist). "We'll call it—Newfoundland!" I roared. There was silence. The twin horns of Thorkell's helmet pierced the sky, his eyes were like stones, "Thorkell-land," he said.

We voted. The Thorkells had it, 9 to 4.

For two and a half weeks we plumbed the coast, catching conies, shooting deer, pitching camp on islands or guarded promontories. I'd like to tell you it was glorious—golden sunsets, virgin forests, the thrill of discovery and all that—but when your business is sacking and looting, a virgin forest is the last thing you want to see. We grumbled bitterly. But Thorkell son of Thorkell the Misaligned was loath to admit that the land to which he'd given his name was uninhabited— and consequently of no use whatever. We forged on. Then one morning he called out from his place at the tiller: "Hah!" he said, and pointed toward a rocky abutment a hundred yards ahead. The mist lay on the water like flocks of sheep. I craned my neck, squinted, saw nothing. And then suddenly, like a revelation, I saw them: three tall posts set into the earth and carved with the figures of men and beasts. The sight brought water to my eyes and verse to my lips (but no sense in troubling you with any dilatory stanzas now—this is a climactic moment).

We landed. Crept up on the carvings, sly and wary, silent as stones. As it turned out, our caution was superfluous: the place was deserted. Besides the carvings (fanged monsters, stags, serpents, the grinning faces of a new race) there was no evidence of human presence whatever. Not even a footprint. We hung our heads: another bootyless day. Ofeig—the berserker—was seized with his berserker's rage and wound up hacking the three columns to splinters with his massive stoke-dealing sword.

The Thorkells were of the opinion that we should foray inland in search of a village to pillage. Who was I to argue? Inland we went, ever hardy and bold, up hill and down dale, through brakes and brambles and bogs and clouds of insects that rushed up our nostrils and down our throats. We found nothing. On the way back to the ship we were luckier. Thorkell-neb stumbled over a shadow in the path, and when the shadows leaped up and shot through the trees, we gave chase. After a good rib-heaving run we caught what proved to be a boy, eleven or twelve, his skin the color of copper, the feathers of birds in his hair. Like the Irish, he spoke gibberish.

Thorkell Son of Thorkell the Misaligned drew pictures in the sand and punched the boy in the chest until the boy agreed to lead us to his people, the carvers of wood. We were Norsemen, and we always got our way. All of us warmed to the prospect of spoils, and off we went on another trek. We brought along our short-swords and disemboweling spears—just in case—though judging from the boy's condition (he was bony and naked, his eyes deep and black as the spaces between the stars) we had nothing to fear from his kindred.

We were right. After tramping through the under- and overgrowth for half an hour we came to a village: smoking cook pots, skinny dogs, short and ugly savages, their hair the color of excrement. I counted six huts of branches and mud, the sort of thing that might excite a beaver. When we stepped into the clearing— tall, hardy and bold—the savages set up a fiendish caterwauling and rushed for their weapons. But what a joke their weapons were! Ofeig caught an arrow in the air, looked at the head on it, and collapsed laughing: it was made of flint. Flint. Can you believe it? Here we'd come Frigg knows how many miles for plunder and the best we could do was a bunch of Stone Age aborigines who thought that a necklace of dogs' teeth was the height of fashion. Oh how we longed for those clever Irish and their gold brooches and silver-inlaid bowls. Anyway, we subdued these screechers as we called them, sacrificed the whole lot of them to the gods (the way I saw it we were doing them a favor), and headed back to our terrible swift ship, heavy of heart. There was no longer any room for debate: Ireland, look out!

As we pointed the prow east the westering sun threw the shadow of the new land over us. Thorkell the Old looked back over his shoulder and shook his head in disgust. "That place'll never amount to a hill of beans," he said.

And then it was gone.

Days rose up out of the water and sank behind us. Intrepid Norsemen, we rode the currents, the salt breeze tickling our nostrils and bellying the sail. Thorkell Flat-Nose was our navigator. He kept two ravens on a cord. After five and a half weeks at sea he released one of them and it shot off into the sky and vanished—but in less than an hour the bird was spotted off starboard, winging toward us, growing larger by turns until finally it flapped down on the prow and allowed its leg to be looped to the cord. Three days later Flat-Nose released the second raven. The bird mounted high, winging to the southeast until it became a black rune carved into the horizon. We followed it into a night of full moon, the stars like milk splattered in the cauldron of the sky. The sea whispered at the prow, the tiller hissed behind us. Suddenly Thorkell Ale-Lover cried, "Land ho!" We were fell and grim and ravenous. We looked up at the black ribbon of the Irish coast and grinned like wolves. Our shoulders dug at the oars, the sea sliced by. An hour later we landed.

Ofeig was for sniffing out habitations, free-booting and laying waste. But dawn crept on apace, and Thorkell Son of Thorkell the Misaligned reminded him that we Norsemen attack only under cover of darkness, swift and silent as a nightmare. Ofeig did not take it well: the berserker's rage came on him and he began to froth and chew at his tongue and howl like a skinned beast. It was a tense moment. We backed off as he grabbed for his battle-axe and whirred it about his head. Fortunately he stumbled over a root and began to attack the earth, gibbering and slavering, sparks slashing out from buried stones as if the ground had suddenly caught fire. (Admittedly, berserkers can be tough to live with—but you can't beat them when it comes to seizing hearts with terror or battling trolls, demons or demiurges.)

Our reaction to all this was swift and uncomplicated: we moved up the beach about two hundred yards and settled down to get some rest. I stretched out in a patch of wildflowers and watched the sky, Ofeig's howls riding the breeze like a celestial aria, waves washing the shore. The Thorkells slept on their feet. It was nearly light when we finally dozed off, visions of plunder dancing in our heads.

I woke to the sound of whetstone on axe: we were polishing the blade edges of our fearsome battle weapons. It was late afternoon. We hadn't eaten in days. Thorkell-neb and Skeggi stood naked on the beach, basting one another with black mud scooped from a nearby marsh. I joined them. We darkened our flaxen hair, drew grim black lines under our eyes, chanted fight songs. The sun hit the water like a halved fruit, then vanished. A horned owl shot out across the dunes. Crickets kreeked in the bushes. The time had come. We drummed one another about the neck and shoulders for a while ("Yeah!" we yelled. "Yeah!"), fastened our helmets, and then raced our serpent-headed ship into the waves.

A few miles up the coast we came on a light flickering out over the dark corrugations of the sea. As we drew closer it became apparent that the source of light was detached from the coast itself—could it be an island? Our blood quickened, our lips drew back in anticipation. Ravin and rapine at last! And an island no less—what could be more ideal? There would be no escape from our pure silent fury, no chance of secreting treasures, no hope of reinforcements hastily roused from bumpkin beds in the surrounding countryside. Ha!

An island it was—a tiny point of land, slick with ghostly cliffs and crowned with the walls of a monastery. We circled it, shadows on the dark swell. The light seemed to emanate from a stone structure atop the highest crag—some bookish monk with his nose to the paper no doubt, copying by the last of the firelight. He was in for a surprise. We rode the bosom of the sea and waited for the light to fail. Suddenly Thorkell the Old began to cackle. "That'll be Inishmurray," he wheezed. "Fattest monastery on the west coast." Our eyes glowed. He spat into the spume. "Thought it looked familiar," he said. "I helped Thorir Paunch sack it back in '75." Then the light died and the world became night.

We watched the bookish monk in our minds' eyes: kissing the text and laying it on a shelf, scattering the fire, plodding wearily to his cell and the cold gray pallet. I recited an incendiary verse while we waited for the old ecclesiast to tumble into sleep:

> *Eye-bleed monk,*
> *Night his bane.*
> *Darkness masks*
> *The sea-wound,*
> *Mickle fell,*
> *Mickle stark.*

I finished the recitation with a flourish, rolling the mickles like thunder. Then we struck.

It was child's play. The slick ghostly cliffs were like rolling meadows, the outer wall a branch in our path. There was no sentry, no watchdog, no alarm. We dropped down into the courtyard, naked, our bodies basted black, our doughty death-dealing weapons in hand. We were shadows, fears, fragments of a bad dream.

Thorkell Son of Thorkell the Misaligned stole into one of the little stone churches and emerged with a glowing brand. Then he set fire to two or three of the wickerwork cells and a pile of driftwood. From that point on it was pandemonium—Ofeig tumbling stone crosses, the Thorkells murdering monks in their beds, Skeggi and Thorkell the Old chasing women, Thorkell Ale-Lover waving joints of mutton and horns of beer. The Irish defended themselves as best they could, two or three monks coming at us with barbed spears and pilgrim's staffs, but we made short work of them. We were Norsemen, after all.

For my own part, I darted here and there through the smoke and rubble, seized with a destructive frenzy, frightening women and sheep with my hideous blackened features, cursing like a jay. I even cut down a doddering crone for the sake of a gold brooch, my sweetheart Thorkella in mind. Still, despite the lust and chaos and the sweet smell of anarchy, I kept my head and my poet's eye. I observed each of the principal Thorkells with a reporter's acuity, noting each valorous swipe and thrust, the hot skaldic verses already forming on my lips. But then suddenly I was distracted: the light had reappeared in the little chapel atop the crag. I counted Thorkells (no mean feat when you consider the congeries of legs and arms, sounds and odors, the panicked flocks of sheep, pigs and chickens, the jagged flames, the furious womanizing, gourmandizing and sodomizing of the crew). As I say, I counted Thorkells. We were all in sight. Up above, the light grew in intensity, flaming like a planet against the night sky. I thought of the bookish monk and started up the hill.

The night susurrated around me: crickets, katydids, cicadas, and far below the rush of waves on the rocks. The glare from the fires behind me gave way to blackness, rich and star-filled. I hurried up to the chapel, lashed by malice aforethought and evil intent—bookish monk, bookish monk—and burst through the door. I was black and terrible, right down to the tip of my foreskin. "Arrrrr!" I growled. The monk sat at a table, his hands clenched, head bent over a massive tome. He was just as I'd pictured him: pale as milk, a fringe of dark pubic hair around his tonsure, puny and frail. He did not look up. I growled again, and when I got no response I began to slash at candles and pitchers and icons and all the other superstitious trappings of the place. Pottery splashed to the floor, shelves tumbled. Still he bent over the book.

The book. What in Frigg's name was a book anyway? Scratchings on a sheet of cowhide. Could you fasten a cloak with it, carry mead in it, impress women with it, wear it in your hair? There was gold and silver scattered round the room, and yet he sat over the book as if it could glow or talk or something. The idiot. The pale, puny, unhardy, unbold idiot. A rage came over me at the thought of it—I shoved him aside and snatched up the book, thick pages, dark characters, the mystery and magic. Snatched it up, me, a poet, a Norseman, an annihilator, an illiterate. Snatched it up and watched the old man's suffering features as I fed it, page by filthy page, into the fire. Ha!

We are Norsemen, hardy and bold. We mount the black waves in our doughty sleek ships and we go a-raiding. We are Norsemen, tough as stone. We are Norsemen.

(1977)

THE CHAMP

Angelo D. was training hard. This challenger, Kid Gullet, would be no push-over. In fact, the Kid hit him right where he lived: he was worried. He'd been champ for thirty-seven years and all that time his records had stood like Mount Rushmore—and now this Kid was eating them up. Fretful, he pushed his plate away.

"But Angelo, you ain't done already?" His trainer, Spider Decoud, was all over him. "That's what—a piddling hundred and some–odd flapjacks and seven quarts a milk?"

"He's on to me, Spider. He found out about the ulcer and now he's going to hit me with enchiladas and shrimp in cocktail sauce."

"Don't fret it, Killer. We'll get him with the starches and heavy syrups. He's just a kid, twenty-two. What does he know about eating? Look, get up and walk it off and we'll do a kidney and kipper course, okay? And then maybe four or five dozen poached eggs. C'mon, Champ, lift that fork. You want to hold on to the title or not?"

First it was pickled eggs. Eighty-three pickled eggs in an hour and a half. The record had stood since 1941. They said it was like DiMaggio's consecutive-game hitting streak: unapproachable. A world apart. But then, just three months ago, Angelo had picked up the morning paper and found himself unforked: a man who went by the name of Kid Gullet had put down 108 of them. In the following weeks Angelo had seen his records toppled like a string of dominoes: gher-kins, pullets, persimmons, oysters, pretzels, peanuts, scalloped potatoes, feta cheese, smelts, Girl Scout cookies. At the Rendezvous Room in Honolulu the

Kid bolted 12,000 macadamia nuts and 67 bananas in less than an hour. During a Cubs–Phillies game at Wrigley field he put away 43 hot dogs—with buns—and 112 Cokes. In Orkney it was legs of lamb; in Frankfurt, Emmentaler and schnitzel; in Kiev, pirogen. He was irrepressible. In Stelton, New Jersey, he finished off 6 gallons of borscht and 93 four-ounce jars of gefilte fish while sitting atop a flagpole. The press ate it up.

Toward the end of the New Jersey session a reporter from ABC Sports swung a boom mike up to where the Kid sat on his eminence, chewing the last of the gefilte fish. "What are your plans for the future, Kid?" shouted the newsman.

"I'm after the Big One," the Kid replied.

"Angelo D.?"

The camera zoomed in, the Kid grinned.

> *"Capocollo, chili and curry,*
> *Big Man, you better start to worry."*

Angelo was rattled. He gave up the morning paper and banned the use of the Kid's name around the Training Table. Kid Gullet: every time he heard those three syllables his stomach clenched. Now he lay on the bed, the powerful digestive machinery tearing away at breakfast, a bag of peanuts in his hand, his mind sifting through the tough bouts and spectacular triumphs of the past. There was Beau Riviere from Baton Rouge, who nearly choked him on deep-fried mud puppies, and Pinky Luzinski from Pittsburgh, who could gulp down 300 raw eggs and then crunch up the shells as if they were potato chips. Or the Japanese sumo wrestler who swallowed marbles by the fistful and throve on sashimi in a fiery mustard sauce. He'd beaten them all, because he had grit and determination and talent—and he would beat this kid too. Angelo sat up and roared: "I'm still the champ!"

The door cracked open. It was Decoud. "That's the spirit, Killer. Remember D. D. Peloris, Max Manger, Bozo Miller, Spoonbill Rizzo? Bums. All of them. You beat 'em, Champ."

"Yeah!" Angelo bellowed. "And I'm going to flatten this Gullet too."

"That's the ticket: leave him gasping for Bromo."

"They'll be pumping his stomach when I'm through with him."

Out in L.A. the Kid was taking on Turk Harris, number one contender for the heavyweight crown. The Kid's style was Tabasco and Worcestershire; Harris was a mashed-potato and creamed-corn man—a trencherman of the old school. Like Angelo D.

Harris opened with a one-two combination of rice and kidney beans; the Kid countered with cocktail onions and capers. Then Harris hit him with baklava—400 two-inch squares of it. The Kid gobbled them like hors d'oeuvres, came back with chiles rellenos and asparagus vinaigrette. He KO'd Harris in the middle of the fourth round. After the bout he stood in a circle of jabbing microphones, flashing lights. "I got one thing to say," he shouted. "And if you're out there, Big Man, you better take heed:

I'm going to float like a parfait,
Sting like a tamale.
Big Man, you'll hit the floor,
In four."

At the preliminary weigh-in for the title bout the Kid showed up on roller skates in a silver lamé jumpsuit. He looked like something off the launching pad at Cape Canaveral. Angelo, in his coal-bucket trousers and suspenders, could have been mistaken for an aging barber or a boccie player strayed in from the park.

The Kid had a gallon jar of hot cherry peppers under his arm. He wheeled up to the Champ, bolted six or seven in quick succession, and then held one out to him by the stem. "Care for an appetizer, Pops?" Angelo declined, his face dour and white, the big fleshy nostrils heaving like a stallion's. Then the photographers posed the two, belly to belly. In the photograph, which appeared on the front page of the paper the following morning, Angelo D. looked like an advertisement for heartburn.

There was an SRO crowd at the Garden for the title bout. Scalpers were getting two hundred and up for tickets. ABC Sports was there, Colonel Sanders was there, Arthur Treacher, Julia Child, James Beard, Ronald McDonald, Mamma Leone. It was the Trenching Event of the Century.

Spider Decoud and the Kid's manager had inspected the ring and found the arrangements to their satisfaction—each man had a table, stool, stack of plates and cutlery. Linen napkins, a pitcher of water. It would be a fourteen-round affair, each round going ten minutes with a sixty-second bell break. The contestants would name their dishes for alternate rounds, the Kid, as challenger, leading off.

A hush fell over the crowd. And then the chant, rolling from back to front like breakers washing the beach: GULLET, GULLET, GULLET! There he was, the Kid, sweeping down the aisle like a born champion in his cinnamon-red robe with the silver letters across the abdomen. He stepped into the ring, clasped his hands, and shook them over his head. The crowd roared like rock faces slipping deep beneath the earth. Then he did a couple of deep knee bends and sat down on his stool. At that moment Angelo shuffled out from the opposite end of the arena, stern, grim, raging, the tight curls at the back of his neck standing out like the tail feathers of an albatross, his barren dome ghostly under the klieg lights, the celebrated paunch swelling beneath his opalescent robe like a fat wad of butter-ball turkeys. The crowd went mad. They shrieked, hooted and whistled, women kissed the hem of his gown, men reached out to pat his bulge. ANGELO! He stepped into the ring and took his seat as the big black mike descended from the ceiling.

The announcer, in double lapels and bow tie, shouted over the roar, "Ladies and Gentlemen—" while Angelo glared at the Kid, blood in his eye. He was choked with a primordial competitive fury, mad as a kamikaze, deranged with hunger. Two days earlier Decoud had lured him into a deserted meat locker and bolted the door—and then for the entire forty-eight hours had projected porno-graphic food films on the wall. Fleshy wet lips closing on éclairs, zoom shots of masticating teeth, gulping throats, probing tongues, children innocently suck-ing at Tootsie Roll pops—it was obscene, titillating, maddening. And through it all a panting soundtrack composed of grunts and sighs and the smack of lips. Angelo D. climbed into the ring a desperate man. But even money nonetheless. The Kid gloated in his corner.

"At this table, in the crimson trunks," bellowed the announcer, "standing six foot two inches tall and weighing in at three hundred and seventy-seven pounds . . . is the challenger, Kid Gullet!" A cheer went up, deafening. The an-nouncer pointed to Angelo. "And at this table, in the pearly trunks and standing five foot seven and a half inches tall and weighing in at three hundred and twenty-three pounds," he bawled, his voice rumbling like a cordon of cement trucks, "is the Heavyweight Champion of the World . . . Angelo D.!" Another cheer, perhaps even louder. Then the referee took over. He had the contestants step to the center of the ring, the exposed flesh of their chests and bellies like a pair of avalanches, while he asked if each was acquainted with the rules. The Kid grinned like a shark. "All right then," the ref said, "touch midriffs and come out eating."

The bell rang for Round One. The Kid opened with Szechwan hot and sour soup, three gallons. He lifted the tureen to his lips and slapped it down empty. The Champ followed suit, his face aflame, sweat breaking out on his forehead. He paused three times, and when finally he set the tureen down he snatched up the water pitcher and drained it at a gulp while the crowd booed and Decoud yelled from the corner: "Lay off the water or you'll bloat up like a blowfish!"

Angelo retaliated with clams on the half shell in Round Two: 512 in ten min-utes. But the Kid kept pace with him—and as if that weren't enough, he sprin-kled his own portion with cayenne pepper and Tabasco. The crowd loved it. They gagged on their hot dogs, pelted the contestants with plastic cups and peanut shells, gnawed at the backs of their seats. Angelo looked up at the Kid's powerful jaws, the lips stained with Tabasco, and began to feel queasy.

The Kid staggered him with lamb curry in the next round. The crowd was on its feet, the Champ's face was green, the fork motionless in his hand, the ref counting down. Decoud twisting the towel in his fists—when suddenly the bell sounded and the Champ collapsed on the table. Decoud leaped into the ring, chafed Angelo's abdomen, sponged his face. "Hang in there, Champ," he said, "and come back hard with the carbohydrates."

Angelo struck back with potato gnocchi in Round Four; the Kid countered with Kentucky burgoo. They traded blows through the next several rounds, the Champ scoring with Nesselrode pie, fettuccine Alfredo and poi, the Kid lashing back with jambalaya, shrimp creole and herring in horseradish sauce.

After the bell ending Round Eleven, the bout had to be held up momentarily because of a disturbance in the audience. Two men, thin as tapers and with beards like Spanish moss, had leaped into the ring waving posters that read REMEMBER BIAFRA. The Kid started up from his table and pinned one of them to the mat, while security guards nabbed the other. The Champ sat immobile on his stool, eyes tearing from the horseradish sauce, his fist clenched round the handle of the water pitcher. When the ring was cleared the bell rang for Round Twelve.

It was the Champ's round all the way: sweet potato pie with butterscotch syrup and pralines. For the first time the Kid let up—toward the end of the round he dropped his fork and took a mandatory eight count. But he came back strong in the thirteenth with a savage combination of Texas wieners and sauce diable. The Champ staggered, went down once, twice, flung himself at the water pitcher while the Kid gorged like a machine, wiener after wiener, blithely lapping the hot sauce from his fingers and knuckles with an epicurean relish. Then Angelo's head fell to the table, his huge whiskered jowl mired in a pool of béchamel and butter. The fans sprang to their feet, feinting left and right, snapping their jaws and yabbering for the kill. The Champ's eyes fluttered open, the ref counted over him.

It was then that it happened. His vision blurring, Angelo gazed out into the crowd and focused suddenly on the stooped and wizened figure of an old woman in a black bonnet. Decoud stood at her elbow. Angelo lifted his head. "Ma?" he said. "Eat, Angelo, eat!" she called, her voice a whisper in the apocalyptic thunder of the crowd. "Clean your plate!"

"Nine!" howled the referee, and suddenly the Champ came to life, lashing into the sauce diable like a crocodile. He bolted wieners, sucked at his fingers, licked the plate. Some say his hands moved so fast that they defied the eye, a mere blur, slapstick in double time. Then the bell rang for the final round and Angelo announced his dish: "Gruel!" he roared. The Kid protested. "What kind of dish is that?" he whined. "Gruel? Whoever heard of gruel in a championship bout?" But gruel it was. The Champ lifted the bowl to his lips, pasty ropes of congealed porridge trailing down his chest; the crowd cheered, the Kid toyed with his spoon—and then it was over.

The referee stepped in, helped Angelo from the stool and held his flaccid arm aloft. Angelo was plate-drunk, reeling. He looked out over the cheering mob, a welter of button heads like B in B mushrooms—or Swedish meatballs in a rich golden sauce. Then he gagged. "The winner," the ref was shouting, "and still champion, Angelo D.!"

(1977)

BLOODFALL

It started about three-thirty, a delicate tapping at the windows, the sound of rain.
No one noticed: the stereo was turned up full and Walt was thumping his bass
along with it, the TV was going, they were all stoned, passing wine and a glowing pipe, singing along with the records, playing Botticelli and Careers and Mo-
nopoly, crunching crackers. I noticed. In that brief scratching silence between
songs, I heard it—looked up at the window and saw the first red droplets
huddled there, more falling between them. Gesh and Scott and Isabelle were
watching TV with the sound off, digging the music, lighting cigarettes, tapping
fingers and feet, laughing. On the low table were cheese, oranges, wine, shiny
paperbacks, a hash pipe. Incense smoked from a pendant urn. The three dogs
sprawled on the carpet by the fireplace. Siamese cats curled on the mantel, the
bench, the chair. The red droplets quivered, were struck by other, larger drops
falling atop them, and began a meandering course down the windowpane. Alice
laughed from the kitchen. She and Amy were peeling vegetables, baking pies,
uncanning baby smoked oysters and sturgeon for hors d'oeuvres, sucking on
olive pits. The windows were streaked with red. The music was too loud. No one
noticed. It was another day.

When I opened the door to investigate, the three dogs sprang up and ran to
me, tails awag; they stopped at the door, sniffing. It was hissing down now, a
regular storm: it streamed red from the gutter over the door, splashing my pantleg. The front porch smelled like raw hamburger. My white pants were spotted
with red. The dogs inched out now, stretching their necks: they lapped at the red
puddle on the doorstep. Their heads and muzzles were soon slick with it. I
slammed the door on them and walked back into the living room. Gesh and

Scott were passing the pipe. On the TV screen were pictures of starving children: distended bellies, eyes as big as their bony heads, spiders' arms and spiders' legs: someone was laughing in the kitchen. "Hey!" I shouted. "Do you dig what's happening outside?" Nobody heard me. The windows were smeared with red: it fell harder. Gesh looked up to pass the pipe. "What happened to you?" he said. "Cut yourself?"

"No," I said. "It's raining blood."

Gesh was in the shower when the TV screen went blank. Earlier, when everybody had crowded around the open door, holding out their hands to it as it dripped down from the eaves, wowing and cursing and exclaiming, Gesh had pushed through and stepped out, down the stairs and out under the maple tree. His white pants, shirt and shoes turned pinkish, then a fresh wet red, the color of life. "It's fantastic out here!" he yelled. We held back. In a minute or two he came back up the steps, his face a mosaic mortared in blood, the clotted hair stuck to his forehead. He looked like the aftermath of an accident, or a casualty of war. "How do I look?" he said, licking the wet red from his lips. "Like the Masque of the Red Death or something? Huh?" Scott was taking pictures with his Nikkormat. The smell when Gesh stepped in reminded me of a trip I took with my mom and dad when I was in the third grade. An educational trip. Every weekend we took an educational trip. We went to the slaughterhouse. Gesh smelled like that when he came in. Amy made him take a shower with baby shampoo and peppermint soap. She laid out a fresh white shirt and pants for him, and his white slippers. Scott ran downstairs to the darkroom to develop his pictures. Basically he does black and whites of slum kids in rakish hats giving him the finger; old slum women, the fingers stewed to the bone; old slum men, fingering port pints in their pockets. These he enlarges and frames, and hangs about the house. One of them hangs in the corner over Alice's Reclino Love-Chair with the dyed rabbit-fur cover; another hangs in the dining room over my 125-gallon aquarium. The rabbit fur is dyed black.

Walt took a break for a minute to change records and adjust the treble on his amp. In the ringing silence that ensued, we realized that the TV was emitting a thin high-pitched whistle. There was no picture. "What the fuck?" said Isabelle. She jumped up, flipped through the channels. All gray, all emitting the same whistle. Isabelle's eyes were bleared. "Let's try the radio!" she said. It too: the same insidious whine. "The phone!" she shouted. The phone hummed softly in her ear, my ear, Walt's ear, Amy's ear. It was the same sort of hum you get from an empty conch shell. "It's dead," I said. We stood there mute, staring at the receiver suspended from its cord, clickless and ringless. We theorized:

Maybe it's a National Emergency—
Maybe it's D-day—

Maybe it's the Nuclear Holocaust—
Maybe it's Judgment Day—
Maybe it's the Rockets they're sending up—
But we all suspected the soundness of these extrapolations. Probably it was just some new form of pollution, and a few wires down in the storm. Gesh appeared in fresh white, smelling like a candy cane. He walked deliberately to the pipe, thumbed in a chunk of hash, and sucked the flame of a match through it. Isabelle, quickly sedated, picked out a couple of albums and Walt ducked under the embroidered shoulder strap of his bass—the blast of music sealed the room, stopped the ticking at the panes. Alice brought in the hors d'oeuvres, and a comforting smell of exotic dishes abubble in the kitchen. I sat, smoked, and ate.

In the morning I slipped early from the warmth of the nest (Alice's tender buttock, Gesh's hairy satyr's foot framed there beneath the sheets), wrapped my white robe over my white pajamas, stepped into my fluffy white slippers, and went downstairs, as I always do on Saturdays, to watch cartoons. My mind was a tabula rasa, wire-brushed with intoxicants; my dreams had been of cool colors, the green of the forest, the cerulean of the summer sky. In the living room, a pinkish light suffused the slats of the blinds. The window was like stained glass. In the early morning quiet, the red splashes drummed against it. I was stunned; and all alone there, at that early hour, frightened. Then I heard the scratching at the door: the dogs had been out all night. Without thinking, I opened the door and they rushed in, great living lumps of raw flesh, skinned carcasses come to life, slick with blood, their bellies bloated with it. "No, no, get down!" But they were already up on their hind legs, pawing affectionately at me, their fetid breath in my face. Their teeth were stained red, blood hung even in the sockets of their eyes. "Get down, goddamnit!" My robe, my pajamas, my fluffy white slippers were ruined: the blood crept through the white cotton like a stain in water. I kicked out at the dogs. They backed off and shook themselves—a fine bloodmist spotted the walls, the white rugs of the hallway, the potted plants. The dogs grunted, eased themselves down and licked their paws. Blood seeped from beneath them. I felt sick from the stink of it, and so upset with the mess that tears began to crowd my eyes—exasperated, hopeless tears. The hallway looked like a sacrificial altar, my arms like the gory High Priest's. I would wash and go back to bed, face life later.

In the bathroom I stepped carefully out of my clothes in an effort to avoid staining the bathmat. It was no use. Blood oozed from the fluffy red slippers. I wiped my hands and face on the lining of the robe, bundled everything together and stuffed it into the hamper. Seven electric toothbrushes, seven cups, and seven hotcombs hung on the rack over the sink. We kept the seven electric shavers, each in its own carrying case, stacked neatly in the cabinet. I stepped into the shower, the tap of blood against the bathroom window loud in my ears, and turned on hot, full force. Eyes pressed tight, face in the spray, I luxuriated in the warm pure rush of the water. I'd always taken a great deal of pleasure in showering and bathing, in being clean—it reminded me of my mom and the baths she used to give, sponging my crotch, kissing my wet little feet . . . but there was something wrong—that odor—good God, it was in the water supply! Horrified, I leaped from the shower. In the steamed-over mirror I was newborn, coated in blood and mucus, pulled hot from the womb. Diluted blood streamed down my body, puddled at my feet. I lifted the toilet seat and puked into the red bowl. Hung my head and puked: puked and cried, until Amy came down and found me there.

Gesh sat back in the stuffed chair. He wore his white robe with the gold monogram, and his slippers. The bloodfall hammered on. "We've got to look at the precedents," he said. There was a pie and a soufflé in the oven. We were in the living room, sipping apricot nectar, munching buns. Alice, in the entrance hall with detergent and scrub brush, was muttering like Lady Macbeth over the carpet stains. "What precedents?" I asked.

"Like all of that shit that went down in Egypt about thirty-five hundred years ago."

Walt was tuning his bass: *dzhzhzhzhtt. dzhzhzhzhtt.* He picked a rumbling note or two and looked up. "You're thinking of frogs, brother. Millions of frogs. Frogs under the bed, frogs in the flour, frogs in your shoes, clammy frogs' flippers slapping at your ass when you take a shit."

"No, no—there was something about blood too, wasn't there?"

"Yeah," said Walt. "Christ turned it into water. Or was it wine?"

"You know what happened in Egypt?! You want to know?" My voice cracked. I was getting hysterical. A cat jumped into my lap. I tossed it over my shoulder. Everything in the room had a red cast, like when you put on those red cellophane glasses as a kid, to read 3D comic books.

Gesh was staring at me: "So what happened?"

"Never mind," I said.

Amy howled from the basement. "Hey you guys, guess what? The stuff is ankle-deep down here and it's ruining everything. Our croquet set, our camping equipment, our dollhouse!" The announcement depressed us all, even Gesh. "Let's blow a bowl of hash and forget about it," he suggested.

"Anyhow," said Walt, "it'll be good for the trees." And he started a bass riff with a deep throbbing note—the hum of it hung in the air even after the lights went out and the rest of his run had attenuated to a thin metallic whisper. "Hey!" he said. From the kitchen: "Oh shit!" A moment later, Isabelle came in wringing her hands. "Well. The breakfast's ruined. We've got a half-baked pie and a flat soufflé sitting in the oven. And a raw-eggy blob purporting to be eggnog in the blender."

There was a strange cast to the room now. Not the gloom-gray of a drizzly day, but a deep burgundy, like a bottle of wine.

"Well? What am I going to do with it all—give it to the dogs?"

The dogs glanced up briefly. Their hair was matted and brown with dried blood. They were not hungry.

Scott whined: "I'm hungry."

I was scared. I'd been scared all along, scared from the moment I'd noticed the first drops on the window. I looked at Gesh, our leader: he was grinning in that lurid light, sucking reflectively on the pipe. "Don't hassle it, Iz," he said. "Mark and me'll pop down to the deli and get some sandwiches."

"I don't want to go out there—I'll lose my lunch."

"Come on, don't be such a candy ass. Besides, it'll give us a chance to talk to somebody, find out what's going on." He stood up. "Come on, Mark, get your boots."

Outside was incredible. Red sky, red trees, red horizon: the whole world, from the fence to the field to the mountains across the river, looked like the inside of some colossal organ. I felt like an undigested lump of food—Jonah in the belly of the whale. There was the stench of rotting meat. The bloodfall streamed down hard as hail. Under the eaves, on the porch, we were fooling with our rain hats, trying to get up the nerve to run for the car. Gesh too, I could see, was upset. Yesterday it had been a freak, today a plague. "Well, what do you think, bro—make a run for it?" he said.

We ran—down the steps and into the mud. I slipped and fell, while Gesh hustled off through the blinding downpour. It was deeper now, lying about the low spots in nasty red-black puddles. I could feel it seeping in, trickling down my leg, inside the boot: warm, sticky, almost hot. The smell of putrefaction nauseated me. I choked back the apricot nectar and biscuits, struggled up, and ran for the car. When I got there Gesh was standing beside the door, blooddrops thrashing about him. "What about the seats?" he said. "If we stain 'em with this shit, it'll never come off."

"Fuck it. Let's just get out of this—"

"I mean I got a lot of scratch invested in this here BMW, bro—"

The wind-whipped blood flailed our yellow slickers, dripped from the flapping brims of our silly yellow rain hats. We both climbed in. The engine started smooth, like a vacuum cleaner; the wipers clapped to and fro; the windshield smeared. "Let's drive to the desert . . . the Arizona desert, and get away from this . . . shit," I said. My voice was weak. I felt ill. Automatically I reached for the window. "Hey—what the fuck you doing?" Gesh said. It streamed down the inside of the glass, bubbled over the upholstered door, puddled in the ashtray on the armrest. I rolled the window up. "I feel sick," I said. "Well for christsake, puke outside." I didn't. The thought of hanging my head out in that insane unnatural downpour brought it up right there. In the sealed compartment the bouquet of the vomit and the stink of the mud-blood on our shoes was insupportable. I retched again: then dry-retched. "Oh shit," said Gesh.

"I'm going back in," I said, the edge of a whimper in my voice.

Five minutes later, Gesh returned, cursing. Scott was on his way out the door, three cameras strung round his neck, to get some color slides of the dripping trees. "What's the matter," he said. "You back already?"

"Couldn't see a fucking thing. I got down the end of the drive and smacked into the stone wall. The wipers are totally useless—they just smear the crap all over the windshield. It's like looking through a finger painting."

"So what happened to the car?"

"It's not too bad—I was only going about two miles an hour."

Alice emerged from the kitchen, a pair of lighted candles in her hand, egg-walking to avoid spilling the hot wax. "Gesh! Take your slicker off—you're dripping that shit all over the floor. . . . Couldn't make it, huh?"

"No."

"What are we going to do for food?" she asked.

"Scoop it up!" Walt shouted from the living room. "Scoop it up and pour it into balloons. Make blood pudding."

I was sitting in a chair, weak, stinking, blood crusting the lines of my hands. "I'm fed up with it," I said. "I'm going up to lie down."

"Good idea," said Gesh. "Think I'll join you."

"Me too," said Alice. "Can't do anything here—can't even read or listen to music."

"Yeah," said Walt. "Good idea. Save me a pillow."

"Me too," said Amy.

Scott stepped from beneath the cameras, strung them across the back of my chair. He yawned. Isabelle said it would be better if we all went to bed. She expressed a hope that after a long nap things would somehow come to their senses.

I woke from fevered dreams (a tropical forest: me in jodhpurs and pith helmet—queasy-faced—sharing a draft of warm cow's blood and milk with tree-tall Masai warriors) to a rubicund dimness, and the gentle breathing of the rest of the crew. They loomed, a humpbacked mound in the bed beside me. My ears were keen. Still it beat on the roof, sloshed in the gutters. Downstairs, somewhere, I heard the sound of running water, the easy soughing gurgle of a mountain stream. I sat up. Were we leaking? I slipped into Amy's slippers, lit a candle, crept apprehensively down the stairs. I searched the hallway, living room, dining room, kitchen, bathroom: nothing. A cat began wailing somewhere. The basement! The cat bolted out when I opened the door, peered down the dark shaft of the stairway. The flood was up nearly to the fifth step, almost four feet deep, I guessed, and more churning audibly in. The stench was stifling. I slammed the door. For the

first time I thought of the dike: why 'sblood! if the dike went—it must be straining at its foundations this very minute! I envisioned us out there, heroically
stacking sandbags, the wind in our faces, whipping our hair back, the rising level
of the flood registered in our stoic eyes—then I thought of the tepid plasma
seething in my nose, my mouth, my eyes, and felt ill.

Gesh came down the stairs, scratching himself sleepily. "How's it?" he said. I
advised him to take a look at the cellar. He did. "Holy shit! We've got to do
something—start making barricades, strapping floatables together, evacuating
women and children—and dogs!" He paused. "I'm starving," he said. "Let's go
see what we got left, bro." From the kitchen I could hear him taking inventory:
"Two six-packs of warm Coke; a jar of Skippy peanut butter, crunchy—no bread;
ten cans of stewed tomatoes; half a box of granola; a quart of brown rice; one
tin of baby smoked oysters. Not a fuck of a lot. Hey Mark, join me in a late-
afternoon snack?"

"No thanks. I'm not hungry."

We sat around the darkened living room that night, a single candle guttering, the
sound of bloodfall ticking at the windows, the hiss of rapids rushing against the
stone walls of the house, an insidious sloshing in the basement. Seepage had begun at the front door, and Isabelle had dumped a fifty-pound bag of kitty litter
there in an attempt to absorb the moisture. Atop that was a restraining dike of
other absorbent materials: boxes of cake mix, back issues of *Cosmopolitan*, electric blankets, Italian dictionaries, throw pillows, three dogs, a box of Tampax. A
similar barricade protected the basement door. When Gesh had last opened the
window to look, the red current eddying against the house had reached almost to
the windowsill. We were deeply concerned, hungry, bored.

"I'm bored," said Amy.

"I'm hungry," whined Scott. "And I'm sick of Coke. I want a hot cup of
Mu tea."

"It stinks in here," carped Isabelle. "Reminds me of when I was fifteen, working in the meat department at the A & P."

"My teeth are gritty," Alice said. "Wish the water and the damned toothbrushes would work."

Blood began to drip from the windowsill in the far corner of the room. It
puddled atop the thirty-six-inch Fisher speaker in the corner. One of the cats began to lap at it.

Walt paced the room, a man dislocated. Deprived of his bass, he was empty,
devoid of spirit, devoid of personality. He was incapable now of contributing to
our meaningful dialogue on the situation. Gesh, however, tried to amuse us, take
our minds off it. He said it was just a simple case of old mother earth menstruat-
ing, and that by tomorrow, the last day of the moon's cycle, it would no doubt
stop. He passed around a fifth of Châteauneuf and a thin joint. The pool beneath

the door began to spread across the floor, creeping, growing, fanning out to where we sat in a small circle, the candlelight catching the blood in our flared nostrils. Shocked silent, we watched its inexorable approach as it glided out from the barricade in fingerlike projections, seeking the lowest point. The lowest point, it appeared, was directly beneath the Naugahyde pillow upon which my buttocks rested. Slowly, methodically, the bulbous finger of blood stretched toward me, pointed at me. When it was about a foot away, I stood. "I'm going to bed," I said. "I'm taking two Tuinals. Try not to wake me."

It was morning when I woke. Gesh sat in a chair beside the bed, smoking a cigarette. The others slept. "It stopped," he said. He was right: the only sound was a sporadic drip-drip beyond the windows, a poststorm runoff. The celestial phlebotomy had ceased. "Good," was all I could manage. But I was elated, overjoyed, secure again! Life returned to normal!

"Hey—let's slip down to the deli and get some sandwiches and doughnuts and coffee and shit, sneak back, and surprise the rest of the crew," Gesh said.

Curiosity stirred me, and hunger too. But my stomach curdled at the thought of the gore and the stink, the yard like a deserted battlefield. I stared down at my pajama sleeve. Amy's sleeping wrist lay across mine. I studied the delicate contrast of her white wrist and the little pink and brown figures of cowboys on my pajamas. "Well? What do you say?" asked Gesh. I said I guessed so. We pulled on our corduroys, our white rubber boots, our mohair sweaters.

Downstairs the blood had begun to clot. In the hallway it was still sticky in places, but for the most part crusted dry. Outside a massive fibrinogenification was taking place under a dirt-brown sky. Scabs like thin coats of ice were forming over the deeper puddles; the mud was crusting underfoot: fresh blood ran off in streams and drainage ditches; the trees drooled clots of it in the hot breeze. "Wow! Dig that sky, bro—" Gesh said. "Brown as a turd."

"Yeah," I said, "it's weird. But thank christ it stopped bleeding."

Gesh started the car while I broke the scab-crust from the windshield; it flaked, and crumbled in dusty grains. I climbed in, laid some newspaper over the day-old vomit on the floor, steeled myself against the stench. Gesh accelerated in an attempt to back out from the wall: I could hear the wheels spinning. I poked my head out. We were stuck up to the frame in mud and gore. "Fuck it," Gesh said. "We'll take Scott's car." We started up the drive toward the other car. It was then that the first pasty lumps of it began to slap down sporadically; we reached the shelter of the porch just as it began to thunder down, heavy, feculent, and wet.

Upstairs we carefully folded our sweaters, pulled on our white pajamas, and sought out the warm spots in the huddled sleeping mass of us.

(1972)

RUPERT BEERSLEY AND THE BEGGAR MASTER OF SIVANI-HOOTA

It was on a dark, lowering day during one of the interstices of the monsoon that His Royal Highness Yadavindra Singh, nawab of the remote Deccan state of Sivani-Hoota, began to miss his children. That is, the children began to turn up missing, and to an alarming degree. It began with little Gopal, who had been born with a mottled, pale birthmark in the shape of a half moon under the crease of his left buttock. Miss Elspeth Compton-Divot, the children's English governess, whose responsibility it was to instruct her wards in the dead language and living literature of Greece and to keep watch over them as a shepherd keeps watch over his flock (flock, indeed—there were twenty-five sibling Singhs under her care originally), was the first to discover little Gopal's absence. She bowed her way into the nawab's reception room immediately after lessons on that fateful afternoon, the sky so striped with cloud it might have been flayed, to find the nawab and his wife, the third begum, in attendance on several prominent local figures, including Mr. Bagwas the rubber-goods proprietor and Mr. Patel the grain merchant. "Most High, Puissant, Royal and Wise Hegemon Whose Duty It Is to Bring the Word of God and the Will of Just Government to the Peoples of Sivani-Hoota and Environs," she began, "I come before you on a matter of gravest import."

The nawab, a man in late middle age who had attended Oxford in the days of Pater and was given to ejaculations like "What ho!" and *"L'art pour l'art!"* told her to stuff the formality and come to the point.

"It's your third youngest, sir—little Gopal."

"Yes?"

"He seems to have disappeared."

The nawab shifted his bulk uneasily in his chair—for he was a big man, fat-tened on ghee, sweet cream, and chapattis slathered with orange-blossom honey—glanced at his begum and then expelled a great exasperated puff of air. "What a damnable nuisance," he said. "I don't doubt the little beggar's up to some mischief, hiding himself in the servants' pantry or some such rot. Which one did you say it was?"

"Little Gopal, sir."

"Gopal?"

It was then that the begum spoke rapidly to her husband in Tamil and he began almost simultaneously to nod his head, muttering, "Yes, yes, a good boy that. A pity, a real pity."

The governess went on to explain the circumstances of the boy's disappearance—the testimony of the night nurse who'd put him to bed, his eldest-brother-but-six's assertion that they'd played together at cribbage before falling off to sleep, her own discovery of little Gopal's absence early that day, when she commenced morning lessons by comparing her seating chart with the nearly identical moon-shaped grinning brown faces of the nawab's brood.

Mr. Bagwas, who had been silently pulling at a clay pipe through all of this, abruptly pronounced a single word: "Leopards."

But it was not leopards. Though the stealthy cats commonly carried off six or seven of the village's children a night, the occasional toothless grandmother, and innumerable goats, dogs, cows, fowl, royal turtles, and even the ornamental koi that graced the nawab's ponds, they were absolved of suspicion in the present case. After Abha, aged seven, and then the eleven-year-old Shanker vanished on successive nights, the nawab, becoming concerned, called in Mr. Hugh Tureen, game hunter, to put out baits and exterminate the spotted fiends. Though in the course of the ensuing week Mr. Tureen shot some seventy-three leopards, sixteen tigers, twelve wolves, and several hundred skunks, mongeese, badgers, and the like, the nawab continued to lose children. Santha, aged nine and with the mark of the dung beetle on the arches of both feet, vanished under the noses of three night nurses and half a dozen watchmen specially employed to stand guard over the nursery. This time, however, there was a clue. Bhupinder, aged six, claimed to have seen a mysterious shrouded figure hanging over his sister's bed, a figure rather like that of an ape on whom a tent has collapsed. Two days later, when the harsh Indian sun poked like a lance into the muslin-hung sanctuary of the children's quarters, Bhupinder's bed was empty.

The nawab and his begum, who two and a half weeks earlier had been rich in children, now had but twenty. They were distraught. Helpless. At their wits' end. Clearly, this was a case for Rupert Beersley.

We left Calcutta in a downpour, Beersley and I, huddled in our mackintoshes like a pair of dacoits. The train was three hours late, the tea was wretched, and the steward served up an unpalatable mess of curried rice that Beersley, in a fit of pique, overturned on the floor. Out of necessity—Beersley's summons had curtailed my supper at the club—I ate my own portion and took a cup of native beer with it. "Really," Beersley said, the flanges of his extraordinary nostrils drawn up in disgust, "how can you eat that slop?"

It was a sore point between us, the question of native food, going all the way back to our first meeting at Cawnpore some twenty years back, when he was a freshly commissioned young leftenant in the Eleventh Light Dragoons, India Corps, and I a seasoned sergeant-major. "I'll admit I've had better, old boy," I said, "but one must adapt oneself to one's circumstances."

Beersley waved his hand in a gesture of dismissal and quoted sourly from his favorite poem—indeed, the only poem from which he ever quoted—Keats's "Lamia": " 'Not three score old, yet of sciential brain / To unperplex bliss from its neighbor pain.' "

An electric-green fly had settled itself on a congealed lamp of rice that lay on the table before us. I shrugged and lifted the fork to my mouth.

We arrived at the Sivani-Hoota station in the same downpour transposed a thousand miles, and were met by the nawab's silver-plated Rolls, into the interior of which we ducked, wet as waterfowl, while the lackey stowed away our baggage. The road out to the palace was black as the caverns of hell and strewn with enough potholes to take the teeth out of one's head. Rain crashed down on the roof as if it would cave it in, beasts roared from the wayside, and various creatures of the night slunk, crept, and darted before the headlights as if rehearsing for some weird menagerie. Nearly an hour after leaving the station, we began to discern signs of civilization along the dark roadway. First a number of thatch huts began to flash by the smeared windows, then the more substantial stone structures that indicated the approach to the palace, and finally the white marble turrets and crenellated battlements of the palace itself.

As we hurried into the entrance hall, dripping like jellyfish, the nawab, who had lost two more children in the interval between his summons and our arrival, came out to meet us, a distraught begum at his side. Servants sprang up like mushrooms after a rain, turbaned Sikhs with appropriately somber faces, houseboys in white, ladies-in-waiting with great dark staring eyes. "Mr. Beersley, I presume," the nawab said, halting five paces from us and darting his eyes distractedly between Rupert's puggree helmet and my plaid tam-o'-shanter.

"The same," answered Beersley, bowing curtly from the waist and stepping forward to seize the nawab's hand. "Pleased, I'm sure," he said, and then, before pausing either to introduce me or to pay his respects to the begum, he pointed to the wild-haired sadhu seated in the corner and praying over the yellowish flame of a dung fire. "And what precisely is the meaning of this?" he demanded.

I should say at this juncture that Beersley, though undeniably brilliant, tended also to be somewhat mercurial, and I could see that something had set him off. Perhaps it was the beastly weather or the long and poorly accommodated trip, or perhaps he was feeling the strain of overwork, called out on this case as he was so soon after the rigorous mental exercise he'd put into the baffling case of the Cornucopia Killer of Cooch Behar. Whatever it was, I saw to my embarrassment that he was in one of his dark India- and Indian-hating moods, in which he is as likely to refer to a Sikh as a "diaper head" as he is to answer· "Hello" on picking up the phone receiver.

"Beg pardon?" the nawab said, looking puzzled.

"This fellow over here in the corner, this muttering half-naked fakir—what precisely is his function?" Ignoring the shocked looks and dropped jaws of his auditors, Beersley rushed on, as if he were debating in a tavern. "What I mean to say, sir, is this: how can you expect me to take on a case of this nature when I find my very sensibilities affronted by this . . . this pandering to superstition and all the damnable mumbo jumbo that goes with it?"

The beards of the Sikhs bristled, their eyes flared. The nawab, to his credit, made an effort to control himself, and, with his welcoming smile reduced to a tight grim compression of the lips, he explained that the holy man in the corner was engaged in the Vedic rite of the sacred fire, energizer and destroyer, one of the three sacred elements of the Hindu trinity. Twice a day, he would also drink of the *pancha garia,* composed in equal parts of the five gifts of the sacred cow: milk, curds, ghee, urine, and dung. The nawab had felt that the performance of these sacred rites might help cleanse and purify his house against the plague that had assailed it.

Beersley listened to all this with his lip curled in a sneer, then muttered "Humbug" under his breath. The room was silent. I shuffled my feet uneasily. The begum fastened me with the sort of look reserved for the deviates one encounters in the Bois de Boulogne, and the nawab's expression arranged itself in an unmistakable scowl.

" 'Do not all charms fly / At the mere touch of cold philosophy?' " Beersley said, and then turned abruptly on his heel and strode off in the direction the lackey had taken with our baggage.

In the morning, Beersley (who had refused the previous evening to attend the dinner the nawab had arranged in his honor, complaining of fatigue and wishing only that a bit of yogurt and a bowl of opium be sent up to his room) assembled all the principals outside the heavy mahogany door to the nawab's library. The eighteen remaining children were queued up to be interviewed separately, the nawab and begum were grilled in my presence as if they were pickpockets apprehended on the docks at Leeds, the night nurses, watchmen, chauffeurs, Sikhs, gardeners, cooks, and bottle washers were subject to a battery of questions on subjects ranging from their sexual habits, through recurring dreams and feelings about their mothers, to their recollections of Edward's coronation and their perceptions as to the proper use of the nine iron. Finally, toward the end of the day, as the air rose from the gutters in a streaming miasma and the punkah wallah fell asleep over his task, Miss Compton-Divot was ushered into the room.

Immediately a change came over Beersley. Where he'd been officious, domineering, as devious, threatening, and assured as one of the czar's secret police, he now flushed to his very ears, groped after his words, and seemed confused. I'd never seen anything like it. Beersley was known for his composure, his stoicism, his relentless pursuit of the evidence under even the most distracting circumstances. Even during the bloody and harrowing case of the Tiger's Paw (in which Beersley ultimately deduced that the killer was dispatching his victims with the detached and taxidermically preserved paw of the rare golden tiger of Hyderabad), while the victims howled their death agony from the courtyard and whole families ran about in terror and confusion, he never flinched from his strenuous examination of the chief suspects. And now, here he was, in the presence of a comely russet-haired lass from Hertfordshire, as tongue-tied as a schoolboy.

"Miss Compton-Divot," I said, to break the awkward silence. "May I present the celebrated Mr. Rupert Beersley?"

She curtsied and smiled like a plate of buttered scones.

"And may I take this opportunity to introduce myself as well?" I continued, taking her hand. "Sergeant-Major Plantagenet Randolph, retired, at your service. Please have a seat."

I waited for Beersley to begin, but he said nothing, merely sitting there and fixing the governess with a vacuous, slack-jawed gaze. She blushed prettily and looked down to smooth her dress and arrange her petticoats. After an interval, Beersley murmured, " 'And soon his eyes had drunk her beauty up, / Leaving no drop in the bewildering cup, / And still the cup was full.' "

And that was it; he had no more to say. I prompted him, but he wouldn't be moved. Miss Compton-Divot, feeling, I think, the meaning of his stare, began to titter and twist the fabric of the dress in her hands. Finally, heaving an exhausted sigh and thinking ahead to dinner and the nawab's fine Lisbon port, which I'd been pleased to sample the previous evening, I showed her out of the room.

That night, little Govind, aged three and a half, disappeared without a trace.

I found Beersley in the garden the following morning, bending close over a spray of blood-red orchids. Had he found something? I hurried up to him, certain he'd uncovered the minute but crucial bit of evidence from which the entire case would unravel like a skein of yarn, as when he'd determined the identity of the guilty party in the Srinagar Strangler case from a single strand of hair found among countless thousands of others in a barber's refuse bin. Or when an improperly canceled stamp led him to the Benares Blackmailer. Or when half a gram's worth of flaked skin painstakingly sifted from the faded homespun loin-

cloth of a murdered *harijan* put him on the trail of the Leaping Leper of Manga-
lore. "Beersley," I spurted in a barely suppressed yelp of excitement, "are you on
to something, old boy?"

I was in for a shock. When he turned to me, I saw that the lucid reptilian
sheen of his eyes had been replaced by a dull glaze: I might have been staring
into the face of some old duffer in St. James's Park rather than that of the most
brilliant detective in all of Anglo-India. He merely lifted the corners of his mouth
in a vapid smile and then turned back to the orchids, snuffing them with his
great glorious nostrils like a cow up to his hocks in clover. It was the sun, I was
sure of it. Or a touch of the malaria he'd picked up in Burma in 'ought-two.

"Rupert!" I snapped. "Come out of it, old boy!" And then—rather roughly,
I must admit—I led him to a bench in the shade of a banyan tree. The sun
slammed through the leaves like a mallet. From the near distance came the an-
guished stentorian cries of the nawab's prize pachyderms calling out for water.
"Beersley," I said, turning him toward me, "is it the fever? Can I get you a glass
of water?"

His eyes remained fixed on a point over my left shoulder, his lips barely
moved. " 'Some demon's mistress,' " he murmured, " 'or the demon's self.' "

"Talk sense!" I shouted, becoming ever more alarmed and annoyed. Here
we'd been in Sivani-Hoota for some two days and we'd advanced not a step in
solving the case, while children continued to disappear under our very noses. I
was about to remonstrate further when I noted the clay pipe protruding from his
breast pocket—and then the unmistakable odor of incinerated opium. It all became clear in that instant: he'd been up through the night, numbing his perceptions with bowl after bowl of the narcotizing drug. Something had disturbed him
deeply, there was no doubt about it.

I led him straightaway to his suite of rooms in the palace's east end and called
for quinine water and hot tea. For hours, through the long, dreadful, heat-
prostrated afternoon, I walked him up and down the floor, forcing the blood to
wash through his veins, clear his perceptions, and resharpen his wits. By teatime
he was able to sit back in an easy chair, cross his legs in the characteristic brisk
manner, and unburden himself. "It's the governess," he croaked, "that damnable
little temptress, that hussy: she's bewitched me."

I was thunderstruck. He might as easily have confessed that he was a homo-
sexual or the Prince of Wales in disguise. "You don't mean to say that some . . .
some trifling sexual dalliance is going to come between Rupert Beersley and the
pursuit of a criminal case?" My color was high, I'm sure, and my voice hot with
outrage.

"No, no, no—you don't understand," he said, fixing me as of old with that
keen insolent gaze. "Think back, Planty," he said, lifting the teacup to his lips.
"Don't you remember the state I was in when I first came to you?"

Could I ever forget? Twenty-two or -three, straight as a ramrod, thin as a
whippet, the pointed nose and outsized ears accentuated by a face wasted with

rigor, he'd been so silent those first months he might as well have entered the Carthusian monastery in Grenoble as the India Corps. There'd been something eating at him then, some deep canker of the soul or heart that had driven him into exile on the subcontinent he so detested. Later, much later, he'd told me. It had been a woman, daughter of a Hertford squire: on the eve of their wedding she'd thrown him over for another man. "Yes," I said, "of course I remember."

He uncoiled himself from the chair, set down the teacup, and strode to the window. Below, on the polo maidan, the nawab and half a dozen of his retainers glided to and fro on pampered Arabians while the westering sun fell into the grip of a band of monsoon clouds. Beersley gazed out on the scene for half a moment, then turned to me with an emotion twenty years dead quivering in those magnificent nostrils. "Elspeth," he said, his voice catching. "She's her daughter."

That evening the nawab threw a sumptuous entertainment. There was music, dancing, a display of moving lights. Turbaned Sikhs poured French wines, jugglers juggled, the begum beamed, and platter after platter of fine, toothsome morsels was set before us. I'd convinced Beersley to overcome his antipathy to native culture and accept the invitation, as a means both of drawing him out of his funk and of placating the nawab. As we were making our way into the banquet room, however, Beersley had suddenly stopped short and seized my arm. Mr. Bagwas and Mr. Patel were following close on our heels and nearly collided with us, so abruptly did we stop; Beersley waited for them to pass, then indicated a marble bench in the courtyard to our left. When we were alone he asked if I'd seen Miss Compton-Divot as we'd crossed the foyer on our way in.

"Why, yes," I said. She'd been dressed in native costume—a saffron-colored sari and hemp sandals—and had pulled the ginger hair back from her forehead in the way of the Brahman women.

"Did you notice anything peculiar?"

"No, not a bit," I said. "A charming girl really, nothing more."

"Tell me," he demanded, the old cutting edge restored to his voice, "if you didn't see her bent over the fakir for a moment—just the hair of a moment—as we stepped through the door."

"Well, yes, yes, old boy, I suppose I did. What of it?"

"Nothing, perhaps. But—"

At that moment we were interrupted by Mr. Bagwas, who stood grinning before us. "Most reverend gentlemen," he said, drawing back his lips in an idiotic grin that showed off the reddened stumps of teeth ravaged over the years by the filthy habit of betel-nut chewing, "the nawab awaits."

We were ushered to the nawab's table and given the place of honor beside the nawab and his begum, several of the older children, Messrs. Bagwas and Patel, the nawab's two former wives, six of his current concubines, and the keeper of the sacred monkeys. Miss Compton-Divot, I quickly ascertained, was not present. I thought it odd, but soon forgot all about her, as we applauded the jugglers, acrobats, musicians, temple dancers, and trained bears until the night began to grow old. It was then that the nawab rose heavily to his feet, waved his hands for silence, and haw-hawed a bit before making a brief speech. "Even in the darkest hour shines a light," he said, the customary fat pout of his lips giving way to a wistful grin. "What I mean to say, damn it, is that the begum here is pregnant, gravid, heavy with child, that even when we find ourselves swallowed up in grief over our lost lambs we discover that there is a bun in the oven after all."

Beersley gave a snort of withering contempt and was about, I'm sure, to expatiate on the fatuity of the native mind and its lack of proportion and balance— not to mention rigor, discipline, and concentration—when the whole party was thrown into an uproar by a sudden ululating shriek emanating from the direction of the nursery. My companion was up like a hound and out the door before anyone else in the room could so much as set down a water glass. Though I tend to stoutness myself and am rather shorter of breath than I was in my military days, I was nevertheless the fourth or fifth man out the doorway, down the corridor, across the courtyard, and up the jade steps to the children's nursery.

When I got there, heaving for breath and with the sweat standing out on my forehead, I found Beersley kneeling over the prostrate form of one of the watchmen, from between whose scapulae protruded the hilt of a cheap ten-penny nail file. The children had retreated screaming to the far end of the dormitory, where they clutched one another's nightgowns in terror. "Poison," Beersley said with a profound disgust at the crudity of the killer's method as he slipped the nail file from its fatal groove. A single sniff of its bloody, sharpened point bore him out. He carefully wrapped the thing in his handkerchief, stowed it away in his breast pocket, and then leaped to his feet. "The children!" he cried. "Quickly now, line them up and count them!"

The nawab stood bewildered in the doorway; the begum went pale and fell to her knees while her retainers wrung their hands in distress and the children shuffled about confusedly, their faces tear-stained, their nightgowns a collision of sad airy clouds. And then all at once Miss Compton-Divot appeared, striding the length of the room to gather up two of her smaller wards in her lovely arms. "One," she began, "two, three, four . . ." It wasn't until several hours later that we understood what had happened. The murder in the dormitory had been a ruse. A diversion. Vallabhbhi Shiva, aged sixteen, a plump, oleaginous boy who'd sat directly across from Beersley and me during the entertainment, was nowhere to be found.

"A concentrate of the venom of the banded krait," Beersley said, holding a test tube up to the light. It was early, not yet 9:00 A.M., and the room reeked of opium fumes. "Nasty stuff, Planty—works on the central nervous system. I calculate there was enough of it smeared on the nether end of that nail file to dispatch half the unwashables in Delhi and give the nawab's prize pachyderms the runs for a week."

I fell into an armchair draped with one of my companion's Oriental dressing gowns. "Monstrous," was all I could say.

Beersley's eyes were lidded with the weight of the opium. His speech was slow; and yet even that powerful soporific couldn't suppress the excitement in his voice. "Don't you see, old boy—she's solved the case for us."

"Who?"

"The Lamia. It's a little lesson in appearance and reality. Serpent's venom indeed, the little vixen." And then he was quoting: " 'She was a gordian shape of dazzling hue, / Vermilion-spotted, golden, green, and blue . . .' Don't you see?"

"No, Beersley," I said, rising to my feet rather angrily and crossing the room to where the clay pipe lay on the dressing table, "no, I'm afraid I don't."

"It's the motive that puzzles me," he said, musing over the vial in his hand as I snatched the clay pipe from the table and stoutly snapped it in two. He barely noticed. All at once he was holding the nail file up before my face, cradling it carefully in its linen nest. "Do you have any idea where this was manufactured, old boy?"

I'd been about to turn on him and tell him he was off his head, about to curse his narcotizing, his *non sequiturs,* and the incessant bloody poetry-quoting that had me at my wits' end, but he caught me up short. "What?"

"The nail file, old fellow."

"Well, er, no. I hadn't really thought much about it."

He closed his eyes for a moment, exposing the peculiar deep-violet coloration of his eyelids. "Badham and Son, Manufacturers," he said in a monotone, as if he were reading an advertisement. "Implements for Manicure and Pedicure, Number 17, Parsonage Lane"—and here he paused to flash open his eyes so that I felt them seize me like a pair of pincers—"Hertford."

Again I was thunderstruck. "But you don't mean to say that . . . that you suspect—?"

My conjecture was cut short by a sudden but deferential rap at the door. *"Entrez,"* Beersley called, the sneer he cultivated for conducting interrogations or dealing with natives and underlings scalloping his upper lip. The door swung to and a pair of shrunken little houseboys bowed into the room with our breakfast. Beersley, characteristically indifferent to the native distaste for preparing or consuming meat, had ordered kidneys, rashers, eggs, and toast with a pot of tea, jam, and catsup. He moved forward to the table, allowed himself to be seated, and then called rather sharply to the retreating form of the first servant. "You there," he said, pushing his plate away. The servant wheeled round as if he'd been shot, exchanged a stricken look with his compatriot stationed behind the table, and bowed low. "I want the nawab's food taster up here *tout de suite*— within the minute. Understand?"

"What is it, Beersley?" I said, inspecting the plate. "Looks all right to me." But he would say nothing until the food taster arrived.

From beyond the windows came the fiendish caterwauling and great terrible belly roars of the nawab's caged tigers as they impatiently awaited their breakfast. I stared down at the bloodied nail file a moment and then at the glistening china plate with its bulbous kidneys, lean red rashers, and golden eggs. When I looked up the food taster was standing in the doorway. He was a young man, worn about the eyes and thin as a beggar from the pressures and uncertainties of his job. He bowed his way nervously into the room and said in a tremulous voice, "You called for me, sahib?"

Beersley merely indicated the plate. "A bit of this kidney here," he said.

The man edged forward, clumsily hacked off a portion of the suspect kidney, and, closing his eyes, popped it into his mouth, chewed perfunctorily, and swallowed. As his Adam's apple bobbed on the recoil, he opened his eyes and smiled like a man who's passed a harrowing ordeal. But then, alarmingly, the corners of his mouth began to drop and his limbs to tremble. Within ten seconds he was clutching his stomach, and within the minute he was stretched out prone on the floor, dead as a pharoah.

Things had taken a nasty turn. That evening, as Beersley interrogated the kitchen staff with a ferocity and doggedness unusual even for him, I found myself sniffing suspiciously at my bottle of porter, and though my stomach protested vigorously, I refused even to glance at the platter of *jalebis* the nawab's personal chef had set before me. Beersley was livid. He raged, threatened, cajoled. The two houseboys who had brought the fatal kidney were so shaken that they confessed to all manner of peccancies, including the furtive eating of meat on the part of the one, and an addiction to micturating in the nawab's soup on the part of the other—and yet clearly they were innocent of any complicity in the matter of the kidney. It was nearly midnight when Beersley dismissed the last of the kitchen servants—the third chutney spicer's assistant—and turned to me with a face drawn with fatigue. "Planty," he said, "I shall have your kidnapper for you by tea tomorrow."

He was at it all night. I woke twice—at half past three and close on to six— and saw the light burning in his window across the courtyard. He was indefatigable when he was on the scent, and as I plumped the pillows and drifted off, I knew he would prove true to his word. Unfortunately, in the interval the nawab lost two more children.

The whole house was in a state of agitation the following afternoon when Beersley summoned the nawab and his begum, Messrs. Patel and Bagwas, Hugh

Tureen, Miss Compton-Divot, and several other members of the household staff
to "an enlightenment session" in the nawab's library. Miss Compton-Divot, wearing a conventional English gown with bustle, sash, and uplifted bosom, stepped
shyly into the room, like a fawn emerging from the bracken to cross the public
highway. This was the first glimpse Beersley had allowed himself of her since the
night of the entertainment and its chilling aftermath, and I saw him turn sharply
away as she entered. Hugh Tureen, the game hunter, strode confidently across
the room while Mr. Patel and Mr. Bagwas huddled together in a corner over delicate little demitasses of tea and chatted village gossip. In contrast, the nawab
seemed upset, angry even. He marched into the room, a little brown butterball of
a man, followed at a distance by his wife, and confronted Beersley before the latter could utter a word. "I am at the end of my stamina and patience," he sputtered. "It's been nearly a week since you've arrived and the criminals are still at
it. Last night it was the twins, Indira and er"—here he conferred in a brief whisper with his wife—"Indira and Sushila. Who will it be tonight?"

Outside, the monsoon recommenced with a sudden crashing fall of rain that
smeared the windows and darkened the room till it might have been dusk. I listened to it hiss in the gutters like a thousand coiled snakes.

Beersley gazed down on the nawab with a look of such contempt, I almost
feared he would kick him aside as one might kick an importunate cur out of the
roadway, but instead he merely folded his arms and said, "I can assure you, sir,
that the kidnapper is in this very room and shall be brought to justice before the
hour is out."

The ladies gasped, the gentlemen exclaimed: "What?" "Who?" "He can't be
serious?" I found myself swelling with pride. Though the case was as foggy to
me as it had been on the night of our arrival, I knew that Beersley, in his brilliant
and inimitable way, had solved it. When the hubbub had died down, Beersley re-
quested that the nawab take a seat so that he might begin. I leaned back comfortably in my armchair and awaited the denouement.

"First," Beersley said, clasping his hands behind his back and rocking to and
fro on the balls of his feet, "the facts of the case. To begin with, we have a remote, half-beggared duchy under the hand of a despotic prince known for his
self-indulgence and the opulence of his court—"

At once the nawab leaped angrily to his feet. "I beg your pardon, sir, but I
find this most offensive. If you cannot conduct your investigation in a civil and
properly respectful manner, I shall have to ask you to . . . to—"

"Please, please, please," Beersley was saying as he motioned the nawab back
into his seat, "be patient and you'll soon see the method in all this. Now, as I
was saying: we have a little out-of-the-way state despoiled by generations of self-
serving rulers, rulers whose very existence is sufficient to provoke widespread
animosity if not enmity among the populace. Next we have the mysterious and
unaccountable disappearance of the current nawab's heirs and heiresses—that
is, Gopal, Abha, Shanker, Santha, Bhupinder, Bimal and Manu, Govind, Val-

labhbhi Shiva, and now Indira and Sushila—beginning on a moonless night two weeks ago to this day, the initial discovery of such disappearance made by the children's governess, one Miss Elspeth Compton-Divot."

At the mention of the children, the begum, who was seated to my left, began to whimper softly. Miss Compton-Divot boldly held Beersley's gaze as he named her, the two entrepreneurs—Bagwas and Patel—leaned forward attentively, and Hugh Tureen yawned mightily. As for myself, I began to feel rather sleepy. The room was terrifically hot despite the rain, and the glutinous breeze that wafted up from the punkah bathed me in sweat.

"Thus far," Beersley continued, "we have a kidnapper whose motives remained obscure—but then the kidnapper turned murderer, and as he felt me close on his trail he attempted murder once again. And let me remind you of the method employed in both cases—a foul and feminine method, I might add—that is, the use of poison. I have here," he said, producing the nail file, "the weapon used to kill the servant set to watch over the nawab's flock. It is made of steel and was manufactured in England—in Hertford, to be precise." At this point, Beersley turned to the governess and addressed her directly. "Is it not true, Miss Compton-Divot, that you were born and raised in Hertfordshire and that but six months ago you arrived in India seeking employment?"

The governess's face lost its color in that instant. "Yes," she stammered, "It is true, but—"

"And," Beersley continued, approaching to within a foot of her chair and holding the nail file out before him as if it were a hot poker, "do you deny that this is your nail file, brought with you from England for some malignant purpose?"

"I don't!" she shouted in obvious agitation. "Or rather, I do. I mean, yes, it is my nail file, but I lost it—or . . . or someone stole it—some weeks ago. Certainly you don't think that I—?"

"That you are the murderer, Miss Compton-Divot?"

Her face was parchment, her pretty neck and bosom as white as if they'd never seen the light of day.

"No, my dear, not the murderer," Beersley said, straightening himself and pacing back across the room like a great stalking cat, "but are murderer and kidnapper one and the same? But hold on a minute, let us consider the lines of the greatest poet of them all, one who knew as I do how artifice and deceit seethe through the apparent world and how tough-minded and true one must be to unconfound the illusion from the reality. 'There was an awful rainbow once in heaven: / We know her woof,' " he intoned, and I realized that something had gone wrong, that his voice had begun to drag and his lids to droop. He fumbled over the next line or two, then paused to collect himself and cast his unsteady gaze out over the room. " 'Philosophy will clip an Angel's wing, / Conquer all mysteries by rule and line, / Empty the haunted air, and gnomed mine—' "

Here I cut him off. "Beersley," I demanded, "get on with it, old boy." It was the opium. I could see it now. Yes, he'd been up all night with the case and with his pellucid mind, but with his opium bowl too.

He staggered back at the sound of my voice and shook his head as if to clear it, and then, whirling round, he pointed a terrible riveting finger at the game hunter and shrieked: "Here, here is your murderer!"

Tureen, a big florid fellow in puttees and boots, sprang from his chair in a rage. "What? You dare to accuse me, you . . . you preposterous little worm?" He would have fallen on Beersley and, I believe, torn him apart, had not the nawab's Sikhs interceded.

"Yes, Hugh Tureen," Beersley shouted, a barely suppressed rage shaking his voice in emotional storm, "you who've so long fouled yourself with the blood of beasts, you killed for the love of her, for the love of this, this"—and here the word literally burst from his lips like the great Lord's malediction on Lucifer—"Lamia!"

A cry went round the room. "Oh yes, and she—black heart, foul seductress—led you into her web just as she led you," he shouted, whirling on the nawab, "Yadavindra Singh. Yes, meeting with you secretly in foul unlawful embrace, professing her love while working in complicity with this man"—indicating Bagwas—"and your damned ragged fakir, to undermine your corrupt dynasty, to deprive you of your heirs, poison your wife in her sleep, and succeed to the throne as the fourth begum of Sivani-Hoota!"

Everyone in the room was on his feet. There were twenty disputations, rain crashed at the windows. Tureen raged in the arms of the Sikhs, and the nawab looked as if he were in the throes of an apoplectic fit. Over it all came the voice of Beersley, gone shrill now with excitement. "Whore!" he screamed, descending on the governess. "Conspiring with Bagwas, tempting him with your putrid charms and the lucre the nawab gave out in exchange for your favors. Yes, drugging the children and night nurses with your, quote, hot chocolate!" Beersley swung round again, this time to face the begum, who looked as confused as if she'd awakened to find herself amid the Esquimaux in Alaska. "And you, dear sinned-against lady: your little ones are dead, smothered by Bagwas and his accomplice Patel, sealed in rubber at the plant, and shipped in bulk to Calcutta. Look for them there, so that at least they may have a decent burial."

I was at Beersley's side now, trying to fend off the furious rushes of his auditors, but he seemed to have lost control. "Tureen!" he shrieked, "you fool, you jackanapes! You believed in this harlot, this Compton-Divot, this feminine serpent! Believed her when she lay in your disgusting arms and promised you riches when she found her way to the top! Good God!" he cried, breaking past me and rushing again at the governess, who stood shrinking in the corner, " 'Lamia! Begone, foul dream!' "

It was then that the nawab's Sikhs turned on my unfortunate companion and pinioned his arms. The nawab, rage trembling through his corpulent body, struck Beersley across the mouth three times in quick succession, and as I threw myself forward to protect him, a pair of six-foot Sikhs drew their daggers to warn me off. The rest happened so quickly I can barely reconstruct it. There was the nawab, foaming with anger, his speech about decency, citizens of the crown, and rural justice, the mention of tar and feathers, the hasty packing of our bags, the unceremonious bum's rush out the front gate, and then the long, wearying trek in the merciless rain to the Sivani-Hoota station.

Some weeks later, an envelope with the monogram *EC-D* arrived in the evening mail at my bungalow in Calcutta. Inside I found a rather wounding and triumphant letter from Miss Compton-Divot. Beersley, it seemed, had been wrong on all counts. Even in identifying her with the woman he had once loved, which I believe now lay at the root of his problem in this difficult case. She was in fact the daughter of a governess herself, and had had no connection whatever with Squire Trelawney—whom she knew by reputation in Hertfordshire—or his daughter. As for the case of the missing children, she had been able, with the aid of Mr. Bagwas, to solve it herself. It seemed that practically the only suspicion in which Beersley was confirmed was his mistrust of the *sadhu*. Miss Compton-Divot had noticed the fellow prowling about the upper rooms in the vicinity of the children's quarters one night, and had determined to keep a close watch on him. Along with Bagwas, she was able to tail the specious holy man to his quarters in the meanest street of Sivani-Hoota's slums. There they hid themselves and watched as he transformed himself into a ragged beggar with a crabbed walk who hobbled through the dark streets to his station, among a hundred other beggars, outside the colonnades of the Colonial Office. To their astonishment, they saw that the beggars huddled round him—all of whom had been deprived of the power of speech owing to an operation too gruesome to report here—were in fact the children of the nawab. The beggar master was promptly arrested and the children returned to their parents.

But that wasn't all: there remained the motive. When dragged before the nawab in chains and condemned to death by *peine fort et dure,* the beggar master spat forth his venom. "Don't you recognize me?" he taunted the nawab. "Look closer." Understanding animated the nawab's features and a low exclamation escaped his lips: "Rajendra!" he gasped. "Yes," sneered the beggar master, "the same. The man you wronged thirty-five years ago when you set your filthy minions on me, burned my house and barn to the ground, and took my wife for your own first begum. She turned her back on me for your promises, and you turned me out of the state to wander begging the rest of my life. I have had my revenge." The nawab had broken down in tears, the beggar master was hauled off to be tortured to death, and the nine tongueless children were brought home to be instructed in sign language by Miss Compton-Divot, who became engaged to marry Mr. Bagwas the following week.

And so ends the baffling and ever-surprising case of the Beggar Master of

Sivani-Hoota. I did not show the governess's letter to Beersley, incidentally. I felt that he'd been under an unnatural strain over the course of the past several months, and determined instead to take him for a rest cure to a little hotel in the grassy hills of the Punjab, a place that, so they say, bears a striking resemblance to Hertfordshire.

(1983)

THE NEW MOON PARTY

There was a blizzard in the Dakotas, an earthquake in Chile, and a solar eclipse over most of the Northern Hemisphere the day I stepped up to the governor's podium in Des Moines and announced my candidacy for the highest post in the land. As the lunar shadow crept over the Midwest like a stain in water, as noon became night and the creatures of the earth fell into an unnatural frenzy and the birds of the air fled to premature roosts, I stood in a puddle of TV lights, Lorna at my side, and calmly raked the incumbent over the coals. It was a nice campaign ploy—I think I used the term "penumbra" half a dozen times in my speech—but beyond that I really didn't attach too much significance to the whole thing. I wasn't superstitious. I wore no chains or amulets, I'd never had a rabbit's foot, I attended church only because my constituents expected me to. Of portents, I knew nothing.

My awakening—I've always liked to refer to it as my "lunar epiphany"— came at the dog end of a disappointing campaign in the coach section of a DC-10 somewhere between Battle Creek and Montpelier. It was two months before the convention, and we were on our way to Vermont to spill some rhetoric. I was picking at something the airline optimistically called *salade Madrid,* my feet hurt, my digestion was shot, and the latest poll had me running dead last in a field of eight. My aides—a bunch of young Turks and electoral strong-arm men who wielded briefcases like swords and had political ambitions akin to Genghis Khan's—were daintily masticating their rubbery *coq au vin* and trying to use terms like "vector," "interface," and "demographic volatility" in a single sentence. They were dull as doorknobs, dry as the dust on the textbooks that had given them life. Inspiration? They couldn't have inspired a frog to croak. No, it was Lorna, former Rose Queen and USC song girl and the sweetest, lovingest wife a man could want, who was to lift me that night to the brink of inspiration even as I saw myself swallowed up in defeat.

The plane dipped, the lights flickered, and Lorna laid one of her pretty white hands on my arm. "Honey," she whispered, with that soft throbbing City-of-Industry inflection that always made me think of surf caressing the pylons of the Santa Monica pier, "will you look at that moon?"

I stabbed at my salad in irritation, a speech about Yankee gumption, coydog control, and support prices for maple-sugar pinwheels tenting my lap, and took a hasty glance at the darkened porthole. "Yeah?" I said, and I'm sure there was more than a little edge to my voice: Couldn't she see that I was busy, worn out, heartbroken, and defeated? Couldn't she see I was like the old lion with a thorn in his paw, surrounded by wolves and jackals and facing his snaggle-toothed death in the political jungle? "What of it?" I snarled.

"Oh, I don't know," she murmured, her voice dreamy, seductive almost (had she been reading those women's magazines again?). "It just looks so old and shabby."

I squinted through that dark little porthole at the great black fathomless universe and saw the moon, palely glowing, looked at the moon probably for the first time in twenty years. Lorna was right. It did look pretty cheesy.

She hummed a few bars of "Shine On, Harvest Moon," and then turned to me with those big pale eyes—still beautiful, still enough to move me after all these years—and said, "You know, if that moon was a loveseat I'd take it out to the garage and send to Bloomingdale's for a new one."

One of my aides—Colin or Carter or Rutherford, I couldn't keep their names straight—was telling a joke in dialect about three Mexican gardeners and an outhouse, another was spouting demographic theory, and the stewardess swished by with a smell of perfume that hit me like a twenty-one-gun salute. It was then—out of a whirl of thoughts and impressions like cream whipped in a blender—that I had my moment of grace, of inspiration, the moment that moves mountains, solves for x, and makes a musical monument of the "Hymn to Joy," the moment the mass of humankind lives an entire lifetime for and never experiences. "Of course," I blurted, upending the salad in my excitement, "yes," and I saw all the campaign trails of all the dreary, pavement-pounding, glad-handing years fall away beneath me like streamers from heaven, like ticker tape, as I turned to kiss Lorna as if I were standing before the cheering hordes on Inauguration Day.

Colin or Carter or Rutherford turned to me and said, "What is it, George—are you all right?"

"The New Moon," I said.

Lorna was regarding me quizzically. A few of the other aides turned their heads.

I was holding my plastic cup of 7-Up aloft as if it were crystal, as if it were filled with Taittinger or Dom Pérignon. "To the New Moon!" I said with a fire and enthusiasm I hadn't felt in years. "To the New Moon Party!"

The American people were asleep. They were dead. The great, the giving, the earnest, energetic, and righteous American people had thrown in the towel. Rape, murder, cannibalism, political upheaval in the Third World, rock and roll, unemployment, puppies, mothers, Jackie, Michael, Liza: nothing moved them. Their worst fears, most implausible dreams, and foulest conceptions were all right there in the metro section, splashed across the ever-swelling megalopic eye of the TV screen in living color and clucked over by commentators who looked as alike as bowling pins. Scandal and horror were as mundane as a yawn before bed; honor, decency, heroism, and enterprise were looked on as quaint, largely inapplicable notions that expressed an inexcusable naïveté about the way of the world. In short, no one gave a good goddamn about anything. Myself included. So how blame them when they couldn't tell the candidates apart, didn't bother to turn out at the polls, neither knew nor cared whether the honorable Mr. P. stood for Nazi rebirth or federally funded electronic walkers for the aged and infirm?

I'd seen it all, and nothing stirred me, either. Ultraism, conservatism, progressivism, communism, liberalism, neofascism, parties of the right, left, center, left of center, and oblate poles: who cared? I didn't even know why I was running. I'd served my two terms as a fresh-faced, ambitious young representative during the Eisenhower years, fought through three consecutive terms in the senatorial wars, wielded the sword of power and influence in the most armorplated committees on the Hill, and been twice elected governor of Iowa on a platform that promised industrial growth, environmental protection, and the eradication of corn blight through laser technology. And yet, for all that, I wasn't satisfied. I guess, even at sixty-one, I was still afflicted with those hungry pangs of ambition that every boy who can't play center field for the Yankees will never wholly shake: I wanted to be top dog, kick off my shoes in the Oval Office, and stir up a fuss wherever I went; I wanted to climb high atop the mountain and look down on the creeping minuscule figures of queens, rock stars, matinee idols, and popes. It was a cold life in a comfortless universe; I didn't believe in God, afterlife, or leprechauns. I wanted to make my mark on history—what else was there?

And so I—we—came up with the issue that would take the country—no, the world itself—by storm. From the moment of my epiphany on that rattling howling DC-10 I never said another word about taxes, inflation, Social Security, price supports, or the incumbent's lamentable record on every key issue from the decentralization of the Boy Scouts to relations with the Soviet Union. No, I talked only of the New Moon. The moon *we* were going to build, to create, to hurl into the sky to take its place among the twinkling orbs of the night and recover the dignity and economic stability of America in the process. Jupiter had twelve moons, Saturn ten, Uranus five. What were we? Where was our global pride when we could boast but one craggy, acne-ridden bulb blighting the nighttime sky? *A New Moon. A New Moon Soon:* it was on my lips like a battle cry.

In Montpelier they thought I'd gone mad. An audience of thirty-seven had turned out at the local ag school to hear me talk about coydogs and maple-sugar pinwheels, but I gave them a dose of the New Moon instead. I strode out onto the stage like a man reborn (which I was), shredded my prepared speech, and flung it like confetti over their astonished heads, my arms spread wide, the spontaneous, thrilling message of the lunar gospel pouring from me in evangelical fervor. LUNACY, mocked the morning headlines. THORKELSSON MOONSTRUCK. But the people listened. They murmured in Montpelier, applauded lightly—hands chapped and dry as cornhusks—in Rutland. In Pittsburgh, where I really began to hit my stride (I talked of nothing but the steel it would take to piece together the superstructure of the new satellite), they got up on tables and cheered. The American people were tired of party bickering, vague accusations, and even vaguer solutions; they were sick to death of whiz-kid economists, do-nothing legislatures, and the nightmare specter of nuclear war. They wanted joy, simplicity, a goal as grand as Manifest Destiny and yet as straightforward and unequivocal as a bank statement. The New Moon gave it to them.

By the time the convention rolled around, the New Moon was waxing full. I remember the way the phones rang off the hook: would we take a back seat to Fritz, throw our support to John, accept the VP nomination on a split-issue platform? Seven weeks earlier no one had even deigned to notice us—half the time we didn't even get press coverage. But New Moon fever was sweeping the country—we'd picked up a bundle of delegates, won in Texas, Ohio, and California, and suddenly we were a force to reckon with.

"George," Colin was saying (I'm sure it was Colin, because I'd canned Carter and Rutherford to avoid the confusion), "I still say we've got to broaden our base. The one issue has taken us leagues, I admit it, but—"

I cut him off. I was George L. Thorkelsson, former representative, former senator, and current governor of the Mesopotamia of the Midwest, the glorious, farinaceous, black-loamed hogbutt of the nation, and I wasn't about to listen to any defeatist twaddle from some Ivy League pup. "Hey diddle, diddle," I said, "the cat and the fiddle." I was feeling pretty good.

It was then that Gina—Madame Scutari, that is—spoke up. Lorna and I had discovered her in the kitchen of Mama Gina's, a Nashville pasta house, during the Tennessee primary. She'd made an *abbacchio alla cacciatora* that knocked my socks off, and when we'd gone back to congratulate her she'd given me a look of such starstruck devotion I felt like the new Messiah. It seemed that the Madame (who wasn't Italian at all, but Hungarian) was a part-time astrologist and clairvoyant, and had had a minor seizure at the very moment of my epiphany in the DC-10—her left arm had gone numb and she'd pitched forward into a platter of antipasto with the word "lunar" on her lips. She told us all this in a rush of malaproprisms and tortured syntax, while cauldrons of marinara sauce bubbled around her and her faintly mustachioed upper lip rose and fell like a shuttlecock. Then she'd leaned forward to whisper in my ear like a priestess of the oracle. *Leo,* she'd said, hitting my sign on the nose, *Scorpio in the ascendant.* Then she drew up her rouged face and gave me a broad Magyar wink and I could feel her lips moving against my ear: *A New Moon Soon,* she rasped. From that moment on she'd become one of my closest advisers.

Now she cleared her throat with a massive dignity, her heavy arms folded over her bust, and said, in that delicate halting accent that made you feel she could read the future like a Neapolitan menu, "Not to worry, Georgie: I see you rising like the lion coming into the tenth house."

"But George"—Colin was nearly whining—"gimmicks are okay, but they can only take you so far. Think of the political realities."

Lorna and the Madame exchanged a look. I watched as a smile animated my wife's features. It was a serene smile, visionary, the smile of a woman who already saw herself decked out in a gown like a shower of gold and presiding over tea in the Blue Room.

I turned to Colin and tersely reminded him of the political realities his late colleagues were currently facing. "We need no naysayers here," I added. "You're either on the bus or you're off it." He looked at me as if he were about to say something he would regret, but the Madame cut him off, her voice elevated yet soft, the syllables falling together with a kiss that cut through the confusion and the jangling of telephones like a benediction: "Promise them the moon," she said.

The convention itself was child's play. We'd captured the imagination of the country, restored the average workingman's faith in progress, given America a cause to stand up and shout about. We split the thing down the middle and I took my delegates outside the party to form the first significant rump party since the days of Henry Wallace. We were the New Moon Party and they came to us in droves. Had anyone ever stopped to consider how many amateur astrologists there were out there? How many millions who decided their every move—from love affairs to travel plans to stock purchases and the most auspicious time for doing their nails—according to the conjunction of the planets and the phases of the moon? Or how many religious fanatics and sci-fi freaks there were, Trekkies, lunatics, werewolves, extraterrestrialists, saucer nuts, and the like? Not to mention women, who've had to carry that white-goddess baggage around with them since the dawn of time. Well, here was an issue that could unite them all. Nixon had put men on the moon; I was going to bring the moon to men. And women.

Oh, there were the usual cries of outrage and anathema, the usual blockheads, whiners, and pleaders, but we paid them no heed. NASA was behind us, one hundred percent. So were U.S. Steel, the AFL-CIO, the Teamsters, Silicon

Valley, Wall Street and Big Oil, and just about anyone else in the country who worked for a living. A New Moon. Just think of the jobs it would create!

The incumbent—a man twelve years my senior who looked as if he'd been stuffed with sand—didn't stand a chance. Oh, they painted him up and pointed him toward the TV monitors and told him when to laugh or cry or make his voice tremble with righteousness, and they had him recite the usual litany about the rights of the rich and the crying need for new condos on Maui, and they prodded him to call the New Moon a hoax, a technological impossibility, a white elephant, and a liberal-humanist threat to the integrity of the interplanetary heavens, but all to no avail. It almost hurt me to see his bowed head, smeared blusher, and plasticized hair as he conceded defeat to a national TV audience after I'd swept every precinct in the country with the exception of a handful in Santa Barbara, where he'd beaten me by seventeen votes, but what the hell. This was no garden party, this was politics.

Sadly, however, unity and harmony are not the way of the world, and no leader, no matter how visionary—not Napoleon, not Caesar, not Mohammed, Louis XVI, Jim Jones, or Jesus of Nazareth—can hope to stave off the tide of discord, malcontent, envy, hatred, and sheer seething anarchy that inevitably rises up to crush him with the force of a tidal wave. And so it was, seven years later, my second term drawing to a close and with neither hope nor precedent for a third, that I found the waves crashing at my very doorstep. I, who had been the most heralded chief executive in the country's history, I, who had cut across social strata, party differences, ethnic divisions, and international mistrust with my vision of a better world and a better future, was well on my way to becoming the most vilified world leader since Attila the Hun.

Looking back on it, I can see that perhaps my biggest mistake was in appointing Madame Scutari to my Cabinet. The problem wasn't so much her lack of experience—I understand that now—but her lack of taste. She took something truly grand—a human monument before which all the pyramids, Taj Mahals, and World Trade Centers paled by comparison—and made it tacky. For that I will never forgive her.

At any rate, when I took office back in January of '85, I created a new Cabinet post that would reflect the chief priority of my administration—I refer to the now infamous post of secretary for Lunar Affairs—and named Gina to occupy it. Though she'd had little formal training, she knew her stars and planets cold, and she was a woman of keen insight and studied judgment. I trusted her implicitly. Besides which, I was beleaguered by renegade scientists, gypsies, sci-fi hacks (one of whom was later to write most of my full-moon address to the nation), amateur inventors, and corporation execs, all clamoring for a piece of the action—and I desperately needed someone to sort them out. Gina handled them like diners without reservations.

The gypsies, Trekkies, diviners, haruspices, and the like were apparently pursuing a collective cosmic experience, something that would ignite the heavens; the execs—from U.S. Steel to IBM to Boeing to American Can—wanted contracts. After all, the old moon was some 2,160 miles in diameter and eighty-one quintillion tons of dead weight, and they figured whatever we were going to do would take one hell of a lot of construction. Kaiser proposed an aluminum-alloy shell filled with Styrofoam, to be shuttled piecemeal into space and constructed by robots on location. The Japanese wanted to mold it out of plastic, while Firestone saw a big synthetic gold-ball sort of thing and Con Ed pushed for a hollow cement glove that could be used as a repository for nuclear waste. And it wasn't just the big corporations, either—it seemed every crank in the country was suddenly a technological wizard. A retired gym teacher from Sacramento suggested an inflatable ball made of simulated pigskin, and a pizza magnate from Brooklyn actually proposed a chicken-wire sphere coated with raw dough. *Bake it with lasers or something,* he wrote, *it'll harden like rock. Believe me.* During those first few heady months in office the proposals must have come in at the rate of ten thousand a day.

If I wasn't equipped to deal with them (I've always been an idea man myself), Gina was. She conferred before breakfast, lunched three or four times a day, dined and brunched, and kept a telephone glued to her head as if it were a natural excrescence. "No problem," she told me. "I'll have a proposal for you by June."

She was true to her word.

I remember the meeting at which she presented her findings as keenly as I remember my mother's funeral or the day I had my gall bladder removed. We were sitting around the big mahogany table in the conference room, sipping coffee. Gina flowed through the door in a white caftan, her arms laden with clipboards and blueprints, looking pleased with herself. She took a seat beside Lorna, exchanged a bit of gossip with her in a husky whisper, then leaned across the table and cleared her throat. "Glitter," she said, "that's what we want, Georgie. Something bright, something to fill up the sky and screw over the astrological charts forever." Lorna, who'd spent the afternoon redesigning the uniforms of the Scouts of America (they were known as Space Cadets now, and the new unisex uniforms were to feature the spherical New Moon patch over the heart), sat nodding at her side. They were grinning conspiratorially, like a pair of matrons outfitting a parlor.

"Glitter?" I echoed, smiling into the face of their enthusiasm. "What did you have in mind?"

The Madame closed her heavy-lidded gypsy eyes for a moment, then flashed them at me like a pair of blazing guns. "The Bonaventure Hotel, Georgie—in L.A.? You know it?"

I shook my head slowly, wondering what she was getting at.

"Mirrors," she said.

I just looked at her.

"Fields of them, Georgie, acres upon acres. Just think of the reflective power! Our moon, *your* moon—it'll outshine that old heap of rock and dust ten times over."

Mirrors. The simplicity of it, the beauty. I felt the thrill of her inspiration, pictured the glittering triumphant moon hanging there like a jewel in the sky, bright as a supernova, bright as the star of Bethlehem. No, brighter, brighter by far. The flash of it would illuminate the darkest corners, the foulest alleys, drive back the creatures of darkness and cut the crime rate exponentially. George L. Thorkelsson, I thought, light giver. "Yes," I said, my voice husky with emotion, "yes."

But Filencio Salmón, author of *The Ravishers of Pentagord* and my chief speech writer, rose to object. "Wees all due respet, Meeser Presiden, these glass globe goin' to chatter like a gumball machine the firs' time a meteor or anytin' like that run into it. What you wan eeze sometin' strong, Teflon maybe."

"Not shiny enough," Gina countered, exchanging a hurt look with Lorna. Obviously she hadn't thought very deeply about the thing if she hadn't even taken meteors into account. Christ, she was secretary for Lunar Affairs, with two hundred JPL eggheads, selenologists, and former astronauts on her staff, and that was the best she could come up with?

I leaned back in my chair and looked over the crestfallen faces gathered round the table—Gina, Lorna, Salmón, my national security adviser, the old boy in the Philip Morris outfit we sent out for sandwiches. "Listen," I said, feeling wise as Solomon, "the concept is there—we'll work out a compromise solution."

No one said a word.

"We've got to. The world's depending on us."

We settled finally on stainless steel. Well buffed, and with nothing out there to corrode it, it would have nearly the same reflective coefficient as glass, and it was one hell of a lot more resistant. More expensive too, but when you've got a project like this, what's a hundred billion more or less? Anyway, we farmed out the contracts and went into production almost immediately. We had decided, after the usual breast-beating, shouting matches, resignations, and reinstatements, on a shell of jet-age plastic strengthened by steel girders, and a façade—one side only—of stainless-steel plates the size of Biloxi, Mississippi. Since we were only going up about eighty thousand miles, we figured we could get away with a sphere about one-third the size of the old moon: its proximity to earth would make it appear so much larger.

I don't mean to minimize the difficulty of all this. There were obstacles both surmountable and insurmountable, technologies to be invented, resources to be tapped, a great wealthy nation to be galvanized into action. My critics—and they were no small minority, even in those first few euphoric years—insisted that the whole thing was impossible, a pipe dream at best. They were defeatists, of course, like Colin (for whom, by the way, I found a nice little niche in El Salvador as assistant to the ambassador's bodycount man), and they didn't faze me in the least. No, I figured that if in the space of the six years of World War II man could go from biplanes and TNT to jets and nuclear bombs, anything was possible if the will was there. And I was right. By the time my first term wound down we were three-quarters of the way home, the economy was booming, the unemployment rate approaching zero for the first time since the forties, and the Cold War defrosted. (The Russians had given over stockpiling missiles to work on their own satellite project. They were rumored to be constructing a new planet in Siberia, and our reconnaissance photos showed that they were indeed up to something big—something, in fact, that looked like a three-hundred-mile-long eggplant inscribed at intervals with the legend NOVAYA SMOLENSK.) Anyway, as most of the world knows, the Republicans didn't even bother to field a candidate in '88, and New Moon fever had the national temperature hovering up around the point of delirium.

Then, as they say, the shit hit the fan.

To have been torn to pieces like Orpheus or Mussolini, to have been stretched and broken on the rack or made to sing "Hello Dolly" at the top of my lungs while strapped naked to a carny horse driven through the House of Representatives would have been pleasure compared to what I went through the night we unveiled the New Moon. What was to have been my crowning triumph—my moment of glory transcendent—became instead my most ignominious defeat. In an hour's time I went from savior to fiend.

For seven years, along with the rest of the world, I'd held my breath. Through all that time, through all the blitz of TV and newspaper reports, the incessant interviews with project scientists and engineers, the straw polls, moon crazes, and marketing ploys, the New Moon had remained a mystery. People knew how big it was, they could plot its orbit and talk of its ascending and descending nodes and how many million tons of materials had gone into its construction—but they'd yet to see it. Oh, if you looked hard enough you could see that something was going on up there, but it was as shadowy and opaque as the blueprint of a dream. Even with the telescope—and believe me, many's the night I spent at Palomar with a bunch of professional stargazers, or out on the White House lawn with the Questar QM 1 Lorna gave me for Christmas—you couldn't make out much more than a dark circle punched out of the great starry firmament as if with a cookie cutter.

Of course, we'd planned it that way. Right from the start we'd agreed that the best policy was to keep the world guessing—who wanted to see a piecemeal moon, after all, a moon that grew square by square in the night sky like some crazy checkerboard or something? This was no department store going up on West Twenty-third Street—this was something extraordinary, unique, this was the quintessence of man's achievement on the planet, and it should be served up whole or not at all. It was Salmón, in a moment of inspiration, who came up with the idea of putting the reflecting plates on the far side, facing out on the deeps of the universe, and then swinging the whole business around by means of initial-thrust and retro-rockets for a triumphant—and politically opportune—unveiling. I applauded him. Why not? I thought. Why not milk this thing for everything it was worth?

The night of the unveiling was clear and moonless. Lorna sat beside me on the dais, regal and resplendent in a Halston moonglow gown that cost more than the combined gross product of any six towns along the Iowa-Minnesota border. Gina was there too, of course, looking as if she'd just won a fettuccine cook-off in Naples, and the audience of celebrities, foreign ambassadors, and politicos gathered on the south lawn numbered in the thousands. Outside the gates, in darkness, three-quarters of a million citizens milled about with spherical white-moon candles, which were to be lit at the moment the command was given to swing the New Orb into view. Up and down the Eastern Seaboard, in Quebec and Ontario, along the ridge of the Smokies, and out to the verge of the Mississippi, a hush fell over the land as municipalities big and small cut their lights.

Ferenc Syzgies, the project's chief engineer, delivered an interminable speech peppered with terms like "photometric function" and "fractional pore space." Anita Bryant sang a couple of spirituals, and finally Luciano Pavarotti rose to do a medley of "Moon River," "Blue Moon," and "That's Amore." Lorna leaned over and took my hand as the horns stepped in on the last number. "Nervous?" she whispered.

"No," I murmured, but my throat had thickened till I felt I was going to choke. They'd assured me there would be no foul-ups—but nothing like this had ever been attempted before, and who could say for sure?

"When-a the moon-a hits your eye like a big pizza pie," sang Pavarotti, "that's amore." The dignitaries shifted in their seats, Lorna was whispering something I couldn't hear, and then Coburn, the VP, was introducing me.

I stood and stepped to the podium to spontaneous, thrilling and sustained applause, Salmón's speech clutched in my hand, the shirt collar chafing at my neck like a garrote. Flashbulbs popped, the TV cameras seized on me like the hungry eyes of great mechanical insects, faces leaped out of the crowd: here a senator I loathed sitting cheek by jowl with a lobbyist from the Sierra Club, there a sour-faced clergyman I'd prayed beside during a dreary rally seven years earlier. The glowing, corn-fed visage of Miss Iowa materialized just beneath the podium, and behind her sat Coretta King, Tip O'Neill, Barbra Streisand, Carl Sagan, and Mickey Mantle, all in a row. The applause went on for a full five minutes. And then suddenly the audience were on their feet and singing "God Bless America" as if their lives depended on it. When they were finished, I held up my hands for silence and began to read.

Salmón had outdone himself. The speech was measured, hysterical, opaque, and lucid. My voice rang triumphantly through the PA system, rising in eulogy, trembling with visionary fervor, dropping to an emotion-choked whisper as I found myself taking on everything from the birth of the universe to Conestoga wagons and pioneer initiative. I spoke of interstellar exploration, of the movie industry and Dixieland jazz, of the great selfless, uncontainable spirit of the American people, who, like latter-day Prometheuses, were giving over the sacred flame to the happy, happy generations to come. Or something like that. I was about halfway through when the New Orb began to appear in the sky over my shoulder.

The first thing I remember was the brightness of it. Initially there was just a sliver of light, but the sliver quickly grew to a crescent that lit the south lawn as if on a July morning. I kept reading. "The gift of light," I intoned, but no one was listening. As the thing began to swing round to full, the glare of it became insupportable. I paused to gaze down at the faces before me: they were awestruck, panicky, disgusted, violent, enraptured. People had begun to shield their eyes now; some of the celebrities and musicians slipped on sunglasses. It was then that the dogs began to howl. Faintly at first, a primal yelp here or there, but within thirty seconds every damn hound, mongrel, and cur in the city of Washington was baying at the moon as if they hadn't eaten in a week. It was unnerving, terrifying. People began to shout, and then to shove one another.

I didn't know what to do. "Well, er," I said, staring into the cameras and waving my arm with a theatrical flourish, "ladies and gentleman, the New Moon!"

Something crazy was going on. The shoving had stopped as abruptly as it had begun, but now, suddenly and inexplicably, the audience started to undress. Right before me, on the platform, in the seats reserved for foreign diplomats, out over the seething lawn, they were kicking off shoes, hoisting shirt fronts and brassieres, dropping cummerbunds and Jockey shorts. And then, incredibly, horribly, they began to clutch at one another in passion, began to stroke, fondle, and lick, humping in the grass, plunging into the bushes, running around like nymphs and satyrs at some mad bacchanal. A senator I'd known for forty years went by me in a dead run, pursuing the naked wife of the Bolivian ambassador; Miss Iowa disappeared beneath the rhythmically heaving buttocks of the sour-faced clergyman; Lorna was down to a pair of six-hundred-dollar bikini briefs and I suddenly found to my horror that I'd begun to loosen my tie.

Madness, lunacy, mass hypnosis, call it what you will: it was a mess. Flocks of birds came shrieking out of the trees, cats appeared from nowhere to caterwaul along with the dogs, congressmen rolled about on the ground, grabbing for flesh and yipping like animals—and all this on national television! I felt lightheaded, as if I were about to pass out, but then I found I had an erection and there before me was this cream-colored thing in a pair of high-heeled boots and nothing else,

Lorna had disappeared, it was bright as noon in Miami, dogs, cats, rats, and squirrels were howling like werewolves, and I found that somehow I'd stripped down to my boxer shorts. It was then that I lost consciousness. Mercifully.

These days, I am not quite so much in the public eye. In fact, I live in seclusion. On a lake somewhere in the Northwest, the Northeast, or the Deep South, my only company a small cadre of Secret Service men. They are laconic sorts, these Secret Service men, heavy of shoulder and head, and they live in trailers set up on a ridge behind the house. To a man, they are named Greg or Craig.

And as those who read this will know, all our efforts to modify the New Moon (Coburn's efforts, that is: I was in hiding) were doomed to failure. Syzgies's replacement, Klaus Erkhardt the rocket expert, had proposed tarnishing the stainless-steel plates with payloads of acid, but the plan had proved unworkable, for obvious reasons. Meanwhile, a coalition of unlikely bedfellows—Syria, Israel, Iran, Iraq, Libya, Great Britain, Argentina, the Soviet Union, and China among them—had demanded the "immediate removal of this plague upon our heavens," and in this country we came as close to revolution as we had since the 1770s.

Coburn did the best he could, but the following November, Colin, Carter, and Rutherford jumped parties and began a push to re-elect the man I'd defeated in '84 on the New Moon ticket. He was old—antediluvian, in fact—but not appreciably changed in either appearance or outlook, and he was swept into office in a landslide. The New Moon, which had been blamed for everything from causing rain in the Atacama to fomenting a new baby boom, corrupting morals, bestializing mankind, and making the crops grow upside down in the Far East, was obliterated by a nuclear thunderbolt a month after he took office.

On reflection, I can see that I was wrong—I admit it. I was an optimist, I was aggressive, I believed in man and in science, I challenged the heavens and dared to tamper with the face of the universe and its inscrutable design—and I paid for it as swiftly and surely as anybody in all the tragedies of Shakespeare, Sophocles, and Dashiell Hammett. Gina dropped me like a plate of hot lasagna and went back to her restaurant, Colin stabbed me in the back, and Coburn, once he'd taken over, refused to refer to me by name—I was known only as his "predecessor." I even lost Lorna. She left me after the debacle of the unveiling and the impeachment that followed precipitately on its heels, left me to "explore new feelings," as she put it. "I've got to get it out of my system," she told me, a strange glow in her eyes. "I'm sorry, George."

Hell yes, I was wrong. But just the other night I was out on the lake with one of the Secret Service men—Greg, I think it was—fishing for yellow perch, when the moon—the age-old, scar-faced, native moon—rose up out of the trees like an apparition. It was yellow as the underbelly of the fish on the stringer, huge with atmospheric distortion. I whistled. "Will you look at that moon," I said.

Greg just stared at me, noncommittal.

"That's really something, huh?" I said.

No response.

He was smart, this character—he wouldn't touch it with a ten-foot pole. I was just talking to hear myself anyway. Actually, I was thinking the damn thing did look pretty cheesy, thinking maybe where I'd gone wrong was in coming up with a new moon instead of just maybe bulldozing the old one or something. I began to picture it: lie low for a couple years, then come back with a new ticket—*Clean Up the Albedo, A New Face for an Old Friend, Save the Moon!*

But then there was a tug on the line, and I forgot all about it.

(1983)

THE SECOND SWIMMING

Mao flicks on the radio. Music fills the room, half notes like the feet of birds. It is a martial tune, the prelude from "The Long March." Then there are quotations from Chairman Mao, read in a voice saturated with conviction, if a trifle nasal. A selection of the Chairman's poetry follows. The three constantly read articles. And then the aphorism for the hour. Mao sits back, the gelid features imperceptibly softening from their habitual expression of abdominal anguish. He closes his eyes.

FIGHTING LEPROSY WITH REVOLUTIONARY OPTIMISM

Chang Chiu-chu of the Kunghui Commune found one day that the great toe of his left foot had become leprous. When the revisionist surgeons of the urban hospital insisted that they could not save the toe but only treat the disease and hope to contain it, Chang went to Kao Fei-fu, a revolutionary machinist of the commune. Kao Fei-fu knew nothing of medicine but recalled to Chang the Chairman's words: "IF YOU WANT KNOWLEDGE, YOU MUST TAKE PART IN THE PRACTICE OF CHANGING REALITY. IF YOU WANT TO KNOW THE TASTE OF A PEAR, YOU MUST CHANGE THE PEAR BY EATING IT YOURSELF." Kao then inserted needles in Chang's spinal column to a depth of 18 fen. The following day Chang Chiu-chu was able to return to the paddies. When he thanked Kao Fei-fu, Kao said: "Don't thank me, thank Chairman Mao."

Mao's face attempts a paternal grin, achieves the logy and listless. Out in the square he can hear the planetary hum of 500,000 voices singing "The East Is

Red." It is his birthday. He will have wieners with Grey Poupon mustard for breakfast.

How he grins, Hung Ping-chung, hurrying through the congested streets (bicycles, oxcarts, heads, collars, caps), a brown-paper parcel under one arm, cardboard valise under the other. In the brown-paper parcel, a pair of patched blue jeans for his young wife, Wang Ya-chin. Haggled off the legs of a Scandinavian tourist in Japan. For 90,000 yen. In the cardboard valise, Hung's underwear, team jacket, paddle. The table-tennis team has been on tour for thirteen months. Hung thirsts for Wang.

There is a smear of mustard on Mao's nose when the barber clicks through the bead curtains. The barber has shaved Mao sixteen hundred and seven times. He bows, expatiates on the dimension of the honor he feels in being of personal service to the Revolutionary Chairman of the Chinese Communist Party. He then congratulates the Chairman on his birthday. "Long live Chairman Mao!" he shouts. "A long, long life to him!" Then he dabs the mustard from Mao's nose with a flick of his snowy towel.

Mao is seated in the lotus position, hands folded in his lap. Heavy of jowl, abdomen, nates. The barber strops.

"On the occasion of my birthday," says Mao, "I will look more like the Buddha." His voice is parched, riding through octaves like the creak of a rocking chair.

"The coiffure?"

Mao nods. "Bring the sides forward a hair, and take the top back another inch. And buff the pate."

Out on the Lei Feng Highway a cold rain has begun to fall. Chang Chiu-chu and his pig huddle in the lee of a towering monolithic sculpture depicting Mao's emergency from the cave at Yenan. Peasants struggle by, hauling carts laden with produce. Oxen bleat. A bus, the only motorized vehicle on the road, ticks up the hill in the distance. Chang's slippers are greasy with mud. He is on his way to the city to personally thank Mao for the healing of his great toe (the skin has gone from black to gray and sensation has begun to creep back like an assault of pinpricks) and to present the Chairman with his pig. There are six miles to go. His feet hurt. He is cold. But he recalls a phrase of the Chairman's: "I CARE NOT THAT THE WIND BLOWS AND THE WAVES BEAT: IT IS BETTER THAN IDLY STROLLING IN A COURTYARD," and he recalls also that he has a gourd of maotai (120 proof) in his sleeve. He pours a drink into his thermos-cup, mixes it with hot water and downs it. Then lifts a handful of cold rice from his satchel and begins to chew.

He pours another drink. It warms his digestive machinery like a shot of Revolutionary Optimism.

Hung is two blocks from home, hurrying, the collar of his pajamas fastened against the cold, too preoccupied to wonder why he and his class brothers wear slippers and pajamas on the street rather than overshoes and overcoats. He passes under a poster: fierce-eyed women in caps and fatigues hurtling toward the left, bayonets and automatic weapons in hand. It is an advertisement for a ballet: "The Detachment of Red Women." Beneath it, a slogan, the characters big as washing machines, black on red: "GET IN THE HABIT OF NOT SPITTING ON THE GROUND AT RANDOM." The phlegm catches in his throat.

When Hung turns into his block, his mouth drops. The street has been painted red. The buildings are red, the front stoops are red, the railings are red, the lampposts are red, the windows are red, the pigeons are red. A monumental poster of Mao's head drapes the center of the block like an arras and clusters of smaller heads dot the buildings. Hung clutches the package to his chest, nods to old Chiung-hua where she sits on her stoop, a spot of gray on a carmine canvas, and takes the steps to his apartment two at a time.

Wang is in bed. The apartment is cold, dark. "Wang!" he shouts. "I'm back!" She does not rise to meet him, to leap into his arms in her aggressive elastic way (she a former tumbler, their romance a blossom of the People's Athletic and Revolutionary Fitness Academy). Something is wrong. "Wang!" She turns her black eyes to him and all at once he becomes aware of the impossible tumescence of the blanket spread over her. What is she concealing? She bites the corner of the blanket and groans, the labor pains coming fiercer now.

Hung is stung. Drops package and valise. Begins to count the months on his fingers. All thirteen of them. His face shrinks to the size of a pea. "Wang, what have you done?" he stammers.

Her voice is strained, unsteady: "YOU CAN'T SOLVE A PROBLEM? WELL, GET DOWN AND INVESTIGATE THE PRESENT FACTS AND THEIR PAST HISTORY."

"You've been unfaithful!"

"Don't thank me," she croaks, "thank Chairman Mao."

Mao's eyes are closed. His cheeks glow, freshly shaven. In his face, the soapy warm breath of the barber: in his ears, the snip-snip of the barber's silver scissors. His shanks and seat and the small of his back register the faint vibration of the 500,000 voices ringing in the square. A warmth, an electricity tingling through the wood of the chair. Snip-snip.

Mao's dream is immediate and vivid. The sun breaking in the east, sweet marjoram on the breeze, crickets singing along the broad base of the Great Wall, a sound as of hidden fingers working the blades of a thousand scissors. The times are feudal. China is disunited, the Han Dynasty in decline, the Huns (Hsiung-nu) demanding tribute of gold, spices, silk and the soft, uncallused hands of the Emperor's daughters. They wear impossible fierce mustaches stiff-ened with blood and mucus, these Huns, and they keep the rain from their backs with the stretched skin of murdered children. An unregenerate lot. Wallowing in the sins of revisionism and capitalist avarice. Mao, a younger man, his brow shorter, eyes clearer, jowls firmer, stands high atop the battlements supervising the placement of the final stone. The Great Wall, he calls it, thinking ahead to the Great Leap Forward and the Great Hall of the People. Fifteen hundred miles long. Forty feet high, sixteen across.

In the distance, a duststorm, a whirlwind, a thousand acres of topsoil flung into the air by the terrible thundering hoofs of the Huns' carnivorous horses. Their battle cry is an earthquake, their breath the death of a continent. On they come, savage as steel, yabbering and howling over the clattering cannonade of the horsehoofs while Mao's peasants pat the mortar in place and quick-fry won-ton in eighty-gallon drums of blistering oil. Mao stands above them all, the khaki collar visible beneath the red silk robe smoothing his thighs in the breeze. In his hand, held aloft, a Ping-Pong paddle.

The Huns rein their steeds. They are puzzled, their babble like the disquisi-tions of camels and jackals. From a breezy pocket Mao produces the eggshell-frail ball, sets it atop the paddle. The grizzled Hun-chief draws closer, just beneath the rippling Chairman. "Hua?" he shouts. Mao looks down. Cups his hands to his mouth: "Volley for serve."

Chang is having problems with his legs, feet. The left is reluctant to follow the right, and when it does, the right is reluctant to follow suit. To complicate mat-ters the leprous toe has come to life (feeling very much like a fragment of glow-ing iron pounded flat on an anvil), and the pig has become increasingly insistent about making a wallow of the puddled road. A finger-thick brass ring pierces the pig's (tender) septum. This ring is fastened to a cord which is in turn fastened to Chang's belt. From time to time Chang gives the cord a tug, gentle persuader.

Ahead the buildings of the city cut into the bleak horizon like a gap-toothed mandible. The rain raises welts in the puddles, thrushes wing overhead, a man approaches on a bicycle. Chang pauses for a nip of maotai, as a sort of internal liniment for his throbbing toe, when suddenly the pig decides to sit, flip, floun-der and knead the mud of the road with its rump. The cord jerks violently. Chang hydroplanes. Drops his gourd. Comes to rest in a dark puddle abob with what appears to be spittle randomly spat. He curses the animal's revisionist mentality.

There are two framed photographs on the wall over Wang's bed. One a full-face of Mao Tse-tung, the other a profile of Liu Ping-pong, originator of table tennis. Hung tears the Mao from the wall and tramples it underfoot. Wang sings out her birth-pangs. In the street, old Chiung-hua totters to her feet, listening. Her ancient ears, withered like dried apricots, tell her the first part of the story (the raised voice, slamming door, footsteps on the stairs), and the glassy eyes relay the rest (Hung in the crimson street, flailing at the gargantuan head of Mao suspended just above his reach like the proud stiff sail of a schooner; his use of stones, a broom, a young child; his frustration; his rabid red-mouthed dash down the length of the street and around the corner).

Chiung-hua sighs. Mao's head trembles in a gust. Wang cries out. And then the old woman hikes her skirts and begins the long painful ascent of the stairs, thinking of white towels and hot water and the slick red skulls of her own new-born sons and daughters, her spotted fingers uncertain on the banister, eyes clouding in the dark hallway, lips working over a phrase of Mao's like a litany: "WHAT WE NEED IS AN ENTHUSIASTIC BUT CALM STATE OF MIND AND INTENSE BUT ORDERLY WORK."

Mao is planted on one of the few toilet seats in China. The stall is wooden, fitted with support bars of polished bamboo. A fan rotates lazily overhead. An aide waits without. The Chairman is leaning to one side, penknife in hand, etching delicate Chinese characters into the woodwork. The hot odor that rises round him tells of aging organs and Grey Poupon mustard. He sits back to admire his work.

IMPERIALISM IS A PAPER TIGER

But then he leans forward again, the penknife working a refinement. The aide taps at the stall door. "Yes?" says Mao. "Nothing," says the aide. Mao folds the blade back into its plastic sheath. The emendation pleases him.

IMPERIALISM SUCKS

The man lays his bicycle in the grass and reaches down a hand to help Chang from the mud. Chang begins to thank him, but the stranger holds up his hand. "Don't thank me," he says, "thank Chairman Mao." The stranger's breath steams in the chill air. He introduces himself. "Chou Te-ming," he says.

"Chang Chiu-chu."

"Chang Chiu-chu?"

Chang nods.

"Aren't you the peasant whose leukemia was cured through the application of Mao Tse-tung's thought?"

"Leprosy," says Chang, his toe smoldering like Vesuvius.

"I heard it on the radio," says Chou. "Two hundred times."

Chang beams. "See that pig?" he says. (Chou looks. The pig breaks wind.)

"I'm on my way to the city to offer him up to the Chairman for his birthday. By way of thanks."

Chou, it seems, is also en route to the capital. He suggests that they travel together. Chang is delighted. Shakes the mud from his pantlegs, gives the pig's septum an admonitory tug, and then stops dead. He begins tapping his pockets.

"Lose something?" asks Chou.

"My gourd."

"Ah. Maotai?"

"Home-brewed. And sweet as rain."

The two drop their heads to scan the muddied roadway. Chang spots the gourd at the same moment the pig does, but the pig is lighter on its feet. Rubber nostril, yellow tusk: it snatches up the spotted rind and jerks back its head. The golden rice liquor drools like honey from the whiskered jowls. *Snurk, snurk, snurk.*

Old Chiung-hua lights the lamp, sets a pot of water on the stove, rummages through Wang's things in search of clean linen. Her feet ache and she totters with each step, slow and awkward as a hard-hat diver. Wang is quiet, her breathing regular. On the floor, in the center of the room, a brown-paper parcel. The old woman bends for it, then settles into a chair beside the bed. A Japanese-made transistor radio hangs from the bedpost on a leather strap. She turns it on.

ASSISTING MORE DEAF-MUTES TO SING "THE EAST IS RED"

It was raining, and the children of the Chanchai People's Revolutionary Rehabilitation Center could not go out of doors. The paraplegic children entertained themselves by repeating quotations of Mao Tse-tung and singing revolutionary songs of the Chairman's sayings set to music. But one of the deaf-mute children came to Chou Te-ming, a cadre of a Mao Tse-tung's thought propaganda team, in tears. She signed to him that it was her fondest wish to sing "The East Is Red" and to call out "Long live Chairman Mao, a long, long life to him!" with the others. While discussing the problem with some class brothers later that day, Chou Te-ming recalled a phrase of Chairman Mao's: "THE PRINCIPLE OF USING DIFFERENT METHODS TO RESOLVE DIFFERENT CONTRADICTIONS IS ONE WHICH MARXIST-LENINISTS MUST STRICTLY OBSERVE." He was suddenly inspired to go to the children's dormitory and examine their Eustachian tubes and vocal apparatuses. He saw that in many cases the deaf-mute children's tubes were blocked and frenums ingrown. The next morning he operated. By that evening, eighteen of the twenty children were experiencing their fondest desire, singing "The East is Red" in praise of

Mao Tse-tung. This is a great victory of Mao Tse-tung's thought, a rich fruit of the Great Proletarian Revolution.

In the shifting shadows cast by the lamp, old Chiung-hua nods and Wang wakes with a cry on her lips.

When Mao steps out on the balcony the square erupts. Five hundred thousand voices in delirium. "Mao, Mao, Mao, Mao," they chant. Confetti flies, banners wave. Mammoth Mao portraits leap at the tips of upraised fingers. The Chairman opens his arms and the answering roar is like the birth of a planet. He looks down on the wash of heads and shoulders oscillating like the sea along a rocky shoreline, and he turns to one of his aides. "Tell me," he shouts, "did the Beatles ever have it this good?" The aide, an intelligent fellow, grins. Mao gazes back down at the crowd, his frozen jowls trembling with a rush of paternal solicitude. It is then that the idea takes him, then, on the balcony, on his birthday, the grateful joyous revolutionary proletarian class brothers and sisters surging beneath him and bursting spontaneously into song ("The East Wind Prevails Over the West Wind"). He cups a hand to the aide's ear. "Fetch my swimtrunks."

Though the table-tennis team has taken him to Japan, Malaysia, Albania, Zaire, Togoland and Botswana, Hung's mental horizons are not expansive. He is a very literal-minded fellow. When Wang made her announcement from between clenched teeth and dusky sheets, he did not pause to consider that "Thank Chairman Mao" has become little more than a catchword or that virgin births have been known to occur in certain regions and epochs and under certain conditions or even that some more prosaic progenitor may have turned the trick. But perhaps he didn't want to. Perhaps the shock cauterized some vital portion of the brain, some control center, and left him no vent but a species of mindless frothing rage. And what better object for such a rage than that the ice-faced universal progenitor, that kindly ubiquitous father?

The pig is swimming on its feet, drunk, ears and testicles awash, eyes crossed, nostrils dripping. It has torn the cord free from Chang's pants and now trots an unsteady twenty paces ahead of Chang and Chou. Chou is walking his bicycle. Chang, rorschached in mud and none too steady of foot himself, limps along beside him. From time to time the two lengthen their stride in the hope of overtaking the pig, but the animal is both watchful and agile, and holds its liquor better than some.

They are by this time passing through the outskirts of the great city, winding through the ranks of shanties that cluster the hills like tumbled dominoes. The river, roiled and yellow, rushes on ahead of them. Chang is muttering curses under his breath. The pig's ears flap rhythmically. Overhead, somewhere in the thin bleak troposphere, the rain submits to a transubstantiation and begins to fall as snow. Chang flings a stone and the porker quickens its pace.

"But it's snowing—"
   "Thirty degrees—"
   "Your shingles—"
   "Blood pressure—"
   "Hemorrhoids—"
Mao waves them away, his aides, as if they were so many flies and mosquitoes. His face is set. Beneath the baggy khaki swimtrunks, his thin thick-veined legs, splayed feet. He slips into his slippers, pulls on a Mao tunic, and steps down the stairs, out the door and into the crowd.
   They are still singing. Holding hands. Posters wave, banners flash, flakes fall. By the time Mao's presence becomes known through the breadth of the crowd, he has already mounted an elevated platform in the back of a truck. The roar builds successively—from near to far—like mortar rounds in the hills, and those closest to him press in on the truck, ecstatic, frenzied, tears coursing down their cheeks, bowing and beaming and genuflecting.
   The truck's engine fires. Mao waves his cap. Thousands pass out. And then the truck begins to inch forward, the crowd parting gradually before it. Mao waves again. Mountains topple, icebergs plunge into the sea. With the aid of an aide he climbs still higher—to the seat of a chair mounted on the platform—and raises his hand for silence. A hush falls over the crowd: cheers choke in throats, tears gel on eyelashes, squalling infants catch their breath. The clatter of the truck's engine becomes audible, and then, for those fortunate thousands packed against the fenders, Mao's voice. He is saying something about the river. Three words, repeated over and over. The crowd is puzzled. The Chairman's legs are bare. There is a towel thrown over his shoulder. And then, like the jolt of a radio dropped in bathwater, the intelligence shoots through the crowd. They take up the chant. "To the River! To the River!" The Chairman is going swimming.

Chang and Chou feel the tremor in the soles of their feet, the blast on the wind. "They're cheering in the square," says Chou. "Must be the celebration for Mao's birthday." The trousers slap round his ankles as he steps up his pace. Chang struggles to keep up, slowed by drink and toethrob, and by his rube's sense of amaze at the city. Periodically he halts to gape at the skyscrapers that rise from the bank of shanties like pyramids stalking the desert, while people course by on either side of him—peasants, workers, Red Guards, children—all rushing off to join in the rites. Ahead of him, the back of Chou, doggedly pushing at the handlebars of his bicycle, and far beyond Chou, just visible through the thicket of thighs and calves, the seductive coiled tail of the pig. "Wait!" he calls. Chou looks back over his shoulder. "Hurry!" There is another shout. And then another. The crowd is coming toward them!

Straight-backed and stiff-lipped, propped up by his aides, Mao rides the truckbed like a marble statue of himself, his hair and shoulders gone white with a fat-flake snow. The crowd is orderly ("THE MASSES ARE THE REAL HEROES," he is thinking), flowing out of the square and into the narrow streets with the viscous ease of lightweight oil. There is no shoving or toe-stamping. Those in front of the truck fan to the sides, remove their jackets and lay them over the white peach fuzz in the road. Then they kneel and bow their foreheads to the pavement while the black-grid tires grind over the khaki carpet. Light as milkweed, the snow-flakes spin down and whiten their backs.

The sight of the river reanimates the Chairman. He lifts his arms like a con-ductor and the crowd rushes with hilarity and admiration. "Long live," etc., they cheer as he strips off his jacket to reveal his skinny-strap undershirt beneath, the swell of his belly. (At this shout, Hung, who is in the process of defacing a thirty-foot-high portrait of the Chairman in a tenement street three blocks away, pauses, puzzling. It is then that he becomes aware of the six teenagers in Mao shirts and red-starred caps. They march up to him in formation, silent, pure, aus-tere and disciplined. Two of them restrain Hung's hands; the others beat him with their Mao-sticks, from scalp to sole, until his flesh takes on the color and consistency of a fermenting plum.) Mao steps down from the truck, his pudgy hand spread across an aide's shoulder, and starts jauntily off for the shoreline. People weep and laugh, applaud and cheer: a million fingers reach out to touch the Chairman's bare legs and arms. As he reaches the water's edge they begin to disrobe, stripping to khaki shorts and panties and brassieres, swelling hordes of them crowding the littoral, their clothes mounting faster than the languid feath-ery snowflakes.

Two hundred yards up the shore Chou abandons his bike along the roadway and dashes for the water, Chang hobbling behind him, both neck-stretching to catch a glimpse of the Chairman's entourage. Somewhere behind them a band begins to play and a loudspeaker cranks out a spate of Mao's maxims. In the con-fusion, Chang finds himself unbuttoning his shirt, loosing the string of his trousers, shucking the mud-caked slippers. Chou already stands poised in the gelid muck, stripped to shorts, waiting for Mao to enter the water. His mouth is a black circle, his voice lost in the boom of the crowd.

And then, miracle of miracles, Mao's ankles are submersed in the yellow cur-rent, his calves, his knees! He pauses to slap the icy water over his chest and shoulders—and then the geriatric racing dive, the breaststroke, the square brow and circular head riding smooth over the low-lapping waves! The people go mad, Coney Island afire, and rush foaming into the chill winter water—old women, children, expectant mothers, thrilled by Mao's heroic example, charged by the passion to share in the element which washes the Revolutionary Chairman of the Chinese Communist Party.

Chou is in, Chang hesitating on the bank, the snow blowing, his arms prickled with gooseflesh. The water foams like a battle at sea. People fling themselves at the river, shouting praise of Chairman Mao. Chang shrugs and follows them.

The water is a knife. Colder than the frozen heart of the universe. The current takes him, heaves him into a tangle of stiffening limbs and shocked bodies, a mass of them clinging together like worms in a can, the air splintering in his lungs, the darkness below, a thousand hands, the mud, the cold. He does not catch a glimpse of the Chairman's entourage, nor does he have an opportunity to admire the clean stroke, the smooth glide of the Chairman's head over the storm-white waves, forging on.

Wang's features are dappled with sweat. Old Chiung-hua sips white tea and dabs at Wang's forehead with a handkerchief. "Push," she says. "Bear down and heave." At that moment, over the jabber of the radio and the clang of the pipes, a roar, as of numberless human voices raised in concert. Chiung-hua lifts her withered head and listens.

Suddenly the door pushes open. The old woman turns, expecting Hung. It is not Hung. It is a pig, black head, white shoulders, brass ring through the nose. "Shoo!" cries Chiung-hua, astonished. "Shoo!" The pig stares at her, then edges into the room apologetically. The old lady staggers angrily to her feet, but then Wang grabs her hand. Wang's teeth are gritted, her gymnast's muscles flexed. "Uh-oh," she says and Chiung-hua sits back down: a head has appeared between Wang's legs. "Push, push, push," the old woman hisses, and Wang obeys. There is a sound like a flushing toilet and then suddenly the infant is in Chiung-hua's wizened hands. She cuts the cord, dabs the blood and tissue from the puckered red face, and swaddles the tiny thing in the only clean clothes at hand: a pair of patched blue jeans.

Wang sits up and the old woman hands her the infant. She hefts it to look underneath. (A male. Heavy of jowl, abdomen, nates. And with hair on its head—the strangest growth of hair set across the most impossible expanse of brow. Square across.) Wang wrinkles her nose. "That smell," she says. "Like a barnyard."

Chiung-hua, remembering, turns to shoo the pig. But then her ancient face drops: the pig is kneeling.

Out in the street, so close it jars, a shout goes up.

(1976)

DADA

We were organizing the Second International Dada Fair. The first had been held fifty-seven years ago in Berlin. The second, we felt, was overdue. Friedrich had asked Jean Arp's grandson, Guillaume, to exhibit his *Static Hobbyhorse #2*, and Marcel Duchamp's daughter, Lise, had agreed to show her *Nude Descending Escalator*. All very well and fine. But we were stuck for a main attraction, a drawing card, the pièce de résistance. Then Werther came up with a suggestion that slapped us all with its brilliance: waves beat on the rocks, lights flashed in dark rooms. I remember it clearly. We were drinking imported beer in Klaus's loft, laying plans for the Fair. Werther slouched against a molded polyethylene reproduction of Tristan Tzara's *Upended Bicycle*, a silver paper knife beating a tattoo in his palm. Beside him, on the coffee table, lay a stack of magazines. Suddenly he jerked the knife to his lips, shouted "Dada Redivivus!" and thrust the blade into the slick cellulose heart of them. Then he stepped back. The knife had impaled a magazine in the center of the stack: we began to understand.

Werther extracted his prize and flipped back the page. It was a news magazine. Glossy cover. We gathered round. There, staring back at us, between the drum major's braided cap and the gold epaulettes, were the dark pinguid features of Dada made flesh: His Excellency Al Haji Field Marshal and President for Life of Uganda: Idi Amin Dada.

"Crazee!" said Friedrich, all but dancing.

"Épatant!" sang Klaus.

My name is Zoë. I grinned. We had our pièce de résistance.

■ ■ ■

Two days later I flew into Entebbe via Pan African Airways. Big Daddy met me at the airport. I was wearing my thigh-high boots, striped culottes. His head was like a medicine ball. He embraced me, buried his nose in my hair. "I love Americans!" he said. Then he gave me a medal.

At the house in Kampala he stood among his twenty-two children like a sleepy brontosaur among the first tiny quick-blooded mammals. One of the children wore a white tutu and pink ribbons. "This one," he said, his hand on the child's head, "a girl." Then he held out his broad pink palm and panned across the yard where the rest of the brood rolled and leaped, pinched, climbed and burrowed like dark little insects. He grinned and asked me to marry him. I was cagey. "After the Fair," I said.

"The Fair," he repeated. His eyes were sliced melons.

"Dada," I said.

The plane was part of a convoy of three Ugandan 747s. All across Zaire, Cameroon and Mali, across Mauritania and the rocky Atlantic, my ears sang with the keen of infants, the cluck of chickens, the stringy flatulence of goats and pigs. I looked out the window: the wing was streaked with rust. To the right and left, fore and aft, Big Daddy's bodyguards reclined in their reclining seats, limp as cooked spaghetti. High-heeled boots, shades and wristwatches, guns. Each held a transistor radio to his ear. Big Daddy sat beside me, sweating, caressing my fingers in a hand like a boxing glove. I was wearing two hundred necklaces and a turban. I am twenty-six. My hair is white, shag-cut. He was wearing a jumbo jumpsuit, khaki and camouflage, a stiff chest full of medals. I began to laugh.

"Why you laugh?" he said.

I was thinking of Bergson. I explained to him that the comical consists of something mechanical encrusted on the living. He stared at me, blank, his face misshapen as a decaying jack-o'-lantern.

"Dada," I said, by way of shorthand explication.

He grinned. Lit a cigarette. "They do me honor," he said finally, "to name such a movement for me."

The Fair was already under way when we landed at Kennedy. Big Daddy's wives, cattle and attendants boarded five rented buses and headed for Harlem, where he had reserved the fourth floor of the Hotel Theresa. His Excellency himself made a forty-five-minute impromptu speech at Gate 19E, touching on solutions to the energy crisis, inflation and overcrowded zoos, after which I hustled him into a cab and made for Klaus's loft on Elizabeth Street.

We rattled up Park Avenue, dipping and jolting, lights raining past the windows. Big Daddy told me of his athletic and military prowess, nuzzled my ear, pinned a medal to my breast. "Two hundred cattle," he said. "A thousand acres." I looked straight ahead. He patted my hand. "Twenty bondmaids, a mountain of emeralds, fresh fish three days a week."

I turned to look into the shifting deeps of his eyes, the lights filming his face, yellow, green, red, bright, dark. "After the Fair," I said.

The street outside Klaus's was thronged, the hallway choked. The haut monde emerged from taxis and limousines in black tie and jacket, Halston, Saint-Laurent, mink. "Fantastic!" I said. Big D. looked baleful. "What your people need in this country is savannah and hippo," he said. "But your palace very fine."

I knotted a gold brocade DADA sign around his neck and led him up the stairs to a burst of applause from the spectators. Friedrich met us at the door. He'd arranged everything. Duchamp's *Urinal* stood in the corner; DeGroff's soiled diapers decorated the walls; Werther's own *Soir de l'Uganda* dominated the second floor. Big Daddy squeezed my hand, beamed like a tame Kong. There were champagne, canapés, espresso, women with bare backs. A man was strapped to a bicycle suspended from the ceiling.

Friedrich pumped Big Daddy's hand and then showed him to the seat prepared for him as part of the *Soir de l'Uganda* exhibit. It was magnificent. A thousand and one copper tulips against a backdrop of severed heads and crocodiles. Big D. affixed a medal to Friedrich's sweatshirt and settled into his seat with a glass of champagne. Then he began his "People Must Love Their Leaders" speech.

A reporter took me by the arm and asked me to explain the controlling concept of the Fair and of our principal exhibit. It was a textbook question. I gave him a textbook answer. "Any object is a work of art if the artist proclaims it one," I said. "There is static, cerebral art and there is living art, monuments of absurdity—acts of art. And actors." Then he asked me if it was true that I had agreed to become Bid Daddy's fifth wife. The question surprised me. I looked over at the *Soir de l'Uganda* exhibit. Two of the bodyguards were shooting craps against the bank of papier-mâché heads. Big Daddy slouched in his chair, elephantine and black, beleaguered by lords and ladies, photographers, reporters, envious artists. I could hear his voice over the natter of the crowd—a basso profundo that crept into the blood and punched at the kidneys. "I am a pure son of Africa," he was saying. Overhead the bicycle wheels whirred. I turned back to the reporter, an idea forming in my head—an idea so outré that it shot out to scrape at the black heart of the universe. The ultimate act of art. Dada sacrifice!

He stood there, pen poised over the paper.

"Da," I said. "Da."

(1977)

TWO SHIPS

I saw him today. At the side of the road, head down, walking. There were the full-leafed trees, the maples, elms, and oaks I see every day, the snarl of the wild berry bushes, sumac, milkweed, and thistle, the snaking hot macadam road, sun-flecked shadows. And him. An apparition: squat, bow-legged, in shorts, T-shirt, and sandals, his head shaved to the bone, biceps like legs of lamb. I slowed with the shock of seeing him there, with the recognition that worked in my ankles and fingertips like sap, and for a stunned second or two I stared, fixated, as the car pulled me closer and then swept past him in a rush. I was dressed in white, on my way to crack stinging serves and return treacherous backhands in sweet arcing loops. He never looked up.

When I got home I made some phone calls. He was back in the country—legally—the government forgiving, his mind like damaged fruit. Thirty-one years old, he was staying with his parents, living in the basement, doing God knows what—strumming a guitar, lifting weights, putting pieces of wood together—the things he'd been doing since he was fourteen. Erica listened as I pried information from the receiver, a cigarette in the corner of her mouth, polished surfaces behind her.

I was pouring Haig & Haig over a hard white knot of ice cubes. The last of my informants had got off the subject of Casper and was filling me in on the pains in her neck, lips, toes, and groin as I cradled the receiver between ear and shoulder. The smile I gave Erica was weak. When the whiskey-cracked voice on the other end of the line paused to snatch a quick breath, I changed the subject, whispered a word of encouragement, and hung up.

"Well?" Erica was on her feet.

"We've got to move," I said.

I was overdramatizing. For effect. Overdramatizing because humor resides in exaggeration, and humor is a quick cover for alarm and bewilderment. I *was* alarmed. He could stay indefinitely, permanently. He could show up at the tennis courts, at the lake, at my front door. And then what would I do? Turn my back, look through him, crouch behind the door and listen to the interminable sharp intercourse of knuckle and wood?

"Is it really that bad?" Erica said.

I sipped at my Scotch and nodded. It was really that bad.

Twelve years ago we'd been friends. Close friends. We'd known each other from the dawn of consciousness on. We played in the cradle, in the schoolyard, went to camp together, listened to the same teachers, blocked and batted for the same teams. When we were sixteen we declared war on the bourgeois state and its material and canonical manifestations. That is, we were horny adolescents sublimating glandular frustrations in the most vicious and mindless acts of vandalism. We smoked pot, gulped stolen vodka, and drove our parents' cars at a hundred miles an hour. Each night we cruised the back streets till three or four, assaulting religious statues, churches, the slick curvilinear windshields of Porsches and Cadillacs. Indiscriminate, we burned crosses and six-pointed stars. We tore down fences, smashed picture windows, filled Jacuzzis with sand. Once we climbed a treacherous three-hundred-foot cliff in utter darkness so we could drop raw eggs on the patrons of the chic restaurant nestled at its base.

Casper saw the whole thing as a crusade. He was given to diatribe, and his diatribes had suddenly begun to bloom with the rhetoric of Marxism. We would annihilate a dentist's plaster lawn ornaments—flamingoes and lantern-wielding pickaninnies—and he'd call it class warfare. Privately, I saw our acts of destruction as a way of pissing in my father's eye.

We ran away from home at one point—I think we were fifteen or so—and it was then that I had my first intimation of just how fanatical and intransigent Casper could be. I'd never considered him abnormal, had never thought about it. There was his obsession with the bodily functions, the vehement disgust he felt over his parents' lovemaking—*I could hear them,* he would say, his features pinched with contempt, *grunting and slobbering, humping like pigs*—the fact that he went to a shrink twice a week. But none of this was very different from what other fifteen-year-olds did and said and felt, myself included. Now, running away, I saw that Casper's behavior went beyond the pale of wise-guyism or healthy adolescent rebellion. I recognized the spark of madness in him, and I was both drawn to it and repelled by it. He was serious, he was committed, his was the rapture of saints and martyrs, both feet over the line. He went too far; I drew back from him.

We'd planned this excursion with all the secrecy and precision of prison breakers. Twenty miles away, tucked deep in the leafy recesses of Fahnestock

State Park, was a huge cache of canned food, an ax, two six-packs of Jaguar malt liquor, sleeping bags, and a tent. We signed in at school, ducked out the back door, hitchhiked the twenty miles, and experienced freedom. The following day, while we were exploring the park, my father stalked up to the campsite (my brother had broken down under interrogation and given us away) and settled down to wait. My father is a powerful and unforgiving man. He tapped a birch switch against a rock for an hour, then packed up everything he could carry—food, tent, sleeping bags, canteens—and hiked out to the highway. The sight of the barren campsite made my blood leap. At first I thought we were in the wrong spot, the trees all alike, dusk falling, but then Casper pointed out the blackened circle of rocks we'd cooked a triumphant dinner over the night before. I found my father's note pinned to a tree. It was curt and minatory, the script an angry flail.

Casper refused to give in. Between us we had four dollars and twenty cents. He dragged me through swamps and brambles, the darkening stalks of the trees, past ponds, down hills, and out to the highway. Afraid to hitch—my father could be glaring behind each pair of headlights—we skirted the road and made our way to a clapboard grocery where we purchased a twenty-five-pound bag of Ken-L Ration. Outside, it was 29°F. We hiked back up into the woods, drank from a swamp, crunched the kibbled nuggets of glyceryl monostearate and animal fat preserved with BHA, and slept in our jackets. In the morning I slipped away, walked out to the road, and hitchhiked back home.

The state police were called in to track Casper down. They employed specially trained trackers and bloodhounds. Casper's parents hired a helicopter search team for eighty-five dollars an hour. The helicopter spotted Casper twice. Whirring, kicking up a cyclone, the machine hovered over the treetops while Casper's mother shouted stentorian pleas through a bullhorn. He ran. Two weeks later he turned up at home, in bed, asleep.

It was just after this that Casper began to talk incessantly of repression and the police state. He shuffled round the corridors at school with a huge, distended satchel full of poorly printed pamphlets in faded greens and grays: *The Speeches of V. I. Lenin; State and Anarchy; Das Kapital*. The rhetoric never appealed to me, but the idea of throwing off the yoke, of discounting and discrediting all authority, was a breath of fresh air.

He quit college at nineteen and went to live among the revolutionary workers of the Meachum Brothers Tool & Die Works in Queens. Six months later he was drafted. How they accepted him or why he agreed to report, I'll never know. He was mad as a loon, fixated in his Marxist-Leninist phase, gibbering nonstop about imperialist aggressors and the heroic struggle of the revolutionary democratic peoples of the Republic of Vietnam. It was summer. I was living in Lake George with Erica and he came up for a day or two before they inducted him.

He was worked up—I could see that the minute he got off the bus. His feet shuffled, but his limbs and torso danced, elbows jerking as if they were wired, the big knapsack trembling on his back, a cord pulsing under his left eye. He was wearing a cap that clung to his head like something alive, and the first thing he did was remove it with a flourish to show off his bald scalp: he'd shaved himself—denuded himself—every hair plucked out, right down to his mustache and eyebrows. From the neck up he looked like a space invader; from the neck down, rigidly muscled, he was Charles Atlas. He couldn't stop talking. Couldn't sit down, couldn't sleep, couldn't eat. Said he was going into the army all right, but that he'd do everything in his power to subvert them, and that when they shipped him to Vietnam he'd turn his weapon on his own platoon and then join the NLF. I tried to joke with him, distract him—if only for a moment. But he was immovable. He played his one note till Erica and I just wanted to jump into the car and leave him there with the house, the books, the stereo, everything. Someone pulled a knife out of my ribs when he left.

I never saw him again. Until today.

Rumor had it that he'd disappeared from Fort Dix the first week. He was in Canada, he was in Sweden. The Finns had jailed him for entering the country illegally, the Swiss had expelled him. He was in Belize City stirring up the locals, the British had got hold of him and the United States was pressing for his extradition. Rumors. They sifted back to me through my mother, friends, people who claimed they'd seen him or talked to someone who had. I was in law school, student-deferred. There were exams, the seasons changed, Erica visited on weekends, and there were long breathy phone calls in between. In my second year, the packages began to show up in my mailbox. Big, crudely bundled manuscripts— manuscripts the size of phone books—sent from an address in London, Ontario.

There were no cover letters. But, then, cover letters would have been superfluous: the moment I saw the crabbed scrawl across the flat surface of the first package (lettering so small it could have been written with the aid of magnification), I knew who had sent it. Inside these packages were poems. Or, rather, loosely organized snatches of enjambed invective in strident upper-case letters:

> THE FASCIST NAZI ABORTIONIST LOBBY THAT FEEDS
> ON THE TATTERED FLESH OF ASIAN ORPHANS
> MUST BE CIRCUMVENTED FROM ITS IMPERIALIST EXPANSIONIST DESIGN
> TO ENSLAVE THE MASSES AND TURN ARTIFICIALLY NATIONALIZED
> PROLETARIANS AGAINST BROTHER AND SISTER PROLETARIANS
> IN THE INTERNECINE CONFLICT THAT FEEDS
> THE COFFERS
> OF THE REVISIONIST RUNNING DOGS
> OF BOURGEOIS COMPLACENCY!

The poems went on for hundreds of pages. I couldn't read them. I wondered why he had sent them to me. Was he trying to persuade me? Was he trying to justify himself, reach out, recapture some sympathy he'd deluded himself into thinking we'd once shared? I was in law school. I didn't know what to do. Eventually, the packages stopped coming.

Erica and I married, moved back to Westchester, built a house, had a daughter. I was working in a law firm in White Plains. One night, 2:00 A.M., the phone rang. It was Casper. "Jack," he said, "it's me, Casper. Listen, listen, this is important, this is vital—" Phone calls in the night. I hadn't spoken to him in seven years, gulfs had opened between us, I was somebody else—and yet here he was, with the same insistent, demanding voice that wraps you up in unasked-for intimacies like a boa constrictor, talking as if we'd just seen each other the day before. I sat up. He was nearly crying.

"Jack: you've got to do something for me, life and death, you got to promise me—"

"Wait a minute," I said, "wait, hold on—" I didn't want to hear it. I was angry, puzzled; I had to be at work in five and a half hours.

"Just this one thing. You know me, right? Just this: if anybody asks, you stick up for me, okay? No, no: I mean, tell them I'm all right, you know what I mean? That I'm good. There's nothing wrong with me, understand?"

What could I say? The phone went dead, the room was dark. Beside me, in bed, Erica shifted position and let out a sigh that would have soothed all the renegades in the world.

I was busy. The incident slipped my mind. Three days later a man in an elaborately buckled and belted trenchcoat stepped into the anteroom at Hermening & Stinson, the firm that had given me my tenuous foothold in the world of corporate law. No one paid much attention to him until he announced that he was from the FBI and that he wanted to speak with me. The typist stopped typing. Charlie Hermening looked up at me like a barn owl scanning the rafters. I shrugged my shoulders.

The man was big and fleshy and pale, his irises like water, wisps of white hair peeping out from beneath the fedora that hugged his bullet head. When I showed him into my office he flashed his credentials, and I remember wondering if TV producers had studied FBI men, or if FBI men had learned how to act from watching TV. He took a seat, but declined to remove either his hat or trenchcoat. Was I acquainted with a Casper R. Mendelson, he wanted to know. Did I know his whereabouts? When had I seen him last? Had he telephoned, sent anything in the mail? What did I think of his mental state?

"His mental state?" I repeated.

"Yes," the man said, soft and articulate as a professor, "I want to know if you feel he's mentally competent."

I thought about it for a minute, thought about Lake George, the poems, Casper's tense and frightened voice over the phone. I almost asked the FBI man why he wanted to know: Was Casper in trouble? Had he done something illegal? I wanted to gauge the man's response, listen for nuances that might give me a clue as to what I should say. But I didn't. I simply leaned across the desk, looked the man in the eye, and told him that in my estimation Casper was seriously impaired.

That was a year ago. I'd forgotten the man from the FBI, forgotten Casper. Until now. Now he was back. Like a slap in the face, like a pointed finger: he was back.

"What are you afraid of?" Erica asked. "That he'll say hello or shake your hand or something?"

It was dark. Moths batted against the screens; I toyed with my asparagus crêpes and spinach salad. The baby was in bed. I poured another glass of French Colombard. "No," I said, "that's not it." And then: "Yes. That would be bad enough. Think of the embarrassment."

"Embarrassment? You were friends, you grew up together."

"Yes," I said. That was the problem. I sipped at the wine.

"Look, I'm not exactly thrilled about seeing him either—the weekend at Lake George was enough to last me a lifetime—but it's not the end of the world or anything. . . . I mean, nothing says you've got to invite him over for dinner so he can lecture us on the wisdom of Mao Tse-tung or tell us how miserable he is."

She was in the kitchen area, spooning the foam off a cup of cappuccino. "Are you afraid he'll vandalize the house—is that it?"

"I don't know," I said. "I mean, we're not kids anymore—he's not that crazy." I thought about it, listening to the hiss of the coffee maker. The house we'd put up was pretty cozy and dramatic. Modern. With decks and skylights and weathered wood and huge sheets of glass. It called attention to itself, stylish and unique, a cut above the slant-roofed cottages that lined the road. It was precisely the sort of house Casper and I had sought out and violated when we were sixteen. I looked up from my wine. "He might," I admitted.

Erica looked alarmed. "Should we call the police?"

"Don't be ridiculous, we can't—" I broke off. It was futile. I wasn't really afraid of that sort of thing—no, my fears went deeper, deeper than I wanted to admit. He would look at me and he would condemn me: I'd become what we'd reacted against together, what he'd devoted his mad, misguided life to subverting. That was the problem. That's why I didn't want to see him at the tennis courts or at the lake or even walking along the road with his shoulders hunched under the weight of his convictions.

"Hey"—she was at my side, massaging the back of my neck—"why not forget about it, you've got enough worries as it is." She was right. The EPA was filing suit against one of our clients—a battery company accused of dumping toxic waste in the Hudson—and I'd been poring over the regulations looking for some sort of loophole. I was meeting with Charlie Hermening in the morning to show him what I'd come up with.

"You know something—didn't Rose say he'd been back nearly a month already?" She was purring, the cappuccino smelled like a feast, I could feel the alcohol loosening my knotted nerves. "And you only saw him today for the first time? If he was going to come over, wouldn't he have done it by now?"

I was about to admit she was right, finish my coffee, and take a look at the newspaper when there was a knock at the door. A knock at the door. It was nine-thirty. I nearly kicked the table over. "I'm not here," I hissed. "No matter who it is," and I slipped into the bedroom.

There were voices in the hallway. I heard Erica, and then the polite but vaguely querulous tones of—a woman?—and then Erica's voice, projecting: "Jack. Jack, will you come out here, please?"

Mrs. Shapiro, our next-door neighbor, was standing in the doorway. "Sorry to bother you," the old woman said, "but your garbitch is all over the driveway—I can't even get the car through."

Garbage? Her driveway was at least fifty feet from ours. What was she talking about?

The night was warm, redolent of flowers and grass clippings. There was a moon, and the crickets seemed to be serenading it, chirring in the trees like a steel band locked in a groove. I walked beside Mrs. Shapiro to where her car sat rumbling and sputtering, lights flooding the gumbo of vegetable peels, papers, milk cartons, and diapers strewn across her driveway. The cans had been deliberately hauled down the street, upended and dumped—no dog or raccoon could have been so determined or efficient. This was deliberate. As I bent to the mess, I thought of Casper.

"Kids." Mrs. Shapiro, arms folded, stood silhouetted against the headlights. She spat the words out as if she were cursing. "Things just seem to get worse and worse, don't they?"

I worked in silence, embarrassed, digging into the slop with my bare hands, trying not to think about baby stool, maggots, the yielding wet paste of coffee grounds and cantaloupe shells, scooping it up by the armload. When I was finished I told Mrs. Shapiro that I'd have Erica hose down the driveway for her in the morning. The elderly woman merely raised her hand as if to say "Forget about it," tumbled into the car seat, and set the car in motion with a shriek of the steering mechanism and a rumble of rotten exhaust. I watched the taillights trace the arc of her driveway, then hauled the garbage cans back to my own yard, all the while expecting Casper to pop out at me with a laugh. Or maybe he was crouching in the bushes, giggling to himself like a half-witted adolescent. That was about his speed, I thought.

Inside, I washed up, fumed at Erica—"It was deliberate," I kept saying, "I know it was"—and then shut myself up in the study with the brief I'd prepared on the battery manufacturer. I couldn't read a word of it. After a while—it must have been twenty minutes or so—I heard Erica getting ready for bed—running water, brushing her teeth—and then the house went silent. I knew I should go over the brief a couple of times, have a mug of hot Ovaltine, and get a good night's rest. But I was rooted to the chair, thinking about Casper—a grown man, thirty-one years old—sneaking around in the dark dumping people's garbage. What could he be thinking of?

A muffled sound was pulsing through the house. At first it didn't register, and then, with a flash of anger, I realized what it was: someone was knocking at the door. This was too much. If there was garbage in the neighbors' driveway they could damn well clean it up themselves, I thought, storming down the hallway. I wrenched the door back, expecting Mrs. Shapiro.

It was Casper.

He stood there, his head bowed, the moon blanching the stiff bristle of his crown. He was wearing a sleeveless T-shirt, shorts, sandals. The veins stood out in his arms. When he looked up at me his eyes were soft and withdrawn. "Jack," was all he said.

I was at a loss. The worst possible scenario was playing itself out on my doorstep, and I was caught up in it, against my will, suddenly forced to take a part. I felt like an unrehearsed actor shoved out onstage; I felt exhausted and defeated. My initial impulse had been to slam the door shut, but now, with Casper standing there before me, I could only clear my throat, wipe my features clean, and ask him in.

He hesitated. "No," he said, "no, I couldn't do that. I mean, I just came to . . . to say hello, that's all."

"Don't be silly," I said, insistent, already ushering him in. "Here, the living room. Have a seat. Can I get you something: beer? brandy? 7-Up?"

We were standing beside each other in the center of the living room. He took in the potted plants, the umbrella tree, the little Paul Klee my mother had given me. The nearest piece of furniture was the loveseat; he perched on the edge of it, apologetic. "No thanks," he said, eyes on the floor.

I was halfway to the kitchen, needing a brandy. "You sure? It's no trouble at all. I've got liqueur—how about a Drambuie?" It had suddenly become crucially important that I give him something, an offering of some sort, a peace pipe, the communal leg of lamb. "Are you hungry? I've got Brie and crackers—I could make a sandwich—?"

He was still staring at the floor. "Milk," he said, so softly I wasn't sure I'd heard him.

"You want a glass of milk?"

"Yes, thanks—if it's not too much trouble."

I made some deprecatory noises, poured out a brandy and a milk, arranged some Danish flatbread on a platter around the cheese. Two minutes later we were sitting across the room from each other. I was looking into my brandy snifter; he was studying the glass of milk as if he'd never seen anything like it before. "So," I said, "you're back."

He didn't answer. Just sat there, looking at his milk. There was something monkish about him—perhaps it was the crewcut. I thought of acolytes, nuns, the crop-headed Hare Krishnas in airport lounges. "It's been a long time," I offered. No response. It occurred to me to ask about the garbage cans—perhaps we could share the intimacy of the joke—but then I thought better of it: no sense in embarrassing him or stirring up any rancor.

"About the garbage cans," he said, as if reading my thoughts, "I did it."

I waited for an explanation. He stared at me so fixedly I finally looked away, and more as a means of breaking the silence than satisfying my curiosity, I asked him why.

He seemed to consider this. "I don't know," he said finally, took a tentative sip of milk, then downed the glass in a single gulp. He belched softly and settled back in the chair.

I was losing my patience. I had work in the morning. The last thing I wanted to do was sit here with this wacko, on edge in my own living room, mouthing the little platitudes of social formality when I knew both of us were seething. I made another stab at conversation, just because the silence was so inadmissible. "So," I said, "we've wondered about you from time to time, Erica and I. . . . We have a daughter, did you know that? Her name's Tricia."

His arms were rigid, tense with muscle. He was staring down at his interlocked fingers, straining with the tension, as if he were doing an isometric exercise. "I was in the hospital," he said.

The hospital. The syllables bit into me, made something race round the edge of my stomach. I did not want to hear it.

I got up to pour another brandy. "More milk?" I asked, the rigorous host, but he ignored me. He was going to tell me about the hospital. He raised his voice so I could hear him.

"They said it was a condition of giving me a clean slate. You know, they'd rehabilitate me. Eleven months. Locked up with the shit-flingers and droolers, the guys they'd shot up in the war. That was the hospital."

I stood in the kitchen doorway, the brandy in my hand. He was accusing me. I'd started the war, oppressed the masses, wielded the dollar like an axe; I'd deserted him, told the FBI the truth, created the American Nazi Party, and erected the slums, stick by stick. What did he want from me—to say I was sorry? Sorry he was crazy, sorry he couldn't go to law school, sorry Marx's venom had eaten away the inside of his brain?

He was on his feet now. The empty glass flashed in his hand as he crossed the room. He handed it to me. We were inches apart. "Jack," he said. I looked away.

"I've got to go now," he whispered.

I stood at the door and watched him recede into the moonlight that spilled across the lawn like milk. He turned left on the macadam road, heading in the direction of his parents' house.

Erica was behind me in her robe, squinting against the light in the hallway. "Jack?" she said.

I barely heard her. Standing there in the doorway, watching the shadows close like a fist over the lawn, I was already packing.

(1981)

THE LITTLE CHILL

Hal had known Rob and Irene, Jill, Harvey, Tootle, and Pesky since elementary school, and they were all forty going on sixty.

Rob and Irene had been high-school sweethearts, and now, after quitting their tenured teaching jobs, they brokered babies for childless couples like themselves. They regularly flew to Calcutta, Bahrain, and Sarawak to bring back the crumpled brown-faced little sacks of bones they located for the infertile wives of dry cleaners and accountants. Though they wouldn't admit it, they'd voted for Ronald Reagan.

Jill had a certain fragile beauty about her. She'd gone into a Carmelite nunnery after the obloquy of high school and the unrequited love she bore for Harvey, who at the time was hot for Tootle. She lived just up the street from Rob and Irene, in her late mother's house, and she'd given up the nun's life twelve years earlier to have carnal relations with a Safeway butcher named Eugene, who left her with a blind spot in one eye, a permanent limp, and triplets.

Harvey had been a high-school lacrosse star who quit college to join the Marines, acquiring a reputation for ferocity and selfless bravery during the three weeks he fought at Da Nang before taking thirty-seven separate bayonet wounds in his legs, chest, buttocks, and feet. He was bald and bloated, a brooding semi-invalid addicted to Quaalude, Tuinol, aspirin, cocaine, and Jack Daniel's, and he lived in the basement of his parents' house, eating little and saying less. He despised Hal, Rob and Irene, Jill, Tootle, and Pesky because they hadn't taken thirty-seven bayonet wounds each and because they were communists and sellouts.

Tootle had been a cover girl; a macrobiot; the campaign manager for a presidential candidate from Putnam Valley, New York, who promised to push through legislation to animate all TV news features; and, finally, an environmentalist who spent all her waking hours writing broadsides for the Marshwort Preservationists' League. She was having an off/on relationship with an Italian race-car driver named Enzo.

Pesky was assistant manager of Frampold's LiquorMart, twice divorced and the father of a fourteen-year-old serial murderer whose twelve adult male victims all resembled Pesky in coloring, build, and style of dress.

And Hal? Hal was home from California. For his birthday.

Jill hosted the party. She had to. The triplets—Steve, Stevie, and Steven, now seven, seven, and seven, respectively—were hyperactive, antisocial, and twice as destructive as Hitler's Panzer Corps. She hadn't been able to get a baby-sitter for them since they learned to crawl. "All right," Hal had said to her on the phone, "your house then. Seven o'clock. Radical. Really." And then he hung up, thinking of the dingy cavern of her mother's house, with its stained wallpaper, battered furniture, and howling drafts, and of the mortified silence that would fall over the gang when they swung by to pick up Jill on a Friday night and Mrs. Morlock—that big-bottomed, horse-toothed parody of Jill—would insist they come in for hot chocolate. But no matter. At least the place was big.

As it turned out, Hal was two hours late. He was from California, after all, and this was his party. He hadn't seen any of these people in what—six years now?—and there was no way he was going to be cheated out of his grand entrance. At seven he pulled a pair of baggy parachute pants over his pink high-tops, stuck a gold marijuana-leaf stud through the hole in his left earlobe, wriggled into an Ozzie Osbourne Barf Tour T-shirt though it was twenty-six degrees out and driving down sleet, and settled into the Barcalounger in which his deceased dad had spent the last two-thirds of his life. He sipped Scotch, watched the TV blip rhythmically, and listened to his own sad old failing mom dodder on about the Jell-O mold she'd bought for Mrs. Herskowitz across the street. Then, when he was good and ready, he got up, slicked back his thinning, two-tone, forty-year-old hair that looked more and more like mattress stuffing every day, shrugged into his trenchcoat, and slammed out into the storm.

There were two inches of glare ice on the road. Hal thumped his mother's stuttering Oldsmobile from tree to tree, went into a 180-degree spin, and schussed down Jill's driveway, narrowly avoiding the denuded azalea bush, three Flexible Flyers, and a staved-in Renault on blocks. He licked his fingertips and smoothed down his sideburns on the doorstep, knocked perfunctorily, and entered, grinning, in all his exotic, fair-haired, California glory. Unfortunately, the effect was wasted—no one but Jill was there. Hunched in the corner of a gutted sofa, she smiled wanly from behind a mound of soggy Fritos and half a gallon of California dip. "Hi," she said in a voice of dole, "they're coming, they're coming." Then she winked her bad eye at him and limped across the room to stick her tongue in his mouth.

She was clinging to him, licking at his mustache and telling him about her bout with breast cancer, when the doorbell rang and Rob and Irene came hurtling into the room shrieking "My God, look at you!" They were late, they screamed, because the baby-sitter never showed for their daughter, Souka-mathandravaki, whose frightened little face peered in out of the night behind them.

An instant later, Harvey swung furiously up the walk on his silver crutches, Tootle and Pesky staggered in together with reddened noses and dilated pupils, and Steve, Stevie, and Steven emerged from the back of the house on their minibikes to pop wheelies in the middle of the room. The party was on.

"So," Harvey snarled, fencing Hal into the corner with the gleaming shafts of his crutches, "they tell me you're doing pretty good out there, huh, bub?"

Pesky and Tootle were standing beside him, grinning till Hal thought their lips would dry out and stick to their teeth, and Pesky had his arm around Tootle's shoulder. "Me?" Hal said, with a modest shrug. "Well, since you ask, my agent did say that—"

Harvey cut him off, turning to Pesky with a wild leer and shouting, "So how's the kid, what's his name—Damian?"

Dead silence fell over the room.

Rob and Irene froze, clutching Dixie cups of purple passion to their chests, and Jill, who'd been opening their eyes to the in-fighting, petty abuses, and cata-strophic outrages of the food-stamp office where she worked, caught her tongue. Even Steve, Stevie, and Steven snapped to attention. They'd been playfully bind-ing little Soukamathandravaki to one of the dining-room chairs with electri-cal tape, but at the mention of Damian, they looked round them in unison and vanished.

"You son of a bitch," Pesky said, his fingers dug so deep in Tootle's shoulder his knuckles went white. "You crippled fascist Marine Corps burnout."

Harvey jerked his big head to one side and spat on the floor.

"What'd they give him, life plus a hundred and fifty years? Or'd they send him to Matteawan?"

"Hey," Irene shouted, a desperate keening edge to her voice, "hey, do you guys remember all those wild pranks we used to pull back in high school?" She tore across the room, waving her Dixie cup. "Like, like when we smeared that black stuff on our faces and burned the Jewish star on Dr. Rosenbaum's front lawn?"

Everyone ignored her.

"Harv," Hal said, reaching out to take his arm, but Harvey jerked violently away—"Get your stinking hands off me!" he roared—before he lost his balance and fell with a sad clatter of aluminum into the California dip.

"Serves you right, you bitter son of a bitch," Pesky growled, standing over him as if they'd just gone fifteen rounds. "The crippled war hero. Why don't you show us your scars, huh?"

"Pesky," Hal hissed, "leave it, will you?"

Rob and Irene were trying to help Harvey to his feet, but he fought them off, sobbing with rage. There was California dip on the collar of his campaign jacket. Hairless and pale, with his quivering jowls and splayed legs, he looked like a monstrous baby dropped there on the rug.

"Or the time Pesky ran up in front of Mrs. Gold's class in the third grade and did squat thrusts till he passed out, remember that?" Irene was saying, when the room was rent by a violent, predatory shriek, as if someone had torn a hawk in half. It was Tootle. She twisted out from under Pesky's arm and slammed her little white fist into his kidney. "You," she sputtered, "who are you to talk, lording it over Harvey as if he was some kind of criminal or something. At least he fought for his country. What'd you do, huh?" Her eyes were swollen. There was a froth of saliva caught in the corner of her mouth.

Pesky swung around. He was wearing his trademark Levi's—jeans, jacket, sweatshirt, socks, and big-buckled belt. If only they made shoes, he used to say. "Yeah, yeah, tell us about it," he sneered, "you little whore. Peddling your ass just like—"

"Canada, that's what you did about it. Like a typical wimp."

"Hey, hold on," Hal said, lurching out of the corner in his parachute pants, "I don't believe this. We all tried to get out of it—it was a rotten war, an illegal war, Nixon's and Johnson's war—what's the matter with you? Don't you remember?"

"The marches," Irene said.

"The posters," Rob joined in.

"A cheap whore, that's all. Cover girl, my ass."

"Shut up!" Tootle shrieked, turning on Hal. "You're just as bad as Pesky. Worse. You're a hypocrite. At least he knows he's a piece of shit." She threw back a cup of purple passion and leveled her green-eyed glare on him. "And you think you're so high and mighty, out there in Hollywood—well, la-de-da, that's what I say."

"He's an artist," Harvey said from the floor. "He co-wrote the immortal script for the 'Life with Beanie' show."

"Fuck you."

"Fuck you too."

And then suddenly, as if it signaled a visitation from another realm, there was the deep-throated cough of a precision engine in the driveway, a sputter and its dying fall. As one, the seven friends turned to the door. There was a thump. A knock—*dat dat-dat-dat da.* And then: "Allo, allo, anybody is home?"

It was Enzo. Tall, noble, with the nose of an emperor and a weave of silver in his hair so rich it might have been hammered from the mother lode itself. He was dressed in a coruscating jumpsuit with Pennzoil and Pirelli patches across the shoulder and chest, and he held his crash helmet in his hand. "Baby," he said, crossing the room in two strides and taking Tootle in his arms, "ciao."

No one moved. No one said a thing.

"Beech of a road," Enzo said. "Ice, you know." Outside, through the open door, the sleek low profile of his Lazaretto 2200 Pinin Farina coupe was visible, the windshield plated with ice, sleet driving down like straight pines. "Tooka me seventeen and a half minutes from La Guardia—a beech, huh? But baby, at least I'm here."

He looked round him, as if seeing the others for the first time, and then, without a word, crossed the room to the stereo, ran a quick finger along the spines of the albums, and flipped a black platter from its jacket as casually as if he were flipping pizzas in Napoli. He dropped the stylus, and as the room filled with music, he began to move his hips and mime the words: "Oooh-oooh, I heard it through the grapevine . . ."

Marvin Gaye. Delectable, smooth, icy cool, ancient.

Pesky reached down to help Harvey from the floor. Jill took Hal's arm. Rob and Irene began to snap their fingers and Enzo swung Tootle out into the middle of the floor.

They danced till they dropped.

(1987)

A BIRD IN HAND

No, jutty, frieze,
Buttress, nor coign of vantage, but this bird
Hath made his pendent bed and procreant cradle.

—*Macbeth,* I. vi.

1980

They come like apocalypse, like all ten plagues rolled in one, beating across the sky with an insidious drone, their voices harsh and metallic, cursing the land. Ten million strong, a flock that blots out the huge pale sinking sun, they descend into the trees with a protracted explosion of wings, black underfeathers swirling down like a corrupt snow. At dawn they vacate the little grove of oak and red cedar in a streaming rush, heading west to disperse and feed in the freshly seeded fields; at dusk they gather like storm clouds to swarm back to their roost. Ten million birds, concentrated in a stand of trees no bigger around than a city block—each limb, each branch, each twig and bole and strip of bark bowed under the weight of their serried bodies—ten million tiny cardiovascular systems generating a sirocco of heat, ten million digestive tracts processing seeds, nuts, berries, animal feed, and streaking the tree trunks with chalky excrement. Where before there had been leafspill, lichened rocks, sunlit paths beneath the trees, now there are foot-deep carpets of bird shit.

"We've got a problem, Mai." Egon Scharf stands at the window, turning a worn paperback over in his hand. Outside, less than a hundred feet off, ten million starlings squat in the trees, cursing one another in a cacophony of shrieks, whistles, and harsh *check-checks*. "Says here," holding up the book, "the damn birds carry disease."

A muted undercurrent of sound buzzes through the house like static, a wheezing, whistling, many-throated hiss. Mai looks up from her crocheting: "What? I can't hear you."

"Disease!" he shouts, flinging the book down. "Stink, fungus, rot. I say we got to do something."

"Tut," is all she says. Her husband has always been an alarmist, from the day Jack Kennedy was shot and he installed bulletproof windows in the Rambler, to the time he found a single tent-caterpillar nest in the cherry tree and set fire to half the orchard. "A flock of birds, Egon, that's all—just a flock of birds."

For a moment he is struck dumb with rage and incomprehension, a lock of stained white hair caught against the bridge of his nose. "Just a flock—? Do you know what you're saying? There's millions of them out there, crapping all over everything. The drains are stopped up, it's like somebody whitewashed the car— I nearly broke my neck slipping in wet bird shit right on my own front porch, for Christ's sake—and you say it's nothing to worry about? *Just a flock of birds?*"

She's concentrating on a tricky picot stitch. For the first time, in the silence, she becomes aware of the steady undercurrent of sound. It's not just vocal, it's more than that—a rustling, a whisper whispered to a roar. She imagines a dragon, breathing fire, just outside the house.

"Mai, are you listening to me? Those birds can cause disease." He's got the book in his hand again—*The Pictorial Encyclopedia of Birds*—thumbing through it like a professor. "Here, here it is: histoplasmosis, it says. Wind-borne. It grows in bird crap."

She looks inexpressibly wise, smug even. "Oh, that? That's nothing, no more serious than a cold," she says, coughing into her fist. "Don't you remember Permilla Greer had it two years back?"

"Can spread through the reticulo-something-or-other system," he reads, and then looks up: "with a high percentage of mortality."

Three days later a man in a blue Ford pickup with tires the size of tank treads pulls into the driveway. The bed of the truck is a confusion of wires and amplifiers and huge open-faced loudspeakers. Intrigued, Mai knots the belt of her housecoat and steps out onto the porch.

"Well, yes, sure," Egon is saying, "you can back it over that pile of fence posts there and right up under the trees, if you want."

A young man in mirror sunglasses is standing beside the open door of the pickup. He nods twice at Egon, then hoists himself into the truck bed and begins flinging equipment around. "Okay," he says, "okay," as if addressing a large and impatient audience, "the way it works is like this: I've got these tapes of starling distress calls, and when they come back tonight to roost I crank up the volume and let 'em have it."

"Distress calls?"

The man is wearing a T-shirt under his jacket. When he pauses to put his hands on his hips, Mai can make out the initials emblazoned across his chest— KDOG—red letters radiating jagged orange lightning bolts. "Yeah, you know, like we mike a cage full of starlings and then put a cat or a hawk or something in there with them. But that's not when we start the tape. We wait till the cat rips one up, then we set the reels rolling."

Egon looks dubious. Mai can see him pinching his lower lip the way he does when somebody tells him the Russians are behind high fertilizer prices or that a pack of coyotes chewed the udders off twenty dairy cows in New Jersey.

"Don't worry," the man says, a thick coil of electrical cord in his hand, "this'll shake 'em up."

For the next two weeks, at dusk, the chatter of the roosting birds is entirely obliterated by a hideous tinny death shriek, crackling with static and blared at apocalyptic volume. When the Bird Man, as Mai has come to think of him, first switches on the amplifier each night, thirty or forty starlings shoot up out of the nearest tree and circle the yard twice before settling back down again. These, she supposes, are the highstrung, flighty types. As for the rest—the great weltering black mass hunkered down in the trees like all the generations of God's creation stretching back from here to the beginning of time—they go about their business as if wrapped in the silence of the Ages. That is, they preen their wings, cackle, squawl, screech, warp the branches, and crap all over everything, as unruffled and oblivious as they were before the Bird Man ever set foot in the yard.

On this particular evening the racket seems louder than ever, the very windowpanes humming with it. Mai has not been feeling well—she's got a cough that makes her want to give up smoking, and her forehead seems hot to the touch—and she was lying down when the Bird Man started his serenade. Now she gets up and shuffles over to the window. Below, parked in the shadow of the nearest oak, the Bird Man sits in his truck, wearing a set of headphones and the sunglasses he never removes. The hammering shriek of the bird call sets Mai's teeth on edge, assaults her ears, and stabs at her temples, and she realizes in that instant that it is distressing her far more than it distresses the birds. She suddenly wants to bolt down the stairs, out the door and into the pickup, she wants to pull the plug, rake the sunglasses from the Bird Man's face, and tell him to get the hell out of her yard and never come back again. Instead, she decides to have a word with Egon.

Downstairs the noise is even louder, intolerable, as if it had been designed to test the limits of human endurance. She rounds the corner into the den, furious, and is surprised to see Ed Bartro, from the McCracken Board of Supervisors, perched on the edge of the armchair. "Hello, Mai," he shouts over the clamor, "I'm just telling your husband here we got to do something about these birds."

Egon sits across from him, looking hunted. He's got two cigarettes going at once, and he's balancing a double gimlet on his knee. Mai can tell from the blunted look of his eyes that it isn't his first.

"It worked in Paducah," Ed is saying, "and over at Fort Campbell too. Tergitol. It's a detergent, like what you use on your dishes, Mai," he says, turning to her, "and when they spray it on the birds it washes the oil out of their feathers. Then you get them wet—if it rains, so much the better; if not, we'll have the fire department come out and soak down the grove—and they freeze to death in the night. It's not cheap, not by a long shot," he says, "but the country's just going to have to foot the bill."

"You sure it'll work?" Egon shouts, rattling the ice in his glass for emphasis.

"Nothing's for certain, Egon," Ed says, "but I'm ninety-nine and nine-tenths sure of it."

The following night, about seven o'clock, a pair of helicopters clatter over the house and begin circling the grove. Mai is hand-mashing potatoes and frying pork chops. The noise startles her, and she turns down the flame, wipes her hands on her apron, and steps out onto the porch to have a look. Angry suddenly, thinking, *Why must everything be so loud?,* she cups her hands over her ears and watches the searchlights gleam through the dark claws of the treetops. Gradually, she becomes aware of a new odor on the damp night air, a whiff of soap and alcohol undermining the sour ammoniac stench of the birds. It's like a dream, she thinks, like a war. The helicopters scream, the spray descends in a deadly fog, the pork chops burn.

An hour later the firemen arrive. Three companies. From Lone Oak, West Paducah and Woodlawn. The sequence is almost surreal: lights and shouts, black boots squashing the shoots in the garden, heavy-grid tires tearing up the lawn, the rattle of the pumps, coffee for thirty. By the time they leave, Mai is in bed, feeling as if she's been beaten with a shoe. She coughs up a ball of phlegm, spits it into a tissue and contemplates it, wondering if she should call the doctor in the morning.

When Egon comes in it is past midnight, and she's been dozing with the light on. "Mai," he says, "Mai, are you asleep?" Groggy, she props herself up on her elbows and squints at him. He is drunk, trundling heavily about the room as he strips off his clothes, "Well, I think this is going to do it, Mai," he says, the words thick on his tongue. "They knocked off six million in one shot with this stuff over at Russellville, so Ed tells me, and they only used half as much."

She can't make out the rest of what he says—he's muttering, slamming at a balky bureau drawer, running water in the bathroom. When she wakes again the house is dark, and she can feel him beside her, heavy and inert. Outside, in the trees, the doomed birds whisper among themselves, and the sound is like thunder in her ears.

In the morning, as the sun fires the naked fingers of the highest branches, the flock lifts up out of the trees with a crash of wings and a riot of shrieks and cackles. Mai feels too weak to get out of bed, feels as if her bones have gone soft on her, but Egon is up and out the door at first light. She is reawakened half an hour later by the slam of the front door and the pounding of footsteps below. There is the sound of Egon's voice, cursing softly, and then the click-click-click of the telephone dial. "Hello, Ed?" The house is still, his voice as clear as if he were standing beside her. A cough catches in her throat and she reaches for the bottle of cough syrup she'd fished out of the medicine cabinet after the firemen had left.

". . . nothing at all," her husband says below. "I think I counted eighty-six or -seven birds . . . uh-huh, uh-huh . . . yeah, well, you going to try again?"

She doesn't have to listen to the rest—she already knows what the county supervisor is saying on the other end of the line, the smooth, reasonable politician's voice pouring honey into the receiver, talking of cost overruns, uncooperative weather, the little unpleasantries in life we just have to learn to live with. Egon will be discouraged, she knows that. Over the past few weeks he's become increasingly touchy, the presence of the birds an ongoing ache, an open wound, an obsession. "It's not bad enough that the drought withered the soybeans last summer or that the damned government is cutting out price supports for feed corn," he'd shouted one night after paying the Bird Man his daily fee. "Now I can't even enjoy the one stand of trees on my property. Christ," he roared, "I can't even sit down to dinner without the taste of bird piss in my mouth." Then he'd turned to her, his face flushed, hands shaking with rage, and she'd quietly reminded him what the doctor had said about his blood pressure. He poured himself a drink and looked at her with drooping eyes. "Have I done something to deserve this, Mai?" he said.

Poor Egon, she thinks. He lets things upset him so. Of course the birds are a nuisance, she'll admit that now, but what about the man with the distress calls and the helicopters and firemen and all the rest? She tilts back the bottle of cough syrup, thinking she ought to call him in and tell him to take it easy, forget about it. In a month or so, when the leaves start to come in, the flock will break up and head north: why kill yourself over nothing? That's what she wants to tell him, but when she calls his name her voice cracks and the cough comes up on her again, racking, relentless, worse than before. She lets the spasm pass, then calls his name again. There is no answer.

It is then that she hears the sputter of the chainsaw somewhere beyond the window. She listens to the keening whine of the blade as it engages wood—a sound curiously like the starling distress call—and then the dry heaving crash of the first tree.

1890

An utter stillness permeates the Tuxedo Club, a hush bred of money and privilege, a soothing patrician quiet insisted upon by the arrases and thick damask curtains, bound up in the weave of the rugs, built into the very walls. Eugene Schieffelin, dilettante, portraitist, man of leisure, and amateur ornithologist, sits before the marble fireplace, leafing through the *Oologist Monthly* and sipping meditatively at a glass of sherry. *The red-eyed vireo,* he reads, *nests twice a year, both sexes participating in the incubation of the eggs. The eggs, two to four in number, are white with brown maculations at the larger extremity, and measure 5/16 by 2/3 of an inch. . . .* When his glass is empty, he raises a single languid finger and the waiter appears with a replacement, removes the superfluous glass, and vanishes, the whole operation as instantaneous and effortless as an act of the will.

Despite appearances to the contrary—the casually crossed legs, the proprietary air, the look of dignity and composure stamped into the seams of his face—Eugene is agitated. His eyes give him away. They leap from the page at the slightest movement in the doorway, and then surreptitiously drop to his waistcoat pocket to examine the face of the gold watch he produces each minute or so. He is impatient, concerned. His brother Maunsell is half an hour late already—has he forgotten their appointment? That would be just like him, damn it. Irritated, Eugene lights a cigar and begins drumming his fingertips on the arm of the chair while the windows go gray with dusk.

At sixty-three, with his great drooping mustache and sharp, accipiter's nose, Eugene Schieffelin is a salient and highly regarded figure in New York society. Always correct, a master of manners and a promoter of culture and refinement, a fixture of both the Society List and the Club Register, he is in great demand as commencement speaker and dinner guest. His grandfather, a cagey, backbiting immigrant, had made a fortune in the wholesale drug business, and his father, a lawyer, had encouraged that fortune to burgeon and flower like some clinging vine, the scent of money as sweet as jasmine. Eugene himself went into business when he was just out of college, but he soon lost interest. A few years later he married an heiress from Brooklyn and retired to hold forth at the Corinthian Yacht Club, listen to string quartets, and devote himself to his consuming passions—painting, Shakespeare, and the study of birds.

It wasn't until he was nearly fifty, however, that he had his awakening, his epiphany, the moment that brought the disparate threads of his life together and infused them with import and purpose. He and Maunsell were sitting before the fire one evening in his apartment at Madison and Sixty-fifth, reading aloud from *Romeo and Juliet.* Maunsell, because his voice was pitched higher, was reading Juliet, and Eugene, Romeo. "Wilt thou be gone?" Maunsell read, "it is not yet near day: / It was the nightingale, and not the lark, / That pierc'd the fearful hollow of thine ear." The iambs tripped in his head, and suddenly Eugene felt as if he'd been suffused with light, electrocuted, felt as if Shakespeare's muse had touched him with lambent inspiration. He jumped up, kicking over his brandy and spilling the book to the floor. "Maunsell," he shouted, "Maunsell, that's it!"

His brother looked up at him, alarmed and puzzled. He made an interrogatory noise.

"The nightingale," Eugene said, "and, and . . . woodlarks, siskins, linnets,
chaffinches—and whatever else he mentions!"

"What? Who?"

"Shakespeare, of course. The greatest poet—the greatest man—of all time.
Don't you see? This will be our enduring contribution to culture; this is how
we'll do our little bit to enrich the lives of all the generations of Americans to
come—"

Maunsell's mouth had dropped open. He looked like a classics scholar who's
just been asked to identify the members of the Chicago White Stockings. "What
in Christ's name are you talking about?"

"We're going to form the American Acclimatization Society, Maunsell, here
and now—and we're going to import and release every species of bird—every
last one—mentioned in the works of the Bard of Avon.

That was thirteen years ago.

Now, sitting in the main room of the Tuxedo Club and waiting for his
brother, Eugene has begun to show his impatience. He jerks round in his seat,
pats at his hair, fiddles with his spats. He is imbibing his fourth sherry and examining a table enumerating the stomach contents of three hundred and fifty-nine
bay-breasted warblers when he looks up to see Maunsell in the vestibule, shrugging out of his overcoat and handing his hat and cane over to the limp little fellow in the cloakroom.

"Well?" Eugene says, rising to greet him. "Any news?"

Maunsell's face is flushed with the sting of the March wind. "Yes," he says,
"yes," the timbre of his voice instantly soaked up in the drapes and rugs and converted to a whisper. "She's on schedule as far as they know, and all incoming
ships have reported clear weather and moderate seas."

Any irritation Eugene may have shown earlier has vanished from his face. He
is grinning broadly, the dead white corners of his mustache lifted in exultation,
gold teeth glittering. "That's the best news I've heard all week," he says. "Tomorrow morning, then?"

Maunsell nods. "Tomorrow morning."

At eight the following morning, the two brothers, in top hats and fur-lined overcoats, are perched anxiously on the edge of the broad leather seat of Maunsell's
carriage, peering out at the tapering length of the Fourteenth Street pier and the
Cunard steamer edging into the slips. Half an hour later they are on deck, talking
animatedly with a man so short, pale, and whiskerless he could be mistaken for a
schoolboy. It is overcast, windy, raw, the temperature lurking just below the
freezing mark. "They seem to have held up pretty well, sir," the little fellow is

shouting into the wind. "Considering the Cunard people made me keep them in the hold."

"What? In the hold?" Both brothers look as if they've been slapped, indignation and disbelief bugging their eyes, mad wisps of silver hair foaming over their ears, hands clutching savagely at the brims of their hats.

" 'Loive cargo goes in the 'old,' " the little fellow says, his voice pinched in mockery, " 'and Oy'm vewy sowwy, Oy am, but them's the regelations.' " He breaks into a grin. "Oh, it was awful down there—cold, and with all those horses stamping and whinnying and the dogs barking it's a wonder any of the birds made it at all."

"It's a damned outrage," Eugene sputters, and Maunsell clucks his tongue. "How many did you say made it, Doodson?"

"Well, as you'll see for yourself in a minute, sir, the news is both good and bad. Most of the thrushes and skylarks came through all right, but there was a heavy mortality among the nightingales—and I've got just three pairs still alive. But the starlings, I'll tell you, they're a hardy bird. Didn't lose a one, not a single one."

Eugene looks relieved. In what has become a reflex gesture over the past few days, he consults his pocket watch and then looks up at Doodson. "Yes, they're a glorious creature, aren't they?"

Maunsell directs the driver to Central Park East—Fifth and Sixty-fifth—and then settles back in the seat beside his brother. Two cabs fall in behind them, the first containing Doodson and a portion of the transatlantic aviary, the second packed to the roof with bird cages. There is the steady adhesive clap of hoofs, the rattling of the springs. Eugene glances over his shoulder to reassure himself that the cabs—and birds—are still there, and then turns to his brother, beaming, his fingers tapping at the stiff crown of the hat in his lap, an aureole of hair radiating from his head. "When birds do sing, hey ding a ding, ding; / Sweet lovers love the spring," he recites with a laugh, unscrewing the cap of his flask and nudging Maunsell. "I think we've really got it this time," he says, laughing again, the sound of his voice softening the cold clatter of the coach. "I can feel it in my bones."

Outwardly, his mood is confident—celebratory, even—but in fact his high hopes are tempered by the Acclimatization Society's history of failure over the course of the thirteen years since its inception. Eugene has released thrushes, skylarks, and nightingales time and again. He has released siskins, woodlarks, and common cuckoos. All have failed. Inexplicably, the seed populations disappeared without a trace, as if they'd been sucked up in a vacuum or blown back to Europe. But Eugene Schiefflin is not a man to give up easily—oh no. This time he's got a new ace in the hole, *Sturnus vulgaris,* the starling. Certainly not the

Bard's favorite bird—in all the countless lines of all the sonnets, histories, come-
dies, and tragedies it is mentioned only once—but legitimate to the enterprise
nonetheless. And hardy. Doodson's report has got to be looked upon as auspicious: *not a single bird lost in the crossing.* It's almost too good to be true.

He is musing with some satisfaction on the unexpected beauty of the bird—
the stunning metallic sheen of the plumage and the pale butter pat of the beak
revealed to him through the mesh of the cage—when the carriage pulls up along
the curb opposite the park. Before the percussive echo of the horses' hoofs has
faded, Eugene is out of the carriage and shouting directions to Doodson, the two
cabbies, and Maunsell's driver. In one hand he clutches a pry bar; in the other, a
bottle of Moët et Chandon. "All right," he calls, rigorous as a field marshal. "I
want the cages laid side by side underneath those elms over there." And then he
strikes out across the grass, Maunsell bringing up the rear with three long-
stemmed glasses.

It is still cold, a crust of ice stretched over the puddles in the street, the cabbies' breath clouding their faces as they bend to negotiate the wooden cages.
"Here," Eugene barks, striding across the field and waving his arm impatiently,
"hurry it along, will you?" Well-tipped, but muttering nonetheless, the cabbies
struggle with one cage while Doodson—his nose red with cold and excitement—
helps Maunsell's chauffeur with another. Within minutes all eight cages are
arranged in parallel rows beneath the elms, laid out like coffins, and Eugene has
begun his customary rambling speech outlining his and the society's purposes,
eulogizing Shakespeare and reciting quotations relevant to the caged species. As
he stoops to pry the lid from the first cage of thrushes, he shouts out an injunc-
tion from *Hamlet*: "Unpeg the baskets on the house's top," he calls, liberating
the birds with a magisterial sweep of his arm, "Let the birds fly."

The cabbies, paid and dismissed, linger at a respectful distance to watch the
mad ceremony. Deliberate, methodical, the old fellow in the top hat and silk
muffler leans down to remove the tops of the cages and release the birds. There
is a rustle of wings, a cry or two, and then the appearance of the first few birds,
emerging at random and flapping aimlessly into the branches of the nearest tree.
The pattern is repeated with each box in succession, until the old man draws up
to the single remaining cage, the cage of starlings. The other old fellow, the rickety one with the drawn face and staring eyes, steps forward with the glasses, and
then there's the sound of a cork popping. "A toast," the first one shouts, and
they're raising their glasses, all three of them, the two old duffers and the young
cub with the red nose. "May these humble creatures, brought here with goodwill
and high expectation, breed and prosper and grace the land with beauty and
song."

"Hear, hear!" call the others, and the chauffeur as well, though he hasn't
been offered any wine.

Behind the mesh of their cage, the big dull birds crouch in anticipation,
stuffed like blackbirds in a pie, their voices wheezing with a sound of metal on

metal. The cabbies shake their heads. A cold wind tosses the dead black limbs of the trees. Then the old gentleman bends to the cage at his feet, his hair shining in the pale sunlight, and there is a sudden startling explosion as the birds stream from the opening as if propelled, feathers rasping, wings tearing at the air, a single many-voiced shriek of triumph issuing from their throats. En masse, almost in precision formation, they wheel past the spectators like a flock of pigeons, and then, banking against the sun, they wing off over the trees, looking for a place to roost.

(1981)

THE ARCTIC EXPLORER

I. DAY

Departure

Posing in full dress uniform at the bow of the little brig *Endeavor*, rigid as the mast looming behind him, he raises a stiff arm in acknowledgment of the small send-off parties spotting the Kings' shore of the Narrows. With his perfect posture, immaculate uniform and manicured mustache, he looks very much the Hero, a reincarnated admixture of Henry Hudson, John Paul Jones and El Cid.

His solemn eyes scan the bandless, bannerless shore. A paltry crowd, he reflects, for an occasion so momentous. After all, he *is* sailing cheekily off into the frigid unknown, beyond the reaches of men's maps, to probe regions whose very existence is but rumor. Yet such, he supposes, is the lot of Heroes: all but ignored by the self-satisfied Present, revered by Posterity. Glebe cows. If it were up to them Kentucky would be a wilderness still.

Beyond the Narrows, the open Atlantic, rolling pleasantly underfoot to a gentle June breeze. Captain John Pennington Frank (M.D., U.S.N.) breathes deeply, closes his eyes, and removes his cap to let the seabreeze tickle through his hair. As he does so, the last spangles of confetti are sucked up in the wind and shot away to starboard (this the confetti that his mother and two unmarried sisters had solemnly flung at him just half an hour earlier when the brig had been launched at the Brooklyn Naval Yard). Like Ishmael too long a-land, he feels the salt breeze raking up all the old sailor's pluck: Ah! The Open Sea! Adventure! Man against the Elements! It is then that the brig pitches forward and an icy slap intrudes itself upon the Captain's meditations. His eyelids snap-to like the surprise of a stroke and he lurches forward against the rail: the cap sails out from his hand in a graceful arc, to be sucked down by the frothing waves below. When he recovers himself he glances furtively about before digging out the handkerchief, thankful that none of the crew had been watching. The ceremonies over, and the voyage begun, the Captain retires to his cabin, where the crisp and neatly lined pages of the logbook await him.

Of course he knows nothing as yet of the Arctic Night.

Captain's Log, June 2

Set sail from NY Harbor at 1100 hours Eastern Time. Momma, Evangeline and Euphonia saw us off with a not inconsiderable crowd. As we passed the Narrows, quite ten thousand I should think turned out to cheer us. It was heartening thus to witness the deep reverence and goodwill the people of this great nation show for our venture.

My party consists of fifteen: eight officers (myself included); five crewmen; Phillip Blackwark, cook; and Harlan Hawkins, cabin boy. Our stores include a large supply of navy ration salt beef and pork, hard biscuit, flour, some barrels of exsiccated potato, two thousand pounds of pemmican, a quantity of dried fruits, and twelve barrels of pickled cabbage. (Surreptitiously, I laid in a supply of party hats and whistles, to cheer the men during our winter confinement.) It is my expectation to reach the northern coast of Newfoundland by the twentieth. There we will supplement our stores with a few sides of fresh beef, God and Governor Pickpie willing.

Glut at Anoatuk

Kresuk's bare chest is bespattered with blood, his face a smear, the oily black hair at his cheeks congealed with blood and birdfat. His incisors dig at the purple vein along the breastbone, his lips suck at the tatters of pink flesh still clinging to the pink ribs. As he gnaws, the denuded breast and its few dangling particles flap flat against his greasy knuckles. The remains of nine eider-ducks lie beside his bare thigh, a wet neck and ribcage beneath it. His right nostril is crammed white with fat and bits of raw meat.

Ooniak, his woman, patiently cracks auk eggs and drains the contents into the yawning maw of Sip-su, their defective son. Mouth agape, head thrown back, Sip-su is a birdling in the nest, begging the sky for food. Five winters, thinks Kresuk, looking hard at his son. I give him one more. Then he lies back with a sigh, his head buried in a heap of bloodied feathers. He breaks wind. He picks his teeth. And thinks of walrus, bearded seal, narwhal. He does not suspect the existence of New York Harbor 2800 miles to the south, nor does he suspect the existence of the brig *Endeavor*, already making its way north to ripple the placid waters of his life. There are legends telling of tribes of gaunt, pale men, but

Kresuk has no time for legends—the Night, the season of frozen ice, of terror and of want, is over, and the birds have returned to Anoatuk.

Dining at St. John's, Newfoundland

(A dainty tinkle of silverware, china and crystal accompanies the dialogue.)

Oh, excellent, You know I haven't titillated my palate with such northern delicacies as these since—oh, '47 I guess it was, up in Finland.

It's only on special occasions that I can get them myself, you know, Captain. I don't expect you picture me glutting on poached wapiti tongue all the time—

No, no, no. And I'm deeply flattered that you consider our visit one of those special occasions, Governor Pickpie . . . these smell ducky—what are they?

We call them St. John's marbles. The genitalia of the male musk-ox, braised in port. Care for some more wine?

Oh yes, thank you. . . . Quite tasty, these marrrbles. Ho. Ho-ho.

Have you tried the smoked salmon in soured cream? Cochlearia salad?

Um yes. Superb. You know, Governor Pickpie, I think the memory of this feast alone will sustain us through the long winter to come.

You're very kind, sir. At any rate, I wish you greater success than the last party that came through—Sir Regis Norton's expedition.

Oh?

Yes. Their ship was found by a Swedish fellmonger no more than a month ago, frozen solid as a rock into the ice sheet—all hands dead from frost. Preserved like pickles.

Down

Kresuk smiles to himself in the loud sun, mirror-whiteness, bird squabble. He stoops to collect eider-down from around the eider-nests, occasionally pausing to poke a hole in an egg and suck its contents. Ooniak squats on a lichen-crowned rock, stuffing a new walrus sleeping bag with eider-down and the ass feathers of the arctic tern. Nearby Sip-su sits: circular, drooling, eyes focused on nothing. Work a son should be doing, thinks Kresuk. The seal are back. I should hunt. I give him one winter more.

Captain's Log, June 28

Entered Baffin's Bay, bearing to northwest by north, looking for open water. Great bergs like floating mountains hem us in. We keep in sight of the dramatic coastline, navigating from headland to headland—it takes us steadily westward, and always to the north.

The sixty-two Esquimau dogs we purchased at Fiskarnaes are perhaps not even half-a-step removed from their lupine ancestors. One is afraid to go on deck anymore—they surge about one in a snarling pack, nosing about for food, snapping and tearing at each other. Yesterday they pulled down two sides of beef from the rigging, and before Mr. Mallaby could get through the seething pack, they had reduced the rock-hard frozen meat to bare bone, like a swarm of those carnivorous Amazonian fishes. The men complain bitterly of these ravening wolves infesting our decks, and I explain that we shall need them to pull our sledges during the fall and spring explorations. Still the men grumble. Perhaps I shall break out the party hats this evening to brighten their spirits.

UFO

Metek is agitated. He can barely contain himself. Nervously he cuts strip after strip from the walrus carcass and nervously he wedges them in his mouth. Across from him squat Kresuk and Ooniak, their faces slimed with the buttery wet liver that had served as an hors d'oeuvre—they too are now cutting strips of walrus-beef and feeding them into their mouths. Sip-su sits on, an autistic little Buddha. It was big as the floating ice, Metek says finally. No one looks up. The assiduous gorging continues, to the accompaniment of lip-smacks, grunts, booming eructations. It had great white wings, and it flew atop the water like a flock of eider coming in to feed. I saw it from Pekiutlik Lookout where I am hunting. A great creature, of color like the summer fox, and wings that hum like the auk.

Kresuk, without breaking the studied hand-to-mouth rhythm he has established, looks up and utters a single word: *Sealshit.*

Berg-Beleaguered

Like a foundling among wolves, a shot-glass of Wild Turkey among winos, a bridge over the River Kwai, the *Endeavor* drifts among ice peaks that rear malevolently a hundred feet above the water. The bergs are drifting too: battering together like gargantuan rams, shattering the arctic stillness with explosions as the ship-sized blocks thunder down. The brig rocks dizzily in the concussive waves; the men are panic-struck; the sixty-two dogs beshit the decks in fright. But the Captain seems unmoved, absorbed as he is in thinking up names for salient coastal features. Aunt, Aunt, Aunt? he thinks aloud.

Soon the black channel before them vanishes—two titanic bergs roll gently together and lock with a kiss: the open passage has become a cul-de-sac. Accordingly, First Officer Mallaby orders the brig turned 180 degrees. But wait! Even the channel they've just passed through is stoppered tight as a nun's orifices— the brig's wake trails off into the gullets of two implacable bergs, tall and white as the chalk cliffs at Dover. The open sea becomes a lake—no, a pond— inexorably the ring of ice closes in, like a mountain range seen creeping in time-stop photography through ten million years. Captain Frank! shouts Mallaby.

Captain Frank! The Captain looks up, and for the first time assesses the situation. How embarrassing, he mutters, and returns to his notebook, annoyed with the interruption—he'd almost had it, the name he'd been searching for—his great aunt on his mother's side.

Two hours later the *Endeavor* bobs in a puddle, surrounded by the sheer ice faces, kicked about now and again by their feet—the feet which even now, deep in the black and secretive depths, are welding themselves together, freezing across in a grim sort of net.

Five hundred yards distant, from their vantage point in Pekiutlik Lookout, two figures, swathed in the hair of beasts, are watching. One grunts: Hmph. What'd I tell you. The other, incredulous, mouths his reply: Mother of Walrus!

Captain's Log, July 17

It is with great sorrow that I must report the loss of our ship. In searching for a northwest passage we entered a blind bay, became beleaguered by ice, and were finally crushed by the shifting floes. All hands escaped without incident, and due to my own foresight, much of our stores were saved, including a great quantity of wood from the crushed hull. She was a stout little brig, and we all hated to see her go—especially as it means making the eight-hundred-mile journey to Fiskarnaes, on the South Greenland coast, by foot. I have given orders to establish a winter camp here, as the season is so far progressed as to render any attempt at escape impracticable. About five hundred yards from the scene of the *Endeavor*'s demise is an outcropping of greenstone. I have named it Pauce Point, in honor of my great aunt, Rudimenta Pauce. It is in the lee of this cliff that we shall make our winter quarters with the heavy timber salvaged from the brig, insulating the walls and ceilings with packed ice, Esquimau-fashion. God willing, we shall live to see the spring, and other eyes will come to peruse what I have written here—the record of our tribulations.

The Glare

Out on the floes Kresuk is bent over a tiny hole, no more than two inches in diameter. His ear is to the ice, his fist curled round the harpoon. The seal responsible for this hole is at that very moment gamboling about the ice-blue depths, gobbling fish, undulating sealishly through the water, out of breath now, darting back to the airhole for a heaving gasp of oxygen. It will be his last gasp, smiles Kresuk.

Some distance off, the man with rifle and notebook is busy naming headlands, cliffs and glaciers after himself and members of his family. The jagged pencil line of the coast grows northward on the paper as each day he hikes farther, ostensibly in search of game. Soon, he thinks, he will have a team of dogs trained and will be able to cover twice the distance in a sledge—but for now he must walk, and haul back meat for the crew and ravenous dog-pack. Up ahead he catches sight of a movement out on the ice—he strains his eyes, but with the glare, and his sun-blindness, the object drifts and melds with the red and blue spots before his eyes. But isn't it a bear? A fat bear, rich with meat and suet, bent now over a hole in the ice? The man folds the notebook into his parka and begins his stalk. When he gets within two hundred feet he lies flat, braces the rifle on an ice pedestal, takes careful aim, and fires.

Captain's Log, August 15

Have made contact with the Esquimaux. I found one of these savages unconscious on the ice, suffering apparently from shock as a result of a recent flesh wound in the gluteus maximus. With the aid of a sledge drawn by six of the crew (we've not yet been able to train the dogs), I brought the poor fellow back to camp, where I was able to perform a crude operation, dressing his wound and treating the shock with a dose of morphine. He lies asleep now in the main cabin the fellows have constructed from the remains of the *Endeavor*. In appearance, he is very much like his Christianized counterparts to the south, but in size he greatly surpasses them, measuring six feet from toe to crown, and weighing nearly one hundred ninety pounds. He is dressed in rude garments fashioned from the pelts of his prey—he wears a sort of breeches fabricated from the hindquarters of the polar bear, the claws still attached and trailing upon the ground as he stands. His boots are of sealskin and his parka of arctic fox. He exudes a strong odor of urine.

I am quite anxious to speak with our primitive guest (hopefully through the office of my interpreter, Second Officer Moorhead Bone), as information regarding the indigenous Esquimau tribes and their seasonal wanderings should prove invaluable to us in effecting our spring escape.

Gaunt, and Pale

Kresuk awakes groggy, and with a distant ache in his anak, from a dream in which he had harpooned Osoetuk, the great narwhal, God of the Seas, and been dragged through the ice, down to Osoetuk's lair in the icy depths. There Osoetuk had given him a wonderful elixir, the spirit of fishes and heart of walrus, and it had made him warm beneath the ice and the dark waters—warm, and drowsy.

Now he lies still, eyes closed, listening to the beat and wash of a strange tongue, remembering the flank attack and the lost seal. He struggles to open his eyes but the elixir prevents him. It takes all his concentration to crack the heavy lids just enough to catch a glimpse of the ceiling, its wooden beams. Wood! The last thing he'd expect to see at Pekiutlik. Hard and carvable, just the ticket for tools and totems—but up here the best he'd ever done was a forked branch washed up from the south. His conclusion is inevitable: I am dead, he thinks, and lifted into another world. The voices drone. His eyes open, close. He looks again: wood all around him, so precious, so rare, a forest above his heavy lids— the lids which now close as if weighted, while the dream seeps back into his consciousness. When again they open he twists his head in the direction of the voices, strains to see, focuses finally . . . on legends! Men with hair on their faces, gaunt and pale as winter, legends incarnate.

II. NIGHT

Captain's Log, November 7

So cold your axillary hair shatters like glass, and the spittle freezes in your throat.

Captain's Log, November 8

We have just enough light at noon to read the thermometer without aid of a lantern. Temperature at noon today was −38 degrees F., with a stiff breeze kicking up. Mr. Mallaby is lost somewhere out on the floes. At ten this morning he went out to feed the dogs and has not been seen since. I have sent out a search party.

The supply of fresh meat I commissioned from Kresuk in early September is nearly gone. It was well worth the price (some three hundred pounds of walrus and bear in exchange for a string of glass beads and six red wooden buttons). Judging from his look of idiot delight as I dangled the beads before his nose, I think I could have got another six hundred pounds of meat in the bargain. My only complaint is that the savage has not returned since, and we are in dire need of further barter. I presume he is wintering at Etah, the Esquimau village sixty miles south of us.

Captain's Log, November 12

The search party has not returned; no trace either of Mr. Mallaby. I regret to report that of the men remaining (five went out on the search) only four are well enough to be up and about. Frostbite has been our biggest enemy, with scurvy running a close second. All the men suffer from the latter, and to complicate matters, our meager supply of dried fruits has been already exhausted. Even the pickled cabbage is beginning to go quickly—yet all of us show signs of scorbutic weariness and bleeding at the gums.

The incessant hacking and wheezing, and the groaning of the amputees, is trying on my nerves. Besides which I am bored witless—nothing to do but tend the sick and wait for the sun—nearly 140 days distant. Nursing is not exactly my idea of an heroic occupation—I long for the more active fight.

Captain's Log, November 15

The remains of Mr. Mallaby's fur suit have been found by Mr. Bone among the dogs: I can only conjecture his fate. The dog-pack, incidentally, is now down to twenty-seven survivors—it appears they have been eating one another, as we have been unable to provide them with fresh meat, and the pemmican (unpalatable though it is), we must conserve for our own use. Yet Mr. Bone reminds me that without dogs we should be hard-pressed in making our spring trek to civilization. Something must be done.

The search party has not yet returned. I have dispatched a second search party, composed of our three ablest men (Tiggis, Tuggle and Mr. Wright), to search for the missing search party.

Barter

Kresuk returns. His round cheeks, white furs, slit eyes. His shaggy frame in the doorway. The stiff seal flipper clutched in his mittens.

The Captain beckons him in, slamming the door against the wind. A dying wood-fire glows in the corner, shadows mount the walls. The men snuff and wheeze. The Captain nods at Kresuk, smiling. Kresuk nods back, smiling. "Bone!" shouts the Captain. "Bone!"

Mr. Bone lifts himself from his pallet, breath steaming around his head like a pot of coffee, and hobbles out to join his superior. "Mr. Bone, speak with this fellow. I feel certain that he's come to exchange meat for beads, and I don't think I need emphasize how sorely necessitous we are at this juncture." Bone coughs, relieves himself of a wad of sputum. "Wuk noah tuk-ha," he says. Kresuk stares past him for a moment, then turns to sift through the murky low room. He pokes into each cabinet, each bed, beneath each man's pillow. "What's he about, Bone?" demands the Captain. "Here now!"

Kresuk is collecting things: fine glittering knives, pewter mugs, pocket watches, axes. A sack of red wooden buttons. He clatters them down in the center of the room, holds out the seal flipper to Mr. Bone.

Captain's Log, November 21

Kresuk has been back. We exchanged a few of our things for a new, if small, supply of fresh meat. The savage drives a hard bargain. He has us, as they say, over a barrel.

Mr. Bone's great toe has suppurated to such a degree that I fear gangrenous infection if it is not removed. Once again, I think, as the surgical blade splashes through to negotiate the bone in a quick down-and-across stroke, the damnable frost has cost us another part of our bodies. We'll all of us be amputees by the time the sun returns to us—a pack of sniveling, scurvied cripples.

No word from either search party. I would organize a third search party to search for the two missing search parties, but there are just five of us here, and I am the only one with two serviceable legs and feet, arms and hands. Really, I feel like chief attendant at a leper colony.

Captain's Log, November 22

Funeral obsequies for Mr. Mallaby today. My bedridden mates hobbled outside where we gathered round a memorial plaque and sang hymns. What with the coughing and slobbering of the men, and the groans of the wind, it was difficult, but we did manage a fairly respectable job of "Art thou weary, art thou languid?"—one of my personal favorites. Young Harlan Hawkins wept as I read "ashes to ashes, dust to dust, ice to ice" (I thought the insertion quite apposite), and scattered the remaining strands of Mr. Mallaby's furs to the wind. It was a pitiable sight indeed—the poor boy swabbing at the frozen tears with his right stump as the soul of his valiant shipmate was set free to be gathered to the bosom of his Maker. The boy's own soul, I'm afraid, will not be long with us either.

Lost on the Floes

The wind howls a gale, the cold shatters steel, splinters wood, transubstantiates flesh to ice. Misshapen ice-hummocks rear up like bad dreams, gray and ghostly in the perennial dark. All living things perish here: only the ice belt lives on—thrives—in the searing winds and falling temperatures.

The search parties, having found one another, are faced with a secondary problem: finding their way back. Their progress for the past six hours has been geometrical—on feet long dead, they have plodded out the shaky hypotenuses of a dozen right triangles, one atop the other. They are drunk with the cold, enraptured with it; cold no longer, they lie down to rest. Pekiutlik Lookout (known variously as Pauce Point) lies but half a mile south of them. Half a mile through the black moonscape of the Arctic Night.

Natural Selection

In his igloo at the Etah settlement Kresuk and his neighbors are lounging about naked, skin on fur, sunning in the prodigious heat put out by their seal-blubber lamps. At this particular moment Kresuk is bending over to display the tiny circular scar on his anak, the badge of his first encounter with the gaunt men. The badge of his later encounters with the gaunt men dangles beneath his chin: a necklace of red wooden buttons, glass beads and gold pocket watches. His neighbors are threading similar necklaces, chipping away at the icy floor with their steel knives, trying their teeth against the smoky pewter mugs. They look up as Kresuk begins retelling the story of the wound, a story they've heard as many as ninety-seven times. They are fascinated nonetheless. Beads, knives and mugs drop, mouths hang open. And pairs of quick black eyes follow the necklace twisting and slapping against Kresuk's breastbone as he pantomimes the action of his sealhunt. When he speaks, the gibbous cheeks part to reveal his smile, and his eyes flash like headlights beneath the fleshy lids.

When the tale is finished and Metek sits up to tell his story of the great winged whale that brought the gaunt men, the others turn back to their beads, knives, mugs. Kresuk stretches out and begins picking at his sealhaunch. He chews thoughtfully, only half-attending his friend's narrative, his mind on the glory he's won, glory that will pass down through generations. He sees himself a king, his sons princes. It is then that Sip-su raises himself and waddles over to his father, where he squats to deposit a turd, wet and shapeless, on Kresuk's foot. The friends laugh. Ooniak stares down at her toe. And Kresuk explodes, slaps the fat-headed child across the igloo—Sip-su totters, spins off the kotluk, scalds himself, wails. The neighbors look down at their beads and laps, faces elongate, and fight to suppress chuffles and snorts while Kresuk pulls on his furs, orders Ooniak to dress the child. Wordless, he snatches up the screeching Sip-su and crawls out the door. The old men nod.

Outside, in the wind so sharp it takes away the child's squalling breath, Kresuk harnesses the dogs, straps the child to his back, and starts off toward Pekiutlik Lookout, tomb of his ancestors.

Plaint

Driven by the insufferable stench of the accumulated slops, he determines to make a slop-emptying expedition. Doggedly he hefts the slop bucket and doggedly he steps out into the glacial dark: the hairs in his nostrils fuse with his first steaming breath. When he exhales he can hear the vapor crystallize, whisper to the ground in tiny pellets. Already the reeking paste has become a bucket-shaped block, no more offensive than an ice cube. He stops, whale-oil lantern in hand, intent on checking the thermometer for his meteorological records. As he stoops to clear the glass an exceptionally virulent gust extinguishes his light, and brings to his ears the unmistakable plaint, weak and attentuated, of a child in distress.

He drops the bucket, holds his breath, uncovers his ears (the lobes freeze through instantaneously). Yes, there it is again—borne down on the wind from above, up on Pauce Point!

Captain's Log, January 5

The Esquimau child is doing well, fully recovered from the effects of his exposure. I only wish I could say as much for the men. Blackwark and Hoofer are alternately comatose and delirious; young Harlan Hawkins has contracted erysipelas in his left stump; Bone, who could hardly walk in any case, is suffering from a new attack of frostbite. Yesterday he reeled out to chop wood from our scrap heap to keep the fire going. After half an hour I began to wonder what had become of him, and went out searching. I found him asleep in the snow, his cheek frozen fast to the beam he'd been chopping—it was necessary to hack half his beard away in order to extricate the poor fellow. On one of my downward strokes I inadvertently swiped off his left ear. Little matter: I hardly expect the poor beggar to make it through the night.

The child, though about five or six years of age, appears to be defective mentally, from all indications suffering from mongoloidism. He must be hand-fed, and insists on fouling himself. I can only pity the savage heart that left him to the cold.

Captain's Log, January 10

Disaster. The dogs have broken loose and got at our cache of pemmican—practically all we had left, better than two hundred pounds, is gone. I've managed to round up five of them, bloated as they are. Four will pull my sledge (or be whipped raw) and the fifth will grace our table. I can't see how we'll survive—we've almost no provisions left, and the night has barely begun.

Captain's Log, January 11

Bone and Hoofer dead, Blackwark on the brink. I must leave them in their bunks, as I've barely the strength to drag them outside, and I must conserve my resources for the days ahead. With an interior temperature of +35 degrees F., I do not expect an overly rapid decomposition. Temperature outside at noon today was −54 degrees F.

Captain's Log, January 21

Mad with hunger. The last two days we've had nothing to eat but a broth made from bits of wood and the more tender portions of Mr. Bone's boots. Blackwark expired early this morning—there were no hymns, as Harlan Hawkins is in a coma, and the Esquimau child, my only other companion, can do nothing but wail for food and defecate. Clearly, without edibles, there is no hope for us here. As a result, I've come to a decision—I've determined to strap Hawkins and the child to a sledge drawn by the four curs I've spared (what a temptation it's been to roast them!) and make for the Esquimau settlement at Etah. When they see the condition we're in, and when they see the child—one of their own—I trust they'll help us.

Hegira

A Hero indeed! he triumphantly thinks as he brings the lash down across the muzzles of the four dogs. If only Momma and the girls could see me now! But it is dark as Styx-mist and cold as Proserpine's breath—so cold the thoughts begin to freeze in his head. Beneath his feet the ice is a jagged saw's edge, cutting into each agonizing step, overturning the sledge, abrading the hard pads of the dog's paws as if they were wax. Sip-su and the comatose Hawkins are lashed to the sledge, greatly impeding its progress, and from time to time the dogs stop and begin devouring one another and it is all he can do to whip them back to order. But indomitable, he presses on, a navy fight tune frozen in his cerebrum. Ard! he bellows (he had meant to yell "On you Bastards!" but the wind had driven the words back at him, right down his throat and into his shocked lungs). Soon his fingers will become brittle, and the fluid in his eyes will turn to slush.

At Etah

Outside the wind tells of a gale as it sweeps smooth over the glassy surface of the igloo. Inside it is sweating hot, and the three seal-blubber lamps, burning simultaneously, circulate a thick greasy smoke which stings the eyes. In the center of the domed ceiling a black helix winds and dances as it is sucked up through the chimney-piece and out, to rush before the deadly gusts.

Kresuk is sitting on the floor, dressed in furs, breathing heavily, his eyebrows white with frost. The carcass of a big bearded seal is wedged in the narrow entrance passage, its head and whiskers and cold dead eyes at Kresuk's feet. The seal's tail is outside, in the wind and dark, the bloated belly jammed like a cork in the neck of the entranceway. Kresuk turns, tugs at the animal's head. He smiles. He'd been improvident in his early dealings with the gaunt men, trading away half his winter cache of meat for a few buttons and beads. And so he'd been forced out on the dark floes, hungry, hunting. There was no choice about it: Ooniak grumbling, the dogs howling, Metek muttering every time Kresuk stepped next door for dinner. But now he looks down at the seal. And thinks feast.

Then the voices outside: Ooniak, Metek, Metek's woman. Kresuk rises to his knees, works a hand under each flipper and leans back. He can feel the others pushing at the seal's fat flank. There is a moment of inertia, effort in suspension, and then a lewd wet sucking release and Kresuk is on his anak, the seal in his lap, Ooniak and his friends scrambling in: laughing.

Later, his belly full, Kresuk crawls over to Ooniak and lies beside her, the string of beads and watches clacking as he throws himself down. She is rounder than normal. He puts his ear to her stomach, and then barks out a laugh: something is moving, just beneath the skin. He sits up, grinning. Metek says something about sons sturdy as bears. The wind howls. And Kresuk looks down, suddenly startled. Beneath the smooth crystal, inching like an insect, the second hand has begun to trace its way around a watch face, and the watch has begun to tick.

A Soporific

A soporific, it lulls, soothes, spreads its uterine warmth—and you want to lie down on the floes, tired, ineffably tired, impervious now to the sting of it—bed down right there, on the floes. The child and Hawkins are still lashed down, but stiff as flagpoles: a patina of frost glosses their lips. The dogs have given up, ice-blood crusting between their toes: they lie doubled, nose to tail, whimpering, and still in their traces. Have you the strength to crack the whip? Hardly. It's all you can do to grip the sledgehandles, woozy and reeling as you are. But warm, strangely warm, and tired. This is no gale, but gentle windsong, a lullaby in your tired ears. If only to lie down . . . for just a moment . . .

(1973)

RAPTURE OF THE DEEP

"We must go deeper," Cousteau says. He is haggard, worn to bone, his splendid Gallic nose a wedge driven into his face. He uses his utensils to illustrate—his fork has become a crane, his spoon the diving machine, a pool of sauce the ocean. I feel the ship roll under my feet, an undulation as gentle as a breath.

"Mais oui!" a chorus of voices sings out. "Deeper!"

I'm working my way round the cramped table, pouring coffee into a desolation of plates, cutlery, crusts of bread and fish bones. "But why?" I hear myself asking. "Haven't we gone deep enough? What crime have we committed that we don't deserve to see a port, a tree, the inside of a good brasserie?"

Twenty pairs of eyes settle on me. I can see that this last bit about the brasserie is having its effect. Cousteau glances up. "I will never rest," he says, "until I see with my own two eyes what lies on the bottom. Who knows what miracles will be revealed, what kaleidoscopic vistas of the unknown and silent world?"

I bite my tongue, though I could say plenty. Cousteau is getting old. We're all getting old. We've plumbed every body of water on earth, from McMurdo Sound to the Arafura Sea and the Firth of Clyde, we've found every wreck and frolicked with every fish, and I just don't see the point of it anymore. But Cousteau is the perennial Boy Scout, intoxicated with adventure, if not the *cru bourgeois* the *Calypso* carries in her three-ton stainless steel wine tank. For him, everything is "kaleidoscopic," "dreamlike," "phantasmagoric," from the life of the coral reef to the dregs of *vin rouge* left in the bottom of his glass after dinner. The whole watery world is his to embrace, but for me it's the galley and the galley only, for me it's a dwindling supply of veal chops and limp vegetables and nothing but *poisson, poisson, poisson*. Twenty ravenous gastronomes stare up at me from the table each night, and what do I have to offer them? *Poisson.*

The first to break the silence is Saôut. He has bags under his eyes, and his chest, once sculpted and firm with his years of manhandling winches and hawsers, droops like an old woman's. "Bernard has a point," he says. "We've gone over two months now without liberty."

"Two months without women," Didier growls.

"Or meat," Sancerre puts in.

I try to keep from smirking as I lean over the sun-blasted nape of this man or that to pour my bitter black brew. But Cousteau is oblivious. He merely waves the lank flap of his hand and says, "Deeper."

We are anchored—have been anchored for two months now and counting—some 160 miles off the coast of West Africa, hovering over a deep sea canyon that for all intents and purposes has no bottom. Sense and sonar indicate that it is there, somewhere between thirteen and fourteen thousand feet, but because of poor maneuverability, undersea mudslides and senile dementia on the part of captain and crew, we have been unable to locate it. As if it matters. As if we haven't already sounded out the sterile bottoms of a hundred canyons just like it and found absolutely nothing that would change anyone's life one way or the other. The usual complement of scientists is aboard, of course, eager boyish men with pinched features, oversized eyeglasses, clipboards and calculators. They are geniuses. Learned professors. World-renowned authorities on the sponge or the sea cucumber. *Tant pis.* To me they are simply mouths to feed, mouths that tighten perceptibly at the mention of fish.

I am up, as always, an hour before dawn, preparing breakfast. I still have flour—thank God for that or we'd have a full-scale mutiny on our hands—and am busy fashioning crêpes from thin air. I find myself absently filling them with artificial pastry creme and the obscenely flavorless pulp of defrosted strawberries, but what can I do? Even the batter is bastardized, the eggs produced from a tin in the form of a noxious yellow powder that looks like something you'd use in a chemistry experiment. What I wouldn't give for a dozen fresh eggs. Half a dozen. *Merde:* even a single one. But of course there are no chickenhouses on the open sea.

Busy with my whisk, I fail to notice Sancerre creeping into the galley. I hear him before I see him. "Who's there?" I demand, the portholes black with the vestiges of yet another night at sea, the ship undulating beneath my feet in an incipient morning swell.

Sheepish, the sleep still glued to his eyes, Sancerre emerges from the pool of shadow behind the deep freeze. "Me," he says simply.

"What are you doing here?"

I watch as his long mulish face reconstitutes itself in the glare of the galley lights, a face yellowed by the shambling years and the hostility of the sun. He shuffles his big feet, drops his shoulders and spreads his hands wide. "I'm hungry," he says.

"Hungry, eh?"

My first impulse is to toy with him, make him squirm a bit, offer to perhaps fry up a batch of the flying fish that lie stunned on the deck each morning. Fish isn't what he wants. He wants sausage, cheese, croissants pregnant with butter, he wants cold chicken, thick slices of Bayonne ham, beefsteaks and pâté maison spread on crusty rounds of peasant bread. Yes, of course, but he too must suffer through this hell of fish.

"A little something would do," he says almost apologetically. "Just a bite to settle the stomach."

And in that moment, even before I reach for the smoked sausage I keep hidden behind the saucepans, I realize I have an ally.

As soon as breakfast has been tucked away, down goes the bathyscaph, accompanied partway by the *soucoupe plongeant*—our diving saucer—and all hands are hungrily occupied till lunch. Cousteau himself is piloting the bathyscaph, though he's too old to sit for hours in the moist cramped bubble of steel and glass down there in the ultimate hole of the earth, too old by far, just as I'm too old to prepare fillets of *loup de mer* in this straitjacket of a galley or ladle scalding *chaudrée* from the pot in an unsettled sea—and I have the scars to prove it. One of the scientists has gone down with him, an American with big American teeth and a braying American laugh that makes me want to kill every time I hear it. His very name—Dr. Mazzy Gort—sticks in my throat. I wish no one harm, but sometimes I fantasize. What if Cousteau and Dr. Mazzy Gort never come up again? What if the lifeline fails or a mudslide buries them two miles down in ooze a hundred feet thick and they join the fishes forever? It's an evil thought. But it's not my first, nor, I suspect, will it be my last.

For lunch I serve a grouper Falco speared last night. I've taken some care with it, marinated the fine white flesh in olive oil and fennel—the last of my fennel—and a soupçon of pastis. I serve it with fresh bread, the remaining potatoes and defrosted green beans in an explosion of aromas, pretending, for all and sundry, that this is not fish at all, that this is not the open sea, that we are not prisoners of Cousteau's madness. And what do I get for it?

Saôut: "Oh, *merde*, not fish again."

Piccard: "What else?"

Sancerre: "I want my mother."

Didier: "I want a whore. Two whores. One for this—and one for this." (A manual demonstration, very nimble and expressive.)

Afterward, in the interval between morning and afternoon dives, I find my feet directing me to the main deck and the cabin Cousteau used to share with his wife, back in the days when we were young and such things mattered. I am thinking. Talking to myself, actually. Making speeches. In one of the rear compartments of my brain, uninfected by the primordial reek of the sea and the visible evidence of the portholes, is the image of a modest auberge in Cluny or Trévoux, a tasteful little place that specializes in country dishes, viands mostly, heavy on cassoulets, game and sweetbreads, though perhaps, after a year or two on dry land, the chef might consider adding a pike quenelle or a *truite aux amandes* to the bill of fare. In the forefront of my consciousness an argument simmers for Cousteau.

Jacques-Yves, mon vieux, be reasonable, I will tell him. *We are out of butter, eggs, cream, vegetables and herbs, we have less than a gallon of olive oil, no meats to speak of, no shallots or onions or potatoes. Release us. Release me. I'm fed up. Thirty years of clinging to the drainboard while the sea jerks my feet out from under me, thirty years of dicing leeks on a counter that won't stand still, thirty years of racking my brain to come up with new ways and yet more new ways to prepare fish, and I've had it. I want to retire. I want to cook for tourists and the petite bourgeoisie. I want to cook meat, I want an herb garden and a chickenhouse. I want to feel the earth under my feet.*

This is my speech, the one gathering itself on my lips as I seek out Cousteau. Unfortunately, I never get to deliver it. Because by the time I get to Cousteau's cabin and stick my head in the door, he is lost to me, lost to us all, as faraway as if he were on another ship off another coast. The portholes are smothered, the room bathed in shadow: Cousteau is absorbed in the ritual of the voice-over. He sits before the TV monitor, a weird greenish glow on his face, mesmerized by images of the sea. Nothing moves but his lips, his voice murmurous and rapt: "As we go deeper into the somnolent depths, a kaleidoscope of fishes whirling round us like painted stars in a night sky, we cannot help but wonder at the phantasmagoric marvels that await us below. . . ."

That evening, as the grouper appears in the guise of a saffronless bouillabaisse that is short on all ingredients except fish, Sancerre takes me aside. We are in the galley, the ship rolling in a moderate-to-heavy swell, the crew loud and raucous in the main cabin. His skin is the color of a baked yam, his eyes sunk deep in his head. "Bernard," he says, lowering his voice to a whispery rasp, "I've been talking to some of the men. . . ."

The pans rattle. A knife shoots across the expanse of the cutting board and lodges in the wall. I grab hold of the counter to keep from pitching face forward into the dessert. "Yes?" I prompt.

Sancerre's face is like an old boot. The swell doesn't faze him—he might as well be a fly clinging to the wall. "We want to go home," he says finally.

Relief washes over me. I can feel the tears coming to my eyes as I take the blistered hide of Sancerre's hand in mine and give it an affirmative squeeze. "Me too," I say, "me too," and I can hardly contain my emotion.

Sancerre glances over his shoulder, furtive and sly, then comes back to me with a wink. "We were just thinking," he whispers, and it's a strain to hear him over the habitual roar of the sea and the brouhaha of the crew at their sorry dinner, "about what you said last night over coffee, standing up to Cousteau like that—"

The ship dips to port, then jerks back at the long leash of its anchor, which is mired in the muck on top of a submerged mountain five hundred feet down. "Yes," I say, afraid of moving too fast, afraid of scaring him off, "go on."

But he just shrugs, the big idiot, and jams his hands into his pockets even as the swell rocks the deck under his feet.

"Listen," I say, "Sancerre, old friend, could you find room for another little morsel of sausage? And some cheese I've been saving—some Gruyère?"

Sancerre's eyes leap at me like caged beasts. The ship heaves back again and there's a sharp curse from the main cabin followed by the sound of breaking glass. "Cheese? Did you say cheese?"

I am expansive, generous to a fault. Not only do I break out the cheese and sausage but two neat little glasses of the culinary pastis as well, and in the next minute we're seated side by side atop the deep freeze like two old cronies on a country picnic. I wait till he's wolfed down half a dozen wedges of the Gruyère and three plump slices of sausage before I say anything, and when I say it I am already pouring his second glass full to the brim with the clear fragrant liquor. "How many of you are in on it?" I whisper.

"Six of us," he says before he can think.

"And the American?"

A look of disgust creeps across his features, settling finally into the ropy bulge of his lower lip. "The American," he spits, and I know exactly what he means: if push comes to shove, the American will have to be sacrificed, along with anyone else who gets in our way.

"Falco?" I ask.

"He's with the Captain, you should know that. They're like two peas in a pod."

Am I trembling—or is it just the boat rocking under my feet? Are we really sitting here in the galley over a bottomless pit in a rolling swell, contemplating mutiny? The thought thrills me till I feel as if I've been rung like a bell. Strange to say, though, I'm not thinking of Cousteau or fathomless depths or crashing waves or even courts of inquiry, but of forest mushrooms—forest mushrooms growing in sweet pale clumps among the ferns in a deep pool of shade.

It is then that Saôut slips in the door with his old woman's tits and a broken plate held out conspicuously before him, looking secretive, looking like a spy— or a conspirator. His eyes take in the scene and without a word he goes straight for the sausage. One bite, two: he doesn't bother with the knife. I watch his jaws work around the bleached-out bristle of his beard. The ship lurches, but he's glued to the floor. "Are you with us?" he says finally, and as the sea lashes at the porthole and the ship comes back up and shakes itself like an old dog emerging from a bath, I can only nod.

In the morning, though it hurts me to do it, though it goes against every principle I've held sacrosanct since I successfully reduced my first Béarnaise some forty years ago, I serve a breakfast even an American wouldn't eat. The coffee—strained through yesterday's grounds—is the color of turpentine, watery and thin and without benefit of cream. There is no bread. Instead of baking, I made use of the old crusts I've been saving for croûtons, dipping them in a paste made of powdered egg and water and then frying them hard in twice-used oil and serving them with an accompaniment of flying fish poached in sea water and nothing else, not even a dash of pepper or a pass of the bouquet garni. I feel like an imp, a demon, a saboteur. I set out the plates in the main cabin, ring the breakfast bell, and slink away to my berth, heart pounding in my chest.

It doesn't take long. The rumble of outrage spreads through the ship like some seismic event, radiating outward from the epicenter of the main cabin till every last bolt and iron plate thrums with it. I'm taking a calculated risk, and I know it. For the moment, at least, the gastronomic outrage is directed at me, and I'm not surprised when fifteen minutes later a deputation of the crew seeks me out in my bunk. It is led by Piccard and one of the scientists—Laffite, the sponge man—but to my relief, as I look up long-faced from my pillow, I see that Sancerre and Saôut are hovering protectively in the background.

"What's the matter with you, Bernard?" Piccard demands. "Are you sick, is that it? Dizzy spells again?"

The sponge man is more direct: "How could you serve such, such"—he's so overwrought he can barely get the words out—"such offal? It's nothing short of criminal."

I gaze up at them with a composed face, calm as the sacrificial lamb. "Sick, yes," I say. "But not in the body—in my heart."

Laffite is a bomb choking on its own fuse. He is a big man, bloated with his cravings, a priest worshipping at the temple of the gustatory pleasures. "What the hell is that supposed to mean?" he cries. "Get out of that bed, you slacker, you assassin!"

Fortunately, Saôut is able to wrestle hold of his arms, or the first blood might have been spilled right then and there—and it would have been mine. "Calm yourself, Laffite," he growls, and only I detect the quick slice of his wink. I let my eyes fall shut, and the sea, quiet now, rocks me in my cradle. A minute passes, the four of them squabbling like schoolchildren, and then I listen to the retreat of their footsteps. But my ears deceive me: when I open my eyes I see that

Sancerre has stayed behind. He is grinning, and his jaundiced face seems to be lit from within, glowing like a freshly picked lemon. "We are eight," he whispers, and I give him a look. *Who?* I silently mouth.

Sancerre glances over his shoulder. "It's all a charade," he says. "Piccard has capitulated."

Lunch is a triumph of negativity: the selfsame flying fish, baked to the texture of wood pulp, their veiny winglike fins dried to stumps and served in a crimson jacket of American catsup, with canned niblet corn and sweet gherkins desecrating the rest of the plate under a garnish of seaweed. Again I retreat to my berth, again an incensed mob seeks me out. This time Sancerre shepherds Borchardt, Pépin and Fasquelle into my presence, and by the time they leave, we are eleven.

And then the pièce de résistance, the straw that breaks the camel's back, our ticket to freedom: dinner. During the course of the afternoon, Cousteau and Dr. Mazzy Gort have descended again, ever deeper, seeking their solutions in the eternal muck. The crew has worked doggedly beneath an unsympathetic sun, their wizened biceps and arthritic backs straining, stomachs rumbling, the taste of mutiny burning like some bitter potion in their throats. And I? I have made my slow deliberate way through the reefs and shoals of my saucepans, my cruets, my knives and sieves and whisks. For the first time in as long as I can remember, I am working from a recipe, a curiosity from a thin volume left behind ten or fifteen years ago by a scientist from a place called Missouri: *The Show Me State Cookbook*. I do not have the butter, the crème fraîche, the milk, the champignons or the Parmesan, but the tinned tuna, the yellow wax beans and the packets of egg noodles exist in a sedimentary layer at the very bottom of the larder in a box labeled *Emergency Rations*.

Fair enough. I wouldn't want to spoil the thing with any hint of flavor, after all. The sun slides across the porthole. I whistle while I work.

It is past seven by the time the bathyscaph is back on deck and Cousteau and Dr. Mazzy Gort have extricated their cramped limbs from its bowels. The crew steps lively, working furiously to secure everything against the night, lurching across the deck on aching feet, their noses turned optimistically to the air in the hope of catching a whiff of what the prandial hour promises to bring them. I overhear snatches of conversation, Cousteau's voice raised in giddy triumph— they've found something, but not the bottom, not yet—and as the sun swells on the horizon the first cigarettes are lit, the first glasses of wine circulated. This is the hour when an air of festivity prevails aboard the *Calypso*, a time when labors are set aside and the mind drifts toward the simple pleasures to come. And so it is tonight, and yet, as bits and pieces of hushed dialogue float in through the open porthole and as this man or that sticks his head in the galley for a premonitory sniff, I can sense the tension underlying it all, the nasty nagging collective memory of that unforgivable breakfast and the obscenity of a lunch that followed it. They tread lightly. They are afraid. Deeply afraid.

This time I stand my ground. With a grand flourish I set the three big steaming pans down in the center of the table for each man to serve himself: the moment of truth is at hand. I note the sly, guilty looks of my co-conspirators as they suck at their wine glasses like condemned men, resigned to going hungry, and it props up my resolve. A lull falls over the conversation, hands fiddling with cutlery, with napkins, reaching out for the salt shaker, the pepper, the quietly oozing pans of my chef d'oeuvre. And now I have eyes only for the head of the table, where Cousteau sits absorbed in talk of the deeps with Dr. Mazzy Gort, Falco and Laffite. They retract unconsciously into the shells of their bent heads and bunched shoulders; their noses sniff the air warily. Steam rises. The first pan is breached, then the second and third, and all but the conspirators dig in.

Laffite is the first to react. "Good Christ!" he explodes, coughing up a mouthful of the stuff.

"I'm poisoned!" gasps Falco, and all round the table men lurch back from their plates in shock and horror. Even the Captain, whose taste buds must have withered and died long ago, lifts his head to give me a look of astonishment. Only Mazzy Gort seems unaffected, feeding the mucilaginous paste into the slot of his mouth as unconcernedly as if he were at a hot dog stand in some fantastical place like Peoria or Oshkosh.

Through the general tumult that ensues, one voice begins to take command: Laffite's. "Murderer!" he cries, leaping from his seat in a frenzy. "And what do you call this, this, this *shit?!*"

I am a rock, a pillar, the statue of a man in a crisp white toque, arms folded across my chest. "Tuna noodle casserole," I announce, and the place erupts.

Later, after the walls of the main cabin have been scrubbed down and the belligerents separated and sent wheezing to their bunks, Sancerre appears in the doorway to the galley to inform me that the Captain would like to have a word with me. Poor Sancerre. His dried yellow fig of a face is as mournful as a Greek mask, but his bloodied nose and the flapping rags of his eyes show that he isn't licked yet. "What happened?" I ask, not bothering to look up or offer him a portion of the sausage I'm feeding into my mouth, one compulsive slice after another. "I thought you said we were eleven?"

"Son of a bitch," he mutters. "It was Piccard. Did you see him?"

Only too clearly. Piccard stood with the Captain when the fight broke out, and when the food began to fly it wasn't Cousteau who took the brunt of the abuse, but me, as if everything I'd done wasn't for the general good and benefit of all. "What next?" I want to know, my voice a miserable croak. "I've given it everything I have."

Framed in the doorway like some ghost of the larder, Sancerre replies in a voice as miserable as mine. "Give it time," he says. "The men can't hold out much longer. They can't." He steps closer, eyeing my sausage, his hands spread wide in extenuation. "They're sucking on hard candy and drinking wine like it was gravy, they're cracking jars of peanuts, raiding the emergency supplies in the lifeboats. They're in an ugly mood, Bernard. I tell you, if it wasn't for the wine—"

Suddenly we lock eyes. *The wine.* Of course: *the wine.* Deny a Frenchman his bread and he is angry, deny him his foie gras and his truffles and he is savage, but deny him his wine and he is nothing short of homicidal. Sancerre is grinning, and his grin has a country village in it, a kitchen garden, fruit trees, rabbits on a hook. I am grinning too, and my grin contains all that and more. "The wine," I repeat, and though Cousteau awaits and my stomach plunges and everywhere the stink of fish infests my nostrils, I find myself laughing, laughing till the tears begin to stream down my face.

"Bernard," Cousteau intones, and there is nothing left of his face but nose and two huge and liquidly suffering eyes, "I am chagrined. And puzzled too. It almost seems as if you're deliberately trying to provoke the crew."

We are in Cousteau's cabin, a dark void rocking on the night of the sea and lit only by the subaquatic glow of the TV monitor. Finned legs kick across the screen, fish appear. Coral. The deeps. There is a plea on my tongue, a plea for our thirty years, for understanding and compassion, a *mon vieux* and a *mon ami*, but I kill it. "That's right," I say. "I am."

"But what are you thinking?" Here the nose becomes a slash of shadow, the eyes luminous with the reflection of the screen—in this moment he looks like nothing so much as a fish himself. "Don't you realize that we've almost reached our objective?"

"I don't care."

"Don't care? But what of the kaleidoscopic wonders, what of the fishes in their undersea grottoes?"

The sea is calm, the ship motionless beneath us, held fast in a liquid vise. "I'm too old for exploring," I say finally. "My feet hurt. There are no more wonders for me." I look him dead in the eye. "I've cooked my last meal aboard this ship."

And now the look of surprise, of consternation, of a befuddlement so deep you would have thought I was a talking eel or a puffer fish reciting *La Nymphe de la Seine.* "But you can't do that—you've signed the articles. I'd have to, to put you in chains. . . ."

I feel myself giving way—I can't take this anymore, not another minute. I spit my words out, vomit them up, and I don't care, I don't. "Spanish Rice!" I shout. "Chuck Wagon Beans, Tuna Surprise, Macaroni and Cheese!"

■ ■ ■

And so, the next morning, as dawn breaks over the sea, I find myself confined to quarters, Laffite, the sponge man, standing guard over me as if I were some ship-wrecked loon or common provocateur. I can smell from afar the sordid amateur attempts at breakfast, the blackened and fallen bread, the ruined coffee. My stomach stirs as I watch Laffite slump over the farce of his pistol, his heavy face drawn with hunger and fatigue. "What would you give, Laffite," I say, as the morning swell drops us into a trough and buffets us back up again, "for a nice crisply presented *caneton Tour d'Argent* or a *filet de boeuf en croûte?* Eh? How many baskets of your precious sponges? Or would you prefer to eat *them?*"

The big man, with his big head and suffering eyes, looks queasy. "I warn you," he says, and he clutches at the pistol with fat sweating fingers.

"Remember the *petites brioches* I used to make in the mornings, still hot from the oven? The way the butter would sink into them? Or the *pain de campagne,* a loaf per man?"

"Madman," he snarls. "Fiend. Shut up!"

But I go on and on till he's at the breaking point, till he's either going to have to shoot me or give up the charade and let me climb above decks and guide the misguided. He's giving way, I can see it, but then, right in the middle of my loving re-creation of the recipe for roast leg of venison with *poivrade* sauce, there's a shout from above followed almost immediately by the most piteous outpouring of shock and lament I've ever heard. Laffite drops the pistol as if it's suddenly come to life and bitten him and we leap simultaneously to our feet and fling ourselves out the door and up the companionway. A moment later, out of breath, we emerge on deck to a scene of purgatorial despair. Borchardt is beating his head against the rail, Falco striding up and down the boards shouting "All hands on deck!," Piccard hiding his face and weeping like a schoolgirl. The Captain and Dr. Mazzy Gort, huddled by the babyscaph in their deep-sea explorer's costumes, can only blink and stare—they couldn't look any more confused if the ship had hit a reef.

There in the water, all round the ship, is a deep red stain, a stain that might have been the life's blood of a hundred crews, already paling to dissolution in the brine. I look to Sancerre and his reckless smile, to Saôut and his suicidal eyes, and I know that this is not blood, but wine, *cru bourgeois,* five hundred gallons at least. The voyage is over. The bottom will remain inviolate, the fishes undisturbed. Cousteau is defeated.

It is my moment, and I seize it. "Rally round, men!" I cry, my heart contracting like a fist. "Weigh anchor! We're going home!"

No one moves. The wind lifts the hair over our ears, the wine-dark sea heaves at the hull. All eyes turn to Cousteau. Wearily, sunk into the pouches and wrinkles of his obsession, he takes a step forward and burns us all with his eyes. "Deeper," he says, "we must go deeper."

Falco is the first to fracture the tableau. Stooped and sun-blasted, his face un-readable, he breaks ranks with the men to stride across the deck and stand with the Captain. Dr. Mazzy Gort is next. He looks from Falco to Cousteau and then to the rest of us and can't suppress a whinny of apprehension: he may be an American, but he can see what's coming. "It's all over!" I shout. "Give it up!"

Cousteau ignores me. He just pulls on his hood and thermal jacket and climbs into the bathyscaph, that fat sputnik of the deeps suspended from the crane at the stern of the ship. I can see him there, in hawkish profile, fiddling with the controls through the rictus of the open door. He gestures impatiently to Mazzy Gort, but the American hesitates, and in the moment of his hesitation Falco moves to the Captain's side, disappearing aloft in the shadows of the div-ing capsule. The steel doors crank shut.

It's up to me now. Up to me to order the bathyscaph set in motion and dropped over the side into the yawning mouth of the waves, up to me to cut the throats of thirty individual years, one by one, as cleanly and surely as I cut the lifeline with a torch and insure, once and for all, that Costeau finds what he's seeking. For a moment the responsibility paralyzes me. The men—Sancerre, Saôut, Piccard, even Laffite and Dr. Mazzy Gort—watch me in silence, hardly daring to swallow. And then the breeze shifts direction, carrying all the way out from some distant shore, a breeze smelling impossibly of pork roast, of beef, of goose and quail and duck à l'orange, and I know I can do anything, anything at all.

(1995)

56—0

It wasn't the cast that bothered him—the thing was like rock, like a weapon, and that was just how he would use it—and it wasn't the hyperextended knee or the hip pointer or the yellowing contusions seeping into his thighs and hams and lower back or even the gouged eye that was swollen shut and drooling a thin pale liquid the color of dishwater; no, it was the humiliation. Fifty-six to nothing. That was no mere defeat; it was a drubbing, an ass-kicking, a rape, the kind of thing the statisticians and sports nerds would snigger over as long as there were records to keep. He'd always felt bigger than life in his pads and helmet, a hero, a titan, but you couldn't muster much heroism lying facedown in the mud at fifty-six to nothing and with the other team's third string in there. No, the cast didn't bother him, not really, though it itched like hell and his hand was a big stippled piece of meat sticking out of the end of it, or the eye either, though it was ugly, pure ugly. The trainer had sent him to the eye doctor and the doctor had put some kind of blue fluid in the eye and peered into it with a little conical flashlight and said there was no lasting damage, but still it was swollen shut and he couldn't study for his Physical Communications exam.

It was Sunday, the day after the game, and Ray Arthur Larry-Pete Fontinot, right guard for the Caledonia College Shuckers, slept till two, wrapped in his own private misery—and even then he couldn't get out of bed. Every fiber of his body, all six feet, four inches and two hundred sixty-eight pounds of it, shrieked with pain. He was twenty-two years old, a senior, his whole life ahead of him, and he felt like he was ready for the nursing home. There was a ringing in his ears, his eyelashes were welded together, his lower back throbbed and both his knees felt as if ice picks had been driven into them. He hobbled, splayfooted and naked, to the bathroom at the end of the hall, and there was blood in the toilet bowl when he was done.

All his life he'd been a slow fat pasty kid, beleaguered and tormented by his quick-footed classmates, until he found his niche on the football field, where his bulk, stubborn and immovable, had proved an advantage—or so he'd thought. He'd drunk the protein drink, pumped the iron, lumbered around the track like some geriatric buffalo, and what had it gotten him? Caledonia had gone 0–43 during his four years on the varsity squad, never coming closer than two touchdowns even to a tie—and the forty-third loss had been the hardest. Fifty-six to nothing. He'd donned a football helmet to feel good about himself, to develop pride and poise, to taste the sweet nectar of glory, but somehow he didn't feel all that glorious lying there flat on his back and squinting one-eyed at Puckett and Poplar's *Principles of Physical Communications: A Text*, until the lines shifted before him like the ranks of X's and O's in the Coach's eternal diagrams. He dozed. Woke again to see the evening shadows closing over the room. By nightfall, he felt good enough to get up and puke.

In the morning, a full forty hours after the game had ended, he felt even worse, if that was possible. He sat up, goaded by the first tumultuous stirrings of his gut, and winced as he pulled the sweats over each bruised and puckered calf. His right knee locked up on him as he angled his feet into the laceless high-tops (it had been three years at least since he'd last been able to bend down and tie his shoes), something cried out in his left shoulder as he pulled the Caledonia sweatshirt over his head, and then suddenly he was on his feet and ambulatory. He staggered down the hall like something out of *Night of the Living Dead*, registering a familiar face here and there, but the faces were a blur mostly, and he avoided the eyes attached to them. Someone was playing Killer Pussy at seismic volume, and someone else—some half-witted dweeb he'd gladly have murdered if only his back didn't hurt so much—had left a skateboard outside the door and Ray Arthur Larry-Pete damn near crushed it to powder and pitched right on through the concrete-block wall in the bargain, but if nothing else, he still had his reflexes. As he crossed the courtyard to the cafeteria in a lively blistering wind, he noted absently that he'd progressed from a hobble to a limp.

There was no sign of Suzie in the cafeteria, and he had a vague recollection of her calling to cancel their study date the previous evening, but as he loaded up his tray with desiccated bacon strips, mucilaginous eggs and waffles that looked, felt and tasted like roofing material, he spotted Kitwany, Moss and DuBoy skulking over their plates at one of the long tables in the back of the room. It would have been hard to miss them. Cut from the same exaggerated mold as he, his fellow linemen loomed over the general run of the student body like representatives of another species. Their heads were like prize pumpkins set on the pedestals of their neckless shoulders, their fingers were the size of the average person's fore-arm, their jaws were entities unto themselves and they sprouted casts like weird growths all over their bodies.

Ray Arthur Larry-Pete made the long limp across the room to join them, set-ting his tray down gingerly and using both his hands to brace himself as he low-ered his bruised backside to the unforgiving hardwood slats of the bench. Then, still employing his hands, he lifted first one and then the other deadened leg over the bench and into the well beneath the table. He grunted, winced, cursed, broke wind. Then he nodded to his teammates, worked his spine into the swallowing position and addressed himself to his food.

After a moment, DuBoy spoke. He was wearing a neck brace in the place where his head was joined to his shoulders, and it squeezed the excess flesh of his jowls up into his face so that he looked like an enormous rodent. "How you feeling?"

You didn't speak of pain. You toughed it out—that was the code. Coach Tun-dra had been in the army in Vietnam at some place Ray Arthur Larry-Pete could never remember or pronounce, and he didn't tolerate whiners and slackers. *Pain?* he would yelp incredulously at the first hint that a player was even think-ing of staying down. *Tell it to the 101st Airborne, to the boys taking a mortar round in the Ia Drang Valley or the grunts in the field watching their buddies get blown away and then crawling six miles through a swamp so thick it would choke a snake with both their ears bleeding down their neck and their leg gone at the knee. Get up, soldier. Get out there and fight!* And if that didn't work, he'd roll up his pantleg to show off the prosthesis.

Ray Arthur Larry-Pete glanced up at DuBoy. "I'll live. How about you?"

DuBoy tried to shrug as if to say it was nothing, but even the faintest lift of a shoulder made him gasp and slap a hand to the neck brace as if a hornet had stung him. "No . . . big thing," he croaked finally.

There was no sound then but for the onomatopoeia of the alimentary process—food going in, jaws seizing it, throats closing on the load and opening again for the next—and the light trilling mealtime chatter of their fellow stu-dents, the ones unencumbered by casts and groin pulls and bloody toilets. Ray Arthur Larry-Pete was depressed. Over the loss, sure—but it went deeper than that. He was brooding about his college career, his job prospects, life after foot-ball. There was a whole winter, spring and summer coming up in which, for the first time in as long as he could remember, he wouldn't have to worry about training for football season, and he couldn't imagine what that would be like. No locker room, no sweat, no pads, no stink of shower drains or the mentholated reek of ointment, no jock itch or aching muscles, no training table, no trainer—no chance, however slim, for glory. . . .

And more immediately, he was fretting about his coursework. There was the Phys. Comm. exam he hadn't been able to study for, and the quiz the professor would almost certainly spring in Phys. Ed., and there were the three-paragraph papers required for both Phys. Training and Phys. Phys., and he was starting to get a little paranoid about Suzie, one of the quintessentially desirable girls on campus, with all her assets on public view, and what did he have to offer her but the glamour of football? Why had she backed out on their date? Did this mean their engagement was off, that she wanted a winner, that this was the beginning of the end?

He was so absorbed in his thoughts he didn't register what Moss was saying when he dropped his bomb into the little silence at the table. Moss was wearing a knee brace and his left arm was in a sling. He was using his right to alternately take a bite of his own food and to lift a heaping forkful from Kitwany's plate to Kitwany's waiting lips. Kitwany was in a full-shoulder harness, both arms frozen in front of him as if he were a sleepwalker cast in plaster of Paris. Ray Arthur Larry-Pete saw Moss's mouth working, but the words flew right by him. "What did you say, Moss?" he murmured, looking up from his food.

"I said Coach says we're probably going to have to forfeit to State."

Ray Arthur Larry-Pete was struck dumb. "Forfeit?" he finally gasped, and the blood was thundering in his temples. "What the hell do you mean, forfeit?"

A swirl of snow flurries scoured his unprotected ears as he limped grimly across the quad to the Phys. Ed. building, muttering under his breath. What was the Coach thinking? Didn't he realize this was the seniors' last game, their last and only chance to assuage the sting of 56–0, the final time they'd ever pull on their cleats against State, Caledonia's bitterest rival, a team they hadn't beaten in modern historical times? Was he crazy?

It was cold, wintry, the last week in November, and Ray Arthur Larry-Pete Fontinot had to reach up with his good hand to pull his collar tight against his throat as he mounted the big concrete steps brushed with snow. The shooting hot-wire pains that accompanied this simple gesture were nothing, nothing at all, and he barely grimaced, reaching down automatically for the push-bar on the big heavy eight-foot-tall double doors. He nodded at a pair of wrestlers running the stairs in gym shorts, made his way past the woefully barren trophy case (*Caledonia College, Third Place Divisional Finish, 1938* read the inscription on the lone trophy, which featured a bronzed figurine in antiquated leather headgear atop a pedestal engraved with the scores of that lustrous long-ago 6-and-5 season, the only winning season Caledonia could boast of in any of its athletic divisions, except for women's field hockey and who counted that?), tested his knees on the third grueling flight of stairs, and approached the Coach's office by the side door. Coach Tundra almost never inhabited his official office on the main corridor, a place of tidy desks, secretaries and seasonal decorations; of telephones, copiers and the new lone fax machine he could use to instantaneously trade X's and O's

with his colleagues at other colleges, if he so chose. No, he preferred the back
room, a tiny unheated poorly lit cubicle cluttered with the detritus of nineteen
unprofitable seasons. Ray Arthur Larry-Pete peered through the open doorway
to find the Coach slumped over his desk, face buried in his hands. "Coach?" he
said softly.

No reaction.

"Coach?"

From the nest of his hands, the Coach's rucked and gouged face gradually
emerged and the glittering wicked raptor's eyes that had struck such bowel-
wringing terror into red-shirt freshman and senior alike stared up blankly. There
was nothing in those eyes now but a worn and defeated look, and it was a shock.
So too the wrinkles in the shirt that was always pressed and pleated with military precision, the scuffed shoes and suddenly vulnerable-looking hands—even
the Coach's brush cut, ordinarily as stiff and imperturbable as a falcon's crest,
seemed to lie limp against his scalp. "Fontinot?" the Coach said finally, and his
voice was dead.

"I, uh, just wanted to check—I mean, practice is at the regular time, right?"

Coach Tundra said nothing. He looked shrunken, lost, older in that moment
than the oldest man in the oldest village in the mountains of Tibet. "There won't
be any practice today," he said, rubbing his temple over the spot where the military surgeons had inserted the steel plate.

"No practice? But Coach, shouldn't we—I mean, don't we have to—"

"We can't field a team, Fontinot. I count sixteen guys out of forty-two that
can go out there on the field and maybe come out of their comas for four consecutive quarters—and I'm counting you among them. And you're so banged up
you can barely stand, let alone block." He heaved a sigh, plucked a torn battered
shoe from the pile of relics on the floor and turned it over meditatively in his
hands. "We're done, Fontinot. Finished. It's all she wrote. Like at Saigon when
the gooks overran the place—it's time to cut our losses and run."

Ray Arthur Larry-Pete was stunned. He'd given his life for this, he'd sweated
and fought and struggled, filled the bloated vessel of himself with the dregs of
defeat, week after week, year after year. He was flunking all four of his Phys. Ed.
courses, Suzie thought he was a clown, his mother was dying of uterine cancer
and his father—the man who'd named him after the three greatest offensive linemen in college-football history—was driving in from Cincinnati for the game, his
last game, the ultimate and final contest that stood between him and the world
of pay stubs and mortgages. "You don't mean," he stammered, "you don't mean
we're going to *forfeit*, do you?"

For a long moment the Coach held him with his eyes. Faint sounds echoed in
the corridors—the slap of sneakers, a door heaving closed, the far-off piping of
the basketball coach's whistle. Coach Tundra made an unconscious gesture
toward his pant leg and for a moment Ray Arthur Larry-Pete thought he was go-

ing to expose the prosthesis again. "What do you want me to do," he said finally, "go out there and play myself?"

Back in his room, Ray Arthur Larry-Pete brooded over the perfidy of it all. A few hours ago he'd been sick to death of the game—what had it gotten him but obloquy and bruises?—but now he wanted to go out there and play so badly he could kill for it. His roommate—Malmo Malmstein, the team's kicker—was still in the hospital, and he had the room to himself through the long morning and the interminable afternoon that followed it. He lay there prostrate on the bed like something shot out in the open that had crawled back to its cave to die, skipping classes, blowing off tests and steeping himself in misery. At three he called Suzie—he had to talk to someone, anyone, or he'd go crazy—but one of her sorority sisters told him she was having her nails done and wasn't expected back before six. Her *nails*. Christ, that rubbed him raw: where was she when he needed her? A sick sinking feeling settled into his stomach—she was cutting him loose, he knew it.

And then, just as it was getting dark, at the very nadir of his despair, something snapped in him. What was wrong with him? Was he a quitter? A whiner and slacker? The kind of guy that gives up before he puts his cleats on? No way. Not Ray Arthur Larry-Pete Fontinot. He came up off the bed like some sort of volcanic eruption and lurched across the room to the phone. Sweating, ponderous, his very heart, lungs and liver trembling with emotion, he focused all his concentration on the big pale block of his index finger as he dialed Gary Gedney, the chicken-neck who handled the equipment and kept the Gatorade bucket full. "Phone up all the guys," he roared into the receiver.

Gedney's voice came back at him in the thin whistling whine of a balloon sputtering round a room: "Who is this?"

"It's Fontinot. I want you to phone up all the guys."

"What for?" Gedney whined.

"We're calling a team meeting."

"Who is?"

Ray Arthur Larry-Pete considered the question a moment, and when finally he spoke it was with a conviction and authority he never thought he could command: "I am."

At seven that night, twenty-six members of the Caledonia Shuckers varsity football squad showed up in the lounge at Bloethal Hall. They filled the place with their presence, their sheer protoplasmic mass, and the chairs and couches groaned under the weight of them. They wore Band-Aids, gauze and tape—miles of it—and the lamplight caught the livid craters of their scars and glanced off the railway stitches running up and down their arms. There were casts, crutches, braces, slings. And there was the smell of them, a familiar, communal, lingering smell—the smell of a team.

Ray Arthur Larry-Pete Fontinot was ready for them, pacing back and forth in front of the sliding glass doors like a bear at the zoo, waiting patiently until each of them had gimped into the room and found a seat. Moss, DuBoy and Kitwany were there with him for emotional support, as was the fifth interior lineman, center Brian McCornish. When they were all gathered, Ray Arthur Larry-Pete lifted his eyes and scanned the familiar faces of his teammates. "I don't know if any of you happened to notice," he said, "but here it is Monday night and we didn't have practice this afternoon."

"Amen," someone said, and a couple of the guys started hooting.

But Ray Arthur Larry-Pete Fontinot wasn't having any of it. He was a rock. His face hardened. He clenched his fists. "It's no joke," he bellowed, and the thunder of his voice set up sympathetic vibrations in the pole lamps with their stained and battered shades. "We've got five days to the biggest game of our lives, and I'm not just talking about us seniors, but everybody, and I want to know what we're going to do about it."

"Forfeit, that's what." It was Diderot, the third-string quarterback and the only one at that vital position who could stand without the aid of crutches. He was lounging against the wall in the back of the room, and all heads now turned to him. "I talked to Coach, and that's what he said."

In that moment, Ray Arthur Larry-Pete lost control of himself. "Forfeit, my ass!" he roared, slamming his forearm, cast and all, down on the nearest coffee table, which fell to splinters under the force of the blow. "Get up, guys," he hissed in an intense aside to his fellow linemen, and Moss, DuBoy, Kitwany and McCornish rose beside him in a human wall. "We're willing to play sixty minutes of football," he boomed, and he had the attention of the room now, that was for sure. "Burt, Reggie, Steven, Brian and me, and we'll play both ways, offense *and* defense, to fill in for guys with broken legs and concussions and whatnot—"

A murmur went up. This was crazy, insane, practically sacrificial. State gave out scholarships—and under-the-table payoffs too—and they got the really topflight players, the true behemoths and crackerjacks, the ones who attracted pro scouts and big money. To go up against them in their present condition would be like replaying the Gulf War, with Caledonia cast in the role of the Iraqis.

"What are you, a bunch of pussies?" Ray Arthur Larry-Pete cried. "Afraid to get your uniforms dirty? Afraid of a little contact? What do you want—to have to live with fifty-six-to-nothing for the rest of your life? Huh? I don't hear you!"

But they heard him. He pleaded, threatened, blustered, cajoled, took them aside one by one, jabbered into the phone half the night till his voice was hoarse and his ear felt like a piece of rubber grafted to the side of his head. In the end, they turned out for practice the following day—twenty-three of them, even Kitwany, who could barely move from the waist up and couldn't get a jersey on over his cast—and Ray Arthur Larry-Pete Fontinot ascended the three flights to the Coach's office and handed Coach Tundra the brand-new silver-plated whistle they'd chipped in to buy him. "Coach," he said, as the startled man looked up at him from the crucible of his memories, "we're ready to go out there and kick some butt."

The day of the game dawned cold and forbidding, with close skies, a biting wind and the threat of snow on the air. Ray Arthur Larry-Pete had lain awake half the night, his brain tumbling through all the permutations of victory and disaster like a slot machine gone amok. Would he shine? Would he rise to the occasion and fight off the devastating pass rush of State's gargantuan front four? And what about the defense? He hadn't played defense since junior high, and now, because they were short-handed and because he'd opened his big mouth, he'd have to go both ways. Would he have the stamina? Or would he stagger round the field on rubber legs, thrust aside by State's steroid-swollen evolutionary freaks like the poor pathetic bumbling fat man he was destined to become? But no. Enough of that. If you thought like a loser—if you doubted for even a minute—then you were doomed, and you deserved 56–0 and worse.

At quarter to seven he got out of bed and stood in the center of the room in his undershorts, cutting the air savagely with the battering ram of his cast, pumping himself up. He felt unconquerable suddenly, felt blessed, felt as if he could do anything. The bruises, the swollen eye, the hip pointer and rickety knees were nothing but fading memories now. By Tuesday he'd been able to lift both his arms to shoulder level without pain, and by Wednesday he was trotting round the field on a pair of legs that felt like bridge abutments. Thursday's scrimmage left him wanting more, and he flew like a sprinter through yesterday's light workout. He was as ready as he'd ever be.

At seven-fifteen he strode through the weather to the dining hall to load up on carbohydrates, and by eight he was standing like a colossus in the foyer of Suzie's sorority house. The whole campus had heard about his speech in the Bloethal lounge, and by Wednesday night Suzie had come back round again. They spent the night in his room—his private room, for the duration of Malmstein's stay at the Sisters of Mercy Hospital—and Suzie had traced his bruises with her lips and hugged the tractor tire of flesh he wore round his midsection to her own slim and naked self. Now she greeted him with wet hair and a face bereft of makeup. "Wish me luck, Suze," he said, and she clung to him briefly before going off to transform herself for the game.

Coach Tundra gathered his team in the locker room at twelve-thirty and spoke to them from his heart, employing the military conceits that always seemed to confuse the players as much as inspire them, and then they were thundering out onto the field like some crazed herd of hoofed and horned things with

the scent of blood in their nostrils. The crowd roared. Caledonia's colors, char-
treuse and orange, flew in the breeze. The band played. Warming up, Ray Arthur
Larry-Pete could see Suzie sitting in the stands with her sorority sisters, her hair
the color of vanilla ice cream, her mouth fallen open in a cry of savagery and
bloodlust. And there, just to the rear of her—no, it couldn't be, it couldn't—but
is was: his mom. Sitting there beside the hulking mass of his father, wrapped up
in her windbreaker like a leaf pressed in an album, her scalp glinting bald
through the dyed pouf of her hair, there she was, holding a feeble fist aloft. His
mom! She'd been too sick to attend any of his games this year, but this was his
last one, his last game ever, and she'd fought down her pain and all the unimag-
inable stress and suffering of the oncology ward just to see him play. He felt the
tears come to his eyes as he raised his fist in harmony: this game was for her.

Unfortunately, within fifteen seconds of the kickoff, Caledonia was already in
the hole, 7–0, and Ray Arthur Larry-Pete hadn't even got out onto the field yet.
State's return man had fielded the kick at his own thirty after Malmstein's replacement, Hassan Farouk, had shanked the ball off the tee, and then he'd
dodged past the entire special teams unit and on into the end zone as if the Caledonia players were molded of wax. On the ensuing kickoff, Bobby Bibby, a jittery, butterfingered guy Ray Arthur Larry-Pete had never liked, fumbled the ball,
and State picked it up and ran it in for the score. They were less than a minute
into the game, and already it was 14–0.

Ray Arthur Larry-Pete felt his heart sink, but he leapt up off the bench with a
roar and butted heads so hard with Moss and DuBoy he almost knocked himself
unconscious. "Come on, guys," he bellowed, "it's only fourteen points, it's nothing, bear down!" And then Bibby held on to the ball and Ray Arthur Larry-Pete
was out on the field, going down in his three-point stance across from a guy who
looked like a walking mountain. The guy had a handlebar mustache, little black
eyes like hornets pinned to his head and a long wicked annealed scar that
plunged into his right eye socket and back out again. He looked to be about
thirty, and he wore Number 95 stretched tight across the expanse of his chest.
"You sorry sack of shit," he growled over Diderot's erratic snap-count. "I'm going to lay you flat out on your ass."

And that's exactly what he did. McCornish snapped the ball, Ray Arthur
Larry-Pete felt something like a tactical nuclear explosion in the region of his
sternum, and Number 95 was all over Diderot while Ray Arthur Larry-Pete
stared up into the sky. In the next moment the trainer was out there, along with
the Coach—already starting in on his Ia Drang Valley speech—and Ray Arthur
Larry-Pete felt the first few snowflakes drift down into the whites of his wide-
open and staring eyes. "Get up and walk it off," the trainer barked, and then half
a dozen hands were pulling him to his feet, and Ray Arthur Larry-Pete Fontinot
was back in his crouch, directly across from Number 95. And even then, though
he hated to admit it to himself, though he was playing for Suzie and his mother

and his own rapidly dissolving identity, he knew it was going to be a very long afternoon indeed.

It was 35–0 at the half, and Coach Tundra already had his pant leg rolled up by the time the team hobbled into the locker room. Frozen, pulverized, every cord, ligament, muscle and fiber stretched to the breaking point, they listened numbly as the Coach went on about ordnance, landing zones and fields of fire, while the trainer and his assistant scurried round plying tape, bandages and the ever-present aerosol cans of Numzit. Kitwany's replacement, a huge amorphous red-faced freshman, sat in the corner, quietly weeping, and Bobby Bibby, who'd fumbled twice more in the second quarter, tore off his uniform, pulled on his street clothes without showering and walked on out the door. As for Ray Arthur Larry-Pete Fontinot, he lay supine on the cold hard tiles of the floor, every twinge, pull, ache and contusion from the previous week's game reactivated, and a host of new ones cropping up to overload his nervous system. Along with Moss and DuBoy, he'd done double duty through the first thirty minutes—playing offense and defense both—and his legs were paralyzed. When the Coach blew his whistle and shouted, "On the attack, men!" Ray Arthur Larry-Pete had to be helped up off the floor.

The third quarter was a delirium of blowing snow, shouts, curses and cries in the wilderness. Shadowy forms clashed and fell to the crunch of helmet and the clatter of shoulder pads. Ray Arthur Larry-Pete staggered around the field as if gutshot, so disoriented he was never quite certain which way his team was driving—or rather, being driven. But mercifully, the weather conditions slowed down the big blue barreling machine of State's offense, and by the time the gun sounded, they'd only been able to score once more.

And so the fourth quarter began, and while the stands emptied and even the most fanatical supporters sank glumly into their parkas, Caledonia limped out onto the field with their heads down and their jaws set in grim determination. They were no longer playing for pride, for the memories, for team spirit or their alma mater or to impress their girlfriends: they were playing for one thing only: to avoid at all cost the humiliation of 56–0. And they held on, grudging State every inch of the field, Ray Arthur Larry-Pete coming to life in sporadic flashes during which he was nearly lucid and more often than not moving in the right direction, Moss, DuBoy and McCornish picking themselves up off the ground at regular intervals and the Coach hollering obscure instructions from the sidelines. With just under a minute left to play, they'd managed (with the help of what would turn out to be the worst blizzard to hit the area in twenty years) to hold State to only one touchdown more, making it 49–0 with the ball in their possession and the clock running down.

The snow blew in their teeth. State dug in. A feeble distant cheer went up from the invisible stands. And then, with Number 95 falling on him like an avalanche, Diderot fumbled, and State recovered. Two plays later, and with eight seconds left on the clock, they took the ball into the end zone to make it 55–0, and only the point-after attempt stood between Caledonia and the unforgivable, unutterable debasement of a second straight 56–0 drubbing. Ray Arthur Larry-Pete Fontinot extricated himself from the snowbank where Number 95 had left him and crept stiff-legged back to the line of scrimmage, where he would now assume the defensive role.

There was one hope, and one hope only, in that blasted naked dead cinder of a world that Ray Arthur Larry-Pete Fontinot and his hapless teammates unwillingly inhabited, and that was for one man among them to reach deep down inside himself and distill all his essence—all his wits, all his heart and the full power of his honed young musculature—into a single last-ditch attempt to block that kick. Ray Arthur Larry-Pete Fontinot looked into the frightened faces of his teammates as they heaved for breath in the defensive huddle and knew he was that man. "I'm going to block the kick," he said, and his voice sounded strange in his own ears. "I'm coming in from the right side and I'm going to block the kick." Moss's eyes were glazed. DuBoy was on the sidelines, vomiting in his helmet. No one said a word.

State lined up. Ray Arthur Larry-Pete took a deep breath. The ball was snapped, the lines crashed with a grunt and moan, and Ray Arthur Larry-Pete Fontinot launched himself at the kicker like the space shuttle coming in for a landing, and suddenly—miracle of miracles!—he felt the hard cold pellet of the ball glancing off the bandaged nubs of his fingers. A shout went up, and as he fell, as he slammed rib-first into the frozen ground, he watched the ball squirt up in the air and fall back into the arms of the kicker as if it were attached to a string, and then, unbelieving, he watched the kicker tuck the ball and sprint unmolested across the goal line for the two-point conversion.

If it weren't for Moss, they might never have found him. Ray Arthur Larry-Pete Fontinot just lay there where he'd fallen, the snow drifting silently round him, and he lay there long after the teams had left the field and the stands stood empty under a canopy of snow. There, in the dirt, the steady drift of snow gleaming against the exposed skin of his calves and slowly obliterating the number on the back of his jersey, he had a vision of the future. He saw himself working at some tedious, spirit-crushing job for which his Phys. Ed. training could never have prepared him, saw himself sunk in fat like his father, a pale plain wife and two grublike children at his side, no eighty-yard runs or blocked points to look back on through a false scrim of nostalgia, no glory and no defeat.

No defeat. It was a concept that seemed all at once to congeal in his tired brain, and as Moss called out his name and the snow beat down, he tried hard, with all his concentration, to hold it there.

(1992)

THE BIG GARAGE

For K.

B. stands at the side of the highway, helpless, hands behind his back, the droopy greatcoat like a relic of ancient wars. There is wind and rain—or is it sleet?—and the deadly somnolent rush of tires along the pavement. His own vehicle rests on the shoulder, stricken somewhere in its slippery metallic heart. He does not know where, exactly, or why—for B. is no mechanic. Far from it. In fact, he's never built or repaired a thing in his life, never felt the restive urge to tinker with machinery, never as a jittery adolescent dismantled watches, telephone receivers, pneumatic crushers. He is woefully unequal to the situation at hand. But wait, hold on now—shouldn't he raise the hood, as a distress signal? Isn't that the way it's done?

Suddenly he's in motion, glad to be doing something, confronting the catastrophe, meeting the challenge. He scuttles round to the front of the car, works his fingers under the lip of the hood and tugs, tugs to no effect, slips in the mud, stumbles, the knees of his trousers soaked through, and then rises to tug again, shades of Buster Keaton. After sixty or seventy seconds of this it occurs to him that the catch may be inside, under the dashboard, as it was in his late wife's Volvo. There are wires—bundles of them—levers, buttons, handles, cranks and knobs in the cavern beneath the steering wheel. He had no idea. He takes a bundle of wire in his hand—each strand a different color—and thinks with a certain satisfaction of the planning and coordination that went into this machine, of the multiple factories, each dominating its own little Bavarian or American or Japanese town, of all the shifts and lunch breaks, the dies cast and what do you call them, lathes—yes, lathes—turned. All this—but more, much more. Iron ore dug from rock, hissing white hot vats of it, molten recipes, chromium, tall rubber trees, vinyl plants, crystals from the earth ground into glass. Staggering.

"Hey pal—"

B. jolted from his reverie by the harsh plosive, spasms of amber light expanding and contracting the interior of the car like the pulse of some predatory beast. Looking up into a lean face, slick hair, stoned eyes. "I was ah trying to ah get the ah latch here—"

"You'll have to ride back in the truck with me."

"Yeah, sure," B. sitting up now, confused, gripping the handle and swinging the door out to a shriek of horns and a rush of air. He cracks something in his elbow heaving it shut.

"Better get out this side."

B. slides across the seat and steps out into the mud. Behind him, the tow truck, huge, its broad bumper lowering over the hood of his neat little German-made car. He mounts the single step up into the cab and watches the impassive face of the towman as he backs round, attaches the grappling hook and hoists the rear of the car, spider and fly. A moment later the man drops into the driver's seat, door slamming with a metallic thud, gears engaging. "That'll be forty-five bucks," he says.

A white fracture of sleet caught up in the headlights, the wipers clapping, light flashing, the night a mist and a darkness beyond the windows. They've turned off the highway, jerking right and left over a succession of secondary roads, strayed so far from B.'s compass that he's long since given up any attempt at locating himself. Perhaps he's dozed even. He turns to study the crease folded into the towman's cheek. "Much farther?" he asks.

The man jerks his chin and B. looks out at a blaze of light on the dark horizon, light dropped like a stone in a pool of oil. As they draw closer he's able to distinguish a neon sign, towering letters stamped in the sky above a complex of offices, outbuildings and hangars that melt off into the shadows. Eleven or twelve sets of gas pumps, each nestled under a black steel parasol, and cars, dark and driverless, stretching across the whitening blacktop like the reverie of a used-car salesman. The sign, in neon grid, traces and retraces its colossal characters until there's no end and no beginning: GARAGE. TEGELER'S. BIG. GARAGE. TEGELER'S BIG GARAGE.

The truck pulls up in front of a deep, brightly lit office. Through the steamed-over windows B. can make out several young women, sitting legs-crossed in orange plastic chairs. From here they look like drum majorettes: white calf boots, opalescent skirts, lace frogs. And—can it be?—Dale Evans hats! What is going on here?

The towman's voice is harsh. "End of the road for you, pal."

"What about my car?"

A cigarette hangs from his lower lip like a growth, smoke squints his eyes.

"Nobody here to poke into it at this hour, what do you think? I'm taking it around to Diagnosis."

"And?"

"Pfft." The man fixes him with the sort of stare you'd give a leper at the Inaugural Ball. "*And* when they get to it, they get to it."

B. steps into the fluorescent blaze of the office, coattails aflap. There are nine girls seated along the wall, left calves swollen over right knees, hands occupied with nail files, hairbrushes, barrettes, magazines. They are dressed as drum majorettes. Nappy Dale Evans hats perch atop their layered cuts, short-and-sassies, blown curls. All nine look up and smile. Then a short redhead rises, and sweet as a mother superior welcoming a novice, asks if she can be of service.

B. is confused. "It . . . it's my car," he says.

"Ohhh," running her tongue round her lips. "You're the Audi."

"Right."

"Just wait a sec and I'll ring Diagnosis," she says, high-stepping across the room to an intercom panel set in the wall. At that moment a buzzer sounds in the office and a car pulls up to the farthest set of gas pumps. The redhead jerks to a halt, peers out the window, curses, shrugs into a fringed suede jacket and hurries out into the storm. B. locks fingers behind his back and waits. He rocks on his feet, whistles sotto voce, casts furtive glances at the knee-down of the eight majorettes. The droopy greatcoat, soaked through, feels like an American black bear *(Ursus americanus)* hanging round his neck.

Then the door heaves back on its hinges and the redhead reappears, stamping round the doormat, shaking out the jacket, knocking the Stetson against her thigh. "Brrrr," she says. In her hand, a clutch of bills. She marches over to the cash register and deposits them, then takes her seat at the far end of the line of majorettes. B. continues to rock on his feet. He clears his throat. Finally he ambles across the room and stops in front of her chair. "Ahh . . ."

She looks up. "Yes? Can I help you?"

"You were gong to call Diagnosis about my car?"

"Oh," grimacing. "No need to bother. Why, at this hour they're long closed up. You'll have to wait till morning."

"But a minute ago—"

"No, no sense at all. The Head Diagnostician leaves at five, and here it's nearly ten. And his staff gets off at five-thirty. The best we could hope for is a shop steward—and what would he know? Ha. If I rang up now I'd be lucky to get hold of a janitor." She settles back in her chair and leafs through a magazine. Then she looks up again. "Listen. If you want some advice, there's a pay phone in the anteroom. Better call somebody to come get you."

The girl has a point there. It's late already and arrangements will have to be made about getting to work in the morning. The dog needs walking, the cat feeding. And all these hassles have sapped him to the point where all he wants from life is sleep and forgetfulness. But there's no one to call, really. Except possibly Dora—Dora Ouzel, the gay divorcée he's been dating since his wife's accident.

One of the majorettes yawns. Another blows a puff of detritus from her nail file. "Ho hum," says the redhead.

B. steps into the anteroom, searches through his pockets for change, and forgets Dora's number. He paws through the phone book, but the names of the towns seem unfamiliar and he can't seem to find Dora's listing. He makes an effort of memory and dials.

"Hello?"

"Hello, Dora?—B. Listen, I hate to disturb you at this hour but—"

"Are you all right?"

"Yes, I'm fine."

"That's nice, I'm fine too. But no matter how you slice it my name ain't Dora."

"You're not Dora?"

"No, but you're B., aren't you?"

"Yes . . . but how did you know?"

"You told me. You said: 'Hello, Dora?—B.' . . . and then you tried to come on with some phony excuse for forgetting our date tonight or is it that you're out hooching it up and you want me—if I was Dora and I bless my stars I'm not—to come out in this hellish weather that isn't fit for a damn dog for christsake and risk my bones and bladder to drive you home because only one person inhabits your solipsistic universe—*You* with a capital Y—and *You* have drunk yourself into a blithering stupor. You know what I got to say to you, buster? Take a flyer. Ha, ha, ha."

There is a click at the other end of the line. In the movies heroes say "Hello, hello, hello," in situations like this, but B., dispirited, the greatcoat beginning to reek a bit in the confines of the antechamber, only reaches out to replace the receiver in its cradle.

Back in the office B. is confronted with eight empty chairs. The redhead occupies the ninth, legs crossed, hat in lap, curls flaring round the cover of her magazine like a solar phenomenon. Where five minutes earlier there were enough majorettes to front a battle of the bands, there is now only one. She glances up as the door slams behind him. "Any luck?"

B. is suddenly overwhelmed with exhaustion. He's just gone fifteen rounds, scaled Everest, staggered out of the Channel at Calais. "No," he whispers.

"Well that really is too bad. All the other girls go home at ten and I'm sure any one of them would have been happy to give you a lift. . . . You know it really is a pity the way some of you men handle your affairs. Why if I had as little common sense as you I wouldn't last ten minutes on this job."

B. heaves himself down on one of the plastic chairs. Somehow, somewhere along the line, his sense of proportion has begun to erode. He blows his nose lugubriously. Then hides behind his hands and massages his eyes.

"Come on now." The girl's voice is soft, conciliatory. She is standing over him, her hand stretched out to his. "I'll fix you up a place to sleep in the back of the shop."

The redhead (her name is Rita—B. thought to ask as a sort of quid pro quo for her offer of a place to sleep) leads him through a narrow passageway which gives on to an immense darkened hangar. B. hunches in the greatcoat, flips up his collar and follows her into the echo-haunted reaches. Their footsteps clap up to the rafters, blind birds beating at the roof, echoing and reechoing in the darkness. There is a chill as of open spaces, a stink of raw metal, oil, sludge. Rita is up ahead, her white boots ghostly in the dark. "Watch your step," she cautions, but B. has already encountered some impenetrable, rock-hard hazard, barked his shin and pitched forward into what seems to be an open grease pit.

"Hurt yourself?"

B. lies there silent—frustrated, childish, perverse.

"B.? Answer me—are you all right?"

He will lie here, dumb as a block, till the Andes are nubs and the moon melts from the sky. But then suddenly the cavern blooms with light (a brown crepuscular light, it's true, but light just the same) and the game's up.

"So there you are!" Arms akimbo, a grin on her face. "Now get yourself up out of there and stop your sulking. I can't play games all night, you know. There's eleven sets of pumps out there I'm responsible for."

B. finds himself sprawled all over an engine block, grease-slicked and massive, that must have come out of a Sherman tank. But it's the hangar, lit like the grainy daguerreotype of a Civil War battlefield, that really interests him. The sheer expanse of the place! And the cars, thousands of them, stretching all the way down to the dark V at the far end of the building. Bugattis, Morrises, La Salles, Daimlers, the back end of a Pierce-Arrow, a Stutz Bearcat. The rounded humps of tops and fenders, tarnished bumpers, hoods thrown open like gaping mouths. Engines swing on cables, blackened grilles and punctured cloth tops gather in the corners, a Duesenberg, its interior gutted, squats over a trench in the concrete.

"Pretty amazing, huh?" Rita says, reaching out a hand to help him up. "This is Geriatrics. Mainly foreign. You should see the Contemp wings."

"But what do you do with all these—?"

"Oh, we fix them. At least the technicians and mechanics do."

There is something wrong here, something amiss. B. can feel it nagging at the edges of his consciousness . . . but then he really is dog-tired. Rita has him by the hand. They amble past a couple hundred cars, dust-embossed, ribs and bones showing, windshields black as ground-out eyes. Now he has it: "But if you fix them, what are they doing here?"

Rita stops dead to look him in the eye, frowning, schoolmarmish. "These things take time, you know." She sighs. "What do you think: they do it overnight?"

The back room is the size of a storage closet. In fact, it *is* a storage closet, fitted out with cots. When Rita flicks the light switch B. is shocked to discover three other people occupying the makeshift dormitory: two men in rumpled suits and a middle-aged woman in a rumpled print dress. One of the men sits up and rubs his eyes. His tie is loose, shirt filthy, a patchy beard maculating his cheeks. He mumbles something—B. catches the words "drive shaft"—and then turns his face back to the cot, already sucking in breath for the first stertorous blast: *hkk-hkk-hkkkkkkgg.*

"What the hell is this?" B. is astonished, scandalized, cranky and tired. Tools and blackened rags lie scattered over the concrete floor, dulled jars of bolts and screws and wing nuts line the shelves. A number of unfolded cots, their fabric stained and grease-spotted, stand in the corner.

"This is where you sleep, silly."

"But—who?"

"It's obvious, isn't it? They're customers, like yourself, waiting for their cars. The man in brown is the Gremlin, the one with the beard is the Cougar—no, I'm sorry, the woman is the Cougar—he's the Citroën."

B. is appalled. "And I'm the Audi, is that it?"

Suddenly Rita is in his arms, the smooth satiny feel of her uniform, the sticky warmth of her breath. "You're more to me than a machine, B. Do you know that I like you? A lot." And then he finds himself nuzzling her ear, the downy ridge of her jawbone. She presses against him, he fumbles under the cheerleader's tutu for the slippery underthings. One of the sleepers groans, but B. is lost, oblivious, tugging and massaging like a horny teenager. Rita reaches behind to unzip her uniform, the long smooth arch of her back, shoulders and arms shedding the opalescent rayon like a holiday on ice when suddenly a buzzer sounds—loud and brash—end of the round, change classes, dive for shelter.

Rita freezes, then bursts into motion. "A customer!" she pants, and then she's gone. B. watches her callipygian form recede into the gloom of the Geriatrics Section, the sharp projection in his trousers receding with her, until she touches the light switch and vanishes in darkness. B. trundles back into the closet, selects a cot, and falls into an exploratory darkness of his own.

■ ■ ■

B.'s. breath is a puff of cotton as he wakes to the chill gloom of the storage closet and the sound of tools grating, whining and ratcheting somewhere off in the distance. At first he can't locate himself—What the? Where?—but the odors of gas and kerosene and motor oil bring him back. He is stranded at Tegeler's Big Garage, it is a workday, he has been sleeping with strangers, his car is nonfunctional. B. lurches up from the cot with a gasp—only to find that he's being watched. It is the man with the patchy beard and rancid shirt. He is sitting on the edge of a cot, stirring coffee in a cardboard container, his eyes fixed on B. My checkbook, my wallet, my wristwatch, thinks B.

"Mornin'," the man says. "My name's Rusty," holding out his hand. The others—the man in brown (or was it gray?) and the Cougar woman—are gone.

B. shakes the man's hand. "Name's B.," he says, somewhere between wary and paranoid. "How do I get out of here?"

"Your first day, huh?"

"What do you mean?" B. detects an edge of hysteria slicing through his voice, as if it belonged to someone else in some other situation. A pistol-whipped actress in a TV melodrama, for instance.

"No need to get excited," Rusty says. "I know how disquieting that first day can be. Why Cougar here—that woman in the print dress slept with us last night?—she sniveled and whimpered the whole time her first night here. Shit. It was like being in a bomb shelter or some frigging thing. Sure, I know how it is. You got a routine—job, wife at home, kids maybe, dog, cat, goldfish—and naturally you're anxious to get back to it. Well let me give you some advice. I been here six days already and I still haven't even got an appointment lined up with the Appointments Secretary so's I can get in to see the Assistant to the Head Diagnostician, Imports Division, and find out what's wrong with my car. So look: don't work up no ulcer over the thing. Just make your application and sit tight."

The man is an escapee, that's it, an escapee from an institution for the terminally, unconditionally and abysmally insane. B. hangs tough. "You expect me to believe that cock-and-bull story? If you're so desperate why don't you call a cab?"

"Taxis don't run this far out."

"Bus?"

"No buses in this district."

"Surely you've got friends to call—"

"Tried it, couldn't get through. Busy signals, recordings, wrong numbers. Finally got through to Theotis Stover two nights ago. Said he'd come out but his car's broke down."

"You could hitchhike."

"Spent six hours out there my first day. Twelve degrees F. Nobody even slowed down. Besides, even if I could get home, what then? Can't get to work, can't buy food. No sir. I'm staying right here till I get that car back."

B. cannot accept it. The whole thing is absurd. He's on him like F. Lee Bailey grilling a shaky witness. "What about the girls in the main office? They'll take you—one of them told me so."

"They take you?"

"No, but—"

"Look: they say that to be accommodating, don't you see? I mean, we *are* customers, after all. But they can't give you a lift—it's their job if they do."

"You mean—?"

"That's right. And wait'll you see the bill when you finally do get out of here. Word is that cot you're sitting on goes for twelve bucks a night."

The bastards. It could be weeks here. He'll lose his job, the animals'll tear up the rugs, piss in the bed and finally, starved, the dog will turn on the cat. . . . B. looks up, a new worry on his lips: "But what do you eat here?"

Rusty rises. "C'mon, I'll show you the ropes." B. follows him out into the half-lit and silent hangar, past the ranks of ruined automobiles, the mounds of tires and tools. "Breakfast is out of the machines. They got coffee, hot chocolate, candy bars, cross-ants and cigarettes. Lunch and late-afternoon snack you get down at the Mechanics' Cafeteria." Rusty's voice booms and echoes through the wide open spaces till B. begins to feel surrounded. Overhead, the morning cowers against the grimed skylights. "And eat your fill," Rusty adds, "—it all goes on the tab."

The office is bright as a cathedral with a miracle in progress. B. squints into the sunlight and recognizes the swaying ankles of a squad of majorettes. He asks for Rita, finds she's off till six at night. Outside, the sound of scraping, the putt-putt of snowplow jeeps. B. glances up. Oh, shit. There must be a foot and a half of snow on the ground.

The girls are chewing gum and sipping coffee from personalized mugs: Mary-Alice, Valerie, Beatrice, Lulu. B. hunches in the greatcoat, confused, until Rusty bums a dollar and hands him a cup of coffee. Slurping and blowing, B. stands at the window and watches an old man stoop over an aluminum snow shovel. Jets of fog stream from the old man's nostrils, ice cakes his mustache.

"Criminal, ain't it?" says Rusty.

"What?"

"The old man out there. That's Tegeler's father, seventy-some-odd years old. Tegeler makes him earn his keep, sweeping up, clearing snow, polishing the pumps."

"No!" B. is stupefied.

"Yeah, he's some hardnose, Tegeler. And I'll tell you something else too—he's set up better than Onassis and Rockefeller put together. See that lot across the street?"

B. looks. TEGELER'S BIG LOT. How'd he miss that?

"They sell new Tegelers there."

"Tegelers?"

"Yeah—he's got his own company: the Tegeler Motor Works. Real lemons from what I hear . . . But will you look what time it is!" Rusty slaps his forehead. "We got to get down to Appointments or we'll both grow old in this place."

The Appointments Office, like the reward chamber in a rat maze, is located at the far end of a complicated network of passageways, crossways and counterways. It is a large carpeted room with desks, potted plants and tellers' windows, not at all unlike a branch bank. The Cougar woman and the man in the brown suit are there, waiting along with a number of others, all of them looking bedraggled and harassed. Rusty enters deferentially and takes a seat beside Brown Suit, but B. strides across the room to where a hopelessly walleyed woman sits at a desk, riffling through a bundle of papers. "Excuse me," he says.

The woman looks up, her left iris drowning in white.

"I'm here—" B. breaks off, confused as to which eye to address: alternately one and then the other seems to be scrutinizing him. Finally he zeroes in on her nose and continues: "—about my car. I—"

"Do you have an appointment?"

"No, I don't. But you see I'm a busy man, and I depend entirely on the car for transportation and—"

"Don't we all?"

"—and I've already missed a day of work." B. gives her a doleful look, a look charged with chagrin for so thwarting the work ethic and weakening the national fiber. "I've got to have it seen to as soon as possible. If not sooner." Ending with a broad grin, the bon mot just the thing to break the ice.

"Yes," she says, heaving a great wet sigh. "I understand your anxiety and I sympathize with you, I really do. But," the left pupil working round to glare at him now, "I can't say I think much of the way you conduct yourself—barging in here and exalting your own selfish concerns above those of the others here. Do you think that there's no one else in the world but you? No other ailing auto but yours? Does Tegeler's Big Garage operate for fifty-nine years, employing hundreds of people, constantly expanding, improving, streamlining its operations, only to prepare itself for the eventuality of your breakdown? Tsssss! I'm afraid, my friend, that your arrogant egotism knows no bounds."

B. hangs his head, shuffles his feet, the greatcoat impossibly warm.

"Now. You'll have to fill out the application for an appointment and wait your turn with the others. Though you really haven't shown anything to deserve it, I think you may have a bit of luck today after all. The Secretary left word that he'd be in at three this afternoon."

B. takes a seat beside the Cougar woman and stares down at the form in his hand as if it were a loaded .44. He is dazed, still tingling from the vehemence of the secretary's attack. The form is seven pages long. There are questions about employment, annual income, collateral, next of kin. Page 4 is devoted to physical inquiries: Ever had measles? leprosy? irregularity? The next delves deeper: Do you feel that people are out to get you? Why do you hate your father? The form ends up with two pages of IQ stuff: if a farmer has 200 acres and devotes 1/16 of his land to soybeans, 5/8 to corn and 1/3 to sugar beets, how much does he have left for a drive-in movie? B. glances over at the Cougar woman. Her lower lip is thrust forward, a blackened stub of pencil twists in her fingers, an appointment form, scrawled over in pencil with circled red corrections, lies in her lap. Suddenly B. is on his feet and stalking out the door, fragments of paper sifting down in his wake like confetti. Behind him, the sound of collective gasping.

Out in the corridor B. collars a man in spattered blue coveralls and asks him where the Imports Division is. The man, squat, swarthy, mustachioed, looks at him blank as a cow. "No entiendo," he says.

"The. Imports. Division."

"No hablo inglés—y no me gustan las preguntas de cabrones tontos." The man shrugs his shoulder out from under B.'s palm and struts off down the hall like a ruffled rooster. But B. is encouraged: Imports must be close at hand. He hurried off in the direction from which the man came (was he Italian or only a Puerto Rican?), following the corridor around to the left, past connecting hallways clogged with mechanics and white-smocked technicians, following it right on up to a steel fire door with the words NO ADMITTANCE stamped across it in admonitory red. There is a moment of hesitation . . . then he twists the knob and steps in.

"Was ist das?" A workman looks up at him, screwdriver in hand, expression modulating from surprise to menace. B. finds himself in another hangar, gloomy and expansive as the first, electric tools screeching like an army of mechanical crickets. But what's this?: he's surrounded by late-model cars—German cars— Beetles, Foxes, Rabbits, sleek Mercedes sedans! Not only has he stumbled across the Imports Division, but luck or instinct or good looks has guided him right to German Specialties. Well, ha-cha! He's squinting down the rows of cars, hoping to catch sight of his own, when he feels a pressure on his arm. It is the workman with the screwdriver. "Vot you vant?" he demands.

"Uh—have you got an Audi in here? Powder blue with a black vinyl top?"

The workman is in his early twenties. He is tall and obscenely corpulent. Skin pale as the moon, jowls reddening as if with a rash, white hair cropped across his ears and pinched beneath a preposterously undersized engineer's cap. He tightens his grip on B.'s arm and calls out into the gloom—"Holger! Friedrich!"—

his voice reverberating through the vault like the battle cry of some Mesozoic monster.

Two men, flaxen-haired, in work clothes and caps, step from the shadows. Each grips a crescent wrench big as the jawbone of an ass. "Was gibt es, Klaus?"

"Mein Herr vants to know haff we got und Aw-dee."

"How do you say it?" The two newcomers are standing over him now, the one in the wire-rimmed spectacles leering into his eyes.

"Audi," B. says. "A German-made car?"

"Aw-dee? No, never heard of such a car," the man says. "A cowboy maybe—family name of Murphy?"

Klaus laughs, "Har-har-har," booming at the ceiling. The other fellow, short, scar on his cheek, joins in with a psychopathic snicker. Wire-rims grins.

Uh-oh.

"Listen," B. says, a whining edge to his voice, "I know I'm not supposed to be in here but I saw no other way of—"

"Cutting trew der bullshit," says Wire-rims.

"Yes, and finding out what's wrong—"

"On a grassroot level," interjects the snickerer.

"—right, at the grassroot level, by coming directly to you. I'm getting desperate. Really. That car is my life's breath itself. And I don't mean to get dramatic or anything, but I just can't survive without it."

"Ja," says Wire-rims, "you haff come to der right men. We haff your car, wery serious. Ja. Der bratwurst assembly broke down and we haff sent out immediately for a brötchen und mustard." This time all three break into laughter, Klaus booming, the snickerer snickering, Wire-rims pinching his lips and emitting a high-pitched hoo-hoo-hoo.

"No, *seriously*," says B.

"You vant to get serious? Okay, we get serious. On your car we do a compression check, we put new solenoids in der U joints und we push der push rods," says Wire-rims.

"Ja. Und we see you need a new vertical stabilizer, head gasket and PCV valve," rasps the snickerer.

"Your sump leaks."

                              "Bearings knock."

                                        "Plugs misfire."

B. has had enough. "Wiseguys!" he shouts. "I'll report you to your superiors!" But far from daunting them, his outburst has the opposite effect. Viz., Klaus grabs him by the collar and breathes beer and sauerbraten in his face. "We are Chermans," he hisses, "—we haff no superiors."

"Und dammit punktum!" bellows the snickerer. "Enough of dis twaddle. We haff no car of yours und furdermore we suspect you of telling to us fibs in order maybe to misappropriate the vehicle of some otter person."

"For shame," says Wire-rims.

"Vat shall we do mit him?" the snickerer hisses.

"I'm tinking he maybe needs a little lubrication," says Wirerims. "No sense of humor, wery dry." He produces a grease gun from behind his back.

And then, for the first time in his life, B. is decorated—down his collar, up his sleeve, crosshatched over his lapels—in ropy, cake-frosting strings of grease, while Klaus howls like a terminally tickled child and the snickerer's eyes flash. A moment later he finds himself lofted into the air, strange hands at his armpits and thighs, swinging to and fro before the gaping black mouth of a laundry chute—"Zum ersten! zum andern! zum dritten!"—and then he's airborne, and things get very dark indeed.

B. is lying facedown in an avalanche of cloth: grimy rags, stiffened chamois, socks and undershorts yellowed with age and sweat and worse, handkerchiefs congealed with sputum, coveralls wet with oil. He is stung with humiliation and outrage. He's been cozened, humbugged, duped, gulled, spurned, insulted, ignored and now finally assaulted. There'll be lawsuits, damn them, letters to Congressmen—but for now, if he's to salvage a scrap of self-respect, he's got to get out of here. He sits up, peels a sock from his face, and discovers the interior of a tiny room, a room no bigger than a laundry closet. It is warm, hot even.

Two doors open onto the closet. The one to the left is wreathed in steam, pale shoots and tendrils of it curling through the keyhole, under the jamb. B. throws back the door and is enveloped in fog. He is confused. The Minotaur's labyrinth? Ship at sea? House afire? He can see nothing, the sound of machinery straining at his ears, moisture beading along eyebrows, nostril hairs, cowlick. Then it occurs to him: the carwash! Of course. And the carwash must give onto the parking lot, which in turn gives onto the highway. He'll simply duck through it and then hitchhike—or, if worse comes to worst, walk—until he either makes it home or perishes in the attempt.

B. steps through the door and is instantly flattened by a mammoth, water-spewing pom-pom. He tries to get to his feet, but the sleeve of his coat seems to be caught in some sort of runner or track—and now the whole apparatus is jerking forward, gears whirring and clicking somewhere off in the mist. B., struggling to free the coat, finds himself jerking along with it. The mechanism heaves forward, dragging B. through an extended puddle of mud, suds and road salt. A jet of water flushes the right side of his face, a second pom-pom lumbers out of the haze and pins his chest to the floor, something tears the shoe from his right foot. Soap in his ears, down his neck, sudsing and sudsing: and now a giant cylinder, a mill wheel covered with sponges, descends and rakes the length of his body. B. shouts for help, but the machinery grinds on, squeaking and ratcheting, war of the worlds. Look out!: cold rinse. He holds his breath, glacial runoff coursing over his body, a bitter pill. Then there's a liberal blasting with hot wax, the clouds part, and the machine turns him loose with a jolt in the rear that tumbles him out the bay door and onto the slick permafrost of the parking lot.

He staggers to his feet. There's a savage pain in his lower back and his right shoulder has got to be dislocated. No matter: he forges on. Round the outbuildings, past the front office and on out to the highway.

It has begun to get dark. B., hair frozen to his scalp, shoeless, the greatcoat stiff as a dried fish, limps along the highway no more than a mile from the garage. All around him, as far as he can see, is wasteland: crop-stubble swallowed in drifts, the stripped branches of the deciduous trees, rusty barbed wire. Not even a farmhouse on the horizon. Nothing. He'd feel like Peary running for the Pole but for the twin beacons of Garage and Lot at his back.

Suddenly a fitful light wavers out over the road—a car coming toward him! (He's been out here for hours, holding out his thumb, hobbling along. The first ride took him south of Tegeler's about two miles—a farmer, turning off into nowhere. The second—he didn't care which direction he went in, just wanted to get out of the cold—took him back north about three miles.)

B. crosses the road and holds out his thumb. He is dancing with cold, clonic, shoulder, arm, wrist and extended thumb jerking like the checkered flag at the finish of the Grand Prix. Stop, he whispers, teeth clicking like dice, stop, please God stop. Light floods his face for an instant, and then it's gone. But wait—they're stopping! Snot crusted to his lip, shoe in hand, B. double-times up to the waiting car, throws back the door and leaps in.

"B.! What's happened?"

It is Rita. Thank God.

"R-r-r-r-ita?" he stammers, body racked with tremors, the seatsprings chattering under him. "The ma-ma-machine."

"Machine? What are you talking about?"

"I-I need a r-r-r-ride. Wh-where you going?" B. manages, falling into a sneezing jag.

Rita puts the car in gear, the tires grab hold of the pavement. "Why—to work, of course."

The others smack their lips, sigh, snore, toss on their cots. Rusty, Brown Suit, the Cougar woman. B. lies there listening to them, staring into the darkness. His own breathing comes hard (TB, pleurisy, pneumonia—bronchitis at the very least). Rita—good old Rita—has filled him full of hot coffee and schnapps, given him a brace of cold pills and put him to bed. He is thoroughly miserable of course—the car riding his mind like a bogey, health shot, job lost, pets starved—but the snugness of the blanket and dry mechanic's uniform Rita has found for him, combined with the country-sunset glow of the schnapps, is seducing him off to sleep. It is very still. The smell of turpentine hangs in the air. He pulls the blanket up to his nose.

Suddenly the light flicks on. It is Rita, all thighs and calves in her majorette's outfit. But what's this? There's a man with her, a stranger. "Is this it?" the man says.

"Well, of course it is, silly."

"But who are these chibonies?"

"It's obvious, isn't it? They're customers, like yourself, waiting for their cars. The man in brown is the Gremlin, the one with the beard is the Citroën, the woman is the Cougar and the old guy on the end is the Audi."

"And I'm the Jaguar, is that it?"

"You're more to me than a machine, Jeff. Do you know that I like you? A lot."

B. is mortally wounded. Enemy flak, they've hit him in the guts. He squeezes his eyes shut, stops his ears, but he can hear them just the same: heavy breathing, a moan soft as fur, the rush of zippers. But then the buzzer sounds and Rita gasps. "A customer!" she squeals, struggling back into her clothes and then hurrying off through the Geriatrics hangar, her footsteps like pinpricks along the spine. "Hey!" the new guy bellows. But she's gone.

The new guy sighs, then selects a cot and beds down beside B. B. can hear him removing his things, gargling from a bottle, whispering prayers to himself— "Bless Mama, Uncle Ernie, Bear Bryant . . ."—then the room dashes into darkness and B. can open his eyes.

He fights back a cough. His heart is hammering. He thinks how pleasant it would be to die . . . but then thinks how pleasant it would be to step through the door of his apartment again, take a hot shower and crawl into bed. It is then that the vision comes to him—a waking dream—shot through with color and movement and depth. He sees Tegeler's Big Lot, the ranks of cars, new Tegelers, lines of variegated color like beads on a string, windshields glinting in the sun, antennae jabbing at the sky, stiff and erect, like the swords of a conquering army. . . .

In the dark, beneath the blanket, he reaches for his checkbook.

(1977)

ZAPATOS

There is, essentially, one city in our country. It is a city in which everyone wears a hat, works in an office, jogs, and eats simply but elegantly, a city above all, in which everyone covets shoes. Italian shoes, in particular. Oh, you can get by with a pair of domestically made pumps or cordovans of the supplest sheepskin, or even, in the languid days of summer, with huaraches or Chinese slippers made of silk or even nylon. There are those who claim to prefer running shoes—Puma, Nike, Saucony—winter and summer. But the truth is, what everyone wants—for the status, the cachet, the charm and refinement—are the Italian loafers and ankle boots, hand-stitched and with a grain as soft and rich as, well—is this the place to talk of the private parts of girls still in school?

My uncle—call him Dagoberto—imports shoes. From Italy. And yet, until recently, he himself could barely afford a pair. It's the government, of course. Our country—the longest and leanest in the world—is hemmed in by the ocean on one side, the desert and mountains on the other, and the government has leached and pounded it dry till sometimes I think we live atop a stupendous, three-thousand-mile-long strip of jerky. There are duties—prohibitive duties—on everything. Or, rather, on everything we want. Cocktail napkins, Band-Aids, Tupperware, crescent wrenches, and kimchi come in practically for nothing. But the things we really crave—microwaves, Lean Cuisine, CDs, leisure suits, and above all, Italian shoes—carry a duty of two and sometimes three hundred percent. The government is unfriendly. We are born, we die, it rains, it clears, the government is unfriendly. Facts of life.

Uncle Dagoberto is no revolutionary—none of us are; let's face it, we manage—but the shoe situation was killing him. He'd bring his shoes in, arrange them seductively in the windows of his three downtown shops, and there they'd languish, despite a markup so small he'd have to sell a hundred pairs just to take his shopgirls out to lunch. It was intolerable. And what made it worse was that the good citizens of our city, vain and covetous as they are, paraded up and down in front of his very windows in shoes identical to those he was selling—shoes for which they'd paid half price or less. And how were these shoes getting through customs and finding their way to the dark little no-name shops in the ill-lit vacancies of waterfront warehouses? Ask the Black Hand, Los Dedos Muertos, the fat and corrupt Minister of Commerce.

For months, poor Uncle Dagoberto brooded over the situation, while his wife (my mother's sister, Carmen, a merciless woman) and his six daughters screamed for the laser facials, cellular phones, and Fila sweats he could no longer provide for them. He is a heavyset man, my uncle, and balding, and he seemed to grow heavier and balder during those months of commercial despair. But one morning, as he came down to breakfast in the gleaming, tiled expanse of the kitchen our families share in the big venerable old mansion on La Calle Verdad, there was a spring in his step and look on his face that, well—there is a little shark in the waters here, capable of smelling out one part of blood in a million parts of water, and when he does smell out that impossible single molecule of blood, I imagine he must have a look like that of Uncle Dagoberto on that sunstruck morning on La Calle Verdad.

"Tomás," he said to me, rubbing his hands over his Bran Chex, Metamusil, and decaffeinated coffee, "we're in business."

The kitchen was deserted at that hour. My aunts and sisters were off jogging, Dagoberto's daughters at the beach, my mother busy with aerobics, and my father—my late, lamented father—lying quiet in his grave. I didn't understand. I looked up at him blankly from my plate of microwave waffles.

His eyes darted round the room. There was a sheen of sweat on his massive, close-shaven jowls. He began to whistle—a tune my mother used to sing me, by Grandmaster Flash—and then he broke off and gave me a gold-capped smile. "The shoe business," he said. "There's fifteen hundred in it for you."

I was at the university at the time, studying semantics, hermeneutics, and the deconstruction of deconstruction. I myself owned two sleek pairs of Italian loafers, in ecru and rust. Still, I wasn't working, and I could have used the money. "I'm listening," I said.

What he wanted me to do was simple—simple, but potentially dangerous. He wanted me to spend two days in the north, in El Puerto Libre—Freeport. There are two free ports in our country, separated by nearly twenty-five hundred miles of terrain that looks from the air like the spine of some antediluvian monster. The southern port is called Calidad, or Quality. Both are what I imagine the great bazaars of Northern Africa and the Middle East to have been in the time of Marco Polo or Rommel, percolating cauldrons of sin and plenty, where anything known to man could be had for the price of a haggle. But there was a catch, of

course. While you could purchase anything you liked in El Puerto Libre or Calidad, to bring it back to the city you had to pay duty—the same stultifying duty
merchants like Uncle Dagoberto were obliged to pay. And why then had the government set up the free ports in the first place? In order to make digital audio
tape and microwaves available to themselves, of course, and to set up discreet
banking enterprises for foreigners, by way of generating cash flow—and ultimately, I think, to frustrate the citizenry. To keep us in our place. To remind us
that government is unfriendly.

At any rate, I was to go north on the afternoon plane, take a room under the
name "Chilly Buttons," and await Uncle Dagoberto's instructions. Fine. For me,
the trip was nothing. I relaxed with a Glenlivet and Derrida, the film was *Death
Wish VII*, and the flight attendants small in front and, well, substantial behind,
just the way I like them. On arriving, I checked into the hotel he'd arranged for
me—the girl behind the desk had eyes and shoulders like one of the amazons of
the North American cinema, but she tittered and showed off her orthodontia
when I signed "Chilly Buttons" in the register—and I went straight up to my
room to await Uncle Dagoberto's call. Oh, yes, I nearly forgot: he'd given me an
attaché case in which there were five hundred huevos—our national currency—
and a thousand black-market dollars. "I don't anticipate any problems," he'd
told me as he handed me onto the plane, "but you never know, eh?"

I ate veal medallions and a dry spinach salad at a brasserie frequented by
British rock stars and North American drug agents, and then sat up late in my
room, watching a rerun of the world cockfighting championships. I was just dozing off when the phone rang. "Bueno," I said, snatching up the receiver.

"Tomás?" It was Uncle Dagoberto.

"Yes," I said.

His voice was pinched with secrecy, a whisper, a rasp. "I want you to go to
the customs warehouse on La Avenida Democracia at ten A.M. sharp." He was
breathing heavily. I could barely hear him. "There are shoes there," he said "Italian shoes. Thirty thousand shoes, wrapped in tissue paper. No one has claimed
them and they're to be auctioned first thing in the morning." He paused and I listened to the empty hiss of the land breathing through the wires that separated
us. "I want you to bid nothing for them. A hundred huevos. Two. But I want you
to buy them. Buy them or die." And he hung up.

At quarter of ten the next morning, I stood outside the warehouse, the attaché case clutched in my hand. Somewhere a cock crowed. It was cold, but the
sun warmed the back of my neck. Half a dozen hastily shaven men in sagging
suits and battered domestically made oxfords gathered beside me.

I was puzzled. How did Uncle Dagoberto expect me to buy thirty thousand
Italian shoes for two hundred huevos, when a single pair sold for twice that? I
understood that the black-market dollars were to be offered as needed, but even
so, how could I buy more than a few dozen pairs? I shrugged it off and buried
my nose in Derrida.

It was past twelve when an old man in the uniform of the customs police
hobbled up the street as if his legs were made of stone, produced a set of keys,
and threw open the huge hammered-steel doors of the warehouse. We shuffled
in, blinking against the darkness. When my eyes became accustomed to the light,
the mounds of unclaimed goods piled up on pallets around me began to take on
form. There were crates of crescent wrenches, boxes of Tupperware, a bin of
door stoppers. I saw bicycle horns—thousands of them, black and bulbous as
the noses of monkeys—and jars of kimchi stacked up to the steel crossbeams of
the ceiling. And then I saw the shoes. They were heaped up in a small mountain,
individually wrapped in tissue paper. Just as Uncle Dagoberto had said. The others ignored them. They read the description the customs man provided, unwrapped the odd shoe, and went on to the bins of churchkey openers and
chutney. I was dazed. It was like stumbling across the treasure of the Incas, the
Golden City itself, and yet having no one recognize it.

With trembling fingers, I unwrapped first one shoe, then another. I saw
patent leather, suede, the sensuous ripple of alligator; my nostrils filled with the
rich and unmistakable bouquet of newly tanned leather. The shoes were perfect,
insuperable, the very latest styles, au courant, à la mode, and exciting. Why had
the others turned away? It was then that I read the customs declaration: *Thirty
thousand leather shoes*, it read, *imported from the Republic of Italy, port of
Livorno. Unclaimed after thirty days. To be sold at auction to the highest bidder.*
Beside the declaration, in a handscrawl that betrayed bureaucratic impatience—
disgust, even—of the highest order, was this further notation: *Left feet only.*

It took me a moment. I bent to the mountain of shoes and began tearing at
the tissue paper. I tore through women's pumps, stiletto heels, tooled boots,
wing tips, deck shoes, and patent-leather loafers—and every single one, every
one of those thirty thousand shoes, was half a pair. Uncle Dagoberto, I thought,
you are a genius.

The auction was nothing. I waited through a dozen lots of number-two pen-
cils, Cabbage Patch Dolls, and soft-white lightbulbs, and then I placed the sole
bid on the thirty thousand left-footed shoes. One hundred huevos and they were
mine. Later, I took the young amazon up to my room and showed her what a
man with a name like Chilly Buttons can do in a sphere that, well—is this the
place to gloat? We were sharing a cigarette when Uncle Dagoberto called. "Did
you get them?" he shouted over the line.

"One hundred huevos," I said.

"Good boy," he crooned, "good boy." He paused a moment to catch his
breath. "And do you know where I'm calling from?" he asked, struggling to keep
down the effervescence in his voice.

I reached out to stroke the amazon's breasts—her name was Linda, by
the way, and she was a student of cosmetology. "I think I can guess," I said.
"Calidad?"

"Funny thing," Uncle Dagoberto said, "there are some shoes here, in the cus-

toms warehouse—fine Italian shoes, the finest, thirty thousand in a single lot—
and no one has claimed them. Can you imagine that?"

There was such joy in his tone that I couldn't resist playing out the game with
him. "There must be something wrong with them," I said.

I could picture his grin. "Nothing, nothing at all. If you're one-legged."

That was two years ago.

Today, Uncle Dagoberto is the undisputed shoe king of our city. He made
such a killing on that one deal that he was able to buy his way into the cartel that
"advises" the government. He has a title now—Undersecretary for International
Trade—and a vast, brightly lit office in the President's palace.

I've changed too, though I still live with my mother on La Calle Verdad and I
still attend the university. My shoes—I have some thirty pairs now, in every style
and color those clever Italians have been able to devise—are the envy of all, and
no small attraction to the nubile and status-hungry young women of the city. I no
longer study semantics, hermeneutics, and the deconstruction of deconstruction,
but have instead been pursuing a degree in business. It only makes sense. After
all, the government doesn't seem half so unfriendly these days.

(1988)

RESPECT

When Santo R. stepped into my little office in Partinico last fall, I barely recognized him. He'd been a corpulent boy, one of the few in this dry-as-bones country, and a very heavyset young man. I remembered his parents—peasants, and poor as church mice—and how I'd treated him for the usual childhood ailments—rubella, chicken pox, mumps—and how even then the gentlest pressure of my fingers would leave marks on the distended flesh of his upper arms and legs. But if he'd been heavy then, now, at the age of twenty-nine, he was like a pregnant mule, so big around the middle he hardly fit through the door. He was breathing hard, half-choked on the dust of the streets, and he was wet through to the skin with sweat. "Doctor," he wheezed, sinking a thumb into the morass of his left pectoral, just above the heart, "it hurts here." An insuck of breath, a dab at the brow, a wince. I watched his bloated pale hand sink to cradle the great tub of his abdomen. "And here," he whispered.

Behind him, through the open door, the waiting room full of shopkeepers, widows and hypochondriacs looked on in awe as I motioned Crocifissa, my nurse, to pull the door closed and leave us. My patients might have been impressed—here was a man of respect, who in the company of his two endomorphic bodyguards had waddled up the stairs and through the waiting room without waiting for anyone or anything—but for my part, I was only alarmed at the state he was in. The physician and his patient, after all, have a bond that goes far deeper than the world of getting and keeping, of violence and honor and all the mess that goes with them—and from the patient's point of view, self-importance can take you only so far when you come face to face with the man who inserts the rectal thermometer.

"Don R.," I said, getting up from the desk and simultaneously fitting the stethoscope to my ears, "I can see that you're suffering—but have no fear, you've come to the right man. Now, let's have a look. . . ."

Well, I examined him, and he was as complete and utter a physical wreck as any man under seventy who has ever set foot in my office. The chest pain, extending below the breastbone and down the left arm to the wrist and little finger, was symptomatic of angina, a sign of premature atherosclerosis; his liver and spleen were enlarged; he suffered from hypertension and ulcers; and if he didn't yet have a full-blown case of emphysema, he was well on his way to developing it. At least, this was my preliminary diagnosis—we would know more when the test results came back from the lab.

Crocifissa returned to inform me that Signora Malatesta seemed to be having some sort of attack in the waiting room, and as the door swung shut behind her, I could see one of Santo's bodyguards bent over the old woman, gently patting her on the back. *"Momento,"* I called out, and turned to Santo with my gravest expression. "You are a very unwell man, Don R.," I told him, "and I can't help but suspect that your style of living has been a contributing factor. You do smoke, do you not?"

A grunt. The blocky fingers patted down the breast pocket of his jacket and he produced an engraved cigarette case. He offered me a Lucky Strike with a gallant sweep of his arm and, when I refused, lit one up for himself. For a long moment he sat meditating over my question with a lungful of tobacco smoke. Finally, he shrugged his shoulders. "Two or three packs a day," he rasped, and appended a little cough.

"And alcohol?"

"What is this, Doctor, the confessional?" he growled, fixing me with a pair of dangerous black eyes. But then he subsided, shrugging again. "A liter of Chianti or Valpolicella with my meals—at breakfast, lunch, evening snack and dinner— and maybe two or three *fiaschi* of brandy a day to keep my throat open."

"Coffee?"

"A pot or two in the morning. And in the evening, when I can't sleep. And that's another problem, Doctor—these pills that Bernardi gave me for sleeping? Well, they have no effect on me, nothing, I might as well be swallowing little blue capsules of cat piss. I toss, I turn. My stomach is on fire. And this at four and five in the morning."

"I see, yes," I said, and I pulled at the little Vandyke I've worn for nearly forty years now to inspire confidence in my patients. "And do you—how shall I put it? Do you exercise regularly?"

Santo looked away. His swollen features seemed to close in on themselves and in that moment he was the pudgy boy again, ready to burst into tears at some real or imagined slight. When he spoke, his voice had sunk to a whisper. "You mean with the women then, eh?" And before I could answer he went on, his voice so reduced I could barely hear him: "I—I just don't seem to feel the urge anymore. And not only when it comes to my wife, as you might expect after ten years of marriage, but with the young girls too."

Somehow, we had steered ourselves into dangerous conversational waters, and I saw that these waters foamed with naked shoals and rocky reefs. "No, no," I said, and I almost gasped out the words, "I meant physical exercise, jogging, bicycling, a regular twenty-minute walk, perhaps?"

"Ha!" he spat. "Exercise!" And he rose ponderously from the chair, his face as engorged and lopsided as a tomato left out to rot in the sun. "That's all I do is exercise. My whole frigging life is exercise, morning to night and back to morning again. I can't sleep, I can't eat, I can't ball the girls in the brothel and my cigarettes taste like shit. And do you know why? Do you?"

Suddenly his voice had risen to a roar and the door popped open so that I could see the burnished faces of the two bodyguards as they clutched at their waistbands for the heavy pistols they wore there. "Bastiano!" he bellowed. "Bastiano Frigging C., that's why. That's my problem. Not the cigarettes, not the booze, not the heart or the liver or the guts, but that bony pussy-licking son of a bitch Bastiano!"

A week later, in the middle of a consultation with Signora Trombetta over her hot flashes and crying spells, the door to my office burst open and there, looking like death in a dishpan, stood Bastiano C. I hadn't seen him in over a year, since I'd last treated him for intestinal worms, and, as with Santo R., I was stunned by his visible deterioration. Even as a boy he'd been thin, the sullen elder child of the village schoolmaster, all legs and arms, like a spider, but now it was as if the flesh had been painted on his bones. At five feet, nine inches tall, he must have weighed less than a hundred pounds. His two bodyguards, expressionless men nearly as emaciated as he, flanked him like slats in a fence. He gave a slight jerk of his neck, barely perceptible, and the widow Trombetta, though she was in her sixties and suffering from arthritis in every joint, scurried out the door as if she'd been set afire.

"Don C.," I said, peering at him through the upper portion of my bifocals, "how good to see you. And how may I help you?"

He said nothing, merely stood there in the doorway looking as if a breeze would blow him away if it weren't for the pistols, shivs and cartridges that anchored him to the floor. Another minute gesture, so conservative of energy, the merest flick of the neck, and the two henchmen melted away into the waiting room, the door closing softly behind them.

I cleared my throat. "And what seems to be the matter?" I asked in my most mellifluous, comforting tones, the tones I used on the recalcitrant child, the boy who doesn't like the look of the needle or the girl who won't stick out her tongue for the depressor.

Nothing.

The silence was unlike him. I'd always known him as a choleric personality, quick to speak his mind, exchange insults, fly into a rage—both in the early days of our acquaintance, when he was a spoiled boy living at home with his parents, and afterward, when he began to make his mark on the world, first as a *campiere* on the Buschetta estate and later as a man of respect. He wasn't one to hold anything back.

I rearranged the things on my desk, took off my glasses and wiped them with my handkerchief. Bastiano C. was twenty-six or twenty-seven years old, somewhere in that range, and his medical history had been unremarkable as far as I could recall. Oh, there had been the usual doses of clap, the knife and gun wounds, but nothing that could begin to explain the physical shambles I now saw before me. I listened to the clock in the square toll the hour—it was 4:00 P.M. and hotter than even Dante could have imagined—and then I tried one last time. "So, Don C., you're not feeling well. Would you like to tell me about it?"

The man's face was sour, the gift of early handsomeness pressed from it like grappa from the dregs. He scratched his rear casually, then took a seat as if he were stuffed with feathers, and leaned forward. "Pepto-Bismol," he said in the moist high-pitched tones that made it seem as if he were sucking his words like lozenges. "I live Pepto-Bismol. I breathe it, drink it by the quart, it runs through my veins. I even shit pink."

"Ah, it's your stomach, then," I said, rising now, the stethoscope dangling from my neck, but he gestured for me to remain seated. He wasn't yet ready to reveal himself, to become intimate with my diagnostic ways.

"I am telling you, Doctor," he said, "I do not eat, drink, smoke; my taste is gone and my pleasure in things is as dead as the black cat we nailed over Miraglia Sciacca's door. I take two bites of pasta with a little butter and grated Romano and it's like they stabbed me in my guts." He looked miserably at the floor and worked the bones of his left wrist till they clicked like dice thrown against a wall. "And do you know why?" he demanded finally.

I didn't know, but I certainly had a suspicion.

"Santo R.," he said, slowing down to inject some real venom into his voice. "The fat-ass bastard."

That night, over a mutton chop and a bowl of bean soup, I consulted my housekeeper about the situation. Santuzza is an ignorant woman, crammed from her toes to her scalp with the superstitious claptrap that afflicts the Sicilian peasantry like a congenital defect (I once caught her rubbing fox fat on her misshapen feet and saying a Salve Regina backwards in a low moaning singsong voice), but she has an uncanny and all-encompassing knowledge of the spats, feuds and sex scandals not only of Partinico but of the entire Palermo province. The minute I leave for the office, the telephone receiver becomes glued to the side of her head—she cooks with it in place, sweeps, does the wash and changes the sheets, and all the while the pertinacious voice of the telephone buzzes in her ear. All day long it's gossip, gossip, gossip.

"They had a falling-out," Santuzza said, putting a loaf in front of me and re-filling my glass from the carafe on the sideboard. "They were both asked to be a go-between in the dispute of Gaspare Pantaleo and Miraglia Sciacca."

"Ah," I murmured, breaking off a crust and wiping it thoughtfully round the rim of my plate, "I should have known."

As Santuzza told it, the disaffection between Pantaleo and Sciacca, tenant farmers on the C. and R. estates, respectively, arose over a question of snails. It had been a dry year following hard on the heels of the driest year anyone could remember, and the snails hadn't appeared in any numbers during the previous fall. But recently we'd had a freak rain, and Gaspare Pantaleo, a poor man who has to do everything in his power to make ends meet, went out to gather snails for a stew to feed his children. He knew a particular spot, high on the riverbank where there was a tumble of stones dumped to prevent erosion, and though it was on private property, the land belonged neither to the C. nor R. family hold-ings. Miraglia Sciacca discovered him there. Apparently Sciacca knew of this spot also, a good damp protected place where the snails clumped together in bunches in the cracks between the rocks, and he too had gone out to collect snails for a stew. His children—there were eight of them, and each with an iden-tical cast in the right eye—were hungry too, always hungry. Like Pantaleo, he lived close to the bone, hunting snails, frogs, elvers and songbirds, gathering borage and wild asparagus and whatnot to stretch his larder. Well, they had words over the snails, one thing led to another, and when Miraglia Sciacca came to he was lying in the mud with maybe a thousand snails crushed into his groin.

Two days later he marched up to the Pantaleo household with an antiquated carbine and shot the first two dogs he saw. Gaspare Pantaleo's brother Filippo retaliated by poisoning the Sciacca family's pig, and then Rosario Bontalde, Mi-raglia Sciacca's uncle by marriage, sent a fifteen-pound wheel of cheese to the Pantaleos as an apparent peace offering. But the cheese was hexed—remember, this is Santuzza talking—and within the week Girolama Pantaleo, Gaspare's el-dest daughter and one of the true and astonishing beauties of the province, lost all her hair. Personally, I suspected ringworm or perhaps a dietary deficiency, but I didn't want to distract Santuzza, so I ate my soup and said nothing.

Things apparently came to a head when Gaspare Pantaleo stormed up the road to the Sciacca place to demand that the hex be lifted—the cheese they'd dis-posed of, but in such cases the hex, Santuzza assured me, lingers in all who've eaten of it. At the time, Miraglia Sciacca was out in the yard, not five paces from the public street, splitting olive wood so he could stack it against the fence for the coming winter. "You're a fraud and a pederast," Gaspare Pantaleo accused in a voice the neighbors could hear half a mile away, "and I demand that you take the hex off that cheese."

Miraglia's only response was a crude epithet.

"All right then, you son of a bitch, I'll thrash it out of you," Gaspare roared, and he set his hand down on the fence post to hoist himself over, and that was when Miraglia Sciacca, without so much as a hitch in his stroke, brought the ax down and took Gaspare Pantaleo's right hand off at the wrist. That was bad enough, but it wasn't the worst of it. What really inflamed the entire Pantaleo clan, what drove them to escalate matters by calling in Don Bastiano C. as mediator, was that the Sciaccas wouldn't return the hand. As Santuzza had it from Rosa Giardini, an intimate of the Sciaccas, Miraglia kept the hand preserved in a jar on the mantelpiece, taking it down at the slightest pretext to show off to his guests and boast of his prowess.

Three weeks passed and the sun held steady in the sky, though by now we should have been well into the rains, and I heard nothing of the feuding parties. I saw Santo R. one evening as I was sitting in the cafe, but we didn't speak—he was out in the street, along with his two elephantine bodyguards, bending painfully to inspect the underside of his car for explosives before lumbering into the driver's seat, firing up the ignition and roaring away in a cyclone of leaves and whirling trash. It was ironic to think that snails had been the cause of all this misunderstanding and a further burden to the precarious health of the two men of respect, Don Santo R. and Don Bastiano C., because now you couldn't find snails for love or money. Not a trattoria, cafe or street vendor offered them for sale, and the unseasonable sun burned like a cinder in the sky.

It was a festering hot day toward the end of November, no rain in sight and the sirocco tearing relentlessly at the withered branches of the trees, when Santo R. next showed up at my office. Business was slow—the season of croup and bronchitis, head colds and flu depended upon the rains as much as the snails did—and I was gazing out the window at a pair of buzzards spiraling over the slaughterhouse when he announced himself with a delicate little cough. "Don R.," I said, rising to greet him with a smile, but the smile must have frozen on my face—I was shocked at the sight of him. If he'd looked bad a month ago, bloated and pale and on the verge of collapse, now he was so swollen I could think of nothing so much as a sausage ready to burst its skin on the grill.

"Doctor," he rasped, and his face was like chalk beside the ruddy beef of the bodyguard who supported him, "I don't feel so good." Through the open door I could see Crocifissa making the sign of the cross. The second bodyguard was nowhere to be seen.

Alarmed, I hurried out from behind the desk and helped the remaining henchman settle Don R. in the chair. Don R.'s fingers were so puffed up as to be featureless, and I saw that he'd removed the laces of his shoes to ease the swelling of his feet—this was no mere obesity, but a sign that something was desperately wrong. Generalized edema, difficulty breathing, cardiac arrhythmia—

the man was a walking time bomb. "Don R.," I said, bending forward to listen to the fitful thump and wheeze of his heart, "you've been taking your medication, haven't you?" I'd prescribed nitroglycerine for the angina, a diuretic and Aldomet for hypertension, and strictly warned him against salt, alcohol, tobacco and saturated fats.

Santo's eyes were closed. He opened them with a grunt of command, made eye contact with the bodyguard and ordered him from the room. When the door had closed, he let out a deep, world-weary sigh. "A good man, Francesco," he said. "He's about all I have left. I had to send my wife and kids away till this blows over, and Guido, my other man, well"—he lifted his hand and let it drop like a guillotine—"no one lives forever."

"Listen to me, Don R.," I said, stern now, my patience at an end, "you haven't been taking your medication, have you?"

No reaction. I might as well have been addressing a stump, a post in the ground.

"And the alcohol, the cigarettes, the pastries and all the rest?"

A shrug of the shoulders. "I'm tired, Doctor," he said.

"Tired?" I was outraged. "I should think you'd be tired. Your system's depleted. You're a mess. You're taking your life in your hands just to mount a flight of stairs. But you didn't come here for lectures, and I'm not going to give you one—no, I'm going to lift up that telephone receiver on the desk and call the hospital. You're checking in this afternoon."

The eyes, which had fallen shut, blinked open again. "No, Doctor," he rasped, and his words came in a slow steady procession, "you're not going to touch that telephone. Do you know how long I'd last in a hospital? Were you born yesterday? Bastiano'd have me strung up like a side of beef before the night was out."

"But your blood pressure is through the roof, you, you—"

"Fuck blood pressure."

There was a silence. The sirocco, so late for the season, rattled the panes of the window. The overhead fan creaked on its bearings. After a moment he spoke, and his voice was thick with emotion. "Doctor," he began, "Doctor, you've known me all my life—I'm not thirty yet and I feel like I'm a hundred. Do you know what it takes to be a man of respect in this country, do you?" His voice broke. "All the beatings, the muggings, the threats and kidnappings, cutting off the heads of the dogs and horses, nailing the cats to the walls . . . I tell you, Doctor, I tell you: it takes a toll on a man."

He was about to go on when a noise from the outer room froze him—it was nothing, barely audible above the wind, the least gurgle in the throat, but it was enough. With a swiftness that astonished me, he was up from the chair, the pistol clenched in his hand. I heard Crocifissa suddenly, a truncated cry, and then the door flew open and there stood Bastiano C., one hand clutching a gleaming silver snub-nosed revolver, the other pinned to his gut.

This was the longest moment of my life. It seemed to play out over the course of an hour, but in reality, the whole thing took no more than a minute or two. Behind Bastiano, I could make out the sad collapsed form of Santo's bodyguard, stretched out like a sea lion on the beach, a wire garrote sunk into the fleshy folds of his throat. Beneath him, barely visible, lay the expiring sticklike shadow of Bastiano's remaining bodyguard—Bastiano too, as it turned out, had lost one to the exigencies of war. Crocifissa, wide-eyed and with a fist clamped to her mouth, sat at her desk in shock.

And Bastiano—he stood there in the doorway nearly doubled over with abdominal pain, more wasted even than he'd been three weeks earlier, if that was possible. The pistol was leveled on Santo, who stood rigid at the back of the room, heaving for breath like a cart horse going up the side of Mount Etna. Santo's pistol, a thing the size of a small cannon, was aimed unflinchingly at his antagonist. "Son of a whore," Bastiano breathed in his wet slurping tones. There was no flesh to his face, none at all, and his eyes were glittering specks sunk like screws in his head.

"*Puttana!*" Santo spat, and he changed color twice—from parchment white to royal *pomodoro*—with the rush of blood surging through his congested arteries.

"Now I am going to kill you," Bastiano whispered, even as he clutched with his left hand at the place where his ulcers had eaten through the lining of his stomach and the surrounding vessels that were quietly filling his body cavity with blood.

"In a pig's eye," Santo growled, and it was the last thing he ever said, because in that moment, even as he wrapped his bloated finger round the trigger and attempted to squeeze, his poor congested fat-clogged heart gave out and he died before my eyes of a massive coronary.

I went to him, of course, my own heart pounding as if it would burst, but even as I bent over him I was distracted by a noise from Bastiano—a delicate little sigh that might have come from a schoolgirl surprised by love—and I glanced up in confusion to see his eyes fall shut as he pitched face-forward onto the linoleum. Though I tried with all my power, I couldn't revive him, and he died that night in a heavily guarded room at the Ospedale Regionale.

I don't know what it was, and I don't like to speculate, being a man of science, but the rains came three days later. Santuzza claimed it was a question of propitiating the gods, of bloodletting, of settling otherworldly accounts, but the hidebound and ignorant will have their say. At any rate, a good portion of the district turned out for the funerals, held on the same day and at the same cemetery, while the rain drove down as if heaven and earth had been reversed. Don Bastiano C.'s family and retainers were careful not to mingle with Don Santo R.'s, and the occasion was somber and without incident. The snails turned out, though, great snaking slippery chains of them, mounting the tombstones in their legions and fearlessly sailing the high seas of the greening grass. The village priest intoned the immortal words, the widows wept, the children huddled beneath their umbrellas and we buried both men, if not with pomp and circumstance, then at least with a great deal of respect.

(1992)

FILTHY WITH THINGS

He dreams, amidst the clutter, of sparseness, purity, the wheeling dark star-haunted reaches beyond the grasp of this constrained little world, where distances are measured in light-years and even the galaxies fall away to nothing. But dreams get you nowhere, and Marsha's latest purchase, the figured-mahogany highboy with carved likenesses of Jefferson, Washington and Adams in place of pulls, will not fit in the garage. The garage, designed to accommodate three big chromium-hung hunks of metal in the two-ton range, will not hold anything at all, not even a Japanese fan folded like a stiletto and sunk to the hilt in a horizontal crevice. There are no horizontal crevices—nor vertical, either. The mass of interlocked things, the great squared-up block of objects, of totems, of purchases made and accreted, of the precious and unattainable, is packed as tightly as the stones at Machu Picchu.

For a long moment Julian stands there in the blistering heat of the driveway, contemplating the abstract sculpture of the garage while the boy from the Antique Warehouse rolls and unrolls the sleeves of his T-shirt and watches a pair of fourteen-year-old girls saunter up the sidewalk. The sun and heat are not salutary for the colonial hardwood of which the highboy is composed, and the problem of where to put it has begun to reach critical proportions. Julian thinks of the storage shed behind the pool, where the newspapers are stacked a hundred deep and Marsha keeps her collection of Brazilian scythes and harrows, but immediately rejects it—the last time he was back there he couldn't even get the door open. Over the course of the next ten seconds or so he develops a fantasy of draining the pool and enclosing it as a sort of step-down warehouse, and it's a rich fantasy, richly rewarding, but he ultimately dismisses it, too. If they were to drain the pool, where would Marsha keep her museum-quality collection of Early American whaling implements, buoys and ship's furniture, not to mention the two hundred twelve antique oarlocks currently mounted on the pool fence?

The boy's eyes are vapid. He's begun to whistle tunelessly and edge back toward the van. "So where'd you decide you want it?" he asks listlessly.

On the moon, Julian wants to say. Saturn. On the bleak blasted ice plains of Pluto. He shrugs. "On the porch, I guess."

The porch. Yes. The only problem is, the screened-in porch is already stacked to the eaves with sideboards, armoires, butter churns and bentwood rockers. The best they can do, after a fifteen-minute struggle, is to wedge the thing two-thirds of the way in the door. "Well," says Julian, and he can feel his heart fluttering round his rib cage like some fist-sized insect, "I guess that'll have to do." The laugh he appends is curt with embarrassment. "Won't have to worry about rain till November, anyway."

The boy isn't even breathing hard. He's long-lipped and thin, strung together with wire, and he's got one of those haircuts that make his head look as if it's been put on backwards. For a long moment he leans over the hand truck, long fingers dangling, giving Julian a look that makes him feel like he's from another planet. "Yeah, that's right," the boy finally murmurs, and he looks at his feet, then jerks himself up as if to drift back to the van, the freeway, the warehouse, before stopping cold again. He looks at Julian as if he's forgotten something, and Julian digs into his pocket and gives the boy three dollars for his efforts.

The sun is there, a living presence, as the boy backs the van out of the driveway, and Julian knows he's going to have to do something about the mahogany highboy—drape a sheet over it or maybe a plastic drop cloth—but somehow he can't really seem to muster the energy. It's getting too much for him—all these things, the addition that was filled before it was finished, the prefab storage sheds on the back lawn, the crammed closets, the unlivable living room—and the butt end of the highboy hanging from the porch door seems a tangible expression of all his deepest fears. Seeing it there, the harsh light glancing off its polished flanks, its clawed feet dangling in the air, he wants to cry out against the injustice of it all, his miserable lot, wants to dig out his binoculars and the thin peeling ground cloth he's had since he was a boy in Iowa and go up to the mountains and let the meteor showers wash him clean, but he can't. That ancient handcrafted butt end represents guilt, Marsha's displeasure, a good and valuable thing left to deteriorate. He's begun to move toward it in a halfhearted shuffle, knowing from experience that he can squeeze it in there somehow, when a horn sounds breathlessly behind him. He turns, condemned like Sisyphus, and watches as Marsha wheels into the drive, the Range Rover packed to the windows and a great dark slab of furniture lashed to the roof like some primitive landing craft. "Julian!" she calls. "Julian! Wait till you see what I found!"

■ ■ ■

"I've seen worse," the woman says, and Julian can feel the short hairs on the back of his neck begin to stiffen—she's seen worse, but she's seen better, too. They're standing in the living room—or rather on the narrow footpath between the canyons of furniture that obscure the walls, the fireplace, even the ceiling of what was once the living room—and Julian, afraid to look her in the eye, leans back against a curio cabinet crammed with painted porcelain dolls in native costume, nervously turning her card over in his hand. The card is certainly minimalistic—*Susan Certaine*, it reads in a thin black embossed script, *Professional Organizer*, and it gives a telephone number, nothing else—and the woman herself is impressive, brisk, imposing, even; but he's just not sure. Something needs to be done, something radical—and, of course, Marsha, who left to cruise the flea markets an hour ago, will have to agree to it, at least in substance—but for all his misery and sense of oppression, for all the times he's joked about burning the place down or holding the world's biggest yard sale, Julian needs to be reassured, needs to be convinced.

"You've seen worse?" he prompts.

"Sure I have. Of course I have. What do you take me for, an amateur?"

Julian shrugs, turns up his palms, already on the defensive.

"Listen, in my business, Mr. Laxner, you tend to run across the hard cases, the ones anyone else would give up on—the Liberaces, the Warhols, the Nancy Reagans. You remember Imelda Marcos? That was me. I'm the one they called in to straighten out that mess. Twenty-seven hundred pairs of shoes alone, Mr. Laxner. Think about that."

She pauses to let her eyes flicker over the room, the smallest coldest flame burning behind the twin slivers of her contact lenses. She's a tall, pale, hovering presence, a woman stripped to the essentials, the hair torn back from her scalp and strangled in a bun, no cheeks, no lips, no makeup or jewelry, the dress black, the shoes black, the briefcase black as a dead black coal dug out of the bottom of the bag. "There's trouble here," she says finally, holding his eyes. "You're dirty with things, Mr. Laxner, filthy, up to your ears in the muck."

He is, he admits it, but he can't help wincing at the harshness of the indictment.

She leans closer, the briefcase clamped like a breastplate across her chest, her breath hot in his face, soap, Sen-Sen, Listerine. "And do you know who I am, Mr. Laxner?" she asks, a hard combative friction in the back of her throat, a rasp, a growl.

Julian tries to sound casual, tries to work the hint of a smile into the corners of his mouth and ignore the fact that his personal space has suddenly shrunk to nothing. "Susan Certaine?"

"I am the purifying stream, Mr. Laxner, that's who I am. The cleansing torrent, the baptismal font. I'll make a new man of you."

This is what she's here for, he knows it, this is what he needs, discipline, compulsion, the iron promise, but still he can't help edging away, a little dance of the feet, the condensing of a shoulder. "Well, yes, but"—giving her a sidelong glance, and still she's there, right there, breathing out her Sen-Sen like a dental hygienist—"it's a big job, it's—"

"We inventory everything—*everything*—right down to the paper clips in your drawers and the lint in your pockets. My people are the best, real professionals. There's no one like us in the business, believe me—and believe me when I tell you I'll have this situation under control inside of a week, seven short days. I'll guarantee it, in fact. All I need is your go-ahead."

His go-ahead. A sudden vista opens up before him, unbroken beaches, limitless plains, lunar seas and Venusian deserts, the yawning black interstellar wastes. Would it be too much to ask to see the walls of his own house? Just once? Just for an hour? Yes, okay, sure, he wants to say, but the immensity of it stifles him. "I'll have to ask my wife," he hears himself saying. "I mean, consult with her, think it over."

"Pah! That's what they all say." Her look is incendiary, bitter, the eyes curdling behind the film of the lenses, the lipless mouth clenched round something rotten. "Tell me something, Mr. Laxner, if you don't mind my asking—you're a stargazer, aren't you?"

"Beg pardon?"

"The upstairs room, the one over the kitchen?" Her eyes are jumping, some mad electric impulse shooting through her like a power surge scorching the lines. "Come on now, come clean. All those charts and telescopes, the books— there must be a thousand of them."

Now it's Julian's turn, the ball in his court, the ground solid under his feet. "I'm an astronomer, if you want to know."

She says nothing, just watches him out of those burning messianic eyes, waiting.

"Well, actually, it's more of a hobby really—but I do teach a course Wednesday nights at the community college."

The eyes leap at him. "I knew it. You intellectuals, you're the worst, the very worst."

"But, but"—stammering again despite himself—"it's not me, it's Marsha."

"Yes," she returns, composing herself like some lean effortless snake coiling to strike, "I've heard that one before. It takes two to tango, Mr. Laxner, the pathological aggregator and the enabler. Either way, you're guilty. Don't *ask* your wife, tell her. Take command." Turning her back on him as if the matter's been settled, she props her briefcase up against the near bank of stacked ottomans, produces a note pad and begins jotting down figures in a firm microscopic hand. Without looking up, she swings suddenly round on him. "Family money?" she asks.

And he answers before he can think: "Yes. My late mother."

"All right," she says, "all right, that's fine. But before we go any further, perhaps you'd be interested in hearing a little story one of my clients told me, a journalist, a name you'd recognize in a minute. . . ." The eyes twitch again, the eyeballs themselves, pulsing with that electric charge. "Well, a few years ago he was in Ethiopia—in the Eritrean province—during the civil war there? He was looking for some refugees to interview and a contact put him onto a young couple with three children, they'd been grain merchants before the war broke out, upper-middle-class, they even had a car. Well, they agreed to be interviewed, because he was giving them a little something and they hadn't eaten in a week, but when the time came they hung back. And do you know why?"

He doesn't know. But the room, the room he passes through twenty times a day like a tourist trapped in a museum, seems to close in on him.

"They were embarrassed, that's why—they didn't have any clothes. And I don't mean as in 'Oh dear, I don't have a thing to wear to the Junior League Ball,' but literally no clothes. Nothing at all, not even a rag. They finally showed up like Adam and Eve, one hand clamped over their privates." She held his eyes till he had to look away. "And what do you think of that, Mr. Laxner, I'd be interested to know?"

What can he say? He didn't start the war, he didn't take the food from their mouths and strip the clothes from their backs, but he feels guilty all the same, bloated with guilt, fat with it, his pores oozing the golden rancid sheen of excess and waste. "That's terrible," he murmurs, and still he can't quite look her in the eye.

"Terrible?" she cries, her voice homing in, "you're damned right it's terrible. Awful. The saddest thing in the world. And do you know what? Do you?" She's even closer now, so close he could be breathing for her. "That's why I'm charging you a thousand dollars a day."

The figure seizes him, wrings him dry, paralyzes his vocal apparatus. He can feel something jerking savagely at the cords of his throat. "A thousand— dollars—a day?" he echoes in disbelief. "I knew it wasn't going to be cheap—"

But she cuts him off, a single insistent finger pressed to his lips. "You're dirty," she whispers, and her voice is different now, thrilling, soft as a lover's, "you're filthy. And I'm the only one to make you clean again."

The following evening, with Julian's collusion, Susan Certaine and her associate, Dr. Doris Hauskopf, appear at the back gate just after supper. It's a clear searing evening, not a trace of moisture in the sky—the kind of evening that would later lure Julian out under the stars if it weren't for the light pollution. He and Marsha are enjoying a cup of decaf after a meal of pita, tabbouleh and dolma from the Armenian deli, sitting out on the patio amidst the impenetrable maze of lawn furniture, when Susan Certaine's crisp penetrating tones break through the muted roar of freeway traffic and sporadic birdsong: "Mr. Laxner? Are you there?"

Marsha, enthroned in wicker and browsing through a collectibles catalogue, gives him a quizzical look, expecting perhaps a delivery boy or a package from the UPS—Marsha, his Marsha, in her pastel shorts and oversized top, the quintessential innocent, so easily pleased. He loves her in that moment, loves her so fiercely he almost wants to call the whole thing off, but Susan Certaine is there, undeniable, and her voice rings out a second time, drilling him with its adamancy: "Mr. Laxner?"

He rises then, ducking ceramic swans and wrought-iron planters, feeling like Judas.

The martial tap of heels on the flagstone walk, the slap of twin briefcases against rigorously conditioned thighs, and there they are, the professional organizer and her colleague the psychologist, hovering over a bewildered Marsha like customs inspectors. There's a moment of silence, Marsha looking from Julian to the intruders and back again, before he realizes that it's up to him to make the introductions. "Marsha," he begins, and he seems to be having trouble finding his voice, "Marsha, this is Ms. Certaine. And her colleague, Dr. Doris Hauskopf—she's a specialist in aggregation disorders. They run a service for people like us . . . you remember a few weeks ago, when we—" but Marsha's look wraps fingers around his throat and he can't go on.

Blanching, pale to the roots of her hair, Marsha leaps up from the chair and throws a wild hunted look round her. "No," she gasps, "no," and for a moment Julian thinks she's going to bolt, but the psychologist, a compact woman with a hairdo even more severe than Susan Certaine's, steps forward to take charge of the situation. "Poor Marsha," she clucks, spreading her arms to embrace her, "poor, poor Marsha."

The trees bend under the weight of the carved birdhouses from Heidelberg and Zurich, a breeze comes up to play among the Taiwanese wind chimes that fringe the eaves in an unbroken line, and the house—the jam-packed house in which they haven't been able to prepare a meal or even find a frying pan in over two years—seems to rise up off its foundation and settle back again. Suddenly Marsha is sobbing, clutching Dr. Hauskopf's squared-up shoulders and sobbing like a child. "I know I've been wrong," she wails, "I know it, but I just can't, I can't—"

"Hush now, Marsha, hush," the doctor croons, and Susan Certaine gives Julian a fierce, tight-lipped look of triumph, "that's what we're here for. Don't you worry about a thing."

The next morning, at the stroke of seven, Julian is awakened from uneasy dreams by the deep-throated rumble of heavy machinery. In the first startled moment of waking, he thinks it's the noise of the garbage truck and feels a sudden stab of regret for having failed to put out the cans and reduce his load by its weekly fraction, but gradually he becomes aware that the sound is localized, static, stalled at the curb out front of the house. Throwing off the drift of counterpanes, quilts and granny-square afghans beneath which he and his wife lie entombed each night, he struggles through the precious litter of the floor to the bedroom window. Outside, drawn up to the curb in a sleek dark glittering line, their engines snarling, are three eighteen-wheel moving vans painted in metal-flake black and emblazoned with the Certaine logo. And somewhere, deep in the bowels of the house, the doorbell has begun to ring. Insistently.

Marsha isn't there to answer it. Marsha isn't struggling up bewildered from the morass of bedclothes to wonder who could be ringing at this hour. She isn't in the bathroom trying to locate her toothbrush among the mustache cups and fin-de-siècle Viennese soap dishes or in the kitchen wondering which of the coffee drippers/steamers/percolators to use. She isn't in the house at all, and the magnitude of that fact hits him now, hard, like fear or hunger.

No, Marsha is twenty-seven miles away, in the Susan Certaine Residential Treatment Center in Simi Valley, separated from him for the first time in their sixteen years of marriage. It was Dr. Hauskopf's idea. She felt it would be better this way, less traumatic for everyone concerned. After the initial twilit embrace of the preceding evening, the doctor and Susan Certaine had led Marsha out front, away from the house and Julian—her "twin crutches," as the doctor put it—and conducted an impromptu three-hour therapy session on the lawn. Julian preoccupied himself with his lunar maps and some calculations he'd been wanting to make relating to the total area of the Mare Fecunditatis in the Southeast quadrant, but he couldn't help glancing out the window now and again. The three women were camped on the grass, sitting in a circle with their legs folded under them, yoga style, while Marsha's tiki torches blazed over their heads like a forest afire.

Weirdly lit, they dipped their torsos toward one another and their hands flashed white against the shadows while Marsha's menagerie of lawn ornaments clustered round them in silent witness. There was something vaguely disquieting about the scene, and it made Julian feel like an interloper, already bereft in some deep essential way, and he had to turn away from it. He put down his pencil and made himself a drink. He flicked on the TV. Paced. Finally, at quarter to ten, he heard them coming in the front door. Marsha was subdued, her eyes downcast, and it was clear that she'd been crying. They allowed her one suitcase. No cosmetics, two changes of clothing, underwear, a nightgown. Nothing else. Not a thing. Julian embraced his wife on the front steps while Susan Certaine and Dr. Hauskopf looked on impatiently, and then they were gone.

But now the doorbell is ringing and Julian is shrugging into his pants and looking for his shoes even as Susan Certaine's whiplash cry reverberates in the stairwell and stings him to action. "Mr. Laxner! Open up! Open up!"

It takes him sixty seconds. He would have liked to comb his hair, brush his teeth, reacquaint himself with the parameters of human life on the planet, but there it is, sixty seconds, and he's still buttoning his shirt as he throws back the door to admit her. "I thought . . . I thought you said eight," he gasps.

Susan Certaine stands rigid on the doorstep, flanked by two men in black jumpsuits with the Certaine logo stitched in gold over their left breast pockets. The men are big-headed, bulky, with great slabs of muscle ladled over their shoulders and upper arms. Behind them, massed like a football team coming to the aid of a fallen comrade, are the uncountable others, all in Certaine black. "I did," she breathes, stepping past him without a glance. "We like to keep our clients on their toes. Mike!" she cries, "Fernando!" and the two men spring past Julian and into the ranked gloom of the house. "Clear paths here"—pointing toward the back room—"and here"—and then to the kitchen.

The door stands open. Beyond it, the front lawn is a turmoil of purposefully moving bodies, of ramps, ladders, forklifts, flattened boxes in bundles six feet high. Already, half a dozen workers—they're women, Julian sees now, women cut in the Certaine mold, with their hair shorn or pinned rigidly back—have begun constructing the cardboard containers that will take the measure of his and Marsha's life together. And now others, five, six, seven of them, speaking in low tones and in a language he doesn't recognize, file past him with rolls of bar-code tape, while out on the front walk, just beyond the clutter of the porch, three men in mirror sunglasses set up a gauntlet of tables equipped with computers and electric-eye guns. Barefooted, unshaven, unshowered, his teeth unbrushed and his hair uncombed, Julian can only stand and gape—it's like an invasion. It *is* an invasion.

When he emerges from the shower ten minutes later, wrapped only in a towel, he finds a small hunched Asian woman squatting on her heels in front of the cabinets under the twin sinks, methodically affixing bar-code stickers to jars of petroleum jelly, rolls of toilet paper and cans of cleanser before stacking them neatly in a box at her side. "What do you think you're doing?" Julian demands. This is too much, outrageous, in his own bathroom no less, but the woman just grins out of a toothless mouth, gives him the thumbs-up sign and says, "A-OK, Number One Charlie!"

His heart is going, he can feel it, and he tries to stay calm, tries to remind himself that these people are only doing their job, doing what he could never do, liberating him, cleansing him, but before he can get his pants back on two more women materialize in the bedroom, poking through the drawers with their ubiquitous stickers. "Get out!" he roars, "out!" and he makes a rush at them, but it's as if he doesn't exist, as if he's already become an irrelevance in the face of the terrible weight of his possessions. Unconcerned, they silently hold their ground, heads bowed, hands flicking all the while over his handkerchiefs, underwear, socks, over Marsha's things, her jewelry, brassieres, her ashtray and lacquered-box collections and the glass case that houses her Thimbles of the World set.

"All right," Julian says, "all right. We'll just see about this, we'll just see," and he dresses right there in front of them, boldly, angrily, hands trembling on button and zipper, before slamming out into the hallway in search of Susan Certaine.

The only problem is, he can't find her. The house, almost impossible to navigate in the best of times, is like the hold of a sinking ship. All is chaos. A dark mutter of voices rises up to engulf him, shouts, curses, dust hanging in the air, the floorboards crying out, and things, objects of all shapes and sizes, sailing past him in bizarre array. Susan Certaine is not in the kitchen, not on the lawn, not in the garage or the pool area or the guest wing. Finally, in frustration, he stops a worker with a Chinese vase slung over one shoulder and asks if he's seen her. The man has a hard face, smoldering eyes, a mustache so thick it eliminates his mouth. "And who might you be?" he growls.

"The owner." Julian feels lightheaded. He could swear he's never seen the vase before.

"Owner of what?"

"What do you mean, owner of what? All this"—gesturing at the chaotic tumble of carpets, lamps, furniture and bric-a-brac—"the house. The, the—"

"You want *Ms.* Certaine," the man says, cutting him off, "I'd advise you best look upstairs, in the den," and then he's gone, shouldering his load out the door.

The den. But that's Julian's sanctuary, the only room in the house where you can draw a breath, find a book on the shelves, a chair to sit in—his desk is there, his telescopes, his charts. There's no need for any organizing in his den. What is she thinking? He takes the stairs two at a time, dodging Certaine workers laden with artifacts, and bursts through the door to find Susan Certaine seated at his desk and the room already half-stripped.

"But, but what are you doing?" he cries, snatching at his Velbon tripod as one of the big men in black fends him off with an unconscious elbow. "This room doesn't need anything, this room is off-limits, this is mine—"

"*Mine,*" Susan Certaine mimics, leaping suddenly to her feet. "Did you hear that, Fernando? Mike?" The two men pause, grinning wickedly, and the wizened Asian woman, at work now in here, gives a short sharp laugh of derision. Susan Certaine crosses the room in two strides, thrusting her jaw at Julian, forcing him back a step. "Listen to yourself—'mine, mine, mine.' Don't you see what you're saying? Marsha's only half the problem, as in any codependent relationship. What did you think, that you could solve all your problems by depriving her of *her* things, making *her* suffer, while all your precious little star charts and musty books and whatnot remain untouched? Is that it?"

He can feel the eyes of the big men on him. Across the room, at the bookcase, the Asian woman applies stickers to his first edition of Percival Lowell's *Mars and Its Canals*, the astrolabe that once belonged to Captain Joshua

Slocum, the Starview scope his mother gave him when he turned twelve. "No, but, but—"

"Would that be fair, Mr. Laxner? Would that be equitable? Would it?" She doesn't wait for an answer, turning instead to pose the question to her henchmen. "You think it's fair, Mike? Fernando?"

"No gain without pain," Mike says.

"Amen," Fernando chimes in.

"Listen," Julian blurts, and he's upset now, as upset as he's ever been, "I don't care what you say, I'm the boss here and I say the stuff stays, just as it is. You— now put down that tripod."

No one moves. Mike looks to Fernando, Fernando looks to Susan Certaine. After a moment, she lays a hand on Julian's arm. "You're not the boss here, Julian," she says, the voice sunk low in her throat, "not anymore. If you have any doubts, just read the contract." She attempts a smile, though smiles are clearly not her forte. "The question is, do you want to get organized or not? You're paying me a thousand dollars a day, which breaks down to roughly two dollars a minute. You want to stand here and shoot the breeze at two dollars a minute, or do you want action?"

Julian hangs his head. She's right, he knows it. "I'm sorry," he says finally. "It's just that I can't . . . I mean I want to do something, anything—"

"You want to do something? You really want to help?"

Mike and Fernando are gone, already heading down the stairs with their burdens, and the Asian woman, her hands in constant motion, has turned to his science-fiction collection. He shrugs. "Yes, sure. What can I do?"

She glances at her watch, squares her shoulders, fixes him with her dark unreadable gaze. "You can take me to breakfast."

Susan Certaine orders wheat toast, dry, and coffee, black. Though he's starving, though he feels cored out from the back of his throat to the last constricted loop of his intestines, he follows suit. He's always liked a big breakfast, eggs over easy, three strips of bacon, toast, waffles, coffee, orange juice, yogurt with fruit, and never more so than when he's under stress or feels something coming on, but with Susan Certaine sitting stiffly across from him, her lips pursed in distaste, disapproval, ascetic renunciation of all and everything he stands for, he just doesn't have the heart to order. Besides which, he's on unfamiliar ground here. The corner coffee shop, where he and Marsha have breakfasted nearly every day for the past three years, wasn't good enough for her. She had to drive halfway across the Valley to a place *she* knew, though for the life of him he can't see a whole lot of difference between the two places—same menu, same coffee, even the waitresses look the same. But they're not. And the fact of it throws him off balance.

"You know, I've been thinking, Mr. Laxner," Susan Certaine says, speaking into the void left by the disappearance of the waitress, "you really should come over to us. For the rest of the week, I mean."

Come over? Julian watches her, wondering what in god's name she's talking about, his stomach sinking over the thought of his Heinleins and Asimovs in the hands of strangers, let alone his texts and first editions and all his equipment—if they so much as scratch a lens, he'll, he'll . . . but his thoughts stop right there. Susan Certaine, locked in the grip of her black rigidity, is giving him a look he hasn't seen before. The liminal smile, the coy arch of the eyebrows. She's a young woman, younger than Marsha, far younger, and the apprehension hits him with a jolt. Here he is, sharing the most intimate meal of the day with a woman he barely knows, a young woman. He feels a wave of surrender wash over him.

"How can I persuade you?"

"I'm sorry," he murmurs, fumbling with his cup, "but I don't think I'm following you. Persuade me of what?"

"The Co-Dependent Hostel. For the spouses. The spoilers. For men like you, Mr. Laxner, who give their wives material things instead of babies, instead of love."

"But I resent that. Marsha's physically incapable of bearing children—and I *do* love her, very much so."

"Whatever." She waves her hand in dismissal. "But don't get the impression that it's a men's club or anything—you'd be surprised how many women are the enablers in these relationships. You're going to need a place to stay until Sunday anyway."

"You mean you want me to, to move out? Of my own house?"

She lays a hand on his. "Don't you think it would be fairer to Marsha? She moved out, didn't she? And by the way, Dr. Hauskopf tells me she passed a very restful night. Very restful." A sigh. A glance out the window. "Well, what do you say?"

Julian pictures a big gray featureless building lost in a vacancy of smog, men in robes and pajamas staring dully at newspapers, the intercom crackling. "But my things—"

"Things are what we're disburdening you of, Mr. Laxner. Things are crushing you, stealing your space, polluting your soul. That's what you hired me for, remember?" She pushes her cup aside and leans forward, and the old look is back, truculent, disdainful. He finds himself gazing into the shimmering nullity of her eyes. "We'll take care of all that," she says, her voice pitched low again, subtle and entrancing, "right on down to your toothbrush, hemorrhoid cream and carpet slippers." As if by legerdemain, a contract has appeared between the creamer and the twin plates of dry unadulterated toast. "Just sign here, Mr. Laxner, right at the bottom."

Julian hesitates, patting down his pockets for his reading glasses. The original contract, the one that spelled out the responsibilities of Certaine Enterprises with respect to his things—and his and Marsha's obligations to Certaine Enterprises—had run to 327 pages, a document he barely had time to skim before signing, and now this. Without his reading glasses he can barely make out the letterhead. "But how much is it, per day, I mean? Marsha's, uh, treatment was four hundred a day, correct? This wouldn't be anywhere in that ballpark, would it?"

"Think of it as a vacation, Mr. Laxner. You're going away on a little trip, that's all. And on Sunday, when you get home, you'll have your space back. Permanently." She looks into his eyes. "Can you put a price on that?"

The Susan Certaine Co-Dependent Hostel is located off a shady street in Sherman Oaks, on the grounds of a defunct private boys' school, and it costs about twice as much as a good hotel in midtown Manhattan. Julian had protested—it was Marsha, Marsha was the problem, she was the one who needed treatment, not him—but Susan Certaine, over two slices of dry wheat toast, had worn him down. He'd given her control over his life, and she was exercising it. That's what he'd paid for, that's what he'd wanted. He asked only to go home and pack a small suitcase, an overnight bag, anything, but she refused him even that—and refused him the use of his own car on top of it. "Withdrawal has got to be total," she says, easing up to the curb out front of the sprawling complex of earth-toned buildings even as a black-clad attendant hustles up to the car to pull open the door, "for *both* partners. I'm sure you'll be very happy here, Mr. Laxner."

"You're not coming in?" he says, a flutter of panic seizing him as he shoots a look from her to the doorman and back again.

The black Mercedes hums beneath them. A bird folds its wings and dips across the lawn. "Oh, no, no, not at all. You're on your own here, Mr. Laxner, I'm afraid—but in the best of hands, I assure you. No, my job is to go back to that black hole of a house and make it livable, to catalogue your things, organize. *Organize,* Mr. Laxner, that's my middle name."

Ten minutes later Julian finds himself sitting on the rock-hard upper bunk in the room he is to share with a lugubrious man named Fred, contemplating the appointments. The place is certainly Essene, but then, he supposes that's the idea. Aside from the bunk bed, the room contains two built-in chests of drawers, two mirrors, two desks and two identical posters revealing an eye-level view of the Bonneville Salt Flats. The communal bathroom/shower is down the checked linoleum hallway to the right. Fred, a big pouchy sack of a man who owns a BMW dealership in Encino, stares gloomily out the window and says only, "Kind of reminds you of college, doesn't it?"

In the evening, there's a meal in the cafeteria—instant mashed potatoes with gravy, some sort of overcooked unidentifiable meatlike substance, Jell-O—and Julian is surprised at the number of his fellow sufferers, slump-shouldered men and women, some of them quite young, who shuffle in and out of the big room like souls in purgatory. After dinner, there's a private get-acquainted chat with Dr. Heiko Hauskopf, Dr. Doris's husband, and then an informational film about acquisitive disorders, followed by a showing of *The Snake Pit* in the auditorium. Fred, as it turns out, is a belcher, tooth grinder and nocturnal mutterer of the first degree, and Julian spends the night awake, staring into the dark corner above him and imagining tiny solar systems there, hanging in the abyss, other worlds radiant with being.

Next morning, after a breakfast of desiccated eggs and corrosive coffee, he goes AWOL. Strides out the door without a glance, calls a taxi from the phone booth on the corner and checks into the nearest motel. From there he attempts to call Marsha, though both Susan Certaine and Dr. Doris had felt it would be better not to "establish contact" during therapy. He can't get through. She's unavailable, indisposed, undergoing counseling, having her nails done, and who is this calling, please?

For two days Julian holes up in his motel room like an escaped convict, feeling dangerous, feeling like a lowlife, a malingerer, a bum, letting the stubble sprout on his face, reveling in the funk of his unwashed clothes. He could walk up the street and buy himself a change of underwear and socks at least—he's still got his credit cards, after all—but something in him resists. Lying there in the sedative glow of the TV, surrounded by the detritus of the local fast-food outlets, belching softly to himself and pulling meditatively at the pint of bourbon balanced on his chest, he begins to see the point of the exercise. He misses Marsha desperately, misses his home, his bed, his things. But this is the Certaine way—to know deprivation, to know the hollowness of the manufactured image and the slow death of the unquenchable Tube, to purify oneself through renunciation. These are his thirty days and thirty nights, this is his trial, his penance. He lies there, prostrate, and when the hour of his class at the community college rolls round he gives no account of himself, not even a phone call.

On the third night, the telephone rings. Absorbed in a dramedy about a group of young musician/actor/models struggling to make ends meet in a rented beach house in Malibu, and well into his second pint of bourbon, he stupidly answers it. "Mr. Laxner?" Susan Certaine's hard flat voice drives at him through the wires.

"But, how—?" he gasps, before she cuts him off.

"Don't ask questions, just listen. You understand, of course, that as per the terms of your agreement, you owe Certaine Enterprises for six days' room and board at the Co-Dependent Hostel whether you make use of the facilities or not—"

He understands.

"Good," she snaps. "Fine. Now that that little matter has been resolved, let me tell you that your wife is responding beautifully to treatment and that she, unlike you, Mr. Laxner, is making the most of her stay in a nonacquisitive environment—and by the way, I should caution you against trying to contact her again; it could be terribly detrimental, traumatic, a real setback—"

Whipped, humbled, pried out of his cranny with a sure sharp stick, Julian can only murmur an apology.

There's a pause on the other end of the line—Julian can hear the hiss of gathering breath, the harsh whistle of the air rushing past Susan Certaine's fleshless lips, down her ascetic throat and into the repository of her disciplined lungs. "The good news," she says finally, drawing it out, "is that you're clean. Clean, Mr. Laxner. As pure as a babe sprung from the womb."

Julian is having difficulty putting it all together. His own breathing is quick and shallow. He rubs at his stubble, sits up and sets the pint of bourbon aside. "You mean—?"

"I mean twelve o'clock noon, Mr. Laxner, Sunday the twenty-seventh. Your place. You be there."

On Sunday morning, Julian is up at six. Eschewing the religious programming in favor of the newspaper, he pores methodically over each of the twenty-two sections—including the obituaries, the personals and the recondite details of the weather in Rio, Yakutsk and Rangoon—and manages to kill an hour and a half. His things have been washed—twice now, in the bathroom sink, with a bar of Ivory soap standing in for detergent—and before he slips into them he shaves with a disposable razor that gouges his face in half a dozen places and makes him yearn for the reliable purr and gentle embrace of his Braun Flex Control. He breakfasts on a stale cruller and coffee that tastes of bile while flicking through the channels. Then he shaves a second time and combs his hair. It is 9:05. The room stinks of stir-fry, pepperoni, garlic, the sad reek of his take-out life. He can wait no longer.

Unfortunately, the cab is forty-five minutes late, and it's nearly ten-thirty by the time they reach the freeway. On top of that, there's a delay—roadwork, they always wait till Sunday for roadwork—and the cab sits inert in an endless field of gleaming metal until finally the cabbie jerks savagely at the wheel and bolts forward, muttering to himself as he rockets along the shoulder and down the nearest off-ramp. Julian hangs on, feeling curiously detached as they weave in and out of traffic and the streets become increasingly familiar. And then the cab swings into his block and he's there. Home. His heart begins to pound in his chest.

He doesn't know what he's been expecting—banners, brass bands, Marsha embracing him joyously on the front steps of an immaculate house—but as he climbs out of the cab to survey his domain, he can't help feeling a tug of disappointment: the place looks pretty much the same, gray flanks, white trim, a thin sorry plume of bougainvillea clutching at the trellis over the door. But then it hits him: the lawn ornaments are gone. The tiki torches, the plaster pickaninnies and flag holders and all the rest of the outdoor claptrap have vanished as if into the maw of some brooding tropical storm, and for that he's thankful. Deeply thankful. He stands there a moment, amazed at the expanse of the lawn, plain simple grass, each blade a revelation—he never dreamed he had this much grass. The place looks the way it did when they bought it, wondering naively if it would be too big for just the two of them.

He saunters up the walk like a prospective buyer, admiring the house, truly admiring it, for the first time in years. How crisp it looks, how spare and uncluttered! She's a genius, he's thinking, she really is, as he mounts the front steps fingering his keys and humming, actually humming. But then, standing there in the quickening sun, he glances through the window and sees that the porch is empty—swept clean, not a thing left behind—and the tune goes sour in his throat. That's a surprise. A real surprise. He would have thought she'd leave something—the wicker set, the planters, a lamp or two—but even the curtains are gone. In fact, he realizes with a shock, none of the windows seem to have curtains—or blinds, either. What is she thinking? Is she crazy?

Cursing under his breath, he jabs the key in the lock and twists, but nothing happens. He jerks it back out, angry now, impatient, and examines the flat shining indented surface: no, it's the right key, the same key he's been using for sixteen years. Once again. Nothing. It won't even turn. The truth, ugly, frightening, has begun to dawn on him, even as he swings round on his heels and finds himself staring into the black unblinking gaze of Susan Certaine.

"You, you changed the locks," he accuses, and his hands are trembling.

Susan Certaine merely stands there, the briefcase at her feet, two mammoth softbound books clutched under her arms, books the size of unabridged dictionaries. She's in black, as usual, a no-nonsense business suit growing out of sensible heels, her cheeks brushed ever so faintly with blusher. "A little early, aren't we?" she says.

"You changed the locks."

She waits a beat, unhurried, in control. "What did you expect? We really can't have people interfering with our cataloguing, can we? You'd be surprised how desperate some people get, Mr. Laxner. And when you ran out on your therapy . . . well, we just couldn't take the chance." A thin pinched smile. "Not to worry: I've got your new keys right here—two sets, one for you and one for Marsha."

Her heels click on the pavement, three businesslike strides, and she's standing right beside him on the steps, crowding him. "Here, will you take these, please?" she says, dumping the books in his arms and digging into her briefcase for the keys.

The books are like dumbbells, scrap iron, so heavy he can feel the pull in his shoulders. "God, they're heavy," Julian mutters. "What are they?"

She fits the key in the lock and pauses, her face inches from his. "Your life,

Mr. Laxner. The biography of your things. Did you know that you owned five hundred and fifty-two wire hangers, sixty-seven wooden ones and one hundred and sixty-nine plastic? Over two hundred flowerpots? Six hundred doilies? Potholders, Mr. Laxner. You logged in over one hundred twenty—can you imagine that? Can you imagine anyone needing a hundred and twenty potholders? Excess, Mr. Laxner," and he watches her lip curl. "Filthy excess."

The key takes, the tumblers turn, the door swings open. "Here you are, Mr. Laxner, *organization,*" she cries, throwing her arms out. "Welcome to your new life."

Staggering under the burden of his catalogues, Julian moves across the barren porch and into the house, and here he has a second shock: the place is empty. Denuded. There's nothing left, not even a chair to sit in. Bewildered, he turns to her, but she's already moving past him, whirling round the room, her arms spread wide. He's begun to sweat. The scent of Sen-Sen hangs heavy in the air. "But, but there's nothing here," he stammers, bending down to set the catalogues on the stripped floorboards. "I thought . . . well, I thought you'd pare it down, organize things so we could live here more comfortably, adjust, I mean—"

"Halfway measures, Mr. Laxner?" she says, skating up to him on the newly waxed floors. "Are halfway measures going to save a man—and woman—who own three hundred and nine bookends, forty-seven rocking chairs, over two thousand plates, cups and saucers? This is tabula rasa, Mr. Laxner, square one. Did you know you owned a hundred and thirty-seven dead penlight batteries? Do you really need a hundred and thirty-seven dead penlight batteries, Mr. Laxner? Do you?"

"No, but"—backing off now, distraught, his den, his den—"but we need the basics, at least. Furniture. A TV. My, my textbooks. My scopes."

The light through the unshaded windows is harsh, unforgiving. Every corner is left naked to scrutiny, every board, every nail. "All taken care of, Mr. Laxner, no problem." Susan Certaine stands there in the glare of the window, hands on her hips. "Each couple is allowed to reclaim one item per day from the warehouse—anything you like—for a period of sixty days. Depending on how you exercise your options, that could be as many as sixty items. Most couples request a bed first, and to accommodate them, we consider a bed one item—mattress, box spring, headboard and all."

Julian is stunned. "Sixty items? You're joking."

"I never joke, Mr. Laxner. Never."

"And what about the rest—the furniture, the stereo, our clothes?"

"Read your contract, Mr. Laxner."

He can feel himself slipping. "I don't want to read the contract, damn it. I asked you a question."

"Page two hundred and seventy-eight, paragraph two. I quote: 'After expiration of the sixty-day grace period, all items to be sold at auction, the proceeds going to Certaine Enterprises, Inc., for charitable distribution, charities to be chosen at the sole discretion of the above-named corporation.' " Her eyes are on him, severe, hateful, bright with triumph. This is what it's all about, this—cutting people down to size, squashing them. "You'd be surprised how many couples never recall a thing, not a single item."

"No," Julian says, stalking across the room, "no, I won't stand for it. I won't. I'll sue."

She shrugs. "I won't even bother to remind you to listen to yourself. You're like the brat on the playground—you don't like the way the game goes, you take your bat and ball and go home, right? Go ahead, sue. You'll find it won't be so easy. You signed the contract, Mr. Laxner. Both of you."

There's a movement in the open doorway. Shadow and light. Marsha. Marsha and Dr. Hauskopf, frozen there on the doorstep, watching. "Julian," Marsha cries, and then she's in his arms, clinging to him as if he were the last thing in the world, the only thing left her.

Dr. Doris and Susan Certaine exchange a look. "Be happy," Susan Certaine says after a moment. "Think of that couple in Ethiopia." And then they're gone.

Julian doesn't know how long he stands there, in the middle of that barren room in the silence of that big empty house, holding Marsha, holding his wife, but when he shuts his eyes he sees only the sterile deeps of space, the remotest regions beyond even the reach of light. And he knows this: it is cold out there, inhospitable, alien. There's nothing there, nothing contained in nothing. Nothing at all.

(1992)

Grateful acknowledgment is made to the following magazines where these stories were first published: *Antaeus, The Antioch Review, The Atlantic Monthly, Epoch, Esquire, Fiction, Fiction International, Gentleman's Quarterly, The Georgia Review, Granta, Harper's, Interview, The Iowa Review, The New Yorker, The North American Review, Oui, The Paris Review, PEN Syndicated Fiction Project, Penthouse, Playboy, Quest/77, Quest/78, Rolling Stone, The South Dakota Review, The Transatlantic Review, TriQuarterly,* and *Wigwag.*

Most of the selections appeared in the following short story collections of Mr. Boyle, all published by Penguin Books: *Descent of Man* (1979), *Greasy Lake* (1985), *If the River Was Whiskey* (1989), and *Without a Hero* (1994).

Acknowledgment is made for permission to reprint excerpts from the following copyrighted works:

"I Shot the Sheriff," written by Bob Marley. Copyright © 1974 Fifty-Six Hope Road Music, Ltd., and Odnil Music, Ltd. Used by permission. All rights reserved.

"Poem Without a Hero," by Anna Akhmatova from *Poems of Akhmatova*, translated by Stanley Kunitz and Max Hayward. © 1972 by Stanley Kunitz and Max Hayward. By permission of Darhansoff & Verrill Literary Agency.

"Don't Be Cruel," by Otis Blackwell and Elvis Presley. Copyright © 1956 by Unart Music Corporation. Rights assigned to CBS Catalogue Partnership. All rights controlled and administered by CBS Unart Catalog, Inc. All rights reserved. International copyright secured. By permission of CBS Songs, a Division of CBS Inc.

"Hound Dog," by Jerry Leiber and Mike Stoller. Copyright © 1956 by Elvis Presley Music and Lion Publishing Company, Inc. Copyright renewed, assigned to Gladys Music, Inc., and MCA Music. Administered in the U.S.A. by Chappell & Co., Inc. (Intersong Music, Publisher). International copyright secured. All rights reserved. By permission of Chappell/Intersong Music Group–USA.

"Heartbreak Hotel," by Elvis Presley, Mae Boren Axton, and Tommy Durden. Copyright © 1956 by Tree Publishing Co., Inc. Copyright renewed. International copyright secured. All rights reserved. By permission of Tree Publishing Co., Inc.

"Whales Weep Not!" from *The Complete Poems of D. H. Lawrence*, collected and edited by Vivian de Sola Pinto and F. Warren Roberts. Copyright © 1964, 1971 by Angelo Ravagli and C. M. Weekley, Executors of the Estate of Frieda Lawrence Ravagli. Used by permission of Viking Penguin, a member of Penguin Putnam Inc.

"Spirit in the Night," by Bruce Springsteen. Copyright © 1972 by Bruce Springsteen. All rights reserved. By permission of Bruce Springsteen/Jon Landau Management, Inc.

"I'm a King Bee," by Slim Harpo, reprinted by permission of Excellorec Music.

"Stones in My Passway," "Phonograph Blues," and "Hellbound on My Trail," words and music by Robert Johnson. © (1978) 1991 King of Spades Music. All rights reserved. Used by permission of King of Spades Music.

"That's Amore," by Jack Brooks and Harry Warren. Copyright © 1953 by Paramount Music Corporation and Four Jays Music. Copyright renewed 1981 by Paramount Music Corporation and Four Jays Music. By permission of Paramount Music Corporation.

Some of "The Extinction Tales" was suggested by material in Jay Williams's *Fall of the Sparrow* (Oxford, 1951).